PENGUIN BOOKS

Noonday

'Bold, hard-hitting, unforgettable . . . a virtuoso rendition of the bombing, as huge swathes of London blaze away with the brightest of bright lights. Barker shows us how the city's finest moment was indubitably also its most terrifying, with luminous and unsparing insight' *Independent on Sunday*

'Barker's command of detail and gift for metaphor are as sharp as ever: her evocation of the bombed city is terrific, and every night patrol is steeped in drama . . . as a tribute to those who dared and suffered on the home front, *Noonday* is in the first rank' *Mail on Sunday*

'Tremendously good' *Daily Mail*

'Ambitious, vivid, sharp . . . she writes with precision about distinct effects on the senses . . . Barker's chronological leap is a sophisticated bridge between the drama of the present and the haunted history of the past . . . the closer you get to the end, the more lives need saving and the more thwarted and complicated the domestic backdrop' *Daily Telegraph*

'The narrative fizzes with energy . . . the novel's point of view swivel[s] like a torchbeam to illuminate London's devastated streets' *Independent*

'*Noonday*'s Blitz-era setting gives Barker ample opportunity to do what she does best: intent descriptions of splayed limbs that are sometimes engaged in the act of love, occasionally the subjects of paintings or, more often, casualties of war' *Spectator*

'Powerful and vivid, with nuanced characters and Barker's unerring eye for detail' *Women and Home*

'A fine and satisfying novel . . . despite the misery and madness of war, there is a tiny flare in the darkness that Barker softly fans as the novel moves towards its powerful and compassionate end' *Financial Times*

'Many strokes of genius from Barker . . . accessible and moving'
Sunday Times

'This is so well done. From guilt at finding evacuees unappealing, to the marriages that disintegrate as people seek a quick and urgent comfort from strangers, Barker takes us to the dark heart of London during the Blitz' *Bookseller*

ABOUT THE AUTHOR

Pat Barker was born in 1943. Her books include *Another World*, *Border Crossing*, *Double Vision* and the highly acclaimed Regeneration trilogy: *Regeneration* (1991), which was made into a film of the same name; *The Eye in the Door* (1993), which won the *Guardian* Fiction Prize; and *The Ghost Road* (1995), which won the Booker Prize. More recently she has published a second fiction trilogy comprising *Life Class*, *Toby's Room* and the final novel in the series, *Noonday*. Pat Barker lives in Durham.

Noonday

PAT BARKER

PENGUIN BOOKS

PENGUIN BOOKS

UK | USA | Canada | Ireland | Australia
India | New Zealand | South Africa

Penguin Books is part of the Penguin Random House group of companies
whose addresses can be found at global.penguinrandomhouse.com.

First published by Hamish Hamilton 2015
Published in Penguin Books 2016
001

Copyright © Pat Barker, 2015

Typeset in Dante by Palimpsest Book Production Limited, Falkirk, Stirlingshire
Printed in Great Britain by Clays Ltd, St Ives plc

A CIP catalogue record for this book is available from the British Library

ISBN: 978-0-241-96603-7

www.greenpenguin.co.uk

MIX
Paper from
responsible sources
FSC
www.fsc.org
FSC® C018179

Penguin Random House is committed to a
sustainable future for our business, our readers
and our planet. This book is made from Forest
Stewardship Council® certified paper.

For Finn, Niamh, Gabe and Jessie

One

Elinor was halfway up the drive when she sensed she was being watched. She stopped and scanned the upstairs windows – wide open in the heat as if the house were gasping for breath – but there was nobody looking down. Then, from the sycamore tree at the end of the garden, came a rustling of leaves. Oh, of course: *Kenny*. She was tempted to ignore him, but that seemed unkind, so she went across the lawn and peered up into the branches.

'Kenny?'

No reply. There was often no reply.

Kenny had arrived almost a year ago now, among the first batch of evacuees, and, although this area had since been reclassified – 'neutral' rather than 'safe' – here he remained. She felt his gaze heavy on the top of her head, like a hand, as she stood squinting up into the late-afternoon sunlight.

Kenny spent hours up there, not reading his comics, not building a tree house, not dropping conkers on people's heads – no, just watching. He had a red notebook in which he wrote down car numbers, the time people arrived, the time they left . . . Of course, you forgot what it was like to be his age: probably every visitor was a German spy. Oh, and he ate himself, that was the other thing. He was forever nibbling his fingernails, tearing at his cuticles, picking scabs off his knees and licking up the blood. Even pulling hair out of his head and sucking it. And, despite being a year at the village school, he hadn't made friends. But then, he was the sort of child who attracts bullying, she thought, guiltily conscious of her own failure to like him.

'Kenny? Isn't it time for tea?'

Then, with a great crash of leaves and branches, he dropped at her feet and stood looking up at her, scowling, for all the world like a small, sour, angry crab apple. 'Where's Paul?'

'I'm afraid he couldn't come, he's busy.'

'He's always busy.'

'Well, yes, he's got a lot to do. Are you coming in now?'

Evidently that didn't deserve a reply. He turned his back on her and ran off through the arch into the kitchen garden.

Two

Closing the front door quietly behind her, Elinor took a moment to absorb the silence.

Facing her, directly opposite the front door, where nobody could possibly miss it, was a portrait of her brother, Toby, in uniform. It had been painted, from photographs, several years after his death and was frankly not very good. Everybody else seemed to like it, or at least tolerate it, but Elinor thought it was a complete travesty. *Item: one standard-issue gallant young officer, Grim Reaper for the use of.* There was nothing of Toby there at all. Nigel Featherstone was the artist: and he was very well regarded; you saw his portraits of judges, masters of colleges, politicians and generals everywhere, but she'd never liked his work. Her own portrait of Toby was stronger – not good, she didn't claim that – but certainly better than this.

She resented not having been asked to paint this family portrait: his own sister, after all. And every visit to her sister's house began with her standing in front of it. When he was alive, Toby's presence had been the only thing that made weekends with the rest of her family bearable. Now, this portrait – that blank, lifeless face – was a reminder that she was going to have to face them alone.

She caught the creak of a leather armchair from the open door on her left. *Oh, well, better get it over with.* She went into the room and found Tim, her brother-in-law, sitting by the open window. As soon as he saw her he stood up and let his newspaper slide, sighing, to the floor.

'Elinor.' He pecked her proffered cheek. 'Too early for a whisky?' Evidently it wasn't: there was a half-empty glass by his side. She opened her mouth to refuse but he'd already started to pour. 'How was the train?'

'Crowded. Late.'

'Aren't they all?'

When she'd first met Tim he might've been a neutered tomcat for all the interest he aroused in her. She'd thought him a nonentity, perhaps influenced in that – as in so much else – by Toby, who hadn't liked Tim, or perhaps hadn't found much in him to either like or dislike. And yet Tim had gone on to be a successful man; powerful, even. Something in Whitehall, in the War Office. Which was strange, because he'd never actually seen active service. It had never been clear to her what precisely Tim did, though when she expressed her bewilderment to Paul he'd laughed and said: 'Do you really not know?'

She took a sip of whisky. 'I saw some soldiers in the lane.'

'Yes, they're building gun emplacements on the river.'

'Just over there?'

He shrugged. 'It's the obvious place.'

How easily they'd all come to accept it: searchlights over the church at night, blacked-out houses, the never-ending *pop-pop* of guns on the marshes . . . Such an inconsequential sound: almost like a child's toy. The whisky was starting to fizz along her veins. Perhaps it hadn't been such a bad idea after all. 'Where's Rachel?'

'Upstairs with your mother. Who's asleep, I think.'

'I don't suppose Mrs Murchison's around?'

'Why, do you particularly want to speak to her?'

'More thinking of avoiding her, actually.'

He looked at his watch. 'She generally takes a break about now. I expect she's in her room.'

But she wasn't. She was crossing the hall with a firm, flat-footed step, her shoes making minuscule squeaks on the tiles. 'Ah, Miss Brooke, I thought it must be you.'

Always that barely perceptible emphasis on the 'Miss'. To be fair, she had some reason to be confused. Elinor and Paul had lived together for almost six years before they finally married, very quietly, in Madrid. None of Elinor's family had been invited to the wedding and she'd continued to use her own name professionally – and also, to some extent, socially – ever since. Clearly, Mrs Murchison suspected she was not, in any proper sense, married at all.

'Will you be wanting tea?'

'I'll see what my sister says.'

Elinor picked up her case and carried it upstairs to the spare room. This should have been Mrs Murchison's job, but really the less she had to do with that woman the better. Queuing in the post office once, she'd heard Mrs Murchison whisper to the woman beside her: 'She's a Miss, you know.' Elinor knew exactly what she meant. *Miss*-take. *Miss*ed out. Even, perhaps, *miss*-carriage? No, she was being paranoid: Mrs Murchison couldn't possibly have known about that. Of course there'd always be people like her, people who regarded childless women as hardly women at all. 'Fibroids' – Mr O'Brien had announced a few years ago when Elinor's periods had gone haywire – 'are the tears of a disappointed womb.' Obnoxious little Irish leprechaun, twinkling at her over his steepled fingertips. She'd just gaped at him and then, unable to control herself, burst out laughing.

In the spare room she dumped her suitcase on the bed; she'd unpack later. Quickly, she splashed her face and hands, examined herself in the glass, noting pallor, noting tiredness, but not minding too much, not today at any rate. Through the open window she heard Mrs Murchison calling Kenny in to get washed in time for dinner.

Kenny had a lot to do with Elinor's dislike of Mrs Murchison. Given the task of dealing with his nits, she'd simply shaved his head, without apparently finding it necessary to consult anybody else first. Elinor had gone into the kitchen the morning after he arrived and found him standing there, orange hair lying in coils around his feet. Thin, hollow-eyed, the strange, white, subtle egg shape of his head – he'd looked like a child in the ruins of Guernica or Wieluń. She'd completely lost her temper; she was angrier than she'd been for years. Rachel came running, then Mother, who was still, only a year ago, well enough to come downstairs. 'Elinor.' Mother laid a cool hand on her arm. 'This isn't your house. And that isn't your child.' Which was, undeniably, true. Not her house, not her child, not her responsibility.

Outside, in the garden, Mrs Murchison was still calling: 'Kenny? Kenny?'

Well, she could call till she was blue in the face; he wouldn't come in for her.

A murmur of voices drifted across the landing from her mother's room: so she must be awake. It couldn't be put off any longer, though even now Elinor stood outside the door for a full minute, taking slow, deliberate, deep breaths, before she pushed it open and went in.

A fug of illness rose to meet her: aging flesh in hot sheets, camphor poultices that did no good at all, a smell of faeces and disinfectant from the commode in the far corner. Rachel was sitting on the other side of the bed, her back to the window, her face in shadow. Mother's nightdress was open at the front: you could see her collarbone jutting out and the hollows in her throat. Her chest moved, not merely with every breath, but with every heartbeat. Looking at her, Elinor could almost believe she saw the dark, struggling muscle labouring away inside its cage of bone. Mother's eyes were closed, but as Elinor approached the bed, the lids flickered open, though not completely. They stopped halfway, as if already weighted down by pennies. 'Oh, Elinor.' Her voice was slurred. 'It's you.'

Wrong person. 'Hello, Mother.' She bent and kissed the hollow cheek.

She was about to sit down, but then she saw Rachel mouthing at her. 'Outside.'

Elinor slipped quietly out on to the landing and a few seconds later Rachel joined her. The sisters kissed, Rachel's dry lips barely making contact with Elinor's cheek. They'd never been close. Toby, the middle child, had come between them in every sense. Looking back on her early childhood, Elinor realized that even then she and Rachel had been rivals for Toby; and Elinor had won. An empty victory, it seemed, so many years after his death.

'Has the doctor been?' she asked.

'This morning, yes. He comes every morning.'

'What does he say?'

'You mean how long has she got? No, of course he didn't say. They never do, do they? I don't think they know. She'll hang on till Alex gets back – and then I think it might be very quick.'

'When's he coming?'

'He's hoping they'll let him out tomorrow. But it depends on the consultant, of course.'

Mother had always used her grandson, Alex, as a substitute for Toby. Was 'used' a bit harsh? No, she didn't think so.

'I expect you'd like some tea?' Rachel said.

'Well, yes, but hadn't one of us better sit with her?'

'No, it's all right, I'll get Nurse Wiggins. Oh, you don't know about her, do you? She's our new addition.' A fractional hesitation. 'Very competent.'

'You don't like her.'

'We-ell, you know . . .' Rachel gave a theatrical shudder. 'She *hovers*.'

'You need the help, you're worn out.'

'Wasn't my idea, it was Tim's.'

'Well, good for him.'

Rachel glanced back into their mother's bedroom. 'Ah, she's nodded off again; I thought she might. I'll just nip up and get the Wiggins.'

Tim had retreated to his study, so Elinor went into the drawing room to wait for Rachel. The farmhouse, which had been shabby, even dilapidated, when Rachel first fell in love with it, was now beautifully furnished. Oriental rugs, antique furniture – good paintings too. Nothing of hers, though. She had three in the Tate; none here.

Rachel came in carrying a tray, which she put down on a small table near the window. Out of the corner of her eye, Elinor noticed Kenny scaling along the wall, trying to avoid being seen from the kitchen window. 'I see Kenny's still here?'

'Oh, don't talk to me about Kenny; I'm beginning to think he's a fixture. His mother was supposed to come and get him last Saturday. Poor little devil was sitting at the end of the drive all day. Suitcase packed, everything – and she didn't show up. And he never says anything, you know, never cries.' She pulled a face. 'Just wets the bed.'

'He's still doing that?'

'Every night. I mean, I know you don't like Mrs Murchison, but really, the extra work . . .' She hesitated. 'I don't suppose you could go and see her, could you? His mother?'

Not your house. Not your child.

'I'm actually quite busy at the moment.'

'Busy?'

'Painting.'

'Oh, yes. Painting.'

That was only just not a sneer. The silence gathered. Elinor reminded herself of how tired Rachel must be, how disproportionately the burden of their mother's illness fell on her. 'You know, if you liked, you could have an early night; I'll sit with her.'

'No, there's no need. Nurse Wiggins does the nights.'

So why am I here?

'Would you mind if I phoned Paul tonight?'

'Phone him now if you like.'

'No, he'll be working, I'll leave it till after dinner.'

'How is he?'

'A bit up and down. Kenny was disappointed he hadn't come. I think I'm a very poor substitute.'

'Now that is something you could do. Make sure he turns up for dinner washed and reasonably tidy. He won't do anything for Mrs Murchison and I just don't have the time.'

Kenny. Somehow, whenever she was here, the responsibility for making Kenny behave got passed on to her. Still, it was the least she could do. So after Rachel had gone back upstairs, Elinor went into the garden, first to the sycamore tree and then into the kitchen garden where he'd built himself a den behind the shed. No luck there either. The night nursery was the next most likely place.

As she climbed the stairs, Elinor was remembering her first sight of Kenny, almost a year ago, the day the children arrived. A busload of them, carrying suitcases, paper parcels and gas masks, with luggage labels fastened to their clothes.

She and Rachel had arrived late at the church hall. It was rather like a jumble sale, all the good stuff disappearing fast, except that here the stuff was children. Pretty little blonde-haired girls were popular and not always with the obvious people. You could see why the Misses Richards might want one, but Michael Ryan, who'd lived alone at Church Farm ever since his parents died and seemed barely able to look after himself, let alone a child, why was he so keen? Big, strapping lads, strong enough for farm work, they were snapped up. Older girls went quickly too. A twelve-year-old, provided she was clean and tidy – and not too slow on the uptake – was virtually a free housemaid. And then there were the children nobody wanted: families of four or five brothers and sisters. They'd have to be split up, of course. In fact, it was happening already. Some of the smaller children were wide-eyed with shock and grief.

Then she saw him. Pale, thin, his face slum-white, disfigured by freckles, orange hair, coppery-brown eyes. His trousers were too short, his sleeves too: he had unusually knobbly wrist bones. And a rather long, thin neck. For some reason, that made him seem vulnerable, like an unfledged bird, though closer to – she'd begun to walk towards him now – she revised her impression. Yes, he looked like a chick, but the chick of some predatory bird: an eagle or a falcon. Not an attractive child, but even so, he should've been picked by now – he was the right age for farm work.

And then she saw the lice. She'd never seen anybody with a head that lousy. His hair was moving. Made desperate by their overcrowded conditions, lice had started taking short cuts across his forehead. She was about to speak to him – though she had no idea what to say – when Rachel came up behind her.

'They want me to take three. *Three*. How on earth am I supposed to manage three?'

'What about him?'

Rachel peered at the boy. She was short-sighted and too vain to wear glasses. 'Well, at least there's only one of him . . . Yes, all right, I'll see what she says.'

Rachel went off to speak to the billeting officer, Miss Beatrice Marsh, who regularly made a mess of the church flower-arranging roster. They seemed to be having an extremely animated discussion. The boy showed no interest in the outcome. His gas-mask case was on a long string: Elinor noticed a sore patch on the side of his knee where the case had chafed against the skin. He had placed a battered brown suitcase between his legs and was gripping it tight, so at least he'd have something, a change of clothes, a favourite toy. But he'd lost his luggage label.

'Which school are you with?'

He shook his head.

You did it on purpose, she thought. *You threw it away*. Not that there was anything sinister in that. There were many reasons why a child might choose to slip off the end of one school crocodile and attach himself to a different one entirely. A teacher he didn't like, a gang of bigger boys bullying in the playground . . . Whatever the reason, he'd arrived in the village with no name, no history. Something about that appealed to Elinor. Bundled up, parcelled off . . . and in the middle of it all, the chaos, the confusion, he'd taken off his label and thrown it away.

Only of course it couldn't go on like that. He had to give Rachel his name, his address, because he wanted his mother to be able to find him. He wanted her a good deal more than she appeared to want him.

Elinor tapped on the nursery door. Kenny was playing with his toy soldiers – Alex's, originally, now his – hundreds of tiny grey and khaki figures spread across a vast battlefield, many of them lying on their backs, already wounded or killed. He looked up from the game, but didn't smile or speak.

'It's dinner time. Have you washed your hands?'

He shook his head.

'Well, will you go and do it now, please?'

Still silent, he got up and left. Now and then it was brought home to her that Kenny hardly spoke – except, oddly enough, to Paul. And in the past year he'd scarcely grown at all. She looked round the chaotic room, decided to leave the toy soldiers undisturbed, but knelt to close the dolls' house.

Officially, Kenny despised the house and the dolls – wouldn't have been seen dead playing with them – and yet whenever she came into the room the dolls were in different positions and the furniture had been rearranged. She both loved and hated this house, which had once been hers. Her eighth-birthday present. She could still remember the mixture of delight and uneasiness she'd felt when the wrapping paper fell away and she saw that the dolls weren't just ordinary dolls: they were Father and Mother and Rachel and Toby and her. And the toy house was an exact copy of the house they lived in, right down to the piano in the drawing room and the pattern of wallpaper on the bedroom walls. It had always had pride of place in her bedroom, but she hadn't played with it much. She picked up the Toby doll, held it between her thumb and forefinger, and felt a pang of grief so intense it squeezed her heart. She remained kneeling there, on the cold lino, waiting for the pain to pass, then laid the little figure on its bed.

Rachel came in. 'Ken—' She stopped when she saw Elinor. 'Still playing with dolls?'

'I never did, if you remember.'

'No, you didn't, did you? You were always out with Toby. I think I played with that more than you did.'

Elinor went on putting the dolls to bed. One moment, she was looking through a tiny window, the next, she saw her own face peering in: huge, piggy nostrils, open-pored, grotesque. Then, immediately, she was back in the nursery, looking down at the last doll in her hand: Mother.

'Are you all right?' Rachel asked.

'Fine.'

'Only you've gone quite pale.'

'No, I'm fine.' She fastened the front of the house and stood up. 'Kenny's getting washed; at least I think he is. What about Mother, is she awake?'

'No, and anyway the Wiggins is there. Come on, I need a drink.'

As they were going downstairs the telephone in the hall started to ring, and Rachel went to answer it. When she came into the drawing room a few minutes later, she was glowing with excitement. 'That was Alex; he's coming home tomorrow. I'll go and tell Tim.'

Left alone, Elinor thought: *Yes, good news*. But she couldn't stop thinking about her mother lying upstairs, dying, but clinging on to life so she could see Alex again, one last time. This was what they'd all been waiting for: Alex's arrival; the end.

Three

Alex arrived the following afternoon, straight out of hospital with the smell of it still on his skin. Elinor witnessed his meeting with his father. Tim stuck out his hand and then, realizing too late that Alex was unable to take it, blushed from the neck up and let the hand drop. She sensed a great tension in Alex: something coiled up hard and tight. His face softened when Rachel came into the room, but otherwise he seemed merely impatient, anxious to get this visit over and move on.

Thinking he would like time alone with his parents, Elinor fetched a drawing pad from her room and went into the garden. She sat under the birch tree, her back pressed hard against its scaly bark, staring up through the branches at yet another flawlessly blue sky. The aeroplanes were active today, little, glinting, silver minnows darting here and there. Earlier, she'd started trying to draw a cabbage and it was sitting on a low stone wall, waiting for her, yellower and flabbier than she remembered. She gazed at it without enthusiasm, then forced herself to begin. *Draw something every single day*, Professor Tonks used to say. *Doesn't matter what it is: just draw*.

All the upstairs windows were open. Behind that one on the far left her mother lay dying, attended, at the moment, by Nurse Wiggins, a great, galumphing, raw-boned creature with a jolly, professional laugh and downy, peach-perfect skin. Her laugh, so obviously designed to keep fear and pain at bay, grated on Elinor. And yes, she did *hover*. But she was good at her job, you had to give her that, though her presence added to the tension in the house. Rachel, in particular, seemed to find it difficult to relax.

Elinor held the drawing at arm's length. Not good. Cabbages are shocking if you get them right, especially those thick-veined outer leaves: positively scrotal. Only she couldn't draw them like that, not here, surrounded by her family. She was unconsciously censoring herself, and it wasn't just what she drew, either. It was what she let herself see. This was one of the reasons she'd left home early, and refused, even after Toby's death, to go back. Her mother needed care and company: it had been obvious to everybody that Elinor, the then unmarried daughter, should stay at home and provide it.

Obvious to everybody except Elinor, who'd refused, and gone on refusing. It was Rachel, in the end, who'd found their mother a cottage within walking distance of her own home.

The caterpillar on the leaf
Repeats to thee thy mother's grief.

What the hell was that about? It was true, though. She'd have liked to do the drawing that would be the equivalent of those lines.

Voices from an upstairs window: Rachel and Alex. She'd be taking him up to his room. Elinor looked at the brown lawn, the wilting shrubs and flowers; everything seemed to be suspended. Was that the war? Possibly. Even the roses, this summer, looked as if they were expecting to be bombed. But no, it was more than that: closer. *She* was waiting: for something to happen or, more likely, for something to be said; but though Mother's thick, white tongue came out at intervals to moisten her cracked lips she stayed silent, drifting in and out of sleep.

Elinor glanced up, caught by some movement other than the ceaseless circling of aeroplanes in the sky, and there was Alex, in a white shirt with the sleeves rolled up, coming towards her over the lawn. 'Aunt Elinor, I thought I'd find you here.'

Flattering as always, implying he'd been looking especially for her. Alex was a devil with women, though his affairs never lasted long. It was the chase that interested Alex; the girls, once caught, quickly bored him. He bent down to kiss her, briefly cutting off the light.

Elinor was extremely fond of Alex, but wary of him too. He was tall, broad-shouldered and, despite his convalescent state, exuded virility. Beside him, she felt like a spindle-shanked elderly virgin, while knowing of course that she was nothing of the sort, but perhaps that's what middle age does to you? Makes you – women, perhaps, particularly – vulnerable to the perceptions other people have of you? She thought Alex might see her like that. He flirted with her rather as he might have done with a schoolgirl too young to be considered a possible conquest.

He sat cross-legged on the grass beside her, squinting through his spread fingers at the sky. More and more planes, great clusters of them, like midges over a stagnant pond.

'Been busy all day,' she said.

'Yes, it's certainly hotting up. No raids though?'

'Not here. There was one near the coast, Rachel says, a few days ago. Thirteen people killed.'

He was looking at the window of his grandmother's room. 'Strange, isn't it, how private life just goes on? People get married, have babies. *Die*. And all the time . . .'

'I find I alternate,' she said. 'You know, I'll have days when I think about nothing except the war and how terrible it is and are we going to be invaded . . . and then suddenly, for no reason – nothing's changed – it all disappears. And I think: Well, we're still here. We're still the same people we've always been.'

'Oh, I don't know about that.'

Something in his voice made her turn to look at him. She saw lines around his eyes and mouth that hadn't been there before. Suddenly, he did actually look like Toby; Toby as he'd been when he'd first come home on leave. So much had been made of Alex's resemblance to Toby, especially by her mother, but also by Rachel, that Elinor had always resisted seeing it. Alex was different, she told herself: brash, coarser. But now she saw how alike they really were, and it stopped her breath.

'How's the, er . . .?' *Wound*, she meant.

He held out his arm. Suntanned skin, the tan fading a little now, after the long weeks in hospital. A dusting of blond hairs. 'Not a lot to see, really. I got it in the elbow. The funny bone. Oh my God it was hilarious – and apparently there's some damage to the nerves.' His fingers were curled over, the tips almost touching the palm. 'I haven't got a lot of sensation here. Or here.'

'So you're out of it, then?'

'Not if I can help it.' He was flexing his hand as he spoke. 'Though I don't know what I can do.'

'Is it painful?'

'Can be.'

Voices floated over the lawn towards them. Somewhere in the house a door opened and closed.

'Have you been in to see her?'

'Not yet. The nurse is in there doing something so I thought I'd leave it a bit. God, it's hot.'

'I think I know where there's some lemonade.'

And that, Elinor thought, crossing the lawn, was an appropriately maiden-auntish thing to say.

Outside the kitchen door, she paused to listen, but Mrs Murchison was having her post-lunch break, so she opened the door and walked in. A porcelain sink, with two buckets underneath, a range that had to be black-leaded every morning, and a long table, scarred with overlapping rings where hot plates and saucepans had been put down. Above the table, a rack with bunches of dried herbs, ready for the winter, though at the moment there were still masses of thyme, parsley, sage, rosemary and bay in the kitchen garden – and hundreds of bees feasting on them.

The pantry opened off the kitchen. The lemonade jug sat on the top shelf underneath the one tiny window, its muslin cover weighed down by blue beads. She picked up the jug and two glasses and returned to Alex.

'Auntie Elinor, you're an angel.'

This was going from bad to worse: aunt*ie*, now. He got up and dragged a small iron table closer. They were in deep shade: the shadow of a branch fell across Elinor's bare ankle so sharply it suggested amputation. The lemonade was cloudy, but relatively cold and sweet. Almost immediately wasps started hovering, drawn away from the easy pickings of windfall apples in the long grass of the orchard.

Elinor didn't feel like talking and evidently Alex felt the same, but there was no awkwardness in their silence. It was born of heat and exhaustion, and, on his side, recent illness and possibly pain. He kept batting wasps away. 'Don't,' she said. 'It only makes them worse.' *Why couldn't men leave things alone?* After a while she left him to it, leaned back against the tree and closed her eyes.

There were so many insect sounds – the hum of bees, the whirring of gnats, the petulant buzz of wasps – that at first she didn't notice one particular drone growing louder. A shadow swept across her closed lids. Opening her eyes, she saw a huge plane above the house, black, or at least it looked black against the sun. 'Is it one of ours?' she asked. She knew it wasn't – the German crosses on its wings were very clear – only her brain refused to accept what her eyes saw. The plane banked steeply; at first she thought it was going away, but it circled and came back again, this time much lower. She got up to run to the house, but Alex caught her arm. '*No.*' He pulled her back into the shadow of the tree. 'Better not cross the lawn.' She felt sick. There was a popping sound, curiously unimpressive, like a child bursting paper bags or balloons. Alex dragged her to the ground, face down, and lay on top of her. 'Don't clench your teeth.' *What?* Pale faces appeared at the kitchen door. 'Stay there!' Alex shouted, waving them back. He knew about this, they didn't, so automatically they obeyed. The plane veered away in the direction of the coast, falling, always falling, until it dipped below the level of a hill. The pressure on the back of her neck eased. She saw a ladybird, an inch away from her eyes, on the top of a grass stalk, waving its front legs, as if it didn't understand why the stalk had come to an end and there was only air. Now more planes were circling overhead – two? Three? She was afraid to look. 'Ours,' Alex said, letting go of her arm. She saw red marks where his fingers had been. *That'll bruise.* Slowly, she began to breathe more deeply, to direct weak, foolish smiles at the faces in the kitchen doorway: Rachel, Tim, Mrs Murchison, Joan Wiggins. Everybody must've rushed down when they heard the engine directly overhead. Beyond the hill, a column of black smoke was rising. The British planes circled, then banked steeply and headed towards London. Alex helped her to her feet and she wobbled on boneless legs into the house.

'Jerry right enough.' Tim gave a little cough, reclaiming status

17

from his son. Then, abruptly, he turned on Rachel, his face contorted with anger. 'What on earth possessed you?'

Elinor realized Rachel must've tried to run across the lawn to get to her son. Tim sounded so angry, but Alex was angry too: both of them, angry with the women because they hadn't been able to protect them. But then, gradually, everybody started to calm down. Mrs Murchison put the kettle on for tea. 'Oh, I think we can do better than that,' Tim said, and went to fetch the whisky.

Mrs Murchison turned to Nurse Wiggins. 'You'll have a cup, Joan?'

'No, I'll be getting back.'

In the turmoil of the last few minutes, the dying woman had been completely forgotten. Only now, conscience-stricken, Rachel remembered and ran upstairs.

Four

Elinor heard her mother wanting to know what was going on. She sounded wide awake, no doubt wrenched into full consciousness by the roar of the plane. A second later, there were footsteps on the landing and Rachel appeared, leaning over the bannisters. 'You can come up now.'

She was speaking to Alex, who grimaced and put down his glass. Elinor smiled, tried to look encouraging. She wondered what it was like to be Alex, to have seen so many men his own age and even younger killed, and then to come back into this other world, where an old woman dying in her own bed, surrounded by people who loved her, was treated as a tragedy. *They never really come back*, she thought, looking at Alex, thinking of Toby. Wondering if the same might not be true of Paul.

'You too, Elinor.'

She didn't want to go; she thought Alex would want time alone with his grandmother – they'd been so close – but evidently Rachel thought otherwise. For whatever reason, she'd decided the whole family should all be there together.

Alex was sitting with his back to the door when she entered the room, his left hand resting on his grandmother's wrinkled arm, her dead-white skin and his brown hand shockingly contrasted against the pale blue coverlet. It imprinted itself on her mind, that image; she knew she would always remember it. Mother was smiling, though she could only smile with one side of her face; the other was twisted into a permanent droop or sneer. And she was struggling to speak.

'It's all right, Gran.' Alex obviously meant don't bother, don't try to speak, but the old woman's mouth worked and worked at the words that wouldn't come. Then: 'Toby,' she said. 'I knew you'd come.'

Elinor saw Alex flinch. Rachel, who was standing on the other side of the bed, leaned forward as if to protect her son. Too late for that, Elinor thought. You should have been doing that years ago.

Shortly afterwards, Mother drifted off to sleep again. She seemed contented; happy, even. They listened to her breathing, waiting, and perhaps – some of them – longing, for a change in the rhythm, but, though the gaps between one breath and the next seemed sometimes impossibly long, her chest still rose and fell with the same remorseless regularity. This might go on for days.

I can't bear it, Elinor thought. And then: *Don't be stupid, of course you can.*

In the end the prolonged silence became too revealing. 'I'll get Nurse Wiggins,' Elinor said. She didn't know what Nurse Wiggins could do, but she felt the family atmosphere needed diluting. She ran quickly upstairs and tapped on the door at the end of the corridor. Nurse Wiggins appeared, bleary-eyed from lack of sleep, all that fresh, jolly hardness gone. 'Yes, of course I'll come.' She stifled a yawn, then yawned again. Moist, pink, catlike interior; huge tonsils.

Beginning to relax slightly, Elinor went first to her own room to splash her face with tepid water – no water was really cold this summer – was tempted to lie down for half an hour, but decided she ought to go downstairs. When she reached the bottom step she saw Alex and Rachel standing under Toby's portrait in the hall. Something about their attitude suggested the talk was private, so she retreated a few steps and settled down to wait.

Rachel was saying in a low, urgent voice, 'You will stay, won't you?'

'Tonight? Yes.'

'Only one night? I hoped you . . .'

'Yes?'

'Well, I hoped you'd stay till the end.'

'Don't you think I've done enough?'

'You've only been here a couple of hours.'

'I don't mean *now*.'

'Look, it'll only be a day or two. If that.'

'I've got things to do in town.'

'Can't they wait?'

'I've got a life.'

'She loved you more than anybody.'

'*Me?*'

He jerked his head at the portrait, then walked out into the garden, the front door banging shut behind him. Rachel stood for a moment, looking after him, and then, head down, crossed the hall into the drawing room.

Elinor lingered on the stairs for a minute, then went to stand where they'd been standing. *Killed in action*, she read, looking at the plaque, and even that wasn't true. She was remembering an incident when Alex had been five or six years old. He'd come running in from the garden, had stopped under the portrait, and pulled his sweater over his head. 'Christ, it's hot!' She remembered him saying it, she'd thought it so funny at the time, his chubby red face struggling out of the neck hole, first one ear, then the other, almost as if the sweater were giving birth to him. Then, suddenly, he stopped, one arm still in the sleeve, and stared at the portrait. 'It wasn't my fault!' Yelling, right at the top of his voice. Then, freeing his arm, he threw the sweater at the painting. There'd been something disturbing about the little boy shouting at the painted face of a man he couldn't remember. She'd wanted to ... intervene, protect him somehow – but from what? *It wasn't my fault*. She hadn't known what it meant, then, and she wasn't sure she knew now. Of course, it might have been a reference to some childish game he was in the middle of, perhaps he'd been accused of breaking the rules, something like that, but no, it had been very definitely directed at the portrait. At Toby. So what was it? A repudiation of the grief that hung over the house like a pall of black smoke and wouldn't go away? A refusal to feel guilt – and how guilty they all felt, then and now. Especially now, when another generation of young men was dying. *We dropped the catch*, she thought. *Our generation*. Wondering why she'd suddenly strayed into cricket: the memory of Alex's white sweater, perhaps. *And Alex's generation is paying the price*.

She looked across the hall and saw him still standing there, the angry little boy. And then he turned and ran out into the garden, where the dazzling light swallowed him, like the skin on a sunlit sea.

Crossing the hall, she was about to follow that flitting shadow into the garden, when she stopped, for there, pacing up and down the lawn, smoking furiously, was the adult Alex. As she watched, he turned towards the house and stared straight at her. She raised a hand to wave, then realized that he couldn't see her. From where he stood, the hall would be in darkness.

She couldn't imagine what he felt, now the old woman who'd loved him and used him as a substitute for her dead son was herself dying. Loss? Relief? Or did he perhaps no longer care much either way? His face really had aged; she'd noticed it earlier, but it struck her again, now, with renewed force. When he was talking, the play of expression on his face softened the lines around his eyes and mouth, but now, in repose, they looked as if they'd been scored in with a knife. She remembered the identical transformation in Toby; how, suddenly, from being two years older, he was five, ten, fifteen years older. Out of reach.

As Alex was. He was his own man now. The war that had taken so much away from him, had given him that, at least.

Five

Elinor woke early from confused dreams of Paul. She'd telephoned twice the previous night, had listened to the phone ring in their empty house, walked in memory through the familiar rooms, seeing the dented cushions, hearing the affronted silence. What on earth could he be doing? He couldn't be on duty every night, but he certainly wasn't at home. Working late in his studio, she guessed, perhaps even sleeping there – he did that sometimes when she was away from home – but there was no telephone in the studio so she had no way of contacting him.

Throwing back the bedclothes, she went to the window and looked out, feeling the morning air cool on her sleep-swollen face. Five or six jackdaws were strutting across the lawn – little storm troopers – rapacious beaks jab-jabbing at the soil in search of worms. Drops of dew glinted in the grass. It was still only half light.

Something had woken her. She listened. Footsteps on the landing? No, no, it was much too early for anybody to be about. But then, the front door opened and Alex came out, carrying a suitcase, followed by Tim. She looked down at the tops of their heads, Alex's thick blond hair, Tim's pink scalp showing through carefully combed mouse-brown. They got into the car, moving heavily, not speaking, grey shapes in the grey light. Doors clunked, the engine coughed and choked before settling down to a steady hum, spinning wheels scattered gravel and away they went. She wondered if her mother was awake to hear it, and whether if she heard it she'd realize that Alex had gone.

By late afternoon the heat had become intolerable. Taking a break from the sickroom, Elinor went into the garden and watered the plants. Unlike Rachel – and their mother too, for that matter – she was no gardener, but watering was one job she did enjoy.

She took off her shoes and let her white London feet explore the crumbly, moist soil. By the time she'd finished, all the paths were shining wet, and yet, even before she'd coiled the hose and restored it to its place by the tap, they were starting to dry. Steam rising from them, here and there.

Before dinner she went back to her mother's room, to the sour smell from the commode that no amount of bleach seemed able to remove. *And so it ends.* She'd been thinking things like that all day: vague, trite little phrases, trying to nudge herself into feeling the appropriate emotions, and never quite succeeding. The truth was that, like Rachel, she was too tired to feel anything very much. During the evening, Nurse Wiggins took over for a few hours; the sisters sat on the terrace in the breathy, moth-haunted darkness, smoking and talking – about nothing very much. Everything was subsumed in waiting.

Elinor was going to sit with their mother for the first half of the night. Neither of the sisters wanted her to be with a stranger when she died. At bedtime they went upstairs together, but outside their mother's door, Rachel lingered. 'You will wake me, won't you?'

'Of course I will. Go on now, shoo. *Shoo.*'

Sitting beside the bed, Elinor read for an hour, taking nothing in, listening to her mother's uneven breaths. Without realizing, she started to match her own breathing to her mother's, becoming in the process slightly light-headed. After a while, she gave up pretending to read and switched off the lamp. At least, now, she could open the blackout curtains and lean out of the window into the hot, still night.

Even flowers and grass no longer smelled fresh; it was as if everything had been singed. Searchlights fingered the underbelly of clouds, coming together sometimes to form a pyramid of light over the church tower. They seemed, in their constant, quivering, hyper-sensitive movement, to be living things, like the antennae on a moth.

A rustle behind her. Quickly, she pulled the blackout curtains across and groped her way back to her chair.

'Is that you, Elinor?'

'Yes.' Elinor put her hand over her mother's eyes to shield them before switching on the lamp. 'Would you like me to call Rachel?'

'No, let her sleep.'

Another breath. And another. After each dragging pause, the skeletal chest expanded again. *Let go, just let go*. Elinor almost said it aloud, only she was too ashamed, knowing it was her own deliverance she was pleading for.

The old woman looked around the room, bewildered. 'I thought Toby was here.'

'When?'

'Just now.'

'That was Alex, Mother. Yesterday.'

'*No*, just now.' The old woman's eyes focused on the empty space beyond the foot of the bed. 'He was standing just there.'

She's wandering, Elinor thought, resisting the temptation to turn round and check there was nobody there. But then her mother surprised her by turning towards her a gaze that was sharp, alert, even slightly malicious: a glimpse of the woman she'd once been. The thick, white tongue came out and moistened her cracked lips. Elinor bent forward to hear.

'I knew.'

Humour her. 'What did you know?'

'You and Toby.' Her chest rattled – she might even have been trying to laugh. 'Bed creaking, night after night, you must've thought I was stupid, I knew whose room it was coming from.'

Elinor daren't acknowledge that she'd heard, still less that she'd understood. Instead, she asked, 'Would you like some water?'

A reluctant nod. Elinor held the glass to her lips and watched the wasted throat working as she drank. After a while she waved it away. 'Did you really think I didn't know?'

'We used to play, that's all.'

'*Play*.'

Elinor dabbed her mother's mouth with a folded handkerchief and settled the grey head back on to the pillow. She said, brightly, 'Alex is coming again at the weekend.'

'Alex?'

So Alex had stopped existing, which seemed rather hard on Alex, whose whole childhood had been warped by his supposed resemblance to Toby. How many other families were like this? The chair at the dining-room table that nobody ever sat in, the bedroom kept as it had always been: school books, toys . . . On the mantelpiece or the piano, photographs of a face that didn't age. Other people's lives moulding themselves around the gap.

Another pause in her mother's breathing. Longer? 'I'll get Rachel.'

This time there was no protest. Blindly, Elinor stumbled across the landing and tapped on Rachel's door. After waiting a few moments, she pushed it open and peered into the darkness. That familiar married smell, male and female scents combined. 'Rachel?'

A hump under the bedclothes heaved and muttered. Then Rachel, still half asleep, staggered to the door, struggling to get her arms into the sleeves of her wrap. 'What's the matter? Is she worse?'

'No, I don't think so, she's awake, that's all. I thought you'd want to be there.'

'Yes, of course. Oh God, I didn't think I'd get to sleep at all and I must've gone really deep.'

Elinor continued along the landing to the bathroom.

'You are coming back?' Rachel sounded frightened.

'Yes, I just want to splash my face, I was starting to nod off in there.'

In the bathroom, she stood for a moment with her back against the door, then went to the basin and turned on the cold water. Cupping her hands, she threw water over her face, neck, chest, before finally filling the bowl to the brim and pushing her head underneath the surface. Water slopped on to the floor, but no matter. She looked at her dripping face in the mirror, coils of wet hair stuck to her forehead, haunted eyes. Her nightdress was soaked. Her nipples showed through the white cotton like a second pair of eyes. *I look mad*, she thought.

Now, when it was too late, she wanted to argue. Once. It had happened *once*. It was all nonsense saying the bed creaked 'night after night'. As children, she and Toby had often crept along the passage to each other's rooms. The only way to stop them was to lock them in, and even then Toby had crawled along the ledge outside their bedrooms, careless of the forty-foot drop on to the terrace below. Only after his death had she looked down at that ledge and realized the risk he'd run. As a child, ten, eleven years old. Why? Why that need? It hadn't been sexual then, couldn't have been; he was too young. All that came later. And it happened *once*. Though, of course, saying you'd slept with your brother only once was a bit like saying you'd committed murder *only once*. It wasn't really much of an excuse.

Back in her bedroom, she changed into a fresh nightdress before going to the window and peering round the blinds. Searchlights illuminating steep cliffs and chasms of cloud. Then, as she strained to hear, there came that curiously unimpressive *pop-pop* from the marshes. A couple of weeks from now there might be German tanks parked on the village green – mid-September seemed to be everybody's best guess for the invasion – and yet here she was, remembering two children playing in the dark.

She needed Paul, not to talk to – she'd never told him about Toby, never told anybody – no, simply to have him here, his weight and warmth beside her in the bed. As for tonight . . . Well, she had to go back, see it through to the end, there was no choice. But on the landing she paused, still reluctant to go in. Through the half-open door, she saw a halo of soft light around the lamp, her sister's heavy shadow. *Not long now. Please God, not long.*

Six

All the normal routines of the house had broken down, though food – mainly cold meats and salad – still appeared at mealtimes, laid out on the sideboard in the dining room. Elinor and Rachel ate – when they ate at all – in their mother's room. Paul, newly arrived from London, sat in solitary splendour at the dining-room table or, more often, took bread and cheese wrapped in a napkin and went out to sketch on the marshes. He'd responded to Elinor's plea for help; though, in fact, there was very little he could do, apart from just be there when she needed to talk. The only practical, useful thing he could do was spend time with Kenny, who seemed, for some extraordinary reason, to have become quite attached to him.

Returning late one afternoon from a sketching trip, he found Kenny loitering at the end of the drive. He'd been hoping for a visit from his mother, though nobody seemed to know whether he had any reason to expect one.

'Wishful thinking, I'm afraid,' Rachel said. 'I've no patience with the woman. I mean, I know she's probably having a hard time but then, frankly, so are we.'

Paul found the sight of the boy mooching about at the end of the drive almost intolerable. The last bus had been and gone; she wouldn't be coming now – if she'd had any intention of coming at all. Kenny sometimes invented these visits because he wanted them so badly, though there had been times when she'd arranged to come and then just not shown up. 'You all right, Kenny?' Paul asked, turning into the drive. He got a sort of smile in return, though he thought from the boy's swollen eyelids that he might have been crying. *Bloody woman.* He went into the house and poured himself a drink – Tim was still in London – but he couldn't settle so, in the end, he fetched a football from Kenny's room and they spent an hour in the lane behind the house kicking the ball around, using old coats he found in the under-stairs cupboard as goalposts. The sun sank lower in the sky, its blood-red smears widening to a flood, and still they played. Paul's shadow lengthened till it threatened to envelop Kenny, while, at the same time, the boy's shadow fled away.

They played until Paul was too tired to go on. 'Come on, let's go and get something to eat.' Kenny dragged his feet, complaining all the way, but then burst into the hall, eyes glowing, pupils dilated, looking like a little fox cub, with his thin, sharp face and orange hair. He even smelled strong and musky like a wild animal. Paul cut them each a slice of veal and ham pie and settled down to eat. Soon Kenny was yawning uncontrollably, tired out by the misery of his long wait as much as by the football; but at least he'd sleep. Ought to, anyway.

After Kenny had gone upstairs to bed, Paul got his sketchbook out and looked through the drawings he'd done that day, but after a while his eyes became so tired he switched off the lamp and simply sat in darkness, listening to the drone of planes. Somewhere close at hand an owl screeched.

Disturbed by the sight of Kenny loitering at the end of the drive, he'd started to remember going to the asylum to see his own mother, and how, by the end of four years, he'd known every stop on the journey, which always ended with him walking up a long grey corridor towards his mother, who stood waiting at the end. A fat woman in a hideous grey smock. He almost didn't recognize her, she'd put on so much weight. This strange woman, who felt different, looked different, even smelled different, who was always touching him, stroking his hair, fondling him . . . Now, when he didn't need it, when he was merely embarrassed by it. For the most part, he just stood there, putting up with it, but once, and he was almost sure it was the last visit, he just couldn't bear it any more and pushed her away. Really quite hard; she stumbled and might have fallen if his father hadn't caught her.

Had that rejection led directly to her suicide? It had happened not long afterwards. Did it seem to her that since her only child had turned against her there was nothing left worth living for?

No point in asking questions like that. He would never know the truth, and besides, he had, somehow or other, to forgive himself.

After all, he'd been fourteen years old; not a child, admittedly, but certainly not a man. You have to learn not to be too hard on your own younger self. Most of the time he dealt with it by forgetting it. Only Kenny, his obvious misery, his separation from his mother, threatened to disinter these long-buried memories. But there was no point. Absolutely no point at all. Getting up, he poured himself a generous glass of whisky, selected a book at random from the shelves and threw himself on to the sofa to begin reading. He'd go back to the drawings later.

That night, the old woman sank into unconsciousness. There was no question, now, of taking turns in the sickroom; the sisters sat on either side of the bed, each of them holding one of their mother's hands, Rachel, pink and blurry with tears, Elinor, hard and white, defiantly unfeeling. The long hours passed. Mother gave no sign of knowing them. Once Elinor gripped her hand and said: 'Squeeze if you're in pain.' A slight, but unmistakable, pressure in return. So the doctor came to give morphine. And the wait went on. It was like watching a great liner begin to go down, lighted windows darkening one after another. Her breathing had changed; and then, in the last few minutes – only they didn't know they were the last – she started to vomit. They stared at the stains on the sheets. Elinor thought: *That's not vomit; it's shit*. A few minutes later, the death throes started. All her life, Elinor had believed death throes were some kind of poetic invention. Evidently not. The sisters held on to her, talking, trying to think of soothing things to say, until eventually she went slack.

'Is that it?' Rachel was still waiting for the next breath, but the old woman's chest didn't move. They looked at each other; the silence went on . . . 'I think she's gone.'

Rachel went to get Nurse Wiggins, who confirmed what by now they were both beginning to believe. In her deep, inviolable silence, their mother was still the dominant figure in the room. But then, Nurse Wiggins pushed the drooping head back – it had fallen forward so her chin was resting on her chest – and so her mouth fell open. Suddenly, she looked dead. Nurse Wiggins said she'd have to fasten up the jaw. And then there were sheets to be changed, the body to be washed . . .

The sisters sat together on the bed in Rachel's room while the nurse finished the laying-out. Rachel was twisting a handkerchief round and round in her fingers. 'Why is it such a shock? It's not as if we weren't expecting it.'

'Look, why don't you go back to bed and try to get some sleep? It's not as if you can do anything.'

Before parting, they went back to their mother's room. She lay there, grey and remote, penny weights on her eyelids, her jaw bound up with a white cloth. Nurse Wiggins had put a posy of flowers between the clasped, brown-spotted hands. Immediately, Elinor wanted to snatch them away, it seemed so false somehow, but then Mother had always loved flowers. Rachel touched the cooling face and whispered, 'Goodbye, Mum.' Crying, she turned away.

Elinor went to her own room, also grieving, not for what she'd lost, but for what she'd never had, and never could have now. As she climbed into bed, Paul half woke and reached out to her, so she cried in his arms and let him soothe her to sleep.

When, a few hours later, she woke she heard her mother's voice say, as loud and clear as if she'd been in the same room: *I knew*. And from that moment, Elinor ceased to feel anything Rachel, or anybody else for that matter, would have recognized as grief.

The next day she hardly thought at all; she made telephone calls, sent telegrams, worked her way through her mother's address book, coming across the names of relatives and friends dimly remembered from childhood, but often finding, when she set out to contact them, that they'd died years ago. Her mother's eldest sister was so frail she might not be able to make it to the funeral, but her two younger sisters certainly would, along with various other relatives, nieces, nephews and cousins, and then of course there were the grandchildren. Gabriella, though heavily pregnant, had decided she would come. Rachel wanted to keep Mother at home till the funeral – it was the family tradition – but Tim, who'd arrived from London in the early afternoon, said: 'No, not in this heat' – and the undertaker backed him up. So the sisters held on to each other in the drawing room, while the undertaker's men sweated and strained to negotiate the stairs.

A great deal had been achieved in a short time, only now there was emptiness. Mrs Murchison was busy in the kitchen, preparing, for the first time in over a week, a proper sit-down dinner. She'd managed to get river trout for the main course, with potatoes and other vegetables from the garden, and she'd made an apple pie. 'I don't know who she thinks is going to eat *that*,' Elinor said, though Paul thought he might. And no doubt Kenny as well, if he chose to appear. He was being elusive, even by his own impressive standards. The last few days he'd simply raided the kitchen whenever Mrs Murchison's back was turned and eaten whatever scraps of food he managed to find behind the garden shed or out on the marshes. He was becoming almost feral and nobody seemed to give a damn about it except Paul.

When dinner time came, Kenny was, predictably, missing.

'Paul, do you think you could find him?' Rachel asked.

'I thought I heard him come in just now.'

'Well, he's not here.'

Paul went first into the garden and looked up at the sycamore tree. Alex had used this tree as a refuge when he was a boy: the 'safety tree' he used to call it. It interested Paul that Alex, with his privileged background, had felt the same need for a refuge from the adult world as Kenny did, who was so much more obviously disadvantaged. Oh, Paul didn't underestimate the psychological pressures on Alex. Nobody could grow up in Toby Brooke's shadow and not be distorted in some way; deformed, even. Paul's view of Alex was a good deal less favourable than either Rachel's or Elinor's.

'Kenny? Kenny? Dinner time.'

It was growing dark; he'd almost certainly have come in by now. So Paul trailed to the top of the house, knocked on the nursery door and went in. Kenny was kneeling on the floor beside his bed, playing with toy soldiers. He'd laid them out, hundreds of them, khaki and grey, facing each other across No Man's Land: an appropriately mud-coloured stretch of lino. The soldiers had belonged to Alex. As a child, he'd been obsessed with fighting the last war, convinced he could do a better job than the generals. *And who am I to argue?* Paul thought, persuading his stiff leg to bend. But really there was no time to get involved in this particular game. 'Dinner time, Kenny.'

He didn't even look up. 'Too hot.'

'Apple pie? Custard?'

No answer. Paul picked up two of the little soldiers and laid them on the palm of his hand. Officers, wearing the dated uniform of the last war: tunics, peaked caps, breeches, puttees. He remembered the advice supposedly given to German snipers: *Look for the thin knees. Take out the chain of command.* They'd changed the uniform later, made it slightly more difficult to pick out the officers. He felt a sudden impulse to talk to somebody who'd been there; no, not even talk – just be with him. Share what there was to share, in silence. Nobody here he could do that with: certainly not Tim, who'd spent the last war behind a desk in Whitehall.

His silence caught the boy's attention. Kenny was adept at screening out nagging and shouting: he simply didn't hear it. Any more than he heard his own name being called. Attention means trouble, and trouble comes fast enough. But now, looking across the battlefield, Paul found those curious, copper-coloured eyes fixed on him. Purple shadows underneath. He looked tired; tired of life. No child should look like that.

'Who's winning?' Paul asked, searching for a point of contact.

'Us.'

'That's good.'

'You won't tell them, will you?'

'Tell them what?'

'That I got the soldiers.'

Paul was shocked. 'Nobody minds, Kenny. You play with anything you like. It must be really boring, with nobody to play with. At least at school –'

'*School's* boring. I hate it.'

'What about it? What don't you like?'

'The way they pick on us.'

'The other boys?'

'Yeah – and the teachers.'

'Why do you think that is?'

'Dunno. I don't talk like them? And . . .' A sudden, painful, disfiguring blush. 'Me hair.'

'But it's all grown back.'

'Doesn't stop 'em shouting, "Baldy, don't sit by him, he's got nits." '

'You haven't got nits.'

'Doesn't stop 'em saying it.'

'Perhaps if Auntie Rachel went down –'

'You joking? I'd really get me head kicked in then.'

As he spoke he was scooping up handfuls of tiny khaki soldiers and dropping them into a wooden box. Heavy losses for one small square of lino. Perhaps they'd been defending a salient. Paul turned the two little figures over and over in the palm of his hand. Suddenly, he glanced up and saw the boy watching him.

'Were you in it?'

'The war?' Paul looked down at the battlefield. 'Yes.'

'Were you wounded?'

'Ye-es.'

'Whereabouts?'

'Knee. Since you ask.'

'Thought so, you got a limp, haven't you?' He hesitated, but only for a second. 'Can I see?'

'There's nothing to see. And no, you can't.'

'What was it like? Being wounded.'

'Not very nice. Why do you want to know about that?'

'Just interested.'

'But why are you?'

'I like hearing about people getting hurt.'

Oh, do you indeed? 'I was unconscious most of the time.'

'Did you win a medal?'

'No.'

'Why not?'

'I was never very brave.'

The boy looked at him. 'Bet you were.'

'Bet I wasn't.'

Kenny considered this, then unexpectedly laughed. 'I'm going to be a soldier when I grow up.'

'Well, if it goes on long enough you mightn't have much choice.'

'Nah, won't last that long.'

'We said that last time. Oh, unless we get invaded . . . Be over in no time then.'

'Cheerful sod, aren't you?' Another handful went into the box. 'Some people think we already have been.' He glanced cautiously from side to side and whispered: '*Nuns*.'

Oh, yes. Nuns on buses paying the fare with surprisingly masculine hands. 'I shouldn't worry about that, Kenny. It's just a story. Newspapers'll print anything.'

'You could kill one of them if you had a pitchfork.'

'I suppose you could, though you'd need to make sure it wasn't a real nun first.'

'S'easy, you just put your hand up his skirt and see if he's got a willy.'

Mental note: Keep Kenny away from nuns. Suddenly tired of the whole business, Paul heaved himself to his feet. His stiff knee meant he had to get up like a toddler, pushing himself up with his hands, and he didn't like to be watched doing it. Looking down, he saw a neat parting in the orange hair revealing the dead white of the scalp, and felt a stab of pain, for the boy, for himself, for the whole bloody stupid business. 'Come on, now. Dinner time.'

'I've got to wash me hands.' He held them up as proof.

'All right, but *hurry up*.'

Paul went slowly downstairs. Crossing the hall, he stopped in front of Toby Brooke's portrait. Nigel Featherstone, no less. Now why on *earth* was he so successful? He'd never done anything that wasn't completely bland. Perhaps that was why. Who wants disturbing truths in the portrait of a loved one? Elinor's portrait of Toby, though not, in her own view, a complete success, was better than this. It caught something of the reality, the power, of that slim, voracious ghost.

Paul became aware of Kenny standing by his side. 'Now he *was* brave.' Toby, he knew from several accounts, had been a whole lot of things, but brave was certainly one. 'See that?' Paul pointed to the canvas. 'That's the MC, the Military Cross.' He looked down at Kenny, who was staring intently at the medal. 'Come on, they're all in there waiting. You must be hungry; I know I am.'

Putting his hand on the boy's shoulder, he steered him towards the dining room.

Seven

Next day was a Saturday. At eleven o'clock, the vicar came to offer condolences and talk about hymns and readings. Then there were wreaths to be ordered, flowers for the church, cars to be booked – but how many cars? Rooms to be got ready for those who'd need to stay over. And they hadn't even started thinking about food and drink. By mid-afternoon, Rachel was exhausted. The rest would just have to wait, she said. 'You forget how much work there is.'

They decided to have tea on the lawn. All the leaves were limp, folded in on themselves in a desperate attempt to conserve moisture. There was a sweet, sickly smell of rotten apples lying in the grass. Drunken bees toppled from flower to flower.

'Where's Kenny?' Elinor said, resigned to another search.

He'd gone out early with a catapult, a slice of veal and ham pie wrapped in a table napkin, and a bottle of warm, flat lemonade. Nobody had seen him since.

Tim, Elinor and Paul perched on uncomfortable iron chairs and watched the shadows lengthen on the grass. Unmentioned by anybody, but dominating all their thoughts, was the stripped bed that had lately and for so many months held the dying woman. Mrs Murchison carried out the teapot and plates of sandwiches but nobody felt able to start eating. Rachel was still indoors talking to Nurse Wiggins, who'd packed her suitcase and was preparing to depart. They were straining their ears for the sound of her car driving away, which somehow, they all felt, would mark the end of the whole long-drawn-out, miserable episode.

What a small part we play in other people's lives, Paul thought. *How quickly the water closes over us*. And almost immediately realized he didn't believe that at all. He'd been thinking about his mother a lot in the last few months, more than he'd done for years. He was haunted by images of her, some of actual events – the moment in the hospital, when he'd pushed her away – others imagined. Above all, he saw her walking across the mudflats to a tidal river, leaving a trail of footprints behind her. There were other markings too: rats' tails trailing across the mud, leaving lines and curves as indecipherable as the hieroglyphs on an ancient tomb, but carrying, he felt, some urgent hidden meaning, if only they could be understood. No, his mother was certainly not slipping away into oblivion; if anything, his relationship with her had gone on changing. He was older now than she'd ever been, and that realization brought with it a kind of tenderness, as if he were the adult now and she the child. Nothing to be gained by thinking like this. He closed his eyes and let his thoughts dissolve into the orange glow behind his lids.

When he opened them again, Kenny was walking towards him across the lawn.

'Thought so,' Tim said, in that jocular, avuncular way of his. 'Thought his belly would bring him back.'

Kenny flicked a glance at him. Like most of Kenny's glances it seemed exclusively designed to establish that he was not about to be hit, and then he sat down, cross-legged, at Paul's feet. *Why me?* Paul thought, in equal measure flattered and exasperated. Above the creased shirt, the nape of the boy's neck stuck out – a dingy white, and far too thin for the size of his head. He reminded Paul of a baby blackbird: 'gollies', they used to call them. The word brought back bird-nesting trips when he was a boy, Kenny's age or even younger, in the mythic golden summers before the last war.

At that moment they heard Nurse Wiggins's little car puttering away down the drive and Rachel appeared round the corner of the house, puffing her lips out in a pantomime of relief. 'I thought she'd never go.'

'She was all right,' Tim said.

'Oh, I know *you* liked her,' Rachel said.

Elinor shook her head. 'She was all right, but it's never comfortable, is it, having strangers in your house.'

'Servants are strangers,' Tim said.

'Ye-es,' Rachel said, 'but you don't have to treat them as family. The trouble with Wiggins was she was here all the time.'

Paul looked down at the top of Kenny's head, wondering how much of this he was taking in. He was such an obvious cuckoo in the nest himself, but fortunately he didn't seem to be listening.

Rachel and Elinor passed round plates of sandwiches. Tim said: 'Shall I be Mother?' and poured the tea. Wasps kept up their priggish, bad-tempered whine around the jam and sugar bowls. One settled on Rachel's shoulder, causing a huge commotion until Tim picked up a napkin and flicked it away.

Elinor took another napkin and spread it over the gooseberry tart. 'Trouble is they get sleepy. It's nearly always autumn when people get stung.'

Rachel looked surprised. 'It's not autumn.'

'It's September,' Paul said.

For a moment, Rachel looked completely bewildered, and they understood how, for her, the whole summer had been swallowed up in her mother's dying. And immediately the shadows creeping towards them over the grass seemed longer and darker.

'Gooseberry tart,' Rachel said. 'Elinor, could you help Mrs Murchison with the plates?'

The gooseberry tart, cut into huge slabs and drizzled with cream, was amazing: Mrs Murchison had surpassed herself. The wasps certainly thought so. Paul was waiting for somebody to suggest they do the obvious common-sense thing and move indoors; he might have suggested it himself, only at that moment he heard a different kind of buzzing, and, almost simultaneously, the sirens set up their disconsolate wail.

Even then, the little group on the lawn was reluctant to move. Lethargy, caused by the emotional upheaval of the past few days, and the need, shared by everybody this summer, to make the most of every last glimmer of sunshine, kept them pinned to their chairs. Only Paul, who still, so many years after the last war, reacted rather differently from most people, jumped to his feet. Splaying his fingers, he peered through them at the sky. 'My God, look at them.'

A formation of bombers was coming towards them, fighter planes circling around them like gnats. Enemy fighter planes, there to protect the bombers from attack. Nobody moved; reluctant, even now, to take shelter from a threat they only half believed in. There'd been several raids in the last few months, but most of those on the coast; one or two on the outskirts of London. 'Nuisance raids', the papers were calling them, though presumably they were more than a nuisance to the relatives of those who'd been killed.

Elinor was on her feet too now, shielding her eyes. 'I don't think I've ever seen so many.'

'They'll be heading for London,' Tim said. 'For the docks. I suppose I ought to think about getting back.'

Rachel turned on him. 'Why? What on earth can you do about it?'

It seemed impossible the planes should keep on coming, but come on they did. Kenny became tremendously excited and ran round and round the lawn pretending to be a Spitfire, which did rather underline the fact that there were no actual Spitfires in the air.

'Not much resistance, is there?' Elinor said.

'They're waiting.' Tim didn't sound at all confident. 'Being held in reserve.'

'For what?'

Everybody knew something out of the ordinary was happening, but at the same time it seemed unreal, less threatening than the solitary plane that had flown low over the garden only five days ago.

'They'll split up, won't they?' Rachel asked.

Tim shook his head. 'I don't think so, I think this is it.'

Paul looked at Elinor. 'I ought to go back.'

'I doubt you'll be able to,' Rachel said.

'He might,' Tim said. 'All the traffic's going to be coming the other way.'

'What, refugees?' Rachel sounded alarmed.

'Why not? Civilians under fire, there's always the possibility of panic.'

'Well, as long as they don't land on us.'

'Not very patriotic,' Elinor said.

'I've done my bit.'

It was so obvious what Rachel meant they all looked round for

Kenny, but he'd seized the opportunity to take the last two slices of gooseberry tart and was nowhere to be seen.

'I wouldn't have thought there's much point going back tonight.' Tim was looking at Paul. 'It'll be over by the time you get there.'

It was easy, once the drone of bombers had receded, to accept what he said, settle back and enjoy the last of the sun. The shadows now had swallowed more than half the lawn. A single star clung to the topmost branches of the fir tree, and the sky above the distant hill, where the stricken German plane had gone down, was fading to a pale translucent green.

'This is perfect,' Elinor said.

But then, a short time later, a plague of midges descended on bare arms and legs and they were glad to pick up their plates and cups and run for the shelter of the house. Only then, surrounded by the familiar walls and furniture, did the reality of the war reassert itself.

'I wonder if there's any news,' Tim said.

They all gathered round the wireless, while Tim fiddled with the knobs, producing a great buzzing and crackling interspersed with short bursts of music. After a while, he gave up and tried to telephone several people in London, but it was impossible to get through. He was starting to look uneasy. 'I'll drive up in the morning, see what's going on.'

As if that was going to make a difference, they all silently thought. They went through into the drawing room, where they decided the sun had definitely fallen over the yardarm and it was high time they had a drink.

Two glasses of whisky later, Rachel was already slightly slewed. She squinted at Elinor, as if a sea-fret had suddenly blown into the drawing room. 'You're not really going to drive an ambulance, are you?'

'Ye-es.'

'But, Elinor, you can't drive.'

'I can, actually.'

'She's rather good,' Paul said. *Well, decisive, anyway.*

'I simply can't imagine it.'

'They wouldn't let her do it if she wasn't competent.'

Poor Elinor. When he'd first met her family, Paul had been inclined to think her complaints about them were unjustified, but over the years, he'd seen how consistently her mother and sister undermined her, though he didn't quite know why she was singled out for criticism in this way.

Mrs Murchison appeared in the doorway. 'I'm off now, madam.'

'Oh, yes, thank you. Where's Kenny? Is he in bed?'

'I don't know, madam. I thought he was in here with you.'

'I expect he's still in the garden. Elinor . . .?'

'He won't be out there now,' Elinor said. 'It's dark.'

Rachel waved a hand vaguely at the blacked-out window. 'He catches moths.'

'God, yes, and he uses a lamp.' Tim made an unconvincing show of getting out of his armchair. 'We'll have the air-raid warden down on us like a ton of bricks.'

Rachel said, 'Frightful little man, always looking for something he can tell me off about, he just can't wait.'

Paul put his glass down. Elinor said, 'No, look, you stay here, I'll go.'

It was a relief to get out of the house. Rachel had been starting to needle her, as she always did when she'd had a few drinks.

The moonlight and the blacked-out windows behind her made the garden seem a wild, even dangerous, place. She could see the attraction being out here at night would have for a child. At Kenny's age, she and Toby had been great bug hunters: soaking sheets of purple paper in sugar water then arranging them around an oil lamp under the trees. Moths had been Toby's speciality. She remembered herself as a girl in a white dress with moths fluttering all around her, a blizzard of moths, and Toby saying: *'Keep still.'* She froze, instantly, and he pointed to a huge dark moth that was clinging to her chest. He bent to look more closely, his pupils in the lamplight tiny pinpricks of black. 'Do you know, I think it's a Death's Head?' 'I don't care what it is, get it off me.' Jigging up and down, afraid to touch the moth that clung and clung and rubbed its *things* together. 'No, keep still, they're rare.' So she kept still, while he came closer and closer until she could feel his breath on her neck, almost as if he were the moth and she the flame . . .

But it wasn't fair. Middle-aged, now, searching through a moonlit garden for a child who wasn't hers, she wanted to protest: he was older than me. Two years older. How could I possibly have known? Decades too late for that. *Forget*, she told herself. Some things can only be forgotten.

'Kenny?'

No reply. She walked round the side of the house to the gate and looked up and down the lane. The moon was bright enough for her to see the black squares of gun emplacements on the river banks. No guns fired tonight, though; no fighter planes in the sky.

Paul came out of the house. 'Any luck?'

'No, he might just have gone to bed.'

'No, I've checked.' He joined her by the gate. 'I hope the little bugger hasn't run off. Bet he has.'

'No, I don't think –'

'There was too much talk at teatime about the East End being bombed. His mother's there, for God's sake.'

Rachel had come to the door. 'No sign?'

'No.' Elinor was trying not to sound worried.

'He'll have gone to the station,' Paul said.

'Well, he'll be out of luck, then.' Tim, peering over Rachel's shoulder. 'There'll be no trains running tonight.'

'Would he have any money?' Elinor asked.

'*Oh, yes,*' Rachel said.

Tim explained: 'He steals.'

'When did we last see him?' Elinor asked.

On the lawn at teatime, that was the general opinion. Nobody could be more precise than that.

'So he's been gone for hours,' Paul said.

Elinor chafed her bare arms as if the night had suddenly grown colder. 'I think he's still here. He's probably up there now, laughing at us.'

'I'll just check the station,' Paul said.

'Hang on, I'll come with you.'

'No, you stay with Rachel.' He lowered his voice. 'And for God's sake, try to get her to lay off the booze, she's half-cut already.'

'You won't be long?'

'No, you go on in, I'll be all right.'

Reluctantly, she let go of his arm and went back into the house.

Driving down the long tunnel of trees with only the thin beams of blackout headlights to guide him, Paul felt a small sense of relief at getting away from the house and the empty bedroom upstairs. To have something concrete to do – find the little bugger and bring him back – helped enormously. He told himself he wasn't seriously worried: a boy that age couldn't have got far. On the other hand, Kenny wasn't most boys.

At the station, Paul parked in a great spray of gravel and ran on to the platform. Despite Tim's certainty, there might still be some local trains running and if he'd got on one of those he could be anywhere by now. The platform was deserted. Standing on the edge, Paul looked up the line towards London, where an ominous red glow was lighting the underbelly of the clouds. His fear, now – because his fears kept shifting – was that Kenny had come to the station, realized there were no trains, and had simply jumped down on to the track and started walking. That would solve one problem: finding his way. Walk along that line and, yes, you would reach London, in the end. He could be miles away by now. Or – *let's be optimistic* – he might have decided to wait till morning.

Finding the door of the waiting room unlocked, Paul went in and flashed the dim needlepoint of his blackout torch around the walls. Posters advertising day trips to the seaside: children building sandcastles on beaches, buckets, spades, swings, roundabouts: all as innocent and far away as childhood itself. Only one poster, newer than the rest, warned of the dangers of careless talk. No Kenny. It was beginning to look as if he had set off to walk. Paul closed the door and went to the end of the platform. The more he thought about it the more obvious it seemed: Kenny would simply follow the lines.

Paul jumped down on to the track and started to walk, his footsteps loud on the gravel. Moonlight sliding along the rails beside him made him feel as if he were wading through water. He was treading on the heels of his own faint shadow. At the bend in the line, he stopped, the tracks stretching out ahead of him into the far distance. It was pointless to go on, when he didn't even know whether Kenny had chosen this route or not.

He turned and started to go back, but then a movement in the buddleia bushes by the side of the track caught his eye. There was no wind to account for the movement, but it could be an animal, a fox out hunting, though something in the waiting silence felt human. Quickly, he darted up the bank and dragged out a struggling Kenny, a little, yelping, spitting ball of fury who kicked at his shins and, finally, bit his hand. 'Ouch, you little sod.'

Kenny went still. 'I'm not going back.'

'What you going to do, then? Stay here?'

'Getting the train.'

'Not tonight you're not.'

'There'll be one in the morning.'

'All right, then, but what's the point of staying here tonight? When you could be sleeping in your own bed?' A mulish silence. 'Look, why don't we talk about it in the morning? Just let's get you home and –'

The boy wrenched himself free. '*That's* home.' He jabbed his finger at the red glare in the sky.

It was Paul's turn to be silenced. At that moment, he knew he had to take Kenny to see his mother. Not necessarily to stay with her, but at least to see her. 'She'll be all right, you know.'

'No, she won't, she's only got a shelter in the backyard and she won't even go in it.'

'Why won't she?'

'She says she can't breathe, she just –' He shook his head, on the verge of tears.

'Tell you what, come back now and –'

'*No.*'

'*Listen.* I'll take you to see her.'

'Now?'

'No, in the morning, it's too –'

'She could be dead by then.'

Deep breath. 'Kenny, you can't go tonight.'

Kenny heaved a great sigh of resignation, his shoulders dropped and he started to trudge back towards the station.

Paul relaxed. 'There's a good lad.'

Then, without warning, Kenny dodged round him and raced away along the track. *Oh for God's sake*. Paul set off after him, lurching from side to side, gritting his teeth against the pain in his knee – running on gravel was almost impossible. *Mad*, he thought. *And dangerous*. Local trains might still be running and like everything else these days they operated with dimmed lights. If there was one on the other side of the bend, it could be on you before you knew it. And Kenny was already well ahead.

'Kenny, all right!'

The boy looked over his shoulder, tripped and fell. But he was up on his feet again in a minute, brushing gravel from his knees, by the time Paul came panting up.

'You stupid little bugger, if a train had come round that bend you wouldn't've stood a chance.'

'Thought you said there weren't any.'

'*Local* trains.'

'Well, why can't I get on one of them, then, and walk the rest of the way?'

'Because it's *miles*.'

He realized Kenny had no idea where he was, or London was, or – supposing he ever got to London – where the docks were . . . Nothing. Not a bloody thing. And yet, if Paul forced him back to the house, he'd just wait for the first opportunity and run away again. He needed to see his mother.

'Look, all right, we'll go tonight, but you've got to go back and tell everybody, do it properly. Right?'

Kenny nodded. 'You promise, though?'

'I promise.'

'All right.'

They found the family still in the drawing room, slumped in armchairs with the dazed, disorientated look of the recently bereaved and the totally pissed.

'I'm taking him home,' Paul said.

Elinor looked up. 'You mean, to our house?'

'No. Well, yes, that first. Then his.'

She shook her head. 'You can't do that.'

'He wants to go.'

'And that's a reason? Paul, it's mad. Oh, all right, if he wants to see his mother, fair enough . . . But surely it can wait till morning?'

Paul felt the boy's eyes on him. 'No, it's got to be tonight. I promised.'

'Then you shouldn't have done!'

Rachel stood up. 'I'll just pack a few things.'

Holding on to the backs of chairs, she made it to the door. She was making no effort to postpone their departure, nor even to assert her right to take the decision. The truth was, she was as keen to get rid of Kenny as he was to go. And Tim said nothing. It was all rather disgraceful, but it did at least confirm Paul's view that the boy would be better off with his own family. While Rachel moved around upstairs, Paul and Elinor stood a few feet away from each other, Elinor with her bare arms clasped across her chest, Paul smoking furiously.

'You will ring when you get there?' she asked.

'If I can get through.'

A few minutes later, Rachel came down with a small battered suitcase, the same one Kenny had arrived with a year ago, though the clothes inside were all new. She'd given him a few *Boy's Own* annuals and the toy soldiers. Kenny's eyes widened when he opened the paper bag and saw them.

'What do you say?' Elinor asked.

'Thank you.'

He was hugging them to his chest as if they might be taken back at any moment.

'Come on, then,' Paul said.

Kenny went round the circle, shaking hands. 'Thank you for having me.'

It was an oddly stilted performance, heart-breaking in a way. It brought tears to Paul's eyes. Perhaps Kenny had, after all, grown fond of this family who'd taken him in so reluctantly?

But he didn't look back or wave as they drove away.

Eight

As they were leaving the village, Paul glanced sideways at Kenny. 'I'd try to get some sleep if I were you. It's a long way.'

But Kenny was wide awake, both hands resting on the seat, surreptitiously stroking the leather. Of course, he wouldn't have been in a car very often, if at all. Even in these circumstances it was a treat to be savoured. He leaned against the glass, peering at passing trees and fields. Once or twice, Paul thought he might have nodded off, but no. Kenny's eyes were strained wide with excitement. No hope of sleep there.

He didn't seem to want to talk, which was probably just as well: Paul needed to concentrate on the road. So far, he'd managed to avoid blackout driving altogether. In London, if he had to be out late, he took a taxi or walked. Now, he drove slowly, his headlights casting narrow beams of bluish light in which moths and insects constantly danced. On either side of the lane, hedges and ditches shelved steeply into darkness. He crouched over the wheel, straining his eyes to see into the gloom. So far the blackout had killed more people than the raids; and no wonder: you couldn't see people until you were right on top of them. But the trouble with staring into darkness, if you do it long enough, is that you start seeing things. Like looking into No Man's Land in the last war: in the end, you could imagine anything lurking out there. *Don't look straight at it*, he used to tell sentries, the young, inexperienced ones who were almost too terrified to blink. *You'll see more if you look slightly to one side*. Unfortunately, looking slightly to one side of the road wasn't an option. Though there was this to be said for it: the need to concentrate stopped him thinking about the possible idiocy of what he was doing. *Possible?* Elinor might have asked. And he had to admit it: this did feel like driving into a trap.

He looked at Kenny. *Ha*, eyelids drooping, and about time too.

He went on driving as smoothly as he could until, at the next bend, the boy slid sideways and slumped against his arm. Asleep, at last.

Central London was reassuring. The streets, though quiet, seemed almost normal, or what passed for normal these days. The few cars he saw had little, piggy, red eyes; they puttered cautiously along, while taxis careered past, as if they owned the entire city – as indeed they did. Petrol rationed for private cars, buses scarce. This was what you saw everywhere. The change was in the sky: beyond the black ridges of the rooftops, a red, sullen glare was growing and spreading, lit at intervals by the orange flashes of exploding bombs. Searchlights everywhere, but no fighter planes that he could see; and no guns.

He parked the car and persuaded Kenny to get out. At first the boy was groggy with sleep, but Paul knew he'd need to keep an eye on him. Kenny was wound up to such a pitch of excitement he was quite capable of slipping away and trying to reach home tonight. He'd have no trouble finding the docks; all he'd have to do was walk straight towards that red glow. But into what kind of hell?

Paul tried several times to turn the front-door key, but it no longer quite fitted. Perhaps the wood had warped, something like that; you couldn't get a locksmith for love nor money. He sucked the key, pursing his lips against the sourness of the metal, but when he tried again, it turned. A breath of cool, stale air. The house had been empty only a few days and yet already it had started to forget them. Letters and newspapers littered the mat. Stooping, he picked them up and put them, unopened, on the hall table. Kenny stepped over the threshold as cautiously as a cat. Now the drive was behind him, Paul felt suddenly very tired.

Closing the door on the merciless moonlight, he went round the drawing room checking the blackout curtains were in position and switching on the lamps. Then he turned to look at Kenny, who was staring blankly around the strange room. *Now what? What on earth am I supposed to do with him?* The sirens were sounding for the second time that night. They ought, really, to go to one of the public shelters, but he couldn't face going out again and he didn't think Kenny could either.

'We'll sleep in the hall,' he said. 'We'll be safe enough there.' A few weeks ago, when the nuisance raids started, he and Elinor had dragged a double mattress downstairs. They'd lined the walls with other mattresses and cushions from the sofa and he'd made sure all the windows were taped against blast. Of course, none of this would protect them from a direct hit, but then neither would most of the shelters. 'Why don't you settle yourself down? I'll see if I can find us something to eat.' *And drink.*

In the kitchen, he opened and shut cupboards, found half a loaf of bread (stale, but it would have to do), a couple of wizened apples, a slab of Cheddar just beginning to sweat and a bottle of orange juice. Then he poured himself a large whisky and carried the tray into the hall.

Kenny had tipped the toy soldiers out of the bag and was arranging them on a strip of wooden floor between the mattress and the drawing-room door. He looked up, white-faced, on the verge of tears again but blinking them back hard. 'Why can't we go tonight?'

'Because it'll be absolute chaos and we'll only get in the way.'

'We could help.'

'I don't think so. Anyway, I doubt they'd let us anywhere near.' Thumps and bangs in the distance. 'Look, I'll take you first thing in the morning, soon as it's light. Sorry, Kenny, best I can do.' A nearer thud shook the door. 'Come on, have something to eat, it'll make you feel better.'

Kenny was tearing off a chunk of bread with his teeth. 'We could play.'

'Play?'

Kenny nodded towards the soldiers. Well, why not? It would take his mind off it. So they munched apples, cheese and bread, drank whisky and orange juice, moved cohorts of little figures here and there until, eventually, even Paul became absorbed in the game. The background clumps and thuds blended in really rather well. Kenny was the officer, of course. Paul was a not-very-bright NCO. Now and then, an explosion rattled the window frames – and, yes, he was afraid. Nothing like the fear he'd experienced in the trenches; though, in one way, it was worse: he was experiencing this fear in the safety of his own home, and that meant nowhere was safe. More than once, he was tempted to go out and try to see what was happening, but he didn't want to interrupt the game – it was so obviously helping take Kenny's mind off the bombs – and so they played on, metal armies advancing across strips of parquet floor, rather more quickly than they'd done in life; Passchendaele and the Somme played out on the floor of a house in Bloomsbury. 'Yes, sir!' Drifting clouds of smoke obscured the salient. 'Right you are, sir!' A shell landing in a flooded crater sent sheets of muddy water thirty feet into the air. 'Going out to take a look, now, sir!'

Kenny would have to sleep soon, his eyes were rolling back in his head, but my God he fought it. Finished his orange juice, asked for more . . . This time, Paul tipped a little whisky into the glass and, although Kenny wrinkled his nose at the funny taste, he drank it all down and shortly afterwards curled up on the mattress and went to sleep.

Paul began to clear the soldiers away, then stopped, selected two and looked at them, lying side by side on the palm of his hand. Somehow, last time he'd seen them, he hadn't quite realized what it meant. *My God*, he thought. *We've become toys.* He wanted to share the moment, the shock of it, but there was nobody who'd understand.

He slipped the little figures into his pocket, lay down beside Kenny and went to sleep.

In the middle of the night, Kenny woke up and shook Paul's arm. 'You hear that?'

Paul struggled to wake up; he must've gone very deep, he could hardly force his eyes open. They lay listening to the thuds until one blast louder than the rest made Kenny cry out. He was too big to ask for reassurance, too young not to need it. Paul touched his arm. 'Don't worry, it's all right.'

'Is it true, you don't hear the one that hits you?'

'*Yes.*' Said very firmly indeed, though he'd certainly heard the shell that had hit him; he'd heard it shrieking all the way down. Still did.

Kenny was sitting up, wide-eyed, quivering like a whippet at the start of a race. 'Can we go now?'

'Soon as it's light.'

'What time is it?'

'Three thirty. Come on, go back to sleep.'

'I can't sleep.'

Nor could Paul.

'You know, we mightn't be able to get there. There won't be any buses or taxis. And I'm not driving through that.'

'We can walk.'

No point arguing. And anyway he didn't know. No more than Kenny could he guess what they would have to face. 'Well, I'm going back to sleep,' he said. 'And if you've got any sense at all you'll do the same.'

He turned on his side and lay in darkness, waiting for the change in Kenny's breathing. Only when he was sure Kenny was asleep did he let his own eyes close.

The All Clear went at four thirty. Kenny woke instantly, alert and wary, more like an animal than a child. Paul fetched the last of the orange juice for Kenny and two cups of black tea, one for each of them. 'Here, drink this. No, I know it doesn't taste very nice but you need something hot.'

Paul stepped across the mattress and opened the front door; his eyes, gritty with tiredness, flinched from the sudden light. Yet another monotonously blue sky, but over there above the docks, the red glow lingered, mixed in with plumes of billowing black smoke. Even at this distance he could smell burning.

Kenny joined him on the step. 'Look,' Paul started to say, wanting to warn him again that it mightn't be possible to get anywhere near his house, but the words dribbled into vacancy before the boy's fixed, hard stare. He was going, no question; no hope of deflecting him either.

'Come on,' Paul said. 'Let's get your case.'

A cabbie agreed to take them part of the way. When a warden waved at them to turn back, Paul and Kenny got out and walked for a while before Paul begged a lift in an ambulance from Derek James, one of the drivers Elinor worked with.

Oily black smoke drifted across the wet roads. Many of the warehouses were still on fire, dwarfing the exhausted crews who still, hour after hour, directed white poles of water into the heart of the blaze. Other buildings had been reduced to charred and smouldering ruins in which, at any moment, you felt a fire could break out again. So many streets lay in ruins he couldn't understand how Kenny was finding his way, and yet he rarely hesitated. Bodies lay by the side of the roads, lifeless, sodden heaps of rags. No child should be seeing this, but then, some of the bodies were children.

Once, he tried to persuade Kenny to turn back, but the boy just shook his head, 'No, no, it's just along here.' He grabbed Paul's sleeve and started dragging him along. He had such a strange, haunted look on his face that Paul was frightened for him, though at least the intensity of his drive to get home seemed to prevent his taking in the horrors on either side. They were walking along the river now, or as close to it as they could get. On the opposite bank, a wall of flame half a mile long leapt into the lowering sky. In midstream, burning barges, loose from their moorings, drifted hither and thither with the shifting of the tide.

Ahead of them a cluster of little terraces, still apparently more or less intact, ran up to the dock gates, like a row of piglets suckling a sow's teats. As they got closer, they saw that most of the houses were badly damaged and a few had collapsed altogether, leaving gaps through which further destruction showed. 'Kenny . . .'

'No, it's not far. Just along there.'

As they turned into the first street Paul heard Kenny's intake of breath. It seemed, at first sight, as though all the houses had been hit. Kenny began to run, weaving his way around piles of rubble until at last he stopped in front of one of the houses. The windows had been blown in, a mattress hung out of an upstairs room, most of the roof had gone. Paul tried to push the front door open. It was a struggle – the door was jammed shut by debris from a fallen ceiling – but he managed it at last.

Kenny pushed past him and was clambering across the mess of bricks and plaster in the passage.

'Don't,' Paul called out. 'It's not –'

Safe, he had been going to say, but the word meant nothing here. He followed Kenny into the devastated sitting room, through the almost-untouched kitchen and out into the yard at the back. Fleeting glimpses along the way of where and how Kenny had lived.

'Mam?' Kenny was calling. 'Mam?'

A body was lying outside the coalhouse door, a woman's body, face down, and for a moment Paul thought: *Oh God it's her*, but Kenny paid it no attention. Further along, by the yard door, a man's head rested on the concrete, severed neatly at the neck, one eye closed. Kenny pushed it to one side with his foot and opened the door into the alley. A big jump down and he was on the cobbles, staring up and down a row of washing lines, from some of which, incredibly, shirts and pillowcases still hung. Dazed-looking people were wandering up and down, lost, waiting for somebody to get hold of them and tell them where to go. A few, braver or harder than the rest, were rescuing their possessions from ruined houses, carrying tables and chairs into the alley and setting them down, with sheets and blankets and pots and pans, small heaps of possessions fiercely guarded. Somebody had stuck a Union Jack on a pile of rubble, but most of these people were too exhausted and shocked for gestures of that kind.

Kenny looked around him. 'It's all gone.'

Paul opened his mouth, but had no idea what to say. He was about to suggest that Kenny should come back inside the house, when, at the far end of the street, they saw a woman walking towards them with a baby in her arms. Kenny ran towards her shouting, 'Mam! Mam!' She stopped, but then came on more quickly. Her clothes were black and torn, her face blackened too. She might even be burnt, Paul thought. At any rate she'd lost her eyebrows. She looked dully at Kenny. 'Oh, it's you.'

A dark-haired, cadaverous man with yellow skin and deep furrows in his cheeks followed along behind, holding a tiny red-haired girl by the hand. 'What you doing here?'

Kenny ignored this and went on tugging at the woman's sleeve, but she shook him off. It's the shock, Paul thought, she'll be all right in a minute, and indeed, a few seconds later, she pressed the boy's head against her side and ran her fingers distractedly through his hair. But then, immediately, she looked accusingly at Paul. 'What you brought him back for? I can't have him – you can see for yourself there's nothing left.'

'Kenny.' Paul put his hand on the boy's shoulder but he squirmed away and burrowed his head deeper into his mother's side. 'Your mam's right. I think you'd better come back with me, just till your mam gets a bit more settled.'

'I'm not going.' He looked up at his mother. 'You can't make me go with him, he's been mucking me about.'

It took Paul a moment to realize what he meant. 'You little toad. You know bloody well that's not true.'

'Mam, it is, Mam. He's been putting whisky in me orange juice and all sorts. Ask him. No, go on, ask him. *And* we slept in the same bed last night.'

'Kenny? No-o, Kenny, look at me, look me in the eye and say it, go on.' When there was no response, Paul looked directly at the mother. 'It's not true.'

'No, I know, it's all right, he's always making things up.' She leaned in closer. With a slight shock he saw the moist, puckered anemone of the baby's mouth tugging at a huge brown nipple. Almost whispering, she said, 'The thing is, he doesn't get on with his stepdad.' She glanced over her shoulder, then made a sharp, sideways gesture with her free hand: *hopeless*.

The cadaverous man was starting to take an interest in the conversation – perhaps thinking there might be a fiver in it for him, if he played his cards right. And why not? Plenty of girls, and not a few boys, changed hands for a lot less than that. This was not quite the family reunion Paul had been expecting.

'Where are they taking you?' he asked.

'I don't know.' She looked helplessly at a small crowd that was gathering a few feet away at the end of the alley.

'School on Agate Street!' somebody shouted.

'Is it far?' Paul called back.

''Bout a mile.'

A hell of a distance for these shattered people – some injured, some with minor burns, many in pyjamas and dressing gowns – to walk. He looked down at their feet. Not all of them had shoes; some limped over the cobbles, blood-shod.

He turned back to Kenny's mother. 'Look, I'll help you carry.' He was desperate to do something, anything.

'I've got a suitcase packed,' she said.

So Paul followed her into the house and dragged it out of its hiding place under the stairs. God knows what she'd got in there. Lifting it almost wrenched his arm out of the socket, but he wasn't going to give in. If they could bear this, so could he.

Air-raid wardens, white-faced with plaster dust, had already started shepherding the crowd along.

So they walked. And what a rabble they were. Red eyes stared out of grey faces; some ranted and raved, others were hysterical or mute with shock. He'd witnessed all these reactions in Casualty Clearing Stations in France and Belgium, only he'd never thought to see them here. *London's burning, London's burning* . . . Bloody tune skittered round and round his brain as he lugged and tramped, try as he might he couldn't get rid of it, so he made himself look outwards, to notice and remember.

They walked along rubble-strewn roads, through puddles of water filmed with oil, over fire hoses that lay across the black and glistening pavements as grey and flaccid as drowned worms. On their right, buildings blazed out of control; others, black and skeletal, wavered in the heat. Once, looking ahead, he saw the tarmac come to life and move. He thought it must be a trick of the light then realized it was a colony of rats, thousands of them, fleeing a burning warehouse. Sometimes the ground underfoot was hot and the people whose feet were lacerated or burned cried out as they limped across it. The really terrifying thing, the one he knew he'd never forget, was when the road behind them suddenly ignited in a long, slow, leisurely lick of flame.

The things people carried. An old lady's wrinkled forearms covered in claw marks, beaded with blood. A tabby cat, its pupils wildly dilated, peered out from the neck of her dressing gown. A clock.

Photographs – yes, of course you'd try to save those, but a black hand grasping a bunch of plastic lilies of the valley? Or an elephant's tusk in a brown leather sling?

At last they reached the school. After twenty minutes' hanging about, they were guided down into the basement. They found a place by the wall and Paul was finally able to relinquish the suitcase and chafe his hands to get the blood flowing again. 'I'll see if I can find out what's going on.'

Pushing his way through the crowd, he saw how packed the basement was. The smell of hot human bodies mingled with the fumes from oil lamps snagged in his throat. Wardens were setting up latrine buckets behind a screen of blankets, men one end of the corridor, women the other, though how people were supposed to get to them through the crush . . . He spoke to one of the wardens who said buses were coming to take everybody away that afternoon. 'Where to?' The man didn't know; nobody knew. But it was some consolation to know they weren't going to have to endure these conditions for more than a couple of hours.

When he got back Kenny's mother was sitting on the suitcase feeding the baby, a tiny, wizened little mite with a bright orange face and a shock of straight black hair. Two weeks old, apparently, and he hadn't been due till mid-October. Looking away to give her some privacy, Paul caught the expression on Kenny's face. Love? Yes, that certainly. But also the pain of exclusion. A gap of twelve years or more between him and these children, and that sallow-skinned, silent man was very obviously not his father. Had they sent him to the country for his own safety, or because the family worked better without him there?

All around them people were settling down, arranging bags and coats, staking out small territories, though as more and more people pushed down the stairs these fragile boundaries were being continually breached. 'Where are we going?' was the question on everybody's lips. 'Where are they taking us?' But there were no answers from the wardens or anyone else, only offers of more tea. Nobody knew. People were guessing Kent, the hop fields, where there was accommodation for migrant workers. 'I've had some good holidays there,' Kenny's mother said. The thought of the hop fields seemed to cheer her up. She really didn't look at all well.

More and more people crammed themselves into the airless space. Many people had lit cigarettes and a bluish pall of smoke hung on the stagnant air. The wardens shouted at them to put them out, but only a few did. Along with sweat, cigarette smoke, dirty nappies and latrine buckets, were all the smells they'd brought with them on their clothes: burnt brick, charred wood, the carrion stench of high explosive. Paul's chest was tightening all the time, but he didn't feel he could just walk away.

He found the chief warden and offered to help with first aid, though with no clean water or bandages there was very little he or anybody else could do. Wardens and voluntary workers were everywhere, trying to help, but the press of bodies defeated them. By now, moving was almost impossible. No Underground train at the height of the rush hour had ever been as packed as this. He could see Kenny and his mother, who now had the grizzling toddler in her arms, at the other end of the main corridor, but there was no hope of reaching them. He pointed to the stairs, mouthing: *Got to go*. Kenny raised his hand to wave goodbye, then turned to his baby sister, who stopped crying and held out her arms.

At first, getting upstairs against the crush of people surging down seemed impossible, but then somebody at the top started organizing those coming down on to the left. Paul and another warden edged up step by step, persuading people to move to one side. At the top of the stairs Paul looked around for somebody in authority. An exhausted little man with a grey, bristly moustache bleated, 'What am I supposed to do? They can't stay up here, it's not safe.'

When, finally, Paul struggled out of the playground into the street he held on to the railings and watched the stream of the shocked and homeless going through the gates. It wasn't all bad. That basement was deep enough to withstand even a direct hit. But then, just as he was about to leave, he noticed the building was already bomb-damaged. One wall had a crack running from the roof down to the ground. Immediately, he wanted to go back and get them out, but it was impossible and anyway they'd be all right, the buses would be here in another hour, the wardens would get everybody organized and they'd be off to Kent, and safety. And Kenny was back with his mother, where he'd wanted, and needed, to be.

Nine

Back at the house he picked his way across the mattress in the hall, remembering Kenny's outrageous accusation: And *we slept in the same bed last night*. It was difficult not to feel a certain reluctant admiration for the boy's single-minded and utterly unscrupulous determination to get what he wanted. *Little toad*.

He ought really now to go straight to his studio and start work but he was finding it unusually difficult. That walk with the suitcase had taken a lot out of him. So he went out, bought milk and bread and made himself a pot of tea and toast. He was just finishing the last mouthful when he heard the front door open.

'Elinor?'

It had to be: the only other person who had a key was the housekeeper, who'd gone to stay with her sister in Dorset and God alone knew when she'd be back. He went upstairs to the ground floor and found Elinor in front of the hall mirror, unpinning her hat. She raised her cheek for him to kiss.

'This is a surprise.'

'Yes, Tim gave me a lift; I thought it was too good an opportunity to miss. And I need some more clothes anyway.'

'Oh, you're going back?'

She pulled a face. 'Well, I've got to, really. I can't leave Rachel to do it all.'

'I thought Gabriella was supposed to be coming?'

'Yes, but she's eight months pregnant. She's not going to be doing a lot of running around. Where's Kenny?'

Paul looked surprised. 'With his mother.'

'So you took him back?'

'Well, yes, of course. That was the point.'

'Are they all right?'

'So-so. The house was bombed, but they're being evacuated this afternoon.'

'Was she pleased to see him?'

That was not a comfortable question. It forced him to weigh his impressions. 'No, not very. I don't think he gets on with his step-father and she's got two younger children.'

'And she kept them with her?'

'Well, yes, obviously.'

'I wonder what Kenny thinks about that.'

'He doesn't seem to fit in, but on the other hand, he obviously loves them.'

'I don't think you should've taken him back.'

'He wanted to go.'

'He's a *child*. Anyway, it wasn't your decision.'

'No, it was Rachel's. And Tim's. Tim said bugger-all and Rachel couldn't wait to see the back of him.'

She turned back to the mirror and started fluffing up her hair where the hat had flattened it.

'You think it was about me, don't you? *My* mother?'

She met his eyes in the glass. 'Wasn't it?'

The conversation disturbed Paul. Kenny had wanted more than anything to be back with his mother. Wasn't that justification enough? He remembered the way her soot-blackened arm had come round to press his head into her side. No, absolutely, he didn't regret it. A lot of this uneasiness was no more than the shapeless anxiety that comes from extreme tiredness, and he couldn't afford to give in to it. He was on duty tonight, and the next night. And the next. No, he'd taken the decision, and now he just had to forget about it and move on.

By the end of the second night on duty tiredness had become another dimension. He snatched an hour or two of dozing on the bed between coming off duty and walking round to his studio, but during the long, golden, sludgy afternoon he had to force himself to go on painting; it was dangerous even to think about sleep.

On the morning after his third night, he was standing in the kitchen, drinking a cup of hot sweet tea and idly flicking through the newspapers. There was a certain grim fascination in seeing how officialdom packaged the destruction of the night before. He was about to turn a page when a headline about a direct hit on a school in the East End caught his eye. Seventy-three people dead. Well, there must be hundreds of schools in the East End. Under the headline there was a grainy photograph of the ruined building with a heap of rubble breaking through iron railings on to the pavement. *Was* that Agate Street? Well, even if it was, Kenny and his family would have long since moved on.

He opened the door, intending to walk round to his studio as he did every morning. Another fine day, though the smell of burnt brick dust tainted the bright air. Further along the street, an old man was sweeping up the first of the autumn's fallen leaves, a sight you saw every year around this time, only this September the familiar rustle was sharpened by the scratching of broken glass. If you closed your eyes, it sounded exactly like waves seething between the pebbles of a shingle beach. Only he daren't close his eyes. Even the action of blinking brought with it the strong, dark undertow of sleep.

A crowd had gathered at the entrance to a side street, people who'd spent the night in shelters returning to find access to their homes denied. He looked across the road. From where he stood, the tape cordoning off the street was invisible, so the people seemed to be pressed against a glass wall – like insects splatted across a windscreen. Lured by the attraction of that forbidden space, he crossed the road and stared up the empty street. At first nobody spoke, and then a few whispers began to break the cathedral hush. There was a time bomb in the street. Nobody was allowed to go home and, after the long night in a cramped, foul-smelling shelter, that was hard. Some of the group were in pyjamas and dressing gowns; one of the women had thrown a mackintosh over her nightdress. An old lady with her hair in thin, grey plaits was trembling with shock, or perhaps it was just the general frailty of age, and yet she seemed positively cheerful; defiant, even. She touched his sleeve – her hand as skeletal as a dead leaf on a bonfire, but God how she crackled and sparked as the flames licked round her. 'That's my house,' she said, pointing. 'The one with the blue door.'

It was odd; when he'd crossed the road to join the little group staring into the sunlit silence of the cordoned-off street, he'd fully intended going to his studio to do a normal day's work, and yet, minutes later, as he turned away, he knew he had to go to Agate Street. At the corner of the road, he turned and looked back. There they still were, haloed in light, as if the air had somehow solidified in front of them. How would you paint them – convey that sense of suspended motion – or of an infinitely slow, noiseless collision – when there was nothing visible to account for it?

He took a taxi as far as he could, then walked. All around were signs of last night's destruction. A burst water main with a group of boys egging each other on to run through it, their shrieks, sharp as seagulls' cries, slicing the crisp air. Further along, he passed a broken shop window with mannequins inside, all prudishly shrouded in brown paper, one leaning out into the street, arm and wrist elegantly posed, smirking at devastation. All the time, now, you noticed these oddities. What survived; what didn't. And that first feeling of indecency at peering into other people's lives – their bedrooms, their bathrooms, their toilets – had already begun to fade.

As he walked, he thought not about Kenny – he still felt there was no real reason for anxiety – but about that cordoned-off street, the way a perfectly ordinary road acquired, merely because access to it had been denied, an air of mystery. He remembered looking through a periscope into No Man's Land: the inhabitation of rats and eels, and of the corpses, submerged in flooded craters, whose slow, invisible decomposition sent strings of bubbles spiralling to the surface. But, no, that wasn't it. It wasn't the obvious horrors that made the hairs on the nape of your neck stand up. It might be a country lane: not bombed, not devastated, pretty, even; but a lane you couldn't walk down, because it was enemy territory. And that lane, merely by being forbidden, acquired depth, mystery and terror. It seemed shocking to him that now there were streets and squares in

London that aroused the same prickling of unease. He'd never before felt that he wanted to paint London, or any other built-up area, and yet those roped-off, silent squares and streets had started to haunt him. Perhaps because blacked-out and bombed London felt less and less like a city?

Agate Street wasn't difficult to find. A corkscrew of black smoke twined into the sky above it, almost like a question mark reversed. This was the school in the photograph. Even before he turned the corner, he knew that.

Despite the coil of smoke, the fire service must have declared the building safe, because teams of rescue-squad workers, wearing overalls and tin hats, were clambering over a scree of rubble, slipping and slithering as they tried to get a footing. The school seemed to have imploded; there was a crater at the centre where the roof had crashed through on to the floors below. Whoever had been in the basement when the upper floors collapsed was dead now. Nobody could have survived tons of brick landing on them like that.

The scene in front of Paul was oddly static. Heat and dust everywhere, but no sense of urgency. The rescue workers with their covering of white dust might have been carvings on an antique frieze: a funeral procession, though, not a wedding feast. There was no sound. Four ambulances were parked by the side of the road, the drivers leaning against their vehicles, smoking, occasionally wiping sweat from foreheads or lips. They looked as if they'd been there for hours.

Still wearing his warden's coat and tin hat, Paul ducked under the tape and strode confidently towards the ambulances. A tin hat could take you almost anywhere. Close to, it was obvious the drivers had been there all night. Red-eyed, exhausted, stubble sprouting from their chins, lips parched from the long hours of chain-smoking, none of them looking as if they expected to be going anywhere in the next few hours. As he approached, the door of one of the vehicles opened and a figure he recognized jumped down on to the road. Derek James.

'My God,' Paul said. 'They're keeping you busy.'

'Twelve bloody hours I've been stuck here.'

'What's happening?'

'You can see what's happening – bugger-all.' He fished a packet of Woodbines from his pocket and offered it. 'What you doing here anyway?'

'You know that lad I was with when you gave us a lift – Sunday?'

'Yeah?'

'Well, it turned out his house had been bombed and they were sent here.' He could tell from James's face that something was wrong. 'That was Sunday. They were just waiting for the buses to take them away.'

'Bloody long wait.'

Paul stared at him.

'They didn't come. Apparently, there was some mix-up over the address, Canning Town, Camden Town, God knows. And then, when they finally did show up, a raid started so they decided to post-pone the evacuation. They were still here last night.'

'But that's three days.'

James shrugged. 'Another bloody cock-up. They've had years to get this right. *Years*.'

Paul pictured Kenny and his family at the end of the crowded corridor, how at the last moment the little red-haired girl had turned and held out her arms. 'How many?'

'They're saying seventy-three.'

Paul twisted sharply to one side. 'I was *there*, it was bloody well jam-packed.'

James said, slowly: 'To begin with you could hear them crying out . . . You know? And every now and then they'd call for silence and everybody stopped and listened, and then the last time . . .' He shook his head. 'Mind, we did get two babies out. Tough little bug-gers, babies.'

'Nobody else?'

'Not that I saw.'

The rescue squads had started gathering in small groups around their leaders, the men who'd been climbing across the rubble sliding down and walking across to join them.

James nodded. 'I think they're calling it.'

'What, pulling out?'

'What else can they do? It's going to take weeks to clear that lot. Hundreds of bodies, this heat?'

He was right, of course. Every night these rescue squads were needed to dig out people who could still be saved. How could you possibly justify using them to retrieve dead bodies? No, the only thing to do with this was cement it over. Walk away. Paul patted James's shoulder and walked across to the railings. Now he was closer to the building, he noticed a smell that was not the stench of high explosive. The rescue workers wore masks against the plaster dust, but others, this side of the railings, were pinching their noses and covering their mouths with their hands. No, James was right, that was all you could do, declare it a mass grave. But my God . . . All those people. Kenny, the little girl, the baby. Kenny.

Resting his forehead against the railings, Paul realized he was looking at the small area of playground that was clear of rubble. Somebody, perhaps a teacher but more likely a child, had chalked out squares for a game of hopscotch. He saw, for a moment, with the clarity of hallucination, a stick of yellow chalk gripped in a small, pudgy hand.

Blinking the image away, he looked instead at the wrecked building and above it to the sky, where the corkscrew of black smoke was beginning to change shape. Again, he saw Kenny raise his hand and wave; again the little girl stretched out her arms, while flakes of soot, whirled around on the slight breeze, fell on to his upturned face like snow.

Ten

Crappit heid. Dear God, fancy being reduced to that after all these years. Fishmonger just now give her a funny look – you'd think it was in his own best interest to be civil, wouldn't you, but oh, no. Just stood there in his straw hat and his white coat, fag end stuck to his bottom lip, bloody great turd of ash ready to drop – *and* he was leaning over the fish. 'Cod's head?' he asked. She felt like saying: *You want the business or not?* Didn't, of course, just raked about in her purse for the coppers and handed them across. As she walked away, she felt his gaze stitched to her back, though when she turned round she saw he'd already moved on to the next customer, wasn't watching her at all.

She was sat on a bench in Russell Square on this September afternoon because she didn't know what the fuck else to do. In prison the only fresh air you got was an hour in the exercise yard every day, and even then all you did was trudge round and round, nothing much to look at except the wobbling backside of the woman in front. Still, on the inside, there were people all round you, you could hear them and see them even if you didn't talk to them, and then she come out and there was nobody. Oh, she could've gone back up north, set herself up again in a small way, people's front rooms, that type of thing – she didn't want to go attracting attention to herself. She knew she was going to have to be very, very careful.

So, in the end, she decided she'd make a complete break of it. Plenty of work in London, masses – *and* it was easy reach of the south coast. That's where the real money was, the ports, only she didn't want Gladys and Mrs Buckle getting their fingers in the pot – bloodsuckers, the pair of 'em – so she told them she was packing it in altogether. 'Can't face it without Howard,' she'd said.

'What about Albert?' Gladys asked.

'What about him?'

'What's he going to do?'

'Oh, he'll move on.' Stubborn silence. 'You know as well as I do, Gladys, spirit guides do move on.'

Albert hadn't. He was in and out all the time. Mind you, she hadn't dared risk the ports, though it was a big temptation, that lot at the Temple paid her a pittance. Absolute bloody disgrace, the amount they gave her. She filled the house – they didn't. Hence the frigging cod's head.

Which didn't half pong. Probably ponged a bit herself, to be honest, in this heat. God, it was hot. She could feel the sweat soaking through her dress shields, and the Vaseline she rubbed into her thighs to stop them chafing had long since melted into a claggy mess. No fun being fat this weather – and totally unfair, too. The amount she ate she should be thin as a rake, 'stead of which she was piling it on. It upset her, sometimes, the size she was. So to cheer herself up she started singing. 'Wider still and wider, shall my bounds be set . . .' She was on stage, now, at the Alhambra, belting it out: 'God, who made me mighty, make me mightier yet . . .' Waving her trident at the audience. 'God who made me mighty, MAKE ME MIGHTIER YET!'

She looked around – people always seemed to think it a bit odd when you sang like that – and saw a tall, thin man, with a limp, approaching. Not bad looking, coat a bit shabby, but his shoes were good and he'd given them a bit of a polish. She noticed the limp, she always picked up on things like that, last war, probably, but it wasn't just the limp making him wobbly on his pins. Bugger was pissed, had to be. She pursed her lips disapprovingly, thinking of the bottle of gin under her kitchen sink. Never touched a drop of it before six o'clock. Eh, dear me, the state people let themselves get into. She hoped he wasn't going to sit near her, but, of course, Sod's law, he did.

He was a funny colour, mind. 'You all right?'

'Yes, I'm – all right. Went a bit dizzy there for a minute.'

'Be the heat.'

He agreed that yes, very probably, it would be the heat, then lapsed into silence.

Least he spoke. The way some of them went on down here, you couldn't pass a civil remark without them thinking you were giving them the glad eye or something. Bloody cod's head wasn't half stinking the place out, she only hoped he couldn't smell it, though the way he kept glancing her way she thought he probably could. It reminded her of something, that smell, and she couldn't quite place it – but then suddenly it dawned on her. And all at once she was back in the big classroom at Castle View Board School – skinny little thing with long black hair – nobody would credit it, but she had once been very thin, even a bit *too* thin – looking up at tall, angular Miss Brackenbury who'd been drafted in to deliver her famous domestic science lecture: 'Five Ways to Stuff a Cod's Head for a Penny'. Forty little girls sat on stools and listened; forty little girls who knew their place and never seemed to wonder who was eating the cod's body while they were stuffing the head. But she did. She wondered.

And before she knew what she was doing she was on her feet and telling Miss Brackenbury exactly how she could stuff the cod's head – and where.

Six strokes of the cane she got for that. The minute school was out, she ran all the way along the shore to the castle and stood right on the edge of the cliff, clouds whirling around above her head, the sea boiling and churning in the Egyncleugh beneath her feet. One step. *One step.* She knew there'd be another good hiding when she got home. Nothing more certain. Dad believed in supporting the school. 'Don't you go telling me you did nowt . . . You must've done summat.' And off would come his belt, whipped from round his trousers, fast as a snake.

Eh, dear me. She heaved a sigh and closed her eyes, but then almost immediately opened them again and looked around the square. Amazing how many kids there were. A boy and an older man – dad or granddad – were kicking a ball around the grass. The boy couldn't have been more than twelve or thirteen, still young enough to be evacuated. Another lot, over there, were even younger, charging around having a whale of a time. Nice seeing them.

The lad playing football was a right little ginger nut. Couldn't really tell about the father, he didn't have enough left.

'Nice to see them happy,' she said, with a sidelong glance along the bench. When he didn't reply, she thought at first: *Stuck-up git*; but then she looked more closely, and realized he was in a terrible state. She could feel it, she could feel his misery; it was coming off him in waves. And he was looking so intently at the ginger boy and grinding one clenched fist into the palm of his other hand. Didn't even know he was doing it, you could tell. She wondered for a minute if he wasn't one of the peculiar fellas you get hanging round school playgrounds, but she didn't think it was that. There was hunger on his face – or grief, pretty much the same thing, really – but she didn't think it was that sort of hunger.

'Surprising how many bairns there are.'

She saw him register the word 'bairns' and thought his face softened. He was a northerner.

'Have you seen the posters?'

She shook her head. 'No.'

'There's one that shows Hitler whispering in a mother's ear: *Bring the children back*.'

'A lot have done.'

'Yes, I know. But there's nothing for them here, is there? The schools aren't open, it certainly isn't safe.'

'No, look at that school. Seventy-three dead.'

'And the rest.'

She looked a question.

'Four or five hundred. I was there.'

'My God, doesn't bear thinking about, does it?'

'No.' He was watching the boy again. 'It doesn't.'

She looked from the boy to the man on the bench and back again. Now what was all that about? 'They're right, you know, the mothers – bringing them back. It's bloody bedlam down there, at the minute. You see . . .' She leaned forward, confidentially. 'People think it's like they were taught, pearly gates and harps and St Peter running round with his little list, but it's not. Charing Cross Station in the rush hour more like, people running round like headless chickens, half of 'em don't even know they've passed. No, I say, stick together and if you've got to die, die

71

together. Believe me, you don't want to let go of a child's hand in that.'

He was looking at her rather uneasily. Oh, well. Should've known, should've kept her trap shut, people were frightened, they didn't want to know. And anyway why should she do it for nothing?

Only the expression on his face as he looked at the boy worried her. After that, they sat in silence, but then, a couple of minutes later, she started to hear something, an all too familiar sound: the peevish muttering the dead go in for, whenever they think they're not getting enough attention, which of course is most of the time, poor sods. And then she looked past the man, and there he was. Not very clear, but definitely there.

She had to say something. 'Who's the lad?'

'What lad?'

'The one behind you.'

He started to turn round, but checked himself. There was no space behind the bench for anybody who took up space.

'There's nobody there,' he said.

She went back to watching the children. After a while, she said, 'Skinny, white face, freckles, red hair?'

'That's a description of the boy you're looking at.' The next words seemed to be dragged out of him. 'What does he want?'

She looked, and shrugged. 'Gone now.'

At that, he seemed to lose patience; stood up, walked a few paces, then stopped. Every bit of colour had drained from his face.

'Here, sit down,' she said. 'You're not well.'

She got a hand under his elbow and helped him to sit down, but he was no sooner down than he was up again. 'I think I'll be better walking it off.'

Couldn't wait to get away, although, to be fair, he did smile and thank her as he left. He stumbled several times before he reached the end of the path – he certainly wasn't walking in a straight line – but he kept on going. At the gate he turned and looked back. 'You take care now,' she called out, but he was too far away to hear. A second later he disappeared into the press of people rushing past.

She thought: *I'll be seeing you again.*

No reason to suppose so, in this vast, overcrowded city, but she knew absolutely – no question at all – that she'd see him again.

Eleven

Neville answered the door half naked and slightly drunk. The former was a surprise.

'Tarrant!' He sounded startled, even a little put out, although it was he who'd suggested the meeting.

'I'm not early, am I?'

'No, sorry. Fell asleep in the bath.'

He led the way across the hall, Paul following a trail of wet footprints, averting his gaze from the gyrations of Neville's arse under the damp towel. The hall was lit by a small window, taped against blast, letting in only a dim, stripy light, through which Neville padded like a huge, pink tiger.

Opening a door on the left, he showed Paul into the drawing room, before continuing up the stairs, in search – Paul devoutly hoped – of clothes.

Left alone, Paul looked around the room, his gaze as always drawn first to the paintings. Several good landscapes: the one above the mantelpiece – *Dunstanburgh Castle at Sunset* – was particularly fine. He thought he could identify the exact spot the painter had been standing on. In 1920, a war artist without a war, he'd spent a month in Northumberland scratting and scraping about for inspiration – and not finding it, in Dunstanburgh or anywhere else, not for a long, long time. Meanwhile, Neville, the minute he was released from hospital, left for America in a blaze of publicity. No hesitation, no groping about for inspiration there. Within a couple of years, every boardroom in Chicago and New York seemed to have one or other of Neville's 'vibrant', 'challenging', 'futuristic' cityscapes hanging on the wall. Mind, he hadn't been doing so well recently. Of course, his Great War paintings still hung in galleries alongside Paul's own, but he wasn't getting much critical attention these days. In fact, he was probably better known to the younger generation as a critic than an artist. Paul's reputation as a painter was higher than Neville's now, though they did share a problem: their best work – at least their best-known work – was behind them. It was a strange predicament, to be remembered for what everybody else was trying to forget.

'We should've got ourselves killed,' Neville had said, bitterly, more than once. 'They'd be all over us then.'

On the mantelpiece, there was a framed photograph of a little girl, five or six years old: Neville's daughter, presumably. Anne, was it? No resemblance to Neville, or none that he còuld see, but then he'd almost forgotten what Neville looked like. *Used* to look like. No photograph of Catherine, and he thought he remembered somebody saying they were separated. Where had he heard that?

Feeling suddenly that he was prying, he turned his back on the fireplace and looked around. A pleasant, slightly old-fashioned room, comfortable chairs and sofas: nothing wrong with any of it. Though he couldn't see much trace of Neville's own taste. The one discordant note was a broken blind, which drooped like a half-shut eyelid, making the room look as if it had suffered a stroke.

Footsteps on the landing. A second later, Neville appeared in the doorway, more or less dressed, though still without a tie and bringing with him a swimming-baths smell of damp skinfolds and wet hair.

'Sorry about that. Just nodded off.'

'Bad night?'

'Busy.' He went straight to the drinks table. 'Whisky?'

Paul nodded. 'I've just been admiring your paintings.'

'Job lot, I'm afraid. Dad used to collect them.'

Job lot? Unless he was very much mistaken the one above the fireplace was a Turner. 'I painted Dunstanburgh Castle once.'

'Any good?'

'Not really.'

'I keep meaning to get rid of them, but nothing goes for anything these days; I'd be giving them away.' He handed Paul a glass. 'Same with the house, I wouldn't mind selling it, but . . .'

Paul looked at the ceiling. 'You must rattle around a bit.'

'I do.'

'Catherine not coming over?'

'No, she'll stay in America.'

'You must miss them.'

'I miss Anne.'

Ah.

A slightly awkward pause. Then Neville said: 'Tell you what I've got that might interest you.'

He led the way across the hall into a small study. Above the desk hung a framed pastel portrait of Neville himself, though not Neville as he was now – as he had been when he returned from France in 1917. Striving for some kind of objectivity, Paul looked at the drawing.

An eye like a dying sun sank beneath the rim of a shattered cheekbone, the lips were pulled back to reveal teeth like stumps of dead trees, and right at the centre, where the nose should have been, a crater gaped wide. This was less a face than a landscape: a landscape Paul knew very well.

Neville stood, four-square, nursing his glass. 'Best thing Tonks ever did, those portraits.'

'How did you get it?'

'From Tonks, he gave it to me. I don't think it was his to give, actually; I think it belongs to the War Office. But . . .' He shrugged. 'I suppose he just stretched the rules.'

'Kind of him.'

'Yes, very. Normally all you got was a couple of photographs. Fact, I think I've still got mine somewhere . . .'

The vagueness was a pretence. He went straight to the top-left-hand drawer of the desk, took two photographs out of a brown envelope and handed them across. Paul looked down. One profile, one full face – both utterly shocking. He looked up and found Neville watching him. Keeping his face carefully expressionless, he handed them back. 'This was a parting present?'

'Yes, I think they're meant for if you go in a pub and some silly cow chokes on her drink, you know? You're supposed to whip them out of your pocket, point at your face and say: "You think this is bad, love? Well, just look what they started with." '

'It *is* remarkable, you know, what they did.'

The surgeons, he meant. Was that the right thing to say? Well, if the pursing of Neville's lips was anything to go by – no, it most certainly was not. Paul handed the photographs back. This had been a rather disconcerting episode. It was a relief when Neville led the way back into the drawing room.

'So, what have you been up to?' Neville asked, settling himself into an armchair.

'Oh, you know . . . Working quite hard.'

'Painting?'

'Aeroplanes, you know, dog fights, that sort of thing.'

'Yes, I believe I've seen some of your recent stuff. Vapour trails?'

Why was it, when Neville said 'vapour', Paul heard 'vapid'? Because Neville bloody well meant him to, that's why.

A silver clock on the mantelpiece began to chime. Immediately, Neville put his glass down. 'Blackout.'

He crossed to the windows and began pulling down blinds, each tug of the cords contributing to a premature descent of night until finally only a sliver of sunlight remained. Paul felt a small stab of grief as that, too, was extinguished.

Neville was now merely a moving column of deeper shadow. There was a rasp to his breathing, a side effect of surgery, perhaps; you noticed it more in the dark. He was going from table to table, switching on lamps. As he bent over a side table near Paul's chair every scar and suture line showed. And yet what Paul had just said was true: the surgeons had done a remarkable job.

Only it was not his face, just as this was not his room.

'So . . .' Neville picked up his glass. 'Where were we?'

Starting to needle each other, Paul thought. Painting wasn't a safe area. Yes, it was what they had in common, but it was also what divided them. Time for a change of subject. 'I had a rather strange experience this afternoon. I think I met the Witch of Endor . . .'

Quickly, he told Neville about his meeting with the fat woman in Russell Square, emphasizing the absurdity of the occasion, recounting it, more or less, as a joke against himself.

Neville was amused, but he was also good at detecting pain.

'Well,' he said, when Paul had finished, 'she certainly got you rattled.'

'No –'

'Oh, come *on*.'

'No, really; actually, I felt quite sorry for her.'

'I don't see why. I mean, you say yourself she was describing the boy you were looking at. She just picked up on it, that's all. She was obviously having you on.'

'But that's just it, you see, I'm not sure she was. Oh, I'm not saying she actually saw anything but . . . Oh, I don't know. She was . . . she was . . . doing *something* – and I'm not quite sure what it was.'

'I suppose the real question is, why have you suddenly got interested in boys?'

Paul didn't want to talk about Kenny but he could see an explanation was required, and once he'd started it was surprisingly easy to go on. When, at last, he stopped, Neville said, 'There's no doubt he's dead?'

'None at all. Nobody got out.'

'Still, you mustn't let that woman get to you.'

'I don't think she was trying to, to be fair.'

'Oh, of course she was! If you'd gone along with it she'd have been asking for money in no time at all. I can't stand the way these people crawl out of the woodwork whenever there's a war on, battening on people's grief – it's horrible. Do you know, my mother used to hold seances in the last war – in the dining room just along there. And I mean she was a *highly* intelligent woman, very forward-thinking in all kinds of ways, and yet she couldn't seem to see through it. I actually went to one of them –' He shuddered. 'Appalling stuff. "Auntie Maud likes your curtains." I'm glad I didn't die, it would've been me coming back to say I liked the curtains. You don't seriously think –?' He threw up his hands in disgust. 'It's all *fraud*.'

He came over to refill Paul's glass. As he bent down, the lamp threw his shadow across the far wall. Bull neck, massive shoulders, a whiff of the Minotaur's stable. The beast in the brain. But it wasn't just his physical bulk. It was that impression of baffled pain. An animal's pain. That invitation to go and see the Tonks portrait had been decidedly odd. It was almost as if he'd been reaching out, trying to get past the rivalry that had always prevented them from being, in any simple or uncomplicated way, friends.

No sooner had he finished pouring than the siren set up its nightly wail.

'What do you do in a raid?' Neville asked. 'You know, if you're not on duty?'

'I walk.'

'Not all night?'

'You might be surprised.'

'What does Elinor think about that?'

'Well, I don't do it when she's here.'

'We haven't seen much of her recently.'

'No, she's still in the country, helping her sister sort things out.'

The siren had stopped wailing. In its absence the silence of the deserted streets began to ooze through cracks in doors and window frames, a silence so deep the whisper of blood in your ears became more and more difficult to ignore. And then they heard it: that awful, desperate, edge-of-darkness buzzing, the sound a kettle makes when it's about to boil dry.

'Ours,' Neville said.

'No, it's not.'

And immediately, from Hampstead Heath close by, came the hysterical yapping of the guns. A thud, followed by another, closer, the end of the next street, perhaps. Above their heads, the chandelier gave out a soft, silvery chime.

Paul said, 'You need to get that bloody thing bagged up.'

'Spoken like a true air-raid warden.' Neville got to his feet. 'Well, unless you want to stay inside . . .?'

'I never want to stay in.'

In the hall, there was a brief hiatus as Neville fumbled for his keys. Paul was starting to feel dizzy again. He'd been suffering from episodes of vertigo ever since a particularly nasty bout of flu in January. Inflammation of the labyrinth, the doctor said. Nothing to worry about, he'd said, most people get over it quite quickly; only an unlucky few get stuck. It was beginning to look as if Paul was one of the few. The walls spun round him; Neville's breath grated in his ears. He put a hand out to steady himself. Neville had switched the light out before he opened the door and, for some reason, the dizziness was always worse in the dark.

'Bloody key.'

He got the door open at last. They collected hats and gas masks from the hall table and stepped out into the noisy night.

They were shown to a quiet table in the corner of the restaurant. Menus were produced, a bottle of wine ordered. It was all really rather pleasant, except Paul's appetite seemed to have deserted him. The soup went down easily enough, but he struggled with the game pie, refused a pudding and merely picked at the cheese, content to let Neville do most of the talking. He could be very amusing, when he chose: scurrilous gossip about other painters, bizarre goings-on at the Ministry of Information . . . 'Complete loony bin.'

'For God's sake, keep your voice down.'

Neville looked round the room and shrugged. Nobody was paying them any attention, and actually, to be fair, he'd said virtually nothing about his work – while contriving to imply his contribution to the war effort was second only to Winston Churchill's. But then – he was well into the second bottle by now – he embarked on a great rant about Kenneth Clark and the War Artists Advisory Committee. None of the commissioned artists had any talent whatsoever, *not a glimmer*. Moore, Sutherland, Piper: all rubbish. Clark was the problem, of course – Clark and his coterie of arse-licking toadies.

'He's commissioned one or two women as well,' Paul said, hoping to divert the flow of bile.

'Elinor?'

'No, not yet, though –'

'Then she should think herself lucky. It's an insult to be commissioned by that man.'

Paul was one of the people 'that man' had insulted, but obviously it suited Neville to forget that. 'Laura Knight, she's –'

'Poisonous old bat.'

Paul gave up. Let him rant, if it made him feel better, but Neville seemed to have finished with Kenneth Clark, for the time being, at least. He glanced at Paul's plate. 'You're not eating your cheese.'

'No, I've had enough.'

Immediately, a predatory fork descended and impaled the Cheddar. Neville munched in silence for a while.

Paul's vertigo was getting worse. Fresh air, that's what he needed, he'd be all right once he was outside, but the bill was a long time coming. When, finally, he staggered out into the street, the buildings started revolving around his head. He'd gone only a few paces when he found himself sitting on the pavement, trying not to be sick.

Neville stood over him. 'You can't be drunk.'

'Vertigo.'

Even the effort of saying the word made it worse. If only things would *keep still*. He fixed his gaze on a crack in the pavement and, for a moment, the spinning did slow down.

'Can you stand?' Neville offered Paul his hand and then, when that didn't work, went behind and levered him to his feet. 'Come on, my place. You need to get to bed.'

Slowly, with Neville's help, Paul managed to take a few steps. He could walk, though he seemed to have only two paces: so slow he was threatening to sink into the ground, or so fast he was almost running. '*Whoa!*' Neville kept saying, as if to a skittish horse. Now he *was* drunk.

Blotched into a single shadow, they staggered from side to side in the road. Once, the wavering beam of a blackout torch came towards them, nothing of the man behind it visible except the hand holding the torch. An old man's hand, with thick, raised, bluish-grey veins. 'Goodnight!' he said. Seconds later, the murk swallowed him.

Not long after, they arrived back at the house. Neville lowered Paul into an armchair. 'Well. That was a surprise.'

Unable to speak, Paul gripped the arms of the chair and willed the room to stop spinning. Neville stood looking down at him. 'Who was the Witch of Endor anyway?'

'Saul,' he tried to say, but it came out as 'sore'.

Immediately Neville's fingers were round his throat. 'Yes, it will be, your glands are up. Is there anything I can get you?'

'No, I'm all right, thanks.'

'Has it happened before?'

'Off and on since January. I had the flu and this started a few days later. But, you know, I've seen a doctor and he says it's nothing to worry about. It's just the room keeps spinning every time I move my head.'

'That'd worry me. Wouldn't you be better off in bed?'

During the time he'd been sitting in the chair the spinning had slowed down, though he knew it would start again the moment he moved. It was tempting to stay where he was, even to sleep in the chair, but he knew Neville wouldn't be happy leaving him downstairs on his own. 'Yes, probably.'

With Neville behind him, pushing him every step of the way, he managed to get upstairs and across the landing into a guest room where he immediately collapsed on to the bed. Neville's voice came and went, now booming, now barely audible: the effect you can get by pressing your hands rhythmically against your ears. He remembered doing that in the hall at school, a small boy, lost and frightened, dumbfounded by the noise. In, out, loud, soft – and suddenly it was all right, everything was under control.

This wasn't. He just prayed he wasn't going to vomit all over the counterpane. Neville was pulling his shoes off now. *Clunk*: one of them hit the floor. And again: *clunk*. A blurry face bent over him. 'You all right?'

This had gone on quite long enough. 'Yes, thank you.' He enunciated the words with great precision, and immediately, as if in response to his efforts, Neville's face swam into focus, though his voice still boomed and vanished. 'I'll be . . . door . . . don't . . . if you . . . thing.'

Then he switched off the light, and Paul was left alone.

Twelve

Nightmares crawled across each other like copulating toads. He was walking with Neville along a shingle beach, the rasp and roar of waves loud in his ears, but then he realized it wasn't the waves, it was Neville's breathing. Humped shapes lay at intervals along the shore. He assumed they were seals, and expected them to heave and lollop into the water, but they didn't, and as he got closer he saw they were corpses, some stranded on the shoreline, others drifting to and fro on the tide: all too badly burned to be identified. Then, as he probed them, one stood up and seemed about to speak, its lipless mouth struggling to form words . . .

The dream shifted. He was going through the front door at home, throwing his school satchel down on the floor by the stairs. His hand was on the living-room door, but he hesitated, afraid to go in, afraid of what he would find. She'd be standing by the window and, though he knew she'd heard his footsteps, she wouldn't turn round. She never turned round. Always, he had to touch her, pull her back, *make* her notice him. Then, slowly, she would turn – and turn and turn and turn, day after day. He never knew which face he was going to see: blank with misery, blubbery with tears, contracted into a hard, angry knot. Sometimes she didn't turn at all, merely brushed his hand away as if it were an insect crawling across her skin. At other times, but rarely, she managed a smile: always with that curious string of saliva at the corner of her mouth – it should have been repulsive, but it wasn't, not to him; it was one of the things he loved most about her – and then sometimes she'd say his name, but tentatively, as if she couldn't quite remember who he was.

On the day they came to get her, she was sitting in a chair by the fireplace, and so, for a moment, he thought she must be better. But his father was home from work and he shouldn't be – he was working two till ten – and Gran was in the kitchen, banging pots and pans. 'I thought you were going to tea at your Auntie May's?' she said. 'Why, what's happening?' 'Nothing.' He looked at Dad, who just shook his head. It was bad, Paul knew it was. So he went straight to his mother and knelt beside her.

She had tears trickling down her face. Back when things were normal, before the standing-at-the-window began, she used to sing, and so he sang to her now: hymns – she knew hundreds of hymns – music-hall songs – she loved the music hall – and so he sang all her favourites, every single one. He was afraid to stop; he knew if he stopped something bad would happen. He even had a go at the 'Hallelujah Chorus'. 'Jesus Christ!' Gran muttered in the kitchen. At first, it didn't seem as if his mother were listening, but after a while she reached out and squeezed his hand.

A knock on the door. Wiping her hands on her pinny, Gran went to answer it. His father hung back. A horse-drawn wagon had pulled up outside; he caught only one glimpse of it before Dad grabbed him by the shoulders and pushed him into the front room. From the window, he saw them helping her into the wagon. The driver flicked the reins, the wheels started to turn, and, as if realizing what was happening for the first time, she turned to look back.

Meeting him in the street a few weeks later, the vicar said, 'Why've you stopped coming to choir practice, Paul?'

Because. Because, because, because, because . . .

He went on seeing her standing by the window. She lingered like an after-image on the retina, except that after-images fade and this never did. There she stood, looking out on to a yard where nothing grew, where there was nothing to see except brick walls imprisoning a patch of sky. Still, even now, he had to touch her, make her acknowledge him: *Mam, Mam*. Still, he never knew which face he'd see. The angry face was the one he dreaded most: the shout, the slap that sent him flying . . . She was angry now and he was frightened, really frightened this time – only, thank God, he heard Dad coming up the passage, the door opened, and there he was –

'*Dad!*'

A cold hand touched his forehead. He opened his eyes and it

wasn't Dad, it was a man he'd never seen before, a man whose face, like a reflection in ruffled water, slowly settled and resolved into –

'Neville.'

'You were shouting.'

'Was I?' He stared round the room. 'I'm sorry, I –'

'You were shouting, "Dad!" '

'Was I?' He struggled to sit up, but the movement set the vertigo off and he was glad to sink back on to the pillows. 'Poor old Dad, he was never much use when he was alive. What time is it?'

'Ten to four.'

'Oh, I'm sorry. Look, you go back to bed, I'll be all right.'

But he couldn't stop looking at the window, afraid of finding her there, or something there.

'I'll get you some water.'

Even in the few minutes Neville was gone, Paul must have drifted off to sleep for the next time he woke Neville was at the window pulling up the blinds. Hard, scouring light flooded into the room and, like slugs sprinkled with salt, the nightmares shrivelled and died.

'Let's get you into these pyjamas, shall we? You'll feel a lot more comfortable.'

Before helping him into the jacket, Neville took a flannel soaked in tepid water and gave Paul's arms and chest a quick rub. Paul knew it made sense, his skin was slick with sweat, but he hated it all the same, the enforced intimacy, and withdrew, as far as he could, turning his head to one side, disowning the stinking carcass on the bed. When it was finished, though, he did, admittedly, feel a whole lot better.

Neville threw the towel over his shoulder and picked up the bowl. 'I think I should phone Elinor.'

'There's no need, she's got enough on.'

'I think she should know where you are, at least.'

'I'll be home in a couple of hours.'

Neville looked doubtful. 'Let's see how you get on.'

Though the nightmares had gone, their fetid darkness stained the day. Paul kept looking at the window, expecting to see her standing there, or his father coming through the door, shambling and inept. As you get older, you think you're moving further away from your parents, leaving them behind, but it's not like that. There's a trick, a flaw, some kind of hidden circularity in the path, because suddenly, in old age, there they are in front of you again, and getting closer by the day.

This particular day dragged. Neville closed the curtains because the brightness hurt Paul's eyes. He couldn't read: even the movement of his eyes across the page was enough to bring the dizziness back. He could do nothing, in fact, except lie with his eyes closed or every now and then glance apprehensively at the lighter square of grey that was the window.

Surprisingly often, he found himself thinking about the woman in the square. How she must've noticed him watching the ginger-haired boy kicking the football around. No other explanation of what she'd claimed to see was possible. But the woman herself haunted him. Her singing. 'Land of Hope and Glory' of all things, one of the songs he'd sung that day. She'd had remarkable eyes – blue with the merest hint of mauve, the colour of harebells – and all the more remarkable for being sunk in wads of fat. And my God she stank.

Yet, somehow, this ludicrous woman had seen him watching the boy and put her finger – possibly a rather mercenary finger – on his grief.

If 'grief' was the right word. He'd scarcely known Kenny well enough to grieve for him. No, what he felt was regret; guilt, even. Taking Kenny back to his mother had been the wrong decision, arrived at for the wrong reasons. Elinor was right: he hadn't been thinking about Kenny at all. It had been about *himself* and *his* mother. A kind of proxy reconciliation; a reconciliation that in his own life had never been achieved. So he'd failed in the most basic human task: to shield the present from the deforming weight of the past. And now, lying in a strange bed, in the hot, close darkness of a strange room, his condemnation of himself was absolute.

By mid-afternoon he was starting to feel hot again. Neville brought him a cup of tea, but he couldn't drink it. *Sleep*, that was the thing – and no more nightmares, please God. Throwing off the covers, he tried to ignore the images that clung to the inside of his skull, thousands of them – black, furry, insistent, clicking . . .

'*Ridiculous.*'

'What's ridiculous?'

'This. Me.'

'Blame the Witch of Endor.'

'Oh, so you think I'm cursed, do you?'

Neville tapped him on the head. 'Go to sleep.'

And, abruptly, as if he'd been waiting for that word of command, he fell asleep.

Thirteen

The bell's doleful clanging brought Kit to the door. Elinor wasted no time on small talk. 'How is he?'

'Asleep.'

He turned and led the way upstairs. Paul was lying with his eyes closed, propped up on three pillows. The pyjama jacket – Kit's presumably – was open and each breath delineated the structure of ribs and sternum. Sitting on the bed, she clasped his slippery fingers in hers and, after a while, he seemed to feel her presence. His eyes dragged open. 'Oh, hello, I didn't expect to see you.'

She kissed him. 'I'd have come sooner, only I was down at the cottage and nobody told me you'd rung.'

'That was Neville, I didn't want to bother you.'

Standing just inside the door, Kit stirred. 'Elinor, would you like a drink?'

'Tea would be lovely.'

He left the room. They were silent for a moment, listening to his footsteps going heavily downstairs. Paul said, 'He's been very good.'

That sounded like a plea: *Don't be nasty to Kit*. Well, no, of course she wouldn't be. 'Thing is, can we get you home?'

'There's only one way to find out.'

Pushing the covers back, he swung his legs over the side of the bed – and sat there, motionless, swallowing hard. She reached out to help, but he waved her away. After several attempts to stand up, he admitted defeat and lay back on the pillows. 'Dunno what's wrong with me.'

'Well, don't force it. Why don't you have a sleep?'

'Because I've been sleeping all day.'

'Perhaps that's what you need . . .'

'What I need is to go home.'

But his eyelids were already closing, and by the time Kit

reappeared with the tea he was asleep. Kit put the tray down, glanced at the bed, and mouthed: 'See you downstairs.'

Left alone, Elinor poured herself a cup of tea and settled back to drink it. *Damn*, she was thinking. Paul obviously wasn't well enough to be moved, but she couldn't just leave him here – and that meant her spending an evening with Kit. Something she'd so far managed to avoid. Her relationship with Kit, never easy, seemed to become more and more complicated. He'd been serving with Toby in the months leading up to Toby's death, but he'd never written to her about it, and when she wrote to him, he hadn't replied. An omission Paul had described at the time as 'unforgivable'. Later, he'd told Paul as much as he knew about Toby's death – or as much as he could bring himself to tell – but he'd never directly told *her* anything. She'd found that hard to forgive, and for a long time, even after he married Catherine, her closest friend, she'd seen as little of him as possible. Avoiding him had not been too difficult, since she and Paul spent a lot of time in Spain whereas he and Catherine had lived in Germany for a number of years before finally settling in America. An occasional encounter in London or New York – strained civility – and that was it: friendship over.

Only now Kit was back in London, working as an ambulance driver in the same Tottenham Court Road depot as Elinor. This proximity added a new dimension to what had always been a difficult – well, what could you call it? Association? They were now members of the same team: they'd trained together, grumbled together, drunk endless cups of stewed tea together; and now – almost nightly, when she was in London – faced danger together. All this inevitably produced a sense of comradeship that was both intense and impersonal. But it was the same with all the drivers. It hardly seemed to matter whether you liked the person or not. You just jogged along together, because you had to. This was something altogether new in Elinor's experience, though she supposed the men were familiar with it from the last war. Even so, she'd managed to avoid anything in the way of direct contact with Kit. If they went to the pub, it was always in a group of five or six other people. Sitting around in the depot, waiting for calls, she talked to Violet or

Dana. She doubted if she'd exchanged a single personal word with him in the last few months – nor had she wanted to. So she wasn't particularly looking forward to this evening, but it needn't last long; she could always say she was tired and needed an early night.

On her way downstairs, she paused to peer into an aquarium that stood in a recess on the half-landing, but, though well stocked with plants, it seemed to be empty. Kit had come out of a door on the right and was looking up at her.

'I can't see any fish.'

'That's because there aren't any.' He came upstairs and took the tray from her. 'It's all for him.' He pointed to a small terrapin lurking at the bottom of the tank.

'Oh, I didn't see him.'

'No, well, he's very well disguised, isn't he?' He hesitated. 'When I was a child I used to think that was me.'

'What, rattling around on your own?'

'Felt like it sometimes.' He nodded towards the stairs as if to emphasize the size of the house.

'Must feel a little bit like that now.'

'It does, rather. I mean, I suppose I could live at the club, but . . . Oh, I don't know.' He led the way into the drawing room. 'Would you like a drink?'

She suppressed a smile: he so obviously *needed* her to have a drink. 'What are you having?'

'Whisky.'

'Go on, I'll join you.'

The glass he handed her was rather large. Never mind, she could always take it slowly. He was busy drawing the blinds.

She took a sip of whisky and recoiled from the peaty taste. Kit didn't seem to have heard of water. 'Don't you think the blackout's worse in summer? In winter you can kid yourself it feels cosy, but . . .'

'I don't think I ever managed that.' He sat down, about as far away as he could get while remaining in the same room. 'How did you find him?'

'Not good.'

'He had a bad night. *We* had a bad night.'

'No, he's not been sleeping well.'

'What's wrong?'

'Did he tell you about the dizziness?'

'He didn't have to, he fell over.'

'Oh, as bad as that?'

'He said something about flu.'

'Yes, that's when it started. Apparently there's nothing much wrong. I mean, we were terrified at first – well, you can imagine – but it's nothing like that. Nothing serious.'

'What do you think's causing it?'

'Well, like the doctor said – flu.'

'You don't believe that.'

She hesitated. 'No, I don't, not really. I mean, it's certainly worse if he gets upset about something.'

'He was upset last night.'

'Was he?'

'Yes, he was hiding it well, but looking back, I think he was in quite a state. He met some sort of weird woman in the square – the one weird sister, I think – and she said she could see a ginger-haired boy standing behind him. But Paul was actually looking at a ginger-haired boy at the time – staring at him, in fact – and she obviously picked up on that.'

'Did he tell you about Kenny?'

'He did, yes.'

She closed her eyes. 'Oh, poor Paul. That's the last thing he needed.'

'As I say, he was in quite a state.' He raised his empty glass, asking her if she'd like another. When she shook her head, he got up and refilled his own. 'Are you back in town now?'

'Yes – though there's an awful lot of sorting out still.'

'I was sorry to hear about your mother.'

She thanked him, and then the talk turned to other things. Not, as she'd expected, their shared experiences of driving an ambulance. No, by mutual, unspoken consent, they went right back to their student days at the Slade, before the last war, before his silence after

Toby's death divided them. Rather to her surprise, Elinor began to enjoy it. All those fancy-dress parties, what was all that about? And they'd put so much effort into it . . .

'Do you remember the last one?' she asked. 'We must have been sewing costumes for a week.'

'Was that the one where you and Catherine went as Harlequin?'

She smiled. 'Yes, both of us.'

'And you wouldn't take your masks off, or say anything, so nobody could tell which was which. And you danced with each other all evening, wouldn't let any of the men break in.'

'Funny, Paul remembers that too.'

'Elinor, every man who was *there* remembers that.'

'Yes, you were all standing round the edge of the dance floor with your tongues hanging out.'

'Ah, so you did know? Thought you did.'

'Wasn't why we were doing it though . . .'

'No, you never took your eyes off each other – all evening.'

Elinor looked down into her glass. 'How is she?'

'Pretty good. Well, as far as I know.'

'I'm sorry.'

'Don't be. I've never regretted the marriage. It gave me Anne.'

'How old is she now?'

'Six. She's got two gaps in her front teeth. Just here.' He tapped his own teeth. 'She's very proud of them; she was one of the last people in her class to get them. I think she thought it was never going to happen.'

'It's a nice age,' Elinor said, vaguely. She found it hard to imagine Kit as a father.

'Do you know, I was thinking the other evening – well, the middle of the night, really – the last time the three of us were together – I mean, under the same roof – was the start of the last war.'

'Yes, we went for a bike ride. To see the Doom.'

'And I fell off.'

'So you did.'

'And asked you to marry me.'

An awkward pause. 'So you did.'

'God, that was so humiliating.'

'Oh, don't be silly, Kit, you didn't mean it . . .'

'No, I meant falling off. Poor old Dad, he used to take me round and round the heath, must've run miles. And the minute he let go, off I came. I never did get the hang of it.'

'Well, you seem to have got the hang of proposing.'

'E-vent-u-al-ly.' He moved the lamp a few inches further away from his face. 'Oh, and by the way, I did mean it.'

She shook her head.

'I was trying to remember who else was there. Paul, of course, and, er –'

'Toby.'

Abruptly, it was between them: Toby's death; Kit's long silence. But then, just as he was about to speak, the siren set up its awful tooth-jarring wail and so she never did find out what he was going to say.

Sitting like this in silence, listening to the sirens, you felt the darkness deepen. Even with every lamp in the room lit, you were aware of it, pushing against the windowpanes, seeping through cracks in doors and walls, dragging the city back into barbarism. London: no longer one of the world's great centres of civilization, but merely a settlement on a river, lit by guttering candles after dark.

'I've just realized something,' he said, as the banshee howl wound down into silence. 'You're the only person who still calls me "Kit".'

'Really?' How impossibly self-centred men were. No, she corrected herself: not 'men'. *This* man.

'Since my mother died, yes.'

'How extraordinary. What does Catherine call you?'

' "You". If Anne's there, "Daddy" – or, if I'm really in the dog-house: "Your father".'

Elinor didn't know how to respond to that and was glad when it was time to go through into the dining room to eat. Cold cuts on the sideboard, a surprising amount of meat. Apparently his house-keeper knew somebody. *Oh, yes*, Elinor thought, restored to something of her original dislike: Kit's housekeeper would know somebody. Over the meal, he talked about his time in Germany.

Catherine hadn't wanted to leave, though she seemed perfectly happy in America. In fact, she was probably more American than he was. Perhaps that was why the marriage had broken down? Elinor wasn't sure she believed in all this 'drifting apart' nonsense. There was always a reason.

Outside the raid went on, various thuds and bumps, none very close. Her glass seemed to be emptying itself rather quickly. The clock ticked towards midnight. She thought it had been an altogether strange evening, full of emotional undercurrents, things said, things left unsaid, she didn't know what to make of it. But at least it ended in laughter. They'd been reminiscing about the dances they used to go to when they were students, when – it was a shock to remember – they'd been, actually for quite a long time, each other's best friend. They'd spent virtually every evening together, in fact: going to exhibitions, theatres, music halls . . . But, above all, dancing.

'Do you remember the turkey trot?' Kit asked. 'We used to go in for competitions.'

She put her hands over her eyes. 'Oh my God, yes. The turkey trot. What were we thinking?'

Kit stood up, spread his legs – more frog than turkey – and hopped a few paces to the left . . . Then, tucking his thumbs into his braces, a few paces to the right. He looked so ridiculous she burst out laughing. He joined in, but then stopped and looked at her.

'Do you think we could still do it?'

'No, of course we couldn't.'

'Bet you we could.'

He was holding out his hand and, for a second, anything seemed possible – she was on the verge of getting up – but then she smiled and shook her head, and turned away.

Fourteen

Paul hated the Underground stations that had been turned into shelters. For a long time, the authorities had resisted using the Underground in this way, but after the destruction of the school in Agate Street, people took things into their own hands: they forced their way in. And so at night the Underground became almost indistinguishable from the underworld, with hundreds of people asleep or inert under their blankets. You had to clamber over them. And always, for Paul, there were memories of other tunnels: humped bodies in half-darkness, sleeping or dead. Increasingly, the two worlds – France, then; London, now – met and merged. It was a relief to escape the fetid darkness of the shelters into the tumult of the upper air.

Darkness was falling, a hot, clammy darkness that made it hard to breathe. He still didn't feel well, though the dizziness had gone; and he was constantly afraid. He quickened his steps. The only solution to fear was other people. A few jokes, a game of cards, and things didn't look quite so bad.

At the corner of Guilford Street, he bumped into Walter Harris, who was just going out on patrol.

'What's happening?'

'Nothing much,' Walter said. 'Very quiet.'

Incendiaries were drifting down like huge yellow peonies. The two of them stood at the centre of a web of shadows, reluctant to part. People clung to each other these days, as if the mere fact of being known, recognized, addressed by name, could protect you from the random destruction of bombs and blast. But after a few minutes, Walter ground his fag out, said, 'So long' – nobody these days risked saying 'Goodbye' – and set off in the direction of Russell Square.

As Paul turned the corner, he saw a stick of bombs come

down the beam of a searchlight on to a building fifty yards ahead, an extraordinary sight, like a worm's-eye view of somebody shitting. He was close enough to feel the blast wave suck at his eyeballs, but already he'd started to run, arriving on the scene in a smog of black smoke. Charlie Web was there and Brian Temple and shortly afterwards Nick Hendry came shambling up.

As Paul turned to greet him, there was another explosion further down the street. The windows behind them shattered and they crouched down, shielding their faces and arms from a shower of broken glass. 'Bloody hell,' Charlie said. 'You all right, lad?' This was directed at Nick, who was looking more dazed than frightened.

Cautiously, Paul straightened up. The road was filling with civilians, swarming out of the burning buildings, many of them barefoot, treading on broken glass, impervious to pain. There must've been a shelter in one of the basements. Sandra Jobling, bent double, was leading a group out, waving at them to come on. *Come on.* There was another shelter not far away in Gray's Inn Road, but it was going to be a terribly long walk for some of those people.

Within half an hour, Sandra was back. 'All right, love?' Charlie asked. She nodded, without speaking. It was difficult to tell how she was, or how anybody was. They were all white with plaster dust, their eyelids crusted and inflamed. Nick was in a bad way. Charlie pointed to the basement of a nearby house. 'There's an old man lives down there, I think we ought to check on him.'

'No, he's in hospital,' Brian Temple said.

'Nope, came out yesterday.'

Nobody questioned it: Charlie knew everything and everybody on his patch.

'Won't he have gone to a shelter?' Paul asked.

'Can't walk.'

'*Bloody* hell.'

They found him in the living room. Plaster had fallen from the ceiling and lay in clumps all over the floor, but the old man didn't seem to be injured. He was sitting on the edge of a sofa bed, stick-thin, rodent-faced, a plastic bag full of urine dangling from his side, but as they helped him to the door he was positively cackling with triumph. Apparently, they'd told him in the hospital he might never walk again. 'And look at me now.' He paused for breath, hanging on to Charlie's arm. 'Shows how much the fuckers know.'

'*Oi*, you, language.' Charlie jabbed his finger at Sandra. '*Lady*.'

'Sorry, love. Didn't see you.'

Sandra smiled. ''S'all right.'

'Thought she was a lad,' they heard him say, as Charlie pushed his skinny arse up the stairs. 'They all wear trousers these days, you can't tell hes from shes.'

They got him into one of the ambulances that had drawn up on the other side of the road and were just turning away when somebody said there was a man trapped on the second floor of a building further down the street. 'Why the fuck wasn't *he* in a shelter?' Brian asked. It didn't matter why; they still had to go in. Inside, there was total devastation, illuminated at intervals by flares that shone through the broken windows. A crater, twenty foot deep, had opened up at the centre of the building and they were having to edge around its rim. 'Like that school in Agate Street,' Brian said. Twenty yards further on, they heard a slithering thump, exactly like snow falling off a roof in a rapid thaw. They looked at each other, as the seconds ticked past. Charlie had stopped, mid-stride, one hand raised. He seemed to be on the point of turning back, but then he lowered his hand and they started to move forward again.

They found a man on the first-floor landing, his head and shoulders sticking out of the rubble, eyes glazed, that unmistakable look of nobody at home. But was this the man they'd been told about, or was there somebody else? No way of knowing. Charlie decided to press on. Paul swept the torch from side to side, training the light on their feet, as they crept up the stairs, each tread complaining under their combined weight. At any moment, now, you felt the whole bloody staircase was coming down. Paul opened his mouth to say they ought to think about going back, but at that moment Charlie raised his hand again.

A man was lying across the top of the stairs, unconscious, barely breathing, short, middle-aged, with a paunch that strained his shirt buttons, and cheeks like a hamster's full of nuts. Brian blew his whistle, and the sound carried Paul back to the trenches. *Stretcher-bearers!* Trying to fix himself in the present, he swung the torch over gilt picture frames and velvet curtains. 'Keep it steady, mate,' Charlie said. 'Can't see what I'm doing here.'

No stretcher-bearers appeared in response to Brian's whistle; nobody had seriously thought they would. 'All right then?' Charlie said, and they positioned themselves at the unconscious man's head and feet.

It took them an hour to get him out. Paul helped the woman ambulance driver lift him on to the top bunk. The bunk below was already occupied, by a terrified man who kept whimpering that he'd broken his arm and it was a disgrace – an absolute bloody disgrace – that he hadn't been taken to the hospital straight away. 'There's plenty worse than you,' the driver said, in a ferociously clipped accent. 'If you don't keep quiet I'll dump you in the road.'

'I'd do as I was told if I were you,' Paul said. 'I think she means it.'

The driver slipped off her right gauntlet and held out her hand. Automatically, Paul took it, though it seemed an odd gesture in the circumstances.

'Thank you,' she said. 'Bit of a dead weight, wasn't he?'

Or just dead. 'It's Miss Tempest, isn't it?'

'Oh, Violet, please. I trained with Elinor.'

'Yes, I remember.'

He was just about to jump down into the road when she took hold of his sleeve. Puzzled, he glanced down and saw the cloth was stiff with blood. 'Oh, it's all right,' he said. 'It's not mine.'

She pulled the edges of the tear apart and peered inside. 'I think you'll find it is.'

Immediately, his arm began to throb, though up to that moment he'd felt no pain. 'I'd no idea.'

'No, I'm serious, now, you go and get that seen to.'

He looked at her. A painfully thin, wiry, indestructible woman in late middle age. Far too old to be driving an ambulance, but nobody had the nerve to tell her that. Before the war she'd taught – classics, was it? At Cambridge. Very ivory-tower, the sort of woman whom normally he might not have taken seriously, but in the confusion of the moment any sufficiently firm suggestion acquired the force of a command. He sketched a salute. 'Yes, ma'am.'

He thought he might as well get the cut seen to, though he didn't think it was anything serious and felt a bit of a fraud, crunching along Gower Street over a river of broken glass. This same route he'd taken every morning as a student at the Slade. Now, shocked people huddled in doorways or wandered around in the middle of the road, purgatorial shadows with their white, dust-covered faces and dark clothes. Some, in pyjamas and dressing gowns, limped along on bloodied feet.

Reaching his station at the School of Tropical Medicine, he staggered down into the basement where he found Nick Hendry being treated for a cut to his forehead. Lucky lad – another inch and it would've been his eye.

When Paul's turn came, he rolled up his shirtsleeve and discovered, as he'd rather expected, that the cut, though still oozing blood, was not deep. 'Looks worse than it is,' the first-aid worker said. 'Go and have a cup of tea.'

He retreated to one of the two battered sofas that lined the walls. Nick Hendry was stretched out on the other and was snoring softly, his upper lip vibrating with every breath. Paul tried to read a newspaper, but couldn't concentrate. He forced down a cup of orange tea, and though his stomach rose in revolt, immediately began to feel better.

After a brief respite, he started to feel he was shirking and forced himself to go out on patrol again. One good thing, he hadn't suffered any spells of dizziness all night and that was reassuring because this was his first night back on duty, and he'd been half expecting it to return.

Two hours later, he returned to the station, eyelids gritty with tiredness, yawning and scratching his neck. Nick was still on the sofa, face averted, though Paul could tell from his breathing he wasn't asleep. A few minutes later, Sandra Jobling came in and took off her helmet, bending forwards to run her fingers through her sweaty hair. Her face was still covered in plaster dust, but at some time during the night she must have reapplied her lipstick without the aid of a mirror, because she now had two huge, glossy, smiling, red lips, with smears of lipstick all over her cheeks and chin. She waved to Paul, then went straight through to the cloakroom next door.

Charlie Web and Brian Temple came in not long after. Charlie put his mug of tea on the table and pulled up a chair. 'Gone quiet.'

'Not long now,' Paul said.

They waited for the All Clear with hardly less tension than they'd waited for the warning sirens the night before. Charlie jerked his head in Nick's direction. 'He's making the most of it.' He slurped a mouthful of tea. 'What about that old geezer, then, the one with the plastic bag? Bloody thing burst, you know. I was lifting him on to the top bunk and . . . *Pish*. All over me. Could've done with a bloody umbrella.'

Nick sat up, ostentatiously rubbing his eyes.

'Hey up,' Charlie said. 'Sleeping Beauty's back. How are you, mate?'

He carried his mug across to the sofa and sat down. Nick had seemed very jittery all night; Charlie had been virtually carrying him. Their voices sank to a low murmur. Paul was already nodding off to sleep when a hand on his shoulder jerked him awake.

Charlie: 'I'm taking Nick round the corner for a pasty. You coming?'

Brian stood up at once, but Paul shook his head. 'No thanks, I think I'll be getting off home.'

But it was hard to make himself get going. He'd only just levered himself to his feet when Sandra came back into the room, her face pink and shining, forehead plastered with tendrils of wet hair. She came straight over to him. 'I don't know. *Men*.'

'What have we done now?'

'How could you let me walk round like that?'

'Like what?'

'Lipstick plastered all over me face.'

He smiled. 'I thought you looked amazing.'

'I looked like a clown.'

It seemed the easiest, most natural thing in the world to grab her by the shoulders and kiss her. Only when it was too late, when she'd taken a step back and was gawping at him, did he realize what he'd done. *My God*. He tried to come up with something to say, something that would shrink the kiss, turn it into a friendly, casual, comradely gesture, the sort of thing he might have done to Charlie or Brian, but the words wouldn't come. To his relief, he saw she was looking amused rather than offended. 'I'm –'

Sorry, he was going to say, but at that moment a voice at the door said, 'Is there any tea left in that pot?'

Walter Harris, grey-faced, ready to drop.

Sandra felt the curve of the pot. 'Past its best, I'm afraid. Yeah, no, you can't have that. I'll put the kettle on.'

Walter lowered himself into a chair. 'Thanks, love.'

'Well,' Paul said, deliberately including both of them. 'I'd better be off. See you tomorrow.'

'You not on tonight, then?' Walter said. 'Jammy bugger.'

Paul waited for Sandra to say something, but she was busy at the sink. 'See you?'

She looked over her shoulder. 'Yeah, right.'

Outside on the pavement, breathing the tainted air, he relived the kiss. Had there been a second's yielding before she pulled away? *Nah, wishful thinking. No fool like an old fool, et-bloody-cetera.* He began to walk home, but slowly, in no hurry to get there, noticing cordoned-off streets, gaps in terraces, some new, some already familiar. Relief at having survived the night fizzed in every vein.

But it was Sandra he thought about, as he walked along. Sandra, with her long, coarse, dark hair, the fringe that was always getting into her eyes, so she had to keep pushing it back. What with that and her short, stocky, little legs, she reminded him of a Shetland pony. Oh, she wasn't pretty, but he thought she had something better than prettiness: it was almost impossible to look at her without smiling. He wanted – oh, very badly, he wanted – to lie naked with her in a bed, to feel her young, strong, firm body under his. And, at first, he thought, sheer exhaustion might make lovemaking difficult, but then, in small touches and movements, the heat between them would grow, until at last sex became not merely possible, but urgent, necessary, unavoidable.

He was close to home now, but walking more slowly all the time, until at last, turning into the square, he was forced to acknowledge the truth: that he didn't want to go home at all.

Fifteen

Over the last few weeks, Neville's dislike of the Ministry of Information had become an almost hysterical loathing. He dated the change to one apparently endless afternoon when it first occurred to him that the ministry was alive; that its corridors were the intestines of some flabby, flatulent beast farting memos, reports and minutes that always had to be initialled and passed on, though as far as he could tell no action was ever taken.

Once you started thinking the building might be alive, the evidence for it rapidly accumulated. It was always on the move, always changing shape. Literally, from one Friday afternoon to the following Monday morning, whole corridors would appear or disappear. His own room, which was hardly big enough for one – though he shared it with two other people – had been carved out of another, much larger, room. The half-window let in scarcely any light, and the partition kept out no noise at all. So he was privy to the conversation of half a dozen shorthand typists, listening in – involuntarily, if not reluctantly – as they talked about their boyfriends, nightclubs they were going to, which dresses they were going to wear . . . How far they were going to go. 'Who is it tonight?' he heard one girl say. 'Somebody nice?' Giggles all round. 'Is it somebody you want to die with?'

That shook him. It made him think: *Who would I want to die with? Nobody*; but even as he said, or rather thought, 'nobody' he was back in the dining room with Elinor, holding out his hand, inviting her to dance with him. Totally unexpected, that evening they'd spent together. At first, he'd experienced no more than a slight awkwardness, a few tweaks of nostalgia perhaps, and yet by midnight it had been far more than that. When she smiled and turned away, he was immediately back on a dusty road with his head in her lap, seeing, as she bent over him, how her nipples formed two dark circles

103

against the thin white lawn of her blouse, as unexpected and mysterious as fish rising to break the smooth surface of a lake.

Hilde sat next to him: a sad Austrian woman. He'd have liked to practise his German on her, but, except when discussing the finer points of a translation, she stuck resolutely to English. The only other inhabitant of the room was an old man with the streaming white hair of an Old Testament prophet, Bertram Somebody-or-other, but he appeared less and less frequently. They were supposed to be translating a series of pamphlets collectively entitled *Life under the Nazis*, but progress was slow, and the material unpromising. Hilde, he suspected, knew far more about life under the Nazis than any of the authors did.

Every morning, as he entered the building, along with hundreds of other identically dressed men carrying identical briefcases, his spirits sank. By mid-afternoon, he was desperate, his eyes full of grit, his mouth dry, every muscle aching. As the golden light crept across the parquet floor, he daren't think about sleep. To try to keep himself awake, he went along the corridor to the Gents, where he splashed his face with cold water. There was a mirror behind the washbasin, but he avoided looking at his reflection. He'd long ago mastered the art of washing, combing his hair and even shaving by touch alone. Each basin had a cheap plastic nailbrush chained to the wall behind the taps, for all the world as if they were priceless medieval Bibles. The irritation this caused him was out of all proportion; he wanted to wrench the bloody things off the wall, but of course he didn't. Though as he walked back to the stuffy little room, he was nursing fantasies of escape. After all, he wasn't obliged to stay here. He could leave – leave London, for that matter – go somewhere else, anywhere else, and paint. Accident had made him a journalist and a critic – and a good one, too – but it was not who he was.

Hilde hardly looked up when he came back into the room. She wore her hair pinned up in a rather untidy bun; as he squeezed past he looked down at the nape of her neck and wondered why it should be that exhaustion increased the desire to fuck. Logically, it should have had the opposite effect, but it never did, not with him anyway. In fact, a lot of his time in this room was spent weaving fantasies about Hilde or the typists next door or . . . Well, anybody really. There was nothing to take his mind off it. When talking to Tarrant he'd emphasized the importance of his work, but really anybody with fluent German could have done it. Yes, he dealt with classified information, but only because all information here was classified. The lowest classification was 'Secret' and that was applied to the requisitioning of toilet rolls. Sighing, he sat down, pulled a stack of files towards him and began to sort through it.

The clock ticked towards six. The Indian-summer afternoon was slipping away and that mattered so much these days, when people lay in the parks and squares basking in the sun like lizards, or stood in doorways and windows, raising their eyes to the light, storing it up against the blackout. Nobody dared think about the coming winter when days would be shorter and air raids longer. As he crouched over the files, he could hear Hilde's stocking-clad legs – where did she get them? – whispering to each other as she walked across to the filing cabinet. She bent to pull out the lower drawer and he gazed hungrily at her backside. A minute later, she found the file she was looking for and straightened up. As she turned, their eyes met and he saw her flinch as she registered the full force of his melancholy lust. Quickly, not looking at him, she returned to her desk.

Ah, well. She wasn't even noticeably attractive, though to him at the moment almost all women were attractive, at least to some degree. On his last free night, he'd gone out walking. It was one of the paradoxes of his present exhausted state that on the nights when he wasn't on duty, he sometimes found it difficult to sleep. After tossing and turning for an hour, he thought: *To hell with it* and went out. Though he was London born and bred, he found the blacked-out streets not only startling, but confusing. More than once he got lost. Piccadilly, after dark, felt particularly strange, because in peacetime it had always been so brightly lit. He stopped to light a cigarette and heard the tapping of a prostitute's heels on the pavement. High heels, on these lightless nights, always sounded erotic, but a prostitute's especially so because they hammered tacks into the heels and toes, to make them stand out. And stand out they certainly did, beating an urgent, unmistakable tattoo. This wasn't the only way prostitutes defeated the blackout. Another, was to lurk in shop doorways and, whenever a man approached, shine their blackout torches on exposed breasts or the triangle of darkness at the apex of their thighs. He found these spotlit body parts disturbing: they reminded him of an incident he'd attended near King's Cross where a railway arch, being used as an unofficial shelter, had suffered a direct hit. When the ambulances got there, heavy rescue squads were pulling arms, legs, heads, hands, feet from the rubble, lining them up on the pavement. Somebody had flashed a torch along the line and it was exactly like this. Revulsion and a kind of excitement. The girl whose *tap-tapping* footsteps he'd heard – he could see her now, walking towards him, or at least he could see the shape of her, which was all he needed or wanted to see. As he came closer, she shone her torch down on to her slim legs – the ankles almost fever-ishly thin. They found each other in a shop doorway. He pushed up her skirt, his fingers snagging on her stocking tops, slipping across her bare thighs into the warm, moist darkness between, moaning now, gasping for breath, over in seconds, laughing shakily as he withdrew. From beginning to end, he hadn't seen her face.

Promptly at six, Neville closed the file he was working on and reached for his hat. Hilde was already putting on her jacket. They walked to the lift together, or if not together then at least not osten-tatiously apart, but then she met one of the secretaries from the room next door and stopped to chat so he waved and went on alone.

The lift took ages to arrive; it always did at this time of day. He killed time by looking at the paintings on the wall, which were quite possibly, for all he knew, selected by Kenneth Clark himself. His office was further down the corridor. One, in particular, Neville objected to: a landscape, a beauty spot somewhere in the Lake District, precisely the sort of painting that had no reason to exist. A bit like some of Tarrant's early stuff. Oh my God, it might even be a Tarrant. He peered at the signature, but it was illegible, and then stood back, determined to give the painting a fair chance. *No*, noth-ing there at all, just a picture-postcard view of a lake. Couldn't even tell which one. Ullswater? *Wet*, anyway.

The sight of that scrawled, illegible signature – *was* that a 'T'? – reminded him he was having supper with the Tarrants that night. Probably not a good idea. The continued silence from Kenneth Clark had begun to prey on his mind. Of course it shouldn't matter that he – Neville – was being continually passed over. Every night when on duty he saw lives ended prematurely, people injured, mutilated, in terrible pain. What possible importance could personal ambition have in such a context? Oh, but it did, it *did*. It hurt that Tarrant's reputation had overtaken his. And yet somehow the friendship survived, though it was an odd relationship. Sometimes it hardly seemed like friendship at all.

Whatever it was, he was in for a whole evening of it. The original invitation – when they finally managed to hit on a date when nobody was on duty – had been for dinner at their house, but then Elinor had telephoned to say the house had been damaged by blast – kitchen window blown in, something like that – so now they were going to a restaurant in Dean Street instead.

Elinor was already at the bar when he arrived. She raised her cheek for him to kiss and then they settled down to wait for Tarrant, who'd been unavoidably delayed. No sirens yet.

'So you've been bombed?' he asked.

'Just blast. Kitchen window came in, I've been running round all day trying to find a glazier . . .'

'Still, you've got it boarded up all right?'

'Oh, yes, no problems there, it's secure.'

'Well, that's the main thing.'

'The clocks have stopped. And the electric went off for a time but it's back on now.'

She was looking tired, he thought. Understandably. 'Shall we have a drink while we wait?'

'Oh, yes, please.'

While the barman poured, she sat clasping and unclasping her hands. 'You know, I was expecting Paul to be upset. About the clocks, I mean. He's very fond of them, he's always polishing them and winding them up, and he wasn't at all. In fact, he was rather excited. "We're outside time," he said.'

'Is that why he's late?'

'No, he'll be painting.'

'How has he been?'

'Not too bad, he's not falling over or anything, but he does seem very unsettled. You know that woman he met –?'

'The Witch of Endor, yes.'

'He keeps talking about her.'

'I'm surprised he doesn't see through it.'

'It's Kenny; he blames himself. I don't know what to say any more, he's got me at my wits' end.'

Tarrant arrived a few minutes later, wearing an open-necked blue shirt and a shabby, expensive jacket. 'Sorry.' He settled into the chair beside Elinor. 'I lost track of time.'

Oh dear me. The artist at work.

'You still have an outside studio?'

'God, yes, I couldn't work at home, never could.'

'I've got a room in the attic,' Elinor said.

Neville raised his hand to summon the waiter. 'What'll you drink, Tarrant?'

'I think I'll stick to wine.'

'Well, make the most of it. I drink whisky all the time now. No chance of that running out. Unless he invades Scotland first.'

'Oh, don't talk about invasion,' Elinor said. 'Do you know Violet's got a cyanide capsule? She has, she showed me.'

Bloody hell. It had come to something when middle-aged, dried-up old spinsters took to carrying cyanide capsules. What did she think was going to happen to her, for Christ's sake?

'She's a Communist. Was, anyway.'

'*Violet?*'

Elinor bristled. 'Why not?'

'You never really know people, do you?'

The waiter brought them a menu, which showed a surprising range of choice. 'They're good here,' Tarrant said.

Elinor began reminiscing about food in Spain. 'It's so easy, you know, you go to the market every day, everything's so fresh.'

'It's becoming a bit of a legend, our time out there,' Tarrant said.

'Yes,' Elinor said. 'It is a bit; it's our Land of Lost Content. Well, mine, anyway.'

'When did you come back?'

'We gave the place up in '36,' Tarrant said. 'A man we knew very well – he used to keep an eye on the house when we were in England – was shot in the marketplace and nobody was charged though everybody knew who'd done it – so we thought: Right, that's it, time to go.'

'I still think about sitting out on the terrace in the early morning, having coffee; the sun used to catch the top of the church and everywhere else was still dark.' She seemed to be on the verge of tears.

Tarrant said, quite sharply, 'I think we can be just as happy here.' No response. 'Elinor's inherited her mother's cottage and it's . . . Well, it's really rather nice.'

'Roses round the door.'

Tarrant put his glass down. 'I think you'd like it if you'd only give it a chance.'

Elinor seemed to become aware that Neville was being virtually excluded from the conversation – excluded, but also used as an audience. She said lightly, or with an attempt at lightness, 'Paul wants to pack me off to the country, away from all the nasty bombs.'

'Yes. I do – and I'm not ashamed of it either.' He looked directly at Neville. 'I'd just find everything so much easier if I knew she was safe.'

'She? I am still here, you know.'

Tarrant was looking increasingly exasperated. 'People didn't take their wives into the trenches with them.'

'No, but the trenches didn't run through the family living room.'

'And now they do?'

'Paul, the kitchen window was blown in last night! Anyway, I'm not going and that's that.'

A tense silence.

'You'd be missed,' Neville said. Not perhaps the most tactful thing he could have said, but true all the same.

She looked at him and smiled, and immediately he was back in the country lane, seeing her nipples, hearing a loud *plop* as a frog, affronted by the invasion of his territory, leapt to safety in a ditch . . . And for all the hope *he* had of kissing the princess, he might as well have been the fucking frog. All the same, this marriage was in trouble. Oh, they'd both deny it, but all the same it was. He knew the signs.

Fortunately, at that moment, the waiter arrived to tell them their table was ready, and over the meal the talk took a less abrasive turn.

Going home in the taxi, Elinor said, 'I wish you hadn't mentioned the cottage.'

'Why?'

'Because I don't want him telling the other drivers and them thinking I'm suddenly going to not show up or something.'

'I don't think he'll do that.'

'He's a gossip.'

'No, he's not. He's not interested enough in other people to be a gossip.' He gave her a sidelong glance. 'Tell you one thing, though, he's a bit in love with you.'

A yelp of disbelief. When she saw he was serious, she said: 'Actually, I used to think he was a bit in love with you.'

'What, Neville? No, he's not like that.'

She shrugged and stared out of the window, though there was little to be seen except a circle of blue warning lights around a crater in the road.

While Paul paid the driver, Elinor opened the front door and went through into the drawing room where she was immediately confronted by the carriage clock on the mantelpiece, its hands stopped at twenty past three. Oddly enough, the grandfather clock on the upstairs landing disagreed, putting the time of the explosion at twenty-five to four.

She remembered how strange Paul had been, how almost . . . elated. She'd watched him bending over the clock, shaking it gently to see if it would start, getting out the key, trying to wind it up. She'd been so sure he'd be upset, even perhaps disproportionately upset, but when he turned to face her his eyes were shining. *We're outside time*, he'd said.

She heard the taxi pull away and a moment later Paul came into the room. 'Do you fancy another drink or . . .?'

'No, I think I'll go up now.'

Undressed, stretched about between the sheets, she waited for him to join her, worrying about the broken window and where, in this city of broken glass, she was going to find a glazier willing to take on a small domestic job. Paul got undressed quickly, and as soon as he got into bed turned on his side away from her. Cautiously, not sure if she'd be welcome or not, she rested her cheek between his shoulder blades, feeling a raised mole pressing into her skin. She could have drawn, from memory, the position of every mole on his back. She rested her hand on his hip, then let it slide across his stomach until she was gently cupping his balls. His breath quickened, but he didn't turn to face her, or, in any other way, respond, and after a while she took her hand away.

Sixteen

Elinor came off duty, her hair grey with dust and her trousers sticking uncomfortably to the backs of her thighs. She'd tried shampooing her hair in the showers, but it didn't work. If you weren't careful you risked turning the plaster dust into a paste. People were aged by it, the dust in their hair, that and the rings of exhaustion under their eyes. Women who, before the war, had worn no make-up plastered themselves with it now. Even Violet had been seen dabbing girlishly pink lipstick on her mouth. Dana, like Elinor, went the whole hog: vanishing cream, powder, rouge, eye shadow, the lot.

Elinor walked quickly. She wanted to get home, make tea, have a bath, fall into bed and snatch a couple of hours' sleep before starting on the shopping and cooking and the hundred and one other things that had to be fitted in as if everything were normal. Painting? Ah, well. Somehow, in these changed circumstances, Paul went on painting. She didn't.

The sun was only just rising over the rooftops of the still-intact buildings, casting a cruel light on ruins that had already become familiar, no longer novelties to be gawped at. There was a gap on the corner, and it was an effort to remember which shop used to be there, though it couldn't be more than a week since that bomb fell. Everywhere, there was the crunch of glass under tramping feet as people came up out of the shelters, blinked, took deep breaths, tried to decide between heading home or going straight to work. The streets glittered, hurting her eyes.

Further along, she stopped, then almost ran the rest of the way, because now she could see yellow tape stretched across the entrance to the square. Somebody's house must've been hit, and though really it was no more than a nameless, mouth-parching fear, the conviction grew on her that this time her luck had run out, this time it was her house that had gone.

A group of people, among them many of her neighbours, was standing at the tape. An old man with white hair tried to duck under it, but a warden yelled at him to get back. There was a time bomb at the centre of the square, under the grass, and another in the middle of the road. She could see a sort of boil under the tarmac. Until those bombs were dealt with, nobody was going home.

From this angle, she couldn't quite see her house, though she could see that a house three doors further up had been virtually demolished – that must be where the bomb had fallen. So her house – hers and Paul's – had to be badly damaged. It couldn't not be.

Everybody stood looking into the familiar square that seemed as strange now as the cratered surface of the moon. People whispered. Why? There was no reason for it, and yet not one person spoke at a normal pitch. A deadly silence emanated from the broken houses, the piles of rubble, that menacing blister in the surface of the road. Men clambered across the ruins like black beetles. A woman lit a cigarette and a warden shouted at her to put it out. Gas mains had burst, did she want the whole bloody street to go up? The woman blushed, pinched the cigarette between thumb and forefinger and replaced the tab end in the packet.

Elinor looked round for Paul and saw him approaching, with that distinctive loping stride of his. He hadn't seen her yet, hadn't seen the yellow tape. When he did, he stamped out his cigarette and broke into a run. They met and embraced and she started crying, which surprised her because she hadn't known till then how close she was to tears.

Paul pulled on her elbow, indicating they should walk round to the back of the square: they might be able to see their house more clearly from there. She followed him, stumbling over bricks, hardly able to keep up with him: he was striding ahead as if his life depended on it. Now, she could get a closer look at the house that had received the direct hit. It had been sliced in half with almost surgical precision. On the first floor, a green brocade armchair cocked one elegant cabriole leg over the abyss. There was a bathroom with a washbasin and toilet, looking somehow vulnerable, touching even, like a fleeting, accidental glimpse of somebody's backside. You wanted to cover it up, restore its dignity, but there was no way of doing that.

She knew the three girls who lived in the basement flat – they didn't go to any of the public shelters. They were all young nurses working at University College Hospital. She remembered their laughter on summer evenings, the parties that used to go on half the night, how irritated she'd been. Now she felt her additional years, the years they wouldn't have, as a sagging of the skin, a weight pulling her down, and she was ashamed.

'Can you see what's happened?' she asked.

'No, but I'm going to find out.'

Of course, Paul knew all the local wardens. He simply put his tin hat on and ducked under the tape. She watched him stride across to the man who seemed to be in charge, heard a mutter of conversation, then saw Paul walk on a few steps and peer up the street. He stood staring for a minute, then turned and came back to her.

'There's no hope of getting back in tonight. We're going to have to find somewhere to sleep.'

'Could you see the house?'

He pulled a face. 'Not good. The roof's caved in. I don't think they're going to let us live there, even after they've dealt with the bombs.'

'But it's still standing?'

'Well, just about. Basically, it's collapsed in a V shape.' His hands were making the shape as he spoke. 'We might be able to get something out, depends how stable it is. But it's not looking good.'

Instantly, Elinor felt smaller, less competent, as dependent on Paul as a small child might have been. 'Where shall we go?'

'Oh, there's plenty of B&Bs around. Look, why don't I put you in a café while I go and book us in somewhere? At least then we'll know where we're going to be. Or . . .' He turned to face her. 'I could take you to the station and you could stay with Rachel, just for a few nights, then you can move into the cottage. Have your own place.'

'What about you?'

'I'm all right, I can sleep in the studio.'

'But I don't want to leave you.'

'Well, yes, all right. First thing is, to find a room. And there's clothes . . . You know, you've still got a few things at Rachel's . . .'

'No, absolutely not.'

'All right.'

He sighed, the slump of his shoulders telling her she'd become a problem, something he had to worry about, a distraction from other, arguably more important, matters. That sigh weakened her, undermined her, as almost nothing else could have done.

'Come on,' she said. 'We'll find somewhere together.'

The room they found, in one of the side roads off Oxford Street, was small with yellowish-brown paper on the walls. The one window looked out into a basement yard so at all times of the day they were in semi-darkness. Their faces loomed pale in the brown-spotted mirror, like fish in a badly maintained tank.

By day, Elinor had nowhere to go – it was almost impossible to stay in the room – so she spent a lot of time just wandering around, always drawn back to the square where she'd spent so many years of her life. It was still cordoned off; she stood, with other lost souls, looking across the tape at the bulge in the road, and the wrecked houses. Apparently quite a few of them would have to be demolished, including, Paul seemed to think, their own.

She couldn't face going on duty from the B&B or leaving it to go to one of the public shelters. So when Paul was on duty, she simply lay on the bed and waited for him to return. But then, on the fourth night, she gave herself a good talking-to and reported to the ambulance depot, as usual. Dana and Violet welcomed her with open arms, and other people too – people who in normal circumstances she would probably never have met – went out of their way to be kind. They seemed to care about her – as she did about them.

Next morning, exhausted, but determined to spend the day looking for more permanent accommodation, she went back to Oxford Street and found the B&B had been bombed. So there they were, for the second time in a week, homeless.

Or rather, she was. Paul could always move into his studio, which – as he never tired of pointing out – wasn't big enough for two.

They stood in a doorway on Oxford Street surrounded by yet another group of shocked, disorientated people. The newly risen sun glinted on the silver barrage balloons and silhouetted the broken outline of bombed and partially demolished buildings. The usual smell of charred timber and burning bricks. On the other side of the tape was sunlit emptiness. A man, standing halfway up the road, shimmered in the heat from a still-smouldering building. He seemed almost to be walking on water. The woman standing next to Elinor had long, Rapunzel-like hair, loosely plaited, reaching to her waist, though it was iron-grey. Elinor noticed these things, but blankly, unable to attach any meaning to what she saw.

Paul stood beside Elinor, his elbow lightly touching hers. She realized, without the need for speech, that this second bomb had settled the argument. She would go to Rachel's and then to the cottage, not because she thought it was the right thing to do, but because her tired mind couldn't come up with an alternative. In front of them, closer to the tape, a young girl was brushing her long black hair, trying to get rid of the dust, but soothing herself too, perhaps. As she bent and swayed, her whole body followed the movement of her arm. How slender and supple her waist was. Elinor was aware of Paul following the girl's every movement, and she'd never felt more distant from him than she did at that moment.

'I want to go back to the house.'

'Is that a good idea?'

'I'll go to the cottage, but I want to see the house first.'

'All right, I'll see if I can find a taxi.'

Even in a few days, her memory of the square had started to fade. She struggled now to remember what number 35 had looked like, what colour its front door had been. Next year she supposed buddleia and rosebay willow herb would throng the empty spaces where people had once lived. She closed her eyes. Everywhere – every step she took, every step anybody took – was the crunch of broken glass.

The time bombs' detonation had inflicted further damage on their house, but at least they were allowed access to the square. They could see at first hand the extent of the damage by climbing cautiously over the outer fringes of the rubble. She could even see into her kitchen. The dresser had somehow become jammed at an angle to the wall. She caught a glint of knives and forks, the blue-and-white fragments of a serving dish. They would be able to get a few things out, but it wasn't pots and pans she wanted, it was the paintings from her attic studio, the portraits of her father and Toby. All gone. And, with them, so much of her past.

She and Paul picked their way around the ruin separately. At one point, she saw him straighten up and look around, and the expression on his face was, unmistakably, one of relief.

She slid down the last slope of rubble and waited for him in the road.

'Well,' he said, coming across to join her. 'Worse than you thought?'

She couldn't look at him. 'I don't think I can face another B&B. I think I'd be better off in the country.'

A hint of satisfaction. 'I'm sure that's right.'

Straggling apart, they walked away from their house, past the crater where two nights ago one of the time bombs had exploded. Trudging along with her eyes on the road, Elinor was startled by an unexpected flash of light, and looked up to see sunshine streaming through a gap in the terrace. The light gilded the tops of trees and bushes that only a week ago had been struggling to survive in deep shade. Oh, yes, all kinds of opportunities for new growth. Only not for her.

She stopped and looked around her, wanting to remember the moment. Then, needing reassurance, she glanced at Paul, but against that dazzling shaft of light he'd become merely a silhouette, featureless.

It might have been anybody standing there.

Seventeen

Left alone in London, Paul felt increasingly restless. Partly this was because of his constant involuntary searching for Kenny. He scanned the faces of children he passed in the streets, and somehow, despite the raids, London seemed to be full of children. He watched them during the day, playing in the parks – the schools were still closed – or queuing outside the Underground stations. Children were often sent on ahead to claim the family's favourite spot; you would see them, laden with sleeping bags and blankets, sometimes laughing and messing about, but waiting for hours.

Paul's studio was only ten minutes' walk from his station, so on the nights when he was on duty he went straight to the School of Tropical Medicine basement after finishing work, and played cards or darts till the sirens went and it was time to go out on patrol.

The evenings when he was not on duty were more of a problem, because he found it quite impossible to stay indoors during a raid. He could remember feeling exactly like this during the last war. Very often at night he'd shunned the comparative safety of the dug-out for walks between sentry posts. Anything was better than the dank, grave-smelling murk of life underground, where a single candle, guttering in the blast from an exploding shell, would send panic-stricken shadows fleeing across the walls. The dugout was safer, yes, but it never *felt* safe. Now, he felt the same way about the public shelters. On the nights when he wasn't on duty, he walked miles through the blacked-out city, sometimes not getting home till two or even three in the morning, by which time he was too exhausted not to sleep.

The darkness turned London into a palimpsest. That knot of bois-terous young men by the crush barriers, they were probably soldiers home from Dunkirk, or just possibly stragglers from Boudicca's army. After all, from the perspective of the poor bloody infantry, one cock-up's pretty much like another. You had a sense on these nights of long-buried bones working their way to the surface: London's dead gurgling up through the drains. Perhaps in these thronging shadows the living and the dead met in fleeting, unconscious encounters. Why not? *How would you know?*

On one of these walks, he found himself in a side street near Coram's Fields. On the corner there was a pawnshop, its three brass balls suspended over the pavement, a symbol so evocative of his youth he had to cross the road for a closer look. In the window, as he'd expected, were rows and rows of little white cards offering rings – most poignantly, wedding rings – for sale. Probably they'd been pawned over and over again until some worsening of an already desperate situation meant they couldn't be redeemed. Ah, *redeemed*. The religious language of pawnbroking had always fascinated him.

When he was a boy, his grandmother had owned a pawnshop, conducting business with her usual rapacity. Many of her clients were pawning goods in order to pay the rent on the ramshackle properties she owned. Yet Gran hadn't been the bloated capitalist of socialist theory, but a half-literate working-class woman who'd got many a black eye from her handsome, philandering husband until she stopped loving him and learned to hit back – or rather, since she was a tiny, bird-like woman, to wait till he was too pissed to know what he was drinking and then jollop him till his arse bled.

Paul's first job had been behind the counter of her shop: he'd done his homework in between customers. When he leaned forward, he could see his reflection in wood that had been polished to a hard conker-shine by the weight of human misery that passed over it. But it was a job, a proper job, and he had been proud of it.

God, how it all came flooding back. He was about to move on, when he saw a notice in the bottom-right-hand corner of the window. Bertha Mason, materialization medium, would be giving a seance at eight o'clock this evening. The accompanying photograph was creased and grainy – obviously cut from a newspaper – but there could be no mistaking the woman. It was the Witch of Endor, no less. He bent down to make sure, but, yes, it had to be. There couldn't be two women in London who looked like that. Eight o'clock – just time for a pint of beer and a sandwich. He thought he might as well give it a go, as much from nostalgia as anything else, though he was curious about the woman who had made a disagreeable but powerful impression on him. He wasn't finding her easy to forget.

Returning an hour later, he stepped into a shop whose smells stripped away the intervening years till he was fourteen years old again. A single bulb cast a pallid light over the detritus of hopeless lives: musty-smelling clothes hung from racks, some, with pink tickets, waiting to be redeemed; others, with blue tickets, up for sale. Racks of shoes pressed out of shape by other people's bunions, dresses with other people's sweat stains under the arms, a hatstand from which hung a solitary bowler hat, shiny with age. Despite the downtrodden, shabby air of it all, he kept experiencing exquisitely painful tweaks of nostalgia. Not for when he was a child serving in the shop for the first time – no; for a year or so later, when he was a pimply adolescent with hairs on the palms of his hands. The hairs hadn't been real hairs, of course – they were what you were threatened with if you didn't stop doing *it* – and try as he might he never could stop. There were some mornings when he could virtually have combed those hairs.

There'd been a girl called Gemma Martin who'd come in every Monday morning on her way to work to pawn her father's Sunday suit. Long blonde hair, the greenish colour of unripe wheat, and slightly prominent blue eyes. Gran didn't like the Martins. 'I knew her mam when her knickers were that raggy she was ashamed to hang them on the line. And as for her nan – she used to sew bacon fat in her vest and bloomers every December, didn't take them off till March. I've seen dogs follow her down the street.' The Martins, he gathered, gave themselves airs: a worse crime than murder in Gran's book.

What with Gran's beady eyes and vitriolic tongue, it had taken him nearly six months to summon up the courage to ask Gemma out. Oh, but it was worth it. And the reason he found all these smells erotic, was that one evening, hours after the shop had closed, he'd managed to persuade Gemma to go nearly all the way, on a pile of unredeemed coats.

It was five to eight; he ought to be taking his seat. A thin man with round spectacles appeared and guided him past the racks of clothes and up a rickety staircase. At the top was a small landing packed with people waiting to buy tickets. More people were coming up the stairs behind him. Since that basement in Agate Street he'd hated overcrowded spaces and might have left, only at that moment the couple in front moved on, and he was level with the table. A woman with mournful brown eyes was taking the money, attempting to look deeply spiritual while counting notes with the help of spit on a well-practised thumb. He handed over a ten-shilling note, was given a ticket and asked to surrender his blackout torch.

'Why?'

She looked at him. 'When the medium's in a trance, her eyes are very sensitive to light.'

'But there's hardly any light.' Blackout torches were notoriously dim.

Rolling the notes into a wad, she snapped an elastic band tight around them. '*Very* sensitive.' He gave her the torch.

The seance room was cramped and stuffy, lit only by three small, red-shaded lamps set at intervals along the far wall. An usher guided him to a seat near the back, though he noticed there was a whole row of vacant seats at the front. It was so dark he could hardly see to get to his seat and had to apologize constantly for trampling on people's toes. When, finally, he was settled, he took a deep breath and looked around. Eight rows of chairs faced a stage on which stood some kind of cabinet, not unlike a nightwatchman's box. Black curtains had been pulled back to reveal a wooden chair with arms. He noticed another chair near the front of the stage, which seemed to have black clothes draped over the back. The room was about two thirds full, and it was well past eight o'clock, but for a long time nothing happened, except whispers and coughing and more muttered apologies as late arrivals tripped over people's feet.

He could see slightly better now. In the third row, he noticed a middle-aged shelter warden, Angela Langdale, very jolly-hockey-sticks, but rather nice, with a lot of mousey-fair down on her upper lip and a genius for organization. When he was on patrol, he often called in at her shelter for a cup of tea and a cigarette. Next to her was Sandra Jobling. Now that was a surprise. He didn't think of Sandra as the sort of person who went to seances, but then he didn't think of himself as that sort of person either.

The thought of a cigarette, once planted, quickly blossomed into a craving, though when he looked around he saw that nobody else was smoking. Perhaps the organizers were so wedded to darkness that even the striking of a match seemed threatening? He tried to ignore the craving, but it wouldn't go away, so he repeated the stumbling and apologizing, receiving in return some decidedly disgruntled looks.

Downstairs, he found the front door locked, but there'd be a back entrance and almost certainly a yard. He pushed between the racks of clothes, releasing a smell of mothballs which made him want to sneeze, and found himself in another much smaller room, hardly more than a passage really, with three doors opening off. The first door led into a broom cupboard containing an ironing board, a bucket and a mop. The next door opened on to a room where at last, *at last*, there was enough light to see by, though what he saw defied belief. He stood, rooted to the ground, jaw unhinged, gawping like an idiot.

Bertha Mason sat, naked, on a table, facing him, surrounded by three middle-aged women, all dressed in black, but he had eyes for nobody but her. The sheer size of her: chins, neck, breasts, belly – all pendulous – the sagging, wrinkled abdomen hanging so low it almost hid the fuzz of black hair beneath. Like a huge, white, half-melted candle she sat, eyes glazed, a fag end glued to her bottom lip. She made no move to cover herself, just sat there, breathing noisily through her open mouth. He stared, he couldn't stop himself, until one of the women darted forward and slammed the door in his face.

Dazed, he opened the third door and blundered out into a small yard where he lit a cigarette, dragging smoke into his lungs like oxygen. What he felt was neither pity nor revulsion, but something altogether more complex. An image was taking shape in his mind: the Willendorf Venus. That featureless face beneath elaborately styled hair, vestigial arms, roll upon roll of fat, each roll resting on the one below, vestigial legs, no feet. But it's not negative: she has no eyes because she contains the world; she has no feet because everything comes to her. It's an image of power.

At least Bertha Mason had a face, though it had been completely blank. Was she in a trance? Had to be, something like that. He crushed the remains of the cigarette beneath his foot, taking his time, grinding it away to nothing, then went back upstairs to the crowded room where a buzz of expectation was running along the rows.

His seat had been taken. The back rows were full so he crept down the aisle and took a seat on the end of the front row. Nobody challenged him, though he saw that all these seats were marked 'Reserved'. Evidently only known supporters were allowed as close to the platform as this.

The lady of the ten-shilling notes mounted the stairs and announced in a markedly nasal voice that she would now invite a member of the audience – 'chosen at random' – to step up and examine the medium's clothes. The randomly chosen one, who'd been sitting in one of the reserved seats on the front row, shook the clothes, turned them inside out, ran her fingers ostentatiously along every seam, and then, with a brisk nod, handed them back. The garments were ceremoniously carried out and returned, shortly afterwards, with Mrs Mason inside them, wheezing from the climb upstairs. Her breathing was so bad Paul was inclined to shout: *Oh for God's sake, stop messing about, call a doctor!* She had to be helped on to the platform. Once there, she took a moment to get her breath, then entered the cabinet, where she lowered herself into the chair and let her head fall back, shortly afterwards emitting a succession of grunts and snorts as the curtains, with a great rattling of brass rings, were pulled across. Raggedly at first, then with more conviction, the audience began to sing 'Abide with Me'.

Paul didn't know what to expect. Fraud, yes, of course: only he'd thought it would be subtle. Skilled. What followed was fraud all right, but blatant, crude, embarrassingly unconvincing fraud. He didn't understand how anybody could possibly be taken in by it, but people were. One woman looked positively radiant as she recognized the face of her dead son, though, to Paul, the returning spirit was very obviously a papier mâché head stuck on the end of a broomstick and draped in cheesecloth; cheesecloth which smelled strongly of fish.

Mrs Mason had two spirit guides. The one who appeared most frequently, who acted as a kind of impresario, was Albert, who'd apparently seen service on the Western Front, and had passed over, as he put it, on the first day of the Somme. Albert's voice was convincingly masculine; his public-school accent much less so. This was no more than a music-hall imitation of a toff and even that was starting to slip a bit. The other guide, who popped up from time to time, was a little girl of truly awful sweetness who would keep bursting into song: Shirley Temple, but without the talent. Paul was sickened by it. No, quite literally: he felt sick. Probably he should have walked out, but the memory of that naked figure, the wheeze of her laboured breathing, held him back. Instead he closed his eyes, determined to detach himself from the proceedings.

But then the curtains were drawn back. Mrs Mason, looking decidedly the worse for wear, announced she would give a few individual messages. The audience leaned forward: this was the moment they'd been waiting for. Their turn.

It was the usual trite, banal rubbish. At one point she looked directly at Paul, and he tensed, afraid she was going to give him one of her messages, afraid, irrationally afraid, of what the message might be. At that moment he realized this visit of his was not curiosity about Mrs Mason, or a trip down memory lane, but something more driven, less rational: part of the endless, exhausting search for Kenny, which still went on even though he knew there was no hope of finding him. He wasn't detached from this: he was just like all the other people here.

He was afraid of her. It was a relief when she turned her attention to the back row, to yet another middle-aged woman with a missing son. A voice began to speak, every bit as convincing as Albert, but offering no banal message of comfort: no reassuring platitudes. The beach at Dunkirk, dunes being sprayed with bullets, sand kicked up into the air, cracked lips, no water, his friend dead in the sand beside him – not a British plane in sight. Where were they? Where were the British planes? The words dwindled to an angry mutter before finally winding down into silence. Seconds later, along came Shirley Temple and 'The Good Ship Lollipop'.

But now, suddenly, a commotion broke out near the back of the room. People started turning round, trying to peer into the darkness, one or two of them even stood on their chairs. A tall woman, wearing mannish tweeds, strode down the aisle, shining a forbidden torch on the stage – and not a blackout torch either: a proper pre-war flashlight. Mrs Mason ran back into the cabinet and, with a rattle of brass rings, pulled the curtains across. No sooner had she disappeared than the tall woman leapt on to the platform, pulled the curtains apart and revealed an empty chair. Mrs Mason was on her knees, waving a doll with some kind of vest or camisole attached, and still prattling away in that awful cutesy-pie voice as if unable to grasp what was happening.

The tall woman grabbed the doll, Mrs Mason refused to let go, and an ugly tug of war ensued in which the doll's head came off. Everybody was on their feet now, riveted by the squalid battle. At last, Mrs Mason managed to wrench herself free and again ran back into the cabinet where she could be seen trying to stuff the doll's head up her skirt. At that moment the overhead lights came on, dazzling everybody. Transfixed by the sudden glare, Mrs Mason was still for a moment, then leapt out of the cabinet, roaring with anger.

The tall woman took a step back, but persisted. 'Come on, give it me, I know you've got it. Come on, I want to see what you've got up there.'

'What, and show everybody me knickers? I will *not*. There's men in here, case you haven't noticed.'

The tall woman had been joined on the platform by three

men, who crowded round Mrs Mason, demanding to see the doll. Turning swiftly, she picked up the chair and began wielding it as a battering ram. 'I'll brain the whole bloody lot of you, bloody buggering bastards!' And then she simply yelled, a great battle cry that seemed to require neither words nor intake of breath.

Paul was pushing his way up the steps on to the platform. Perhaps he should have been pleased to see such cynical fraud exposed, but three men jostling one woman was altogether too much like bullying for his taste. Surprising himself, he fought his way to her side. 'Mrs Mason.' Her eyes stared at him without recognition. So she had been in a trance – there was no other way she could have forgotten that encounter downstairs. 'Calm down, now. Deep breaths.' He turned. 'And you lot, back off. Can't you see the state she's in?'

After a while, she seemed to grow calmer. She would get undressed, she said, but only if the men left the room.

The three men who'd been crowding her looked at each other, but made no move. A few others, Paul included, retreated a few paces, though nobody moved very far. Mrs Mason squatted down and pulled her dress and petticoat over her head. Tangled up in the folds, was the doll's head, which fell and rolled across the floor, its china-blue eyes startling in the bristling light. Mrs Mason tried to kick it behind the cabinet, but was too slow. The tall woman pounced, scooped up the doll's head, and held it up for all to see. 'There.'

The sight seemed to enrage Mrs Mason, who began tearing at her clothes. One enormous breast, the size of a savoy cabbage, escaped her camisole and, despite swearing no man on earth should ever see her knickers, she was now whirling them about above her head, looking, Paul thought, like a corpulent version of Liberty leading the people.

'I'm keeping this.' The tall woman waved the doll's head at her. 'It's evidence.'

'You give that here, it's mine.' And, seizing the chair again, Mrs Mason launched another attack.

Paul tried to restrain her, but she was so beside herself he was beginning to think the whole farcical episode might end in murder.

A short, stocky man with a military moustache said: 'Why doesn't somebody ring the police?'

'No,' Mrs Mason said. 'There's no need for that.'

Slowly, she put down the chair and, after a minute or so, began to get dressed. Her lips were blue. Then, just as everybody started to relax, she charged again, seized the doll's head and ran out of the room.

Paul followed her and found her in the downstairs room, with a group of supporters gathered round her, like drones round a termite queen. One woman pressed a cup of tea into her hands; another fanned her with a copy of *Spiritualist News*, while the randomly chosen one held out a dress for her to put on.

There was a stir in the shop. The forces of law and order had arrived in the form of one bewildered police constable with a fresh, young, freckly face. There wasn't a great deal he could do. Nobody wanted to press charges, though the one man she'd caught a glancing blow with the chair was still bleeding. The tall woman introduced herself as Miss Pole, which amused Paul, though no one else seemed to think it was funny. Fraud was mentioned. Mrs Mason turned her eyes to the ceiling. 'As God is my witness, I know nothing about it.'

'What do you mean, you know nothing about it?' Miss Pole demanded. 'You had a doll's head in your knickers.'

Wisely, Mrs Mason burst into tears. One of the attendant women touched Paul's arm. 'Eh, dear God, that poor woman, she's a martyr, she is. She's been to prison, you know.'

Paul could quite believe it.

People were starting to leave. Nobody asked for their money back, perhaps feeling that one way or another they'd had a good show. The policeman left. Somehow, in all the turmoil, the doll's head had vanished, no doubt safely ensconced in somebody else's knickers. And not only the doll; cheesecloth, broomsticks, papier mâché heads: all spirited away. Miss Pole glared at Mrs Mason; Mrs Mason smirked. She'd got away with it, not for the first time, nor probably the last.

Paul looked around for Angela and Sandra, but they'd gone, so he set off to walk alone. A raid had started, so there was no question of going back to the studio just yet. He was alternately amused and nauseated by the events of the evening, or so at first he told himself, but then as he walked, he realized he was once more separating himself from the experience which at times he'd found deeply disturbing. Albert's voice, the young man dying on the beach at Dunkirk, stood out from what would otherwise have been blatant fraud, and nothing else but fraud. Papier mâché heads on broomsticks, fishy cheesecloth – fishy in every sense of the word – but was that the whole truth? He didn't think so. He thought she'd been doing something else, though he didn't believe the something else had much to do with contacting the dead.

He'd been afraid she'd tell him about Kenny, describe his last moments in the basement of the school. How could he be so frightened of something he didn't believe was possible? How could that woman, who was in so many ways pathetic – and also, it had to be said, repulsive – have such power? He remembered seeing her in the downstairs room, naked, eyes glazed, fag end stuck to her bottom lip, an image by turns embarrassing, pitiable and nightmarish. He tried to erase it from his mind, but it drew strength from darkness. As he walked from street to street, he found it easy to believe they were leading him to a secret chamber, right at the heart of the blacked-out city, where a white, bloated figure sat enthroned, a grotesque Persephone, claiming to speak for millions of the mouthless dead.

Eighteen

You weren't supposed to talk to the patients. The one time they'd caught her at it, Sister Matthews had come down on her like a ton of bricks. '*You* are a *ward maid.*' Lips pursed like a cat's arse. 'The patients are nothing to do with you.'

Aye, right. But when there'd been a rush on, after Dunkirk, she'd done all sorts, changed beds, emptied bedpans, pushed trolleys full of filthy sheets down to the laundry in the basement – and none of that was her job. Oh, and in between times, yes, she'd talked to the lads, and nobody pulled her up over it. Poor sods, they'd nowt to do all day except watch shadows moving on the walls, check the time to see how long it still was till visiting, strain to hear familiar footsteps coming up the ward.

Once things had settled down a bit, they played cards, talking through lips that hardly moved about stuff that had happened, some of the things they'd seen. Guardsmen forced to shave in seawater before they'd been allowed to get on a boat. 'Only in England,' one lad said. And then on the train coming back how people had thrown cigarettes in at the windows, treated them like conquering heroes, but they weren't heroes, not in their own estimation. Bloody cock-up – that was the general verdict. She'd never seen so many men so angry.

This poor lad here. Babbling away, but not making a lot of sense, poor soul. God knows what was going on in his head – and his breathing. And she thought hers was bad. First time she clapped eyes on him, she thought: *You're not long for this world, son.* But he had, he'd hung on. And he'd talked, my God he had, how they'd lain in the open under the hot sun, no water, not a British plane in sight. Chap next to him showed him a silk scarf he'd bought for his fancy bit – 'bought, my eye, bloody nicked it' – and then he'd died, lying there in the sand. 'And I took the scarf. Wasn't stealing, was it?' ''Course it wasn't, love. It was no good to him.'

And that's when Sister Matthews had pounced. Things were back to normal now, apparently. She was just the maid.

So now, though he went on babbling, she turned her back on him, kept herself busy polishing the taps, only then he said the one word that would have made any woman turn round. 'Mam.'

He was staring round him, wild-eyed, not a clue where he was, poor lad. 'Mam?'

She put her hand over his. 'It's all right, son. You go off to sleep, now, it's all right.'

He closed his eyes. A few minutes later the fluttering behind his lids stopped, and his mouth fell slightly open. Had he gone? Still touching his hand, she watched his chest, saw the almost-imperceptible rise. No, not yet, but it wouldn't be long.

Mam. She knew it was stupid, but the word kept catching in her throat. He could be, she told herself – well, just about. Her son had been born bang in the middle of the last war, so what would that make him, what – twenty-four, twenty-five? About right. Of course, it wasn't him, she knew that, but . . . Well, no, actually, come to think of it, you couldn't *know*, could you? Not for certain, you couldn't. She needed to go back and see him again, look for resemblances, but she couldn't. There was another ward to clean, and another. Far too many. Seemed to think you could work bloody miracles.

So she trudged from bed to bed, basin to basin, ward to ward. All the time, floating in front of her eyes, was the memory of the purple, howling dwarf they'd torn out of her all them years ago. She'd never seen a newborn baby before. Little babies, yes, a few days old, but not newborn. And my God it come as a shock, she'd no idea they looked like that.

She'd gone into the home the minute she started showing. For a long time you could cover it up with cardigans and jumpers, but not for ever – and you weren't allowed to work in the munitions factory if you were pregnant, something to do with the chemicals, so she more or less had to go in the home. Where was she going to find another job with a belly on her like that? No, it was the home, or starve.

They put her to work in the laundry – laughable, really – lifting buckets, twelve-hour shifts, wonder they didn't all lose their babies – and probably better if they had. But at least the work tired you out. She was asleep the minute her head touched the pillow. And what a lumpy pillow it was. The pillowcase was always spotless – matron saw to that – but the pillow smelled of other people's hair, all the girls who'd slept on it before her. But there it was, lumps or not, she'd drop off to sleep like falling over a cliff, only she didn't stay asleep, not properly asleep. She was aware all the time of the ward: the iron bedsteads, humped bodies under pale green coverlets, grey light seeping through threadbare curtains – and then it all faded, and she was somewhere else.

A place she seemed to know. For some reason, in her dreams – well, she supposed she was dreaming, she didn't know what else to call it – it was always winter. Men huddled under waterproof capes, sheltering from the sleety rain that fell ceaselessly from the evil, yellow sky. On cold nights their eyebrows were rimed with frost. After a while, she found she could hear them speak, taste the chlorine in their tea, feel the heat of the fire – even tell from the sound a shell made as it was coming over how close it was going to land. They weren't aware of her, these men. Stared straight through her. *She* was the ghost.

And then, one night, it all changed. She was with them, watching them, as usual, but now a dark man with heavy eyelids was looking back at her. Watching her. She was so used to being the watcher, it came as quite a shock. At first she didn't believe it, but then, when deliberately she moved a few yards to the right, he turned his head to follow her. She was so new to this, so ignorant, it took her a long time to cotton on that he'd passed.

Next morning, she washed her face as usual, brushed her hair, clumped across the yard to the laundry where the steamy heat made her nose run. Exactly the same as every other morning, except this time she didn't go alone.

She didn't know Howard then, otherwise she might have sorted it out a bit sooner. Though Howard got things wrong too. He always said Albert was an officer, that he'd been killed on the first day of the Somme. But it was always winter when she saw him, and he wasn't an officer: he crawled out of a funk hole in the side of the trench every morning along with all the other men. Anyway, whoever he was, whenever he died, from that night on he was part of her. Not that he was there all the time, she could go days without a squeak out of him, but he generally took over when things were bad. Gave her a bit of a break – and my God she needed it, because the last few weeks in the home things were very bad.

Mind you, bugger didn't show up when she was in labour. He kept well out of the way then.

Lifting buckets of water all day long, her back ached that much she didn't even realize she'd started till her waters broke. The supervisor told her to walk – *walk*? Was she joking? – across the yard to the infirmary, where she got undressed and hauled herself on to the bed. Sister Mortimer stood at the end, watching her. 'Not as much fun getting it out as it was putting it in, is it?' *Wasn't that much bloody fun putting it in*, she wanted to say. Didn't, of course. Oh, and you didn't dare groan. 'Shut that noise up. You'll be worse before you're better.' Not a shred of sympathy, not a grain. Oh, she could've told them a thing or two, might've done, only another pain was building, and she needed every bit of breath . . . And then, amazingly, all in a great rush, there he was.

Purple. Was he supposed to be that colour? Oh, but what a pair of lungs, couldn't be that much wrong with him. She wanted to hold him, but they wouldn't let her. She watched as he was wrapped, expertly, in a white cotton blanket and taken away. She caught one more glimpse of him, just the top of his head, as Sister Mortimer turned to push the door open with her hip, and she whispered, but only to herself: *Good luck, son*.

Back on the streets, with leaking breasts and a craving for sweetness no amount of cake could satisfy, she palled up with a lass called Millie and they went to Glasgow together. Back in munitions, earning good money, she thought Albert might disappear, just fade away, but he didn't. If she got upset – oh, and she did, she couldn't stop thinking about the baby – Albert was there. Some days he was in and out that often she lost track of things. There were holes in her memory, so many holes it was like lace, or a cabbage leaf when the caterpillars have been at it.

But then she met Howard. The best thing that ever happened to her. And the worst. In the twinkling of an eye – Howard's eye, needless to say – she was pregnant, only this time she knew what to do. Howard was more or less disabled – *gas*, he said, though forty fags a day didn't help much, either the budget or his lungs – so she had to work. So there she was, walking round the back streets looking for an address. Mucky old woman come to the door, you could've planted a row of tatties in her neck – now there was a warning – but really there was no choice. Up on the bed, spread your legs. Sometimes, looking back on her life, she thought she'd never done anything else. Well, yes, she had – she'd opened her mouth and let the dead speak through her.

Five days after, she collapsed in the street. Temperature sky high. 'You silly, silly, *silly* girl,' the ward sister said. Bit more sympathetic than most.

No more babies after that. Not that Howard minded – he was a baby himself.

Last bed now, last basin. She was free to go, get her hat and coat from the cupboard. Nice hat, she was very fond of it, it always made her feel good – and it hadn't cost a lot, she'd picked it up for a penny in a jumble sale. Still, with a bit of green ribbon and some artificial roses it didn't look too bad. Cheered her up, anyway – she could see the roses bobbing as she walked. She was passing the door of *his* ward now. Perhaps she better leave it? Just walk past? But no, she couldn't do that.

The bed was empty, stripped, the screens folded and pushed back against the wall. Of course, she'd known he was going – but still, it was a shock. For a minute, she just stood and stared, then rested one hand lightly on the mattress. *Mam.* Probably the last thing he'd ever said. Ah, well. Never any hope, not with a head wound like that, the only mystery was why he'd lasted as long as he had. She patted the bed and turned away.

She was just leaving the ward when Sister Wilkinson caught up with her. 'Would you mind taking this down to the laundry?'

'This' was a trolley loaded with soiled sheets. *His* sheets, probably. She could've said: *'Course I bloody well mind, I'm off duty*. Still, it paid to stay on the right side of the sisters – and Wilkie was nicer than most.

So she took the trolley and began trundling it along the main corridor. Like a lot of the trolleys, it had a mind of its own and would keep veering to the left. Like a bloody wrestling match, sometimes. So she lurched and swayed along, the roses in her hat bobbing, thinking how nice it would be to put her feet up when she got home, have half an hour on the bed . . . At least, though, she could take the lift – you were allowed to, if you had a trolley.

She hated the basement: so dark, gloomy and deserted, though not, of course, the laundry: that was the same hellhole of hissing steam and clanking buckets she remembered from the home. As she pushed the swing doors open and pulled the trolley through, she was breathing in smells of soap and disinfectant, her eyes were watering – horrible stuff, that disinfectant – and she was remembering the girl whose waters had broken all over the damp floor. *And* they'd made her mop it up. Had they? Now she come to think of it, she wasn't sure. She didn't always remember things right, on account of Albert.

'Can I help you?'

The supervisor, drying her red, wet hands on a towel. Friendly words, but not a friendly tone, no, not at all. Bertha pushed the trolley in her direction and turned, wordlessly, away. Outside, in the corridor, she stopped to consider. No conveniently empty trolley to take back to the ward, so she was going to have to face the stairs. And she was feeling a bit peculiar, the way she sometimes did when Albert was on his way. Perhaps she could chance the lift? No, better not. She started to walk the length of the corridor towards the staircase at the far end. No windows, no natural light, the strip light overhead kept flickering, keeping time with the pulsing in her head. She had a headache starting – always one-sided, her headaches. The throbbing turned to muttering, low, at first, but getting louder. She must be passing the morgue. Normally, she'd have said: *Sorry, love, not working*. But not today. After a second's hesitation, standing outside the door, she pushed it open and walked in.

A barred window set high in the opposite wall let in a grudging light, but enough to see three figures, draped in white sheets, and lying stretched out on slabs like huge dead fish. A fan churned up the heavy, lifeless air. The muttering had stopped, probably because he'd heard the door open, but then it started again. It was coming from the nearest slab.

As she walked towards him, she saw the sheet wasn't quite long enough to cover him. He'd grown tall, her boy. Reaching out, she touched the thick yellow soles of his feet. Her fingertips, rasping over hard skin, found no lingering warmth, but further up, in the folds of his groin, he was warm still. At last, standing by his head, but with no recollection of getting there, she pulled back the sheet and looked into his face. Smiling a little, she waited for his eyes to open, for the moment when he'd know her again, and say it, say that word: *Mam*.

'And what the hell do you think you're doing?'

A man in a white coat, Adam's apple jerking in his throat. Dumbly, she stared, then forced herself to say something, anything. *Laundry*, she managed to get out at last. She'd been sent to fetch clean laundry.

'Well, you won't find any in here. The laundry's back there.'

She could tell he didn't believe her. Dropping the sheet, she said, 'I thought he moved.'

'Moved? Good God, woman, are you mad?' Then, when she didn't answer: 'Where do you work?'

'I'm a ward maid.'

Shouldn't've said that. Now he'd report her to matron and she'd get the sack. There'd been several complaints about her work, already – she was on borrowed time here. She started to edge past him, hardly breathing till she reached the door. He didn't try to follow her or ask any more questions, just stood and watched her go. As the door closed behind her, she looked back, seeing his accusing face narrow to a crack and finally disappear.

She stood for a minute, gasping for breath. The lift? No, she'd be seen, she was in enough trouble already. Instead, she walked in the other direction, turned right along a side corridor and out through the double doors at the end. There was a ramp leading up to a yard in which the mortuary vans turned, but it was a steep climb. She had to keep stopping to get her breath.

'You all right, love?' one of the drivers asked.

She nodded and, not wanting to attract any more attention, took shelter behind a parked van. Well, that's me job down the drain, she thought. But perhaps not; he hadn't asked for her name. Nah, but they'd know who she was. She wasn't exactly easy to miss. What the hell was she supposed to do now? If she lost the job, she'd be depending on the seances, and it wasn't enough. Would've been if she got her fair share of the house, but she didn't. Blood-sucking bastards. No, the only way she was going to make money was to go back to the ports, and give them what they wanted: spirits they could see and touch. More cheesecloth up her fanny. Whatever they'd done to her insides that time, it had left a bloody big hole. Which was . . . convenient. She mightn't have been much use giving birth to the living, but my God she was a dab hand giving birth to the dead.

All this time, while she was worrying about money and paying the rent, she'd been feeling the soles of his feet, how hard and cold they were, and, at the same time, seeing that purple, howling, convulsed dwarf, whose long, delicate fingers had clawed the air. That's it. When you come right down to it, what else matters? *Oh, my boy. My poor, poor boy.*

Nineteen

The raids came thick and fast, all night, every night. Paul had more or less made up his mind he was going to die and this acceptance freed him from fear and moral scruple. Nothing quite like the proximity of death to make you feel entitled to grab anything that's going. What he wanted, though, was not easily got. He didn't want casual sex, still less commercial sex; he wanted precisely what he couldn't have. The girls he'd kissed and fumbled when he was a boy, the excitement of those first encounters, back home, before he left for London.

Gemma, especially – he thought a lot about her. Buying fish and chips from Sweaty Betty's, newspaper dark with grease and vinegar, kissing her goodnight on her doorstep, tasting salt on her lips, pushing her not-entirely-reluctant fingers down on to his groin, then her dad throwing open the bedroom window and demanding to know what sort of time they thought this was. Slinking away, after a final, clumsy kiss, exhilarated, sticky and ashamed.

Living, as he now did, in one room with a gas ring and a bathroom down the stairs, it was easy to feel like a student again. Everything: his clothes, his towels, even, for all he knew, his hair and skin smelled of oil paint and turps. Every morning, when he came off duty, he made himself a cup of tea and went to look out of the window at the sunlit street. The houses had a dazed look, as if buildings, no less than people, could marvel at another day of life. But then – unless he was so tired he really had to sleep – he started work, and he worked most of the day. Sleep was for later, for the afternoon, when the light was changing.

On one particularly fine morning, he opened the window and leaned out into the street. No bombs had fallen here last night, so no clouds of billowing black smoke marred the flawless beauty of this day. And there, in one of the houses opposite, was a girl. She was looking out into the street, exactly as he was doing, chafing her bare arms against the morning chill. As she leaned further out, he realized she was almost naked, no more than a skimpy camisole half covering her breasts. He felt a delight in looking at her that was both sensual and innocent, and then she turned in his direction and he saw that it was Sandra Jobling. At the same moment, she recognized him. He expected her to withdraw in confusion, but instead, to his amazement, she leaned even further out, raised her arm and waved.

He remembered kissing her, though now it seemed like an episode in a dream. They'd been going off duty, the All Clear had only just sounded, and he'd been light-headed with exhaustion and relief. Kissing her then had seemed the most natural thing in the world. He remembered the dryness of her lips, the mingled smell of smoke and soap on damp skin. That was only eight or nine days ago, though it seemed much longer. With the destruction of his house, a door had clanged shut, cutting him off from his previous life. From his adult life – curiously, his youth seemed to become more and more vivid every day.

With a final wave, Sandra withdrew into the darkness of her room. From then on, it was a matter of waiting to go on duty. But he worked as usual until the light changed, then snatched an hour or so of sleep, before setting off to walk the short distance to Russell Square. He often spent the last hours before going on duty lying on the grass, watching the sun dip below the trees.

Despite the continuing hot weather, there were signs of autumn everywhere. Rows of abandoned deck chairs lined the grassy open spaces, some of them nursing lapfuls of dead leaves. Ignoring them, he lay on the ground, wanting to smell cut grass and crumbly soil, slept for another twenty minutes or so, then dry-mouthed and sun-sozzled, set off in search of a drink.

The streets were emptying fast, the day's spaciousness narrowing to a single crack of light. Soon would come blackout and the wail of sirens, and people were hurrying home to face another night. He was about to turn into the Russell Hotel when a voice hailed him from the other side of the road. Sandra. Oh my God. For a moment he saw her objectively: a stocky, fearless young woman, bright, amused eyes peering through an overgrown fringe. Not pretty, oh no, God, not pretty. What did he care? She was amazing.

She ran across the road, arriving in front of him, breathless. 'Fancy a drink?'

There wasn't an ounce of flirtatiousness about her, but then they were colleagues, co-workers, comrades. Asking a colleague to go for a drink means precisely nothing. He was going to have to play this very carefully.

He nodded towards the hotel. 'I was just going in there.'

'Bit posh, isn't it?'

'No, it's all right.'

'I think I'd rather sit out.'

They found a pub that had put benches on the pavement. She asked for a Guinness, though normally she drank bitter: in fact, she could sink a pint of beer as fast as any man on the team. The area round the bar was packed with businessmen, snatching one last drink before returning to wives and children in the safety of the country. He carried the drinks outside and sat opposite her. They didn't speak much at first, just sat in the sunshine, looking around them with the smugness of stayers-on. It had become a big part of your identity, whether you spent your nights in London or merely came in during the day to work. More important now than sex or class: whether you got on that evening train. Or not.

'Didn't I see you at the seance?' he asked, feeling the silence had gone on long enough.

'Yes, Angela wanted to go.'

'Funny, I hadn't got her down as a –'

'As a what?'

Superstitious, neurotic loony. 'I just didn't know she was interested.'

'Just curious, I think. I was surprised to see you there.'

'I met her, in this square, actually, a couple of weeks ago. I was curious. What about you?'

'She used to come to the Spiritualist Church near us, before the

139

war. Me mam goes now and then. It's not a big thing with her. You know, if she gets a message from me nanna she's pleased, but she doesn't make a lot of it. More of a night out, really. She always says if it wasn't for the spuggies, she wouldn't get out.'

How easy it was to settle back. 'What about you?'

'What about me?'

'Well, do you think there's anything in it?'

'Not really, though there are one or two things you can't quite explain. I mean, for example, me mam and Auntie Ethel went to a seance – Mrs Mason – and me Auntie Ethel really doesn't believe in it – I think she's quite frightened of it, though – anyway, me nanna came through loud and clear. "I'm surprised," she said, "to see you sat there, our Ethel, being as how you took the ring off my finger as I lay in the coffin." Well, Auntie Ethel nearly passed out. And as they were going home she says to me mam, "You told her that. There's no way she could've known. You told her, didn't you?" And me mam just went very quiet. And then she says, "How could I have told her? You were alone in the room." So that was a dead give-away. And you've got to admit, it is odd, isn't it? I mean, how could Mrs Mason have known?'

Well. If Auntie Ethel was flashing the ring round every pub in Middlesbrough and some friend of the dead woman happened to recognize it . . . He nodded. 'It is odd.'

'It was the finish of me mam and Auntie Ethel, they've not spoken since.'

Good old Mrs Mason, spreading havoc . . . 'Can I get you another drink?'

'Aye, go on.'

When he sat down again, she said, 'I hear you've been bombed.'

'Yes, a week ago.'

'Bad?'

'Pretty bad. Not liveable in.'

'So where's your wife?'

'In the country. We did go to a B&B, but . . .' He shrugged. 'We got bombed out of that too. That's twice in one week.'

'Will she stay there, do you think?'

'Oh, I think so. The second bomb was a shock.'

Sandra's tongue came out and deftly removed a moustache of foam from her upper lip. '*Good*.'

He was left wondering what, exactly, she meant. 'You know, the funny thing is, I worked really hard for that house. And do you know, when I looked at it, the only thing I felt was relief? It was like this huge weight . . .' He flexed his shoulders. 'I still feel it. I mean, to be honest, I wish it had been completely flattened because then I wouldn't have to keep going back.'

'What does your wife think?'

'Oh, she's devastated.' A pause. 'I'm not saying I'm proud of it.'

'You can't help the way you feel.'

'I know one thing, I'm not going to go and live in a bloody cottage in the country.'

'No, of course not.' She batted away a wasp that was hovering over her glass. 'You say you keep going back?'

'Yes, you know, rescuing a few things.'

'So it is stable?'

'Not really.'

He'd spent hours clambering through the ruins, picking up anything he could find, mainly things belonging to Elinor. He had no great desire to rescue his own possessions. At the weekend, he'd piled it all into the boot of the car and driven down to the cottage to lay what he'd managed to salvage at Elinor's feet. Expiating a guilt he had no reason to feel. *Yet*.

He caught Sandra looking at him, puzzled by his sudden abstraction. 'Anyway, that's enough about me. How've you been?'

'Oh, you know.' She gave a little laugh. 'Busy. Tired.'

She wasn't at ease talking about herself. He could see her making an effort to go on, to reciprocate.

'You missed a few duties.'

'Yes, I went back home for a bit.'

'Nice to have a break . . .'

She seemed to come to a decision. 'Actually, I didn't really enjoy it all that much, but I just thought I ought to go. Me mam's not been very good, worried sick about me brother.'

'Where is he? Do you know?'

'Not a clue. He's in the Marines . . .'

'Has he just joined up?'

'Oh, no, before the war. He couldn't get work and when he went down the Labour Exchange they told him he wasn't entitled to anything because his mother and his sister were working. "Is that right?" he says. And off he goes and joins the Marines. Just like that. And me mam will listen to Lord Haw-Haw. I've told her not to, I'm tired of telling her. "Where is His Majesty's ship *Repulse*? His Majesty's ship *Repulse* is at the bottom of the sea." Oh God, that *voice* – it's like scraping your fingernails down a blackboard. Do you listen?'

'No.'

'Somebody should shoot the bugger. Oh, and the other thing was . . .' She hesitated. 'I had a boyfriend, we weren't engaged or anything, and he was posted missing at Dunkirk. Of course his mam's convinced he's still alive – though I can't help thinking the Red Cross would've found him by now – and of course I have to go and see her, I can't not, and to be honest . . . Well, you know. I don't think we'd ever have got married, but there it is, in her mind we were going to get married, and we still are. I feel such a hypocrite.'

'Well, you've no reason to.'

'No, I know. Anyway, I just thought I can't go on like this, so what did I do?' She raised her glass. 'Took a leaf out of me brother's book.'

'And joined the Marines?'

She laughed. 'Nah. Joined the Wrens.' She drained her glass. 'I joined up.'

'Good God. I think you deserve another drink.' He picked up the glasses and stood looking down at her. 'Something stronger?'

'I'll have a port and lemon.'

In the last twenty minutes the crowd round the bar had thinned considerably, so he wouldn't have long to wait. He could see her through the open door. She was tracing a pattern in a puddle of spilled beer, the sunshine finding auburn glints in her brown hair.

So she was leaving, then, probably in a couple of weeks. Right from the start the affair, if there was going to be an affair, would be limited; in time and in commitment. Well. He picked up the glasses. That was the one thing necessary to make her utterly irresistible.

He put their drinks down on the table, sat on the bench beside her, closer than before. 'Well, there is this: you'll be a helluva lot safer in the Wrens than you are here.'

She smiled and they clinked glasses.

'By the way, have you told anybody yet?' He meant other members of the team.

'I told bloody Nick. Do you know what he said?'

'Let me guess. "Up with the lark, to bed with a Wren." '

Nick was a strange lad. At times he seemed almost simple-minded, but he could spell any word backwards, and tell you in a second how many letters there were. He never looked you in the eye, so it was difficult to know whether you were making contact or not. And he was especially awkward around young women. He'd sidle up to them, make remarks he clearly intended to be flirtatious, but which many of the girls found offensive, even, some of the younger girls particularly, intimidating. No doubt about it, Nick was a problem.

'I hate all that,' Sandra was saying. 'You know, the ATS being "officers' groundsheets" – and the Waaf "pilots' cockpits". It's just not true. I know a lot of girls who've joined up and none of them are like that.'

'No, I'm sure they're not.' He hoped Nick's stupid innuendo wasn't going to produce a backlash of propriety in Sandra. If it did, he'd personally strangle the little sod. 'I think a girl who wants to join up should be entitled to respect, same way as a man.'

She smiled at him. 'I suppose you were in the last war?'

'Ye-es.' He wasn't altogether happy to see the conversation turning to his age. 'Long time ago.'

Twenty minutes till blackout. A noisy group at the bar were bidding each other goodnight, setting off to the station, to wives and children and safety. Paul slid his hand along the bench towards her and let it lie there, palm upwards. Silence. He felt a pressure in his throat, he couldn't breathe. After a while she glanced sideways, smiled again and covered his hand with her own.

Twenty

Bloody desperate, this. Picking up her bag, Bertha braced herself to face the stairs. Never liked coming home. Every morning, she plunged on to the streets craving light and space. Every afternoon, she crept back, cowed by the vast expanse of sky. Mind, she wasn't as bad as she used to be. When she first come out, she used to hide in shop doorways, because the bustle was more than she could stand. You didn't get much bustle in prison, only the one hour a day in the exercise yard, trudging round and round in a bloody circle. You weren't supposed to talk to the other women, not that she'd have lowered herself, the riff-raff you got in there.

Needed to do something, cheer herself up. Sing. 'Oh Danny boy, the pipes, the pipes are calling . . .' Singing always cheered you up. 'But when ye come back, and all the flowers are dying, if I am dead, as dead I well may be . . .' Well, not always. What lifted her spirits was the spirits she had in her bag, but it was a bit early to be starting on that. Gin and cod's head – dear God, what a combination. Hated bloody cod's head, but it was cheap, and if it was a choice between food and gin – and these days it quite often was – gin every time. She was turning into a right old gin-lizzie – her mam would've been horrified. Though, truth be told, she'd liked a tipple herself. She'd been thinking a lot about her mam recently. Well, childhood, really. School. Didn't do to think too much about that. Or anything else back then, really. Only she loved her mam.

Landing. Pause for breath – up we go again. Bloody stairs – they'd be the death of her. Still, the seances were picking up, partly because she was pushing the limits. All the time now. But forty people, ten bob a ticket, not bad, not that she'd see anything like her fair share of it. Howard would have told them. To be fair, whatever his faults, he was the one pushing her along. He'd seen the opportunities – she hadn't. And the first few seances, my God . . . Every bloody spirit who showed up – *manifested*, Howard said – he was always correcting her – was fighting mad. *Furious*. 'No use blaming the spirits, love,' Howard said. 'It's you, you're attracting it.' 'Oh, so it's my fault, is it?' 'Well, it's not exactly your fault, but you're going to have to calm it down a bit, love. Nobody's going to pay good money to get whacked over the head with a chair.'

Last lap now. She was looking down at her feet – plod, plod, plod – so she didn't see him at first. But she heard breathing, so she stopped and peered into the darkness. Couldn't see a bloody thing, somebody had nicked the light bulbs on the stairs, but then a long shadow peeled itself off the wall.

'Oh,' she said. 'You.'

'Now, now, no need to be like that.'

He was smiling, big yellow teeth bared in a grin. She wanted to tell him to bugger off, but she didn't dare. Feet squarely planted, he stood waiting for her to unlock the door. Bloody key wouldn't work, her hands were shaking, and all the time he stood there, watching. Weasel-faced little shit. Said his name was Payne. Didn't believe it. Said he was a policeman – didn't believe that either. She could smell police a mile off, but – and this was the alarming bit – if he wasn't police, what was he?

As soon as she got the door open, he followed her into the room, took his hat off, looked all round, taking his time, finally pulled out a chair and sat down.

'Make yourself at home, why don't you?'

'Well, Mrs Mason. What a pleasure to see you again.'

She wasn't going to dignify that with a reply, so she went over to the window and pulled the blackout curtain across. Attic windows were always fiddly, but at least it give her a minute to think. She switched on the light, checked to see the chamber pot was well tucked under the bed, and turned to face him. 'What do you want?'

'You did a seance last night.'

'*Gave*.'

'What?'

'You don't *do* seances, you *give* them.'

'Bit rich, isn't it, seeing you charge the poor buggers ten bob?'

'Oh, you were there, were you?'

'No, heard about it, though.'

'Oh, from Miss Pole, I suppose? I noticed she was there again.'

'Nothing to do with me. I believe she calls herself a "psychic investigator".'

'She can call herself whatever the hell she likes, she's still a twat.'

'Ah, Mrs Mason, I *have* missed you.'

He was leaning forward, elbows on his knees, twirling his hat, a battered trilby, round and round in nicotine-stained fingers. She could see dark stains on the sweatband. His trousers, stretched tight across his bony knees, were shiny, almost threadbare. He had such a seedy, lonely, hangdog look about him – put you in mind of rooms in lodging houses with cracked washbasins and fanny hairs on the bottom sheet. And yet he was a clever man – perhaps 'clever' wasn't the right word – *fly*, that was it. It occurred to her, suddenly, that he might be the Devil. In a long and varied career she'd met quite a lot of people who'd seen the Devil and what always impressed her about them was that they described him in exactly the same way – not so much the Prince of Darkness, more a commercial traveller down on his luck. She was reminded of the men you used to see after the last war, selling silk stockings door to door, twitching that much they could hardly count out the change.

She sat down on the bed, folded her arms across her breasts. 'It's not against the law.'

'Taking money under false pretences is. And you're not seriously claiming you talk to the dead, are you?'

She sat, mute.

'Pull the other one, it's got bells on. No, Mrs Mason, what you do is fraud. *Fraud.*'

That word, it put her right back in the dock with that wretched little creep of a man telling everybody they'd got a doctor to examine her. 'Every orifice,' he'd said. 'Every orifice. *And* the rolls of fat on her belly.' He'd looked across at the jury and smirked. 'You could hide a rat in there.'

She looked at Payne, who was also smirking. 'I need the money.'

'You've got a job. Oh, no, sorry, you haven't, have you? You got the sack. Well, get another one then.'

'Where? There aren't any.'

'There's always cleaning.'

'Too many houses boarded up, and besides it pays peanuts. Nobody could live on that.'

'Not with the gin and fags *you* get through.'

Bastard knew everything. 'What am I supposed to have done this time?'

'Well, it's more of an accumulation, really, isn't it? The boy sailor from the *Royal Oak*? And then there was that soldier on the beach at Dunkirk. No air cover. Remember that. And then last night the boy from the school.'

'What about him?'

'You said there were seven hundred dead.'

'*He* said, and he didn't say seven hundred, he just said "hundreds".'

'The official figure's seventy-three.'

'And do you know anybody who believes it? I don't.'

'Look, it's one thing to say it in private, it's quite another to say it in public.'

'I don't control what gets said.'

''Course you bloody do!' He was leaning towards her again. 'Look, Mrs Mason, I'm going to say something that might surprise you – I don't give a bugger where it comes from, you could be getting it all from the Devil for all I care, the point is: *You can't say it.*'

She caught a flicker in his eye. 'This frightens you, doesn't it?'

'*You* frighten me. I think you're a very stupid and *very* dangerous woman. And no, I don't think you talk to the dead. I think you keep your ear to the ground, you ferret around for gossip and speculation and rumour and . . . *Muck*. And you spout it out without stopping to think about security or other people's feelings or public morale or . . . or anything. Except money.'

'I tell the truth.'

'You wouldn't know the truth if it bit you on the arse. Do you know, I'd have more respect for you if you stood on a street corner and peddled your fanny.'

She was up on her feet now. 'I think you've stayed quite long enough.'

'Think about it.'

'What, peddling me fanny?'

'No, keeping the other hole shut.'

She couldn't look at him. At the door he paused and looked back. 'Because if you don't, it mightn't be fraud next time. It might be witchcraft.'

'What you gunna do, burn me?'

'No, I'm serious. You think about it now.'

After he'd left, she waited a few minutes then went out on to the landing to check he'd really gone, and wasn't still there, in the darkness, hiding. She was trembling all over – back in the dock, back in prison. They could do it. But not witchcraft – that didn't make any sense. And it was all true what she'd told him. She didn't control what was said. Once Albert took over, the most she ever heard was a kind of echo.

She switched the light off, pulled the blackout curtains back and lay on the bed. Awkward shape, that window. They'd had one just like it in Newcastle. The night the bailiffs come and took every last stick of furniture, she'd lain on the floor, on a borrowed mattress – Howard snoring beside her – and seen a hand pressed hard against the glass. Her mam's hand. She recognized it straight away from the scars on the palm, scars she'd got in the herring-gutting sheds in Seahouses. And she'd known straight away her mam had passed.

And she'd known something else too: that the dead came to her, sought her out, and there wasn't a bloody thing she could do about it.

She needed to think, but when she closed her eyes and tried to concentrate, she was back in the dock. *Every* orifice, he'd said, smirking. '*And* the rolls of fat on her belly. You could hide a rat in there.' The faces in the courtroom had become a pink blur, she was back on the couch with her legs in stirrups, eyes shut, praying for Albert to come, but Albert didn't come though she called and called for him. And when they let her sit up – take a breather, they said – she pushed them away and ran down into the street. Clinging to the railings, shouting and crying with the pins coming out of her hair and a woman in a fur coat come across to her and said, 'What's the matter, love? Are you all right?'

Of course, she had to go back in. Howard said it would look bad if she didn't. So on it went: stomach, throat, nose, ears, fanny, arse-hole, and yes, the rolls of fat on her belly. The least of her problems, that day . . . Howard sat outside in the waiting room. She went quiet towards the end, refusing to see the doctor's face, the glint of glasses on his nose, refusing to feel the leather couch that made her back and thighs sweat, refusing to hear the chink of instruments in the bowl . . . And still Albert didn't come.

But he was coming now. The room grew dim as she sank further and further into the hole that was opening up at the centre of her being. At first she went slowly, but then faster and faster, swirling round, no longer able to see the window or feel the bed, down down down until at last the darkness covered her.

Bertha came to herself an hour later, with no sense of time having passed, though the square of sky in the window had faded from blue to white.

She was lying on the bed, though it seemed to have moved several feet across the floor. When she raised her head, she saw a chair lying on its side, plates and cups broken and a grey, sticky mess where the cod's head had been stamped into the rug. Oh God. She didn't blame Albert, not entirely, but didn't he have a shred of common sense? Where was she going to find the money to buy new plates? And that rug was going to have to be thrown out. Of course he hated cod's head, but so did she. Only, when Albert hated something, he went berserk. Always had done, probably always would. And of course, as per bloody usual, he left her to clear up the mess.

Tell you what, she wouldn't be going to the shelter tonight, not with all this lot to clear up – no, not if it pissed bombs.

Twenty-one

After the first few hours you lost track of time. He thought it was about three in the morning, but he couldn't see his watch. In the doorway of a building opposite, a group of people, bombed out of a church basement, was waiting to be found space in other shelters. The usual purgatorial shadows. One of them, a woman, detached herself from the rest and gestured to him to come closer. He crunched towards her over broken glass. She pointed to a house further down the street, the house she lived in – what was left of it. Her mouth was so caked with dust she had to moisten her lips several times before she could make herself understood. 'There's somebody still on the top floor.'

Brian Temple joined him and peered up at the house. 'Well, whoever it is they're a goner.' He was pointing to the side of the roof that had caved in. 'If there *is* anybody.'

'She seems pretty definite.'

Charlie nodded. 'Don't see how we can ignore it.'

'I bloody do,' Brian said. 'I'm sick to death of wild goose chases.'

'We'll just have a look, right?'

They fetched a stretcher from the back of an ambulance and pushed the front door open. 'Rescue-squad job, this,' Brian said. Charlie ignored him. He began creeping up the unlit stairs, testing every tread to make sure it would bear his weight. Brian was probably right, but then every available rescue squad had been called to Malet Street where a bomb had fallen on a hostel. And the building seemed stable enough, nowhere near as bad as the houses on either side. At intervals, Charlie held up his hand and they stopped to listen. Creaks, an occasional louder crack, the grumbling of an injured building.

'I don't think there's anybody here,' Charlie said.

But then, on the third landing, they heard a groan and realized it was coming from a room above the attic stairs. These were narrow, room for only one person, and so steep it would be more like climbing a ladder. Charlie gestured to the others to stay back. Halfway up, there was a bend, and there he had to stop: a beam had fallen across the staircase, leaving only the narrowest of apertures. He shone his torch down on to their faces. 'So who's the thinnest?' This was a joke. He was grinning at Paul.

Right. Paul took off his coat and helmet, lay down, poked his head under the beam and started pushing with his heels, wriggling into the airless tunnel, inch by painful inch – a bit like being born but in reverse. Once, he got stuck and called back, 'This isn't going to work,' but then Charlie gave his backside a tremendous shove, his left shoulder broke through and he found extra space. Burrowing into the dusty darkness, mouth and nostrils choked with dust, eyes smarting, he wasn't sure how much longer he could go on, but then, unexpectedly, he felt cool air on his face and neck and guessed the room beyond was open to the sky.

At least, now, he could see, and what he saw, when he finally managed to crawl into the room, was a woman with her nightdress rucked up to her thighs, lying across a mound of rubble. One leg was dark, covered in dried blood, the other fish-white. He couldn't see her face or upper body, but the size of the thighs alone told him she was heavy, quite possibly a dead weight. She wasn't moving. He tried not to hope she was dead. Dead, she could wait till morning. Alive, she was a nightmare.

As he'd thought, the roof was open to the sky. Searchlights probing banks of cloud cast a shifting light across the debris. Table, more or less intact – she must have been sheltering under that when the ceiling came in – bed broken, chair smashed, sink smashed, chamber pot mysteriously intact – and feathers everywhere. A blizzard of feathers. Bright orange flashes – three as he watched – lit up the room, each accompanied by the thud of high explosive. The walls shook. A saucepan skittered across the floor and came to rest by the sink.

Still not knowing if she were alive or conscious, he started saying the usual comforting words. 'Don't worry, love, we'll soon have you out.' Reaching her ankle, he thought he detected warmth. Not much, but then for God knows how long she'd been lying in a room open to the sky. He crawled along her side till he was level with her shoulders and felt for a pulse in her neck. Irregular, but no mistaking it – she was alive. He tried to assess how badly injured she was, calling out to Charlie on the stairs that he thought she might have broken her leg. He didn't like the angle of that knee.

Her eyes flickered open. 'Hello, love,' he said. 'Well, this is a right pickle, isn't it?' A moan from the white-crusted lips. 'Do you think you can stand?'

Before she could answer, a lump of plaster fell from the ceiling, narrowly missing his head. '*Fucking* hell.'

Charlie from the stairs: 'You all right?'

'Never better.'

'We're going to have to dig you out.'

They'd never get her down the stairs, not without moving that beam. Lying flat on his back, he stared through the hole in the roof. Flares blossomed and faded, each casting a trembling light across the floor. He listened to the sounds of scuffling and scraping on the stairs, then, propping himself up on his elbow, found himself gazing straight into her eyes. Christ, she was sweating, a slippery, cold sheen bringing with it the stench of fear and pain. 'Not long now, love. They've just gone to get the shovels, they'll have us out in no time.' No response. 'I'm Paul. What's your name?'

'Bertha.'

Was it her? My God, it was. He remembered her laboured breathing as she climbed on to the platform, and thought: *She's not going to last.*

A few minutes later came a renewed scrabbling on the stairs and Charlie's hand appeared, waving a bottle of water. Paul crawled across to get it, and trickled some into her open mouth until she choked and turned her head away. Then he moistened his own lips. He'd have liked to take a good swig but he didn't know how long he'd have to make the bottle last. He could hear shovels now, digging into the rubble. By rights, they should have left the building and waited for a rescue squad, but he knew they wouldn't do that. They wouldn't rest till they got her out.

Bertha lay motionless, her eyes closed, breathing through her open mouth. He'd wriggled into the narrow space between her and the wall and now lay pressed against her vast bulk. The film of sweat between his body and hers was acutely unpleasant. In the circumstances they were in, that shouldn't have mattered, but it did. He tried to ease himself away from her, but there was no room, and whenever he moved she groaned.

'Yeah, I know,' a man's voice said. 'She turns my stomach too – all that *lard*.'

Paul froze, then made himself turn towards the voice. She looked different. Where before, there'd been only double chins and flabby cheeks, there was now the suggestion of a jaw. How could anybody change physically, like that?

'So, you know, go easy on her.' The voice was beginning to slur into silence. 'She's a poor beggar.'

Charlie's voice from the stairs. 'Paul, that you?'

So he'd heard it too. 'Yes, don't worry, it's all right.'

Paul struggled to sit up, to free himself from the slime of sweat. Looking down at the fat, pallid face, he was inclined to doubt the evidence of his ears. His eyes. She seemed to be unconscious. He pushed up one eyelid, even shone the torch into her eyes, but there was no response.

'Paul, you still in there?' Brian this time.

'No, I've died and gone to heaven.'

'Don't worry, mate. Soon have you out.'

It was what they said over and over again to people who were injured or trapped, only now they were saying it to him. He'd become a victim, no longer one of the team.

'You OK? Only we thought –'

'Fine!' he shouted back. Easier to say that than try to explain what he didn't understand anyway. More questions; ignoring them, he turned back to her. Her lips moved, but the voice was, once again, not hers. Even in this hot, stuffy darkness, he was drenched in a cold sweat, his own this time. It was a relief when she fell silent.

It took nearly an hour of heaving and shovelling to clear the stairs. They were almost through when a rescue squad arrived and tried to take over. A row broke out as to why the wardens were in the building at all. Paul heard a squeaky, querulous voice laying down the law, or trying to, then Charlie: 'You can go fuck yourself, mate, we're not budging.'

All this time, Paul had been listening to a constant trickle of plaster dust, the minute creaks and rustles and sudden heart-stopping lurches as the stricken building shifted its centre of gravity. Another bottle of water was passed through. He gave some to her, relieved when she seemed to be swallowing, before taking several huge swigs himself. Grit everywhere: between his teeth, in his nostrils, in his eyes. He seemed to be breathing dust. A voice from the past: a doctor he'd consulted a few years ago in Harley Street, after one particularly bad winter. 'You have to take better care of your chest. Have you thought of spending the winter abroad?' He was laughing, still laughing when Charlie's head appeared, level with the floor. 'Glad you think it's funny, mate.'

Paul could cheerfully have kissed him. Charlie inched forward, pressing down hard with his hands before trusting his weight to another foot of sagging floor. When, finally, he reached Paul, he clapped him on the shoulder, then looked down incredulously at the prone woman. 'By heck, the size of her.' He was whispering, but the sound registered on her face.

'Do you think we can get her down?' Paul asked.

'Bloody got to, mate. Can't leave her here.'

'Get some of the others?'

Charlie shook his head. 'Floor won't take it.' He crawled round to Bertha's other side and wiggled his hands underneath her till his fingers were clasping Paul's in a desperate, painful grip. 'Right. Count of three.'

As soon as they tried to move her, she started to moan but also, embarrassingly, to apologize. 'I'm sorry, I'm sorry,' she kept saying. 'I'm sorry.'

'Not your fault, love,' Charlie said. 'Blame Hitler.'

Finally, they managed to drag her further away from the wall.

Paul got behind her, put his hands under her armpits and heaved her into a semi-upright position, aware, but in a totally detached way, that at one point they formed a perfect, if grotesque, pietà. Then they half dragged, half carried her across the floor, and lowered her through what remained of the doorway into Brian's waiting arms. Still, in between screams and moans, she kept apologizing for her weight. 'I'm sorry, I'm so heavy,' she said. 'I can't help it, I hardly eat a thing.' 'Sure you don't, love,' Brian said. He'd make a joke of it later, but he was tender with her now.

At last, the top of her head disappeared into the darkness and they were able to stand up. Charlie indicated to Paul that he should go down the stairs first.

'No, you go.'

Left alone, he took a last look round the room at the detritus of poverty and squalor that had once been a home, then turned and followed Charlie down the stairs.

Then things began to move quickly. Bertha was heaved on to a stretcher and carried downstairs, not easily – it took four men, and even then they grunted and strained. Mercifully, she'd stopped apologizing and lay with her eyes closed, unconscious or dead. Behind them, Charlie was still arguing with the man with the squeaky voice. In the end he simply turned his back and walked away. 'Bloody little Hitler.'

Outside, fire hoses snaked across the street and pools of black water reflected the sullen, red glare in the sky. Paul followed the stretcher across to the ambulance. He recognized Neville's bull-necked shape as he jumped down from the cab and came round to open the door. They exchanged a few words; terse, impersonal. At the last moment, Paul turned back. 'Where you taking her?'

'Guy's.'

Paul raised a hand in acknowledgement, splashing through a puddle of stinking water on his way to rejoin the team.

The All Clear went just after five o'clock. Back at the depot, they stared into thick white cups of dark orange tea and found little to say. Paul tried to look back over the events of the night, but everything before Bertha and after Bertha was a blur. Of course everything would be carefully timed and tabulated in the incident log, but it certainly wasn't tabulated in his brain.

After a few minutes, Charlie stirred and stretched his legs. 'You know what the Chinese say, don't you?'

'No,' Paul said, obligingly. 'What do the Chinese say?'

'If you save somebody's life it belongs to you. I mean, like you become responsible for that person. Mind, I think it might just be if you stop them killing themselves, I'm not sure. But it's not a very nice thought, is it, when you think of some of the people we've saved? I mean, that poor old bugger pissing in a bag, imagine having him around for the rest of your life.'

'He was all right,' Brian said. 'Happy as Larry. No, the one that'd worry me is that woman tonight. God, the size of her. *And* she'd pissed herself.'

'I've met her before,' Paul said. 'She's a medium.'

'Is she?' Charlie said. 'Me mam was a great one for the spuggies. Couldn't see anything in it meself.' He looked up. 'Ah, here they are. We thought you'd got lost.'

Walter came towards them, rubbing his hands, his cheeks purplish with cold. 'By heck, it's nippy out there.'

Paul finished his tea. He didn't fancy going round to the van for pasties with the others. The ambulance drivers went to the same van and he didn't much fancy bumping into Elinor's friends. Outside, he stood on the pavement taking in deep gulps of air. Alive. It wasn't so much a thought as a pulse that throbbed in every vein in his body. His heart was beating so hard he could see the quiver in his fingertips. A voice hailed him: Sandra. Had she been waiting for him? The thought that perhaps she had, produced more throbbing, but further down.

'Bad night?' she asked.

'So-so. How about you?'

She shrugged. 'All right.'

People were watching them. He saw Charlie and Brian exchange a sly grin, then look away, but he didn't care. His previous – very minor – infidelities had been conducted with iron discretion, but not this one. Part of the feeling of being outside time was that nothing seemed to matter very much. Nothing he said or did now would have consequences. If he'd stopped to think about it, even for a second, he'd have known at once it wasn't true, but he *felt* it to be true.

So they linked arms and walked the few hundred yards to his studio. Neither of them said very much. He was amazed by the new day, intensely aware of all those for whom it had never dawned: the dead, lined up on mortuary slabs or lying, still unrecovered, under mountains of rubble. He felt their bewilderment, the pain of truncated lives. So what right did he have to despise Mrs Mason, her ignorance, her superstition, when in his own experience he knew how porous was the membrane that divides the living from the dead?

Leading the way up to his studio, he remembered the stairs to Bertha Mason's room, the moment when he'd realized he couldn't move, that in all probability he was going to die there, without dignity, without purpose, like a fox in a stopped earth, and the minute he unlocked the door he turned and caught Sandra in his arms, his mouth groping for hers. They fell on to the rumpled divan and there the long night ended, in kisses and cries and, finally, at last, at long last, sleep.

Twenty-two

He couldn't get her out of his head.

Not Sandra; he'd loved every minute of their time together, but after she'd put on her clothes and gone home, he scarcely thought of her. No, it was Bertha Mason he couldn't forget. Bertha, on the table, blank-eyed, fag end stuck to her bottom lip; Bertha, on the platform, whirling black silk bloomers around above her head; Bertha, in his arms, piss dripping down her legs and forming a puddle on the floor. And that voice: the voice in the darkness that couldn't have been hers, and couldn't not have been hers. There she was: old, fat, mad, quite possibly dying – utterly repulsive – and he couldn't forget her.

You know what the Chinese say, don't you?

Perhaps Charlie's remark about becoming responsible for the life you save was preying on his mind. Whatever the reason, he knew he had to see her again. She might, of course, be dead by now, or she could have been discharged from hospital, sent to some hostel for people made homeless by the bombing, but on the whole he didn't think so. She'd been in too bad a state for that. No, with any luck she'd still be in Guy's. If she was alive.

Arriving at the hospital in the late afternoon, he was directed to the third floor. Grim corridors, no natural light, though great efforts were being made to cheer things up: there was even a vase of flowers on a table at the centre of the ward. A nurse pointed to a screened-off bed at the far end. Pushing the screen slightly to one side, he saw Bertha sitting up in bed with her head bandaged, looking like a huge, abandoned baby.

'Hello, Mrs Mason. How are you?'

He'd brought some flowers from the garden of his ruined home: bronze and yellow chrysanthemums, past their best. He couldn't see a vase to put them in, so simply laid them at the foot of her bed, where their graveyard smell quickly spread and filled the small space inside the screens.

At first glance, he thought she looked better than he'd expected: she'd lost that lard-white colour; but when he looked more closely, he realized the redness of her cheeks and chin was anything but healthy. He touched her hand – shaking it seemed too formal – and found her flesh hot and clammy. He said, 'I don't know if you remember me, I was one of the –'

'Yes, hello.'

He could tell she wasn't sure. 'I was in the room with you the other night. After the bomb.'

Her eyes widened. 'So you were. You asked me what I was frightened of.'

He couldn't remember asking her that. In fact, he was sure he hadn't. It wasn't the kind of thing you said to injured people in an air raid.

'People think, oh, she knows a lot about the afterlife, she believes in it, so what's she got to be frightened of? If they knew what it's like down there at the moment they'd be bloody frightened. Bedlam, bloody bedlam. People running round in circles, half of 'em don't even know they've passed.'

She'd said that the first time he'd met her, only now it made more of an impression. She must've received a Christian education – of some kind – and yet she'd ended up with a view of the afterlife hardly distinguishable from Homer's. Shades, shadows; people who'd rather have life on any terms than endure the insubstantial misery of the underworld.

'They haven't been,' she said.

'Who haven't?'

'Mr and Mrs Lowe. You know, from the Temple?'

The Temple, he supposed, must be the pawnbroker's. 'They probably don't know where you are.'

'They didn't come to see me when I was in the nick either, they knew where I was then.' She was making curious mumbling motions with her lips: chewing a vile and bitter cud. 'Howard didn't come either, said he was ill, I knew he wasn't, he was with his fancy woman.'

'Howard's your husband?'

'I wasn't supposed to know about her, but I did, of course, there's always some kind person'll tell you.' She looked at him, and her eyes were suddenly sharp. 'Won't be long before somebody tells your wife about you.'

'Is there anything I can get you?'

'No, I've got everything I want, thank you. Peace and quiet, that's all any of us really want, isn't it?'

Paul stood up at once.

'No, not you. *Him*.'

He glanced round. 'Who?'

She was looking at the chair on the other side of the bed, although her eyes seemed to be focused not on the chair itself but on its occupant. Only there was nobody there.

'Is it Howard?'

''Course it bloody isn't. Bugger never bloody come when he was alive, he's not gunna show up now, is he? No, it's that fella, he keeps coming round, Payne, whatever he calls himself. Telling me what I should and shouldn't say – only it's not me saying it – it's Albert – and I just can't get him to *see*.' She was staring at the chair, pleading, justifying herself.

'Why don't you get Albert to talk to him? Well, he'd understand then, wouldn't he?' She didn't seem to have heard. 'Is he here now? Albert?'

'God only knows, he's a law unto himself. I'm fed up with it.' She lay back against the pillows and closed her eyes.

Paul glanced round again, thinking: *I should go*, but somehow he couldn't just walk out and leave her here like this. He looked again and saw her face was changing: the jaw becoming firmer, the brow ridges more prominent. *How could she do that?* She couldn't, of course. Nobody could. But then how did she change the way he saw her?

Albert's voice: 'I'm here all the time, it just doesn't register; to be honest, not a lot does register, these days. You should see the amount of gin she gets through.'

'She's not well, is she?' Paul wondered if he was doing the right thing, going along with the pretence – if pretence it was. But he didn't know what else to do. 'She's not a good colour.'

'She's a goner, if you ask me.'

'Is she really that bad?'

'You've only got to look at her.'

Paul nodded towards the empty chair. 'Does he really exist?'

'Oh God yes, he's the one got her put inside – and he's been nosing around again. Told her she could be tried as a witch, scared the shit out of her. She couldn't face prison again, nearly killed her last time.'

In the seance a great deal had been made of Albert's long service on the Western Front, his officer status, but this was a music-hall version of an upper-class accent, and even that was slipping fast. 'You know, I met her in Russell Square once.'

'I remember. We're not all sozzled on gin.'

'She told me there was a boy standing behind me.'

'Well, there is, isn't there?' Albert sounded bored. 'I mean, it's not as if you don't know he's there.'

His voice had begun to slur, vowel sounds elongating until the words became incomprehensible. Paul watched Bertha's face become puddingy again, a doughy, undifferentiated mass in which once-pretty features were submerged in fat. It had never struck him before, but now he thought that in her youth she must have been beautiful. Was she asleep? She was breathing noisily through her open mouth, her eyes half closed, the whites unnervingly visible.

He could do nothing for her, neither save her life nor wrest her back to sanity. Indeed, the longer he stayed with her the more his own grip on reality would slacken. Reaching an abrupt decision, he stood up and retrieved his hat from the foot of her bed. Yet, even now, he lingered. Suddenly he became aware that in the last few minutes he'd unconsciously changed the rhythm of his breathing until it exactly matched hers.

Quickly then, he turned on his heel and walked out.

*

Bertha listened to the footsteps dying away into the darkness. Somebody had been there, just now – they'd brought flowers – but she couldn't remember who. Be glad to get out of this place. Talk about haunted, she'd never in her life experienced such a cluster of unquiet spirits. Now that was a point. Why did they cluster? Something to do with the place, the actual building? Had to be – unless, of course, they recognized a sensitive and were crowding round *her*. But no, that couldn't be true, the night sister said they'd been here years.

Bertha had been surprised when she was on the toilet wrestling with constipation. The door was thrown open without so much as a by-your-leave and a woman came in wearing the dated uniform of a nursing sister in the last war. 'Hurry up, now,' she'd said. 'We haven't got all day.' She'd been talking to somebody at the sink, totally oblivious to her, Bertha, sat there, needing a bit of privacy.

There was a child as well, a boy who came in and out of a wall where a door had once been. You could see the outline of the door under the paint. She felt sorry for him, he looked so lost, as did the young man in Victorian dress who sat with his back to the wall in the main corridor, sobbing his heart out, poor soul. She'd have helped them if she could, but they just stared through her. The spirits who came to her in seances – *manifested* – bloody Howard – wanted to make contact. These ones didn't even know she was there.

The trouble was, *she* saw them all the time, whereas other people just caught glimpses now and then – the majority, not even that. Though she had once seen a doctor step aside to avoid the small boy as he came through the wall, and she'd thought: *You don't even know you did that*. But he had, he'd stepped aside.

Payne was back. She thought it might actually *be* Payne this time, though she hadn't heard him come in. On the other hand, she had been dozing, on and off, all day – she could easily have missed him. He was – well, not exactly talking, but words formed in her mind. On and on he bloody went. The school: how did she know how many people had died? Every bugger knows, she said. Just 'cos *you* say something's secret doesn't mean it is. And the boy-sailors on the *Royal Oak*, how did she know they were dead, when nobody had said the ship had been attacked? And the young men on the beaches of Dunkirk; the men she'd seen crawl out of funk holes in the trenches . . . 'Oh, piss off and leave me alone.' She didn't know whether she meant the spirits or him.

Somewhere in the lower regions Albert stirred. She was half inclined to let him come to the surface, give Payne a right good bollocking, bloody little pipsqueak. God, just look at him, objectionable little man. 'Seedy' – that was the word. *Seedy*. She honestly did believe he could be the Devil, because he wasn't fixed. Whenever you looked at him, he seemed to be a different shape and size. She felt herself start to sink, a sure sign Albert was on his way. She didn't really know where she went when Albert was here, except sometimes it looked a bit like her bedroom at home. At night, when she was huddled up in the narrow bed, with the sheets over her head, she'd hear footsteps on the stairs and see the knob begin to turn, and then, as he came in, a tall, thin shadow would climb the wall behind the bed, and she'd hear a voice whispering: *It's all right, don't cry.* He loved her. He always said he did.

But tonight, letting herself sink didn't seem to work. The thing in the chair, whoever he was – *what*ever – wouldn't let go. She forced herself to go on looking at him. Neat moustache, reddish-brown with a few white hairs, nicotine-stained fingertips twirling his trilby, round and round, round and round, stains on the sweatband, shiny patches on his knees where the cloth had worn thin – oh, yes, he was down on his luck, this one, in spite of his airs and graces.

I see through you, she thought. And immediately, as in a dream, found she could do exactly that. He was still there, very much there, but reduced to an outline, like a child's drawing. Where the solid mass of his face and body had been there was now only a string of rising bubbles, like you get in a pond when something's rotting underneath. She couldn't put her finger on the change, because she could still see him, only now there was a sense that his apparent solidity was a delusion, and the reality was this constant flux. And he was getting smaller; his feet no longer quite reached the floor. He was child-sized now, and still shrinking fast, but somehow this didn't reduce the force of his presence. If anything it increased it. The more he shrank, the more he was reduced to his essence, the more powerful he became.

She wanted to cry out, call for help, but there was no help, not against this, because he was liquid. He could change shape endlessly, fit himself into anything, flow through every crack in every barrier. And flow he does, drenching her in slime.

Look away. She looks instead at her left arm, which is lying on top of the coverlet, but it doesn't seem to belong to her any more. She focuses on her hand, tries to wiggle the fingers, but they won't move. It's too heavy, too stiff, she can't do anything with it. She feels a spurt of hostility towards it. Is it even hers? It doesn't feel like hers. Is it his hand? Her whole body feels cold along that side and so heavy, so leaden, the bed must surely soon start to tilt. She won't look at the chair. Her right eye can't see anything anyway, but she closes the one eye that still obeys her. Spit drools from the corner of her mouth, she can't wipe it away; she tries to wipe it away with her other hand. The sheets are briefly warm, then cold, oh God she's wet the bed again, she won't half get wrong for that. But she keeps her eye closed, she won't look at the chair. She won't look at the chair.

Voices now, in the ward behind the screens, feet come flapping; a light shines in her eye. *Stroke*, she hears, *stroke*, but makes no sense of it. Nobody's stroked her, not for a long, long time. Oh, six strokes of the cane, yes, she remembers that, remembers running out of school the second the bell rang, along the beach and up the hill to the castle, its towers black against the sky as the sun sinks down behind it. Running across the courtyard, now, stones hard under her feet, flecks of foam drifting like blossom across the grass, her head, her ears, even the marrow in her bones filled with the roaring of the sea. Queen Margaret's tower behind her, she stands on the edge of the cliff. Close, so close she's blinded by the spray and the sea boiling and churning in the Egyncleugh beneath her feet. Oh, and it's nothing now to step forward, to take another step, and then another, to walk on air, and see, in the last moment before the water closes over her head, high above her on the cliff, Dunstanburgh's broken crown.

Twenty-three

Elinor's Diary

14 October 1940

I think. The trouble with my life at the moment is that every day's the same so I end up losing track and forgetting what day it is.

I haven't kept a diary for years and I'm in two minds about it now. I suppose, because I associate it with adolescence, all that endless self-absorption which I'm vain enough to think I've grown out of, though I've no doubt there'd be plenty of people to disagree with me. My entire family, for a start.

So why now? Because I'm lonely. No Paul. No Rachel either – the farmhouse is empty. Rachel's gone to stay with Gabriella, who's had her baby now – a little girl – and Tim's staying at his club, an easy walking distance from the War Office. Rachel's given me a key and told me to take anything I need from the kitchen garden – after all, as she says, it'll only go to waste – she's even told me to raid her wardrobe, though since she's expanded over the years and I've contracted, I can't think that's going to be much use. Still, I'll give it a go. One thing about all that sewing I used to do, I'm quite good at altering clothes.

I found this notebook – completely blank – sitting in the bottom-right-hand drawer of Mother's desk, and I find myself wondering why she bought it, what she intended it for, because it's not at all the kind of thing she'd buy. There are scrapbooks in the kitchen with recipes cut out of magazines and pasted in. They're thick, those books, and they smell of paste, and her thumb- and finger-prints are all over them. Looking through them, I can spot her favourite recipes because those pages are more daubed and crusted than the rest. I can remember the tastes too. Oh, and the ingredients . . . They're like little messages from another world. But this notebook? No, I've no idea what it was for – and evidently she didn't know either, since it was never used. Another mystery, and not one I'm likely to solve now.

I keep tripping over her presence. Everything here is hers, hers, not mine. The dressing table in the back bedroom . . . She used to look into that mirror every evening when she was getting ready for dinner. When I was a child, I used to sit on her bed in our old house and watch, though I knew my presence irritated her. Lots of hair-brushing, dabs of scent, the merest dusting of face powder – it was all a great mystery to me, what grown-up ladies did, and I felt I could never be part of it. (Oh, and how right I was!)

The sofa. I sit here in the evenings staring at the fire (lit for company, not warmth – it's still very mild) and if I close my eyes I can actually feel my legs, skinny, little-girl legs, sticking straight out over the edge. It's like one of those trick photographs where a child appears giant-sized because the proportions of the room are abnormal – or rather the reverse, since here I feel dwarfed by giant furniture, though really it's the same size it always was. Only I don't belong with it any more.

I wonder what Paul's doing. Whether he's on duty. I wonder who he's with. I wonder if Rachel has these thoughts about Tim – well, yes, of course she does, though in her case I'm pretty sure she's right to be suspicious. I wonder if she minds.

Every time Paul visits, he brings me something, something he's retrieved from the house. He says the house is stable, that there's no risk, though I'm not sure I believe him. If it was stable we'd be allowed back in. I wish these little parcels didn't feel so much like peace offerings. Last Friday, he brought two big portfolios of drawings, which had somehow survived, wedged in between the kitchen dresser and the wall, though I haven't had the heart to look at them yet. Can't open the portfolios. Can't paint. Can't do anything.

I'm a pinprick, a speck, a bee floating and drowning on a pool of black water, surrounded by ever-expanding, concentric rings of

*silence. I rub my wings together, or do whatever it is bees do that
makes a noise, but there's no buzzing. And no echo either, no sound
comes back.*

15 October 1940

*Today I walked as far as the river. It came on to rain, a sudden
downpour. I stood and watched raindrops pocking the surface,
rings, bubbles, little spurts of water leaping up. And I thought of
Paul's mother putting bricks in her pockets and wading in and
tried to imagine her last moments, bubbles of water escaping
from slackened lips, hair swaying to and fro in the currents, like
weeds. And an iron band around the chest, the involuntary
struggle for breath – and then, nothing. We have to hope:
nothing.*

*Back at the cottage, I took my wet slacks off in front of the fire
and my skin was all grey and purple, goosepimply, and I thought
why wouldn't he prefer firm, young flesh? Isn't that what all men
prefer, when you get right down to it?*

*I miss my house. It's like grief for a person – an actual physical
craving – and yes, I know it's only bricks and mortar and it shouldn't
matter when every day – or rather every night – so many more
important things are being lost. Lives, for God's sake. And yet I can't
talk myself out of it. There's a particular place – was a particular
place – at the bottom of the basement stairs. You turn left and there's a
small window looking out on to the back garden and it has a cupboard
underneath. I used to keep a jug of flowers there. We bought the jug in
Deià, very cheap, but beautiful, and the flowers came from the garden
in summer, in winter it was twigs and leaves, hemlock, I used to get it
from the river bank here, catkins . . . Nothing cost more than a few
pennies, but in that particular place, at particular times of day – late
afternoon when the sun struck the window at a slight angle and
shone through the leaves, delineating every vein on every leaf, it was
perfection.*

One of the things you notice about getting older is that every loss picks the scab off previous losses. The house is gone, so I miss Toby more. Mad, but true. I feel him all the time now – and I hope that doesn't mean I'm about to join him, because I'm not ready to die just yet.

I think about Violet and her cyanide capsule. She actually offered to get me one, but I said no. I don't want to go to bed at noon.

16 October 1940

Yesterday I got into such a state of gloom and despondency that in the end I just ran out of patience with myself. So I made myself sit down and open the two portfolios Paul brought back last week.

A lot of drawings from last year and the year before, looking rather dated I thought, but then nothing's quite so dated as the recent past. A few shelter drawings, one or two of them quite promising – I might work on those, I suppose. There's one of children queuing outside Warren Street tube station that I rather like, though one of the boys at the front looks exactly like Kenny. I didn't mean it to, but there he is – the resemblance is unmistakable.

I want to go back to London. I don't know what stops me, except I feel I need to get Paul's agreement – consult him at least. I even went up into the loft this morning and got a suitcase down. It'd take me literally minutes to pack. These days I'm like a snail: I carry my house on my back. And though most of the time I feel dreadful, just now and then I get a glimpse of something else, a frisson of something . . . Lightness. Freedom, I suppose.

But I haven't put anything into the suitcase yet, and I don't know what's holding me back. Partly it's fear: going back into that nightly horror, but that's an impersonal fear, shared by everybody. No, I think what I'm really afraid of is being alone, just me, no longer half of a couple. A cold draught blowing down my side where Paul used to be. I don't feel it so much here, because I'm surrounded by all *these relics of my childhood, the before-Paul time. But I know in London I'd feel it badly.*

Almost enough to keep me here, but I think not quite.

17 *October* 1940

Another bright, sunny, gritty day, no wind. Water on the marshes steel blue, reflecting light back at the sky, the reeds a vicious yellow-green, the sort of colour you feel can't possibly occur in nature, but there it is, you're looking at it.

I came back home to a rare event – a letter, readdressed from the house, of course – just before we left we added our new, separate, addresses to the noticeboard at the end of the street. People don't write to each other much these days, we've all shrunk into our little colonies, the people we see every day, but this was an official letter. And as soon as I saw the Ministry of Information stamp I guessed who it was from. One quick scan of the page, there was his signature: Kenneth Clark, chairman of the War Artists Advisory Committee. Would I . . .? Could I . . .? With a view to discussing, etc. . . . . Oh, I would, I could. I will, I can. Though I'm going to have to be quick about it, because the interview's tomorrow morning, the letter having been delayed by the change of address.

If I get a commission – actually, I don't think there's much 'if' about it, but let's be cautious – if I get a commission, it'll be on a painting-by-painting basis. Men – Paul, for example – are salaried; women aren't. And I've got a pretty good idea of what he'll want me to do – rosy-cheeked children, safely evacuated from the bombed cities, merrily playing on ye olde village greene. There's a big drive on to get children back into the country, an awful lot of them have gone home. Though we didn't know it at the time, Kenny was one of thousands. Oh, and land-girls, that'll be the other thing. Come to think of it, probably mainly land-girls – something about girls' bums in breeches appeals to the male visual imagination as almost nothing else can – as long as the girl's young and pretty and the bum not so gigantic it fills the whole canvas.

Still, I don't mind, as long as I can do the things I really want to do as well. It'll give me access to materials, and that's no small thing, these days, because they're getting awfully expensive, and scarce. And of course I've lost a lot of mine. Then there's the licence – I'll be able to go (almost) anywhere and draw (almost) anything. Status, recognition . . . I'd love to be able to say they don't matter, but they do. Hear Kit Neville on the subject!

The interview's at ten, so by half past I ought to know one way or the other.

Then what? Go to see Paul, I suppose. It'll feel odd seeing him again in London. I can't tell him I'm coming – there's no telephone in the studio – I'll just have to hope I catch him in.

Twenty-four

Two or three days later (I could probably work out the date if I really tried but I've been awake all night and I can't bloody well be bothered)

I caught him all right.

But I'm not going to plunge straight into that, because there's Kenneth Clark and the War Artists Advisory Committee and, arguably, that's now more important than Paul.

I know Clark vaguely, as I suppose everybody on the art scene does. He came to the door of his office to greet me, looking taller and broader-shouldered than he actually is – it's amazing what a first-rate tailor can achieve – and shook hands with me very warmly, I think without seeing me at all. Women of my age are invisible to Clark, but, given his tastes, I've probably been invisible for the last twenty-five years at least – so there's no point getting upset about it now!

He started by saying the War Artists Advisory Committee was determined to recruit the largest, most varied, most representative array of talent possible, and as part of this endeavour they were commissioning some of the most distinguished women artists. It was, he said, particularly important that the visual record of the war should include work that conveys the uniquely feminine vision that only women artists can supply. Etc. I've no idea if he really thinks there's a 'uniquely feminine vision', or whether he just thought that would go down well. Rather to my surprise, I found myself arguing against the idea. I said I didn't believe women were necessarily more compassionate than men . . . He just sat there looking cool and amused, and when I'd finished pointed out that my best-known paintings are, nevertheless, of women and children. True, of course. Of the three paintings I've got in the Tate, one's a mother feeding her baby on the night-ferry crossing to Belgium, another's of convent schoolgirls in a park, and the other's one of a series of winter landscapes I painted after Toby's death. (Not the best one either!) And then he started explaining that women were paid on a commission-by-commission basis, unlike men, who get a salary. (Part of the 'uniquely feminine vision' perhaps: we don't need to be paid.)

And then we moved on to suitable subjects. Children, but only in safe areas well away from the raids; land-girls, bums not specified; women in the forces, though obviously not in any aggressive capacity, definitely no guns; factories, etc.

All very much as I expected, and of course I said yes. So – looking forward to a long and productive relationship, etc. – we shook hands again and off I went. I felt an enormous sense of relief getting out of that building; I can quite see why Kit hates it.

Though I must say, standing there on the pavement, I felt better than I've felt since the house was destroyed. Solider. That awful snail-without-a-shell feeling had gone. I was moving back to London, I was absolutely determined on that, but I also felt I owed it to Paul – and myself – to have one last go at persuading him to rent somewhere big enough for both of us. Not a house, necessarily. A flat would do.

So I set off to walk to his studio. And this is the difficult bit. I'd only just turned the corner when I saw him on the pavement in a dressing gown, accompanied by a girl, a stocky, little figure with long dark hair and short legs. She was standing on tiptoe, reaching up to kiss him. She was so short it was almost like a child reaching up to kiss her father, but there was nothing fatherly about the kiss. His arms were round her, he was laughing, pretending to ward her off, she was tugging at his sleeve, trying to persuade him to go back into the house. He kept shaking his head, pretending to be reluctant, but then, with a shrug of mock defeat, he let himself be led back inside – and the door closed behind them.

I walked a little further along the road, and then I just stood and stared at the door. My brain was whirring away, trying to come up with an innocent explanation. I just wanted it to go away. Only of course there was no explanation except the obvious, and I couldn't bear to think about that, so in the end I didn't think at all, just tottered off, feeling ancient, frail, as if my bones had turned to glass.

Now I wonder why I didn't bang on the door, force my way up the stairs. But it never occurred to me to do that.

Instead, I went to the house, which was probably the worst thing I could've done. All the outer walls are intact, but the roof's in a bad way, ceilings collapsed on the floors below. And open to the weather because of the roof, so it's bound to deteriorate quite rapidly. I cried. But also I was following Paul and the girl upstairs, into the studio, on to the bed. We made love on that bed once. I wonder if he remembers that when he's rolling round on it with her?

I felt naked, shivering in the sunlight, everything stripped away, not just the house, Paul as well – all gone. And if you take away all the relationships, the possessions, the achievements of somebody's adult life, what they're left with – what I'm left with – isn't youth. I noticed I was walking differently – more slowly, a bit hunched over. I had to force myself to straighten up.

It was a mistake to go to the house – or perhaps not – perhaps I needed that final brutality to be able to stop feeling. Because I did stop. I went to a Lyons Corner House and sat over a pot of tea and gradually the numbness spread. I remembered the first weeks after Toby died, how unfeeling I was, how ruthlessly efficient. I don't think I've ever been as efficient as that in my entire life. Well – until now.

I drank the tea, paid the bill, checked to see how much money I had in my purse and set off. Two hours later, I'd found a flat on the top floor of a house in Gower Street, two doors down from where I used to live as a student. Huge rooms; one of them, at the back, has wonderful light. I can imagine myself painting in there. Then there's a living room, a bedroom, a kitchen, a bathroom, all good-sized – and it's unbelievably cheap. Of course it's cheap because it's lethal, right at the top of the house, in an area that's seen a lot of bombing, but I don't care about that.

I'm quite clear. This is about survival now. This has the power to destroy me and I'm not going to let it.

But I keep replaying that scene. Paul and the girl kissing, the pretended tug of war, his mock surrender, them going back into the house together. Oh, and then I follow them up the stairs . . . It's like a film I'm being forced to watch, but there's no emotion. I seem to have run out of that.

It's a strange feeling. Rather like the cordoned-off roads and squares where a time bomb's fallen. You look across the tape at sunlit emptiness, but you're not allowed in. And you know there are other quiet, roped-off places, all over London, but you also know the life of London goes on, the people, the traffic, all that roar and bustle forcing itself down side streets and alleys, finding new channels, new ways through. And I think my life's going to be like that. I'm not going to be roped off.

It would have been so easy after seeing Paul and that girl to creep back to the cottage, try to pretend it hadn't happened, convert my mother's bedroom into a studio and paint there. Happy children removed to safety, playing on the village green. Do what Paul wants. Do what Clark wants. Hide. And I think: No. This is my place, my city, and I'm not going to let anybody force me out of it.

Twenty-five

He thought perhaps it was the third incident of the night, but could never afterwards be sure. A pub had been hit – he remembered that. They'd got it roped off and were waiting for a heavy rescue squad to arrive. Three houses adjoining the pub had collapsed and there was minor damage to several others further up the road. The people who lived in these houses were safe in shelters, presumably; though in for quite a nasty shock when they came out.

Then somebody called from across the street to say there was an old couple living in one of the damaged houses. They turned to see a stout, middle-aged woman with her hair in neat rows of curlers, the metal glinting in the light of flares, as aggressive as shark's teeth.

'She's got arthritis, walks with a stick.'

Charlie said: 'We'd better just have a look.' She was so obviously the sort of woman who knows everybody's business they couldn't afford to ignore it.

Stopping outside the house, Charlie bent and shouted through the letter box. No answer.

'They'll be in there.' The woman had followed them and was still watching from the other side of the road.

'You get yourself under cover, Missis!' Charlie shouted back. He turned to Paul. 'What do you think?'

Paul shrugged. 'She'll know.'

Charlie nodded, blew out his lips hard, then wrapped his hand in his coat and smashed the window. He reached through and fiddled with the catch. Often they were jammed under layers of paint, but this one opened. They climbed in, and found themselves in a neat front room. A vase of red plastic roses stood on a sideboard between photographs of children, a boy and a girl, in school uniform. Flashing his torch, Charlie led the way into the passage and opened the door into the back room.

Charlie went in, Paul followed. And there they were, lying side by side on a bed, the counterpane pulled up to their chins; not curled up, as people normally are when they sleep, nor lying chest to back, spoon-fashion, as so many married couples do. No, they lay on their backs, stretched out, an oddly formal position. Stiff. They might have been lying in a double grave. As indeed they were. They'd have woken by now, if this was sleep.

Paul and Charlie looked at each other, Charlie still breathless after scrabbling through the window. Brian followed them in, grumbling as always, though the words died on his lips as he sensed the intensity of their silence. The three of them moved closer to the bed. The old couple lay there, so married, so ordinary – the woman's stick had been hooked over the bedpost so she could reach it easily during the night – and yet infinitely remote, like a medieval knight and lady on a tomb, their blank eyes staring at the vaulted ceiling, unmoving, unchanging, as the slow, murderous centuries pass. Paul felt something like reverence and he thought the others did too. Even Charlie was silenced, and nothing ever stopped Charlie cracking jokes.

Automatically, Paul touched their necks, felt for a pulse, shook his head. What had killed them? There were no obvious wounds. Gently, feeling he was invading their privacy, he pulled the bedclothes back and saw, with a stab of pity, that they were holding hands.

'Shock?' Charlie said. He had to clear his throat to produce the word.

Paul shrugged. 'Suppose so.'

He'd seen people die of shock before: healthy young men lying at the bottom of a trench with not a mark on them anywhere. Charlie, who he knew had served in France, must have seen it too. Had the old couple heard the bomb come shrieking down? Had he reached out and held her hand to comfort her in the last seconds before it fell? So peaceful, they were. So quiet. Their silence was a force spreading out around them, trivializing the yapping of the guns and the thud of exploding bombs.

Nick had come in through the window and was pushing to the front, eager to see.

'I'd stay back if I were you,' Paul said.

He was tense, expecting Nick to say something utterly crass, but instead he stooped, picked up a cardigan that had slipped on to the floor and, for some reason, draped it carefully over the back of a chair. The others, turning their heads to witness this strange ritual, caught themselves reflected in a mirror, and stood like that, motionless, as if the stillness of the couple on the bed had reached and enfolded everybody in the room.

How long they might have stayed like that Paul never knew. The silence was broken by a whimper that seemed, for one horrific moment, to be coming from the couple on the bed. They looked at each other. The sound did seem to be coming from the bed. Paul shuffled along the wall and felt along the floor. Almost immediately his exploring fingers encountered something disgustingly warm and moist, and he snatched his hand back. Nick, meanwhile, was on his knees peering under the bed. 'Come on, boy. Come on.' He slapped his thighs, and a small, white-and-brown Jack Russell terrier, ears flattened against its head, crept towards him on its belly. It must have been there all the time, hiding between the bed and the wall, reaching up to lick a still-warm hand.

'Oh, you've got a friend there all right,' Charlie said, as the dog leapt up and tried to lick Nick's mouth.

'Gerroff.' Nick shoved the dog inside his coat and looked at Charlie, obviously expecting disagreement. 'Well, we can't leave it here.'

The dog peered out, its sharp face and bright, amber eyes glinting in the light from Charlie's torch.

'All right, but it's your responsibility, mind.' He turned to Paul and Brian. 'Come on, there's nothing we can do here.'

As they closed the door behind them, Nick pointed a stern finger at the dog. 'Piss on me, you little fucker, and you're dead.'

The All Clear sounded early that night; the raid had not been a particularly bad one. And yet, meeting at the wardens' station at the end of the shift, everybody seemed subdued. Nick was slumped in an armchair, staring into space. Charlie came up carrying two steaming mugs of tea and put one on the table in front of him.

'What about that dog, then?' He nudged Nick's arm, trying to rouse him, but Nick turned on him a totally blank stare. 'What dog?'

Charlie and Paul exchanged glances. Somebody shouted across to Paul: did he want a cup of tea? But he shook his head. More than on most mornings, he was glad to get away.

At the top of the steps, he paused for a moment, wondering what he should do. No Sandra now. She'd left two days ago, to his mingled sadness and relief. He knew he wouldn't be able to sleep. He'd seen so many more horrific things than that old couple, but he knew they were going to haunt him, possibly for quite a long time. Do something – that was the thing. Keep busy. Perhaps he might have a walk round to the house, see what else he could find in the rubble. He was driving down to the cottage at the weekend and it was always nice to have something to give to Elinor.

Scrambling around among the broken bricks and charred timbers, he unearthed some knives and forks – apostle teaspoons, she was quite fond of those – but the real treasures were the paintings – and quite a few of them had survived. No time for that today though. Something was niggling at the back of his mind and he couldn't think what it was. He thought about the old couple – but no, it wasn't that. It was something more recent, something he'd noticed. He straightened up and looked down the street. An elderly man in an antiquated tweed overcoat had stopped in front of the noticeboard and was jotting down one of the addresses. That was it, something on the noticeboard. He threw down the brick he was holding and went to see.

And there it was. Elinor's handwriting. An address in Gower Street. At first, he couldn't take it in. He knew perfectly well she wanted to return to London – they'd argued about it only last weekend – but it had never occurred to him that she might move without consulting him. Or even telling him. It was – well, impossible. Unless . . .

There's always some kind person'll tell you. Won't be long before somebody tells your wife about you.

Who could've told her? Well, almost anybody – he hadn't been particularly discreet. Anybody, really, who was sufficiently malicious, or perhaps just incensed on her behalf. Neville knew. No, he wouldn't.

It didn't matter who. He had to think straight; he had to get this right. He didn't know for a fact that Elinor was aware of his affair with Sandra, or that moving back to London was an expression of her anger. There were all kinds of reasons why she might have decided to return. His affair with Sandra had receded so rapidly into the past he felt it was hardly worth bothering about. The two days since their last meeting might have been years for all he cared. It was easy to think that, because it was over and had meant so little, it couldn't have any impact on his life – or Elinor's. No, it was equally likely she'd just grown tired of the constant arguments and had decided to present him with a fait accompli. *That* was entirely possible.

His first impulse was to rush round to Gower Street and ask her, but if she knew about the affair this would inevitably lead to a confrontation, and he didn't feel ready to face that. No, perhaps he should wait, get rested – that was the most important thing – and then this evening, he'd come back here and find something – ideally, not knives and forks – a painting or a drawing – and lay it at her feet. That would be the best, the wisest, thing to do.

Twenty-six

21 October 1940

I'd forgotten what living in furnished rooms feels like – the smell of other people's lives: transient lives, passing through. The way the silver plating's always worn off the forks, the cracks in the bone handles on the knives. Oh, I can't put my finger on it exactly, except here I'm a student again. Single. Oh, yes, single.

I've put my address on the board by the house. If Paul's still trying to retrieve stuff he's almost bound to see it and then he'll realize I haven't told him about the move. He'll know I've found out about her.

I lived two doors down from here when I was a student at the Slade. Sometimes when I'm walking down the street I fancy I see her coming towards me, that girl. The girl who lived for days on end on packets of penny soup, made her own clothes, walked everywhere. She doesn't seem so far away now. In fact, I walk through her ghost every time I cross the floor.

And this wallpaper. She'd have had that off the wall in no time. She'd have hated it, the dreary, dingy Victorian fussiness of it, the horrible yellow pattern – paisley, I suppose, a sort of cross between a flower and a praying mantis. No, she'd have been sloshing wallpaper stripper all over that, scraping away at it till her hands ached. How much energy I must have spent over the years, battling with Victorian wallpaper. Well, not any more. Let it stay. You see wallpaper like this all over London where the sides have been ripped off houses. The Luftwaffe's doing a much better demolition job than I ever could.

And I'd like to talk to Paul about it but, of course, there is no Paul.

I had to go to the shelter last night. While the house was still standing, I could use the hall, convince myself it was safe. Not here: it's a death trap, so off to the shelter I must go.

The usual crowd, mainly women. There's an old couple who play chess. Rather sweet, really. Oh, and there's the major, a military gentleman with peppery, blue eyes. No nonsense, no emotion, none of that. Only he has this absolutely marvellous moustache – a beautiful red-gold colour. Titian. He takes tremendous care of it, not in public, of course, but you can imagine him, in private, combing and trimming it. In some strange way – in defiance of biology – all the major's feminine qualities, his vulnerability, his gentleness, are distilled into that moustache. The rest of him is very properly hard, masculine, decisive. And of course he thinks he's boss. Angela, the shelter warden, manages him very well. She always consults him, very deferentially, before going on to do exactly what she was planning to do anyway.

Angela's tremendous. I wouldn't like her job. The facilities are totally inadequate. We're still using latrine buckets behind blanket screens – why didn't they realize? Paul says they thought the raids would be quite short, though very destructive – thousands dead. Instead of which we have long raids – thousands homeless.

But it really is high time I stop referring to Paul as the great authority.

On the rare occasions when I've been here before – generally because Paul bullied me into it – there was an immensely fat woman with very beautiful blue eyes – harebell blue. You don't see that very often. But she wasn't there last night. She used to tell fortunes on top of a suitcase, ordinary cards, not tarot. Always good news: unexpected letters, legacies, tall, dark, handsome strangers.

I used to feel sorry for her, especially in the heat. It can't be much fun. And the latrine bucket was harder for her than for most. Her knees wouldn't take the weight, she had a terrible time of it. I don't think I've ever seen anybody quite as fat. I think you can always tell if somebody's always been fat. And she hadn't. There was a thin girl in there. I thought, when she looks in a mirror she doesn't see herself. A bit like Kit, in a way.

Anyway, she wasn't there last night – Bertha, that's her name
– and apparently she hasn't been for quite a while. I asked Angela if
she knew what had happened to her. She looked round and lowered
her voice. 'She got bombed, they took her to hospital, but she died a
few days later. Poor woman, she was in no state to stand up to
anything.' I think of her lying upstairs in a pokey little room
somewhere, frightened but too tired or too breathless to get to the
shelter. Or too embarrassed. I hope she didn't die because she
couldn't use the bucket, but it's only too probable. If I'd known
where she was I'd've gone to see her.

Our other notable personality is Dorothea Stanhope, who's using
the shelter at the moment because she's having the cellar plastered,
and a new floor laid. It's going to be wonderful when it's finished,
only she can't get the workmen so it's taking longer than she
thought. There she sits, with her jewellery case clasped in skeletal
hands, diamonds worth an absolute fortune dangling from long,
leathery earlobes. She has two daughters. Actually, I think it's an
unmarried daughter and a daughter-in-law. The daughter, fresh-
faced but no longer young – what can one say? A complete doormat
– having failed in what, I suspect, for Dorothea, is the sole business
of a girl's life: getting a rich husband. 'Gel', as Dorothea says. I
don't know if she says 'Injun' because I've never managed to bring
the conversation round to the Wild West, but I'd bet quite a bit of
money she does.

Dorothea's favourite is her granddaughter. Six years old, and
very good, she's no bother, a lot less trouble than some of the
adults. There was one particularly bad raid when she screamed –
but then the rest of us nearly screamed too. The door was shaking
with every blast; we thought it was coming in. Dorothea remained
totally calm. There's a whiff of the Raj about Dorothea; she's very
grand, but also a couple of decades out of date. Anyway, the
cellar's finally finished, according to Angela, so we won't be seeing
her again.

I slept in this morning, tried to work but couldn't seem to get
started, and then the afternoon was so warm I just couldn't bear to
stay indoors. So I went and sat in the garden of my old house on a

kitchen chair I pulled out of the rubble, no doubt looking very
eccentric and rather pathetic but I don't care.

I love my garden. I'm no use at gardening, unlike Mother – or
Rachel, for that matter – but some things seem to grow in spite of
me. I have Michaelmas daisies and sunflowers peering over the fence
into the next garden, almost as if nothing had happened, even
though there's ruin all around them. Paul went through a phase
of painting sunflowers. He used to say they were absolutely
extraordinary, different from any other flower, because they're as
tall as a man, you look them in the face – or they look you in the
face – and they move. Measurably, in the course of a single day,
following the sun. And then they age in the same way as people.
They develop a stoop, a sort of dowager's hump, and the seed heads
fold in on themselves, like an old man's mouth without teeth.

Paul, Paul, bloody Paul. Just as I was getting thoroughly
exasperated with myself, I felt a shadow falling across me. Looked
up and there he was. He was holding the notice with my new
address on it. 'I hope you're going to put that back,' I said.

'Well,' he said.

I wasn't going to help him out, but eventually he did manage to
get going, all by himself. It was very sudden, he said. It really was
rather a shock, he said. Was I sure I was doing the right thing? Had
I really thought it through?

What I heard, loud and clear, was the one question he didn't ask:
WHY? He didn't dare ask, because then I might have told him. And
then the whole business about the girl would be dragged into the
open and he's probably fooling himself it needn't be. Not now, and
possibly not ever. I suppose I could have forced the issue, but really I
couldn't be bothered.

He hung about. There was only the one chair, so after a while he
sat in the grass at my feet, but that put him at a disadvantage so he
stood up again, muttering something about if I wasn't happy I
should have said. Meaning the cottage, I suppose. I did say; he
wasn't listening. Anyway, it's not about the cottage. It was awful.
Really, really awful. I was glad when he gave up and went away.

I just sat there, after he'd gone, looking at the ruin of our life together. Love affairs don't need much – you can manage the whole thing on moonlight and roses, if you have to. But a marriage needs things, routines, a framework, habits, and all of ours were ripped away. I could forgive him the girl – well, no, not yet, but one day perhaps. What I can't forgive, what I'm afraid I may never be able to forgive, is the look of relief on his face when all this was destroyed.

Twenty-seven

Neville walked as far as Russell Square before stopping to look back at the Ministry of Information: a brutal grey mass dominating the skyline. Then he selected a bench where he could sit with his back to it and began enjoying the last warmth of the sun as best he could through his heavy clothes. A few feet away, a pigeon crooned and preened, puffed out its neck feathers, gave its inane, throaty chuckle. He aimed a kick at the bird. 'Why don't you do something useful? Piss off up there and shit on it?' The pigeon lifted off, flapped a few yards further away, and settled contemptuously on the grass.

'Kicking pigeons now, are we?'

He spun round to see Elinor sitting on the grass. She was looking up at him, so amused, so, in a way, *accepting*, that he had to get up and go to her. Then, feeling he couldn't conduct even a brief conversation looking down on her like this, lowered himself on to the prickly grass. 'Sorry.'

'What for? Wasn't me you kicked.'

'Language.'

'Shouldn't worry, I don't suppose it understood.'

All around, people were sitting or lying in couples or singly on the grass, the girls still in their summer dresses. The brilliant summer had given way to a golden and apparently endless autumn, almost as if the bombs that stopped the clocks had power to stop the seasons as well.

Elinor was stretched out, her eyes closed. It pleased him that she didn't feel the need to sit up, to make conversation. Slowly, he lay back himself, enjoying the warmth of the sun on his lids. Lying here like this, they had no past – or none that had the power to hurt them now – and, quite possibly, no future; but that didn't seem to matter. He knew from gossip at the depot that she was living alone. And he knew about Paul and Sandra. Some men would have seized the opportunity, but he'd always been held back by diffidence, the knowledge that he wasn't attractive. Long before the injury to his face, he'd felt that. Years of reconstructive surgery had merely confirmed what he already knew: that his place was in the dark, listening to the *tap-tap* of approaching feet, a muffled voice, a face he couldn't see, and didn't want to see.

After a while, though, he felt he ought to say something. 'How's Paul?'

'Pretty well, I think. As far as I know . . .'

He pricked alert, listening not to the words, but to the tone. 'It's just, I haven't seen him around much.' This was a lie: he'd seen Paul 'around' fairly frequently – and once or twice with Sandra.

'We're separated.'

'Really?'

'Yes, he's having an affair.'

'Actually, I –'

'You knew?' Immediately hostile.

'Somebody said something, but you know what it's like, gossip, I didn't pay much attention.' He rolled over on to his elbow. 'Do you know the girl?'

'I'm glad you said "girl". Every day of twenty-three.'

'He's a fool.'

'Most men wouldn't think so.'

'I'm not most men.'

Her face softened. 'No, you're not, are you?'

He might, at this point, have told her that Sandra Jobling had left London, since she appeared not to know; but he chose not to. 'Are you on duty tonight?'

'Yes, in fact . . .' She glanced at her watch. 'I should probably be going.'

But she made no move. She'd rolled over on to her stomach and was idly picking the grass. He was afraid to speak, afraid of disturbing the intimacy of the moment. After a minute or so, she turned on to her back again, raising one arm to shield her eyes from the light that seemed to become only more dazzling as the sun sank behind the trees.

A memory had begun nibbling at the corners of his mind. A year or two before the last war, smarting from one of Professor Tonks's more withering comments on his work, he'd walked as far as Russell Square, intending to calm down or, failing that, play truant, go to the British Museum instead. And there she was: Elinor Brooke, whom he passed every day in the corridors of the Slade and watched, covertly, during drawing sessions in the Antiques room, but whom – despite all the brash self-confidence of his public persona – he'd never yet summoned up the courage to approach.

Until that afternoon . . .

'Do you remember –?'

She smiled. 'Warm lemonade.'

'Oh God, yes.' He'd forgotten the lemonade.

'There was a hut over there.' She pointed behind her, but without turning her head.

So she did remember. He tried to pin down what he thought about that, but all thought was dissolved in warmth and light. He let his eyes close, aware all the time of how ridiculous he must look in his dark suit and polished shoes and his briefcase lying on the grass beside him. Lying side by side like this, they must look like an established couple, too tired, too jaded, to be bothered to touch each other, and yet so firmly bonded they couldn't bear to be more than an inch apart. In a word, married.

As always, when he was close to Elinor, memories of their student days drifted into his mind. He'd proposed to her, once, on a summer's day a long, long time ago, and this heat, the prickly grass, the tickle of sweat on his upper lip, reminded him forcefully of that day. Riding a bike, of all things, on his way to see the Doom in the local church – and a very fine painting it was too, though his pose as a Futurist had not permitted him to say so. And then, on the way back, he'd hit a bump in the road, soared over the handlebars and landed hard on the gravelly tarmac, cutting his hands and knee and sustaining quite a sharp blow to the head.

Tarrant, who'd been there, of course, waiting to grab Elinor for himself at the earliest opportunity, had gone for help, and he'd lain with his head in her lap. Briefly, when he struggled to sit up, the back of his head had touched her breasts – not entirely accidentally. And he'd asked her to marry him, and then when she refused, or rather laughed, he'd told her that being in love with her was like loving a mermaid. That must have hurt. Or perhaps not. Perhaps she'd just found him as ridiculous as he'd feared he was.

He didn't want to think about that day, but in this merciless, unseasonable heat, things resurfaced, like the spars of a submerged boat in a lake that was drying out. He saw Toby Brooke, in the conservatory, helping his friend Andrew revise for an anatomy exam. Toby, stripped to the waist, arms stretched out on either side, and painted on to his skin: ribs, lungs, liver, heart; all the internal organs. 'Living anatomy', it was called. But standing there, in the sickly golden light of late afternoon, Toby had looked like a man turned inside out. It had disturbed him then in ways he'd never fully understood, and it disturbed him now. He felt a sudden chill, as if a shadow had fallen across his face, though when he opened his eyes there was nobody there, and the sky was the same ruthless blue it had been for months.

What an autumn it had been. What a year. He closed his eyes again and almost immediately something unexpected happened. He began to feel Elinor – not merely sense her presence; this was actual physical contact – all along the side that was closest to her. He raised his head and looked at her, needing to reassure himself that she had not, as in some libidinous dream, moved closer and was actually touching him. Of course she hadn't, one arm was still across her face, the other lying on the grass, an inch away from his own. He tried to think of something to say, to make her look at him, to dispel this strange hallucination. Could you hallucinate touch? Well, obviously, yes, since he'd just been doing it. And when he lay back and closed his eyes, the sensation came back. So, in the end, he simply surrendered to it, lying beside her on the grass, touching and not touching, soaking up the last of the sun.

Twenty-eight

The moment she turned the corner into Gower Street, Elinor stopped, for there, on the steps of her new home, was a familiar shape: Paul. No more than a silhouette in the darkness, but she'd have known him anywhere. He was dressed to go on duty, his shabby uniform recalling the long, black, obviously second-hand coat he'd worn at the Slade, always managing to look supremely elegant – in sharp contrast to Kit, who'd looked like a sack of potatoes in his expensive Savile Row suits. Paul hadn't even been aware of the contrast, which in Kit's eyes had rather added to the offence. The prince in Act Two, she'd called Paul once, teasing. All these memories, bobbing to the surface, merely sharpened her sense of betrayal.

He had propped a large parcel, wrapped in brown paper, against the railings, and was carrying another, much smaller, package under his arm. 'I brought these.'

The larger parcel had to be one of her lost paintings. She wanted to rip the paper off, find out which one, but she restrained herself. Confused now, for this obliged her to be grateful – he'd have gone to considerable trouble to get it and possibly some risk – she opened the door, and gestured to him to step inside.

She led the way upstairs. 'A long haul, I'm afraid.'

'You're on the top floor?' He waited until they'd finished their climb and she was opening the flat door. 'Not very safe.'

'I go to the shelter. Besides, it's cheap.' She nodded at the parcel. 'Which one?'

'Me, I'm afraid.'

They looked at each other, and she turned away, unable to share the irony that, in other circumstances, would have had them both laughing. 'Well, I look forward to that.' She pulled the blackout curtains across and lit a lamp. 'Sit down.'

'There's two.'

'Toby?'

'Yes. A bit damaged. Not too bad.'

She couldn't bring herself to thank him.

'I think that's it, I don't think there's a lot left. A couple of parcels, you know, big brown envelopes with strong, coarse string round them, but I couldn't reach them. I'll have another go tomorrow.'

It was imperative to thank him. 'No, well, it's lovely to have these. Thank you.'

The words stuck in her throat. An awkward silence fell. So far there'd been no mention of why they were here, in this strange room.

He cleared his throat. 'So you decided you couldn't stand the cottage after all?' The cough was a nervous tic; he was inching his way forward.

'I need a London base.'

Innocuous enough, on the surface, but 'I need' was the language of separation and they both knew it. A few days ago this would have been a joint decision. He looked at the fireplace, at the empty grate. 'I hear you've been commissioned.'

'Yes, I went to see Clark.'

'Congratulations.'

'Who told you?'

'Neville.'

'I don't know how he knew.'

'He always knows; he's eaten up with jealousy.'

He was inviting her to gang up against Kit, which at some points in the past she would have been very ready to do. But not any more. 'I saw you,' she said. 'With that girl.'

'Ah.'

After waiting a few seconds, she let out an incredulous laugh, only just not a yelp. 'Is that it?'

'I don't see what else I can say.'

'You could – oh, I don't know . . . *Explain?*'

'It just happened.'

'It just happened?'

He spread his hands.

'Oh, I *see*. The war, the nasty bombs – everybody jumping into bed with everybody else. So you thought you had to jump too?'

'I'm not saying I'm proud of it.'

'*Hallelujah!*'

Silence. His almost-unnaturally long, slim fingers were beating a tattoo on the arm of the chair.

'So what happens now?' she asked.

'What do you mean?'

'Well, are you going to live together? Do you want a divorce?'

He looked startled. 'No, of course not, it's over. She's gone.'

'Well, that's convenient.'

'It didn't . . . Well, frankly, it wasn't all that important. Not to me.'

'And you think that makes it better?'

He clearly didn't know what to say.

'Do you know, Paul, I'd actually rather you were breaking your heart over her. I wish you were in love with her; I wish you were suffering the torments of the damned, because then it would mean something. Better that than an itch in the groin you couldn't resist scratching.'

The clock on the mantelpiece ticked, stitching the silence. The sound seemed to penetrate his brain, at last. 'You bought a clock.'

'Yes.' She turned to look at it. 'Which reminds me, I'm due on duty in a few minutes.'

'Do you have anywhere you can paint?'

'Through there.'

'North facing?'

She stood up. What did one say in these circumstances? It was hardly a normal parting: twelve hours from now one or other of them might be dead. She felt a tide of desolation sweep over her for the lostness of the one who would be left; never again to have the opportunity of saying what needed to be said. Well, here was the opportunity. Here. Now. And yet she couldn't speak.

He stood up. 'There's no need to see me out.'

She shook her head. Going down the stairs, they didn't speak at all. As she opened the front door on to the steps, she tried to think of something to say, but her mind had gone blank.

On the pavement he turned and looked at her. 'Take care.'

She nodded. 'And you.'

It wasn't much, but it would have to do.

Twenty-nine

The first call came just before one in the morning. Elinor had been lying on one of the sofas reading grubby, tattered magazines, unable to sleep, thinking about Paul, the look on his face, the way he'd walked off down the street. She'd known he'd stop at the corner and look back and she'd gone inside so he wouldn't see her standing there. A petty power-play, a means of hurting, of establishing control: she and Paul had never carried on like that, and now they did. Sad. Her mouth was dry and stale; she was too tired to think straight. It was almost a relief when the telephones started to ring.

She was working with Dana Kresberg tonight. She liked Dana, and was rather intrigued by her. As an American, Dana could so easily have sat out these nights very comfortably in the Savoy; she could have gone out on to the balcony after dinner, with a number of American journalists, watching the night's raid almost as if it were a firework display. And why not? This was not, after all, their war: or not yet. But Dana had chosen, instead, to become involved, to risk life and limb night after night, driving an ambulance through bombed and burning streets, and Elinor had never asked her why. Hatred of fascism? A love of adventure? Compassion for trapped and suffering people? An addiction to danger, perhaps? Everybody's motives were a great mixture, but, unlike Londoners, Dana didn't have the most basic motivation: defending your home. And that made her stand out in the team of drivers working out of the depot in Tottenham Court Road.

Dana's great advantage was that she was outside the English class system. Elinor watched, with some amusement, as Dana negotiated its various ravines and rapids with the assurance of a sleepwalker. She even got on with Derek James, whose years as a taxi driver had given him an encyclopaedic knowledge of London's back streets, which was invaluable. But he had a chip on his shoulder. Well, it was more like a log, really. 'Timber yard,' said Kit, whose public-school accent made him the preferred butt of Derek's not-always-funny jokes. But Derek accepted Dana totally; was, in fact, almost mesmerized by her.

Tonight, though, Elinor and Dana were working together. Around about 12.45 a.m., their turn came. They grabbed their tin hats – very useful for shielding exposed wounds from plaster dust or putting out an incendiary, but almost certainly useless at protecting the brain from falling bricks – and pulled on the black greatcoats that reached to their ankles and impeded their movements much as a suit of cardboard armour might have done. It was Elinor's turn to drive and that pleased her. She and Dana each thought the other drove like a lunatic, and possibly they were both right. But then, perhaps, in these conditions there was no other way to drive. Oncoming vehicles were mere pinpricks of light, little, piggy, red eyes looming out of the night. Crashes were frequent in the early part of the evening, before burning fires illuminated the streets. Dana kept ringing the bell, its *clang-clang* adding to the baying and yapping of anti-aircraft guns. Elinor crouched over the wheel, peering through the windscreen for new craters that had not yet been marked by blue warning lights. Dust sifted in through the open windows and settled on their shoulders. More seriously, it formed a film over the windscreen, blurring what little vision they had. But even in this darkness, Elinor recognized the familiar streets. She was driving along the route she'd walked three hours before, turning the corner, now, into Bedford Square.

'This is it,' Dana said.

Elinor pulled up at the kerb. They clambered down on to the road and started walking towards the scene of the incident. Two blue lights stood on the rubble-strewn pavement and the usual crowd had gathered. One house had been badly hit. The houses on either side were damaged, but they'd been empty, a warden told them. One belonged to an old couple who'd gone to stay with their married daughter in the country; the other to a middle-aged couple, but they definitely wouldn't be in there, he knew for a fact they always went to the shelter. 'It's an old lady lives in that one. Two daughters and a –'

'Yes, I know,' Elinor said.

It was Dorothea Stanhope's house. She knew the names of the younger women and the child, but in the stress of the moment they escaped her.

A handful of men was edging warily on to a scree of rubble. Nothing was visible of them but dark backs and bent shoulders; they were all hunched over as if that could protect them from falling ceilings. Elinor pushed to the front, trying to see what was going on. She noticed the mean, sneaky smell of domestic gas, mixed with the stench of high explosive. Paul said it was very like the stink of decomposing bodies on a battlefield, and she wondered what it did to him to smell that here. At home. In London. And then she thought: *Bugger Paul.* Everybody was coughing and covering their mouths. That smell got into your lungs, irritating the mucous membranes of nose and mouth, and then there was the fine dust that repeated blasts sent swirling invisibly into the air.

One of the men on the scree raised his hand, calling for silence. Everybody stood and listened, they hardly seemed to be breathing. Nothing. They started to look at each other, shoulders beginning to slump, but then it came again. Somebody inside the ruined house, from under the collapsed floors and ceilings, was crying out: a thin, reedy wail; an old woman's voice, by the sound of it, although fear and weakness could make anybody sound old.

Work began again, with renewed vigour. Elinor and Dana ducked underneath the tape and stood on the opposite pavement from the wrecked house. Elinor looked at the bent backs of the men heaving away at the rubble; they were working more methodically now, loading buckets with bricks and lumps of fallen plaster, passing them down a chain. As one of them turned to hand a bucket on, she caught a glimpse of his face and recognized Kit. Somebody touched her arm. She turned and saw Violet, looking haggard, wisps of grey hair escaping from under her tin hat. The gutter was running with water from a burst main, turning plaster dust into a claggy paste that would set hard on every inch of exposed skin. 'They're alive,' Violet said. The tension of that knowledge, the need to work harder and faster, was in every face you saw. At intervals, the rescue-squad leader raised his hand and everybody stopped what they were doing and strained to listen. Violet was right: the frail voice under the rubble had been joined by other voices. One was crying: 'My daughter, my baby, where is she?' – edging up into hysteria. They couldn't afford to let it affect them. The hand fell and they got back to work. The burst water main had turned the road into a slick of slimy mud. A rescue-squad worker, running up to help, slipped and fell.

Bombers went on droning overhead, bursts of orange light obliterating the stars. The men were sawing through a beam that had fallen across a mound of rubble and was impeding progress. Another voice started up inside – not the child's voice though – they hadn't heard the child. It was impossible to go on doing nothing. Elinor ran across the road and, clambering up the lower slope, began to talk to the women inside. She felt rather than saw Kit turn at the sound of her voice. She was telling them they'd be all right, they'd soon have them out, no need to worry, not long now . . . It was what you always said, what you had to say, though in the time she'd been standing there no visible progress had been made. But at least they were alive, or the women were. 'My baby, my poor baby,' the mother kept calling out, and the child's name: Libby? Lizzie? No, Livvy, *Livvy*, that was it, she remembered now: the little girl was called Olivia. 'Livvy, are you there? Where are you, Livvy?' And then again: 'My baby, my poor baby.' On and on it went. Unbearable, you'd have said, except that they all bore it.

'All right, love, we're getting there,' the rescue-squad leader called out. 'Not long now.'

Once the beam was out of the way, they were able to start tunnelling into the rubble, but it was slow, arduous work since the tunnel had to be shored up and made safe every few yards or so. Elinor thought – she couldn't be sure – that the rescue workers had managed to pass bottles of water through a gap. If true, it might help the women go on a bit longer, but there was so much rubble to shift, tons of it, she didn't see how the old woman could possibly survive the night.

At one point, she and Dana were sent to answer another call. One incident led to another, through the long hours of darkness – she could never afterwards remember the precise sequence of events – though there were flashes of acute clarity. Her and Dana leaning against the ambulance, shoulders shaking, bent double, laughing till they whooped for breath. And the joke? They'd been asked to deliver four bodies to a mortuary, but when they got there – after rather a difficult journey – the attendant refused to take them: no death certificates. Off they went to the nearest hospital, where an exhausted doctor who'd been toiling all night in an overcrowded, badly lit basement flatly refused to stop work and sign death certificates for corpses that were nothing to do with him. Back to the mortuary. 'Not without a death certificate,' the angry little man insisted, trying to impose his own order on the chaos that was descending from the skies. 'He's going to have a heart attack,' Elinor said, as they left. 'Oh I *do* hope so,' Dana replied. In the end, they appealed for help from a couple of passing air-raid wardens and unloaded the bodies in an alley that ran between two department stores. There they lay, lined up on the cobbles, at a decent distance from the dustbins. There was nothing to cover them with, but Elinor and Dana closed their eyes, and the wardens did the best they could to straighten their remaining limbs.

As she turned to go, Elinor was half embarrassed, half grateful to see one of the wardens do what she couldn't do – cross himself and say a prayer.

Dana had stayed behind to thank the wardens. Elinor waited by the ambulance for her to come back, saw her shoulders shaking as she approached and reached out to comfort her, only to realize she was laughing. 'What? *What?*' Elinor said. ' "Not without a death certificate." Oh my God, that is so funny.' Tears were streaming down her face, making rivulets in the beige dust.

By four in the morning, they were back outside the house in Bedford Square. Not long after their arrival, a bomb fell on the other side of the square and the buried women, hearing the crash and feeling the rubble above their heads begin to slide, screamed in shock and fear. Elinor half thought she'd cried out herself, only the bulge in her throat convinced her the cry was still trapped inside. A burst of flame from the fresh bomb site sent shadows fleeing across the square. A third rescue squad arrived, and then a fourth. Kit relinquished his place in the chain that was passing buckets of rubble from the tunnel to the pavement, and came and stood beside her. 'Who's in there?' he asked. 'Do you know?'

'Dorothea Stanhope. Do you remember, her husband was viceroy, no, he wasn't viceroy, something like that . . . Daughter, daughter-in-law. And a little girl, the granddaughter.'

'How old?'

'Six.'

He said nothing, merely turned to stare at the rubble and the bent, labouring backs. There was nothing they could do now except wait for the rescue squad to break through and start pulling people out. The old woman's cries were growing weaker, but the voices of the two younger women were still strong, and seemed – unless this was wishful thinking – to be getting louder. The chief rescue-squad leader held up his hand. 'Careful. Slow down now.'

Elinor craned forward, as the workers paused. For a long moment nobody moved, but then the teams began inching forward again. A hole had opened at the centre of the rubble and the two halves of the beam had been used to reinforce the sides. Then came another long, familiar, shrieking descent. The ground shook and a cataract of loose bricks and mortar cascaded down the sides of the slope. One of the rescue workers threw back his head and yelled, 'FUCK YOU!' at the sky. Then he caught sight of Violet standing there. 'Sorry,' he said. 'Didn't see you, love.' 'Oh, *please* don't apologize,' Violet said, in her daughter-of-the-vicarage accent. 'My sentiments *precisely*.'

The old woman's cries seemed to be getting louder again – either the rescue squad was getting closer or her own sense that help was at hand had renewed her strength. Perhaps, after all, she'd be the first one out. Suddenly, they all went quiet again. Men with sweat-streaked faces stopped and stared at each other, white eyes startling in their grimy faces. A child's head had appeared through a hole in the rubble. Nobody moved. For a long time, it seemed, nobody moved. Then the rescue-squad leader fell to his knees and, placing his hands on either side of the head, gently persuaded it to rotate, so that first one shoulder then the other and then, in a great rush, the whole body fell out of the hole. Still, no cry. People looked at each other, unable to accept the truth, but the body was small and floppy and it made no sound.

Dana, one hand across her mouth, ran to fetch a stretcher. Elinor followed to help. Only when they returned, did they see the dead child lying on the pavement. They knelt on either side of her and, not looking at each other, prepared to lift her on to the stretcher. Nobody spoke. From inside the ruined building, a voice cried out: 'Livvy? My baby. Oh, my baby.'

Neville looked down at the little body. 'My daughter's that age.' It sounded almost casual: the sort of remark you might make outside the school gates. Then, bending swiftly down, he gathered her into his arms and carried her to the ambulance.

The mother was brought out half an hour later, thickly coated in dust, bleeding from a deep cut to her head, but otherwise surprisingly uninjured. 'My baby,' she kept saying. 'Where's my baby?' 'Won't be long now, love,' one of the rescue workers said. Elinor wrapped a blanket round her shoulders, thinking she and Dana should take her to hospital rather than let her travel in the back of Neville's ambulance with her dead child. But Elinor didn't know what to do. She didn't know what she would have wanted if this unimaginable pain had come to her. Neville took the decision for her. 'You take the mother,' he said. 'I'll stay here.' He gripped the woman's arm and helped her up the steps. 'Come on, let's get you to hospital.'

'But my daughter?'

'Don't you worry, love. They'll soon have her out.'

Wrapped in a red blanket, too shocked to argue, she sat down on the bench. Dana climbed in beside her and put an arm round her shoulders.

At the last moment she started to struggle, trying to throw off the blanket and jump down into the road. 'I want Livvy.'

Dana restrained her. 'I know, I know.'

The All Clear sounded as it started to get light. The dawn wind, tainted by the smell of high explosive, brought with it the assurance they were still alive. The rescue workers breathed deeply once or twice, then got back to work.

Elinor and Dana, returning from the hospital, stood shivering against the garden railings, taking in, for the first time, the full extent of the devastation. In this thin light it looked worse than anything they'd imagined in the dark, and yet both knew that in a few days, a week at most, they might walk along this terrace and hardly notice the gap.

A warden came up and stood beside them, watching the rescue workers still passing chains of buckets down the line. He was sucking something, a boiled sweet, perhaps, or else just his gums. 'It's all very well saying Londoners can take it,' he said. 'But can they? How much more of this can anybody take?'

It was the forbidden question; neither of them answered it.

The old woman was brought out an hour later, garrulous with shock, but unhurt. Her daughter, injured but alive, was pulled out a few minutes later.

'Where's my granddaughter?' the old woman kept asking. She was still clutching her jewellery box, bright, acid-drop sunshine showing up the age spots on the backs of her hands. Dana tried to wrap a blanket round her thin shoulders, but she wasn't having any of that. 'Where's my granddaughter?'

'She'll be all right,' somebody said. 'They've taken her to hospital.'

Dorothea obviously didn't believe it. She stood looking from face to face. 'I hope she didn't suffer.'

Elinor said, 'I think it would have been very quick.'

The old woman looked at her and nodded. Then she turned to her daughter, held out her hand and together the two of them climbed into the ambulance. Elinor got into the driver's seat, checking with Dana that the two women were securely fastened in before bumping along the brick-strewn road in the direction of University College Hospital. There, she and Dana helped the two women into the entrance and handed them over to the porters, before walking out again into gritty sunshine and a song of birds.

Elinor stumbled as they walked back to the ambulance. As she reached up to open the door, Dana pushed her gently to one side. 'My turn,' she said. 'And I'll drop you off.'

Standing on the pavement outside her new home, Elinor thought only about having a bath and falling into bed. Her skull seemed to have been rinsed in icy, bone-numbing water. She was incapable of thinking, or feeling, anything.

Thirty

At some point he must have slept. He woke to find a cup of tea going cold on the table beside him and his tongue sticking to the roof of his mouth. For a moment, it was a normal day. He lay, gazing placidly at what little he could see of the ceiling, but then memories of the night before began to surface. Out of a vortex of darkness emerged the broken body of a small child lying on the pavement. He'd picked her up, yes, and carried her to the ambulance. Her mouth had fallen open to reveal the two adult teeth at the front, not quite through yet, still shorter than the baby teeth on either side. He remembered Anne at that stage: the 'wobbly tooth' she'd insisted he feel half a dozen times a day, long before it was actually wobbly at all.

And then there was the gap, the all-important gap, the visit from the tooth fairy, Anne smiling, baring her teeth to show her friends. She'd been late losing her baby teeth. And for a long time afterwards, he'd noticed her running her tongue along the edge of the grown-up tooth, which was uneven, not smooth as adult teeth are after years of biting and grinding. That little girl, last night – Livvy, was it? Her two precious grown-up teeth would never be worn smooth.

He lay in bed in the darkened room and thought of Anne, whom he hadn't seen now for over a year. She sent him letters, of course, in the neat, joined-up writing she was so proud of, and drawings that were becoming more accurate and less imaginative all the time, but none of that made up for the lack of her physical presence. She used to get into bed with him in the mornings and her freshly baked smell made him ashamed of the sourness of his early-morning breath. 'I'm smooth because I'm new,' she said. 'And you're wrinkly because you're old, but it doesn't matter, I still love you.' All this in an American accent, which never failed to take him by surprise.

Somehow, he'd always assumed she'd speak in the same way as her parents, but she didn't: she sounded exactly like the children she played with in kindergarten. He was smiling to himself, as he thought about the strangeness of it: his little American daughter.

Until last night, it hadn't occurred to him that he might die and never see her again. Now, suddenly, all that ungrounded confidence disappeared, swirled away like dirty water down a plughole, leaving only a gleaming white emptiness that was the certainty of his own death.

Get up. He was doing no good lying here. And it was late, oh my God, it was late.

Downstairs, in the kitchen, he made himself a pot of tea, swishing the first gulp of hot liquid round his mouth before spitting it out. No use, he could still feel grit between his teeth. The sun strengthened, casting his shadow behind him across the tiles. God, he was tired, he was never not tired, he couldn't remember what it was like not to be tired, and yet when he closed his eyes all he saw was the child lying on the dirty pavement. Some kind of pattern on her nightdress, he couldn't quite remember: pink bows, was it, or teddy bears? Rags twisted into her hair. Anne hated rags – but then next day you had ringlets, like Shirley Temple, and that was still the way little girls wanted to look. Only for Livvy there'd been no next day.

He wondered about Elinor, how she was managing to cope with it. And then he thought: *Why not go and see her?* After all, she was single now. And even if she hadn't been, they worked together; there was no reason he shouldn't go to see her in exactly the same way he might have arranged to meet one of the men for a drink. Yes, it was a good idea. He'd tidy himself up a bit and go.

An hour later, he was standing outside Elinor's house. A shaft of sunlight, breaking through a gap in the terrace opposite, twinkled on the doorknocker. Across the road, an old man was setting off to walk his dog, a busy, bright-eyed terrier that stopped to sniff at every lamp post. Unexpectedly, Neville felt a spurt of exhilaration. At one point the previous night, while he was working on the scree, clawing at the bricks with his bare hands, a landslip had started. A lump of flying brick had struck him on the forehead. Nothing much, hardly worth bothering about, but it could have been. And now here was sunlight streaming through a gap in the terrace, a gap where no gap should have been. All over London, now, were little patches of illicit gold. Plants long stunted by deep shade sprouted new leaves, grew and changed shape in the unexpected light. Something lawless about all this: as there was about the interiors of houses, where a bomb ripped off the front or side of a building, leaving bedrooms, toilets, bathrooms recklessly exposed.

He rang the doorbell, wondering, now he was on the brink of seeing her, whether he was doing the right thing. She'd be asleep, almost certainly asleep, and not thank him for waking her, but then he heard her voice. Backing off a few paces, he looked up at the top of the house and there was Elinor, her head and bare shoulders framed in an open window.

'Kit.' Her voice was blurry with sleep.

'I hope I didn't wake you?'

'No, don't worry, I should've been up long since. Is anything the matter?'

'No, I just thought we deserved some of this.' He held up a bottle of whisky.

'What, at this hour?'

'It's nearly one o'clock.'

'Good Lord, is it really?' She looked across the road where the old man with the dog was showing an interest. 'Look, I'll come down.'

She came to the door wearing a navy-blue silk wrap, her hair slightly damp and brushed straight back. 'Come in. Mind the glass.'

'When did this happen?'

'Last night. It's only the landing window. The landlady's supposed to be finding somebody to board it up. I'm just glad it's her problem, not mine.'

'You must be freezing.'

'No, not really. It's only cold at night and I'm not here then. Anyway, I think I'd rather be cold than live behind boarded-up windows.'

He knew what she meant. Many of the rooms in his house –

those he didn't use every day – had blackout curtains permanently drawn, and the darkness seemed to soak into the walls. He followed her upstairs, past the broken window that had a scurf of dead flies on the sill. The wrap glided over her skin as she moved, the silk a touch of pre-war luxury incongruous among the splinters of broken glass that had been swept hastily to either side of the stairs.

Outside her door, she turned to face him. 'Is Paul all right?'

'Yes; well, as far as I know.' He was surprised she asked. How would he know? 'I haven't seen him around for a while.'

'I just thought you –'

She'd thought he was bringing bad news. 'No, the last time I saw him he was with Sandra Jobling.' No harm in reminding her of that. *Do you still love him?* he wanted to ask, as he followed her into the living room.

She turned to face him, pushing her hair out of her eyes. 'I'd better get dressed.'

'No, don't –' He meant: *Don't bother*; or at least he thought he did. But almost immediately, he realized the words were open to misinterpretation, and blushed. He was behaving like a schoolboy.

'No, it's time I was up.'

He heard her moving around the bedroom, edged closer to the half-open door and caught, briefly, a glimpse of nakedness in the dressing-table mirror. Ashamed, he turned away.

A few minutes later she came back into the room, wearing slacks and a jumper. The plum-coloured wool picked up the shadows underneath her eyes and emphasized them. She looked absolutely shattered.

'Well, can I get you a cup –? I suppose there's not much point offering you tea?'

'Not really,' he said. 'I've had tea. How did you sleep?'

'I got off all right, but then the traffic woke me and it took me a while to get back. And then of course I went deep.'

'Yes, you do, don't you? If I let myself go back, I sleep through the alarm and everything.'

He saw her noticing the cut on his forehead. 'That looks nasty,' she said.

'No, it's all right.'

She leaned in closer. 'You should probably have had that stitched.'

'No, really, it's nothing.' *In comparison with the rest*, he wanted to say, but it would've sounded self-pitying, not light, as he meant it to be. 'It's just a bit of broken brick. I think they got most of it out.'

She put a finger gently on the edge of the cut. 'I don't think they did. Hang on, I'll get my tweezers.'

She went into what he supposed was the bathroom. While she was out of the room, he prowled around restlessly, picking things up and putting them down. Being treated as an invalid was the last thing he needed . . .

She came back carrying a bowl of warm water, a wad of cotton wool and the tweezers. 'Come across to the window.'

Resigned, he sat on the arm of a chair. Out of the corner of his eye he could see the street three floors below, cars and people going past. This must be the window she'd looked out of a few minutes earlier, and he'd have been standing just there at the bottom of the steps. Looking down, he saw himself through her eyes. *Methinks I see thee, now thou art below, as one dead in the bottom of a tomb* . . . He shivered.

'Keep still.'

'Yes, ma'am!'

Morbid nonsense. They were a long way from Verona and both of them too old for balcony scenes. And yet that sudden reversal of perspective, the foreshadowing of his own death, sharpened his desire – and his determination. As she bent over him, he felt the warmth of her body through the fine wool of her sweater, her breath on his face. She was frowning with concentration as she dabbed and tweaked, her upper teeth biting her bottom lip. It was incredibly erotic and yet, at the same time, impersonal, almost clinical. And there was something of childhood in it too. Children look at grazes on each other's knees with just that same intent, sexless curiosity. His cousin Blanche, on that holiday in Devon when he was five or six years old: *I'll show you mine if you show me yours*. Laughter bubbled in his throat.

'*Kit*.'

'Sorry.'

Her leg between his thighs, her breasts level with his eyes. And then she straightened up. 'There.'

Brisk, bossy. Very much the nanny, the nurse, the mother. He wasn't having any of it. In one fluid, unconscious motion he stood up, grasped her thin shoulders and kissed her. She stiffened and tried to pull away, and of course he let her go at once, but for the merest sliver of a second her lips had softened under the pressure of his own.

'What was that about?' She sounded curious rather than affronted.

'You know . . .'

'No, I don't know.'

'Yes, you do. I've always loved you.'

She was shaking her head. 'Kit, we've hardly been in touch for twenty years. And during that time – *No*.' She held up a hand to stop him speaking. '*During that time* you married my best friend and had a child with her. *For God's sake*.'

'I loved you the minute I saw you.'

'You can't just turn the clock back like that, nobody can. The fact is, we're two middle-aged people who ought to know better.'

'What about Paul knowing better? He could be living here with you now – if he wanted to – he *chooses* not to.'

'No, he doesn't *choose* not to – he hasn't been invited.'

'I'm sorry, I . . .'

'No, it's all right.'

She looked so downcast he had to touch her again, but this time he simply placed the palm of his hand along the side of her face, more than half expecting her to pull away. Instead she let his hand lie there and covered it with her own. He lowered his head and kissed her again, a long, deep kiss. He was afraid of the moment when it would end. When, finally, they separated, he saw that she was working her tongue against her teeth to get rid of a piece of grit.

'Sorry,' he said. 'It gets everywhere.'

She looked amused. 'Oh, I hope not *every*where.'

He'd never expected, or even hoped, to see that expression on her face. Heart thudding against his ribs, he let himself be led through the door into her bedroom. She pulled the covers back and, for some reason, plumped up the pillows to get rid of the hollow her sleeping head had left.

They were nervous now, both of them, gabbling, postponing the longed-for and feared moment. She went across to the window and pulled the blackout curtain across. A wind had got up and was blowing in gusts so the curtain, now sucked against the frame and now released, seemed to be gasping for breath. The bed seemed huge. She kicked off her shoes, then sat on the side, shuffling along to make room for him. He unlaced his cumbersome boots. Something about this nightly routine: undoing laces, setting the boots down, side by side – clump, and then another clump – peeling off his socks to reveal moist, white feet – all these actions, by their very domestic ordinariness, emphasized the enormity of his transgression. Elinor was married. Paul was his friend.

But then, her exploring hand found a space between his shirt buttons – her fingertips small, hot points on his cold skin – and then he was fumbling with her jumper, trying to tug it out of her slacks, and suddenly none of that mattered. 'Elinor –'

A hand on his mouth. 'Ssh, don't talk.' She swung her legs on to the bed and pulled him down beside her.

Later, he poured them both glasses of whisky, hers well diluted in deference to the hour. She lay on the pillow, looking up at him, her eyes in this half-light unreadable tunnels of darkness. He reached for his cigarettes and offered to light one for her, but she waved it away.

'Did you know this was going to happen?' She sounded faintly accusing.

'No, I just thought we deserved a drink after last night. That poor child.'

They were silent a moment, thinking back. But that was yesterday and the pressure of their lives, the exhaustion, the nightly raids, meant they'd already started to move on. An apparent callousness very familiar to him from the last war, but he thought it would be new to her, and disturbing.

'Did you know about Paul?' he asked.

'And that girl? No. I think I was probably the last person to know.'

'I wouldn't have told you.'

'No, I know. Men stick together, don't they? The Boys' Brigade.'

'That isn't why.'

'Nobody told me; I saw them leaving his studio, having obviously both spent the night there. I just wish somebody *had* told me; it wouldn't have been so much of a shock. It's one of the worst things, knowing everybody knew except me.' She pulled herself up until she was leaning against the headboard. 'I think I will have that cigarette.'

He lit it for her and handed it across. Her eyes closed as she inhaled. 'You know what Paul said? He said it didn't matter. She wasn't important.' A snort of derision. 'Why do men think that makes it better? It doesn't; it makes it worse.'

'Has it happened before? I mean, him –?'

'Once. We-ell, once *that I know about*. One of his students. He was going through a bad patch with his painting, and of course she thought everything he did was absolutely wonderful. Well, I think a lot of what Paul does is wonderful, but you see, I *know*. And he knows I know.' She pulled a face. 'Not the same, is it? Her admiration was – Oh, I don't know . . . reassuringly automatic.'

'But you took him back?'

'He never left – she didn't matter either. The minute I found out, he dropped her. You know, the first time he asked me to marry him, I said no –'

'Yes, well, you were good at that.'

'He said it was probably just as well because he wouldn't have been faithful.' She shook her head. 'I don't think I believed him. I don't *think* I did; I can't remember.'

Neville was wondering what the last hour in bed had meant to her – if anything. A chance to get back at Paul? They seemed to have been talking about him ever since. 'So, do you think you'll get back together again?'

'No.' She looked steadily at him. 'No.'

He drew on his cigarette, creating a small red planet that hovered in the gloom. 'Everybody's doing it, Elinor.' He couldn't think why he'd said that. Why would he want to excuse Paul's behaviour when her hurt and anger had been so delightfully convenient for him?

'Oh, don't worry, I know. It's like *A Midsummer Night's Dream*, isn't it, everybody getting mixed up, swapping partners?' She laughed. 'Goering as Puck – now there's a thought. In tights.'

'Only they woke up, didn't they?' He waited. 'Is that what's going to happen, do you think? We wake up?'

'Who knows what's going to happen?'

She swung her legs to the side of the bed, leaned forward to reach for her wrap, and he thought – the artist's eye unexpectedly reasserting itself – that the human spine was one of the most remarkable sights on earth.

'When can I see you again?'

'I don't know. I'm going to the cottage this weekend, I might stay a few days – I really do need to get some work done.'

'When you get back, then?'

A barely perceptible hesitation, then she nodded. He felt she was waiting for him to go. He'd just got to his feet and was reaching for his trousers when the doorbell rang, and rang again. She crossed to the window and pulled the blackout curtain to one side. 'Oh my God, it's Paul.'

His heart thumped. 'You don't have to let him in.'

'I'm afraid the nurses already have. They're on the ground floor, they let everybody in. I keep telling them.' She turned to face him. 'Look, you stay in here, I'll get rid of him.'

'Can't you pretend you're not in?'

'I think he just saw me.'

A minute later, he heard Paul's voice at the door of the flat. He started to get dressed, pulling on his trousers, snapping his braces into place, fumbling with socks and the laces of his boots, feeling all the time like a character in a farce. Elinor, who seemed to be talking to Paul in the living room now, sounded cool, confident, amused – not like anybody he'd ever met. Dressed, he sat on the side of the bed, his hands loosely clasped between his knees, feeling humiliated and resentful. Why was he being made to feel like a stage adulterer?

It wasn't meant to be like this. The voices went on and on at a low murmur; he couldn't hear the words. Would Paul ever go? But he was beginning to feel slightly less alarmed. After all, there was no reason for Paul to come in here; all he had to do was keep quiet and wait. He tiptoed across and listened at the door: something about the house, photographs, a package Paul had rescued. But the voices were still very low, hardly more than whispers. They must be sitting side by side on the sofa. Well, why not? They were married, after all. He felt sad, old, fat, disillusioned – and very much alone.

At last, sounds of movement from the other side of the door. For one horrible moment, he thought he heard footsteps coming towards him. *They were*. He put his hands flat on the door, feeling Paul on the other side, inches away, but then Elinor said something, a floorboard creaked, and Paul moved away.

A few seconds later, Elinor's voice called 'Goodbye' from the top of the stairs. Neville could breathe normally at last, though it took a while for his heart to slow down. He wiped his palms on the front of his trousers.

Elinor came into the room, pale but composed.

'What did he want?'

'Oh, nothing, he just brought me these.' She was holding a brown envelope from which she pulled out a sheaf of photographs. The top one had been taken on a picnic, one of the annual outings the Slade had arranged for its students; he saw himself sitting beside Elinor, surrounded by faces he recognized, Henry Tonks's skeletal form visible in the back row. He had no memory of the occasion, but there they all were.

He wished he hadn't seen it. Elinor grimaced and put the envelope down on her dressing table. 'He keeps bringing me things; it's very good of him, really – it can't be easy – but . . . Oh, I don't know, sometimes I think he's returning our married life to me in instalments.' She smiled, as if to soften the bitterness. 'I don't think we should go on drinking, do you? I'll put the kettle on.'

While she was busy in the kitchen, he combed his hair, straightened his tie, looked around for something to do, something to postpone the moment when he would have to think. He noticed a couple of paintings stacked against the wall – presumably another of Paul's 'instalments'. Kneeling down, he turned the nearer painting round to face him.

Paul. A full-length nude study; shocking, as nude portraits tend to be. How very much too thin he was, that was Neville's first reaction. The elongated arms and legs hardly seemed to belong with the slightly rounded, middle-aged belly and the scrotum's sweaty sag. Kit's gaze roamed all over the body before settling on the face, the eyes. He forgot, sometimes, how good Elinor was, but he was reminded of it now. Paul was here in the room. And had been all along, staring out of the canvas while they thrashed and heaved on the bed. Nonsense, of course. Absolute nonsense, of course he hadn't. But the sense of Paul's presence in the room with them remained. He couldn't talk himself out of it and it disturbed him so deeply and at so many different levels that in the end he just wanted to get away and be alone.

The door opened as he was turning the painting round to face the wall. Elinor came into the room. 'Here you are.' She handed him a cup. 'Shall we sit through there?'

'Actually, I think I'd better be going.'

'Are you all right?'

'Yes, I'm fine, I just think I . . .'

He didn't know what he just thought, but he and Elinor were of one mind. They both wanted him to leave. And when, a scant five minutes later, he did, the memory he carried with him down the stairs and out on to the street was not Elinor's naked body on the bed, but Paul's painted eyes staring out of a canvas. That, and the sense of him standing, silent, on the other side of the bedroom door.

Thirty-one

He'd have known the sound of Neville's breathing anywhere, even on the other side of a bedroom door: that unmistakable rasp. No, it couldn't have been anybody else.

But it seemed so improbable. He knew of course that they'd been great friends in their student days – perhaps even a bit more than that – but Neville's behaviour after Toby's death had caused an inevitable breach. Never absolute – they'd met from time to time, but it had always been slightly awkward. In fact sometimes it was a struggle to get Elinor to be polite to him.

No, it made no sense. And yet there it was: the breathing. And he knew he hadn't imagined it.

That night, on duty, he walked up and down Gower Street as often as he could, always stopping to look at Elinor's windows. He knew she wouldn't be there – nobody with any sense stayed on the top floor of a house during a raid – but still he looked. He knew it wasn't his business. His own actions had made it not his business. But images of Elinor and Neville naked in a bed drifted about in front of him constantly, like floaters in his eye, distracting him from the outside world. And his imagination busied itself supplying the details . . . Creased and rumpled sheets, pillows tossed aside, clothes scattered over the floor . . . He kept reminding himself he had no right to be angry, but all the time his skin felt tighter. And tighter. Like a membrane stretched over a swelling boil.

When, late the following day, he encountered Neville again, it was at the National Gallery, at an exhibition of war artists' work. Paul hadn't wanted to go, but really he had no choice. Two of his recent paintings – the 'vapid' ones, as Neville would undoubtedly have said – were on display. But he left it as late as he could to set off and arrived to find the gallery already crowded. Any event offering free drinks and nibbles attracted a crowd these days, though to be fair many of these people were hungry for culture as well. The gallery's paintings had been removed to safety and you were aware, somehow, of the blank walls and echoing emptiness all around. This one brightly lit room, lined with paintings and drawings, seemed to be floating like a bubble on a dark tide.

He got himself a glass of wine from a trestle table near the door and looked around. Clark's extravagantly domed forehead he recognized at once, and Henry Moore's stocky, no-nonsense, I-come-from-Yorkshire build and demeanour. Piper was here, and Featherstone, and – Oh my God, everybody. One quick circuit, he promised himself, a chat with Clark to make sure his presence had been noted, and then he would leave.

Laura Knight appeared in front of him. Good grief, what *was* she wearing? He liked Laura, he enjoyed her scurrilous views on agents and galleries and advisory committees – she had something of Neville's bite, but without his venom – so he stayed and talked to her, before moving on to Clark, who was so distracted by the pretty blonde topping up their glasses that he replied to Paul's remarks almost at random before setting off in blatant pursuit. It was all very much as usual.

He was just beginning to think he'd done enough and could go, when he saw Neville. He was on the other side of the room, standing well back from a painting – not, thank God, one of Paul's – and almost imperceptibly shaking his head. After a few minutes, he moved on. Paul retreated to a corner and watched his progress round the room, noticing how he created a ring of silence around him wherever he went. People were afraid of Neville. Everybody cringed before that vitriolic pen, though they all repeated – sometimes with glee – his contemptuous dismissals of other artists. They all took a vicarious pleasure in the pain inflicted, never quite knowing whether to hope that they themselves would be pilloried or ignored. Neville's reviews were long, prominent and *read*. So although pilloried was bad, arguably being ignored was worse.

Neville moved from painting to painting, pausing now and then to jot down notes or peer short-sightedly at some detail of a composition. He wasn't short-sighted: the whole thing was a performance. Now and then, somebody would come up to him, generally the artist whose work he was currently scrutinizing, but they invariably retreated after a few minutes' exposure to that basilisk stare. Oh, he was powerful, all right. Only Paul, who knew him better, probably, than anybody else in the room, understood that what would matter to Neville, at this moment, more than anything else, was that he hadn't a single painting on these walls.

Watching him, Paul felt something akin to hate: an intimate hatred, as physical as desire. Neville was at the other end of the gallery, much too far away for Paul to see the smear of shaving soap in the crease of his left ear, but see it he did. And he could smell him too: soap, shaving cream, cologne, whisky, tobacco; and under it all, the musky odour of his body.

Paul knew he was overreacting, *wildly* overreacting, but he couldn't seem to stop himself. Gradually, he began to work his way towards Neville, but he was always edging away, confirming what Paul had already begun to suspect: that Neville had seen him and was actively avoiding him. People were still arriving. It was becoming difficult to move around, let alone see the paintings, unless of course you were Neville and your reputation created its own space. As gently as possible, Paul threaded his way between the groups. He needed to confront Neville, to see his eyes as they came face to face, but then, just when he was almost within reach, a whole crowd of newcomers obscured his view, and, when he could see clearly again, Neville was gone.

Craning his neck, Paul checked to see if Neville was anywhere in the room, then caught sight of him standing in the hall. He was being detained, obviously against his will, by an angular young man, Clive Somebody-or-other, with a thrusting jaw and a reputation to make, not battle-scarred yet, not yet understanding what reason he had to be afraid. *Keep him talking*, Paul pleaded silently, pushing his way to the door, but by the time he'd got there Neville had disappeared.

He went outside and looked around. People were coming up the steps towards him and there was a queue of taxis at the kerb. No

Neville, though. But it was raining, and Paul couldn't remember if Neville had been wearing a coat, so he went inside to check the cloakroom. Not there either, but suddenly he saw him, saw somebody, a bulky figure slipping through the doors on the far side of the hall into the darkness of an empty gallery.

Paul followed him. No lights: probably the bulbs had been removed. No paintings either. They'd been shared out to stately homes across the country or, some people said, stored at the bottom of mine shafts in Wales. He stood just inside the door, listening, and thought he caught the sound of footsteps in the next gallery, but the absence of paintings changed the acoustics and it was hard to locate the sound.

He began to walk across the unlit gallery, directing the thin beam of his blackout torch at the walls where dust squares and rectangles delineated the shapes of vanished masterpieces. He felt the absence of the paintings as a positive force. A strange sensation – he couldn't put his finger on it. His footsteps echoed round the hall, but the echo was weirdly mismatched so that when he stopped – as he did frequently, to listen – there was always another step. Always one more step than there should have been, so he no longer knew whether he was pursuing or being pursued. The sound of his breathing slithered all over the gallery, little worms of sound chasing each other round the walls. And, abruptly, it was back: the vertigo that had plagued him, on and off, for most of the year. The darkness spun. He groped his way to the nearest wall and let himself slide down it.

At least, now, sitting with his back to the wall, he felt safe from falling. He directed his torch at a particular point on the floor and tried to focus on that, but the beam quivered with the beating of his heart. He trained the light on to his left hand, where there was a minute scar, a half-moon of whiter flesh, on the ball of his thumb, the memento of some childish scrape. He stared unblinkingly at it, and gradually the spinning stopped. After a while, he was able to stand and retrace his steps, the pencil beam wavering over the floor ahead of him.

He should have left it there, but he couldn't. He hadn't gone to the gallery searching for Neville, but the pursuit, once started, acquired a momentum of its own, beyond reason. He had no idea what he would say, or do, when they met, but he knew the meeting had to happen. It was – an odd word came to mind – 'obligatory'. The meeting had become obligatory.

Leaving the gallery, he took a taxi straight to Neville's house. The sirens sounded just as he was walking up the path, but he had no inclination to seek shelter. The bell clanged loud and deep, but brought no sound of footsteps coming to the door. He banged with his clenched fists, put his ear to the letter box and listened, but he had no sense of Neville, or anyone else, hearing the ringing or knocking and deciding not to answer. No, wherever Neville was, he hadn't come home. On duty? Well, yes, it was possible. In which case he'd be out all night. But he could be anywhere. He could be with Elinor now. In her flat.

That sent all the floaters into a manic dance: dented pillows, stained sheets, Neville's arse bobbing up and down between Elinor's spread thighs . . . For a moment, he thought he'd have to go there, but he managed to talk himself out of it. He'd no real reason to suppose Neville was there. Whereas, sooner or later, he would have to come home.

And so he settled down to wait. Total darkness, no moon, no stars, just searchlights on the heath and the roar of ack-ack guns. Perhaps it was a long time he waited, perhaps short, he had no sense of time passing. He might even have dropped off to sleep. Like everybody else, he was permanently exhausted; he could sleep anywhere. He probably had dropped off because he didn't hear the taxi draw up, or Neville's voice as he paid the driver; he didn't hear his footsteps coming up the drive, or his key turning in the lock. He heard his breathing, though.

Paul made no sound, didn't move or speak, but somehow Neville became aware of his presence.

'Tarrant?' Peering into the shadows. 'What are you doing here?' He sounded nervous, even alarmed, but he disguised it well. 'Come in.'

Paul followed him inside. Neville slammed the door shut and then, for a moment, they simply stood together, in the darkness of the hall, Paul listening to Neville's laboured breaths. Then Neville switched the light on. Chairs, table, hatstand, door, walls bristled into life.

'Come through.'

Very much the jolly, welcoming host. Once in the drawing room, he took off his coat and threw it over the back of a chair. Underneath, he was wearing a dinner jacket.

'Good night?' Paul asked.

'Not bad. Well, you know, the Savoy . . .' Vaguely, he looked around. 'Would you like a drink?'

'Whisky, if you've got it.'

If he'd got it. Like asking Dracula if he had blood. Paul unbuttoned his coat and sat down, still feeling slightly dazed with sleep.

Neville had obviously been drinking, but he handed Paul a generous glass before pouring at least the equivalent for himself. 'I must say, I can't stand the Savoy. All that standing on the balcony, watching the raids. It's ghoulish.'

He was attempting to treat Paul's arrival on his doorstep as a normal social call, though it was past midnight and they'd never been in the habit of dropping in on each other unannounced. And yet it seemed, for a time, that the pretence would be maintained. Neither of them could think of anything else to do. So they talked about the Savoy. Paul was thinking how typical of Neville to say he hated the place, while spending, Paul suspected, quite a lot of time there. He'd had exactly the same love–hate relationship with the Café Royal in the last war.

At last the conversation dribbled into silence. Neville said: 'Is anything the matter?'

'You tell me.'

The clock ticked. Neville cleared his throat.

'Do you know,' Paul said. 'Just now, in the garden, I couldn't see a thing, but I knew it was you. Because I heard you breathing. You see, Neville, I'd know your breathing anywhere.'

'Well, yes, I –'

'Even through a bedroom door.'

'Ah.'

Paul asked, on a note of dispassionate curiosity, as if he were only moderately interested in the answer: 'What the hell do you think you're doing? Fucking my wife?'

'Well. Just that, I suppose.'

If he'd been anywhere near Neville at that moment he'd have hit him, but Neville had retreated to the far side of the fireplace. And even in his present state of mind Paul thought he might have found it difficult to punch Neville in the face. Kicking him in the balls might feel good though.

'You don't deny it?'

'No, of course I don't, why should I? Aren't you forgetting something? *Sandra?*'

'Oh, don't worry, I know I've lost the high ground a bit.'

'Totally, I'd say. You dump Elinor in the country – No-o, *listen*. You could perfectly well have found a flat and gone on living together – you *chose* not to.'

'I wanted her to be safe.'

'You wanted her out of the way.'

'That's not quite true.'

'Oh, of course it is. And why? So you could make a complete bloody fool of yourself sniffing round a girl young enough to be your daughter. Do you really think everybody isn't sniggering about it? Because let's face it you weren't particularly discreet, were you? Elinor's friends all knew before she did. The people she works with. How do you think that made her feel?'

'Oh, and you rushed round to console her? How very kind.'

'I did, actually. Though not about you.'

'How many times?'

'Do you know, I might be wrong – but I really don't think that's any of your business.'

They stared at each other. There'd been several times already when Paul had felt like hitting Neville, but he hadn't done it. And now, somehow, they'd got past it. Though not into safer territory. It came to him that he had no idea at all how the night would end.

He said, sounding to his own ears rather pathetic, 'I thought we were friends.'

'Did you?'

None of this was true. So far neither of them had said a single true word. Somehow, he had to find the anger again, because at least that wasn't false. It was there, he could feel it, hear it almost, a drone at the back of his head. It was only when he saw Neville glance at the ceiling that he realized the droning was a real sound in the real world.

'They don't usually fly this low,' Neville said. 'The guns on the heath force them up.'

This one was very low indeed. There was that awful drone, as intolerable as the sound of a dentist's drill, in the end so insistent he and Neville simply sat and listened. After a while, it seemed to go further away, and they relaxed.

Neville looked at his empty glass. 'Is she all right?'

'You mean you don't know?'

'I haven't seen her. She's at the cottage, I think. I thought you might have gone down there.'

'No.'

'So, anyway, Sandra's a thing of the past, is she?'

'Joined the Wrens.'

'You ditched her.'

'I didn't, actually, it was never meant to be permanent. She was engaged – sort of.'

'Fair enough; you were married – sort of.'

'You can talk.'

'I'm divorced.'

'So what do you think's going to happen now?'

'I don't know. I can tell you one thing though: if you force Elinor to choose between us, she'll choose herself.'

'Well, obviously, it's her choice.'

'No, I mean she'll choose her *self*. Don't you see?' Out of nowhere, an immense burst of anger: 'IT'S WHAT SHE DOES!'

From somewhere uncomfortably close came the sound of a long, shrieking descent and the chandelier above their heads rocked and jangled.

'I see you still haven't got that bl-oo-dy th-in—'

The words elongated and vanished into air as the walls buckled and rushed towards them. Then, nothing.

Somewhere nearby, a tap was dripping. He could feel random drops plopping on to his face and trickling down his neck. Something had fallen across his legs. He tried to bring his arms up to push whatever it was away, but they seemed to be trapped too. After a while, by arching his back and heaving himself off the floor, he managed to shift the weight a little. Another nightmare; he was fed up with them. The ones where you knew you were asleep, you knew you were dreaming, and you still couldn't wake up were the worst of the lot. This one was particularly vivid. He seemed to be in a kitchen. There were fragments of blue-and-white pottery scattered over the floor. He couldn't see much because his head was pinned down; he could only look sideways. *Dunstanburgh Castle at Sunset* was propped against a chair. Turner. Seeing it like that, it was very obviously a Turner. Why would anybody want to hang a Turner in a kitchen? The *steam* . . .

He couldn't make out where the light was coming from. Twisting his neck a painful inch to the right, he saw trees and branches wave. If he could only get out there . . . He tried wriggling his fingers, then his toes, and found he could move both. The pain, the pressure, was mainly in his chest. Something he couldn't even see was pinning him down. Flares blossomed and trembled. He was lying out in No Man's Land, waiting for the flares to die so he could scramble back into the lines. It made sense, more sense than lying squashed like a cockroach on the floor of a basement kitchen.

He heard a movement. Somebody knelt beside him, cutting off the draught of cool air.

'Are you all right?'

He forced himself to find words. 'Yes, I think so.'

With the sound of his own voice came a clearer sense of his situation. Not a nightmare, not No Man's Land, a real place, *now*. He was in Neville's house. They'd been talking, shouting, Neville had shouted something, but he couldn't remember what it was – or why they were in the kitchen.

'Can you move your feet?'

He tried again. 'Yes.'

'Well, that's a relief. I think there's a spade in the garden shed. We're going to have to dig you out. I could go and get it, I suppose.'

'Wouldn't it be quicker to go for help?'

'Oh. No rush.'

No rush?

And suddenly he was afraid. As if sensing his fear the voice went on: 'Do you know, I could kill you now? Nobody would be any the wiser. I could pick up this brick – and why not? It's a perfectly good brick – and bash your head in.'

He couldn't breathe. 'Why would you want to do that?'

'Why not?'

'There's got to be a reason.'

'No-o, don't think so. *Because I can*. How could anybody prove it hadn't just landed on your head? Of course I'd have to do it in one blow. Can't have the same brick landing twice.' He giggled.

More than the words, the giggle terrified Paul, because it was not a sound Neville could ever possibly make. Arching his back, he tried again to lift whatever was pinning him down. Neville made no move to help, but neither did he leave – he seemed to be indifferent to his own safety. And there was real danger – the building could come down on top of them at any minute.

The words 'I could kill you now' hung over them.

'Well, your decision,' Paul said. 'I suppose.'

Paul closed his eyes and lay still. There was nothing he could do – and anything he said, anything at all, would feed Neville's rage just as everything fed the London fires. So he gazed sidelong across the floor at the scattered fragments of blue-and-white pottery, wondering where the real cockroaches were and thinking they'd probably survive. It wasn't looking too good for him.

Not that it mattered. And yet the need to understand remained. 'Is this so you can have Elinor?'

Neville had switched his torch on and the beam was shining on the brick in his right hand. Paul tried again to heave the weight off his chest, but pain forced him to stop. Another bomb exploded, not nearby, at the end of the next street, perhaps, but still close enough to shift the balance in the rubble hanging over them. A hissing had started, water spraying from a burst pipe – or gas. 'Whole bloody thing's coming down,' Neville said, but dispassionately.

Paul tried to say something in reply, but his mouth was full of dust and, anyway, what was there to say? He closed his eyes and listened to Neville's laboured breath.

A minute later, he became aware of a light moving across his face. Neville, shining the torch into his eyes, wanting him to respond, to plead. But when Paul opened his eyes the beam was moving haphazardly across the room, fluttering moth-like over collapsed walls and broken furniture. Footsteps clambering over bricks and rubble, and a voice: 'Anybody in there?'

The neighbourhood warden, his face a pale blur behind the torch. A long, still moment. Then Neville stood up. 'Yes, there's somebody trapped, but I don't think you'll need a rescue squad. I think we can get him out between us.'

He sounded brisk, ordinary. The torch shone full in Paul's face again, and he closed his eyes, but not before he'd seen Neville glance down at the brick in his hand, as if surprised to find it there, and toss it casually away.

Thirty-two

1 November 1940

A plane crashed here last week, on a hill about two miles outside the village. It's still there, the wreckage, they haven't started clearing it away. The fuselage is mottled black and grey like one of those city moths, and there's ribbon tape all round it. Children wait till dark then slip under the tape, scavenge whatever they can find to take into school and show around the playground. Mrs Murchison, whom I met this morning in the post office – I think she's quite lonely now with Rachel and the family away; she must be lonely if she stops and speaks to me – says one of the little horrors turned up at school with the pilot's thumb in his gym bag. 'That's lads for you!' And then suddenly we were thinking of Kenny, and a silence fell.

A lowering sky today, scrawls of black cloud, wind rattling dry leaves around. I worked all morning and well into the afternoon. In London, the afternoons are always a dead time, but not here. Here – apart from walks and pauses to chop up vegetables for yet another nourishing stew – I work all day. Around about six, my eyes start burning with tiredness, and then it's blackout time, nothing to do but light the fire and settle down with a book, only I can't concentrate, I'm listening all the time for the nightly drone, for the window frames to start bumping, knowing all the time that any one of those bumps could be the end of somebody I love. I mean Paul, of course. Always Paul.

So why? That's the question I keep tiptoeing round. Because he betrayed me. And it was a betrayal. That girl, so young, so unmarked by life. Oh, and the one before too, the art student. People told me about her, and I'd feel my mouth twist into a little, wry, sophisticated smile – a sort of oh-well-you-know smile – which seemed to get stuck on my face for hours, getting heavier all the time until my cheeks sagged. That's why my periods went haywire. It was nothing to do with 'the tears of a disappointed womb' – it was the strain of pretending, even to myself, that I didn't mind. When, in reality, I minded so much I wanted to scream.

So, yes, that's why.

Though it still leaves another question: why Kit? Why him, of all people? Because he's the person who'd hurt Paul most? But that only makes sense if I tell Paul. Because Kit loved me when I was young and I want those years back? Sweep two world wars away? Oh, yes, why not? Easy: just jump into bed with your childhood sweetheart. We-ell, not childhood exactly, though we were very young. And not sweethearts either, not really, though he certainly wanted us to be. His head lying in my lap on that country lane all those years ago. The weight of it, the warmth. The way when he tried to get up he deliberately brushed the back of his head against my breasts and I wanted to laugh. I still do. Smile, anyway.

When he looks at me, Kit sees me. Or he sees that girl – and perhaps that's the same thing, or I want it to be. Paul doesn't. I don't think Paul's seen me for years.

2 November 1940

Today I walked miles along the river bank. The painting, the one of the little girl on the pavement, is finished. At least, I think it's finished. I need to get right away, then go back and look at it with fresh eyes.

A blustery day, sunny spells, but mixed in with frequent heavy showers, one or two real downpours. Rooks whirling about above the bare elms like the scraps of burnt paper that drift down from London's incinerated offices.

I was trudging along, looking at my feet, thinking about the painting, my fingers still feeling the imprint of the brush, smelling of paint, probably daubed with it as well, but it hardly matters;

I meet nobody on these walks. And then I glanced up and noticed a curious seething movement in the grass on the other side of a long field. I couldn't make out what it was: some reflection of the clouds, I thought at first, but then I realized the river was coming to meet me. It had burst its banks and flooded the low ground. I don't know what I felt – a kind of exhilaration, I suppose. It was so beautiful: fractured reflections of clouds dissolving and re-forming as the water advanced. And all at once a great spray-burst of seagulls wheeling about and settling on the water.

Now it's evening – every joint aches – but the painting is finished. And it's good – I'm almost sure it's good. Kenneth Clark's probably going to hate it. Bad for morale. Though, actually, if one of his aims is to persuade people to send their children to safety – or leave them there – you could hardly imagine a painting better calculated to get the message across. No message, though. I don't do messages. Anyway, it's done – and I'm not going to spend the rest of the evening double-guessing what Clark might say.

It's blowing a gale outside. The windows thump and for once it's not a raid; the glass streams. I'm going to make carrot soup and light a fire.

3 November 1940

As I expected, I'm paying for that walk. I sat on the side of the bed this morning feeling like an old woman, bracing myself for the trip across the landing to the bathroom. I'm so stiff I can hardly move. Actually, though, it's quite a relief to have physical pain to contend with. Takes your mind off the other sort.

Because last night, too tired to read, I got Paul's envelopes out, intending to spend a pleasant, nostalgic hour sorting through old photographs. I thought I'd buy an album and stick them in. Oh, quite a cosy little evening I had planned! What I didn't know was that the envelopes contain letters as well as snaps. And the first letter to fall out was the one Toby wrote to me a day or two before he was killed.

It was a shock, seeing that familiar handwriting again after so many years. Neat, regular, forward slanting . . . You looked at Toby's handwriting and your first thought was: how easy it would be to read. Only when you looked more closely did you realize it was virtually indecipherable. A bit like Toby himself.

I started reading automatically, before I had time to prepare myself. And there he was, instantly, his voice, as clear and strong as if he'd been standing beside me in the room.

Elinor – I've had two goes at this already, so this is it, has to be, because we're moving forward soon and there'll be no time for writing after that. There's no way of saying this without sounding melodramatic, and I really don't think I am. In fact, I feel rather down-to-earth and matter-of-fact about it all. I don't think I would even mind very much, except I know it's going to be a shock to you – and I can't think of any way of softening the blow.

I won't be coming back this time. This isn't a premonition or anything like that. I can't even explain why. I used to think officers' letters weren't censored, but they are sometimes, not by the people here, but back at base. They do random checks or something, and I can't afford to risk that. I hate not being able to tell you. If you ever want to know more, I suggest you ask your friend Kit Neville – assuming he survives, and I'm sure he will. ~~He's been no friend to me.~~ I know you'll take care of Mother as best you can. Father'll be all right, I think – he's got his work. And Rachel's got Tim and the boys. I don't know what to say to you. Remember

How easy it is to feel superior to the dead: we know so much more than they did. I didn't look after Mother. Father wasn't all right – he died of a heart attack in the back of a taxi on his way to work less than two years after Toby's death. He never even looked like 'getting over it' – whatever that means.

Toby's last letter. Unfinished, not signed. Never sent. It survived only by accident because there was a hole in his tunic pocket and it had slipped through into the lining. And the sentence about Kit had been crossed out. As Paul said at the time: a crossed-out sentence in a letter never finished, never signed, never sent. What possible significance can you attach to that? But I did attach significance to it. And I was right.

But there's no point going over all that now. Now, the only word that matters is: 'Remember'.

But I didn't remember. If I'd remembered, I could never have gone to bed with Kit. I talk about Paul betraying me and use it to justify a far worse betrayal. Because it wasn't Paul I betrayed – I don't owe Paul any more loyalty than he's shown me, and God knows, that's been little enough – no, it was Toby I betrayed.

I look at his photograph, the one of him in uniform when he first joined up. It's the one Featherstone used to do that awful portrait. He's young, so much younger than I am now, but it's not an unformed face, not by any means. There's great strength there, great determination, but no trust. I don't think I've ever seen a more guarded expression. I miss him.

Kit. I can't say, as Paul said about that girl – Sandra, whatever her name was – that it wasn't important. That it didn't matter. It was important. It does matter. But it can't go on. And I've no idea what I'm going to say to him. I do know one thing: I don't want to rake over the past, or try to explain why it's impossible. We'd only start arguing about things that can't be helped.

No. I think by far the easiest thing – well, easiest for me, and I hope for him – is just to let it slide. Not get in touch and – Well, I'd like to say: not see him again; but of course there's no hope of that. There'll be times when we're working the same shift, however hard I try to avoid it. I'll just have to be – cool, I suppose. And after all I might be imagining a problem where there isn't one. I mean, for all I know, he's regretting it every bit as much as me.

London again, tomorrow. So I suppose I'll soon know.

Thirty-three

This was supposed to be a job interview, but it didn't feel like one. Half an hour into the meeting, wreaths of cigarette smoke hung stagnant on the air, swirling a little when a secretary came in with tea and biscuits, before settling into new patterns, rather like the marbled endpapers of books. A lot of people had been 'interviewed for jobs' here: Neville could smell them. Essence of anxiety lingered on the air.

The questions focused mainly on his knowledge of German. The time he'd spent in Germany between the wars. His German wife. All the way back to his father's allegedly pro-Boer sympathies in the Boer War.

'He wasn't pro-Boer,' Neville said. 'He was anti-concentration camp, which at the time *we* were running. I think you can safely assume his sympathies with Hitler would have been zero.'

His answers became increasingly acerbic as the questioning went on, though they produced no response beyond a brisk nod and occasionally a smile. And then the next question. 'Why do you speak German so fluently?'

He'd have liked to say: *Because of the brilliant foreign-language teaching at Charterhouse*, but decided not to. 'I had a German nursemaid when I was a child.'

'Really?'

'Yes, really.'

'Why?'

'How should I know? My mother didn't consult me about the domestic arrangements.'

'So you were fluent before you met your wife?'

God, this was exasperating. 'Look, I can translate German, I can do everything I'm required to do here. And yes, I can hold a conversation fairly easily. Parachute me into Berlin? No, I wouldn't last five minutes. But that isn't what this is about, is it?'

Dodsworth was tapping the papers in front of him into a neat pile. He looked up. 'Nobody's accusing you of anything.'

But Neville *felt* accused. On the way back to his office, he became increasingly angry. What right did Dodsworth, who'd been too young for the last war and seemed to be driving a desk in this one, have to question his loyalty? *Nobody's accusing you of anything*. Bollocks. It was an investigation, couldn't be anything else, and he found it insulting. He'd returned to England voluntarily and he'd volunteered to work in the fucking, bloody ministry. He wasn't one of the people who queued up for jobs here to get out of joining the army. No, he'd been entirely motivated by . . . Insanity. Only insanity could account for somebody volunteering to work here.

But then, look at it from Dodsworth's point of view. If Neville was a German spy, what would he do? Get back to England as fast as possible and use his knowledge of German to secure a job at the Ministry of Information, where he'd have constant access to classified files. Perhaps he should just clear out. Go and live at the back of beyond somewhere and paint pretty little pictures of lakes and things. Get Dodsworth off his back, if nothing else.

He was passing Kenneth Clark's office. Never an easy moment. Still no letter, no invitation to tea and biscuits in the great man's office, though God knows that bloody little exhibition of his could have done with an infusion of talent. He'd almost made it to the other side of the landing when the door opened and Clark came out, accompanied by – oh my God – Nigel Featherstone. Now that really was scraping the barrel. Featherstone's 'paintings' – and that was stretching the term till it sagged like a whore's knicker elastic – hung in every major public building in the country. You noticed them, if you noticed them at all, only to remark on how completely they blended into their surroundings – like frightfully well-chosen sofa cushions. Neville turned to face the wall, giving them plenty of time to get past because this was more than a brisk handshake and nice-to-see-you. As they walked towards the lift, Clark's hand rested momentarily between Featherstone's shoulder blades.

Neville found himself looking at Ullswater again. Was it one of Tarrant's? It had to be by somebody distinguished because it was positioned directly opposite Clark's door, though, looking at it again, Neville was inclined to acquit Tarrant. It pained him to admit it, but Tarrant was better than this. At the moment, any thought of Tarrant was painful. He was out of hospital – five or six cracked ribs, but apparently there's not a lot you can do about them, other than bind up the chest and wait for them to heal. Neville hadn't been to see him in hospital. It would have been awkward. His memories of that night were chaotic, but he remembered enough to know his behaviour had been a bit odd. But of course he'd been in shock, and people in shock do and say the most extraordinary things.

Behind his back, he heard Clark and Featherstone laughing, then the lift doors rattled open. They exchanged a few more words – he was too far away to hear – and then, thank God, they were gone. He was free to move again.

Hilde looked up as he came into the room. Bertram's empty desk had been pushed against the wall, so they had slightly more space to move around. Bertram hadn't appeared for three weeks now. Was that significant? Probably not. Suddenly, he thought: *Perhaps there's an oubliette in the basement?* Somewhere they put people whom they want to forget? Perhaps Bertram and all kinds of other people were down there, still vainly protesting their innocence, as their long, white beards grew and grew until they reached the floor . . .

'I'm glad you find it amusing,' Hilde said.

Oh God, he was supposed to be editing her draft translation of *Women under the Nazis*, the latest pamphlet in the series they were working on together.

'Bowling along,' he said, having not taken in a word. All those women under the Nazis. What a waste. Why couldn't at least one of them be under him? He glanced at the clock: *Oh God, another two hours of this. I'm going to leave*, he thought. *I really am going to leave*.

He was tempted to begin clearing his desk there and then. Well, why not? What was stopping him? He lifted his briefcase on to the desk and began filling it with odds and ends. There wasn't much: he hadn't been here long enough to accumulate a load of stuff. Hilde watched him without comment for a time, then, seeing him trying to stick some papers into a file that was slightly too small, came across and held it open for him. Then she cleared her throat in that way she had. 'Have they asked you to leave?'

'Sacked me, you mean? No, quite the opposite, in fact. They've offered me a job.' *Lies, all lies*.

'Here?'

'No, somewhere near Oxford.'

'Will you take it?'

He paused in the act of taking his hat from the peg. 'Do you know, I have absolutely no idea.'

They shook hands. For some reason she blushed and on impulse he leaned forward and kissed her thin cheek.

Then he was off, down the corridor, past the Gents – no, on second thoughts, into the Gents. He splashed his face and hands – that hour in Dodsworth's room had made him feel dirty – then he glanced over his shoulder to check the cubicles were empty, twined his fingers round one of the chains that fastened the plastic nailbrushes to the wall, and pulled. He'd always loathed them. Tightening his grip, he pulled again and this time succeeded in wrenching it off the wall. It hurt like hell; the chain had actually left a weal on the side of his hand. But it was worth it. Then, raising his eyes, he confronted the stranger in the glass.

Would he have done it? The nailbrush rested in the palm of his hand, rough against the skin, rectangular, brick-shaped. Would he have killed Tarrant if that air-raid warden hadn't showed up and started flashing his torch? Ninety-nine per cent of the time, his answer to this question was a resounding no, of course not, never in a million years. But, at other times, when he was fully absorbed in something that needed concentration, not thinking about Tarrant at all, he was aware of a belief taking shape in the shadows of his mind, not that he might have done it, *but that he had done it*. In dreams he relived those moments after the bomb fell, and woke knowing, not with satisfaction but with almost unbearable sorrow, that Tarrant was dead.

He looked down at the brush. A very nice little souvenir, he thought. He'd put it on the mantelpiece, he decided, and then remembered that he didn't have a mantelpiece. The house was boarded up; he was living at his club. A stultifyingly boring place, he was buggered if he was going back there, not until he'd anaesthetized himself in the nearest bar.

Though, walking away from the building – for the last time, *the last time* – he thought he wouldn't go to the pub after all, he'd go to see Elinor, at least see if she was in. She was back in London – he knew that from Dana, who'd had lunch with her – but she hadn't been in touch. He sensed, ringing the bell, and ringing it again, that she was there, but not answering the door. It was starting to look as if their time together, which had meant so much to him, had meant little, or nothing, to her.

Drink. He walked away down the street and knew that he was being watched, that she was at the window behind him. Though he reminded himself sharply that he couldn't know; perhaps he was just being paranoid. God knows, there was enough paranoia about. He turned into the nearest pub; he thought he'd once had a drink with Tarrant in there, but couldn't be sure. There was nobody he knew at the bar. Almost, he missed his evenings with the terrapin, which was now, presumably, dead. Another link with the past broken. But then he wondered: how long did terrapins live? Perhaps his parents, for some extraordinary reason, had kept replacing the terrapin and not told him.

He knocked back the first whisky so fast his eyes watered – and that was saying a lot. Then he ordered the second straight away and sat morosely in a corner. Everything seemed to be conspiring against him. Dodsworth – that was unaccountable. Tarrant's success, his own . . . Well, 'neglect' was hardly the right word, more like a bloody conspiracy. No wonder he couldn't paint. Everybody needs a context, an echo coming back to them – and he didn't have that. He seemed to be living in a vacuum, a glass tank that cut him off from the outside world. There was only Anne, really, to attach him to life. He lived and breathed in the memory of her. The way, when she was a tiny child, just a toddler, she used to come into his bed in the mornings, bouncing up and down, waving her favourite toy, a blue rabbit: *I love Babbit! I love*

Babbit! It had been a small grief for him when, finally, she'd learned to say 'rabbit'.

Lost in his memories, he resurfaced to hear the sirens wailing. Several people immediately left, though he thought the pub had been emptying for the past hour. How many drinks had he had? There seemed to be an impressive array of glasses in front of him, unless of course he was seeing double. He got to his feet easily enough, but found it unexpectedly difficult to weave his way between the tables to the bar.

'Shame again.'

Was that a fractional hesitation? He met the barman's eye.

'Right you are, sir.'

By the time he left, he was . . . Numb. Absolutely clear mentally, though: he did honestly believe there was such a thing as drinking yourself sober. The anger was still there, bubbling away under the surface, but he felt agreeably numbed as he stood swaying on the pavement, buffeted by waves of noise. He might have one last go at seeing Elinor. She wouldn't be in, of course. She'd have taken refuge in one of the shelters, but it was at least worth a try.

Several fires were blazing, the worst of them out of control. Black water lay around in puddles; he sloshed through them, finding it quite difficult to keep a straight line. A fireman was standing in the road holding on to a hose, his eyes glazed with the tedium of what he was doing. By far the worst job, the fire service: equal parts boredom and terror.

Elinor's house was completely blacked out, of course: no way of telling whether she was in or not, but he rang the doorbell anyway. Rather to his surprise it was answered immediately by a young woman wearing a nurse's cap and cape. She was going on duty and had come to the door almost by accident, but that didn't matter – he was in. He thought he might as well go up and see if Elinor was in. If not, fair enough, he'd just go back home, a friendly tap on the terrapin's tank and straight upstairs to bed. Only then he remembered that he couldn't do that. No terrapin, no tank, no home.

He knocked. No answer, as he'd expected, but then he heard a movement inside the room. 'Elinor?'

A second later, the door opened. She was pulling her silk wrap together over her nightdress.

'You should be in a shelter,' he said, accusingly.

'It's late, Kit. What do you want?'

'Just to talk. Please?'

'All right, but not long.' She stepped back. 'Have you been drinking?'

He slumped on to the sofa. "Course I've been bloody drinking, I've had that little pipsqueak Dodsworth on to me again.' He couldn't remember whether he'd told her about Dodsworth – absolutely no idea. Told her again anyway. He was about to explain about Clark and Featherstone and Tarrant's – *possibly* Tarrant's – bloody boring landscape on the wall, and how utterly ludicrous it was that talentless Tarrant and fucking useless Featherstone should have been commissioned as war artists while he, Kit Neville, had been passed over – but he managed to stop himself in time. He was drunk, but not quite as drunk as that.

'I'm sorry about Dodsworth,' she said. 'It is awful.'

He jabbed his index fingers at his face. 'What right does he have to question my loyalty?'

She said, carefully, 'Are you sure you're getting it right? You're sure it's *not* an interview?'

'I don't see how it can be, he keeps going over and over the same ground, doubling back, asking the same questions . . . No, it's got to be an interrogation – can't be anything else.'

She had come across and sat on the sofa, but at the other end. Three feet of dark blue velvet lay between them. No Man's Land. Well, it had taken four fucking years to get across that, and he didn't have that kind of time.

'Elinor, can I stay the night?'

Deep breath. 'No, Kit.'

'Please?'

The sound of his own voice, pleading, released his anger. 'Do you know, I haven't had a squeak out of you for . . . Oh, I don't know. Since you left, anyway.'

'I've been thinking.'

'Huh. Not your strong suit.'

'*What?*' When he didn't reply, she said, 'Kit, it's late and I'm tired.'

'So that's it, then?'

'You know, that day, when it happened, we were neither of us in a particularly good state. I'm not blaming you, I'm not blaming anybody – I'm just saying I'm not *ready*. I think I need to be on my own for a while.'

He didn't believe a word of this. In fact, he felt quite insulted; she was just spouting a load of *Ladies' Home Journal* tripe instead of coming right out and saying what she really felt. At the back of his mind was the fear that she found him as repulsive as he sometimes feared he was.

She wanted him to go – that, at least, was obvious – but he couldn't accept it. People had been saying no to him all his life, taking things away: his marriage, his daughter, his reputation, his house, his FACE, for Christ's sake! Well, no more. As she stood up, he lunged sideways, caught her round the wrist and pulled her down on top of him. She fell across his face. It was easy, so easy, to push the wrap aside, pull her nightdress off her shoulders; he was full of the scent of her, her voice in his ears sounding very far away on the other side of a red mist that rose and covered everything. They were on the floor, he didn't know how they'd got there, but his right knee was between her legs, didn't matter now what she did with her hands, she could flail away with her arms as much as she liked, once he'd got her legs apart his weight did the rest.

After a time, a long time it seemed, but it might have been only minutes, she rolled from under him. Ripped nightdress. White face. Scrabbling to get her wrap closed, she crawled on to the sofa. He should go, go now, before she started screaming. But she didn't seem to think screaming was the appropriate response. She was rocking herself backwards and forwards, but otherwise seemed remarkably composed.

He got up, turned away, fumbled with buttons, retreated to a chair where he sat looking down at his hands. How big they were. 'I seem to have become . . .' He was articulating the words very carefully. 'A bit of a monster.'

'Oh, Kit. You always were.'

The clock on the mantelpiece ticked.

'I should go.'

A brief, hard laugh, indicating, he supposed, agreement. She stood up and let him out.

On the landing, he stopped and looked back at her slim shape silhouetted against the light from the room behind her, then turned and went on, feeling his way down the dark staircase and out into the night.

Thirty-four

Afterwards, it was the horses she remembered, galloping towards them out of the orange-streaked darkness, their manes and tails on fire. One huge black shire horse with frantically rolling eyes came straight at them. Elinor wrenched the steering wheel violently to the left and, a few yards further on, pulled into the kerb. In the rear-view mirror, she saw the horses galloping away, their great, bright, battering hooves striking sparks from the road. She remembered a thud against the side of the ambulance and thought she might have caught one a glancing blow on the shoulder as it careered past.

She sat, breathing heavily, looking at her orange hands on the wheel. Even her skin didn't look like skin.

Beside her, in the co-driver's seat, Neville cleared his throat. 'Would you like me to take over for a bit?'

'No, thank you,' she said, with another glance in the rear-view mirror, preparing to move off. She might have taken that from Dana or Violet, but certainly not from him. 'Actually, Kit, if you want to know what it feels like to have your testicles skewered and roasted over a slow fire *while you watch*, you could try saying that again.'

'Fair enough.'

She risked a sideways glance. His face in the light of the fires was an expressionless mask. Beaten bronze.

For so long she'd contrived to avoid working with Kit. But then, over the Christmas and New Year period, single people like Elinor – and, of course, Kit – had signed up for extra duties so that married people and parents could spend time with their families. Christmas Eve, Christmas Day, Boxing Day had all been quiet – she'd never played so many games of cards in her life – but the unofficial cease-fire was now unmistakably over. Hundreds, if not thousands, of incendiaries must have fallen that night and they were still clattering down. Yes, she'd had a moment of dismay when she'd looked at the duty roster and seen her name and Kit's bracketed together, but she could hardly protest.

As she turned into Gunpowder Court, incendiaries clattered on to the ambulance roof like giant hailstones, and when she looked out of the side window she saw dozens more fizzing and popping all along the pavement. A squad of heavy rescue workers were shouting and jostling each other, like footballers fighting for possession of the ball, as they competed to stamp them out. As she watched, the man nearest to her dived and put his helmet over one of the skittering devices. 'Gotcha, y' little sod!'

Further along the court, two fire engines were parked, taking up almost all the space. Half a dozen hoses snaked across the road, some grey and flaccid, but others very much alive – and she daren't risk driving over those because, for the fireman at the branch, that interruption in the water supply could be dangerous, and the sudden return of water pressure almost equally so. She'd seen firemen injured by a branch writhing and spinning out of control. So: the way ahead was blocked.

She looked at Kit. 'You could try Wine Office Court,' he said. 'Try to get at it from the other side.'

'Is there a way through?'

He shrugged. 'They all lead into one another.'

That was the trouble. They'd both have claimed to know London well, but neither of them was familiar with this particular area: the network of narrow alleys and courts off Fleet Street. Where was Derek when you needed him? Or any one of the other taxi drivers? Still, she wasn't going to give up. They couldn't. They'd been sent to a direct hit on a nurses' hostel and that meant, potentially, dozens of casualties. Unless, of course, they'd all been on duty, or in a shelter as they bloody well ought to have been, but you couldn't rely on that. Increasingly, exhausted people risked everything for the comfort and (spurious) safety of their own beds.

'All right, let's give it a go.'

She reversed fifty yards or so, then pulled over near the entrance to Wine Office Court and stopped again.

They climbed stiffly down from the cab and walked across the narrow road. Elinor felt suddenly sick with tiredness, and cold; she was shivering inside her thick coat. Even the adrenalin rush of fear would have been welcome now, but she felt no fear; she felt nothing. Nothing, after the horses.

Just inside the entrance to the court was a fireman tending a pump, which roared and shook and pulsed grey water down its grey sides, deepening the pool of black water at his feet. He looked glazed, cold, wet, exhausted, bored, but he managed a wave. Kit tried to ask whether there was a way through, but he couldn't make himself heard. They were communicating with the huge pantomimic gestures of people guiding aeroplanes into their hangars. Turning to Elinor, Kit pointed to himself and then along the court, signing that he was going to see if he could find a way through. Elinor shook her head, and made a sharp, dismissive gesture with her hands indicating the court was too narrow. She meant for the ambulance.

Kit mouthed: *Stretcher*. She nodded: *Yes, that might be possible*; then pointed to her chest, meaning: *I'm coming too*. He shook his head, but she ignored him. They began walking along the court, keeping up a brisk pace because speed seemed to offer safety: a moving target, you felt, must be harder to hit. The road was black and gleaming wet, flooded for a stretch where a drain had been blocked by a great wad of charred and sodden newspaper. At first, the roar of the pump was enough to blot out all other noises, but then gradually, as they splashed through the black water, it started to fade, to be replaced by the crackle of burning brick and timber from the building straight ahead. Probably, the blazing building was a printing works or a newspaper office. Scraps of burnt paper whirled down from the glassless windows above their heads. Elinor could see flames and shadows leaping across the inside walls, making it look, unnervingly, as if there were people trapped inside. The two firemen looked dazed with boredom. They'd have been there hours, hands gripping ice-cold metal, doused from head to foot in ice-cold water. One man's lips were moving; she thought he might be trying to say something, but then realized he was singing.

The other man nodded, saw she was a woman, and grinned. 'All right, love?'

She smiled, raising her hand, as she and Kit started to edge along the wall behind them. She felt heat from the blaze scorch her face and neck, though she was still shivering. The branch seemed to be producing a fine, cold spray that blew back into the firemen's faces and soaked everything. She was wet herself now, icy trickles running down under the collar of her coat. Normally, you wouldn't be allowed to get as close to a fire as this. All the other emergency services were supposed to hold back until the fire service declared an area safe, but there could be no question of declaring anywhere safe tonight. She'd just seen the pillars inside St Bride's Church burning like torches. The whole City was on fire.

They walked as fast as they could away from the burning building, their shadows fleeing across the ground ahead of them. She felt like a mouse creeping along the floor of a great canyon, dwarfed by the four- or five-storey buildings on either side. At the end of the court, they turned and looked back. The scene was fitfully lit by the flames leaping from the windows of the burning building, and it was unchanged. That solid-looking pole of white water the firemen were directing at the blaze seemed to be making no difference at all.

She looked at Kit.

'You could get a stretcher past.' His voice was hoarse with shouting. 'That's if we can get to the hostel.'

To their right was another court which seemed at first to be empty, but then they saw two figures walking towards them: an elderly woman, in a pink candlewick dressing gown, and another, much younger, woman who was hobbling along, grimacing with pain at every step. Elinor shone her torch. 'Oh my God, Kit, look.' The girl's feet were burned black. How on earth had she managed to walk this far?

'I'll take her,' Kit said.

No point arguing: it was obvious the girl had to be carried and only Kit could do that. But Elinor was determined to go on and look for more survivors. If these two had got through, there were likely to be others. 'You go with him too,' Elinor said to the older woman.

'Oh, I don't think so, dear.' A reedy, but authoritative, Edinburgh accent. 'I'll be much more use back there.'

Kit had lifted the girl and was looking at Elinor, obviously expecting her to follow, but she shook her head. He nodded, or she thought he did – the shadows leaping and flickering all around him made it difficult to be sure. But he turned, and his bulky, burdened shape disappeared rapidly into the murk.

The girl was mercifully light; just as well too, because he was finding it difficult to keep his footing. Even in the few minutes since he'd last walked along here, the pool of black water around the blocked drain had deepened, and he was splodging through it. He hated leaving Elinor, but this girl was suffering from shock. The burns looked pretty bad; she needed to be in hospital as soon as possible. Which meant he'd have to drive her straight there, then come back for Elinor. He didn't like the idea. They should've stayed together, but Elinor was never going to come trotting meekly along behind him. He was level with the firemen now, and they shuffled forwards a few paces to give him room.

The upper storeys were still blazing, the flames inside leaping and dancing as tauntingly as ever, though the white pole of water was now being directed at another window. And there was a kind of clicking noise. He couldn't think at first where it was coming from, then realized it was the building. It was very like the sound a car makes on a hot day when you've just switched off the engine: the tick of cooling metal. But nothing round here was cooling. He wondered if the firemen had heard it – they must've done, but they were looking at each other and laughing, so evidently it was nothing to worry about. All the same, he tried to walk faster and was glad when the shaking and rattling of the pump drowned out the roar of the flames behind him.

As he emerged from the court, he saw another ambulance had drawn up at the kerb. Bill Morris and Ian Jenkins came towards him.

'Would you mind taking her?' he asked. 'She needs a doctor but I don't want to go and leave Elinor stranded.'

He carried the girl the few yards to their ambulance, and saw her safely stowed inside, wrapped in a blanket, with Ian by her side. Bill said he'd try Bart's first. Apparently, they were still taking people in, though there was some talk of an evacuation. My God, it must be bad.

Neville watched the ambulance bump slowly away towards Fleet Street, then he went back and looked along Wine Office Court. The scene hadn't changed at all; the two firemen might have been carved in bronze. What to do? His first impulse was to follow Elinor, but then suppose she came back by another route and found him gone? If she could get through at all that was quite likely. He lit a cigarette. That was one good thing about tonight: there'd be no officious little pipsqueak of an air-raid warden shouting, 'Put that bloody fag out!' Any leaking gas mains round here had long since exploded. He dragged deeply on the cigarette and then, rather belatedly, offered the packet to the fireman at the pump, who just shook his head and pointed to the cascading water. Poor bugger was drenched. And now, to make things worse, there seemed to be a wind getting up. He could feel it blowing along the court towards him, hot as a dog's breath on his face. At first, he was puzzled because there'd been no wind, no wind all day, and then the truth hit him: he was witnessing the birth of a firestorm.

That wind would carry sparks from building to building faster than a man could run. He was suddenly terribly afraid, and not ashamed of it either. A man who tells you he's not afraid of fire is either a fool or a liar. He lit another cigarette from the stub of the first. There was a strange smell, very sweet. He couldn't think what it was. If he'd had to guess, he'd have said: incense. It didn't smell like war. He thought it might be wood, centuries old, seasoned wood from burning churches. He thought he'd caught a whiff of it just now as they were driving past St Bride's. He tried again to peer into the flame-lit darkness of the court. *Where was she?* The conviction that something terrible had happened to her was growing on him by the minute. He shouldn't have let her set off like that, with only the old woman as a guide, but then what else could he have done? Who'd ever made Elinor do anything she didn't want to do? And then the memory of that evening resurfaced, bobbed up like a turd in a sewer. He had – he'd made her do something she hadn't wanted to do. Oh, given enough time he knew he'd remember the events of that evening differently, smooth over the raw edges, but at the moment he couldn't bear it. At least, it goaded him into action. He'd leave the ambulance, he decided. Go and look for her.

He tried to speak to the fireman by the pump, so he'd be able to tell Elinor what had happened if she returned by another route, but he was signalling to the two men holding the branch. They'd backed away from the wall and seemed to be arguing about what to do. And then, with a great rush of relief, Neville saw her, standing at the other end of the court, waving to him. He started towards her. As the roar of the pump faded, he became aware of yet another sound coming from the burning building. Almost a groan. It sounded so human he thought somebody must be trapped. Was that what the firemen were arguing about? Trying to decide if it was safe to go in? But then he saw them look at each other, laughing, so he knew it was all right, and Elinor was still waving. Jumping up and down now, shouting, but he couldn't hear anything above the roar of flames. She'd been joined by a young man in army uniform, who looked vaguely familiar, but couldn't be, of course; it was just somebody Elinor had roped in to help carry the stretchers. Well, *good girl*. The more young, male muscle there was around, the better.

Whoever it was, he was waving too, or beckoning: *Come on, come on. Hey*, he wanted to say, *I'm coming as fast as I can*, but then, just as he drew level with the firemen, he heard the most stupendous crack, and the whole wall of the building bulged and loomed over him, hung motionless, and then, slowly it seemed, began to fall. He saw everything, in detail, without fear or emotion: the dark mass above him cutting slices out of the sky until only a sliver remained. He couldn't move; he couldn't speak. He heard silence, but then the roar came crashing back and red-hot bricks fell on his face and neck and dashed him to the ground. A cry struggled to his lips, but it was already too late – his mouth was full of dust. He thought: *I won't get to Elinor*. And then he forgot Elinor. What finally crushed his heart, as the avalanche of bricks and mortar engulfed him, was the knowledge that he would never see Anne again, he would never again see his daughter, in this world or any other.

Thirty-five

In Bloomsbury, Paul was having a quiet night. He'd played a game of darts, flipped through yesterday's newspapers and then set out on patrol with Charlie. At the corner of Guilford Street, Charlie stopped to light a cigarette. Shaking the match, he gazed open-mouthed in the direction of the City. Billowing clouds of black smoke, showers of sparks whirled upwards, a broken skyline of buildings stark against furnace red. 'By heck, they aren't half copping it.'

Paul felt the first premonitory tweak of fear. Elinor could be in that. Would be, if she was on duty. Charlie threw away the match and they walked on, their footsteps echoing in the eerie silence. No guns now, no drone of bombers. The All Clear had sounded an hour ago, unusually early. 'Don't worry,' Brian had said. 'They'll be back.'

But they hadn't been. Not yet. And all the time, over the City, that extravagant, melodramatic, stage-sunset grew and spread, and, with it, Paul's fear.

Their patrol over, they decided to get a cup of tea and a pasty from the van in Malet Street. God only knew what was in the pasties – no substance previously known to mankind – but at least they were warm. Paul and Charlie joined the back of the queue, stamping their feet and blowing on their fingers in a vain attempt to keep warm. Three or four places ahead of them, a woman was talking about an ambulance driver who'd been injured. 'Weren't there two of them?' another woman asked. And then a third voice: 'Are you sure they were just injured? I heard they were dead.'

Elbowing people aside, Paul seized her arm. 'Who?' He was shaking her. '*Who?*'

She stared at him, her mouth a scarlet gash in the drained pallor of her face. He tried to calm down. 'It's just, my wife's an ambulance driver.' For some reason the word 'wife' stuck in his throat; it sounded like the sort of thing somebody else would say, and that strangeness, the sudden unfamiliarity of the word, ratcheted up his fear.

'They didn't say. Just two ambulance drivers had been injured, one of them a woman, that's all I heard.'

She was lying – he'd just heard her say they were dead. Of course, it might be another woman – Dana or Violet – but somehow, from the very first moment, he knew it was Elinor.

Tearing himself out of Charlie's restraining grip, he ran all the way to the depot in Tottenham Court Road and down two flights of stairs to the basement, which was deserted, except for three telephonists who fell silent as he entered. They looked nervously at each other. A middle-aged woman, who seemed to be the supervisor, came out of the office and stood in front of them. If he had any doubt, that dispelled it. He'd become somebody to be frightened of, as the bereaved always are.

'We can't be certain, we really don't know who it is.'

He could tell from the way her gaze slithered down his face that she did. 'Where?'

'Wine Office Court, but it's no use going there,' she called after him. 'They'll have taken them to Bart's.'

She followed him into the corridor, shouting something about an ambulance in the yard, so he veered abruptly to the left, burst through the swing doors into the parking area at the back. Sure enough, there was an ambulance about to leave. He ran along beside it, banging with his clenched fist on the door. The vehicle slowed and an elderly man with pouches under his eyes peered down at him.

'Can you give me a lift? My wife works here. Elinor? They've taken her to Bart's.'

To his own ears, he was gobbling, gabbling, not making any sense at all, but the man nodded. 'Oh, yes, I know Elinor. Hop in.' As Paul settled into the co-driver's seat, the man added, 'I'm off to Bart's anyway. They're evacuating. We've all got to go.'

The journey was a blur. Paul leaned forward, willing the driver to go faster, as they bumped slowly along, occasionally swerving to avoid craters in the road. With every mile, after the first, the orange glare grew until the sky was every bit as bright as noon. Everywhere, fires were raging, many of them out of control. Paul couldn't take it in, street after street burning. Only the details registered. Once, he looked down and saw a pigeon flapping about in the gutter with its wings on fire.

A hundred yards from the hospital entrance, the driver slowed to a crawl. Ambulances were queuing bumper to bumper all along the road. At first, Paul thought they might be delivering casualties, but then he saw that most of them were empty. They were here to evacuate the hospital. He reached for the door handle.

'Hang on,' the driver said. 'I'll try and get you a bit closer . . .'

'No, it's OK, I'll be all right.' Paul jumped into the road and raised his hand. 'Thanks, mate.'

As he started running along the line of ambulances, the wind caught him, flattening his trousers against his legs. Looking down the hill, he saw a wall of fire advancing on the hospital – he couldn't understand why it hadn't been evacuated already. The hot wind was snatching up bits of flaming debris and hurling them from one building to the next. At any moment, you felt, the hospital would be engulfed. Elinor. He had to find her and get her out, take her miles and miles away from here.

Inside the entrance, he stared wildly around him, until a passing nurse pointed towards the stairs. No lifts: the doors were all half open, frozen at the point the electricity had failed. He ran upstairs. No lights on the stairs, no lights in the corridor either, except for a couple of smoking oil lamps that signally failed to penetrate the gloom. He groped his way along, a hand on the wall. Nobody seemed to be trying to bring patients down, so evidently the evacuation hadn't started yet.

Bursting through swing doors on to a ward, he was dazzled by the sudden blaze of light. Emergency generator? His brain had time to form the thought, before he realized the truth. The staff had simply thrown open the blinds to let in the light of the blazing City. Doctors, nurses, even surgeons were working in the glare of the firestorm that was roaring up the hill towards them.

Paul ran from bed to bed, thinking: *No, this is wrong, it's all wrong, she can't be here*. These patients had all been admitted, and he knew there wouldn't have been time for that, but he couldn't get anybody to answer his questions, they were all so busy, so *intent*, but then at last he stopped a porter who told him, 'You want to be downstairs, mate. Casualty's in the basement.'

So he skidded down two flights of stairs, along another corridor, and burst into a huge room, lit by dozens of oil lamps whose coils of brown smoke hung heavy on the air. Doors opened off to the left into smaller rooms; he could see beds, wheelchairs, tables, chairs, and torches held in gloved hands casting circles of light on to other gloved hands that were stitching wounds or applying dressings to burns.

Along one side of the main room, the injured were queuing for attention: white-faced, babbling, mute, shaking uncontrollably. The more seriously injured lay on trolleys in a corridor further along, many still and silent, a few writhing with the pain of burns. One – an elderly woman with wispy grey hair and an open mouth – unmistakably dead.

He saw a warden he knew slightly near the back of the queue and asked him if he'd seen Elinor, but the man was too dazed to answer. Paul abandoned him, and began walking up the line, scanning every face, but there was no Elinor – and nobody else he knew to ask. At the head of the queue, he saw there was another smaller room: rows of benches crowded with people. He started walking along the rows, looking at face after face, panicked that when he saw her – *if* he saw her – he wouldn't recognize her. He kept seeing the old woman on the trolley: the open mouth, the staring eyes. Part of him was convinced the corpse was Elinor. It had been nothing like her, and yet he had to stop himself running back to make sure.

Still another room opened off this one. Here, three rows of benches faced a blank wall; people sat staring vacantly into space, waiting for somebody to come and claim them. He heard his voice calling 'Elinor?' over and over again. Perhaps there was an echo, because the walls seemed to bounce the name back at him: *Elinor, Elinor*.

And then he saw her, sitting at the end of a bench, looking straight ahead. 'Elinor?' She seemed to have trouble focusing on him. 'It's me. Paul.' He knelt down and reached for her hands, but she pulled them back. 'Are you all right?'

The question seemed to plop into a deep well. She glanced from side to side and moistened her lips. 'They say I can go.'

Her face was grey; she had the hunched shoulders and anxious expression of smoke inhalation. She wasn't fit to be turned out. He looked round, angrily, but so many of the injuries he saw were worse than hers. And of course with an evacuation imminent they'd be clearing out anybody who could walk. 'Come on,' he said. 'Let's get you home.'

'Where's Kit?'

'Were you working with him?'

She nodded.

'He's fine. Queuing up outside, I think.'

He was thinking he might beg a lift from the ambulance driver who'd brought him here, if he could find him, but in the event he didn't need to. A crowd of frustrated ambulance drivers had gathered outside the hospital entrance, and among them were Dana and Derek, who detached themselves from the group and came towards him. 'Is she all right?' Dana asked.

'She's alive.'

Until he heard himself say the word, he hadn't known it was true, and immediately he was flooded with relief, but he still had to get her home.

'Don't worry,' Dana said. 'We'll take you. If we can get out, that is.'

Paul helped Elinor into the back of the ambulance, then turned to look at Dana, who was waiting to close the door. He mouthed: *Neville?* Dana shrugged, but Derek, who was standing a few feet behind her, shook his head.

It took a great deal of reversing, and not a little shouting, before they were able to get out of the queue. Paul tried to persuade Elinor to lie on the bunk, but she said she couldn't lie flat and so they sat, side by side, jolting and swaying as Dana swerved to avoid obstacles in the road. Lights flashed in the small windows and, once, there was a great clattering on the roof as more incendiaries fell – or perhaps it was just shrapnel from the ack-ack guns that seemed to have started up again, though Paul couldn't remember hearing the sirens.

Nearer home, the orange glow in the windows faded to black, and he was glad of it. Not long after, the jolting and bumping stopped. Footsteps sounded along the side of the ambulance, then Dana opened the door and pulled down the steps. Paul helped Elinor down on to the black, glistening pavement. She looked around her, then up to the windows of her flat. Dana kissed her goodbye, Derek slapped Paul on the shoulder, and then the two of them set off to rejoin the queue outside Bart's. Paul watched the red tail light diminishing into the dark, and the street seemed suddenly very quiet. The guns seemed to have stopped again, so probably it had been a false alarm.

Elinor was still looking up at the windows of her flat. There must have been times in the last few hours when she'd thought she wouldn't see it again. Her hands were so cut and bruised he had to fish the keys out of her pockets while she stood holding her arms away from her body, as helpless as a small child.

He thought she might find the stairs difficult and got behind her to push, but she snapped: 'It's my *hands*, Paul. Not my *feet*.' A brief glimpse of the old Elinor that came as an enormous relief.

Once inside the flat he settled her on to the sofa, then went into the kitchen and filled the kettle for tea. He kept glancing through the open door. She was sitting hunched forward, though more upright perhaps than she had been in the hospital. Her hands were held straight out in front of her. When the kettle boiled, he added a generous dollop of brandy to the tea, and carried the mug through to her.

As she drank, he looked at her more closely. She had several cuts to her forehead, though none very deep. Her hands were worse than her face. He fetched a pillow and blankets from the bed, thinking, as he pulled the counterpane back, that he caught a whiff of Neville, but he couldn't be sure and anyway it hardly mattered now. She snuggled into the blanket, but still wouldn't lie down. She was sitting right on the edge of the sofa, trying now and then to flex her spine, but still with her shoulders rounded.

He kept assessing her, noticing symptoms in a completely detached way. At the same time, he was terrified of losing her, though he knew it wasn't a rational fear. Most of this was shock. At times her eyes went completely blank. Somewhere in the depths of his mind, a thought was forming: that this helplessness of hers might be his opportunity. She needed him now; she'd have to take him back. Only then he looked up and caught her watching him. *Not so fast.* So she came and went: one moment, totally alert; the next, blank and limp.

'What happened?' he asked during one of her more alert spells. He knew she'd have to get it into words, probably tell the story over and over again, until its sting was drawn, but all he got back was a shrug. Too soon. So they sat in silence by the bluish light of the little popping gas fire until he thought he saw her eyelids start to droop. Then, just as she seemed about to drop off, she started awake again. 'There were horses,' she said. 'Galloping towards us. Their manes were on fire.'

Dray horses, they'd be. Probably shire horses, and they were huge. A brewery stables must have caught fire.

For a long time, it seemed that was all she was going to say. He warmed up a tin of soup, but she didn't drink much of it. Her breathing seemed to be getting easier, though, and her colour was definitely better. It might even be possible to get her to bed.

'I kept waving at him: *Go back, go back.*' She pushed her hands repeatedly against the air, and the movement brought on a fit of coughing. When it was over, she went on: 'I could see the firemen were pulling out, but he didn't seem to understand, he just kept coming, and then the wall came down and all I could see was smoke and . . .'

Silence, for a time. Did she know? Feeling his way forward, he asked: 'Did you see him again?'

She shook her head. Then, obviously afraid of the answer, she asked, 'Did Derek say anything?'

'No.'

'I hope he's all right.'

Injecting scorn into his voice, he said: "'Course he's all right! You know Neville – he'll outlive God.'

She seemed willing to accept that, for the time being at least. He took the bowl and spoon from her. 'You know, I think you'd be better off in bed.'

'Yes, I think I would.'

Leaning on his arm, she hobbled into the bedroom and sat on the side of the bed, while he knelt to take off her boots. She was shivering again, with shock or cold, so he got her under the blankets as fast as he could. It took several arrangements of all four pillows to get her comfortably propped up. 'I'll be next door if you need anything.' He hesitated. 'You will call me, won't you . . .?'

She nodded, without opening her eyes.

He went back into the living room, rolled up his overcoat to use as a pillow and stretched out on the sofa. It was too short for him, and lumpy besides – he doubted if he'd get much sleep. He closed his eyes, and saw shire horses galloping towards him with their manes on fire, as if the impossible had happened and the membrane dividing his brain from hers had become permeable. What lovers are supposed to want – except they weren't lovers any more.

Perhaps he'd nodded off, because it seemed only a second later that he felt a jogging at his elbow, and opened his eyes to find her bending over him.

'Oh for God's sake, Paul, you can't possibly sleep like that. Come on, get into bed . . . We are *married*, after all.'

That '*married*' was pure, unadulterated acid. Nevertheless, he got up and followed her.

Lying beside her on the bed he thought perhaps she'd drifted off to sleep, but then she said, 'I keep seeing him walk towards me, you know that walk he has – and then that awful sound. It was like the building was screaming.' She turned her head and looked at him. '*Why* didn't he go back?'

A long silence. He thought, hoped, she'd finished. So they lay, side by side, not speaking, not even looking at each other, while the long hours of darkness passed. He remembered the old couple on the bed, lying there as if they were stretched out on a tomb, with the silence spreading out around, while outside the fires raged and the bombs fell. How he'd pulled back the counterpane and found them holding hands. Elinor's breathing was quieter now. Something of the tension had gone from her shoulders and neck. He closed his eyes and tried to relax. Perhaps he slept. Finally, towards dawn, he became aware that he was awake, and so was she. 'I've been thinking,' he said. 'I might get a little dog.'

'*What?*'

'Just a thought.'

He got out of bed and pulled the blackout curtains back. Sparrows were chirruping and fluttering in the gutters, there were footsteps and voices in the street below, a hum of traffic. Glancing back at the bed, he saw that Elinor was lying with one arm across her face. He waited a moment, hoping she'd take it away and look at him, but she didn't. Then he pushed the windows open, as wide as they would go, letting in the clear, cold air of a new day.

Thirty-six

Ever since the raids ended, she'd been recording the progress of the ruins. If she'd ever thought about ruins at all, before the destruction of her house, she'd have said they were static, unchanging, or if they did change, it would be the work of centuries, decades at least, of wind and rain and scouring ice. But these ruins changed week by week, even day by day. And so, every morning, she set out to draw them; she scribbled notes as well in the margins of the drawings, diary entries, or sometimes just lists, mainly lists of the flowers and plants she found growing in the gardens of wrecked houses, but also, increasingly, out of the walls of the derelict buildings themselves. There seemed to be no crack so narrow, no fissure so apparently barren, it couldn't support the life of some weed or other. She even, as the days lengthened, became attached to particular plants: a clump of bright red flowers growing out of a sagging gutter, too high up to be identified, but bobbing about on the slight breeze, like the flowers in a mad woman's hat. And then, a few doors down – although now there were no doors – a great pool of forget-me-nots caught in the hollow of a wall. *Remember*

These ruins were all close to home; gaps in terraces she'd known intimately as a student, walking every day to and from the Slade. There were far more impressive ruins surrounding St Paul's, most of those created in a single night: the night Kit Neville died. Her grief for Kit was unexpectedly sharp and deep, and she wasn't ready to revisit the courts and alleys they'd walked down together on the night he died.

In good weather, she stayed out all day, filling one sketchbook after another, though she had no idea where this project might be leading, if indeed it was leading anywhere. It was some time now since she'd done a big painting. There'd been the dead child on the pavement, and another ambitious project after that: children

257

queuing outside Warren Street Underground Station to claim their family's place on the platforms. Clark hadn't liked either. 'It's not the quality of the work, it's . . .' And his voice had trailed away into silence.

Every afternoon, around about five o'clock, she packed up and went home, sometimes stopping at one of the barrows at the corner of Store Street to buy vegetables for dinner. There wasn't much choice, but the cauliflowers and carrots were usually all right. And the apples, though wizened and rather small, hardly bigger than crab apples, were good enough for apple pie. Tonight, she was cooking for two, which these days was quite a pleasant experience. Paul was coming to supper. They saw each other regularly, met for drinks or tea and buns, even went on outings to Kew Gardens or Richmond Park, often accompanied by that wretched little dog he'd bought, a brown-and-white Jack Russell terrier, rather unimaginatively called Jack – not even Russell, which might have been marginally better. She knew Paul would have liked more than occasional outings with her. He'd more than once hinted they should start thinking about living together again, but she'd grown to value her independence. Living alone is a skill, and she seemed to have reacquired it. She actually enjoyed having nobody but herself to consult. And yes, of course there were times when loneliness crept up and bit her on the backside, but she had plenty of teeth – and she was learning to bite back.

The barrow boys – always 'boys' though some of them were old men – were mainly market gardeners from Kent. She'd got to know a few of them, though these, today, were new. Two men, one elderly, the other middle-aged – their profiles so similar they could only be father and son – and a ginger-haired boy, white-faced and gangly, with surprisingly big, raw hands. She watched him weighing potatoes, dropping one very small one into the pan to make up the weight. Then he poured them into a paper bag, twisting it briskly to produce two nice, neat ears, and handed it across to the customer. As he did so, he half turned towards her, and she saw that it was Kenny.

It couldn't be.

But it was.

At last it was her turn to be served. She asked for a cabbage and a pound of apples. 'Oh, and carrots,' she said, all the time staring at him, thinking: *No*. He'd grown, my God, he'd grown, and the shape of his face had changed, but he was at the age when boys do change – sometimes almost beyond recognition. He hadn't noticed her yet. He was so busy scooping and weighing and pouring into bags and then giving the bags that final, expert twist. You could see the pride he took in his own skills. There he was: doing a proper job, earning money. In his own estimation, at least: a man among men.

When she came to pay, he looked her in the face for the first time, and suddenly blushed, shedding, in the process, several months of growth.

'Hello, Kenny.'

What to say next? *We thought you were dead?* Well, why not – it was true. Glancing over his shoulder – evidently chatting to the customers was not encouraged – he said, 'Me mam couldn't stick it in there, she couldn't breathe, she got herself into a right old panic, we had to come out . . .'

She whispered, 'Do you know how many people died?'

'Yes, I heard.'

'So what did you do?'

'Walked all the way to me nanna's in Bermondsey. Then she got bombed and we got on the back of a lorry and went to Kent.' He kept looking over his shoulder. 'And I got this job.'

'You're busy.' She handed the money over. 'I'm glad you're all right.'

'Glad' wasn't the word. She could have burst out singing.

At the corner, she stopped and looked back, watching him move on to the next customer, and the next. Then, smiling, she turned into Gower Street and began walking home, burdened by drawing pads and pencil cases and shopping bags, but still quickening her pace until she was almost running. She couldn't wait to get home and tell Paul.

Noonday completes the trilogy of novels by Pat Barker begun with *Life Class* and continued with *Toby's Room*, both available from Penguin Books.

PAT BARKER

LIFE CLASS TRILOGY

Triumphant, shattering, inspiring' *The Times*

A dazzlingly ambitious trilogy about a group of young people living through the chaos of the First and Second World War. Man Booker Prize laureate Pat Barker traces the subtle and lingering legacies of war in the lives of a generation.

Life Class

In spring 1914, Paul Tarrant is taking life-drawing class at the Slade and worrying about his career as an artist. By autumn, war has broken out and Paul enlists in the Belgian Red Cross just as he and fellow student Elinor Brooke admit their feelings for one another. Pat Barker crafts an uncompromising and intimate portrait of a generation broken and transformed by the Great War.

Toby's Room

When her brother Toby is reported 'Missing Believed Killed', unanswered questions cast a lengthening shadow over Elinor Brooke's world: how exactly did Toby die – and why? Elinor is determined to uncover the truth; only then can she finally close the door to Toby's room. Moving from the Slade to Queen Mary's Hospital, this is a dark, compelling examination of human desire, wartime horror and the power of friendship.

Noonday

It is 1940: ex-Slade contemporaries Paul Tarrant, Elinor Brooke and Kit Neville are middle-aged, and another war has begun. As bombs fall on the haunted streets of London one more and old temptations and obsessions return, all of them are forced to make choices about what they really want.

PAT BARKER

LIFE CLASS

Spring, 1914. The students at the Slade School of Art gather in Henry Tonks's studio for his life-drawing class. But for Paul Tarrant the class is troubling, underscoring his own uncertainty about making a mark on the world. When war breaks out and the army won't take Paul, he enlists in the Belgian Red Cross just as he and fellow student Elinor Brooke admit their feelings for one another. Amidst the devastation in Ypres, Paul comes to see the world anew – but have his experiences changed him completely?

'Triumphant, shattering, inspiring' *The Times*

'Barker writes as brilliantly as ever . . . with great tenderness and insight she conveys a wartime world turned upside down' *Independent on Sunday*

'Vigorous, masterly, gripping' Penelope Lively, *Independent*

PAT BARKER

TOBY'S ROOM

Toby has always protected his sister, Elinor, their bond closer than they can acknowledge. Then comes war, and in 1917 on a French battlefield Toby is reported 'Missing, Believed Killed'. Elinor, an artist now involved in helping surgeons reconstruct the faces of injured soldiers, is determined to find out what happened and writes to the horrifically wounded Kit Neville, the last man to see Toby alive. But Neville is in hospital, himself damaged beyond recognition, and he will not talk – until Elinor asks fellow soldier and her former lover Paul Tarrant for help. But are some truths better left concealed ?

'Magnificent; I finished it eagerly, wanting to know what happened next, and as I read, I was enjoying, marvelling and learning' Chimamanda Ngozi Adichie, author of *Half of a Yellow Sun*

'A heart-rending return to the Great War. A superb stylist . . . forensically observant and imaginatively sublime' *Independent*

'The plot unfurls to a devastating conclusion . . . a very fine piece of work' Melvyn Bragg, *New Statesman* Books of the year

PAT BARKER

REGENERATION TRILOGY

'An extraordinary tour de force . . . One of the few real masterpieces of late twentieth-century British fiction' Jonathan Coe

A Booker Prize-winning masterpiece following a group of shell-shocked young poets through the last months of the Great War.

Regeneration

Craiglockhart War Hospital, Scotland, 1917. Army psychiatrist William Rivers is treating shell-shocked soldiers, including poets Siegfried Sassoon, Wilfred Owen and Billy Prior. Rivers' job is to make the men in his charge healthy enough to fight. Yet the closer he gets to mending his patients' minds, the harder becomes every decision to send them back to the horrors of the front.

The Eye in the Door

London, 1918. Billy Prior is working for government intelligence in the war effort. But his private encounters – with pacifists, objectors, homosexuals – conflict with his duties as a soldier, and it is not long before his sense of self begins to break down. Barker paints a heart-rending portrait of the contradictions of war and of those forced to live through it.

The Ghost Road

1918, the closing months of the war. William Rivers is increasingly concerned about the men under in his care – particularly Billy Prior, who is about to return to combat in France with young poet Wilfred Owen. As Rivers tries to make sense of what, if anything, he has done to help these injured men, Prior and Owen await the final battles in a war that has decimated a generation.

GER
?
ELC

BLUEEYEDBOY

BLUEEYEDBOY

Joanne Harris

WINDSOR
PARAGON

First published 2010
by Transworld Publishers
This Large Print edition published 2010
by BBC Audiobooks Ltd
by arrangement with
Transworld Publishers

Hardcover ISBN: 978 1 408 48705 1
Softcover   ISBN: 978 1 408 48706 8

British Library Cataloguing in Publication Data available

Printed and bound in Great Britain by
CPI Antony Rowe, Chippenham and Eastbourne

To Kevin,
who also has blue eyes.

ACKNOWLEDGEMENTS

Some books are easy to write. Some are rather more difficult. And some books are just like Rubik's cubes, with no apparent solution in sight. This particular Rubik's cube would never have been solved without the help of my editor, Marianne Velmans, and my agent, Peter Robinson, who encouraged me to persevere. Thanks, too, to my PA, Anne Riley; to publicist Louise Page-Lund; to Mr Fry for the loan of Patch; to copy-editor Lucy Pinney; to Claire Ward and Jeff Cottenden for the cover art; to Francesca Liversidge; Manpreet Grewal; Sam Copeland; Kate Tolley; Jane Villiers; Michael Carlisle; Mark Richards; Voltaire; Jennifer and Penny Luithlen. Thanks, too, to the unsung heroes: the proofreaders; sales executives; book reps and booksellers who are so often forgotten when it comes to handing out the laurels. Special thanks to my friends in fic and fandom, especially to: gl-12; ashlibrooke; spicedogs; mr_henry_gale; marzella; jade_melody; henry_holland; divka; benobsessed. And, of course, to the man in Apartment 7, whose voice was in my mind from the start.

PART ONE

blue

Once there was a widow with three sons, and their names were Black, Brown and Blue. Black was the eldest, moody and aggressive. Brown was the middle child, timid and dull. But Blue was his mother's favourite. And he was a murderer.

and what i want to know is
how do you like your blueeyed boy
Mister Death
                    e e cummings, 'Buffalo Bill'

You are viewing the webjournal of **blueeyedboy**
posting on:
> badguysrock@webjournal.com

Posted at: *02.56 on Monday, January 28*
Status: *public*
Mood: *nostalgic*
Listening to: *Captain Beefheart:* 'Ice Cream For Crow'

The colour of murder is blue, he thinks. Ice-blue, smokescreen blue, frostbite, post-mortem, body-bag blue. It is also *his* colour in so many ways, running through his circuitry like an electrical charge, screaming blue murder all the way.

Blue colours everything. He sees it, senses it everywhere, from the blue of his computer screen to the blue of the veins on the backs of her hands, raised now and twisted like the tracks of sandworms on Blackpool beach—where they used to go, the four of them, every year on his birthday, and he would have an ice-cream cone, and paddle in the sea, and search out the little scuttling crabs from under the piles of seaweed, and drop them into his bucket to die in the heat of the simmering birthday sun.

Today he is only four years old, and there is a peculiar innocence in the way he carries out these small and guiltless slayings. There is no malice in the act, merely a keen curiosity for the scuttling thing that tries to escape, sidling round and round the base of the blue plastic bucket; then, hours later, giving up the fight, claws splayed, and turning its vivid underbelly upwards in a futile show of surrender, by which time he has long since lost interest and is eating a coffee ice cream (a sophisticated choice for such a little boy, but vanilla has never been his taste), so that when he rediscovers it at the end of the day, when the time comes to empty his bucket and to go home, he is vaguely surprised to find the creature dead, and wonders, indeed, how such a thing could ever have been alive at all.

His mother finds him wide-eyed on the sand, poking the dead thing with a fingertip. Her main concern is not for the fact that her son is a killer, but for the fact that he is suggestible, and that many things upset him in a way that she does not understand.

'Don't play with that,' she tells him. 'It's nasty. Come away from there.'

'Why?' he says.

Good question. The creatures in the bucket have been standing undisturbed all day. He gives it some thought. 'They're dead,' he concludes. 'I collected them all, and now they're dead.'

His mother scoops him into her arms. This is precisely what she dreads. Some kind of outburst: tears, perhaps; something that will make the other mothers look down their noses at her and sneer.

She comforts him. 'It's not your fault. It was just an accident. Not your fault.'

An accident, he thinks to himself. Already, he knows that this is a lie. There was no accident, it *was* his fault, and the fact that his mother denies

4

this confuses him more than her shrill voice and the feverish way she clasps him in her arms, smearing his T-shirt with suntan oil. He pulls away—he hates mess—and she fixes him with a fretful gaze, wondering if he is going to cry.

He wonders whether perhaps he should. Maybe she expects it of him. But he can sense how very anxious she is, how hard she tries to protect him from pain. And the scent of his ma's distress is like the coconut of her suntan oil mixed with the taste of tropical fruit, and suddenly it hits him—*Dead! Dead!*—and he really does begin to cry.

And so she kicks sand over the rest of his catch—a snail, a shrimp, a baby flatfish all landed and gasping, with its little mouth pulled down in a tragic crescent—smiling and singing; *Whoops! All gone!*—trying to make a game of it, holding him tightly as she does, so that no possible taint of guilt may darken the gaze of her blue-eyed boy.

He is so sensitive, she thinks. So startlingly imaginative. His brothers are another race, with their scabbed knees and their uncombed hair and their wrestling matches on the beds. His brothers do not need her protection. They have each other. They have their friends. They like vanilla ice cream, and when they play at cowboys (two fingers cocked to make a gun) they always wear the white hats, and make the bad guys pay.

But he has always been different. Curious. Impressionable. *You think too much*, she tells him sometimes, with the look of a woman too much in love to admit to any real fault in the object of her devotion. He can already see how she worships him, wants to protect him from everything, from every shadow that may pass across the blue skies of

5

his life, from every possible injury, even the ones he inflicts on himself.

For a mother's love is uncritical, selfless and self-sacrificing; a mother's love can forgive anything: tantrums, tears, indifference, ingratitude or cruelty. A mother's love is a black hole that swallows every criticism, absolves all blame, excuses blasphemy, theft and lies, transmuting even the vilest deed into something that is not his fault—

Whoops! All gone!

Even murder.

Post comment:
Captainbunnykiller: *LOL, dude. You rock!*
ClairDeLune: *This is wonderful,* **blueeyedboy**. *I think you ought to write more fully about your relationship with your mother and the way it has affected you. I don't believe that anyone is born bad. We simply make bad choices, that's all. I look forward to reading the next chapter!*
JennyTricks: *(post deleted).*
JennyTricks: *(post deleted).*
JennyTricks: *(post deleted).*
blueeyedboy: *Why, thank you . . .*

> *You are viewing the webjournal of* **blueeyedboy**.
> **Posted at**: *17.39 on Monday, January 28*
> **Status**: *restricted*
> **Mood**: *virtuous*
> **Listening to**: *Dire Straits*: 'Brothers In Arms'

My brother had been dead for less than a minute by the time the news reached my WeJay. That's about how long it takes: six or seven seconds to film the scene on a mobile phone camera; forty-five to upload the footage on to YouTube; ten to Twitter to all your friends—13:06 *OMG! Just saw a terrible car crash*—and after that the caravan of messages to my WebJournal; the texts; the e-mails, the oh-my-Gods.

Well, you can skip the condolences. Nigel and I hated each other from the day we were born, he and I, and nothing he has ever done—including giving up the ghost—has caused any change to my feelings. But he *was* my brother, after all. Give me credit for some delicacy. And Ma must be feeling upset, of course, even though he wasn't her favourite. Once a mother of three, today only one of her children remains. Yours truly, *blueeyedboy*, now so nearly alone in the world—

The police took their time, as usual. Forty minutes, door-to-door. Ma was downstairs, making lunch: lamb chops and mash, with pie for dessert. For months I'd hardly eaten; suddenly now I was ravenous. Perhaps it takes the death of a sibling to really give me an appetite.

From my room, I followed the scene: the police car; the doorbell; the voices; the scream. The sound of something in the hallway recess—the telephone table, at a guess—slamming against the wall as she fell, cradled between two officers, clutching the air with her outstretched hands, and then the smell of burning fat, probably the chops she left under the grill when she went to answer the door—

That was my cue. Time to log off. Time to face the music. I wondered whether I could get away with leaving in one of my iPod plugs. Ma's so used to seeing me wearing them that she might not even have noticed; but the two officers were a different matter, of course, and the last thing I wanted at such a time was for someone to find me insensitive—

'Oh, B.B., the most *terrible* thing—'

My mother's a bit of a drama queen. Contorted face, eyes wide, mouth wider, she looked like a mask of Medusa. Holding out her arms to me as if to pull me under, fingers clawing at my back, wailing into my right ear—defenceless now without my iPod—and shedding tears of blue mascara down the collar of my shirt.

'Ma, please.' I hate mess.

The female officer (there's always one) took over the business of comforting her. Her partner, an older man, looked at me with weary patience, and said:

'Mr Winter, there's been an accident.'

'Nigel?' I said.

'I'm afraid so.'

8

I counted the seconds in my head, whilst mentally replaying Mark Knopfler's guitar intro to 'Brothers In Arms'. I knew I was under scrutiny; I couldn't afford to get this wrong. But music makes things easier, reducing inappropriate emotional responses and allowing me to function, if not entirely normally, then at least as others expect of me.

'I knew it, somehow,' I said at last. 'I had the weirdest feeling.'

He nodded, as if he knew what I meant. Ma continued to rant and rail. *Overdoing it, Ma,* I thought; it wasn't as if they were especially close. Nigel was a ticking bomb; it had to happen sooner or later. And car accidents are so common these days, so tragically unavoidable. A patch of ice, a busy road; almost the perfect crime, you might say, almost above suspicion. I wondered if I ought to cry, but decided to keep it simple. So I sat down—rather shakily—and put my head in my hands. It hurt. I've always been prone to headaches, especially in moments of stress. *Pretend it's just fiction, blueeyedboy. An entry in your WeJay.*

Once more I sought the comfort of my imaginary playlist, where the drums had just come in, ticking gentle counterpoint to a guitar riff that sounds almost lazily effortless. It isn't effortless, of course. Nothing so precise ever is. But Knopfler has curiously spatulate, elongated fingers. Born for the instrument, you might almost say, destined from birth for that fretboard, those strings. If he had been born with different hands, would he have ever picked up a guitar? Or would he have tried it anyway, knowing he'd always be second-rate?

'Was my son alone in the car?'

9

'Ma'am?' said the older officer.

'Wasn't there—a girl—with him?' said Ma, with the special contempt she always reserves for any discussion of Nigel's girl.

The officer shook his head. 'No, ma'am.'

Ma dug her fingers into my arm. 'He never used to be careless,' she said. 'My son was an excellent driver.'

Well, that just shows how little she knows. Nigel brought to his driving the same temperance and subtlety that he did to his relationships. I should know; I still have the marks. But now he's dead, he's a paragon. That hardly seems fair, does it now, after all I've done for her?

'I'll make you a cup of tea, Ma.' Anything to get out of here. I made for the kitchen, only to find the officer obstructing my way.

'I'm afraid we're going to need you to come with us to the station, sir.'

My mouth was suddenly very dry. 'The station?' I said.

'Formalities, sir.'

For a moment I saw myself under arrest, leaving the house in handcuffs. Ma in tears; the neighbours in shock; myself in an orange jumpsuit (really, *not* my colour); locked up in a room without windows. In fic I'd make a run for it: knock out the officer, steal his car and be over the border before the police could circulate my description. In life—

'What kind of formalities?'

'We'll need you to ID the body, sir.'

'Oh. That.'

'I'm sorry, sir.'

Ma made me do it, of course. Waited outside while I put a name to what was left of Nigel. I tried to make it fictional, to see it all as a film set; but even so, I passed out. They took me home in an ambulance. Still, it was worth it. To have him dead; to be free of the bastard for ever—

All this is fic, you understand. I never murdered anyone. I know they tell you to *write what you know*, as if you could ever write what you know, as if *knowing* were the essential thing, when the most essential thing is desire. But wishing that my brother were dead is not the same as committing a crime. It's not my fault if the universe follows my WebJournal. And so life goes on—for most of us— much the same as it ever did, and *blueeyedboy* sleeps the sleep of the just—if not *quite* that of the innocent.

You are viewing the webjournal of **blueeyedboy**.
Posted at: *18.04 on Monday, January 28*
Status: *restricted*
Mood: *blah*
Listening to: *Del Amitri*: 'Nothing Ever
                    Happens'

That was just two days ago. Already we're back to normal, apart from planning the funeral. Back to our comfort rituals, our little everyday routines. With Ma, it's dusting the china dogs. With me, of course, it's the Internet: my WeJay, my playlists, my murders.

Internet. An interesting word. Like something brought up from the deep. A net for something that has been interred, or something as yet to be interred; a holding-place for all the things we'd rather keep secret in our real lives. And yet, we like to watch, don't we? Through a glass, darkly, we watch the world turn: a world peopled with shades and reflections, never more than a mouse-click away. A man kills himself—live, on cam. It's disgusting, but strangely compulsive. We wonder if it was a fake. It could be a fake; anything could. But everything looks so much more real when you're watching it on a computer screen. Thus even the things we see every day—perhaps *especially* those things—gain an extra significance when glimpsed through the eye of a camera.

That girl, for instance. The girl in the bright-red duffel coat who walks past my house nearly every day, windswept and oblivious to the camera's eye that watches her. She has her habits, as do I. She knows the power of desire. She knows that the world turns not on love, or even money, but on *obsession*.

Obsession? Of course. We are all obsessed. Obsessed with TV; with the size of our dicks; with money and fame and the love-lives of others. This virtual—though far from virtuous—world is a reeking midden of mind-trash, mish-mash, slash; car dealerships and Viagra sales, and music and games and gossip and lies and tiny personal tragedies lost in transit down the line, waiting for someone to care, just once, waiting for someone to connect—

That's where WeJay comes in. WebJournal, the site for all seasonings. Restricted entries for private enjoyment; public—well, for everyone else. On WeJay I can vent as I please, confess without fear of censure; be myself—or indeed, someone else—in a world where no one is quite what they seem, and where every member of every tribe is free to do what they most desire.

Tribe? Yes, everyone here has a tribe; each with its divisions and subdivisions, binary veins and capillaries branching out into a near-infinity of permutations as they distance themselves from the mainstream. The rich man in his castle, the poor man at his gate, the pervert with his webcam. No one has to hunt alone, however far from the pack they have strayed. Everyone has a home here, a place where someone will take them in, where all their tastes are catered for—

13

Most people go with the popular choice. They choose vanilla every time. Vanillas are the good guys, common as Coca-Cola. Their conscience is as white as their perfect teeth; they are tall and bronzed and presentable; they eat at McDonald's; they take out the trash; they come with a PG certificate and they'd never shoot a man in the back.

But bad guys come in a million flavours. Bad guys lie; bad guys cheat; bad guys make the heart beat faster—or sometimes come to a sudden stop. Which is why I created *badguysrock*: originally a WeJay community devoted to villains throughout the fictional universe; now a forum for bad guys to celebrate beyond the reach of the ethics police; to glory in their crimes; to strut; to wear their villainy with pride.

Membership is open right now; the price of admission a single post—be it a fic, an essay or just a drabble. Though if there's something you'd like to confess, this is just the place for it: no names, no rules, no colours—but one.

No, *not* black, as you might expect. Black is far too limiting. Black presupposes a lack of depth. But blue is creative, melancholy. Blue is the music of the soul. And blue is the colour of our clan, embracing all shades of villainy, all flavours of unholy desire.

So far, it's a small clan, with less than a dozen regulars.

First comes *Captainbunnykiller*: Andy Scott of New York. Cap's blog is a mixture of jackass humour, pornographic fantasy and furious invective—against niggers, queers, fucktards, the fat, Christians and, most recently, the French—but

14

I doubt he's ever killed anything.

Next comes *chrysalisbaby*. Aka Chryssie Bateman, of California. This one's a typical Body Freak—has been on a diet since she was twelve, and now weighs over three hundred pounds. Has a history of falling for vicious men. Never learns. Never will.

After that there's *ClairDeLune*; Clair Mitchell, to her friends. This one's a local; she teaches a course on creative self-expression at Malbry College (which explains her slightly superior tone and her addiction to literary psychobabble) and runs an online writers' group as well as a sizeable fansite devoted to a certain middle-aged character actor—let us call him Angel Blue—with whom she is infatuated. Angel is an irregular choice, an actor specializing in louche individuals, damaged types, serial killers, and other assorted bad-guy roles. Not A-list, but you'd know his face. She often posts pictures of him on here. Curiously enough, he looks something like me.

Then there's *Toxic69*, aka Stuart Dawson, of Leeds. Left crippled in a motorbike crash, he spends his angry life online, where no one needs to pity him; and *Purepwnage9*, of Fife, who lives for Warcraft and Second Life, oblivious of the fact that his own life is surely but swiftly slipping away; plus any number of lurkers and irregulars—*JennyTricks*; *BombNumber20*, *Jesusismycopilot*, and so on, who exhibit a diverting range of responses to our various entries, from admiration to outrage; from cheeriness to profanity.

And then, of course, there's *Albertine*. Definitely not like the rest, there's a confessional tone to her entries that I find more than a little promising, a

15

hint of danger, a dark undertone, a style perhaps more akin to my own. And she lives right here in the Village, no more than a dozen streets away—

Coincidence?

Not quite. Of course, I have been watching her. Especially so since my brother's death. Not with malice, but with curiosity, even a measure of envy. She seems so self-possessed. So calm. So safely cocooned in her little world, so unaware of what's happening. Her online posts are so intimate, so naked and so oddly naïve that you'd never believe she was one of us, a bad guy among bad guys. Her fingers on the piano keys danced like little dervishes. I remember that, and her gentle voice, and her name, which smelt of roses.

The poet Rilke was killed by a rose. How very *Sturm und Drang* of him. A scratch with a thorn that got infected; a poison gift that keeps on giving. Personally, I don't see the appeal. I feel more kinship with the orchid tribe: subversives of the plant world, clinging to life wherever they can, subtle and insidious. Roses are so commonplace, with their whorls of sickening bubblegum pink; their scheming scent; their unwholesome leaves, their sly little thorns that poke at the heart—

O rose, thou art sick—

Still, aren't we all?

You are viewing the webjournal of **blueeyedboy**.
Posted at: *23.30 on Monday, January 28*
Status: *restricted*
Mood: *contemplative*
Listening to: *Radiohead*: 'Creep'

Call me B.B. Everyone does. No one but the police and the bank ever use my real name. I'm forty-two and five foot eight; I have mousy hair, blue eyes and I've lived here in Malbry all my life.

Malbry—pronounced *Maw-bry*. Even the word smells of shit. But I am unusually sensitive to words, to their sounds and resonances. That's why I don't have an accent now, and have lost my childhood stammer. The predominant trend here in Malbry is for exaggerated vowels and clumsy glottals, coating every word in a grimy sheen. You can hear them on the estate all the time: teenage girls with scraped-back hair, shouting *hiyaaa* in shades of synthetic strawberry. The boys are less articulate, mouthing *freak* and *loser* at me as I pass, in half-broken voices that yodel and boom in notes of lager and locker-room sweat. Most of the time I don't hear them. My life has a permanent soundtrack, provided by my iPod, into which I have downloaded more than twenty thousand tracks and forty-two playlists, one for every year of my life, each with a specific theme—

Freak. They say it because they think it hurts. In

their world, to be labelled a freak is obviously the worst kind of fate. To me, it's just the opposite. The worst thing is surely to be like them: to have married too young; to have gone on the dole; to have learnt to drink beer and smoke cheap cigarettes; to have had kids doomed to be just like themselves, because if these people are good at anything, it's reproduction—they don't live long, but, by God, they populate—and if not wanting any of that has made me into a freak in their eyes—

In truth, I'm very ordinary. My eyes are my best feature, I'm told, though not everyone appreciates their chilly shade. For the rest, you'd hardly notice me. I'm nicely inconspicuous. I don't talk much, and when I do, it's only when strictly necessary. That's the way to survive in this place; to keep my privacy intact. Because Malbry is one of those places where secrets and gossips and rumours abound, and I have to take exceptional care to avoid the wrong kind of exposure.

It's not that the place is so terrible. The old Village is actually very nice, with its crooked York stone cottages and its church and its single row of little shops. There's rarely any trouble here; except perhaps on Saturday nights, when the kids hang around outside the church while their parents go to the pub down the road, and buy chips from the Chinese takeaway and push the wrappers into the hedge.

To the west, there's what Ma calls Millionaires' Row: an avenue of big stone houses shielded from the road by trees. Tall chimneys; four-by-fours; gates that work by remote control. Beyond that there's St Oswald's, the grammar school, with its twelve-foot wall and heraldic gate. To the east, the brick terraces of Red City, where my mother was born, then to the west, White City, all privet and pebble-dash. It's not as genteel as the Village, though I've learnt to avoid the danger zones. This is where you'll find our house, at the edge of the big estate. A square of grass; a flowerbed; a hedge to keep out the neighbours. This is the house where I was born; hardly anything has changed.

I do have a few extra privileges. I drive a blue Peugeot 307, registered in my mother's name. I have a study lined with books, an iPod dock, a computer and a wall of CDs. I have a collection of orchids, most of them just hybrids, but with one or two rare *Zygopetala*, whose names bear the scent of the South American rainforests from which they were sourced, and whose colours are astonishing: violent shades of priapic green, and mottled, acidic butterfly-blue that no chart could possibly duplicate. I have a darkroom in the basement, where I develop my photographs. I don't display them here, of course. But I like to think I have a gift.

At 5 a.m. on weekdays I clock in at Malbry Infirmary—or I did, until very recently—wearing a suit and a blue striped shirt and carrying a briefcase. My mother is very proud of this, of the fact that her son wears a suit to work. What I actually *do* at work is a matter of far less importance to her. I am single, straight, well-spoken, and, if this were a TV drama of the type favoured by *ClairDeLune*, my blameless lifestyle and unsullied reputation would probably make me a prime suspect.

In the real world, however, only the kids notice

me. To them, any man who still lives with his mother is either a paedo or a queer. But even this assumption comes more from habit than real belief. If they thought I was dangerous, they would behave very differently. Even when that schoolboy was killed, a St Oswald's boy, so close to home, no one thought me remotely worthy of investigation.

Predictably, I was curious. A murder is always intriguing. Besides, I was already learning my craft, and I knew I could use any information, any hints that came my way. I've always appreciated a nice, neat murder. Not that many qualify. Most murderers are predictable, most murders messy and banal. It's almost a crime in itself, don't you think, that the splendid act of *taking a life* should have become so commonplace, so wholly devoid of artistry?

In fiction, there is no such thing as the perfect crime. In movies, the bad guy—who is invariably brilliant and charismatic—always makes a fatal mistake. He overlooks the minutiae. He succumbs to vainglory; loses his nerve; falls victim to some ironic flaw. However dark the frosting, in film, the vanilla centre always shows through; with a happy ending for all who deserve it, and imprisonment, a shot through the heart, or better still, a dramatically pleasing—though statistically improbable—drop from a high building for the bad guy, thereby removing the burden to the State, and leaving the hero free of the guilt of having to shoot the bastard himself.

Well, I happen to know that isn't true, just as I know that most murderers are neither brilliant nor charismatic, but often subnormal and rather dull, and that the police force is so buried under its paperwork that the simplest murders can slip through the net—the stabbings, the shootings, the fist-fights gone wrong, crimes in which the perpetrator, if he has left the scene at all, can often be found in the nearest pub.

Call me romantic, if you like. But I do believe in the perfect crime. Like true love, it's just a matter of timing and patience; of keeping the faith; of not losing hope; of carping the *diem*, of seizing the day—

That's how my interests led me here, to my lonesome refuge on *badguysrock*. Harmless interests, to begin with at least, though soon I grew to appreciate the other possibilities. And at the beginning it was just curiosity: a means of observing others unseen; of exploring a world beyond my own, that narrow triangle between Malbry town, the Village and Nether Edge moors, beyond which I have never dared to aspire. The Internet, with its million maps, was as alien to me as Jupiter—and yet, one day, I was simply *there*, almost by chance, a castaway, watching the changing scenery with the slowly dawning awareness that *this* was where I truly belonged; that *this* would be my great escape, from Malbry, my life, and my mother.

My mother. How it resonates. *Mother* is a difficult word; so dense with complex associations that I can barely see it at all. Sometimes its colour is Virgin-blue, like the statues of Mary; or grey like the dust-bunnies under the bed where I used to hide away as a child; or green like the baize of the market stalls; and it smells of uncertainty and loss, and of black bananas gone to mush, and of salt, and of blood, and of memory—

21

My mother. Gloria Winter. She's the reason I'm still here: stuck in Malbry all these years, like a plant too pot-bound ever to thrive. I have stayed with her. Like everything else. Apart from the neighbours, nothing has changed. The three-bedroomed house; the Axminster; the queasy flowered wallpaper; the gilt-edged mirror in the kitchen that hides a hole in the plaster; the faded print of the *Chinese Girl*; the lacquer vase on the mantel; the dogs.

Those dogs. Those hideous china dogs.

An affectation to start with, that since has got totally out of hand. There are dogs on every surface now: spaniels, Alsatians, chihuahuas, basset hounds, Yorkshire terriers (her favourites). There are musical dogs, portraits of dogs, dogs dressed up as people; dogs eager-tongued and lolloping, sitting to attention, paws lifted in silent appeal, heads topped with little pink bows.

I broke one once, when I was a boy, and she beat me—though I denied the crime—with a piece of electrical cord. Even now, I still hate those dogs. She knows it, too—but they are her babies, she explains (with a terrible, girlish coyness), and besides, she tells me, she never complains about all *my* nasty stuff upstairs.

Not that she even knows what I do. I have my privacy: rooms of my own, all of them with locks on the doors, from which she is excluded. The converted loft and study room, the bathroom, the bedroom; and the darkroom in the cellar. I've made a home for myself here, with my books, my playlists, my online friends, while she spends her days in the parlour, smoking, doing crosswords, dusting and watching daytime TV—

Parlour. I always hated that word, with all its fake middle-class resonances, and its stink of citrus potpourri. Now I hate it even more, with her faded chintz and her china dogs and her reek of desperation. Of course, I couldn't leave her. She knew that from the very first; knew that her decision to stay kept me here, chained to her, a prisoner, a slave. And I am a dutiful son to her. I make sure her garden is always neat. I see to her medication. I drive her to her salsa class (Ma drives, but prefers to be driven). And sometimes, when she's not there, I dream . . .

My mother is a peculiar blend of conflicts and contradictions. Marlboros have ruined her sense of smell, but she always wears Guerlain's L'Heure Bleue. She despises novels, but loves to read dictionaries and encyclopaedias. She buys ready meals from Marks & Spencer, but fruit and veg from the market in town—and always the cheapest fruit and veg, bruised and damaged and past their prime.

Twice a week, without fail (even the week of Nigel's death), she puts on a dress and her high-heeled shoes and I drive her to her salsa class at Malbry College, after which she meets up with her friends in town, and has a cup of fancy tea, or maybe a bottle of Sauvignon Blanc, and speaks to them in her half-bred voice about me and my job at the hospital, where I am indispensable (according to her) and save lives on a daily basis. Then at eight I pick her up, although it's only a five-minute walk from the bus stop. *Those hoodies from the estates*, she says. *They'd stab you soon as look at you.*

Maybe she's right to be cautious. The members

23

of our family seem unusually prone to accidents. Still, I pity the hoodie who tries to mess with my mother. She knows how to look after herself. Even now, at sixty-nine, she's sharp enough to draw blood. What's more, she knows how to strike back at anyone who threatens us. She is a little more subtle, perhaps, than in the days of the electrical cord, but even so, it isn't wise to antagonize Gloria Winter. I learnt that lesson very young. In that, if nothing else, I was a precocious pupil. Not as smart as Emily White, the little blind girl whose story has coloured so much of my life, but smart enough to have survived when neither of my brothers did.

Still, isn't that all over now? Emily White is long dead; her plaintive voice silenced, her letters burnt, the blurry flashgun photographs curled away in secret drawers and on bookshelves in the Mansion. And even if she were not, somehow, the Press have almost forgotten her. There are other things to squawk about; newer scandals over which to obsess. The disappearance of one little girl, over twenty years ago, is no longer cause for public concern. Folk have moved on. Forgotten her. Time for me to do the same.

The problem is this. Nothing ends. If ever Ma taught me anything, it is that nothing is ever truly over. It just works its way slyly into the centre, like yarn in a ball. Round and round and round it goes, crossing and re-crossing, until eventually it is almost hidden beneath the tangle of years. But just to be hidden is not enough. Someone will always find you out. Someone is always lying in wait. Drop your guard for even a second and—*wham!* That's when it all blows up in your face.

Take that girl in the duffel coat. The one who

looks like Red Riding Hood, with her rosy cheeks and her blameless air. Would you believe that she is not what she seems? That beneath that cloak of innocence beats the heart of a predator? Looking at her, would you ever think that she could take a person's life?

You wouldn't, would you? Well, think again.

But nothing's going to happen to me. I've thought this out too carefully. And when it *does* go up—as we know it must—*blueeyedboy* will be half a world away, sitting in the shade by a beach, listening to the sound of the surf and watching the seagulls overhead—

Still, that's for tomorrow, isn't it? Right now I have other things on my mind. Time for another fic, I think. I like myself better as a fictional character. The third-person voice adds distance, says Clair; gives me the power to say what I like. And it's nice to have an audience. Even a murderer loves praise. Maybe that's why I write these things. It certainly isn't a need to confess. But I do admit to a leap of the heart every time someone posts a comment, even someone like Chryssie or Cap, who wouldn't know genius if it poked them in the eye.

I sometimes feel like a king of cats, presiding over an army of mice—half-predatory, half in need of those worshipful voices. It's all about approval, you see, and when I log on in the morning and see the list of messages waiting for me I feel absurdly comforted—

Losers, victims, parasites—and yet I can't stop myself from collecting them, as I do my orchids; as I once collected scuttling things in my blue bucket on the beach; as I was once collected.

Yes, it's time for another murder. A public post

25

on my WeJay, to balance these private reflections of mine. Better still, a *murderer*. Because, although I say *he*—

You and I know this is all about *me*.

You are viewing the webjournal of **blueeyedboy** posting on:

badguysrock@webjournal.com

Posted at: 03:56 on Tuesday, January 29
Status: public
Mood: sick
Listening to: Nick Lowe: 'The Beast In Me'

Most accidents occur in the home. He knows this only too well; has spent much of his childhood avoiding those things that might potentially do him harm. The playground with its swings and roundabouts, and the litter of needles along the edge. The fishpond with its muddy banks on which a small boy might so easily slip, to be dragged to his death in the weedy depths. Bikes that might spill him on to the tarmac to skin his knees and hands—or worse, under the wheels of a bus, to be skinned all over like an orange and left in segments on the road. Other children, who might not understand how special he is, how susceptible— nasty boys who might bloody his nose, nasty girls who might break his heart—

Accidents happen so easily.

That's why, if there's anything he should know by now, it's how to create an accident. Maybe a car accident, he thinks, or a fall down a flight of stairs, or a simple, homely electrical fire. But how do you cause an accident—a *fatal* accident, of course—to happen to someone who doesn't drive, who doesn't indulge in dangerous sports, and whose idea of a wild night out is popping into town with her friends (they always *pop*, they never just *go*), for gossip and a glass of wine?

It isn't that he fears the act. What he fears are the consequences. He knows the police will call him in. He knows he will be a suspect, however accidental the deed, and he will have to answer to them, to plead his innocence, to convince them that it isn't his fault—

That's why he has to choose his time. There can be no margin of error. He knows that murder is a lot like sex: some people know how to take their time; to enjoy the rituals of seduction, rejection, reconciliation; the joy of suspense; the thrill of the chase. But most of them just need to *see it done*; to get the need of it out of themselves as quickly as they possibly can; to distance themselves from the horrors of that intimacy; to know release above all things.

Great lovers know it's not about that.

Great murderers know it, too.

Not that he *is* a great murderer. Just an aspiring amateur. With no established modus operandi, he feels like an unknown artist who yet has to find a style of his own. That's one of the hardest things to do—for an artist or for a murderer. Murder, like all acts of self-affirmation, requires a tremendous self-confidence. And he still feels like a novice: shy; uncertain; protective of his talents and hesitant to make himself known. In spite of it all, he is vulnerable; fearing not just the act itself, but also the reception it may have to endure; those people who will, inevitably, judge, condemn and

28

misunderstand—

And of course, he hates her. He would never have planned it otherwise; he is no Dostoyevskian killer, acting at random and thoughtlessly. He hates her with a passion that he has never felt for anything else; a passion that blooms within him like blood; that sweeps him away on a bitter blue wave—

He wonders what it would be like. To be free of her for once and for all; free of the presence that envelops him. To be free of her voice, of her face, of her ways. But he is afraid, and untested; and so he plans the act with care, selecting his subject (he refuses to use the word *victim*) according to the rules, preparing it all with the neatness and precision that he extends to all things—

An accident. That's all it was.

A most unfortunate accident.

To challenge the boundaries, he understands, you first have to learn to follow the rules. To approach such an act, one has to train, to hone one's art on some baser element, just as a sculptor works in clay—discarding anything that is not perfect, repeating the experiment until the desired result is achieved—before creating the masterpiece. It would be naïve, he tells himself, to expect great things of his first attempt. Like sex, like art, the first time is often inelegant, clumsy and embarrassing. He has prepared himself for this. His aim is merely not to be caught. It has to be an accident—and his relationship with the subject must, though real, be distant enough to defy those who will come looking for him.

You see, he thinks like a murderer. He feels its glamour in his heart. He would never harm someone who does not already deserve to die. He may be bad, but he is not unfair. Nor is he degenerate. He will not be a commonplace, bludgeoning, thoughtless, messy, remorse-sodden killer. So many people die futile deaths—but in her case, at least, there will be reason, order and—yes, a kind of justice. One less parasite on the world, making it a better place.

*   *   *

A strident call from downstairs intrudes upon the fantasy. He feels an annoying tremor of guilt. She hardly ever comes into his room. Besides, why should she climb the stairs when she knows that a call will bring him down?

'Who's there?' she says.

'No one, Ma.'

'I heard a noise.'

'I'm working online.'

'Talking to your imaginary friends?'

Imaginary friends. That's good, Ma.

Ma. The sound a baby makes, the sound of sickness, of lying in bed; a feeble, milky, helpless sound that makes him feel like screaming.

'Well, come on down. It's time for your drink.'

'Hang on. I'll be right there.'

Murder. Mother. Such similar words. Matriarch. Matricide. Parasite. *Parricide*, something used to get rid of parasites. All of them coloured in shades of blue, like the blue of the blanket she tucked around his bed every night when he was a boy, and smelling of ether and hot milk—

Night night. Sleep tight.

Every boy loves his mother, he thinks. And his

30

mother loves him so much. *So much I could swallow you up, B.B.* And maybe she has, because that's how it feels, as if something has swallowed him, something slow but relentless, something inescapable, sucking him down into the belly of the beast—

Swallow. There's a blue word. Flying south, into the blue. And it smells of the sea and tastes like tears, and it makes him think of that bucket again, and the poor, trapped, scuttling things dying slowly in the sun—

She's so proud of him, she says; of his job; of his intellect; of his gift. *Gift* means poison in German, you know. Beware of Germans bearing gifts. Beware of swallows flying south. South to the islands of his dreams: to the blue Azores, the Galapagos, Tahiti and Hawaii—

Hawaii. Awayyy. The southernmost edge of his mental map, scented with distant spices. Not that he's ever been there, of course. But he likes the lullaby lilt of the word, a name that sounds like laughter. White sands and palm beaches and blue skies fat with fair-weather clouds. The scent of plumeria. Pretty girls in coloured sarongs with flowers in their long hair—

But really, he knows he'll never fly south. His mother, for all her ambitions, has never been a traveller. She likes her small world, her fantasy, the life she has carved for them piece by piece into the rock of suburbia. She will never leave, he knows; clinging to him, the last of her sons, like a barnacle, a parasite—

'Hey!' She calls to him from downstairs: 'Are you coming down, or what? I thought you said you were coming down.'

31

'Yes, I'm coming down, Ma.'

Of course I am. I always do. Would I ever lie to you?

And the plunge of despair as he goes downstairs into the parlour that smells of some kind of cheap fruit-flavoured air-freshener—grapefruit, maybe, or tangerine—is like going down into the belly of some huge, fetid, dying animal: a dinosaur or a beached blue whale. And the smell of synthetic citrus makes him almost want to gag—

'Come in here. I've got your drink.'

She's sitting in the kitchenette, arms folded across her chest, feet camel-backed in her high heels. For a moment he is surprised, as always, at how very small she is. He always imagines her larger, somehow; but she is smaller than he is by far, except for her hands, which are surprisingly large compared to the bird-bony rest of her, the knuckles misshapen, not just with arthritis, but with the rings she has collected over the years—a sovereign, a diamond cluster, a Campari-coloured tourmaline, a piece of polished malachite and a flat blue sapphire gated with gold.

Her voice is at the same time both brittle and oddly penetrating. 'You look terrible, B.B.,' she says. 'You're not coming down with something, are you?' She says *coming down* with a certain suspicion, as if he has brought it on himself.

'I didn't sleep too well,' he says.

'You need to take your vitamin drink.'

'Ma, I'm fine.'

'It'll do you good. Go on—take it,' she says. 'You know what happens when you don't.'

And take it he does, as he always does, and its taste is a murky, rotten mess, like fruit and shit in

32

equal parts. And she looks at him with that terrible look of tenderness in her dark eyes, and kisses him gently on the cheek. The scent of her perfume—L'Heure Bleue—envelops him like a blanket.

'Why don't you go back to bed for a while? Get some sleep before tonight? They work you so *hard* at that hospital, it's a crime they get away with it—'

And now he's *really* feeling sick, and he thinks that maybe he will lie down, go back to bed and lie down with the blanket pulled around his head, because nothing could be worse than this; this feeling of drowning in tenderness—

'See?' she says. 'Ma knows best.'

Ma-ternal. Ma-stiff. Ma-stodon. The words swim around inside his head like piranhas scenting blood. It hurts, but he already knows that it will hurt much more later; already the edges of things are garlanded with rainbows that in the next minutes will blossom and swell, driving a spike into his skull just behind his left eye—

'Are you sure you're all right?' his mother says. 'Shall I sit beside you?'

'No.' The pain is bad enough, he thinks, but her presence would be so much worse. He forces a smile. 'I just need to sleep. I'll be fine in an hour or two.'

And then he turns and goes upstairs, holding on to the banisters, the filthy taste of the vitamin drink lost in a sudden surge of pain, and he almost falls, but does not, knowing that if he falls, she will come, and she will stay at his bedside for hours or days, for as long as the terrible headache lasts—

He collapses on to his unmade bed. There is no escape, he tells himself. This is the verdict. Guilty as charged. And now he must take his medicine, as

33

he has done every day of his life; medicine to purge him of bad thoughts, a cure for what's hidden inside him—

Night night. Sleep tight.
Sweet dreams, blueeyedboy.

Post comment:
chrysalisbaby: *wow this is awesome*
JennyTricks: (*post deleted*).
ClairDeLune: *This is quite intriguing,*
blueeyedboy. *Would you say it
represents your true inner
dialogue, or is it a character
portrait you're planning to develop
at some later stage? In any case,
I'd love to read more!*
JennyTricks: (*post deleted*).

You are viewing the webjournal of **blueeyedboy**.
Posted at: *22.40 on Tuesday, January 29*
Status: *restricted*
Mood: *vitriolic*
Listening to: *Voltaire:* 'When You're Evil'

The perfect crime comes in four separate stages. Stage One: identification of the subject. Stage Two: observation of the subject's daily routine. Stage Three: infiltration. Stage Four: action.

So far there's no hurry, of course. She is barely at Stage Two. Walking past the house each day, the collar of her bright red coat turned up against the cold.

Red isn't her colour, of course—but I don't expect her to know that. She doesn't know how I like to watch: noting the details of her dress; the way the wind catches her hair; the way she walks with such precision, marking her passage with almost imperceptible touches. A hand against this wall, here; brushing against this yew hedge; pausing to lift her face to the sound of schoolchildren playing in the yard. Winter has stripped the leaves from the trees, and on dry days their percussion underfoot still smells dimly of fireworks. I know she thinks that too; I know how she likes to walk in the park with its alleys and walled gardens and listen to the sound of the naked trees shushing to themselves in the wind. I know how she turns her face to the sky, mouth open to catch the droplets of rain. I know the unguarded look of her; the way her mouth twists when she is upset; the turn of her head when she listens; the way her face tilts towards a scent.

She notices scents especially: lingers in front of the bakery. Eyes closed, she likes to stand by the door and catch the aroma of warm bread. I wish I could talk to her openly, but Ma's spies are everywhere; watching; reporting; examining . . .

One of these is Eleanor Vine, who called round early this evening. Ostensibly to check on Ma, but really to enquire after me, to search for signs of grief or guilt in the wake of my brother's death; to sniff out what was happening at home, and to collect any news that was going.

Every village has one. The local do-gooder. The busybody. The one to whom everyone applies when in need of information. Eleanor Vine is Malbry's: a poisonous toady who currently forms part of the toxic triumvirate that makes up my mother's retinue. I suppose I ought to feel privileged. Mrs Vine rarely leaves her house, viewing the world through net curtains, occasionally condescending to welcome others into her immaculate sanctum for biscuits, tea and vitriol. She has a niece called Terri, who goes to my writing-as-therapy class. Mrs Vine thinks that Terri and I would make a charming couple. I think that Mrs Vine would make an even more charming corpse.

Today she was all sweetness. 'You look exhausted, B.B.,' she said, greeting me in the hushed voice of one addressing an invalid. 'I hope you're taking care of yourself.'

It is common knowledge in the Village that Eleanor Vine is something of a hypochondriac, taking twenty kinds of pills and disinfecting incessantly. Over twenty years ago, Ma used to clean her house, though now Eleanor reserves that privilege for herself, and can often be seen through her kitchen window, Marigolds on standby, polishing the fruit in the cut-glass dish that stands on the kitchen table, a mixture of joy and anxiety on her thin, discoloured face.

My iPod was playing a song from one of my current playlists. Through the earpiece, Voltaire's darkly satirical voice expounded the various virtues of vice to the melancholy counterpoint of a gypsy violin.

> *And it's so easy when you're evil.*
> *This is the life, you see,*
> *The Devil tips his hat to me—*

'I'm quite all right, Mrs Vine,' I said.

'Not sickening for anything?'

I shook my head. 'Not even a cold.'

'Because bereavement can do that, you know,' she said. 'Old Mr Marshall got pneumonia four weeks after his poor wife passed on. Dead before the headstone went up. The *Examiner* called it a double tragedy.'

I had to smile at the thought of myself pining away for Nigel.

'I hear they're missing you at your class.'

That killed the smile. 'Oh yes? Who says?'

'People talk,' said Eleanor.

I'll bet they do. Toxic old cow. Spying on me for Ma, I don't doubt. And now, thanks to Terri, a spy

37

for my writing-as-therapy class, that little circle of parasites and headcases with whom I share—in supposed confidence—the details of my troubled life.

'I've been preoccupied,' I said.

She gave me a look of sympathy. 'I know,' she said. 'It must be hard. And what about Gloria? Is she all right?' She glanced around the parlour, alert for any telltale sign—a smear of dust on the mantelpiece, a speck on any one of Ma's collection of china dogs—to suggest that Ma might be cracking up.

'Oh, you know. She manages.'

'I brought her a little something,' she said, handing me a paper bag. 'It's a supplement I sometimes use when I'm feeling under the weather.' She gave her vinegary smile. 'Looks like you could do with some yourself. Have you been in a fight, or something?'

'Who, me?' I shook my head.

'No. Of course,' said Eleanor.

No, of course. As if I would. As if Gloria Winter's boy could ever be involved in a fight. Everyone thinks they know me. Everyone's an authority. And it always irks me a little to think that she, like Ma, would never believe the tenth of what I am capable—

'Oh, Eleanor, love, you should have come through!' That was Ma, emerging from the kitchen with a tea-towel in one hand and a vegetable peeler in the other. 'I was just making him his vitamin drink. D'you want some tea while you're here?'

Eleanor shook her head. 'I just popped in to see how you were.'

'Holding up all right,' said Ma. 'B.B.'s looking after me.'

Ouch. That was below the belt. But Ma *is* very proud of me. A taste like that of rotten fruit slowly crept into my mouth. Rotten fruit mixed with salt, like a cocktail of juice and sea water. From my iPod, Voltaire declaimed with murderous exuberance:

I do it all because I'm evil.
And I do it all for free—

Eleanor gave me a sidelong glance. 'He must be such a comfort, love.' She turned once more to look at me. 'I don't know how you can hear a word we're saying with that thing in your ear. Don't you ever take it out?'

If I could have killed her then, right then, without risk, I would have snapped her neck like a stick of Blackpool rock without so much as a tremor of guilt—but as it was I had to smile so hard it made my fillings ache, and to take out one of my iPod plugs, and to promise to go back to my class next week, where everyone is missing me—

'What did she mean, go back to your class? Have you been skipping sessions again?'

'No, Ma. Just the one.' I did not quite dare meet her eyes.

'Those classes are for your own good. I don't want to hear you're skipping them.'

Of course, I should have known that sooner or later she would find out. With friends like Eleanor Vine, her net covers all of Malbry. Besides, I quite enjoy my class, which gives me the chance to disseminate all kinds of misinformation—

39

'Besides, it helps you cope with stress.'
If only you knew, Ma.
'OK, I'll go.'

You are viewing the WebJournal of **blueeyedboy**.
Posted at: *01.44 on Wednesday, January 30*
Status: *restricted*
Mood: *creative*
Listening to: *Breaking Benjamin:* 'Breath'

Most accidents occur in the home. I'm guessing that's how I came about; one of three boys, all born within five years. Nigel, then Brendan, then Benjamin, though by then she'd stopped using our real names, and I was always B.B.

Benjamin. It's a Hebrew name. It means *Son Of My Right Hand*. Not so very flattering, really, when you consider what guys actually *do* with their right hand. But then, the man we knew as Dad was hardly a dutiful father. Only Nigel remembered him, and then only as a series of vague impressions: a big voice; a rough face; a scent of beer and cigarettes. Or maybe that's memory doing what it does sometimes, filling in the gaps with plausible detail while the rest turns over in darkness, like a spindle laden with black sheep's wool.

Not that Nigel *was* the black sheep—all of that came later. But he *was* destined to always wear black, and with time, it affected his character. Ma worked as a cleaner in those days: dusting and vacuuming rich people's homes, doing their laundry, ironing their clothes, washing their dishes and polishing their floors. Time spent on our own house was unpaid work, and so of course it took second place. Not that she was slovenly. But time was always an issue with her, and had to be saved at every turn.

And so, with three sons so close to each other in age and so much laundry to do every week, she hit upon an ingenious system. To ensure that items could be easily identified, she allocated to each of her sons a colour, and bought our clothes accordingly from the local Oxfam shop. Thus Nigel wore shades of charcoal, even down to his underwear; Brendan always wore brown and Benjamin—

Well, I'm sure you can guess.

Of course, it never crossed her mind what such a decision might do to us. Colours make a difference; any hospital worker can tell you that. That's why the cancer unit in the hospital where I work is painted in cheery shades of pink; the waiting rooms in soothing green; the maternity wards in Easter-chick yellow—

But Ma never really understood the secret power of colours. To Ma, it was just a practical means of sorting laundry. Ma never asked herself what it might be like to have to wear the same colour day in, day out: boring brown or gloomy black or beautiful, wide-eyed, fairy-tale blue—

But then, Ma always was different. Some boy's mothers are sugar and spice. Mine was—well—she was something else.

Born Gloria Beverley Green, the third child of a factory girl and a steelworker, Ma spent her childhood in Malbry town, in the maze of little brick terraces known locally as Red City. Washing

42

strung across the streets; soot on every surface; cobbled alleyways leading to nothing but blind and litter-lined spray-painted walls.

Ambitious even then, she dreamed of far pavilions, distant shores and working girls rescued by millionaires. Even now, Ma believes in true love, in the lottery, in self-help books, in boosting your word power, in magazine columns and agony aunts and TV advertisements in which the floors are always clean and women always *worth it*—

Of course, she was neither imaginative nor particularly bright—she left school with only five CSEs—but Gloria Green was determined enough to compensate for her failings, and instead turned all of her considerable willpower and energy towards finding a means of escape from the grime and small-mindedness of Red City into that TV world of clean babies and shiny floors and numbers that can change your life.

It wasn't easy, keeping the faith. Red City was all she had ever known. A rat trap, that lures you in, but seldom lets you out again. Her friends all married in their teens; found jobs, had kids. Gloria stayed with her parents, helping her mother keep house and waiting day after tedious day for a prince who never came.

Finally she gave in. Chris Moxon was a friend of her dad's; he ran a fish-and-chip shop and lived on the edge of White City. He wasn't exactly Catch of the Day—being older and balder than she'd planned—but he was kind and attentive, and by then she was getting desperate. She married him at All Saints' Church in white tulle and carnations, and for a while she almost believed that she had somehow escaped the rat trap—

43

But she found that the smell of frying fat crept into everything she owned—her dresses, her stockings, even her shoes. And however many Marlboros she smoked, however much scent she dabbed on to her skin, there was always that stink—*his* stink—underlying everything; and she realized that she *hadn't* escaped the rat trap, she had simply fallen deeper inside.

Then she met Peter Winter at a Christmas party later that year. He worked at a local car dealership and drove a BMW. Heady stuff for Gloria Green, embarking on her first affair with the coolness of a professional poker player. Certainly, the stakes were high. Gloria's Pa thought the world of Chris. But Peter Winter looked promising: he was solvent, ambitious, untroubled, unwed. He spoke of moving out of White City; of finding a house in the Village, perhaps—

It was good enough for Gloria. She made him her personal project. Within twelve months she was divorced, and pregnant with her first child. She swore that the boy was Peter's, of course, and when she was able, she married him, in spite of her family's protests.

This time, there was no fanfare. Gloria had shamed them all. No one attended the ceremony, which was held on a dismal November day at the local Register Office. And when things started to fall apart—when Peter started drinking, when the dealership went broke—Gloria's parents refused to back down, or even to see the little boy that she'd named after her father—

But Gloria was undaunted. She took an evening job in town, as well as her daily cleaning shift; and when she became pregnant again she hid it, wearing a girdle right up until the eighth month, so that she could keep earning money. When her second son was born she took in mending work and ironing too, so that the house was always filled with the steam and the smell of other people's washing. The dream of a house in the Village had become increasingly remote; but at least in White City there were schools, and a park for the kids, and a job at the local laundrette. Things looked good for Gloria, and she faced her new life with optimism.

But two years of unemployment had wrought a change in Peter Winter. Once a charmer, now he'd grown fat, spending his days in front of the TV, smoking Camels and drinking beer. Gloria was carrying him, much to her resentment; and unbeknownst to her, by then she was pregnant once again.

I never knew my real father. Ma seldom spoke of him. He was handsome, though. I have his eyes. I think Gloria secretly thought that he might turn out to be her ticket out of White City. But Mr Blue Eyes had other ideas, and by the time Ma learnt the truth, her ship had sailed for sunnier shores, leaving her to weather the storm.

No one knows how Peter found out. Perhaps he saw them together somewhere. Perhaps someone talked. Perhaps he just guessed. But Nigel remembered the night he left—or at least, he said he did, though he can't have been five years old at the time. A night of broken crockery, of shouted oaths, of insults—and then the sound of the car starting, the slammed door, the squeal of rubber on the road—a sound that to me always conjures up the smell of fresh popcorn and cinema seats.

45

Then, later, the crash, the broken glass, the howl of sirens in the air—

Of course Nigel never heard all that. That was the way she told it, though; that was Ma's version of the tale. Peter Winter took three weeks to die, leaving his widow pregnant and alone. But Gloria Green was tough. She found a childminder in White City and simply worked harder, pushed herself more, and when she left her job at last, two weeks before the baby was due, her employers took a collection that raised a total of forty-two pounds. Gloria spent some of it on a washing machine and banked the rest, to make it last. She was still only twenty-seven.

At this point I think I might have gone home to my parents. She had no job, hardly any savings, no friends. Her looks, too, had begun to fade, and little remained of the Gloria Green who had left Red City with such high hopes. But to crawl back to her family—defeated, with two children, a baby and no husband—was unthinkable. And so she stayed in White City. She worked from home; looked after her sons; washed and ironed and mended and cleaned, while all the time she was searching for another escape, even as her youth left her and White City closed around her like a drowning man's arms.

And then Ma had a stroke of luck. Peter's insurance paid out. Turns out he was worth more dead than he'd ever been worth alive; and finally, Ma had some money. Not enough—there was *never* enough—but now she could see a light ahead. And that piece of good fortune had come along just as her youngest entered the world, making him her lucky charm; her chance at the winning ticket.

In certain parts of the world, you know, blue eyes are thought to be bad luck, the sign of a demon in disguise. But to carry a blue-eye talisman—a glass bead on a piece of string—is to divert the path of malchance, to send back evil to its source; to banish demons to their lair and to bring good fortune in their place—

Ma, with her love of TV drama, believed in easy solutions. Fiction works to formula. The victim is always a pretty girl. And the answers are always right under your nose, to be revealed in the penultimate scene: by accident, or perhaps by a child—tying up all the loose ends in a pretty birthday-party bow.

Life, of course, is different. Life is nothing but loose ends. And sometimes the thread that seemed to lead so clearly into the heart of the labyrinth turns out to be nothing but tangled string, leaving us alone in the dark, afraid and consumed with the growing belief that the *real* action is still going on somewhere without us, just around the corner—

So much for luck. I came very close. Almost close enough to touch before it was taken away from me. It wasn't my fault. But still she blames me. And ever since, I have tried to be everything she expects of me; and still it's never quite enough, never enough for Gloria Green—

Is that what you feel? says Clair, from Group. *Don't you think you're good enough?*

Bitch. Don't even go there.

You're not the first to try it, you know. You women, with your questions. You think it's so easy to judge cause and effect, to analyse and to excuse. Do you think you can fit me into one of your little boxes, a neatly labelled specimen? That, armed with a few choice details, you can pencil in the rest of my soul?

Not much chance of that here, *ClairDeLune*. You people really have nothing on me. You think I'm new to this game? I've been in and out of groups like yours for the greater part of twenty years. As a matter of fact, it's kind of fun: recalling childhood incidents; inventing dreams, spinning straw into fantasy—

In this way, Clair has come to believe that she knows the man behind the avatar. Fat Chryssie— aka *chrysalisbaby*—also thinks she understands. In actual fact, I know more about them than they could ever know about me; knowledge that may come in useful some day if ever I choose to exploit it.

Clair thinks she is trying to help me. I think she is in denial. Clair's therapeutic writing class is really nothing but a disguised attempt at amateur psychoanalysis. And Clair's online fascination for all things damned and dangerous suggests that she, too, feels damaged. I'm guessing an early experience of abuse, perhaps by a family member. Her fixation with the actor Angel Blue—a man so much older than herself—suggests that she may have daddy issues. Well, of course, I can sympathize. But it's hardly reassuring in a lecturer. Plus it makes her so vulnerable. I hope it doesn't end in tears.

As for Fat Chryssie's interest in me—it seems to be purely romantic. Well, it makes a change from her usual posts, which normally consist of a series of lists detailing her calorie consumption—*Diet Coke: 1.5 cals; Skinny Cow: 90 cals; nacho chips, lo-*

fat cheese: prolly about 300 cals—punctuated by agonizing monologues on how ugly she feels, or interminable pictures of skinny, fragile Goth girls that she refers to as *thinspiration.*

Sometimes she posts pictures of herself—always body shots, never the face—taken on a mobile phone in front of the bathroom mirror, and encourages people to rant at her. Very few indulge her in this (with the exception of Cap, who hates fatties), but some of the other girls leave *ana— love*, or saccharine messages of support—*Babe, you're doing great. Stay strong!*—or half-baked advice about dieting.

Thus Chryssie has acquired an almost evangelical faith in the properties of green tea as a metabolism booster, and in 'negative calorie foods' (which to her mind include carrots, broccoli, blueberries, asparagus and many other things that she rarely eats). Her avatar is a manga drawing of a little girl dressed in black with butterfly wings growing out of her shoulders, and her signature line—at the same time hopeful and unutterably sad—reads: *One day I'll be lighter than air . . .*

Well, maybe she will. There's always hope. But not all Body Freaks die thin. Maybe she'll end up as some of them do, dead of a stroke or a heart attack on the porcelain phone to God.

One of her online friends—*Azurechild*—has been urging her to try something called syrup of ipecac. It's a well-known purgative, with potentially fatal side effects, but which causes rapid weight loss. Of course it's irresponsible, one might say downright criminal, to encourage someone with Chryssie's weight problem, and with her already weakened heart, to take such a

49

dangerous substance.

Still, it's her choice, isn't it? No one is forcing her to take the advice. We do not create these situations. All we do is hit the keys. *Control. Alt. Delete.* Gone. A fatal error. An accident —

*   *   *

So—*How Well Do You Think You Know Me Now?*

That's this week's *meme*, posted by Clair, snagged by Chryssie, who always tags me, like a child in a crowded playground trying to summon a circle of friends.

Clair and Chryssie, like so many of our online clan, are addicted to *memes*: Internet chain-letters, whose purpose is to simulate interest and conversation, often in the form of a questionnaire. Sweeping the Net like a schoolyard craze—*Post three facts about yourself! What did you dream about last night?*—passing from one person to another, disseminating information both useful and otherwise; these things behave like viruses, some going global, some dying out, some ending up on *badguysrock*, where talking about oneself—*Me! Me!*—is always a popular pastime.

When tagged, I tend to reciprocate. Not because I enjoy self-promotion, but I find these exercises intriguing for what they reveal—or not—about the recipient. The questions—to be answered at speed—are designed to create the illusion of intimacy, and to answer them correctly sometimes requires a level of detail that might challenge even the closest friend.

Thanks to this medium I know that Chryssie has a cat called Chloë and likes to wear pink socks in

50

bed; that Cap's favourite film is *Kill Bill*, but that he despises *Kill Bill 2*; that Toxic likes black girls with big breasts; and that *ClairDeLune* likes modern jazz and has a collection of ceramic frogs.

Of course, you don't have to tell the truth. And yet, so many people do. The details are designed to be trivial enough to make the lie seem unnecessary—and yet, from those details a picture emerges, the little things that make up a life—

For instance, I know that Clair's computer password is *clairlovesangel*. It's her hotmail password too, which means that now I can open her mailbox. It's so easy to do these things online; and fragments of gleaned information—names of pets, children's birth dates, mothers' maiden names—all make it so much easier. Armed with such seemingly innocuous data, I can access more intimate things. Bank details. Credit cards. It's like nitrogen and glycerine. Each fairly harmless on its own, but pair the two together, and—*Wham!*

Tagged by **chrysalisbaby** *posting on*
badguysrock@webjournal.com
Posted at: *12:54 on Tuesday, January 29*
If you were an animal, what would you be? *A rat.*
Favourite smell? *Petrol.*
Tea or coffee? *Coffee. Black.*
Favourite flavour of ice cream? *Bitter chocolate.*
What are you wearing right now? *A dark-blue hooded top, jeans, blue Converses.*
What are you afraid of? *Heights.*
What's the last thing you bought? *Music for my*

iPod.
What's the last thing you ate? *A toasted sandwich.*
Favourite sound? *Surf on the beach.*
Siblings? *None.*
What do you wear in bed? *Pyjamas.*
What's your pet hate? *The slogan 'Because I'm worth it.' Because you're not, and you know it—*
Your worst trait? *I'm devious, manipulative, and a liar.*
Any scars or tattoos? *A scar across my upper lip. Another on my eyebrow.*
Any recurring dreams? *No.*
Where would you most like to be right now? *Hawaii.*
There's a fire in your house. What would you save? *Nothing. I'd let it all burn.*
When did you last cry? *Last night—and no, I won't tell you why . . .*

See how you think you know me?

As if you could possibly form a judgement on the basis of how I drink my coffee, or whether I wear pyjamas in bed. In fact, I drink tea, and I sleep naked. Has that changed your impression of me? Would it have made a difference if I'd told you that I never cry? That my childhood was bad? That I've never been outside of a hundred-mile radius of the place where I was born? That I'm afraid of physical violence, that I suffer from migraines, that I hate myself?

Some—or all—of those things might be true. All or none of the above. *Albertine* knows some of the truth, although she rarely comments here, and her

WeJay is password-protected so that no one can read her private posts—

But Chryssie will study my answers with care. She will establish a profile from my replies. There's more than enough to intrigue her there, plus there's a hint of vulnerability, which will counterbalance the veiled aggression to which she responds so readily.

And I *do* come across as a bad guy—but I may be redeemable, through love. Who knows? It happens in movies all the time. And Chryssie lives in a rose-tinted world in which a fat girl may find true love with a killer in need of tenderness—

Of course it isn't the real world. I save all that for my writing group. But I like myself so much better as a fictional character. Besides, who is to say that what she sees isn't some fragmentary part of the truth—truth, like an onion, layer upon layer of tissue and skin, wrapped tightly round something that brings tears to your eyes?

Tell me about yourself, she says.

That's how it always starts, you know, with some woman—some girl—assuming she knows the best way to mine the motherlode at the centre of me.

Motherlode. Mother. Load. Sounds like something you'd carry about—a heavy burden, a punishment—

So let's begin with your mother, she says.

My mother? Are you really sure?

See how quickly she takes the bait. Because every boy loves his mother, right? And every woman secretly knows that the only way to win a man's heart is, first of all, to dispose of Ma—

53

You are viewing the webjournal of **blueeyedboy** *posting on:*

badguysrock@webjournal.com

Posted at: *18:20 on Wednesday, January 30*
Status: *public*
Mood: *vibrant*
Listening to: *Electric Light Orchestra*: 'Mr Blue Sky'

He calls her Mrs Electric Blue. Appliances are her thing: novelty door-chimes, CD players, juicers, steamers and microwaves. You have to wonder what she does with so many; her guest bedroom alone contains nine boxes of obsolete hairdryers, curling tongs, foot spas, kitchen blenders, electric blankets, video recorders, shower radios and telephones.

She never throws anything away, keeping them 'for parts', she says, although she belongs to that generation of women for whom technical ineptitude counts as a charming sign of feminine fragility rather than just laziness, and he knows for a fact that she hasn't a clue. She is a parasite, he thinks, useless and manipulative, and no one will grieve very much for her, least of all her family.

He recognizes her voice at once. He has been working part-time in an electrical repair shop a couple of miles from where she lives. An old-fashioned place, rather obsolete now, its small front window packed with ailing TVs and vacuum cleaners, and dusty with the grey confetti of moths who have flown in there to die. She calls him out on his mobile number—at four on a Friday afternoon, no less—to look over her menagerie of dead appliances.

She is pushing fifty-five by now, but can look older or younger according to necessity. Ash-blonde hair, green eyes, good legs, a fluttering, almost girlish manner that can change to contempt at a moment's notice—and she likes the company of nice young men.

A nice young man. Well, that's what he is. Slim in his denim overalls, angular face, slightly over-long brown hair and eyes of that luminous, striking grey-blue. Not the stuff of magazines, but nice enough for Mrs Electric Blue—and besides, at her age, he thinks, she can't afford to be particular.

She tells him at once that she is divorced. She makes him a cup of Earl Grey tea, complains about the cost of living, sighs deeply at her solitude—and at the gross neglect of her son, who works down in the City somewhere, and eventually, with the air of one about to confer an enormous privilege, offers him her collection for cash.

The stuff is totally worthless, of course. He says so as gently as he can, explaining that old electrical goods are fit for nothing but landfill now, that most of her collection doesn't conform to present safety standards, and how his boss will kill him if he pays as much as a tenner for it.

'Really, Mrs B.,' he says. 'The best I can do is dump it for you. I'll take it down to the rubbish tip. The council would charge you, but I've got the van—'

She stares at him with suspicion. 'No, thanks.'

'Only trying to help,' he says.

'Well, if that's the case, young man,' she says in a voice that is crystalline with frost, 'you can *help* by taking a look at my washing machine. I think it's blocked—it hasn't drained for nearly a week—'

He protests. 'I'm due at another job—'

'I think it's the least you can do,' she says.

Of course, he gives in. She knows he will. Her voice still has that blend of disdain and vulnerability, of helplessness and authority, that he finds irresistible . . .

The drive-belt has slipped, that's all. He unbolts the drum, replaces the belt, wipes his hands on his overalls, and in the reflection from the glass door he sees her watching him.

She may have been attractive once. Now you'd call it *well-preserved*; a phrase his mother sometimes uses, and which to him conjures up images of formaldehyde jars and Egyptian mummies. And now he knows she is watching him with a strangely proprietary look; he can feel her eyes like soldering irons pressing into the small of his back—an appraising glance as careless as it is predatory.

'You don't remember me, do you?' he says, turning his head to meet her gaze.

She gives him that imperious look.

'My mother used to clean your house.'

'Did she really?' The tone of her voice is meant to suggest that she couldn't possibly remember all the people who have worked for her. But for a moment she seems to recall *something*, at least— her eyes narrow and her eyebrows—plucked into insignificance, then redrawn in brown pencil half

56

an inch above where they should be—twitch in something like distress.

'She used to bring me with her, sometimes.'

'My God.' She stares at him. '*Blueeyedboy?*'

He's killed it now with that, of course. She'll never look at him again. Not in *that* way, anyhow—her languid gaze moving down his back, gauging the distance between the nape of his neck and the base of his spine, checking out the taut curve of his ass in those faded blue overalls. Now she can *see* him—four years old, hair undarkened by the passage of time—and suddenly the weight of years drops back on her like a wet winter coat and she's old, so terribly *old*—

He grins. 'I think that's fixed it,' he says.

'I'll pay you something, of course,' she says—too quickly, to hide her embarrassment—as if she believes he works for free, as if this might be some kind gesture of hers that will put him for ever in her debt.

But they both know what she's paying him for. Guilt—maybe simple, but never pure, ageless and tireless and bittersweet.

Poor old Mrs B., he thinks.

And so he thanks her nicely, accepts another cup of lukewarm and vaguely fishy tea, and finally leaves with the certainty that he will be seeing a lot more of Mrs Electric Blue in the days and weeks to come.

*　　　*　　　*

Everyone's guilty of something, of course. Not all of them deserve to die. But sometimes karma comes home to roost, and an act of God may

57

sometimes require the touch of a helping human hand. And anyway, it's not his fault. She calls him back a dozen times—to wire a plug, to change a fuse, to replace the batteries in her camera, and most recently, to set up her new PC (God only knows why she needs one, she's going to die in a week or two), which prompts a flurry of urgent calls, which in their turn precipitate his current decision to remove her from the face of the earth.

It isn't really personal. Some people just deserve to die—whether through evil, malice, guilt or, as in the present case, because she called him *blueeyedboy*—

*   *   *

Most accidents occur in the home. Easy enough to set one up—and yet, somehow he hesitates. Not because he is afraid—although he is, most terribly—but simply because he wants to watch. He toys with the idea of hiding a camera close to the scene of the crime, but it's a vanity he can ill afford, and he discards the scheme (not without regret), and instead contemplates the method to use. Understand: he is very young. He believes in poetic justice. He would like her death to be somehow symbolic—electrocution, perhaps, from a malfunctioning vacuum cleaner, or from one of the vibrators that she keeps in her bathroom cabinet (two of them modestly flesh-toned, the third a disquieting purple), amongst the bottles of lotions and pills.

For a moment he is almost seduced. But he knows that elaborate plans rarely work, and firmly dismissing the beguiling image of Mrs Electric

58

Blue pleasuring herself into the grave with the aid of one of her own appliances, on his next visit he sets up the makings of a dull but efficient little electrical fire, and gets back home in time for a snack in front of the TV. While meanwhile, in another street, Mrs Electric gets ready for bed (with or without her purple pal), and dies there sometime during the night, probably of smoke inhalation, he thinks, although, of course, one can only hope—

The police call by the following day. He tells them how he tried to help, how every appliance in the house was some kind of accident waiting to happen, how she was always overloading the sockets with her junk, how all it might take was a little surge—

In fact, he finds them ludicrous. His guilt, he thinks, should be plain for them to see, and yet they do not; but sit on the couch and drink his mother's tea and talk to him quite nicely, as if trying not to cause him distress, while his mother watches suspiciously, alert for any hint of blame.

'I hope you're not saying that was his fault. He works hard. He's a good boy.'

He hides a smile behind his hand. He is trembling with fear, but now laughter overwhelms him, and he has to fake a panic attack before someone realizes that the pale young man with the blue eyes is actually laughing fit to split—

Later, he can pinpoint the moment. It is a thunderous sensation, something like orgasm, something like grace. The colours around him brighten, expand; words take on dazzling new shades; scents are enhanced; he shivers and sobs and the world blisters and cracks like paint, revealing the light of eternity—

The female PC (there's always one) offers him a handkerchief. He takes it and scrubs his face, looking scared and guilty but laughing still, though she, the woman, who is twenty-four and might be pretty out of that uniform, takes his tears as a sign of distress, and puts a hand on his shoulder, feeling strangely maternal—

It's OK, son. It's not your fault.

And that ominous taste at the back of his throat, the taste he associates with childhood, with rotten fruit and petrol and the sickly rose-scent of bubblegum, recedes once more like a bank of cloud, leaving only blue skies in its wake, and he thinks—

At last, I'm a murderer.

Post comment:
chrysalisbaby: *woot woot!* **blueeyedboy** *kicks ass*
Captainbunnykiller: *'Mrs Electric Blue pleasuring herself into the grave . . .' Dude. There's a scene I'd give money to read. How about it, huh?*
Jesusismycopilot: *YOU'RE SICK. I HOPE YOU KNOW THAT.*
blueeyedboy: *I'm aware of my condition, thanks.*
chrysalisbaby: *well i don't care i think ur awesome*
Captainbunnykiller: *Yeah, man. Ignore the troll. Those fucktards wouldn't know good fic if it jumped up and bit them in the ass.*

Jesusismycopilot: *YOU ARE SICK AND YOU WILL BE JUDGED.*

JennyTricks: (*post deleted*).

ClairDeLune:

If these stories upset you, then please don't come here to read them. Thank you, **blueeyedboy**, *for sharing this. I know how hard it must be to express these darker feelings. Well done! I hope to read more of this story as it develops!*

You are viewing the webjournal of **blueeyedboy**.
Posted at: *23.25 on Wednesday, January 30*
Status: *restricted*
Mood: *unrepentant*
Listening to: *Kansas*: 'Carry On Wayward Son'

No, I don't take it personally. Not everyone appreciates the value of a well-written fic. According to many, I am sick and depraved and deserve to be locked up, or beaten to a pulp, or killed.

So, everyone's a critic, right? I get a lot of death threats. Most are rants from the God squad: *Jesusismycopilot* and friends, who always write in capitals, with little punctuation except for a forest of exclamation points that rises above the main text like the upraised spears of a hostile tribe, and who tell me YOUR SICK! (sic) and THE DAY IS AT HAND! and that Yours Truly will BURN IN H*LL (!!!) WITH ALL THE QUEERS AND PEDOPHILES!

Well, thanks. There are headcases everywhere. A newbie, who calls herself *JennyTricks*, has become a regular visitor, posting comments on all of my fics on a rising scale of outrage. Her style is poor, but she makes up for it in vitriol; leaves no term of abuse unused; promises me a world of hurt if ever she gets her hands on me. I doubt she will, however. The Internet is a safe house, close as the confessional. I never post my details. Besides, their anger gives me a buzz. Sticks and stones, dude; stones and sticks.

But seriously, I love the applause. I even enjoy the occasional hiss. To provoke a reaction with words alone is surely the greatest victory. That's what my fiction is for. To incite. To see what reactions I can collect. Love and hate; approval and scorn; judgement and anger and despair. If I can make you punch the air, or feel a little sick, or cry, or want to do violence to me—or to others— then isn't that a privilege? To creep inside another mind, to make you do what I *want* you to do—

Doesn't that pay for everything?

Well, the good news is—apart from the fact that my headache is gone—that I now have more time to indulge. One of the advantages of sudden unemployment is the amount of leisure it provides. Time to pursue my interests, both on and offline. Time, as my mother says, to stop and smell the roses.

Unemployment? Well, yes. I've had some trouble recently. Not that Ma knows *that*, of course. As far as my mother is concerned, I still work at Malbry Infirmary, the details unclear, but plausible—at least to Ma, who barely finished school and whose medical knowledge, such as it is, is taken from the *Reader's Digest* and from the hospital soaps she likes to watch in the afternoons.

Besides, in a way, it's almost true. I *did* work at the infirmary—I worked there for nearly twenty years—though Ma never really knew what I did. Technical operations of some kind—also a partial truth of sorts—in a place in which everyone's job description contains either the word *operator* or *technician*; I was until recently one of a team of hygiene technicians operating two shifts a day and attending to such vital responsibilities as: mopping, sweeping, disinfecting, wheeling out the rubbish bins and general maintenance of toilets, kitchens and public areas.

In layman's terms, a cleaner.

My secondary, even more dangerous job—again, at least, until recently—was that of day carer for an elderly man, wheelchair-bound, for whom I used to cook and clean; on good days I'd read, or play music on scratchy old vinyl, or listen to stories I already knew, and later I'd go looking for *her*, for the girl in the bright-red duffel coat—

As of now, I have more time, and much less chance of being caught in the act. My daily routine hasn't changed. I get up in the mornings as usual, dress for work, care for my orchids, park the car in the infirmary car park, pick up my laptop and briefcase, and spend the day at leisure in a series of Internet cafés, catching up on my f-list, or posting my fiction on *badguysrock* away from my mother's suspicious eye. After four I often drop by at the Pink Zebra café, where there is a minimal chance of my running into Ma or her friends, and which offers Internet access for the price of a bottomless pot of tea.

Given my own choice of venue, I think I'd prefer something a little less bohemian. The Pink Zebra is rather too informal for me, with its wide-mouthed American cups, and its Formica-topped tables, and chalked Specials boards and the noise of its many patrons. And the name itself, that word, *pink*, has a most unfortunate pungency that takes me back to my childhood, and to our family dentist, Mr Pink, and of the smell of his old-fashioned surgery with its sugary, sickly odour of gas. But *she* likes it. She would. The girl in the bright red duffel coat. She likes her anonymity among the café's clientele. Of course, that's an illusion. But it's one I'm willing to grant her—for now. One last unacknowledged courtesy.

I try to find a table close by. I drink Earl Grey—no lemon, no milk. That's what my old mentor, Dr Peacock, drank, and I have acquired the taste myself; not entirely usual for a place like the Pink Zebra, that serves organic carrot cake and Mexican spiced hot chocolate, and acts as a refuge for bikers and Goths and people with multiple piercings.

Bethan—the manager—glares at me. Perhaps it's my choice of beverage, or the fact that I'm wearing a suit and tie and therefore qualify as *The Man*—or maybe today it's just my face—the ladder of suture-strips across one cheekbone, the cuts bisecting eyebrow and lip.

I can tell what she's thinking. I shouldn't be here. She's thinking I look like trouble, though it's nothing she can quantify. I'm clean, I'm quiet, I always tip. And yet there's something about me that unsettles her; that makes her think I don't belong.

'Earl Grey, please—no lemon, no milk.'

'Be with you in five minutes, OK?'

Bethan knows all her customers. The regulars all have nicknames, much the same as my friends online, like Chocolate Girl, Vegan Guy, Saxophone Man and so on. I, however, am just *OK*. I can tell that she would be happier if she could fit me into a category—perhaps *Yuppie Guy*, or *Earl Grey Dude*—and knew what to expect of me.

But I prefer to wrong-foot her sometimes: to turn up in jeans occasionally; to order coffee (which I hate), or, as I did a couple of weeks ago, half a dozen pieces of pie, eating them one by one as she watched, clearly itching to say something, but not quite daring to comment. In any case, she is suspicious of me. A man who will eat six pieces of pie is capable of anything.

But you shouldn't judge by appearances. Bethan herself is an irregular choice, with the emerald stud in her eyebrow and the stars tattooed down her skinny arms. A shy, resentful little girl, who compensates now by being vaguely aggressive with anyone who looks at her askance.

Still, it is to Bethan that I owe much of my information. From the café she notices everything. She seldom speaks to me, of course, but I overhear her conversations. With people like me she is cautious, but with her regulars she is cheery, approachable. Thanks to Bethan I can collect all kinds of information. For instance, I know that the girl in the red duffel coat would rather drink hot chocolate than tea; prefers treacle tart to carrot cake; favours the Beatles over the Stones, and plans to attend the funeral at Malbry Crematorium at 11.30 on Saturday.

Saturday. Yes, I'll be there. At least I'll get to see her away from that wretched café. Maybe—just maybe—she owes me that. Closure, as the Americans say. An end to this parade of lies.

Lies? Yes, everyone lies. I've lied ever since I could remember. It's the only thing I do well, and I think we should play to our strengths, don't you? After all, what is a writer of fiction but a liar with a licence? You'd never guess from my writing that

I'm as plain-vanilla as they come. Vanilla, at least, on the *outside*; the heart is something different. But aren't we, all of us, killers at heart, tapping out in Morse code the secrets of the confessional?

Clair thinks I should talk to her.

Have you tried telling her how you feel? she suggests in her latest e-mail. Of course, Clair only knows what I want her to know: that for an indeterminate time I have been obsessed with a girl to whom I have hardly spoken a word. But maybe Clair identifies with me rather more than she is aware—or rather, with *blueeyedboy*, whose platonic love for an unnamed girl echoes her own unrequited passion for Angel Blue.

Cap's advice is rather more crude. *Just fuck her and get it over with*, he advises, in the world-weary tone of one trying vainly to hide his own inexperience. *When the novelty wears off, you'll see she's just like all those other bitches, and you'll be able to get back to what matters . . .*

Toxic agrees, and pleads for me to write up the intimate details in my WeJay. *The dirtier the better*, he says. *And by the way, what's her cup size?*

Albertine rarely comments. I sense her disapproval. But *chrysalisbaby* responds to what she sees as my hopeless romance. *Even a bad guy needs someone to love*, she says with awkward sincerity. *You deserve it, blueeyedboy, really you do*. She does not offer herself, not yet, but I sense the longing in her words. Any girl would be lucky, she hints, to earn the love of one such as I.

Poor Chryssie. Yes, she's fat. But she has good hair and a pretty face, and I have led her to believe that I prefer the chubby ones.

The problem is that I play it too well. She now

67

wants to see me on webcam. For the past couple of weeks she has been talking to me through WebJournal, sending me personal messages, including photos of herself.

> *Y can't i C U?* she messages.
> *Out of the question,* I reply.
> *Y? U ugly?* ☺
> *Yeah. I'm a mess. Broken nose, black eye, cuts and bruises all over me. I look like I went twelve rounds with Mike Tyson. Trust me, Chryssie. You'd run a mile.*
> *4 real?? What happened?*
> *Someone took exception to me.*
> ☹ *O!!! U mugged?*
> *I guess you could call it that.*
> *!!! Oh, fuck, oh, babe,* ☹ *i just wanna give U a great big hug.*
> *Thanks, Chryssie. You're very sweet.*
> *Does it hurt??*

Dear Chryssie. I can feel the sympathy coming from her. Chryssie loves to nurture, and I like to feed her fantasy. She's not quite in love with me—no, not yet. But it wouldn't take much to draw her in. It's a little cruel, I know. But isn't that what bad guys do? Besides, she brings these things on herself. All I do is enable them. She's an accident waiting to happen, for which no one could possibly hold me to blame.

Babe, tell me what happened, she says, and today I think maybe I'll humour her. Give a little, take a lot. Isn't that the better deal?

All right then—*babe*. Whatever you say. See what you make of *this* little tale.

You are viewing the webjournal of **blueeyedboy**
posting on:
                    badguysrock@webjournal.com
Posted at: *14.35 on Thursday, January 31*
Status: *public*
Mood: *amorous*
Listening to: *Green Day*: 'Letterbomb'

Blueeyedboy in love. What? You don't think a killer
can fall in love? He has known her for ever, and
yet she has never really seen him, not once. He
might have been invisible as far as the woman he
loves is concerned. But he sees *her*: her hair; her
mouth; her small pale face with its straight dark
brows; her bright-red coat in the morning mist like
something out of a fairy tale.

Red is not her colour, of course—but he doesn't
expect her to know that. She doesn't know how he
likes to watch through his telephoto lens; noting
the details of her dress; the way the wind catches
her hair; the way she walks with such precision,
marking her passage with near-imperceptible
touches. A hand against this wall, here; brushing
against this yew hedge, turning her face to catch
the scent as she passes the village bakery.

He is not a voyeur, he thinks. He acts for his
own protection. His instinct for self-preservation
has been honed to a point of such accuracy that he
can sense the danger in her, the danger behind the

sweet face. It may be the danger he loves, he thinks. The fact that he is walking a dangerous line. The fact that every stolen caress through the lens of his camera is potentially lethal to him.

Or it may just be the fact that she belongs to somebody else.

Until now he has never been in love. It frightens him a little: the intensity of that feeling, the way her face intrudes on his thoughts, the way his fingers trace her name, the way everything somehow conspires to keep her always in his mind—

It changes his behaviour. It makes him contradictory; at the same time more accepting, and less so. He wants to do the right thing, but, so doing, thinks only of himself. He wants to see her, but when he does, flees. He wants it to last for ever, but at the same time longs for it to end.

Zooming closer, he brings her face into mystic, near-monstrous proportions. Now she is a single eye, its colour a hybrid of blue and gold, staring sightlessly through the glass like an orchid in a growing-tank—

But through the eye of love, of course, she always appears in shades of blue. Bruise-blue; butterfly-blue; cobalt, sapphire, mountain-blue. Blue, the colour of his secret soul; the colour of mortality.

His brother in black would have known what to say. *Blueeyedboy* lacks the words. But he dreams of them dancing under the stars, she in a ball dress of sky-blue silk, he in his chosen colours. In these dreams he is beyond words, and he can smell the scent of her hair, can almost feel her texture—

And then comes a sharp knock at the door.

Blueeyedboy starts guiltily. It annoys him that he does this; he is in his own home, hurting no one, why should he feel this stab of guilt?

He puts away his camera. The knock is repeated; peremptory. Someone sounds impatient.

'Who is it?' says *blueeyedboy*.

A voice, not well-loved, but familiar, comes to him from the other side. 'Let me in.'

'What do you want?' says *blueeyedboy*.

'To talk to you, you little shit.'

Let's call him Mr Midnight Blue. Bigger by far than *blueeyedboy*, and vicious as a mad dog. Today he is in a violent rage that *blueeyedboy* has never seen before, hammering at the front door, demanding to be let in. No sooner are the safety locks released, than he barges his way into the hall and, with no kind of preliminaries, head-butts our hero right in the face.

Blueeyedboy's trajectory sends him smashing into the hallway table; ornaments and a flower vase fly into shrapnel against the wall. He trips and falls at the bottom of the stairs, and then Midnight Blue is on top of him, punching him, shouting at him—

'Fucking keep away from her, you twisted little bastard!'

Our hero makes no attempt to resist. He knows it would be impossible. Instead he just curls into himself like a hermit crab into its shell, trying to shield his face with his arms, crying in fear and hatred, while his enemy lands blow after blow to his ribs and back and shoulders.

'Do you understand?' says Midnight, pausing to recover his breath.

'I wasn't doing anything. I've never even *spoken* to her—'

'Don't give me that,' says Midnight Blue. 'I know what you're trying to do. And what about those photographs?'

'Ph-photographs?' says *blueeyedboy*.

'Don't even think of lying to me.' He pulls them from one of his inside pockets. '*These* photographs, taken by you, developed right here, in your darkroom—'

'How did you get those?' says *blueeyedboy*.

Midnight gives him a final punch. 'Never mind how I got them. If you ever go anywhere near her again, if you talk to her, write to her—hell, if you even *look* at her—I'll make you sorry you were born. This is your final warning—'

'Please!' Our hero is whimpering, his arms thrown up to protect his face.

'I mean it. I'll kill you—'

Not if I kill you first, *blueeyedboy* thinks, and before he can protect himself, the hateful aroma of rotting fruit fills his throat with its hothouse stench, and a lance of pain drives into his head, and he feels as though he is dying.

'Please—'

'You'd better not lie to me. You'd better not hold out on me.'

'I won't,' he gasps, through blood and tears.

'You'd better not,' says Midnight Blue.

*   *   *

Lying dazed on the carpet, *blueeyedboy* hears the door slam. Warily, he opens his eyes and sees that Midnight Blue has gone. Even so he waits until he hears the sound of Midnight's car setting off down the driveway before slowly, carefully, standing up and going into the bathroom to investigate the damage.

What a mess. What a fucking mess.

Poor *blueeyedboy*; nose broken, lip split, blue eyes blacked and swollen shut. There's blood down the front of his shirt; blood still trickles from his nose. The pain is bad, but the shame is worse, and the worst of it is, this isn't his fault. In this case, he is innocent.

How strange, he thinks, that for all his sins, he should have escaped retribution so far, whereas this time, when he has done nothing wrong, punishment should descend on him.

It's karma, he thinks. Kar-*ma*.

He looks at his reflection, looks at it for a long time. He feels very calm, watching himself, an actor on a small screen. He touches his reflection and feels the answering sting from the abrasions on his face. Nevertheless he feels strangely remote from the person in the looking glass; as if this were simply a reconstruction of some more distant reality; something that happened to someone else many, many years ago.

I mean it. I'll kill you—

Not if I kill you first, he thinks.

And would it be so impossible? Demons are made to be overcome. Maybe not with brute strength, but with intelligence and guile. Already he senses the germ of a plan beginning to form at the back of his mind. He looks at his reflection once more, squares his shoulders, wipes blood from his mouth and, finally, begins to smile.

Not if I kill you first—

Why not?

After all, he has done it before.

Post comment:
chrysalisbaby: *awesome wow was that 4 real?*
blueeyedboy: *As real as anything else I write . . .*
chrysalisbaby: *aw poor* **blueeyedboy** i *just wanna give him a great big hug*
Jesusismycopilot: *BASTARD YOU DESERVE TO DIE.*
Toxic69: *Oh, man. Don't we all?*
ClairDeLune: *This is fantastic,* **blueeyedboy**. *You are finally beginning to come to terms with your rage. I think we should discuss this further, don't you?*
Captainbunnykiller: *Bitchin', dude! This fic pwns. Can't wait to see the payback.*
JennyTricks: (*post deleted*).
JennyTricks: (*post deleted*).
JennyTricks: (*post deleted*).
blueeyedboy: *You're very persistent,* **JennyTricks**. *Tell me—do I know you?*

You are viewing the webjournal of **blueeyedboy**.
Posted at: *01.37 on Friday, February 1*
Status: *restricted*
Mood: *melancholy*
Listening to: *Voltaire*: 'Born Bad'

Well, no. It wasn't *quite* like that. But not too far from the truth, all the same. The truth is a small, vicious animal biting and clawing its way towards the light. It knows that if it wants to be born, something—or *someone*—else has to die.

I started life as a twin-set, you know. The other half—who, if he had lived, Ma would have christened Malcolm—was stillborn at nineteen weeks.

Well, that's the official tale, anyway. Ma told me when I was six that I'd swallowed my sibling *in utero*—most probably at some point between the twelfth and the thirteenth weeks—in the course of some dispute over *Lebensraum*. It happens more often than people think. Two bodies, one soul; floating in Nature's developing fluid, fighting for the right to live—

She kept the memory of him alive as an ornament on the mantelpiece—a statuette of a sleeping dog, engraved with his initials. The same piece, in fact, that I broke as a boy, and tried to lie about to protect myself. For which I was thrashed with the piece of electrical cord and told that I was born bad – a killer, even in embryo – that I owed it to both of them to be good, to make something of my stolen life—

In fact, she was secretly proud of me. The fact that I'd swallowed my twin to survive made her believe that I was strong. Ma despised weakness. Hard as tempered steel herself, she couldn't stand a loser. *Life's what you make it*, she used to say. *If you don't fight, you deserve to die.*

After that I often used to dream that Malcolm— whose name appears to me in sickly shades of green—had won the fight and taken my place. Even now I still have that dream: two little ravenous tadpoles, two piranhas side by side, two hearts in a bloodbath of chemicals just clamouring to beat as one. If he had lived instead of me, I wonder, would Mal have taken my place? Would *he* have become *blueeyedboy*?

Or would he have had his own colour? Green perhaps, to go with his name? I try to imagine a wardrobe in green: green shirts, green socks, dark-green V-necked sweater for school. All of it identical to mine (except for the colour, of course), all of it in my size, as if a lens had been placed on the world, painting my life a different shade.

Colours make a difference. Even after so many years, I still follow my mother's colour schemes. Blue jeans, hoodie, T-shirt, socks—even my trainers have a blue star on the side. A black roll-necked sweater, a birthday present from last year, lies unworn in a bottom drawer, and whenever I think to try it on, there's a sudden stab of unreasonable guilt.

That's Nigel's sweater, a sharp voice says, and although I know it's irrational, I still can't bring

76

myself to wear his colour, not even for his funeral.

Perhaps that's because he hated me. He blamed me for everything that went wrong. He blamed me for causing Dad to leave; blamed me for his stretch in jail; for his breakdown; for his ruined life; resented the fact that Ma liked me best. Well, that, at least, was justified. Without a doubt, she favoured me. Or at least, she did at first. Perhaps because of my dead twin; the anguish of her delivery; perhaps because of Mr Blue Eyes, who was, as she said, the love of her life.

But Nigel made sibling rivalry into a major art form. His brothers lived in terror of his uncontrollable rages. His brother in brown escaped the worst, being vulnerable in so many ways. Nigel held him in contempt, a willing slave when it suited him, a human shield against Ma's wrath, the rest of the time a whipping-boy, taking the blame for everyone.

But bullying Bren was too easy. There was no satisfaction to be gained from hitting such a target. You could punch Brendan and make him cry, but no one ever saw him fight back. Perhaps he'd learnt from experience that the best way to deal with Nigel, as with a charging elephant, is to lie still and play dead, hoping to avoid the stampede. And he never seemed to bear a grudge, not even when Nigel tormented him, confirming Ma's belief that Bren was not the sharpest tool in the box, and that if anyone were to give them their fairy-tale ending, then it would be Benjamin.

Well, yes. Ma liked her clichés. Brought up on tales of the Lottery, of younger sons who end up marrying princesses, of eccentric millionaires who leave all their wealth to the sweet little urchin who

77

captures their heart—Ma believed in destiny. She saw these things in black and white. And though Bren submitted without complaint, preferring safe mediocrity to the treacherous burden of brilliance, Nigel, who was no fool, must have felt a certain resentment to find that he had been cast from birth in the role of the ugly stepsister, perpetually the man in black.

And so, Nigel was angry. Angry at Ma; angry at Ben; even angry at poor, fat Brendan, who tried so hard to be quiet and good, and who found increasing solace in food, as if through the comfort of sweet things he might provide himself with some measure of protection in a world too full of sharp edges.

And so when Nigel was playing outside, or riding his bike around the estate, and Bren was sitting watching TV with a Wagon Wheel in each hand and a six-pack of Pepsi at his side, Benjamin was going to work with his Ma, a duster clutched in one chubby hand, eyes wide at the opulence of other people's houses; at their broad stairs and neat driveways, sprawling sound systems and walls of books; at their well-stocked fridges and hallway pianos and shagpile carpets and bowls of fruit on dining-room tables as shiny and broad as a ballroom floor.

'Look at this, Ben,' she would say, pointing at some photograph of a boy or girl in school uniform, grinning gap-toothed from a leather frame. 'That'll be you in a few years' time. That'll be you, at the big school, making me so proud of you—'

Like so many of Ma's endearments, it sounded eerily like a threat. She was in her thirties by then—already worn down to the canvas by the years.

Or so I thought when I was young. Now, looking at her photographs, I see that she was beautiful, perhaps not in the conventional way, but striking with her black hair and dark eyes, and the full lips and high cheekbones that made her look French, though she was British to the bone.

Nigel looked just like her, with his dark espresso eyes. But I was always different: blond hair that faded to brown with time; a thin and rather suspicious mouth; eyes of a curious blue-grey, so large that they almost ate up my face—

Would Mal and I have been identical? Would he have had my blue eyes? Or do I have his, as well as my own, looking for ever inwards?

In oriental languages, or so Dr Peacock used to say, there is no distinction between blue and green. Instead, there is a compound word, something that expresses both shades, and that translates as 'sky-coloured', or 'leaf-coloured'. It made a kind of sense to me. From my earliest infancy, I'd always thought of blue as being primarily 'Ben-coloured', or brown as 'Brendan-coloured', or black as 'Nigel-coloured', without ever stopping to ask myself if others perceived things differently.

Dr Peacock changed all that. He taught me a new way of looking at things. With his maps and his recordings and his books and his cases of butterflies, he taught me to expand my world, to trust in my perception. For that I'll always be grateful to him, even though he let me down. Let us all down, in the end: me, my brothers, Emily. You see, for all his kindness, Dr Peacock didn't care. When he'd had enough of us he simply threw

79

us back on the pile. *Albertine* understands, even though she never makes any reference to that time; pretends, in fact, to be someone else—

Still, recent events may have changed all that. It's time to check on *Albertine*. Although she may not know it yet, I can read all her entries. No restrictions apply to me; public or private, it's all the same. Of course, she doesn't know this. Hidden away in her cocoon, she has no idea how closely I've been watching her. Looks so innocent, doesn't she, with her red coat and her basket? But as my brother Nigel found out, sometimes the bad guys *don't* wear black, and sometimes a little girl lost in the woods is more than a match for the big, bad wolf . . .

PART TWO

black

1

I've always hated funerals. The noise of the crematorium. The people talking all at once. The clatter of feet on the polished floor. The sickly scent of flowers. Funeral flowers are different from any other kind. They hardly smell like flowers at all, but like some kind of disinfectant for death, somewhere halfway between chlorine and pine. Of course, the colours are pretty, they say. But all I can think of as the coffin goes into the oven at last is the sprig of parsley you get on fish in restaurants: that tasteless, springy garnish that no one ever wants to eat. Something to make the dish look nice; to distract us from the taste of death.

So far, I hardly miss him. I know it's a terrible thing to say. We were friends as well as lovers, and in spite of everything—his black moods, his restlessness, his ceaseless tapping and fidgeting—I cared for him. I know I did. And yet I really don't feel much as his coffin slides into the furnace. Does that make me a bad person?

I think that maybe, yes, it does.

It was an accident, they said. Nigel *was* an appalling driver. Always over the speed limit; always losing his temper, always tapping, rapping, gesturing. As if by his own movements he could somehow compensate for the stolid inactivity of others. And there was always his silent rage: rage at the person in front of him; rage at always being left behind; rage at the slow drivers; rage at the fast drivers, the clunkers, the kids, the SUVs.

No matter how fast you drive, he said—fingers tapping the dashboard in that way that drove me crazy—there's always someone ahead of you, some idiot shoving his back bumper into your face like a randy dog showing its arse.

Well, Nigel. You've done it now. Right at the junction of Mill Road and Northgate, sprawled across two lanes of traffic, overturned like a Tonka toy. A patch of ice, they said. A truck. No one really knew for sure. A relative identified you. Probably your mother, although I have no way of knowing, of course. But it feels like the truth. She always wins. And now she's here, all dressed up, weeping into the arms of her son—her one surviving son, that is—while I stand dry-eyed, at the back of the hall.

There wasn't much left of the car, or of you. Dog food in a battered tin. You see, I am trying to be brutal here. To make myself feel something— *anything*—but this eerie calm at the heart of me.

I can still hear the machinery working behind the curtain; the swish of cheap velvet (asbestos-lined) as the little performance ended. I didn't cry a single tear. Not even when the music began.

Nigel didn't really like classical music. He'd always known what he wanted them to play at his funeral, and they obliged with the Rolling Stones' 'Paint It Black' and Lou Reed's 'Perfect Day', songs that, whilst dark enough in this context, have no power over me.

Afterwards I followed the crowd blindly to the reception room, where I found a chair and sat down away from the mill of people. His mother did not speak to me. I wouldn't have expected her to; but I could sense her presence near by, baleful as a wasps' nest. I do believe she blames me; although it seems hard to imagine how I could have been responsible.

But the death of her son is less of a bereavement to her than an opportunity to parade her grief. I heard her talking to her friends—her voice staccato with outrage:

'I can't believe she's here,' she said. *'I can't believe she had the nerve—'*

'Come on, lovey,' said Eleanor Vine. I recognized her colourless voice. *'Calm down, it isn't good for you.'*

Eleanor is Gloria's friend as well as her ex-employer. The other two in her entourage are Adèle Roberts, another ex-employer of Mother's, who used to teach at Sunnybank Park, and who everyone assumes is French (because of the accent in her name), and Maureen Pike, the bluff and somewhat aggressive woman who runs the local Neighbourhood Watch. Her voice carries most of all; I could hear her rallying the troops.

'That's right. Settle down. Have another piece of cake.'

'If you think I could eat a thing—'

'Cup of tea, then. Do you good. Keep your strength up, Gloria, love.'

Once more I thought of the coffin, the flowers. By now they would be blackening. So many people have left me this way. When will I start caring?

85

*　　　*　　　*

It all began seven days ago. Seven days ago, with the letter. Until then, we—that is, Nigel and I— existed in a soft cocoon of small daily pleasures and harmless routines; two people pretending to themselves that things are normal—whatever *that* means—and that neither of them is damaged, flawed, possibly beyond repair.

And what about love? That too, of course. But love is a passing ship at best, and Nigel and I were castaways, clinging together for comfort and warmth. He was an angry poet, gazing from the gutter at the stars. I was always something else.

*　　　*　　　*

I was born here in Malbry. On the outskirts of this unfashionable Northern town. It's safe here. No one notices me. No one questions my right to be here. No one plays the piano any more, or the records Daddy left behind, or the Berlioz, the terrible *Symphonie fantastique* that still haunts me so. No one talks about Emily White, the scandal and the tragedy. Almost no one, anyway. And all that was so long ago—over twenty years, in fact— that if they think of it at all, it is simply as a coincidence. That one such as I should move into this house—Emily's house—notorious by association, or, indeed, that of all the men in Malbry it should be Gloria Winter's son who found himself a place in my heart.

I met him almost by accident, one Saturday night at the Zebra. Till then I had been almost content, and the house, which had been in need of repair, was finally clear of workmen. Daddy had been dead three years. I'd gone back to my old name. I had my computer; my online friends. I went to the Zebra for company. And if I still sometimes felt lonely, the piano was still there in the back room, now hopelessly out of tune, but achingly familiar, like the scent of Daddy's tobacco, caught in passing down a street, like a kiss from a stranger's mouth—

Then, Nigel Winter came along. Nigel, like a force of Nature, who came and disrupted everything. Nigel, who came looking for trouble, and somehow found me there instead.

There's rarely any unpleasantness at the Pink Zebra. Even on a Saturday, when bikers and Goths sometimes come through on their way to a concert in Sheffield or Leeds, it's nearly always a friendly crowd, and the fact that the place shuts early means that they're usually still sober.

This time was an exception. At ten a group of women—a hen party from out of town—had still not cleared the premises. They'd had a few bottles of Chardonnay, and the talk had turned to scandals past. I pretended not to listen to them; I tried to be invisible. But I could feel their eyes on me. Their morbid curiosity.

'You're her, aren't you?' A woman's voice, a little too loud, divulging in a boozy stage whisper what no one else dared mention. 'You're that What's-her-name.' She put out a hand and touched my arm.

'Sorry. I don't know who you mean.'

'You are, though. I saw you. You've got a Wiki page, and everything.'

'You shouldn't believe what you read on the Net. Most of it's just a pack of lies.'

Doggedly, she went on. 'I went to see those paintings, you know. I remember my mum taking me. I even had a poster once. What was it called? French name. All those crazy colours. Still, it must have been terrible. Poor kid. How old were you? Ten? Twelve? I tell you, if anyone touched one of *my* kids I'd fucking kill the bastard—'

I've always been prone to panic attacks. They creep up on me when I least expect them, even now, after all these years. This was the first I'd suffered in months, and it took me completely unawares. Suddenly I could hardly breathe; I was drowning in music, even though there was no music playing . . .

I shook the woman's hand from my arm. Flailed out at the empty air. For a second I was a little girl again—a little girl lost among walking trees. I reached for the wall and touched nothing but air; around me, people jostled and laughed. The party was leaving. I tried to hold on. I heard someone call for the bill. Someone asked: *Who had the fish?* Their laughter clattered around me.

Breathe, baby, breathe! I thought.

'Are you OK?' A man's voice.

'I'm sorry. I just don't like crowds.'

He laughed. 'Then you're in the wrong place, love.'

Love. The word has potency.

People tried to warn me at first. Nigel was unstable. He had a criminal past, they said; but after all, my own past could hardly be said to bear scrutiny, and it was so good to be with him—to be with someone real, at last—that I ignored the warnings and plunged straight in.

You were so lovely, he told me later. *Lovely and lost*. Oh, Nigel.

That night we drove out to the moors and he told me all about himself, about his time in prison and the youthful mistake that had sent him there; and then we lay for hours on the heath in the overwhelming silence of the stars, and he tried to make me understand about all those little pins of light scattered across the velvet—

There, I thought. Now for the tears. Though not for Nigel as much as for myself and for that starry night. But even at my lover's funeral, my eyes remained stubbornly dry. And then I felt a hand on my arm and a man's voice said:

'Excuse me. Are you all right?'

I'm very sensitive to voices. Every one, like an instrument, is unique, with its own individual algorithm. His voice is attractive: quiet, precise, with a slight pull on certain syllables, like someone who used to stammer. Not at all like Nigel's voice; and yet I could tell they were brothers.

I said: 'I'm fine. Thank you.'

' "*Fine*",' he repeated thoughtfully. 'Isn't that a useful word? In this case, it means: "I don't want to talk to you. Please go away and leave me alone." '

There was no malice in his tone. Just a cool amusement; maybe even a touch of sympathy.

'I'm sorry,' I began to say.

'No. It's me. I apologize. It's just that I hate funerals. The hypocrisy. The platitudes. The food you'd never think of eating at any other time. The ritual of tiny fish-paste sandwiches and mini jam tarts and sausage rolls—' He broke off. 'I'm sorry. Now I'm being rude. Would you like me to fetch

89

you something to eat?'

I gave a shaky laugh. 'You make it sound so appealing. I'll pass.'

'Very wise.'

I could hear his smile. His charm has a way of surprising me, even now, after all this time, and it makes me feel a little queasy to think that at my lover's funeral I talked—I laughed—with another man, a man I found almost attractive . . .

'I have to say, I'm relieved,' he said. 'I rather thought you'd blame me.'

'Blame you for Nigel's accident? Why?'

'Well, maybe because of my letter,' he said.

'Your letter?'

Once more, I heard him smile. 'The letter he opened the day he died. Why do you think he was driving so recklessly? My guess is he was coming for me. To deliver one of his—*warnings*.'

I shrugged. 'Aren't you the perceptive one? Nigel's death was an *accident*—'

'There's no such thing as an accident as far as our family's concerned.'

I stood up much too fast at that, and the chair clattered back against the parquet floor. 'What the hell does *that* mean?' I said.

His voice was calm, still slightly amused. 'It means we've had our share of bad luck. What did you want? A confession?'

'I wouldn't put it past you,' I said.

'Well, thanks. That puts me in my place.'

I was feeling strangely light-headed by then. Perhaps it was the heat, or the noise, or simply the fact of being so close to him, close enough to take his hand.

'You hated him. You wanted him dead.' My

90

voice sounded plaintive, like a child's.

A pause. 'I thought you knew me,' he said. 'You really think I'm capable?'

And now I thought I could almost hear the first notes of the Berlioz, the *Symphonie fantastique* with its patter of flutes and low caress of strings. Something dreadful was on its way. Suddenly there seemed to be no oxygen in the air I was breathing. I put out a hand to steady myself, missed the back of the chair and stepped out into the open. My throat was a pinprick; my head a balloon. I stretched out my arms and touched only empty space.

'Are you OK?' He sounded concerned.

I tried to find the chair again—I desperately needed to sit down—but I had lost my bearings in the suddenly cavernous room.

'Try to relax. Sit down. Breathe.' I felt his arm around me, guiding me gently towards the chair, and once again I thought of Nigel, and of Daddy's voice, a little off-key, saying:

Come on, Emily. Breathe. Breathe!

'Shall I take you outside?' he said.

'It's nothing. It's fine. It's just the noise.'

'As long as it wasn't something I said—'

'Don't flatter yourself.' I faked a smile. It felt like a dentist's mask on my face. I had to get out. I pulled away, sending my chair skittering against the parquet. If only I could get some air, then everything would be all right. The voices in my head would stop. The dreadful music would be stilled.

'Are you OK?'

Breathe, baby, breathe!

And now the music rose once more, lurching

91

into a major key somehow even more dangerous, more troubling than the minor.

Then his voice through the static said: 'Don't forget your coat, *Albertine.*'

And at that I pulled away and ran, regardless of obstacles, and, finding my voice just long enough to shout—*Let me through!*—I fled once more, like a criminal, pushing my way through the milling crowd and out into the speechless air.

> *You are viewing the webjournal of* **blueeyedboy**.
> **Posted at**: *21.03 on Saturday, February 2*
> **Status**: *restricted*
> **Mood**: *caustic*
> **Listening to**: *Voltaire*: 'Almost Human'

So, she finds me almost attractive. That moves me more than words can say. To know that she thinks of me that way—or that she did, for a moment, at least—makes it almost seem worthwhile—

When Nigel came round on the day he died I was developing photographs. My iPod was playing at full blast, which was why I missed the knock at the door.

'B.B.!' Ma's voice was imperious.

I hate it when she calls me that.

'What?' Her hearing is eerily good. 'What are you doing in there? It's been hours.'

'Just sorting out some negatives.'

Ma has a range of silences. This one was disapproving: Ma dislikes my photography, considers it a waste of time. Besides, my darkroom is private; the lock on the door keeps her out. It isn't healthy, so she says; no boy should have secrets from his ma.

'So what is it, Ma?' I said at last. The silence was starting to get to me. For a moment it deepened; grew thoughtful. It is at these moments that Ma is at her most dangerous. She had something up her sleeve, I knew. Something that didn't bode well for me.

'Ma?' I said. 'Are you still there?'

'Your brother's here to see you,' she said.

Well, I'm sure you can guess what happened next. I suppose she felt I deserved it. After all, I had forfeited her protection by keeping secrets from her. It didn't quite happen as it did in my fic, but we have to allow for poetic licence, don't we? And Nigel had a temper, and I was never the type to fight back.

I suppose I could have lied my way out of it, as I have so often before, but by then I think it was too late; something had been set in motion, something that could not be stopped. Besides, my brother was arrogant. So sure of his crude and bludgeoning tactics that he never considered the fact that there might be other, more subtle ways than brute force of winning the battle between us. Nigel was never subtle. Perhaps that's why *Albertine* loved him. He was, after all, so different from her, so open and straightforward; loyal as a good dog.

Is that what you thought, *Albertine*? Is that what you saw in him? A reflection of lost innocence? What can I say? You were wrong. Nigel wasn't innocent. He was a killer, just like me, though I'm sure he never told you that. After all, what would he have said? That for all his pretended honesty, he was as fake as both of us? That he'd taken the role you offered him, and played you like a professional?

*   *   *

The funeral lasted much too long. They always do,

94

and when the sandwiches and the sausage rolls had finally been cleared away, there was still the coming home to endure, and the photographs to be brought out, and the sighs and the tears and the platitudes: as if she'd ever cared for him, as if Ma had cared for anyone in all her life but Gloria Green—

At least it was quick. The Number One, the greatest hit, the all-time favourite platitude, closely followed by such classic tracks as: *At least he didn't suffer,* and *It's wicked, that road, how fast they drive.* The scene of my brother's death now bears a Diana-style floral display—though of somewhat more modest proportions, thank God.

I know. I went on the pilgrimage. My mother, Adèle, Maureen and I; Yours Truly in his colours, Ma regal, all in black, with a veil, reeking of L'Heure Bleue, of course, and carrying, of all things, a stuffed dog with a wreath in its mouth— putting the *fun* into *fun*eral—

'I don't think I can bear to look,' she says, face averted, her eagle eye taking in the offerings at the roadside shrine, mentally calculating the cost of a spray of carnations, a begonia plant, a bunch of sad chrysanthemums picked up at a roadside garage.

'They'd better not be from *her*,' she says, quite unnecessarily. Indeed, there is no indication that Nigel's girl has ever even been there, still less that she brought flowers.

My mother, however, is unconvinced. She sends me to investigate and to purge any gift not bearing a card, and then deposits her stuffed dog by the side of the road with a teary sigh.

Flanked by Adèle and Maureen, who each hold an elbow, she totters away on six-inch heels that

95

look like sharpened pencils, and produce a sound that makes my tastebuds cramp, like chalk against a blackboard.

'At least you've got B.B., Gloria, love.'

Greatest Hits, Number Four.

'Yes. I don't know what I'd do without him.' Her eyes are hard and expressionless. At the centre of each one is a small blue pinprick of light. It takes me some time to realize that this is my reflection. 'B.B. would never let me down. He would never cheat on me.'

Did she really say those words? I may have just imagined it. And yet, that is exactly what she considers this betrayal to be. Bad enough, to lose her son to another woman, she thinks. But to lose him to *that* girl, of all girls—

Nigel should have known better, of course. No one escapes from Gloria Green. My mother is like the pitcher plant, *Nepenthes distillatoria*, which draws in its victims with sweetness, only to drown them in acid later when their struggles have exhausted them.

I ought to know; I've been living with her for forty-two years, and the reason I've stayed undigested so far is that the parasite needs a decoy, a lure: a creature that sits on the lip of the plant to persuade all the others there's nothing to fear—

I know. It's hardly a glorious task. But it certainly beats being eaten alive. It pays to be loyal to Ma, you see. It pays to keep up appearances. Besides, wasn't I her favourite, trained in the womb as a murderer? And, having first disposed of Mal, why should I spare the other two?

I always thought when I was a boy that the

justice system was the wrong way round. First, a man commits a crime. Then (assuming he's caught) comes the sentence. Five, ten, twenty years, depending on the crime, of course. But as so many criminals fail to anticipate the cost of repaying such a debt, surely it makes more sense, rather than crime on credit, to pay for one's felony up front, and to do the time *before* the crime, after which, without prosecution, you could safely wreak havoc at your leisure.

Imagine the time and money saved on police investigations and on lengthy trials; not to mention the unnecessary anxiety and distress suffered by the perpetrator, never knowing if he'll be caught, or has got away with it. Under this system I believe that many of the more serious crimes could actually be avoided—as only a very few would accept to spend a lifetime in prison for the sake of a single murder. In fact, it's far more likely that, halfway through the sentence, the would-be offender would opt to go free—still innocent of any crime, though he might have to lose his deposit. Or maybe by then he would have earned enough time to pay for a minor felony—an aggravated assault, perhaps, or maybe a rape or a robbery—

See? It's a perfect system. It's moral, cheap and practical. It even allows for that change of heart. It offers absolution. Sin *and* redemption all in one; cost-free karma at the Jesus Christ superstore.

Which is just my way of saying this: I've already done my time. Over forty years of it. And now, with my release date due—

The universe owes me a murder.

His brothers never liked him much. Perhaps he was too different. Perhaps they were jealous of his gift and of all the attention it brought him. In any case, they hated him—well, maybe not Brendan, his brother in brown, who was too thick to genuinely hate anyone, but certainly Nigel, his brother in black, who, the year of Benjamin's birth, underwent such a violent personality change that he might have been a different boy.

The birth of his youngest brother was attended by outbursts of violent rage that Ma could neither control nor understand. As for Brendan, aged three—a placid, stolid, good-natured child—his first words on hearing that he had a baby brother were: *Why, Ma? Send him back!*

Not promising words for Benjamin, who found himself thrown into the cruel world like a bone to a pack of dogs, with no one but Ma to defend him and to keep him from being eaten alive.

But he was her blue-eyed talisman. Special, from the day he was born. The others went to the junior school, where they played on the swings and the climbing frames, risked life and limb on the football pitch, and came home every day with grazes and cuts that Ma seemed never to notice. But with Ben, she was always fretful. The smallest bruise, the slightest cough, was enough to awaken his mother's concern, and the day he came home from nursery school with a bloody nose (earned in a fight over control of the sandpit), she withdrew him from the school and took him on her rounds instead.

There were four ladies on Ma's cleaning round, all of them now coloured blue in his mind. All of them lived in the Village; no more than half a mile from each other, in the long tree-lined alleys between Mill Road and the edge of White City.

Apart from Mrs Electric Blue, who was to die so very unexpectedly some fifteen or twenty years later, there was: Mrs French Blue, who smoked Gauloises and liked Jacques Brel; Mrs Chemical Blue, who took twenty kinds of vitamins and who cleaned the house before Ma arrived (and probably after she left); and finally, Mrs Baby Blue, who collected porcelain dolls, and had a studio under the roof, and was an artist, so she said, and whose husband was a music teacher at St Oswald's, the boys' grammar school down the road, where Ma also went to clean and vacuum the classrooms on the Upper Corridor at four thirty every school day, and to run the big old polisher across what seemed miles of parquet floor.

Benjamin didn't like St Oswald's. He hated the fusty smell of it, the reek of disinfectant and floor polish, the low hum of mould and dried-up sandwiches, dead mice, wormy wood and chalk that got into the back of his throat and caused a permanent catarrh. After a while, just the sound of the name—that gagging sound, *Os-wald's*—would conjure up the smell. From the very start he dreaded the place: he was afraid of the Masters in their big black gowns, afraid of the boys with their striped caps and their blue blazers with the badges on them.

But he liked his mother's ladies. To begin with, anyway.

He's so cute, they said. *Why doesn't he smile? Do you want a biscuit, Ben? Do you want to play a game?*

He found he enjoyed being wooed in this way. To be four years old is to wield great power over women of a certain age. He soon learnt how to exploit this power: how even a half-hearted whimper could cause those ladies real concern, how a smile could earn him biscuits and treats. Each lady had her speciality: Mrs Chemical Blue gave him chocolate biscuits (but made him eat them over the sink); Mrs Electric Blue offered him coconut rings; Mrs French Blue, *langues de chat*. But his favourite was Mrs Baby Blue, whose real name was Catherine White, and who always bought the big red tins of Family Circle biscuits, with their jam sandwiches, chocolate digestives, iced rings, pink wafers—which always seemed especially decadent, somehow, by virtue of their flimsiness, like the flounces on her four-poster bed and her collection of dolls, with their blank and somehow ominous faces staring out from nests of chintz and lace.

His brothers hardly ever came. On the rare occasions that they did, at weekends or holidays, they never showed to advantage. Nigel, at nine, was already a thug: sullen and prone to violence. Brendan, still on the cusp of cute, had also once been privileged, but was now beginning to lose his infant appeal. Besides which he was a clumsy child, always knocking things over, including, on one occasion, a garden ornament—a sundial—belonging to Mrs White, which smashed on to the flagstones and had to be paid for by Ma, of course. For which both he and Nigel were punished—Bren for doing the actual damage, Nigel for not preventing him—after which neither of them came round again, and Benjamin was left with the spoils.

What did Ma make of all this attention? Well, perhaps she thought that someone, somewhere, might fall in love; that in one of those big houses might be found a benefactor for her son. Ben's ma had ambitions, you see; ambitions she barely understood. Perhaps she'd had them all along; or perhaps they were born from those long days polishing other people's silverware, or looking at pictures of their sons in graduation gowns and hoods. And he understood almost from the start that his visits to those big houses were meant to teach him something more than how to beat the dust from a rug or wax a parquet floor. His mother made it clear from the start that he was special; that he was unique; that he was destined for greater things than either of his brothers.

He never questioned it, of course. Neither did she. But he sensed her expectations like a halter round his young neck. All three of them knew how hard she worked; how her back ached from bending and standing all day long; how often she suffered from migraines; how the palms of her hands cracked and bled. From the earliest age, they went shopping with her, and long before they got to school they could add up a grocery list in their heads and know just how little of that day's earnings was left for all their other expenses—

She never voiced it openly. But even unvoiced, they always felt that weight on their backs: the weight of their ma's expectations; her terrifying certainty that they would make her sacrifice worthwhile. It was the price they had to pay, never spoken aloud, but implied; a debt that could never be paid in full.

But Ben was always the favoured one. Everything he did strengthened her hopes. Unlike Bren, he was good at sports, which made him suitably competitive. Unlike Nigel, he liked to read, which fostered her belief that he was gifted. He was good at drawing, too, much to the delight of Mrs White, who had no expectations, who'd always wanted a child of her own, and who fussed over him and gave him sweets; who was pretty and blonde and bohemian, who called him *sweetheart*, who liked to dance; and who laughed and cried for no reason sometimes and who all three boys secretly wished could have been *their* Ma—

And the White house was wonderful. There was a piano in the hall, and a big piece of stained glass above the front door, which on sunny days would cast reflections of red and gold on to the polished floorboards. When his mother was working, Mrs White would show Ben her studio, with its stacked canvases and its rolls of drawing paper, and teach him how to draw horses and dogs, and show him the tubes and palettes of paint, and read out their names, like incantations.

102

Viridian. Celadon. Chromium. Sometimes they had French or Spanish or Italian names, which made them even more magical. *Violetto. Escarlata. Pardo de turba. Outremer.*

'That's the language of art, sweetheart,' Mrs White would sometimes exclaim. She painted big, sloshy canvases in sugary pinks and ominous purples, upon which she would then superimpose pictures cut out of magazines—mostly heads of little girls—which she would then varnish heavily on to the canvas and adorn with ruffs of antique lace.

Benjamin didn't like them much, and yet it was from Mrs White that he learnt to distinguish between the colours; to understand that his own colour came in a legion of shades; to span the depths between sapphire and ultramarine, to see their textures, know their scents.

'That one's chocolate,' he would say, pointing out a fat scarlet tube with a picture of strawberries on the side.

Escarlata, the label said, and the scent was overwhelming, especially when placed in sunlight, filling his head with happiness and with motes that shone and floated like magic Maltesers up and away into the air.

'How can red be chocolate?'

By then he was nearly seven years old, and still he couldn't really explain. It just was, he told her stoutly, just as Nut Brown (*avellana*) was tomato soup, which often made him feel anxious, somehow, and *verde Veronese* was liquorice, and *amarillo naranja* was the smell of boiled cabbage, which always made him feel sick. Sometimes just hearing their names would do it, as if the sounds

103

contained some kind of alchemy, teasing from the volatile words a joyous explosion of colours and scents.

At first he'd assumed that everyone had this ability; but when he mentioned it to his brothers, Nigel punched him and called him *freak*; and Brendan just looked confused and said, *You can smell the words, Ben?* After which he would often grin and scrunch up his nose whenever Benjamin was around, as if he could sense things the way Ben could, copying him, the way he often did, though never really in mockery. In fact, poor Brendan envied Ben; slow, tubby, frightened Bren, always lagging behind, always doing something wrong.

Ben's gift didn't make any sense to Ma, but it did to Mrs White, who knew all about the language of colours, and who liked scented candles—expensive ones from France—which Ma said was like burning money, but which smelt wonderful, all the same; in violet and smoky sage and boudoir patchouli and cedar and rose.

Mrs White knew someone—a friend of her husband's, in fact—someone who understood these things, and she explained to Ben's mother that Ben might be special, which his Ma had believed all along, of course, but that secretly he had doubted. Mrs White promised to put them in touch with this man, whose name was Dr Peacock, and who lived in one of the big old houses behind St Oswald's playing fields, on the street Ma always called Millionaires' Row.

Dr Peacock was sixty-one, an ex-governor of St Oswald's, the author of a number of books. We sometimes saw him in the Village, a bearded man in a tweed jacket and a floppy old hat, walking his

104

dog. He was rather eccentric, said Mrs White with a rueful smile, and, thanks to some clever investments, was blessed with rather more money than sense—

Certainly Ma didn't hesitate. Being practically tone-deaf herself, she had never paid much attention to the way her son understood sounds and words, which, when she noticed it at all, she attributed to his being *sensitive*—her explanation for most things. But the thought that he might be gifted soon overcame her scepticism. Besides, she needed a benefactor, a patron for her blue-eyed boy, who was already having trouble at school, and needed a fatherly influence.

Dr Peacock—childless, retired, and, best of all, rich—must have seemed like a dream come true. And so she went to him for help, thereby setting in place a series of events, like filters over a camera lens, that coloured the next thirty-odd years in ever-deepening shades.

Of course, she couldn't have known that. Well, how could *any* of them have known what would come of that meeting? And who could have known it would end this way, with two of Gloria's children dead, and *blueeyedboy* helpless and trapped, like those scuttling things at the seaside that day, forgotten and dying in the sun?

Post comment:
ClairDeLune: *This is quite good*, **blueeyedboy**. *I like your use of imagery. I notice you're drawing on personal anecdotes rather more than usual.*

> *Good idea! I hope to read more!*
> **JennyTricks**: (*post deleted*).
> **blueeyedboy**: *My pleasure . . .*

You are viewing the webjournal of **blueeyedboy**
posting on:
              badguysrock@webjournal.com
Posted at: *01.15 on Sunday, February 3*
Status: *public*
Mood: *serene*
Listening to: *David Bowie*: 'Heroes'

He'd never met a millionaire. He'd imagined a man in a silk top hat, like Lord Snooty in the comic-books. Or maybe with a monocle and a cane. Instead, Dr Peacock was vaguely unkempt, in a tweedy, bow-tied, carpet-slippery way, and he looked at Ben with milk-blue eyes from behind his wire-rimmed spectacles and said: *Ah. You must be Benjamin*, in a voice like tobacco and coffee cake.

Ma was nervous; dressed to the nines, and she'd made Ben wear his new school clothes—navy trousers, sky-blue sweater, something like the St Oswald's colours, although his own school had no uniform code, and most of the other kids just wore jeans. Nigel and Bren were with them, too—she didn't trust them home alone—both under orders to sit still, shut up, and not to dare touch *anything*.

She was trying to make an impression. Ben's first year at junior school had not been a brilliant one, and by then most of White City knew that Gloria Winter's youngest son had been sent home for sticking a compass into the hand of a boy who had called him a *fucking poofter*, and that only his mother's aggressive intervention had prevented him from being expelled.

Whether that information had reached the Village was yet to be determined. But Gloria Winter was taking no risks, and it was a most angelic Benjamin who now found himself on the steps of the Mansion on that mellow October day, listening to the door-chimes, which were pink and white and silvery, and observing the toes of his sneakers as Dr Peacock came to the door.

Of course he had no real understanding of what a poofter actually was. But there was, he recalled, quite a lot of blood, and even though it wasn't his fault, the fact that he hadn't shown any remorse— had actually seemed to *enjoy* the fracas—quite upset his class teacher, a lady we shall call Mrs Catholic Blue, who (quite publicly, it seemed) subscribed to such amusing beliefs as the innocence of childhood, the sacrifice of God's only son and the watchful presence of angels.

Sadly, her name smelt terrible, like cheap incense and horse shit, which was often distracting in lessons, and which led to a number of incidents, culminating at last in Ben's exclusion; for which his mother blamed the school, pointing out that it wasn't his fault that they weren't able to cope with a gifted child, and promising retribution at the hands of the local newspapers.

Dr Peacock was different. His name smelt of bubblegum. An attractive scent for a little boy, besides which Dr Peacock spoke to him as an adult, in words that slipped and rolled off his tongue like multicoloured balls of gum from a sweetshop vending machine.

'Ah. You must be Benjamin.'

He nodded. He liked that certainty. From behind Dr Peacock, where a door led from the porch into the hall, a shaggy black-and-white shape hurtled towards our hero, revealing itself to be an elderly Jack Russell dog, which frolicked about them, barking.

'My learned colleague,' said Dr Peacock by way of explanation. Then, addressing the dog, he said: 'Kindly allow our visitors to gain access to the library,' at which the dog stopped barking at once, and led the way into the house.

'Please,' said Dr Peacock. 'Come on in and have some tea.'

They did. Earl Grey, no sugar, no milk, served with shortbread biscuits, now fixed in his mind for ever, like Proust's lime-blossom tea, a conduit for memories.

Memories are what *blueeyedboy* has instead of a conscience nowadays. That's what kept him here for so long, pushing an old man's wheelchair around the overgrown paths of the Mansion; doing his laundry; reading aloud; making toast soldiers for soft-boiled eggs. And even though most of the time the old man had no idea who he was, he never complained, or failed him—not once—remembering that first cup of Earl Grey tea and the way Dr Peacock looked at him, as if he, too, were special—

*   *   *

The room was large and carpeted in varying tones of madder and brown. A sofa; chairs; three walls of books; an enormous fireplace, in front of which lay

109

a basket for the dog; a brown teapot as big as the Mad Hatter's; biscuits; some glass cases filled with insects. Most curious of all, perhaps, a child's swing suspended from the ceiling, at which the three boys stared with silent longing from their place on the sofa near Ma, wanting, but hardly daring, to speak.

'Wh-what are those?' said *blueeyedboy*, indicating a glass case.

'Moths,' said the doctor, looking pleased. 'So like the butterfly in many ways, but so much more subtle and fascinating in design. This one here, with the furry head'—he pointed a finger at the glass—'is the Poplar hawk-moth, *Laothoe populi*. This scarlet and brown one next to it is *Tyria jacobaeae*, the Cinnabar. And this little chap'—he indicated a ragged brown something that looked like a dead leaf to *blueeyedboy*—'is *Smerinthus ocellata*, the Eyed Hawk-moth. Can you see its blue eyes?'

Blueeyedboy nodded again, awed into silence not merely by the moths themselves, but by the calm authority with which Dr Peacock uttered the words, then indicated another case, hanging above the piano, in which *blueeyedboy* could see resting a single, enormous lime-green moth, all milk and dusty velvet.

'And this young lady,' said Dr Peacock affectionately, 'is the queen of my collection. The Luna moth, *Actias Luna*, all the way from North America. I brought her here as a pupa, oh, more than thirty years ago, and sat in this room as I watched her hatch, capturing every stage on film. You can't imagine how moving it is, to watch such a creature emerge from the cocoon, to see her spread her wings and fly—'

110

She can't have gone far, thought *blueeyedboy. Just as far as the killing jar*—

Wisely, however, he held his tongue. His ma was getting restless. Her hands clicked together in her lap, shooting cheap fire from her rings.

'I collect china dogs,' she said. 'That makes us both collectors.'

Dr Peacock smiled. 'How nice. I must show you my T'ang figurine.'

Blueeyedboy grinned to himself as he saw the expression on Ma's face. He had no idea what a T'ang figurine looked like, but he guessed it was something as different from Ma's collection of china dogs as the Luna moth was from that creature curled up like a dead leaf over its gaudy, useless eyes.

Ma gave him a dirty look, and *blueeyedboy* understood that sooner or later he would have to pay for making her look foolish. But for now, he knew he was safe, and he looked around Dr Peacock's house with growing curiosity. Apart from the cases of moths, he saw that there were pictures on the walls—not posters, but actual paintings. Aside from Mrs White, with her pink and purple collages, he had never met anyone who owned paintings before.

His eyes came to rest on a delicate study of a ship in faded sepia ink, behind which lay a long, pale beach, with a background of huts and coconut palms and cone-shaped mountains adrift with smoke. It drew him; though he didn't know why. Perhaps the sky, or the tea-coloured ink, or the blush of age that shone through the glass like the bloom on a luscious golden grape—

Dr Peacock caught him staring again. 'Do you

111

know where that is?' he said.

Blueeyedboy shook his head.

'That's Hawaii.'

Ha-wa-ii.

'Maybe you'll get to go there some day,' Dr Peacock told him, and smiled.

And that's how, with a single word, *blueeyedboy* was collected.

Post comment:

Captainbunnykiller: *Man, I think you're losing it. Two posts in as many days, and you haven't murdered anyone* ☺

blueeyedboy: *Give me time. I'm working on it . . .*

ClairDeLune: *Very nice,* **blueeyedboy**. *You show genuine courage in writing down these painful memories! Perhaps you could discuss them more fully at our next session?*

chrysalisbaby: *yay I love this so much (hugs)*

You are viewing the webjournal of **blueeyedboy** *posting on*:

badguysrock@webjournal.com

Posted at: *02.05 on Sunday, February 3*
Status: *public*
Mood: *poetic*
Listening to: *The Zombies*: 'A Rose For Emily'

Next he took the three boys out into the rose garden, while their mother drank tea in the library and the dog ran about on the lawn. He showed them his roses and read out their names from the metal tags clipped to the stems. Adelaide d'Orléans. William Shakespeare. Names with magical properties, that made their nostrils tingle and flare.

Dr Peacock loved his roses; especially the oldest ones, the densely-packed-with-petal ones, the flesh-toned, blue-rinse, off-white, old-lady ones that, according to him, had the sweetest scent. In Dr Peacock's garden the boys learnt to tell a moss rose from an Alba, a damask from a Gallica, and Benjamin collected their names as once he had collected the names inscribed on tubes of paint, names that made his head spin, that echoed with more than just colours and scents, from Rose de Recht, a dark-red rose that smelt of bitter chocolate, to Boule de Neige, Tour de Malakoff, Belle de Crécy and Albertine, his favourite, with a musky, pale-pink, old-fashioned scent, like girls in white summer dresses and croquet and iced pink lemonade on the lawn; which, to Ben, smelt of Turkish Delight—

'Turkish Delight?' said Dr Peacock, his eyes alight with interest. 'And this one? Rosa Mundi?'

'Bread.'

'This one? Cécile Brunner?'

'Cars. Petrol.'

'Really?' Dr Peacock said, looking, not angry, as *blueeyedboy* might have expected, but genuinely fascinated.

In fact, everything about Benjamin was fascinating to Dr Peacock. It turned out that most of his books were about something he called *synaesthesia*, which sounded like something they might do to you in hospital, but that was actually a *neurological condition*, so he said, which actually meant that Ma was right, and that Ben had been special all along.

The boys didn't understand it all, but Dr Peacock said that it was something to do with the way the sensory parts of the brain worked: that something in there was cross-wired, somehow, sending mixed signals from those complex bundles of nerves.

'You mean, like a s-super-sense?' interrupted *blueeyedboy*, thinking vaguely of Spider-Man, or Magneto, or even Hannibal Lecter (you see that he was already moving away from the vanilla end of the spectrum into bad-guy territory).

'Precisely,' said Dr Peacock. 'And when we find out how it works, then maybe our knowledge will be able to help people—stroke victims, for instance, or people who have suffered head trauma. The brain is a complex instrument. And in spite of all the achievements of science and modern medicine, we still know so little about it: how it stores and accesses information, how that information is translated—'

Synaesthesia can manifest in so many ways, Dr Peacock explained to them. Words can have colours; sounds can have shapes, numbers can be illuminated. Some people were born with it; others acquired it by association. Most synaesthetes were visual. But there are other kinds of synaesthesia, where words can translate as tastes or smells; or colours be triggered by migraine pain. In short, said Dr Peacock, a synaesthete might see music; taste sound; experience numbers as textures or shapes. There was even mirror-touch synaesthesia, in which, by some extreme of empathy, the subject could actually experience physical sensations felt by *someone else*—

'You mean, if I saw someone getting hit, then I'd be able to feel it too?'

'Fascinating, isn't it?'

'But—how could they watch gangster films, where people get killed and beaten up?'

'I don't think they'd want to, Benjamin. They'd find it too upsetting. It's all about suggestion, you see. This type of synaesthesia would make one very sensitive.'

'Ma says *I'm* sensitive.'

'I'm sure you are, Benjamin.'

*   *   *

By then Benjamin had become increasingly sensitive, not just to words and names, but to

115

voices, too; to their accents and tones. Of course, he'd been aware before of the fact that people had accents. He'd always preferred Mrs White's voice to Ma's, or to the voice of Mrs Catholic Blue, who spoke with a caustic Belfast twang that grated at his sinuses.

His brothers spoke like the boys at school. They said *ta* instead of *thank you*, and *sithee* instead of *goodbye*. They swore at each other in ugly words that stank of the monkey-house at the zoo. His mother made an effort, but failed; her accent came and went depending on the company. It was particularly bad with Dr Peacock—aitches inserted all over the place like needles into a ball of wool.

Blueeyedboy sensed how very hard she worked at trying to impress, and it made him gag with embarrassment. He didn't want to sound like that. He copied Dr Peacock instead. He liked his vocabulary. The way Dr Peacock said: *If you please*; or *Kindly turn your attention to this*; or *To whom am I speaking?* on the phone. Dr Peacock could speak Latin and French and Greek and Italian and German and even Japanese; and when he spoke English he made it sound like a different language, a better one, one that distinguished between *watt* and *what*; *witch* (a green-grey, sour word) and *which* (a sweet and silvery word), like an actor reading Shakespeare. He even spoke like that to the dog, saying: *Kindly desist from chewing the rug*, or *Would my learned colleague like to take a stroll round the garden?* The strangest thing, thought *blueeyedboy*, was that the dog seemed to respond; which made him wonder whether he, too, could be trained to lose his uncouth habits.

116

From his point of view, Dr Peacock was so impressed with Ben's gift that he promised to tutor the boy himself—as long as he behaved at school—to prepare him for the St Oswald's scholarship exam, in exchange for what he called *a few tests*, and the understanding that anything that transpired from their sessions could be used in the book he was writing, the culmination of a lifetime's study, for which he had interviewed many subjects, though none as young or as promising as little Benjamin Winter.

Ma was overjoyed, of course. St Oswald's was the culmination of all her hopes, of her unvoiced ambitions, of all the dreams she'd ever had. The entrance exam was in three years' time, but she spoke as if it were imminent; promised to save every penny she earned; fussed over Ben more than ever before, and made it very clear that he was being given an incredible chance; a chance that he owed it to her to take—

He was less enthusiastic. He still didn't like St Oswald's. In spite of its navy-blue blazer and tie (just perfect for him, she said), he had already seen enough to be conscious of being unsuitable: unsuitable face, unsuitable hair, unsuitable house, unsuitable *name*—

St Oswald's boys were not called *Ben*. St Oswald's boys were called Leon, or Jasper, or Rufus or Sebastian. A St Oswald's boy can pass off a name like Orlando, can make it sound like peppermint. Even Rupert sounds somehow cool when attached to a navy-blue St Oswald's blazer. Ben, he knew, would be the *wrong* blue, smelling of his mother's house, of too much disinfectant and too little space and too much fried food and not enough books and the harsh, inescapable stink of his brothers.

But Dr Peacock said not to worry. Three years was a long time. Time for him to prepare Ben; to make him into a St Oswald's boy. Ben had *potential*, so he said—a red word, like a stretched rubber band, ready to fly into someone's face—

And so, he accepted. What choice did he have? He was, after all, Ma's greatest hope. Besides, he wanted to please them both—to please Dr Peacock, most of all—and if that meant St Oswald's, then he was prepared to take up the challenge.

Nigel went to Sunnybank Park, the big comprehensive at the edge of White City. A series of concrete building blocks, with razor wire along the roof, it looked like a prison. It stank like a zoo. Nigel didn't seem to mind. Brendan, nine and also destined for Sunnybank Park, showed no sign of unusual ability. Both boys had been tested by Dr Peacock; neither seemed to interest him much. Nigel he discarded at once; Brendan, after three or four weeks, finding him uncooperative.

Nigel was twelve, aggressive and moody. He liked heavy rock music and films where things exploded. No one bullied him at school. Brendan was his shadow, spineless and soft; surviving only through Nigel's protection, like those symbiotic creatures that live around sharks and crocodiles, safe from predators by virtue of their usefulness to the host. Whereas Nigel was quite intelligent (though he never bothered to do any work), Bren was useless at everything: hopeless at sports, clueless in lessons, lazy and inarticulate, a prime candidate for the dole queue, said Ma, or, at best, a job flipping burgers—

But Ben was destined for better things. Every other Saturday, while Nigel and Brendan rode their bikes or played with their friends out on the estate, he went to Dr Peacock's house—the house that he called the Mansion—and in the mornings sat at a big desk upholstered in bottle-green leather and read from books with hardback covers, and learnt geography from a painted globe with the names written on it in tiny scrolled lettering—*Iroquois, Rangoon, Azerbaijan*—arcane, obsolete, *magical* names just like Mrs White's paints, that smelt vaguely of gin and the sea, of peppery dust and acrid spices, like an early taste of some mysterious freedom that he had yet to experience. And if you spun the globe fast enough, the oceans and the continents would chase each other so fast that at last all the colours merged into one, into one perfect shade of blue: ocean blue, heavenly blue, Benjamin blue—

In the afternoons they would do other things, like look at pictures and listen to sounds, which was part of Dr Peacock's research, and which Ben found incomprehensible, but to which he submitted obediently.

There were books and books of letters and numbers arranged in patterns that he had to identify. There was a library of recorded sounds. There were questions like: *What colour is Wednesday? What number is green?*—and shapes with intriguing made-up names, but there were never any wrong answers, which meant that Dr Peacock was pleased, and that Ma was always

119

proud of him.

And he *liked* to go to that big old house, with its library and its studio and its archive of forgotten things; records, cameras, bundles of yellow photographs, weddings and family groups and long-dead children in sailor suits with anxious, watch-the-birdie smiles. He was wary of St Oswald's, but it was nice to study with Dr Peacock, to be called *Benjamin*; to listen to him talk about his travels, his music, his studies, his roses.

Best of all, he mattered there. There he was special—a subject, a case. Dr Peacock listened to him; noted down his reactions to various kinds of stimuli; then asked him precisely what he felt. Often he would record the results on his little Dictaphone, referring to Ben as *Boy X*, to protect his anonymity.

Boy X. He liked that. It made him sound impressive, somehow, a boy with special powers—a gift. Not that he *was* very gifted. He was an average pupil at school, never ranking especially high. As for his *sensory gifts*, as Dr Peacock called them— those sounds that translated to colours and smells—if he'd thought about them at all, he'd always just assumed that everyone experienced them as he did, and even though Dr Peacock assured him that this was an aberration, he continued to think of himself as the norm, and everyone else as freakish.

The word serenity *is grey* [says Dr Peacock in his paper entitled 'Boy X and Early Acquired Synaesthesia'], *though* serene *is dark blue, with a slight flavour of aniseed. Numbers have no colours at all, but names of places and of*

120

individuals are often highly charged, sometimes overwhelmingly so, often both with colours and with flavours. There exists in certain cases a distinct correlation between these extraordinary sense-impressions and events that Boy X *has experienced, which suggests that this type of synaesthesia may be partly associative, rather than merely congenital. However, even in this case a number of interesting physical responses to these stimuli may be observed, including salivation as a direct response to the word* scarlet, *which to* Boy X *smells of chocolate, and a feeling of dizziness associated with the colour pink, which to* Boy X *smells strongly of gas.*

He made it sound so important then. As if they were doing something for science. And when his book was published, he said, both he and *Boy X* would be famous. They might even win a research prize.

In fact Ben was so preoccupied with his lessons at Dr Peacock's house that he hardly ever thought about the ladies from Ma's cleaning round who had wooed him so assiduously. He had more pressing concerns by then, and Dr Peacock's research had taken the place of paintings and dolls.

That was why, six months later, when he finally saw Mrs White one day at the market, he was surprised to see how fat she'd got, as if, after his departure, she'd had to eat for herself all the contents of those big red tins of Family Circle biscuits. *What had happened?* he asked himself. Pretty Mrs White had grown a prominent belly;

and she waddled through the fruit and veg, a big, silly smile on her face.

His mother told them the good news. After nearly ten years of trying and failing, Mrs White was finally pregnant. For some reason, this excited Ma, possibly because it meant more hours, but *blueeyedboy* was filled with unease. He thought of her collection of dolls, those eerie, ruffled, not-quite-children, and wondered if she'd get rid of them, now she was getting the real thing.

It gave him nightmares to think of it: all those staring, plaintive dollies in their silks and antique lace abandoned on some rubbish tip, clothes gone to tatters, rain-washed white, china heads smashed open among the bottles and tins.

'Boy or girl?' said Ma.

'A little girl. I'm going to call her Emily.'

Emily. Em-il-y, three syllables, like a knock on the door of destiny. Such an odd, old-fashioned name, compared to those Kylies and Traceys and Jades—names that reeked of Impulse and grease and stood out in gaudy neon colours—whilst hers was that muted, dusky pink, like bubblegum, like roses—

But how could *blueeyedboy* have known that she would one day lead him here? And how could anyone have guessed that both of them would be so close—victim and predator intertwined like a rose growing through a human skull—without their even knowing it?

Post comment:
ClairDeLune: *I really like where this is going. Is it*

part of something longer?
chrysalisbaby: *is that 4 real with the colours?*
how much did U have 2 research
it?
blueeyedboy: *Not as much as you might think* ☺
Glad you liked it, Chryssie!
chrysalisbaby: *aw hunny (hugs)*
JennyTricks: *(post deleted).*

You are viewing the webjournal of **Albertine**.
Posted at: *02.54 on Sunday, February 3*
Status: *restricted*
Mood: *blank*

I cried a river when Daddy died. I cry at bad movies. I cry at sad songs. I cry at dead dogs and TV advertisements and rainy days and Mondays. So—why no tears for Nigel? I know that Mozart's Requiem or Albinoni's Adagio would help turn on the waterworks, but that's not grief; that's self-indulgence, the kind that Gloria Winter prefers.

Some people enjoy the public display. Emily's funeral was a case in point. A mountain of flowers and teddy bears; people wept openly in the streets. A nation mourned—but not for a child. Perhaps for the loss of innocence; for the grubbiness of it all, for their own collective greed, that in the end had swallowed her whole. The Emily White Phenomenon that had caused so much fanfare over the years ended with a whimper: a little headstone in Malbry churchyard and a stained-glass window in the church, paid for by Dr Peacock, much to the indignation of Maureen Pike and her cronies, who felt it was inappropriate for the man to be linked in any way to the church, to the Village, to Emily.

No one really mentions it now. People tend to leave me alone. In Malbry I am invisible; I take pleasure in my lack of depth. Gloria calls me *colourless*; I overheard her once on the phone, back in the days when she and Nigel talked.

I don't see how it can last, she said. *She's such a colourless little thing. I know you must feel sorry for her, but—*

Ma, I do not *feel sorry for her!*

Well, of course you do. What nonsense—

Ma. One more word and I'm hanging up.

You feel sorry for her because she's—

Click.

Overheard in the Zebra one day: *God knows what he sees in her. He pities her, that's all it is.*

How gently, politely incredulous that one such as I might attract a man through something more than compassion. Because Nigel was a good-looking man, and I was somehow *damaged*. I had a past, I was dangerous. Nigel was open wide—he'd told me all about himself that night as we lay watching the stars. One thing he *hadn't* told me, though—it was Eleanor Vine who pointed it out—is that he always wore black: an endless procession of black jeans, black jackets, black T-shirts, black boots. *It's easier to wash*, he said, when I finally asked him. *You can put everything in together.*

Did he call my name at the end? Did he know I was to blame? Or was it all just a blur to him, a single swerve into nothingness? It all began so harmlessly. We were children. We were innocent. Even *he* was, in his way—*blueeyedboy*, who haunts my dreams.

Maybe it was guilt, after all, that triggered yesterday's panic attack. Guilt, fatigue and nerves, that was all. Emily White is long gone. She died when she was nine years old, and no one

125

remembers her any more, not Daddy, not Nigel, not anyone.

Who am I now? Not Emily White. I will not, *cannot* be Emily White. Nor can I be myself again, now that Daddy and Nigel are gone. Perhaps I can just be *Albertine*, the name I give myself online. There's something sweet about *Albertine*. Sweet and rather nostalgic, like the name of a Proustian heroine. I don't quite know why I chose it. Perhaps because of *blueeyedboy*, still hidden at the heart of all this, and whom I have tried for so long to forget . . .

But part of me must have remembered. Some part of me must have known this would come. For among all the herbs and flowers in my garden—the wallflowers, thymes, clove pinks, geraniums, lemon balm, lavenders and night-scented stocks—I never planted a single rose.

> *You are viewing the webjournal of* **blueeyedboy**
> *posting on*:
> **badguysrock@webjournal.com**
> **Posted at**: *03.06 on Sunday, February 3*
> **Status**: *public*
> **Mood**: *poetic*
> **Listening to**: *Roberta Flack*: 'The First Time
>   Ever I Saw Your Face'

Benjamin was seven years old the year that Emily White was born. A time of change; of uncertainty; of deep, unspoken forebodings. At first he wasn't sure what it meant; but ever since that day at the market, he'd been aware of a gradual shift in things. People no longer looked at him. Women no longer wooed him with sweets. No one marvelled at how much he'd grown. He seemed to have moved a step beyond the line of their perception.

His mother, busier than ever with her cleaning jobs and her shifts at St Oswald's, was often too tired to talk to the boys, except to tell them to brush their teeth and work hard at school. His mother's ladies, who had once been so attentive to Ben, flocking around him like hens around a single chick, seemed to have vanished from his life, leaving him vaguely wondering whether it was something he had done, or if it was simply coincidence that no one (except for Dr Peacock) seemed to want him any more.

Finally he understood. He'd been a distraction; that was all. It's hard to talk to the person who cleans around the back of your fridge, and scrubs around the toilet bowl, and hand-washes your lace-trimmed delicates, and goes away at the end of the week with hardly enough money in her purse to buy even a single pair of those expensive panties. His mother's ladies knew that. *Guardian* readers, every one, who believed in equality, to a point, and who maybe felt a touch of unease at having to hire a cleaner—not that they would have admitted it; they were helping the woman, after all. And compensated in their way by making much of the sweet little boy, as visitors to an open farm may *ooh* and *ahh* over the young lambs—soon to reappear, nicely wrapped, on the shelves as (organic) chops and cutlets. For three years he'd been a little prince, spoilt and praised and adored, and then—

And then, along came Emily.

Sounds so harmless, doesn't it? Such a sweet, old-fashioned name, all sugared almonds and rose water. And yet she's the start of everything: the spindle on which their life revolved, the weathervane that moves from sunshine to storm in a single turn of a cockerel's tail. Barely more than a rumour at first, but a rumour that grew and gained in strength until at last it became a juggernaut; crushing everyone beneath the Emily White Phenomenon.

Ma told them he cried when he heard. How sorry he felt for the poor baby; how sorry, too, for Mrs White—who had wanted a child more than anything and, now that she had her wish at last, had succumbed to a case of the baby blues,

128

refusing to come out of her house, to nurse her child, or even to wash, and all because her baby was blind—

Still, that was Ma all over; exaggerating his sensitivity. Benjamin never shed a tear. *Brendan* cried. It was more his style. But Ben didn't even feel upset; only a little curious, wondering what Mrs White was going to do now. He'd heard Ma and her friends talking about how sometimes mothers harmed their children when under the influence of the baby blues. He wondered whether the baby was safe, whether the Social would take her away, and if so, whether Mrs White would want him back—

Not that he needed Mrs White. But he'd changed a lot since those early days. His hair had darkened from blond to brown; his baby face had grown angular. He was aware even then that he had outgrown his early appeal, and he was filled with resentment against those who had failed to warn him that what is taken for granted at four can be cruelly taken away at seven. He'd been told so often that he was adorable, that he was good—and now here he was, discarded, just like those dolls she had put away when her new, living doll had appeared on the scene—

His brothers showed little sympathy at his sudden fall from grace. Nigel was openly gleeful; Bren was his usual, impassive self. He may not even have noticed at first; he was too busy following Nigel about, copying him slavishly. Neither really understood that this wasn't about wanting attention, either from Ma or from anyone else. The circumstances surrounding Emily's birth had taught them that no one is irreplaceable; that even one such as Ben Winter could be stripped unexpectedly of his gilding. Only his sensory peculiarities now set him apart from the rest of the clan—and even that was about to change.

By the time they got to see her at last, Emily was nine months old. A fluffy thing in rosebud pink, furled tightly in her mother's arms. The boys were at the market, helping Ma with the groceries, and it was *blueeyedboy* who saw them first, Mrs White wearing a long purple coat—*violetto*, her favourite colour—that was meant to look bohemian, but made her look too pale instead, with a scent of patchouli that stung at his eyes, overwhelming the smell of fruit.

There was another woman with her, he saw. A woman of his mother's age, in stonewash jeans and a waistcoat, with long, dry, pale hair and silver bangles on her arms. Mrs White reached for some strawberries, then, seeing Benjamin waiting in line, gave a little cry of surprise.

'Sweetheart, how you've grown!' she said. 'Has it really been so long?' She turned to the woman at her side. 'Feather. This is Benjamin. And this is his mother, Gloria.' No mention of Nigel or Brendan. Still, that was to be expected.

The woman she'd addressed as Feather—*What a stupid name*, thought *blueeyedboy*—gave them a rather narrow smile. He could tell she didn't like them. Her eyes were long and wintry-green, devoid of any sympathy. He could tell she was suspicious of them, that she thought they were common, not good enough—

'You had a b-baby,' said *blueeyedboy*.

'Yes. Her name's Emily.'

'Em-i-ly.' He tried it out. 'C-can I hold her? I'll

130

be careful.'

Feather gave her narrow smile. 'No, a baby isn't a toy. You wouldn't want to hurt Emily.'

Wouldn't? blueeyedboy thought to himself. He wasn't as sure as she seemed to be. What use was a baby, anyhow? It couldn't walk, couldn't talk; all it could do was eat, sleep or cry. Even a cat could do more than that. He didn't know why a baby should be so important, anyway. Surely *he* was more so.

Something stung at his eyes again. He blamed the scent of patchouli. He tore a leaf from a nearby cabbage and crushed it secretly into his hand.

'Emily's a—*special* baby.' It sounded like an apology.

'The doctor says *I'm* special,' said Ben. He smirked at Feather's look of surprise. 'He's writing a book about me, you know. He says I'm remarkable.'

Ben's vocabulary had greatly improved thanks to Dr Peacock's tuition, and he uttered the word with a certain flourish.

'A book?' said Feather.

'For his research.'

Both of them looked surprised at that, and turned to stare at Benjamin in a way that was not entirely flattering. He bridled a little, half-sensing, perhaps, that at last he had snagged their attention. Mrs White was *really* watching him now, but in a thoughtful, suspicious way that made *blueeyedboy* uncomfortable.

'So—he's been—helping you out?' she said.

Ma looked prim. 'A little,' she said.

'Helping out financially?'

'It's part of his research,' said Ma.

Blueeyedboy could tell that Ma was offended by

the suggestion that they needed help. That made it sound like charity, which was not at all the case. He started to tell Mrs White that they were helping Dr Peacock, not the other way around. But then Ma shot him a look, and he could see from her expression that he shouldn't have spoken out of turn. She put a hand on his shoulder and squeezed. Her hands were very strong. He winced.

'We're very proud of Ben,' she said. 'The doctor says he has a gift.'

Gift. Gift, thought *blueeyedboy.* A green and somehow ominous word, like radioactivity. *Giffft,* like the sound a snake makes when it sinks its fangs into the flesh. *Gift,* like a nicely wrapped grenade, all ready to explode in your face—

And then it hit him like a slap: the headache, and the stink of fruit that seemed to envelop everything. Suddenly he felt queasy and sick, so sick that even Ma noticed, and relaxed her grip on his shoulder.

'What's wrong now?'

'I d-don't feel so good.'

She shot him a look of warning. 'Don't even think about it,' she hissed. 'I'll give you something to whine about.'

Blueeyedboy clenched his fists and reached for the thought of blue skies, of Feather in a body bag, dismembered and tagged for disposal, of Emily lying blue in her cot with Mrs White wailing in anguish—

The headache subsided a little. Good. The awful smell receded, too. And then he thought of his brothers and Ma lying dead in the mortuary, and the pain kicked back like a wild horse, and his vision was crazed with rainbows—

132

Ma gave him a look of suspicion. *Blueeyedboy* tried to steady himself against the nearest market stall. His hand caught the side of a packing case. A pyramid of Granny Smiths stood, ready to form an avalanche.

'Anything drops on the floor,' said Ma, 'and I swear I'll make you eat it.'

Blueeyedboy withdrew his hand as if the box might be on fire. He knew that this was his fault; his fault for swallowing his twin; his fault for wishing Ma dead. He was born bad, bad to the bone, and this sickness was his punishment.

He thought he'd got away with it. The pyramid trembled, but did not fall. And then a single apple—he can still see it in his mind, with the little blue sticker on the side—nudged against its companion, and the whole of the front of the fruit stall seemed to slide, apples and peaches and oranges bouncing gleefully against each other, then off the AstroTurf apron and rolling on to the concrete floor.

She waited there until he'd retrieved every single piece of fruit. Some were almost intact; some had been trodden into the dirt. She paid for it at the market stall with an almost gracious insistence. And then, that night, she stood over him with a dripping plastic bag in one hand and the piece of electrical cord in the other, and made him eat it: piece by piece; core and peel and dirt and rot. As his brothers watched through the banisters, forgetting even to snigger as their brother sobbed and retched. To this day, *blueeyedboy* thinks, nothing very much has changed. And the vitamin drink always brings it back, and he struggles to stop himself retching; but Ma never notices. Ma thinks

133

he is delicate. Ma knows he would never do anything to anyone—

Post comment:
chrysalisbaby: *Aw babe that makes me want 2 cry*
Captainbunnykiller: *Forget the tears, man, where's the* blood?
Toxic69: *I concur. Roll out those freakin body bags—and by the way, dude, where's the bedroom action?*
ClairDeLune: *Well done,* **blueeyedboy**! *I love the way you tie these stories in with each other. Without wanting to intrude, I'd love to know how much of this ongoing fic is autobiographical, and how much is purely fictional. The third person voice adds an intriguing sense of distance. Perhaps we could discuss it at Group some day?*

You are viewing the webjournal of **blueeyedboy**
posting on:
                          badguysrock@webjournal.com
Posted at: *19.15 on Monday, February 4*
Status: *public*
Mood: *pensive*
Listening to: *Neil Young*: 'After The Gold Rush'

After Mrs Electric Blue, he finds it so much easier. Innocence, like virginity, is something you can only lose once, and its departure leaves him with no feeling of loss, but only a vague sense of wonder that it should have turned out to be such a small thing, after all. A small thing, but potent; and now it colours every aspect of his life, like a grain of pure cyan in a glass of water, dyeing the contents deepest blue—

He sees them all in blue now, each potential subject, quarry or mark. *Mark*. As in something to be erased. *Black mark. Laundry mark.* He is very sensitive to words; to their sounds, their colours, their music, their shapes on the page.

Mark is a blue word, like *market*; like *murder*. He likes it much better than *victim*, which appears to him as a feeble eggy shade, or even *prey*, with its nasty undertones of ecclesiastical purple, and distant reek of frankincense. He sees them all in blue now, these people who are going to die, and despite his impatience to repeat the act, he allows some time for the high to wear off, for the colours to drain from the world again, for the knot of hatred that is permanently lodged just beneath his solar plexus to swell to the point at which he *must* act, *must* do something, or die of it—

But some things are worth the wait, he knows. And he has waited a long time for this. That little scene at the market was well over a decade ago; no one remembers Mrs White, or her friend with the stupid name.

Let's call her Ms Stonewash Blue. She likes to smoke a joint or two. At least, she did, when she was young, when she weighed in at barely ninety-five pounds and never, ever wore a bra. Now, past fifty, she watches her weight, and grass gives her the munchies.

So she goes to the gym every day instead, and to t'ai chi and salsa class twice a week, and still believes in free love, though nowadays even that, she thinks, is getting quite expensive. A one-time radical feminist, who sees all men as aggressors, she thinks of herself as *free-spirited*; drives a yellow 2CV; likes ethnic bangles and well-cut jeans; goes on expensive Thai holidays; describes herself as *spiritual*; reads Tarot cards at her friends' parties; and has legs that might pass for those of a thirty-year-old, though the same cannot be said of her face.

Her current squeeze is twenty-nine—almost the same age as *blueeyedboy*. A blonde and cropped-haired androgyne, who parks her motorbike by the church, just far enough away from the Stonewash house to keep the neighbours from whispering. From which our hero deduces that Ms Stonewash Blue is not quite the free spirit she pretends to be.

Well, things have changed since the sixties. She knows the value of networking, and opting out of the rat race somehow seems far less appealing now that her passion for Birkenstocks and flares has given way to stocks and shares—

Not that he is implying that this is why she deserves to die. That would be irrational. But— would the world really miss her, he thinks? Would anyone really care if she died?

The truth, is, no one really cares. Few are the deaths that diminish us. Apart from losses within our own tribe, most of us feel nothing but indifference for the death of an outsider. Teenagers stabbed over drug money; pensioners frozen to death at home; victims of famine or war or disease; so many of us *pretend* to care, because caring is what others expect, though secretly we wonder what all the fuss is really about. Some cases affect us more profoundly. The death of a photogenic child; the occasional celebrity. But the fact is that most of us are more likely to grieve over the death of a dog or a soap opera character than over our friends and neighbours.

So thinks our hero to himself, as he follows the yellow 2CV into town, keeping a safe distance between them. Tonight he is driving a white van, a commercial vehicle stolen from a DIY retailer's forecourt at six fifteen that evening. The owner has gone home for the night, and will not notice the loss before morning, by which time it will be too late. The van will have been torched by then, and no one will link *blueeyedboy* with the serious incident that night, in which a local woman was run down on the way to her salsa class.

The *incident*—he likes that word, its lemony

scent, its tantalizing colour. Not quite an accident, but something incidental, a diversion from the main event. He can't even call it a hit-and-run, because no one does any running.

In fact, Ms Stonewash sees him coming, hears the sound of his engine rev. But Ms Stonewash ignores him. She locks the yellow 2CV, having parked it just across the road, and steps on to the pedestrian crossing without a look to left or right, heels clicking on the tarmac, skirt hem positioned just high enough to showcase those more-than-adequate legs.

Ms Stonewash subscribes to the view expressed in the slogan of a well-known line of cosmetics and hair products, a slogan he has always despised and which, to him, sums up in four words all the arrogance of those well-bred female parasites with their tinted hair and their manicured nails and their utter contempt for the rest of the world, for the young man in blue at the wheel of the van, no pale horseman by any means, but did she think Death would call by in person just because she's *worth it*?

He has to stop, she thinks to herself as she steps into the road in front of him. He has to stop at the red light. He has to stop at the crossing. He *has* to stop because I'm *me*, and I'm too important to ignore—

The impact is greater than he expects, sending her sprawling into the verge. He has to mount the kerb in order to reverse over her, and by then his engine is complaining vigorously, the suspension shot, the exhaust dragging on the ground, the radiator leaking steam—

Good thing this isn't my car, he thinks. And he

138

gives himself time for one more pass over something that now looks more like a sack of laundry than anything that ever danced the salsa, before driving away at a decent speed, because only a loser would stay to watch; and he knows from a thousand movie shows how arrogance and vanity are so often the downfall of bad guys. So he makes his modest getaway as the witnesses gather open-mouthed; antelopes at the water-hole watching the predator go by—

Returning to the scene of the crime is a luxury he cannot afford. But from the top of the multi-storey car park, armed with his camera and a long lens, he can see the aftermath of the incident: the police car; the ambulance; the little crowd; then the departure of the emergency vehicle, at far too leisurely a pace—he knows that they need a doctor to declare the victim dead at the scene, but there are instances, such as this one, when any layman's verdict would do.

*   *   *

Officially, Ms Stonewash Blue was pronounced dead on arrival.

Blueeyedboy knows that, in fact, she had expired some fifteen minutes earlier. He also knows that her mouth was turned down just like the mouth of a baby flatfish, and that the police kicked sand over the stain, so that in the morning there would be nothing to show that she'd ever been there, except for a bunch of garage flowers Sellotaped to a traffic sign—

How appropriate, he thinks. How mawkish and how commonplace. Litter on the highway now counts as a valid expression of grief. When the Princess of Wales was killed, some months before this incident, the streets were piled high with offerings, taped to every lamp post, left to rot on every wall, flowers in every stage of decay, composting in their cellophane. Every street corner had its own stack of flowers, mouldering paper, teddy bears, sympathy cards, notes and plastic wrappers, and in the heat of that late summer it stank like a municipal tip—

And why? Who was this woman to them? A face from a magazine; a walk-on part in a soap opera; an attention-seeking parasite; a woman who, in a world of freaks, just about qualified as normal?

Was she really worth all that? Those outpourings of grief and despair? The florists did well from it, anyway; the price of roses went through the roof. And in the pub later that week, when *blueeyedboy* dared to suggest that perhaps it was somewhat unnecessary, he was taken into a back street by a punter and his ugly wife, where he was given a serious talking-to—not *quite* a beating, no, but with enough slapping and shoving to bring it close—and told he wasn't welcome, and strongly advised to fuck off—

At which point in the story this punter—shall we call him Diesel Blue?—a family man, a respected member of the community, twenty years older than *blueeyedboy* and outweighing him by a hundred pounds—raised one of his loyal fists and smacked our hero right in the mouth, while the ugly wife, who smelled of cigarettes and cheap antiperspirant, laughed as *blueeyedboy* spat out blood, and said: *She's worth more dead than you'll ever be—*

140

Six months later, Diesel's van is traced through security camera footage to a hit-and-run incident in which a middle-aged woman is killed crossing the road to get to her car. The van, which since has been set on fire, still bears traces of fibre and hair, and although Diesel Blue is adamant that he is not responsible, that the van was stolen the night before, he fails to convince the magistrate, especially in the light of a previous history of drunkenness and violence. The case goes to the criminal court, where, after a four-day trial, Diesel Blue is acquitted, mostly for lack of evidence. The camera footage proves disappointing, failing as it does to confirm the identity of the driver of the van—a figure in a hoodie and baseball cap, whose bulk may be due to an oversized coat and whose face is never visible.

But to be acquitted in court is not everything. Graffiti on the walls of the house; hostile murmurs in the pub; letters to the local Press; all suggest that Diesel Blue got away with it on a technicality, and when, a few weeks later, his house catches fire (with Diesel and his wife inside), no one grieves especially.

Verdict—accidental death, possibly caused by a cigarette.

Blueeyedboy is unsurprised. He'd had the guy down as a smoker.

Post comment:
Captainbunnykiller: *You are totally sick, dude. I love it!*
chrysalisbaby: *woot woot yay for* **blueeyedboy**
ClairDeLune: *Very interesting. I sense your mistrust of authority. I'd love to hear the story behind this story. Is it also based on real life events? You know I'd love to know more!*
JennyTricks: (*post deleted*).

You are viewing the webjournal of **blueeyedboy**
posting on:

badguysrock@webjournal.com

Posted at: *21.06 on Monday, February 4*
Status: *public*
Mood: *prickly*
Listening to: *Poison*: 'Every Rose Has Its
Thorn'

The birth of little Emily White saw a change in
blueeyedboy's Ma. She'd always been quick-
tempered, but by the end of the summer she
seemed perpetually on the brink of some kind of
violent eruption. Part of the cause was financial
stress: growing boys are expensive, and by
unfortunate coincidence, fewer and fewer people
in the Village seemed to need any household help.
Mrs French Blue had joined the ranks of her
ex-employers, and Mrs Chemical Blue, claiming
poverty, had reduced her hours to two per week.
Perhaps, now Ben was back at school, people felt
less charitably inclined to offer work to the
fatherless family. Or perhaps they'd simply had
enough of listening to tales of how talented and
special Ben was.

And then, just before Christmas, they ran across
Mrs Electric Blue near Tandy's in the covered
market, but she didn't seem to notice them, even
when Ma spoke to her.

Perhaps Mrs Electric Blue didn't like being seen so close to the market, where there were always people shouting, and torn-off cabbage leaves on the floor, and everything peppered with brown grease, and where people always called you *luv*. Perhaps all that was too common for her. Perhaps she was ashamed of knowing Ma, with her old coat on and her hair scraped back and her three scruffy boys, and her bags full of shopping that she had to carry home on the bus, and her hands with palms all tattooed with dirt from other people's housework.

'Morning,' said Ma, and Mrs Electric Blue just stared, looking weirdly like one of Mrs White's dolls, half-surprised and half-not-quite alive, with her pink mouth pursed and her eyebrows raised and her long white coat with the fur collar making her look like the Snow Queen, even though there wasn't any snow.

It seemed at first as if she hadn't heard. Ben shot her the smile that had once earned him treats. Mrs Electric didn't smile back, but turned away and pretended to look at some clothes that were hanging on a stall near by, although even *blueeyedboy* could see that they weren't at all the kind of clothes she'd wear, all baggy blouses and cheap, shiny shoes. He wondered if he should call her name—

But Ma went red and said: *Come on*, and started to drag him away by the arm. He tried to explain, which was when Nigel punched him, just above the elbow, where it hurts most, and he hid his face in his cry-baby sleeve, and Ma slapped Nigel across the head. And he saw Mrs Electric Blue walk away towards the shops, where a young man—a *very*

144

young man—dressed in a navy pea coat and jeans, was awaiting her impatiently, and would perhaps have kissed her, he thought, had it not been for the presence of the cleaner and her three kids, one of whom was still watching her with that look of reproach, as if he knew something he shouldn't. And that made her walk a little faster, clipping the ground with her high heels, a sound that smells of cigarettes and cabbage leaves and cheap perfume at knock-off prices.

Then, a week later, she let Ma go—making it sound like a generous gesture, saying that she'd imposed too long—which left just two of her ladies, plus a couple of shifts at St Oswald's per week; hardly enough to pay the rent, let alone feed three boys.

So Ma took another job, working on a market stall, from which she would return frozen and exhausted, but carrying a plastic bag filled with half-rotten fruit and other stuff they couldn't sell, which she would serve up in various guises over the course of the week, or worse still, put in the blender to make what she called 'the vitamin drink', which might be made up of such diverse ingredients as cabbage, apple, beetroot, carrot, tomato, peach or celery, but which always tasted to *blueeyedboy* like a sweet-rotten slurry of sludge-green. The tube of paint might be labelled Nut Brown, but shit smells like shit all the same, and it always made him think of the market, so that in time even the word made him retch—*mark-et*—with its barking twin syllables, like an engine that won't start, and all that was because they happened to see Mrs Electric Blue with her fancy-boy in the market that day.

145

That was why, when they saw her again, six weeks later, in the street, that sickly taste rushed into his mouth, a sharp pain stabbed at his temple, objects around him began to acquire a bevelled, prismic quality—

'Why, Gloria,' said Mrs Electric Blue in that sweetly venomous manner of hers. 'How lovely to see you. You're looking well. How's Ben doing at school?'

Ma gave her a sharp look. 'Oh, he's doing *very* well. His tutor says he's *gifted*—'

It was common knowledge in Malbry that Mrs Electric Blue's son was *not* gifted; that he had tried for St Oswald's, but hadn't got in, then had failed to get into Oxford, in spite of private tutoring. A big disappointment, so they said. Mrs Electric's hopes had been high.

'Really?' said Mrs Electric Blue. She made the word sound like some new and frosty brand of toothpaste.

'Yes. My son's got a tutor. He's trying for St Oswald's.'

Blueeyedboy hid a grimace behind his hand, but not before Ma had noticed.

'He's going to be a scholarship boy.' That was bending the truth a little. Dr Peacock's offer to tutor Ben was payment for his cooperation in his research. His ability remained, as yet, a matter for conjecture.

Still, Mrs Electric Blue was impressed, which was probably Ma's intention.

But now *blueeyedboy* was trying not to be sick as waves of nausea washed over him, flooding him with that market smell, that sludgy-brown stink of the vitamin drink; of split tomatoes gone to white-

146

lipped mush, and half-gone apples (*The brown's the sweetest part*, she'd say), and black bananas and cabbage leaves. It wasn't just the memory, or the sound of her heels on the cobbled street, or even her voice with its high-bred yarking syllables—

It's not my fault, he told himself. *I'm not a bad person. Really, I'm not.*

But that didn't stop the sick smell, or the colours, or the pain in his head. Instead it made it weirdly worse, like driving past something dead in the road and wishing you'd looked at it properly—

Blue is the colour of murder, he thought, and the sick, panicky feeling abated—a little. He thought of Mrs Electric Blue lying dead on a mortuary slab with a tag on her toe, like a nicely labelled Christmas present; and every time he thought of it, the sludgy stink receded again, and the headache dimmed to a dull throb, and the colours around him brightened a little, all merging together to make one blue—oxygen blue, gas-jet blue, circuit-board blue, autopsy blue—

He tried a smile. It felt OK. The rotten-fruit smell had disappeared, although it did come back at regular intervals throughout the whole of *blueeyedboy*'s childhood, as did the phrases his mother spoke that day to Mrs Electric Blue—

Benjamin's a good boy.
We're so proud of Benjamin.

And always with the same, sick knowledge that he was *not* a good boy; that he was crooked in every cell—that, worse still, he *liked* it that way—

And even then, he must have known—

That one day he would kill her.

Post comment:
ClairDeLune: *Very good,* **blueeyedboy!**
chrysalisbaby: *awesome U R so cool*
JennyTricks: (*post deleted*).
JennyTricks: (*post deleted*).

> *You are viewing the webjournal of* **blueeyedboy**
> *posting on*:
>   **badguysrock@webjournal.com**
> **Posted at**: *21.43 on Monday, February 4*
> **Status**: *public*
> **Mood**: *deluded*
> **Listening to**: *Murray Head*: 'So Strong'

That year, things went from bad to worse. Ma was mean, money was tight and no one, not even Benjamin, seemed to be able to please her. She no longer worked for Mrs White, and if Mrs White ever came to her stall at the market, Ma made sure someone else served her instead, and pretended not to notice.

Then there were the rumours that had begun to circulate. *Blueeyedboy* was never sure what exactly was being said, but he was aware of the whispers and of the sudden silences that sometimes fell whenever Mrs White approached, and of the way the neighbours looked at him when he was at the market. He thought it might have something to do with Feather Dunne, a gossip and a busybody who had moved into the Village last spring, who had befriended Mrs White and who often helped out with Emily, although why she should scorn *blueeyedboy*'s ma was still a mystery to him. But whatever it was, the poison spread. Soon, everyone seemed to be whispering.

Blueeyedboy wondered if he should try to talk to Mrs White, to ask her what had happened. He'd always liked her best of Ma's ladies, and she had always been nice to him. Surely, if he approached her, she'd change her mind about letting Ma go, and they could be friends again—

One day he came home from school early and saw Mrs White's car parked outside. A surge of relief came over him. They were talking again, he told himself. Whatever their quarrel had been, it was over.

But when he looked through the window he saw, instead of Mrs White, Mr White standing there beside the china cabinet.

Blueeyedboy had never had much to do with Mr White. He'd seen him in the Village, of course, and at St Oswald's, where he worked, but never like this, never at home, and never without his wife, of course—

He must have come straight from St Oswald's. He was wearing a long coat and carrying a satchel. A man of middle height and build; darkish hair turning to grey; small, neat hands; blue eyes behind his wire-rimmed glasses. A mild, soft-spoken, diffident man, never taking centre stage. But now Mr White was different. *Blueeyedboy* could feel it. Living with Ma had given him a special sensitivity to any sign of tension or rage. And Mr White was angry; *blueeyedboy* could see it in the way he stood, tensed, immobile, under control.

Blueeyedboy edged closer, making sure to keep well out of sight under the line of the privet hedge. Through a gap in the branches he could see Ma, her profile slightly averted, standing next to Mr

150

White. She was wearing her high-heeled shoes—he could tell, they always made her look taller. Even so, her head only reached the curve of Mr White's shoulder. She raised her eyes to his, and for a moment they stood without moving, Ma smiling, Mr White holding her gaze.

And then Mr White reached into his coat and pulled out something that *blueeyedboy* thought at first was a paperback. Ma took it, split the spine, and then *blueeyedboy* realized that it was a wad of banknotes, snappy and fresh and unmarked—

But why was Mr White paying Ma? And why did it make him so angry?

It was then that a thought came to *blueeyedboy*; one of curiously adult clarity. What if the father he had never known—Mr Blue Eyes—was Mr White? What if Mrs White had found out? It would explain her hostility as well as the talk in the Village. It would explain so many things—Ma's job at St Oswald's, where he taught; her open resentment of his wife; and now this gift of money—

Shielded from view by the privet hedge, *blueeyedboy* craned his neck to see; to detect in this man's features the faintest reflection of his own—

The movement must have alerted him. For a moment their eyes met. Mr White's eyes widened suddenly, and *blueeyedboy* saw him flinch—which was when our hero turned and fled. The question of whether Mr White could have been his father or not was entirely secondary to the fact that Ma would certainly flay him alive if she caught him spying on her.

But as far as he could tell, Mr White said nothing to Ma about seeing a boy at the window.

151

Instead Ma seemed in good spirits, and ceased to complain about money, and as the weeks and months passed without any further disruption, *blueeyedboy*'s suspicions increased, at last becoming a certainty—

Patrick White was his father.

Post comment:
ClairDeLune: *I like the way your stories combine 'real-life' events with fiction. Perhaps you'd like to come back to Group and discuss the process of writing this? I'm sure the others would appreciate an insight into your emotional journey.*
JennyTricks: (*post deleted*).
blueeyedboy: *Jenny, do I know you?*
JennyTricks: (*post deleted*).
blueeyedboy: *Seriously*. Do I know you?

You are viewing the webjournal of **blueeyedboy**.
Posted at: *22.35 on Monday, February 4*
Status: *restricted*
Mood: *amused*
Listening to: *Black Sabbath*: 'Paranoid'

Well, if you won't answer me, I'll simply delete your entries. You're on my turf now, *JennyTricks*, and my rules apply. But it feels as if I know you. Could it be that we've met before? Could it be that you're stalking me?

Stalking. Now there's a sinister word. Like part of a plant, a bitter-green stalk that will one day bloom into something sickening. But online, things are different. Online, as fictional characters, we can sometimes allow ourselves the luxury of antisocial behaviour. I'm sick of hearing about how so-and-so *felt so violated* at such-and-such's comments, or how somebody else felt sexually besmirched at some harmless innuendo. Oh, these people with their sensitivities. Excuse me, but writing a comment in capitals *isn't* the same as shouting. Venting a little vitriol isn't the same as a physical blow. So vent away, *JennyTricks*. Nothing you say can touch me. Although I'll admit, I'm curious. Tell me, *have* we met before?

The rest of my online audience shows a pleasing level of appreciation—especially *ClairDeLune*, who sends me a critique (her word) of every single fic I write, with comments on style and imagery. My last attempt, she tells me, is both psychologically intuitive and a breakthrough into a new and more mature style.

Cap, less subtle, as always, pleads for more drama, more anguish, more blood. Toxic, who thinks about sex all the time, urges me to write more explicitly. Or, as he puts it: *Whatever gets your rocks off, dude. Just try to think about mine some time . . .*

As for Chryssie, she just sends me love— adoring, uncritical, slavish love—with a message that says: *Ur made of awesome!* on a banner made up of little pink hearts—

Albertine does not comment. She rarely does on my stories. Perhaps they make her uncomfortable. I hope so. Why post them otherwise?

I saw her again this afternoon. Red coat, black hair, basket over her arm, walking down the hill into Malbry town. I had my camera with me this time, the one with the telephoto lens, and I managed to get a few clear shots from the little piece of waste ground at the top of Mill Road before a man walking his dog forced me to curtail my investigation.

He gave me a suspicious look. He was short, bow-legged, muscular; the type of man who always seems to hate and distrust me on sight. His dog was the same; bandy, off-white; big teeth and no eyes. It growled when it saw me. I took a step back.

'Birds,' I said, by means of explanation. 'I like to come here and photograph birds.'

The man eyed me with open contempt. 'Aye, I'll bet.'

He watched me go with no further comment,

154

but I could feel his eyes in the small of my back. I'll have to be more careful, I thought. People already think I'm a freak—and the last thing I want is for someone to remember later how Gloria Winter's boy was seen lurking around Mill Road with a camera—

And yet, I can't stop watching her. It's almost a compulsion. God knows what Ma would do if she knew. Still, Ma has other fish to fry in the wake (ha!) of Nigel's funeral, though the task of clearing out his flat has fallen to Yours Truly.

Not that there is much to find. His telescope; a few clothes; his computer; half a shelf of old books. Some papers from the hospital in a shoebox under the bed. I'd expected more—a journal, at least—but maybe experience had made him more cautious. If Nigel kept a journal at all, it was probably at Emily's house, where he'd been staying most of the time, and where he could almost certainly rely on its safety from prying eyes.

There is no sign of Nigel's girl here. Not a trace, not a hair, not a photograph. The narrow bed is still unmade, the quilt pulled roughly over the dubious sheet, but she has never slept here. There is no fleeting scent of her, no toothbrush of hers in the bathroom, no coffee cup in the sink bearing the imprint of her mouth. The flat smells of unaired bed, of stale water, of damp, and it will take me less than half a day to clear the contents into the back of a van and to drive it to the refuse site, where anything of value will be sorted and recycled, and the rest consigned to landfill, to the misery of future generations.

It's funny, isn't it, how little a life amounts to? A few old clothes, a box of papers, some dirty plates in the sink? A half-smoked packet of cigarettes, tucked away in a bedside drawer—*she* doesn't smoke, so he kept them here, for those nights when, unable to sleep, he would look out through the skylight with his telescope, trying to see, through the light pollution, the crystal webwork of the stars.

Yes, my brother liked stars. That was pretty much all he liked. Certainly, he never liked *me*. Well, neither of them did, of course, but it was Nigel I feared; Nigel, who had suffered most in the face of Ma's expectations—

Oh, those expectations. I wonder what Nigel made of them. Watching from the sidelines, pallid in his black shirts, bony fists perpetually clenched, so that when he opened up his hands you'd see the little crescents of red that his fingernails had left in his palm, marks he transferred on to my skin whenever he and I were alone—

Nigel's flat is monochrome. Grey sheets under a black-and-white quilt; a wardrobe in shades of charcoal and black. You'd have thought he might have quit that by now, but time has made no difference to my brother's colour scheme. Socks, jackets, sweaters, jeans. Not a shirt, not a T-shirt, not even a pair of underpants that is not the official black or grey—

Nigel was five when Dad left home. I've often wondered about that. Did he remember wearing colours, when he was still the only child? Did he sometimes go to the beach and play on the salty yellow sand? Or did he lie there with Dad at night and point out the constellations? What was he really looking for, scanning the skies with his Junior Telescope (paid for with money from his

156

newspaper round)? Where did his anger come from? Most of all, why was it decreed that *he* should be black, or Ben should be blue? And if our roles had been reversed, would things have turned out differently?

I guess I'll never know now. Maybe I should have asked him. But Nigel and I never really talked, not even back when we were kids. We coexisted side by side, waging a kind of guerrilla war in defiance of Ma's disapproval, each one inflicting as much damage as he could on to the hated enemy.

My brother never knew me, except as the focus of his rage. And the only time I ever found out anything intimate about him, I kept the knowledge to myself, fearing the possible consequences. But if each man kills the thing he loves, must not the opposite also be true? Does each man love the thing he kills? And is love the ingredient that I lack?

I turned on his computer. Skimmed briefly through his favourites. The result was as I'd suspected: links to the Hubble telescope; to images of galaxies; to webcams at the North Pole; to chat rooms in which photographers discussed the latest solar eclipse. Some porn, all of it plain-vanilla; some legally downloaded music. I went into his e-mail—he'd left the password open—but found nothing of interest there. Not a word from *Albertine*; no e-mails, no photographs, no sign that he'd ever known her.

No sign of anyone else, either; no official correspondence, except for the monthly line or two from his therapist; no proof of some clandestine affair; not even a quick note from a friend. My brother had fewer friends than I, and the thought is strangely touching. But now isn't the time to feel sympathy. My brother knew the risks from the start. He shouldn't have got in the way, that's all. It wasn't my fault that he did.

I found the cleanest mug he had and made a cup of tea. It wasn't Earl Grey, but it would do. Then I logged on to *badguysrock*.

Albertine wasn't online. But Chryssie, as always, was waiting for me, her avatar blinking forlornly. Beneath it, an emoticon, coupled with the plaintive message: *chrysalisbaby is feeling sick*.

Well, I'm not entirely surprised. Syrup of ipecac can have some unpleasant side effects. Still, that's hardly my fault, and today I have more pressing concerns.

I glanced quickly through my mailbox. *Captainbunnykiller is feeling good. BombNumber20 is feeling bored.* A meme from Clair entitled: *Try this simple test to know—What kind of a psycho are you?*

Mmm. Cute. And typical Clair, whose knowledge of human psychology—such as it is—is mostly gleaned from cop shows, shows with names like *Blue Murder*, in which feisty female profilers hunt down bed-wetting sociopaths by Getting Inside the Criminal Mind—

So what kind of psycho am I, Clair? Let's look at the results.

Mostly Ds. Congratulations! You are a malignant narcissist. *You are glib, charming, manipulative, and have little or no regard for others. You enjoy notoriety, and are willing to commit acts of violence to satisfy your craving*

158

for instant gratification, although secretly you may harbour feelings of inadequacy. You may also suffer from paranoia, and you have a tendency to live in a dream world in which you are the perpetual centre of attention. You need to get professional help, as you are a potential danger to yourself and others.

Dear Clair. I'm very fond of her. And it's really rather touching that she thinks that she can analyse me. But she has a junior social-worker mentality at best, for all her spit and psychobabble, and besides, she's none too stable herself, as we may discover in due course.

You see, even Clair takes risks online. During what passes for her 'real' work—handing out praise to the talentless and platitudinous comfort to the existentially challenged—she secretly spends hours online updating her fansite on Angel Blue, making banners, searching the Net for pictures, comments, interviews, rumours, guest appearances or any information regarding his current whereabouts. She also writes to him regularly, and has posted on her own website a small collection of his handwritten replies, which are courteous but impersonal, and which only someone truly obsessed would ever take as encouragement . . .

Clair, however, *is* truly obsessed. Thanks to my link to her WeJay, I know that she writes fan fiction about his characters—and sometimes about the man himself—erotic fics that, over the months, are becoming increasingly daring. She also paints portraits of her loved one, and makes cushions on to which she prints his face. Her bedroom at home is filled with these cushions, mostly in pink—her favourite colour—some of them also depicting *her* face next to his, inside a printed heart.

She follows his wife's career, too—an actress to whom he has been happily married for the past five or six years—although recently Clair may have begun to indulge in hopeful speculation. An online friend—who logs on under the name *sapphiregirl* —has informed her of a liaison between Angel's wife and a co-worker on the set of her new film.

This has led to a spate of attacks on Mrs Angel in some of Clair's recent journal posts. Her last post makes her feelings more than clear. She does not want to see Angel hurt; and she is slightly bewildered that a man of his intelligence has not yet come to terms with the fact that his wife is— well, *unworthy*.

The fact that there *was* no such liaison is surely no fault of *sapphiregirl*—these rumours are so easily spread, and how could she possibly have known that Clair would respond so impulsively? It will be interesting to see how Clair reacts if— *when*—Angel's lawyers write to her.

How can I be so sure, you ask? Well, Internet mail can be ignored, but a letter to Mrs Angel's address, and the accompanying box of chocolates (in this case containing an unexpected surprise), all traceable to *ClairDeLune* and posted within five miles of her house—are altogether more sinister.

She will, of course, deny it. But will Angel Blue believe her? And Clair is such a devoted fan: she travels to America to see her idol on the stage; she goes to every convention where she might get a glimpse of him. What might she do on receipt of— let's say, a court order, or even just a rebuke from her man? I suspect her to be volatile—perhaps even slightly deranged. What would it take to make her flip? And wouldn't it be fun to find out?

But for now I have other things on my mind. A man should always clean up after himself. And Nigel is, after all, my mess—my mess, if not my murder.

Does murder run in families? I can almost think it does. Who's next, I wonder? Myself, perhaps, dead of an overdose, maybe, or found beaten to death in an alleyway? A car crash? A hit-and-run? Or will it look like suicide, a bottle of pills by the side of the bath, a bloodstained razor on the tiles?

It could be anything, of course. The killer could be anyone. So play it safe. Don't take any risks. Remember what happened to the other two—

Watch your back, *blueeyedboy*.

You are viewing the webjournal of **blueeyedboy** *posting on*:

badguysrock@webjournal.com

Posted at: *01.22 on Tuesday, February 5*
Status: *public*
Mood: *cautious*
Listening to: *Altered Images*: 'Happy Birthday'

He has always been good at watching his back. Over the years, he has had to learn. Accidents happen so easily, and the men in his family have always been particularly prone to them. It turns out that even his dad, whom *blueeyedboy* had always assumed had simply gone out to buy cigarettes and never bothered to come back, had met with a fatal accident: in his case, a car crash, no one's fault—the kind that the folks at Malbry Infirmary call a *Saturday Night Special*. Too much alcohol; too little patience, maybe a marital crisis and—

—*Wham!*

And so it should come as no surprise that *blueeyedboy* should have turned out this way. No guiding paternal influence; a controlling, ambitious mother; an elder brother who tended to solve all problems with his fists. It's hardly rocket science, is it? And he is more than familiar with the rudiments of psychoanalysis.

Congratulations! You are an Oedipal. *Your unusually close relationship with your mother has stifled your ability to grow into an emotionally balanced human being. Your ambivalence towards her emerges in violent fantasies, often sexual in nature.*

Well—*duh*, as Cap might say.

Nigel may have missed his dad, but the man meant nothing to *blueeyedboy*. He wasn't even *blueeyedboy*'s *real* father—certainly, from his photographs, he sees no resemblance to himself. To Nigel, perhaps: the big, square hands; the black hair falling across the face; the slightly over-pretty mouth, with its hidden threat of violence. Ma often hinted that Peter Winter was possessed of a nasty streak; and if one of them misbehaved, she'd say— whilst wielding that piece of electrical cord—*It's a good thing for you your father's not here. He'd soon sort you out.*

And so the word *father* came to have—shall we say—negative connotations. A loose-lipped, greenish, bilious sound, like the murky water under Blackpool pier, where they used to go on his birthday. *Blueeyedboy* always liked the beach, but the pier itself frightened him, looking as it did like a fossilized animal—a dinosaur maybe—all bones, but still quite dangerous with its muddy feet and broken teeth.

Pier. Peter. *Pierre*, in French. *Sticks and stones may break my bones*—

After seeing Mr White with his ma, our hero's curiosity regarding Patrick White had increased. He found himself watching Mr White whenever he saw him in the Village—walking to St Oswald's

163

with his satchel in one hand and a pile of exercise books in the other; in the park on Sundays with Mrs White and Emily—now two years old and learning to walk—playing games, making her laugh—

It occurred to him that if Mr White were his father, then Emily must be his sister. He imagined himself with a little sister: helping his Ma look after her; reading her stories at bedtime. He began to follow them; to sit in the park where they liked to go, pretending to read a book while he watched—

He hadn't dared ask Ma for the truth. Besides, he didn't need to. He could feel it in his heart. Patrick White *was* his father. Sometimes our hero liked to dream that one day his father would come and take him somewhere far away—

He would have shared, he tells himself. He would have shared him with Emily. But Mr White went out of his way to avoid even having to look at him. A man who, until then, had always greeted him genially in the street; had always called him *young man* and asked how he was doing at school.

It wasn't just because Emily was so much more appealing. There was something in Mr White's face, in his voice whenever our hero approached him; a look of wariness, almost of fear—

But what could Mr White possibly fear from a boy of only nine years old? Our hero had no way of knowing. Was he afraid that *blueeyedboy* might want to harm Emily? Or was he afraid that Mrs White would one day discover his secret?

He started skipping classes at school to hang around St Oswald's. He would hide behind the utility shed and watch the yard as lessons changed:

164

the stream of boys in blue uniforms; the Masters in their flapping black gowns. On Tuesdays it was Mr White who supervised the schoolyard, and *blueeyedboy* would watch him avidly from his hiding-place as he moved across the asphalt, stopping every now and again to exchange a few words with a pupil—

'*String quartet tonight, Jones. Don't forget your music.*'

'*No, sir. Thank you, sir.*'

'*Tuck your shirt in, Hudson, please. You're not on the beach at Brighton, you know.*'

Blueeyedboy remembers one Tuesday, which happened to be his tenth birthday. Not that he expected much in the way of celebration. That year had been especially grim, except for his trips to the Mansion; money was tight; Ma was stressed, and a trip to Blackpool was out of the question—there was too much work to do. Even a birthday cake, he thought, was probably too much to hope for. Even so, that morning, there seemed to be something special in the air. He was ten years old. The big one-oh. His life was in double digits. Perhaps it was time, he told himself, as he headed towards St Oswald's, to find out the truth about Patrick White—

He found him in the schoolyard, a couple of minutes before the end of School Assembly. Mr White was standing by the entrance to the Middle School Quad, his faded gown slung over his arm, a mug of coffee in one hand. In a minute or two the yard would be filled with boys; now it was deserted, except, of course, for *blueeyedboy*, made instantly conspicuous by dint of his lack of uniform, standing beneath the entrance gate with the

165

school's motto emblazoned on it in Latin—*Audere, agere, auferre*—which, thanks to Dr Peacock, he knows means: *to dare, to strive, to conquer.*

Suddenly, our *blueeyedboy* did not feel very daring. He was desperately sure he would stutter; that the words he so badly wanted to speak would break and crumble in his mouth. And even without the black robe, Mr White looked forbidding: taller and sterner than usual, watching our hero's determined approach, listening to the sound of his shoes on the cobbled courtyard—

'What are you doing here, boy?' he said, and his voice, though soft, was glacial. 'Why have you been following me?'

Blueeyedboy looked at him. Mr White's blue eyes seemed a very long way up. 'M-Mr White—' he began. 'I—I—'

Stuttering begins in the mind. It's the curse of expectation. That's why he was able to speak perfectly normally at certain times, while at others his words turned to Silly String, tangling him uselessly in a web of his own making.

'I— I—' Our hero could feel his face turning red.

Mr White regarded him. 'Look, I don't have time for this. The bell's going to ring any moment now—'

Blueeyedboy made a final effort. He *had* to know the truth, he thought. After all, today was his birthday. He tried to see himself in blue: St Oswald's blue, or butterfly blue. He saw the words like butterflies coming out of his open mouth, and said, with barely a stutter at all—

'Mr White, are you my dad?'

For a moment the silence bound them. Then,

166

just as the morning bell sounded through St Oswald's, *blueeyedboy* saw Patrick White's face change from shock to astonishment, and then to a kind of stunned pity.

'Is *that* what you thought?' he said at last.

Blueeyedboy just looked at him. Around them, the courtyard was filling up with blue St Oswald's blazers. Chirping voices all around, circling like birds. Some of the boys gaped at him, a single sparrow in a flock of budgerigars.

After a moment, Mr White seemed to come out of his stupor. 'Listen,' he said in a firm voice. 'I don't know where you got this idea. But it isn't true. Really, it's not. And if I catch you spreading these rumours—'

'You're *n-not* my f-father?' said *blueeyedboy*, his voice beginning to tremble.

'No,' said Mr White. 'I'm not.'

For a moment the words seemed to make no sense. *Blueeyedboy* had been so sure. But Mr White was telling the truth; he could see it in his blue eyes. But then—why had he given money to Ma? And why had he done it in secret?

And then it fell into place in his mind like the moving parts of a Mouse Trap game. He supposed it had been obvious. Ma was blackmailing Mr White—*blackmail*, a sinister word; the Black and White Minstrels under their paint. Mr White had transgressed, and Ma had somehow found out about it. That would explain the whisperings; the way Mrs White looked at Ma; Mr White's anger, and now his contempt. This man was not his father, he thought. This man had never cared for him.

And now *blueeyedboy* could feel the tears

beginning to prick at his eyelids. Terrible, helpless, childish tears of disappointment and of shame. *Please, not in front of Mr White*, he begged of the Almighty, but God, like Ma, was implacable. Like Ma, Our Father sometimes needs that gesture of contrition.

'Are you OK?' said Mr White, reluctantly putting a hand on his arm.

'Fine, thanks,' said *blueeyedboy*, wiping his nose with the back of his hand.

'I don't know how you got the idea that—'

'Forget it. Really. I'm fine,' he said, and very calmly walked away, keeping his spine as straight as he could, although he was a mess inside, although it felt like dying.

It's my birthday, he told himself. *Today, I deserve to be special. Whatever it takes, whatever it costs, whatever punishment God or Ma can possibly inflict on me*—

And that's how, fifteen minutes later, he found himself, not back at school, but at the end of Millionaires' Row, looking towards the Mansion.

*   *   *

It was the first time that *blueeyedboy* had been to the Mansion unsupervised. His visits with his brothers and Ma were always strictly controlled, and he knew that if Ma found out what he'd done, she'd make him sorry he'd ever been born. But today he wasn't afraid of Ma. Today, a breath of rebellion seemed to have taken hold of him. Today, for once, *blueeyedboy* was in the mood for a spot of trespass.

The garden was shielded from the road by a set

of cast-iron railings. At the far end there was a stone wall, and all around, a blackthorn hedge. On the whole, it didn't look promising. But *blueeyedboy* was determined. He found a space through which to crawl, mindful of the twigs and thorns that snagged at his hair and stuck through his T-shirt, and emerged on the other side of the hedge into the grounds of the Mansion.

Ma always called it 'the grounds'. Dr Peacock called it 'the garden', although there was over four acres of it, orchard and kitchen garden and lawns, plus the walled rose garden in which Dr Peacock took so much pride, the pond and the old conservatory, where pots and gardening tools were kept. Most of it was trees, though, which suited *blueeyedboy* just fine, with alleys of rhododendrons that flared brief glory in springtime and in late summer grew skeletal, encroaching darkly across the path, the perfect cover for anyone wishing to visit the garden unseen—

Blueeyedboy did not question the impulse that had driven him to the Mansion. He couldn't go back to St Oswald's, though, not now, after what had happened. He dared not go back home, of course, and at school he'd be punished for being late. But the Mansion was quiet, and secret, and safe. Simply to be there was enough; to dive into the undergrowth; to hear the summery sounds of the bees high up in the leafy canopy, and to feel the beating of his heart slow down to its natural cadence. He was still so immersed in his agitated thoughts that, walking along an alley of trees, he almost ran into Dr Peacock, who was standing, secateurs in hand, shirtsleeves rolled to the elbow, at the entrance to the rose garden.

'And what brings *you* here this morning?'

For a moment *blueeyedboy* was quite unable to answer. Then he looked past Dr Peacock and saw: the newly dug grave; the mound of earth, the rolled square of turf laid aside on the ground—

Dr Peacock smiled at him. It was a rather complex smile; sad and complicit at the same time. 'I'm afraid you've caught me in the act,' he said, indicating the fresh grave. 'I know how this may look to you, but as we grow older our capacity for sentiment expands to an exponential degree. To you it may look like senility—'

Blueeyedboy stared at him with a perfect lack of comprehension.

'What I mean is,' Dr Peacock said, 'I was just bidding a last goodbye to a very loyal old friend.'

For a moment *blueeyedboy* was still unsure of what he'd meant. Then he remembered Dr Peacock's Jack Russell, over which the old man always made such a fuss. *Blueeyedboy* didn't like dogs. Too eager; too unpredictable.

He shivered, feeling vaguely sick. He tried to remember the name of the dog, but all he could think of was *Malcolm*, the name of his would-have-been-sibling, and his eyes filled with tears for no reason, and his head began to ache—

Dr Peacock put a hand on his arm. 'Don't be upset, son. He had a good life. Are you all right? You're shivering.'

'I don't feel so w-well,' said *blueeyedboy*.

'Really? Well, then, we'd better get you in the house, hadn't we? I'll get you something cool to drink. And then perhaps I should call your mother—'

'No! Please!' said *blueeyedboy*.

170

Dr Peacock gave him a look. 'All right,' he said. 'I understand. You don't want to alarm her. A fine woman in many ways, but somewhat over-protective. And besides—' His eyes creased in a mischievous smile. 'Am I correct in assuming that on this bright summer morning, the delights of the school curriculum were not enough to keep you indoors when all of Nature's syllabus demanded your urgent attention?'

Blueeyedboy took this to mean that his truancy had been noted. 'Please, sir. Don't tell Ma.'

Dr Peacock shook his head. 'I see no reason to tell her,' he said. 'I was a boy myself, once. Slugs and snails and puppy-dogs' tails. Fishing in the river. Are you fond of fishing, young man?'

Blueeyedboy nodded, even though he'd never tried it; never would.

'Excellent pastime. Gets you outdoors. Of course, I have my gardening—' He glanced over his shoulder at the mound of earth and the open grave. 'Give me a moment, will you?' he said. 'Then I'll fix us both a drink.'

Blueeyedboy watched in silence as Dr Peacock filled in the grave. He didn't really want to look, but he found that he couldn't look away. His chest was tight, his lips were numb, his head was spinning dizzily. Was he really ill, he thought? Or was it the sound of digging, he thought; the tinny rasp of the spade as it bit, the sour-vegetable scent, the crazy thump as each packet of earth clattered into the open grave?

At last Dr Peacock put down the spade, but he did not turn immediately. Instead he stood by the burial mound, hands in pockets, head bowed, for such a long time that *blueeyedboy* wondered if he

171

had been forgotten.

'Are you all right, sir?' he said at last.

At his voice, Dr Peacock turned. He had taken off his gardening hat, and without it the sunlight made him squint. 'How sentimental you must find me,' he said. 'All this ceremony over a dog. Have you ever kept a dog?'

Blueeyedboy shook his head.

'Too bad. Every boy should have one. Still, you've got your brothers,' he said. 'Bet that's lot of fun, eh?'

For a moment, *blueeyedboy* tried to imagine the world as Dr Peacock saw it: a world where brothers were lots of fun; where boys went fishing, kept dogs; played cricket on the green—

'It's my birthday today,' he said.

'Is that so? Today?'

'Yes, sir.'

Dr Peacock smiled. 'Ah. I remember birthdays. Jelly and ice cream and birthday cake. Not that I tend to celebrate nowadays. August the twenty-fourth, isn't it? Mine was on the twenty-third. I'd forgotten until you reminded me.' Now he looked thoughtfully at the boy. 'I think we should mark the occasion,' he said. 'I can't claim to offer much in the way of refreshments, but I do have tea, and some iced buns, and anyway—' At this he grinned, suddenly looking mischievous, like a young boy wearing a false beard and a very convincing old-man's disguise: 'We Virgos should stick together.'

It doesn't sound much, does it? A cup of Earl Grey, an iced bun and the stub of a candle burning on top. But to *blueeyedboy* that day stands out in memory like a gilded minaret against a barren landscape. He remembers every detail now with

172

perfect, heightened precision: the little blue roses on the cup; the sound of spoon against china; the amber colour and scent of the tea; the angle of the sunlight. Little things, but their poignancy is like a reminder of innocence. Not that he ever *was* innocent; but on that day he approached it; and looking back, he understands that this was the last of his childhood, slipping like sand through his fingers—

Post comment:

ClairDeLune: *I'm glad to see you exploring this theme in more detail,* **blueeyedboy**. *Your central character often appears as cold and emotionless, and I like the way you hint at his hidden vulnerability. I'm sending you a reading-list of books you may find useful. Perhaps you'd like to make a few notes before our next meeting. Hope to see you back here soon!*

chrysalisbaby: *wish i could be there too (cries)*

You are viewing the webjournal of **blueeyedboy**
posting on:
                                badguysrock@webjournal.com
Posted at: *01.45 on Tuesday, February 5*
Status: *public*
Mood: *predatory*
Listening to: *Nirvana*: 'Smells Like Teen Spirit'

After that, Dr Peacock became a kind of hero to
blueeyedboy. It would have been surprising had he
not: Dr Peacock was everything he admired.
Dazzled by his personality, hungry for his approval,
he lived for those brief interludes, his visits to the
Mansion; hanging on to every word Dr Peacock
addressed to him—

All *blueeyedboy* remembers now are fragments
of benevolence. A walk through the rose garden; a
cup of Earl Grey; a word exchanged in passing. His
need had not yet turned to greed, or his affection
to jealousy. And Dr Peacock had the gift of making
them *all* feel special—not just Ben, but his
brothers, too; even Ma, who was hard as nails, was
not beyond the reach of his charm.

Then came the year of the entrance exam.
Benjamin was ten years old. Three and a half years
had passed since his first visit to the Mansion. Over
that time, many things had changed. He was no
longer bullied at school (since the compass
incident, the others had learnt to leave him alone),

but he was unhappy, nevertheless. He had acquired the reputation of being *stuck-up*—a cardinal sin in Malbry—which, added to his early status as a freak and a queer, amounted to social suicide.

It didn't help that, thanks to Ma, word of his gift had got around. As a result, even the teachers had come to think of him differently—some of them with resentment. A different child is a difficult child, or so thought the teachers at Abbey Road, and, far from being curious, many were suspicious, some openly sarcastic, as if his Ma's expectations and his own inability to conform to the mediocrity of the place were somehow an attack on *them*.

Ma, and her expectations. Grown stronger than ever, of course, now that the gift was official, now that there was a name for it—an *official* name, a syndrome, that smelt of sickness and sanctity, with its furry dark-grey sibilants and its fruity Catholic undertint.

Not that it mattered, he told himself. Another year and he would be free. Free to attend St Oswald's, which Ma had painted in such attractive colours for him that he was almost taken in, and of which Dr Peacock spoke with such affection that he had put his fears aside and thrown himself into the task of becoming what Dr Peacock expected of him: to be the son he'd never had, *a chip*, as he said, *off the old block*—

Sometimes Benjamin wondered what would happen if he failed the entrance exam. But since Ma had long ago come to believe that the exam was merely a formality, a series of documents to sign before he entered the hallowed gates, he knew that his worries were best left unvoiced.

His brothers were both at Sunnybank Park. *Sunnybanker. Rhymes with wanker*, as he used to say to them, which made Brendan laugh but infuriated Nigel, who—when he could catch him—would sometimes pin him between his knees and punch him till he cried, shouting—*Fuck you, you little freak!*—until at last he'd exhausted himself, or Ma heard and came running—

Nigel was fifteen, and hated him. He'd hated him from the very first, but by then his hatred had blossomed. Perhaps he was jealous of the attention his brother received; perhaps it was merely testosterone. In any case, the more he grew, the more he turned his whole being towards making his brother suffer, regardless of the consequences.

Ben was skinny and undersized. Nigel was already big for his age, sheathed in adolescent muscle, and he had all kinds of virtually untraceable ways of inflicting pain—Chinese burns, nips and pinches, sly shin-kicks under the table—though when he got angry, he forgot discretion and, without any fear of retribution, laid into his brother with fists and feet—

Telling tales only made it worse. Nigel seemed oblivious to punishment: it simply fed his resentment. Beatings made him worse. If he was sent to bed hungry, he would force-feed his brothers toothpaste, or dirt, or spiders, carefully harvested in the attic and put aside for just such an eventuality.

Brendan, always the cautious one, accepted the natural order of things. Perhaps he was brighter than they'd thought. Perhaps he feared retribution. He was also ridiculously squeamish, and if Nigel or Ben got a hiding from Ma, he would cry just as much as either of them—but at least he wasn't a threat, and sometimes even shared his sweets with Ben when Nigel was safely out of the way.

Brendan ate a lot of sweets, and now it was really beginning to show. A soft white roll of underbelly hung over the waistband of his donkey-brown cords, and his chest was plump and girly beneath his baggy brown jumpers, and although he and Ben might have had a chance if they'd stood together against Nigel, Brendan never had the nerve. And so Ben learnt to look after himself, and to run when his brother in black was around.

Other things had changed as well. *Blueeyedboy* was growing up. Always prone to headaches, now he began to suffer from migraines, too, which began as strobing lights shot through with lurid colours. After that would come the tastes and smells, stronger than any he'd known before: rotten eggs; creosote; the lurking stink of the vitamin drink; and then, at last, the sickness, the pain, rolling over him like a rock, burying him alive.

He couldn't sleep; couldn't think; could hardly concentrate at school. As if that wasn't bad enough, his speech, which had always been hesitant, had developed into a full-blown stammer. *Blueeyedboy* knew what it was. His gift—his sensitivity—had now become a poison to him. A poison creeping slowly through his body, changing him as it went from healthy, wholesome blood and bone to something with which even Ma found it difficult to sympathize.

She called the doctor in, of course, who at first put down the headaches to growing pains, and then, when they persisted, to stress.

'Stress? What has he got to be stressed about?' she cried in exasperation.

His silence annoyed her even more, and finally led to a series of uncomfortable interrogations, which left him feeling even worse. He quickly learnt not to complain; to pretend that there was nothing wrong with him, even when he was sick with pain and almost ready to collapse.

Instead, he evolved his own system of coping. He learnt which medicine to steal from Ma's cabinet. He learnt how to combat the phantom sensations with magic words and images. He took them from Dr Peacock's maps; from books; from the dark places of his heart—

Most of all, he dreamed in blue. Blue, the colour of control. He had always associated it with power, power like electricity; now he learnt to visualize himself encased in a shell of burning blue, untouchable, invincible. There, he was safe from everything. There, he could replenish himself. Blue was secure. Blue was serene. Blue, the colour of murder. And he wrote down his dreams in the same Blue Book in which he wrote his stories.

But there are other ways than fic to cope with adolescent stress. All you need is a suitable victim, preferably one who can't fight back: a scapegoat who will take the blame for everything you've suffered.

Benjamin's earliest victims were wasps, which he'd hated since he'd been stung in the mouth as he swigged from a half-empty can of Coke left unguarded in the summer sun. From then on, all wasps were guilty. His revenge was to catch them using traps made from jars half-filled with sugar water, and later to impale them on the tip of a

178

needle and watch as each creature struggled and died, pumping its pale stinger in and out and writhing its horribly corseted body like the world's most diminutive pole dancer.

He showed them to Brendan, too, and watched him writhe in discomfort.

'Ah, don't, that's disgusting—' said Bren, his face contorted with dismay.

'Why, Bren? It's only a wasp.'

He shrugged. 'I know. But please—'

Ben pulled the needle free of the wasp. The insect, almost severed now, began to turn sticky somersaults. Bren flinched.

'Happy now?'

'It's still m-moving,' Brendan said, his face awry with fear and disgust.

Ben tipped the contents of the jar on to the table in front of Brendan. 'So kill it,' he said.

'Ah, please, Ben—'

'Go on. Kill it. Put it out of its misery, you fat bastard.'

Brendan was almost crying now. 'I c-can't,' he said. 'I just—'

'Do it!' Ben punched him in the arm. 'Do it, kill it, kill it *now*—'

Some people are born to be killers. Brendan was not one of them. And Benjamin revelled sourly in Brendan's stupid helplessness, his whimpering cries as Ben punched him again, his retreat into the corner, arms wrapped around his head. Brendan never tried to fight back. Ben was three years younger, thirty pounds lighter, and still he beat Brendan easily. It wasn't that he hated him; but his weakness was infuriating, making Ben want to hurt him more, to see him squirm like a wasp in

179

a jar—

It *was* a little cruel, perhaps. Brendan had done nothing wrong. But it gave Ben the sense of control that he lacked, and it helped him to manage his growing stress. It was as if by tormenting his brother he could relocate his own suffering; evade the thing that imprisoned him in its cage of scents and colours.

Not that he thought about it much. His actions were purely instinctive, a self-defence against the world. Later, *blueeyedboy* was to learn that this process was called *transference*. An interesting word, coloured a muddy blue-green, that reminds him of the transfers his brothers used to stick on their arms: cheap and messy fake tattoos that stained the sleeves of their school shirts and got them into trouble in class. But somehow, at last, he learnt to cope. First, with the wasp traps, then with the mice, and finally, with his brothers.

And look at your *blueeyedboy* now, Ma. He has exceeded all expectations. He wears a suit to go to work—or at least, to maintain the pretence. He carries a leather briefcase. The word *technician* is in his job title, as is the word *operator*, and if no one knows quite what he does, it is merely because most ordinary people have no idea how complicated these operations can be.

Doctors rely on machines nowadays, Gloria says to Adèle and Maureen, when she meets them on Friday night. *There are millions of pounds invested there in scanners and MRI machines, and* someone *has to operate them—*

Never mind that the closest he has ever come to any one of those clever machines is vacuuming the dust underneath. You see, words *do* have power,

Ma: power to camouflage the truth, to colour it in peacock shades.

Oh, if she knew, she'd make him pay. But she won't find out. He's too careful for that. She may have her suspicions, of course—but he thinks he can get away with it. It's just a question of nerve, that's all. Nerve and timing and self-control. That's all a murderer needs, in the end.

Besides, as you know, I've done it before.

Post comment:
JennyTricks: (*post deleted*).
ClairDeLune: *Jenny, don't you ever get tired of coming here to criticize? This is intriguing,* **blueeyedboy**. *Did you look at the reading-list I sent you? I'd love to know what you thought of it . . .*

You are viewing the webjournal of **Albertine**.
Posted at: *01.55 on Tuesday, February 5*
Status: *restricted*
Mood: *awake*

Nothing in my mailbox tonight. Just a *meme* from *blueeyedboy*, tempting me to come out and play. I'm almost certain he's waiting for me; he often logs on at about this time and stays online into the early hours of the morning. I wonder what he wants from me. Love? Hate? Confessions? Lies? Or is it simply the contact he craves, the need to know I'm still listening? In the small hours of the night, when God seems like a cosmic joke and no one seems to be listening, don't we all need someone to touch? Even you, *blueeyedboy*. Watching me, watching you, through a glass darkly, tapping out on this ouija board my letters to the dead.

Is this why he writes these stories of his, posting them here for me to read? Is it an invitation to play? Does he expect me to answer him with a confession of my own?

Tagged by **blueeyedboy** *posting on*
badguysrock@webjournal.com
Posted at: *01.05 on Tuesday, February 5*

If you were an animal, what would you be? *An eagle soaring over the mountains.*
Favourite smell? *The Pink Zebra café, on a Thursday lunchtime.*
Tea or coffee? *Why have either, when you can have hot chocolate with cream?*
Favourite flavour of ice cream? *Green apple.*
What are you wearing right now? *Jeans, trainers and my favourite old cashmere sweater.*
What are you afraid of? *Ghosts.*
What's the last thing you bought? *Mimosa. It's my favourite flower.*
What's the last thing you ate? *Toast.*
Favourite sound? *Yo-Yo Ma playing Saint-Saëns.*
What do you wear in bed? *An old shirt that belonged to my boyfriend.*
What's your pet hate? *Being patronized.*
Your worst trait? *Evasiveness.*
Any scars or tattoos? *More than I want to remember.*
Any recurring dreams? *No.*
There's a fire in your house. What would you save? *My computer.*
When did you last cry?

Well—I'd *like* to say it was when Nigel died. But both of us know that isn't true. And how could I explain to him that sly, irrational surge of joy that overshadows the bulk of my grief, this knowledge that something is missing in me, some sense that has nothing to do with my eyes?

You see, I *am* a bad person. I don't know how to cope with loss. Death is a heady cocktail of one part sorrow to three parts relief—I felt it with

Daddy, with Mother, with Nigel—even with poor Dr Peacock . . .

Blueeyedboy knew—we both knew—that I was just deluding myself. Nigel never stood a chance. Even our love was a lie from the start, sending out its green shoots like those of a cut branch in a vase; shoots, not of recovery, but of desperation.

Yes, I was selfish. Yes, I was wrong. Even from the start I knew that Nigel belonged to someone else. Someone who never existed. But after years of running away, part of me *wanted* to be that girl; to sink into her like a child into a feather pillow; to forget myself—and everything—in the circle of Nigel's arms. Online friendships were no longer enough. All of a sudden I wanted more. I wanted to be normal: to encounter the world, not through a glass, but through my lips and my fingers. I wanted more than the world online; more than a name at my fingertips. I wanted to be understood, not by someone at a keyboard far away, but by someone I could *touch* . . .

But sometimes a touch can be fatal. I should know; it's happened before. Less than a year later, Nigel was dead, poisoned by proximity. Nigel's girl has proved herself just as toxic as Emily White, sending out death with a single word.

Or, in this case, a letter.

You are viewing the webjournal of **Albertine**.
Posted at: *15.44 on Tuesday, February 5*
Status: *restricted*
Mood: *apprehensive*

The letter arrived on a Saturday, as we were having breakfast. By then Nigel was more or less living here, though he still kept his flat in Malbry, and we had established a kind of routine that almost suited both of us. He and I were nocturnal creatures, happiest at night. Thus Nigel came over at ten o'clock; shared a bottle, talked, made love, slept over and left by nine in the morning. At weekends he stayed longer, sometimes till ten or eleven o'clock, which was why he was there in the first place, and why the letter came to him. On a weekday he wouldn't have opened it, and I could have dealt with it privately. I suppose that, too, was part of the plan. But right then I had no idea of the letter bomb about to explode in our unsuspecting faces—

That morning I was eating cereal, which ticked and popped as the milk sank in. Nigel wasn't eating, or even speaking to me much. Nigel hardly ever ate breakfast, and his silences were ominous, especially in the mornings. Sounds orbiting a central silence like satellites around a baleful planet; the creak of the pantry door; the clatter of spoon against coffee jar; the chink of mugs. A second later, the fridge door opened; rattled; slammed. The kettle boiled; a brief eruption followed by a click of military finality. Then, the clack of the letter box and the stolid double-thump of the post.

Most of my mail is junk mail, though I rarely get mail of any kind. My bills are paid by direct debit. Letters? Why bother. Greetings cards? Forget it.

'Anything interesting?' I said.

For a moment Nigel said nothing at all. I heard the unfolding of paper. A single sheet, unfurled with a dry rasp, like the unsheathing of a sharpened knife.

'Nigel?'

'What?'

He jiggled his foot when he was annoyed; I could hear it against the table leg. And now there was something in his voice; something flat and hard, like an obstacle. He tore the used envelope into halves, then he fingered the single sheet. Stropped it on his thumb, like a blade—

'It isn't bad news, or anything?' I did not speak of what I dreaded most, though I could feel it hanging over me.

'For fuck's sake. Let me read,' he said. Now the obstacle was within my reach; like a sharp-edged table-top in an unexpected place. Those sharp edges never miss; they have a gravity all of their own, pulling me every time into their orbit. And there were so many sharp edges in Nigel; so many zones of restricted access.

It wasn't his fault, I told myself; I would not have had him otherwise. We completed each other in some strange way: his dark moods and my lack of temperament. I am wide open, as he used to say;

186

there are no hidden places in me, no unpleasant secrets. All the better; because deceit, that essentially female trait, is the thing that Nigel despised most of all. Deceit and lies, so alien to him—so alien, he thought, to me.

'I have to go out for an hour or so.' His voice sounded oddly defensive. 'Will you be OK for a while? I have to go to Ma's house.'

Gloria Winter, née Gloria Green, sixty-nine years old and still clutching at the remains of her family with the tenacity of a hungry remora. I knew her as a voice on the line; a rimshot Northern accent; an impatient drumming on the receiver; an imperious way of cutting you off like a gardener pruning roses.

Not that we've ever been introduced. Not officially, anyway. But I know her from Nigel; I know her ways; I know her voice on the telephone and her ominous range of silences. There are other things, too, that he never told me, but that I know only too well. The jealousy; the rancour; the rage; the hatred mixed with helplessness.

He rarely spoke of her to me. He rarely even mentioned her name. Living with Nigel, I soon understood that some subjects were best left alone, and this included his childhood, his father, his brothers, his past and most especially Gloria, who shared, along with her other son, a talent for bringing out the worst in Nigel.

'Can't your brother deal with this?'

I heard him stop on the way to the door. I wondered if he were turning round, fixing me with his dark eyes. Nigel rarely mentioned his brother, and when he did it was all bad. *Twisted little bastard* was about the best I'd heard so far—Nigel never had much objectivity when it came to discussing his family.

'My brother? Why? Has he spoken to you?'

'Of course not. Why would he?'

Another pause. I felt his eyes on the top of my head.

'Graham Peacock's dead,' he said. His voice was curiously flat. 'An accident, by the sound of it. Fell out of his wheelchair during the night. They found him dead in the morning.'

I didn't look up. I didn't dare. Suddenly everything seemed enhanced; the taste of coffee in my mouth; the sound of the birds; the beat of my heart; the table at my fingertips with all its scars and scratches.

'This letter's from your brother?' I said.

Nigel ignored the question: 'It says that the bulk of Peacock's estate—valued at something like three million pounds—'

Another silence. 'What?' I said.

That strangely uninflected voice was somehow more disturbing than rage. 'He's left it all to you,' he said. 'The house, the art, the collections—'

'Me? But I don't even know him,' I said.

'The twisted little *bastard*.'

No need for me to ask who he meant; that phrase was reserved for his brother. So very like him in so many ways, and yet, whenever his name arose, I could almost believe that Nigel could kill a man; could beat him to death with fists and feet . . .

'This must be a mistake,' I said. 'I've never met Dr Peacock. I don't even know what he looks like. Why would he leave his money to me?'

'Well—maybe because of Emily White.' Nigel's voice was colourless.

188

And now the coffee tasted like dust; the birds fell silent; my heart was a stone. That name had silenced everything—except for the buzz of feedback that began right at the base of my spine, erasing all of the past twenty years in a surge of deadly static . . .

I know I should have told him then. But I'd hidden the truth for so long; believing that Nigel would always be there; hoping for the perfect time; not knowing that *this* time was all we had—

'Emily White,' said Nigel.

'Never heard of her,' I said.

You are viewing the webjournal of **Albertine**.
Posted at: *03.15 on Wednesday, February 6*
Status: *restricted*
Mood: *sleepless*

When dealt one of life's terrible blows—the death of a parent, the end of a relationship, the positive test result, the guilty verdict, the final step off the tall building—there comes a moment of light-headedness, almost of euphoria, as the string which tethers us to our hopes is cut and we bounce off in another direction, briefly powered by the momentum of release.

The penultimate movement of the *Symphonie fantastique*—'The March to the Scaffold'—has a similar moment, when the condemned arrives within view of the gallows, and the minor key shifts into a triumphant major, as if at the sight of a friendly face. I know how it feels: that lurch of deliverance, the feeling that the worst has already happened and that the rest is merely gravity.

Not that the worst *had* happened—not yet. But the clouds were gathering. By the time that letter arrived, Nigel had less than an hour to live; and the last thing he ever said to me were the four little syllables of her name, Emily White, like a musical sting performed by the ghost of Beethoven . . .

And Dr Peacock was dead at last. Ex-Master of St Oswald's School, eccentric, genius, charlatan, dreamer, collector, saint, buffoon. Unrelenting in death as in life; somehow it did not surprise me to learn that once more, with the kindest intent, he had torn my life apart.

Not that he could have harmed me. Not intentionally, anyway. Emily always loved him: a large, heavy man with a soft beard and a strangely childlike manner, who read from *Alice in Wonderland* and played old, scratchy records on a wind-up gramophone while she sat on the swing in the Fireplace House and talked about music and painting and poetry and sound. And now the old man was dead at last, and there was no escaping him, or the thing we had helped set in motion.

I don't really know how old Emily was when she first went to the Fireplace House. All I know is that it must have been some time after the Christmas concert, because that is where my memory shorts out for good; one moment I'm there, with the music all around me like some fabulous velvet, the next . . .

Feedback and white noise. A long rush of static, broken occasionally by a sudden burst of perfect sound, a phrase, a chord, a note. I try to make sense of it, but I cannot; too much of it is hidden. Of course there were witnesses; from them I can, if I wish, piece together the variations, if not the fugue. But I trust them less than I trust myself— and besides, I've worked hard to forget all that. Why should I try to remember it now?

When I was a child, and the worst happened— toys broken, affection denied, the small but poignant sorrows of childhood recalled through the mist of adult grief—I always sought refuge in the garden. There was a tree where I loved to sit; I

191

remember its texture, its elephant hide, the sappy, plush scent of dead leaves and moss. Nowadays, when I'm lost and confused, I head for the Pink Zebra. It's the safest place in my world; an escape from myself, a sanctuary. Everything here seems expressly designed to fit my unique requirements.

To begin with, its comfortable size, with every table against a wall. Its menu lists all my favourites. Best of all, unlike the genteel Village, it has no affiliations or pretensions. I am not invisible here, and although that could have its dangers, it's good to be able to walk in and to have people talk *to* you and not *at* you. Even the voices are different here: not reedy like Maureen Pike's or breathy and sour like Eleanor Vine's or affected like Adèle Roberts's, but rich with the tones of jazz clarinet and sitar and steel drums, with lovely calypso rhythms and lilts, so that just sitting here is almost as good as music.

I headed there that Saturday after Nigel had gone. That name on his lips had unsettled me, and I needed a place to think things out. Somewhere noisy. Somewhere safe. The Zebra was always a refuge for me; always filled with people. Today there were more than usual, all waiting outside the café door; their voices surging around me like animals at feeding-time. Saxophone Man's Jamaican accent. The Fat Girl, with her breathy tone. And orchestrating everything, Bethan, with her Irish lilt, cheery, speaking to everyone, pulling it all together:

'Hey, what's going on? You're late. You should have been here ten minutes ago.'

'Hello, darlin'! What'll it be?'

'You got any more of that chocolate cake?'

'Hang on, I'll have a look for you.'

Thank goodness for Bethan, I told myself. Bethan, my coat of camouflage. I don't think Nigel really understood. He resented all the time I spent at the Pink Zebra; wondered how I could so often prefer the company of strangers to his own. But to understand about Bethan, you have to be able to penetrate the many disguises with which she surrounds herself: the voices, the jokes, the nicknames, the cheery Irish cynicism that hides something closer to the bone.

Underneath all that there's someone else. Someone damaged and vulnerable. Someone trying desperately to make sense of something sad and senseless . . .

'There you are, darlin'. Try that for size. Hot chocolate, with cardamom cream.'

The chocolate is one of my favourites. Served with milk in a tall glass, with coconut and marshmallows, or dark, with a clash of chilli.

'Listen to this. Creepy Dude came in to the Zebra the other day. Sat down just where you're sitting. Ordered the lemon meringue pie. I watched him eat it from over there, then he came back to the counter and ordered another. I watched him eat that, then when he'd finished, he called me over and ordered more pie. Honest to God, darlin', your man must have et six pieces of pie in under half an hour. The Fat Girl was sitting right there opposite him, and I thought her eyes were going to pop out of her head, so I did.'

I sipped my chocolate. It was tasteless. But the warmth was comforting. I carried on the conversation without really paying attention to it, against a wall of background noise as meaningless as waves on a shore.

'Hey, babe, lookin' good—'

'Two espressos, Bethan, please.'

'Six pieces of pie. Imagine that. I've been thinking that maybe he's on the run, that he's shot his lover and he's planning to jump off Beachy Head before the police catch up with him, because six pieces of pie—Jesus God!—now there's a man with nothing to lose—'

'And I told her, I said, "I'm not 'avin' *that*—" '

'Be with you in a minute, babe.'

Sometimes in a noisy room you can pick out the sound of a single voice—sometimes even a single word—that clatters against the wall of sound like an out-of-tune violin in an orchestra.

'Earl Grey, please. No lemon, no milk.'

His voice is unmistakable. Soft and slightly nasal, perhaps, with a peculiar emphasis on the aspirates, like a theatre actor, or maybe a man who once stuttered. And now I could hear the music again, the opening chords of the Berlioz, never very far from my thoughts. Why it had to be *that* piece, I don't know; but it's the sound of my deepest fear, and it sounds to me like the end of the world.

I kept my own voice steady and low. No need to disturb the customers. 'You've really done it now,' I said.

'I have no idea what you're talking about.'

'I'm talking about your letter,' I said.

'What letter?'

'Don't bullshit me,' I said. 'Nigel got a letter today. Given the mood he was in when he left, and given the fact that I only know one person capable of winding him up to that level—'

194

'I'm glad you think so.' I heard his smile.

'What did you tell him?'

'Not much,' he said. 'But you know my brother. Impulsive. Always getting the wrong idea.' He paused, and once more I heard his smile. 'Perhaps he was shaken by the news of Dr Peacock's legacy. Perhaps he just wanted Ma to be sure that he knew nothing about it—' He took a sip of his Earl Grey. 'You know, I thought you'd be pleased,' he said. 'It's still a magnificent estate. Perhaps the property's a little rundown. Still, nothing that can't be fixed, eh? Then there's the art. The collections. Three million pounds is conservative. I'd estimate it at closer to four—'

'I don't care,' I hissed at him. 'They can give it to someone else.'

'There isn't anyone else,' he said.

Oh yes there is. There's Nigel. Nigel, who trusted me—

How fragile are these things we build. How tragically ephemeral. In contrast, the house is solid as stone; as tiles and beams and mortar. How could we compete with stone? How could our little alliance survive?

'I have to admit,' he said mildly, 'I thought you might show some gratitude. After all, Dr Peacock's estate is likely to bring you a tidy sum—more than enough to get out of this place and buy yourself somewhere decent.'

'I like my life as it is,' I said.

'Really? I'd kill to get out of here.'

I picked up my empty chocolate cup; turned it round and round in my hands. 'So how *did* Dr Peacock die? And how much did he leave *you*?'

A pause. 'That wasn't very kind.'

I lowered my voice to a hiss. 'I don't care. It's over. Everyone's dead—'

'Not quite.'

No, I thought. *Well—maybe not.*

'So you *do* remember.' I heard his smile.

'Not much. You know how old I was.'

Old enough to remember, he means. He thinks I should remember more; but for me now most of those memories exist only as fragments of Emily, some at best contradictory, others, frankly impossible. But I know what everyone else knows: that she was famous; she was unique; college professors wrote theses on what they had begun to call *The Emily White Phenomenon*.

Memory [says Dr Peacock in his thesis 'The Illuminated Man'], *is, at best, an imperfect and highly idiosyncratic process. We tend to think of the mind as a fully functioning recording machine, with gigabytes of information—aural, visual and tactile—within easy recall. This could not be further from the truth. Although it is true that in theory, at least, I should be able to remember what I had for breakfast on any particular morning of my life, or the precise wording of a Shakespeare sonnet I had to study as a child, it is more probable that without recourse to drugs or deep hypnosis—both methods being, in any case, highly questionable, given the level of suggestibility in the subject— those particular memories will remain inaccessible to me and will finally degrade, like electrical equipment left in the damp, causing short-outs and cross-wiring until finally the system may default into alternative or backup*

196

memory, complete with sense-impressions and internal logic, which may in fact be drawn from a completely different set of experiences and stimuli, but which provides the brain with a compensatory buffer against any discontinuity or obvious malfunction.

Dear Dr Peacock. He always took so long to make a point. If I try hard I can still hear his voice, which was plush and plummy and just a little comic, like the bassoon in *Peter and the Wolf*. He had a house near the centre of town, one of those big, deep old houses with high ceilings, and worn parquet floors, and wide bay windows, and spiky aspidistra, and the genteel smell of old leather and cigars. There was a fireplace in the parlour, a huge thing with a carved overmantel and a clock that ticked; and in the evenings he would burn logs and pine cones in the giant hearth and tell stories to anyone who cared to walk in.

There was constant traffic at the Fireplace House. Students (of course); colleagues; admirers; vagrants on the scrounge for a bite to eat and a cup of tea. Everyone was welcome, as long as they behaved themselves; and as far as I knew, no one had ever abused Dr Peacock's good nature, or caused him any embarrassment.

It was the kind of house where there is something for everyone. There was always a bottle of wine to hand, and a pot of tea standing on the hearth. There was food, too: usually bread and some kind of soup, several fat fruitcakes weighted with plums and brandy, and an enormous barrel of biscuits. There were several cats, a dog called Patch, and a rabbit that slept in a basket under the parlour window.

In the Fireplace House, time stood still. There was no television, no radio, no newspapers or magazines. There were gramophones in every room like great open lilies with tongues of brass; there were shelves and cupboards of records, some small, some as wide as serving dishes, scored close with ancient voices and yawning, scratchy, vinegary strings. There were marbles and bronzes on wobbly tables; strings of jet beads; powder compacts half-filled with fragrant dust; books with autumn pages; globes; fiddly collections of snuffboxes, miniatures, cups and saucers, clockwork dolls. That was home to Emily White, and to think that now I could join her there, a perpetual child in a house of forgotten things, free to do anything I liked . . .

Except, of course, to leave.

I thought I'd managed to get away. To make a new life for myself with Nigel. But I know that was all an illusion now; a game of smoke and mirrors. Emily White never got away. Nor did Benjamin Winter. How could I hope to be different? And do I even understand from what I'm trying to escape?

Emily White?

Never heard of her.

Poor Nigel. Poor Ben. And it hurts, doesn't it, *blueeyedboy?* To be eclipsed by a brighter star, to be ignored and left in the dark, without even a name of your own? Well, now you know how I felt. How I've always felt. How I *still* feel—

'That's all in the past,' I said. 'I hardly remember it any more.'

He poured another cup of Earl Grey. 'It'll all come back eventually.'

'And if I don't *want* it all to come back?'

'I don't believe you'll have the choice.'

Perhaps he was right about that, at least. Nothing ever vanishes. Even after all these years, Emily still shadows me. Now there's an admission, *blueeyedboy*. I'm sure you can see the irony. But the tenor of our relationship is closer in some ways than friendship. Maybe because of the screen that divides us, so like the screen of the confessional.

Perhaps that's what drew me to *badguysrock*. It's a place for people like me, I suppose; a place to confess, if needs be; to tell those stories that ought to be true, even if they are really not. As for *blueeyedboy*—well, I'll admit he draws me too. We fit together so well, he and I; folded together like tissue paper in an album of old photographs, our lives touch in so many ways that we might almost be lovers. And the fiction he writes is so much more true than the fiction on which I have built my life.

I heard his mobile phone beep. In retrospect I think it was the first of those texts of condolence; the messages from his WeJay announcing that his brother was dead.

'Sorry. Got to go,' he said. 'Ma's got lunch on the table. But try to think about what I said. You can't outrun the past, you know.'

When he had gone I considered his words. Perhaps he was right, after all. Perhaps even Nigel would understand. After so many years of seeing the world through a glass darkly, perhaps it was time to face myself; to take back my past and *remember* . . .

But all I can really be sure of now is the impending static in the air, and the first movement of the Berlioz, the 'Rêveries—Passions', gathering like clouds.

PART THREE

white

You are viewing the webjournal of **Albertine** *posting on:*

badguysrock@webjournal.com

Posted at: *21.39 on Thursday, February 7*
Status: *public*
Mood: *tense*

Her first recorded memory is of a chunk of potter's clay. Bland as butter, later drying to a rough scale on her arms and elbows, it smells of the river behind her house, of the rain on the pavements, of the cellar where she must never, *ever* go, where her mother keeps the winter potatoes in their little coffins, growing their long blind eyes up to the light.

Blue clay, her mother says. She squishes it between starfish fingers. *Make something, Emily. Make a shape.*

The clay is soft; beneath her hands it feels like slippery skin. She brings it to her mouth; it tastes like the side of the bathtub when she puts her tongue against it: warm, soapy, a little sour. *Make a shape,* her mother says; and the little girl's hands begin to explore the piece of slippery blue clay, to stroke it like a wet puppy, to fondle and find the shape inside.

But that's nonsense, of course. She doesn't remember the piece of clay. In fact, there are no memories at all of those years that she can altogether trust. She has learnt by imitation; she can reel off every word. And she knows that there *was* a piece of clay; for years it stood in the studio, hard and dense as a fossilized head.

Later, it sold to a gallery, nicely mounted and cast in bronze. Rather overpriced, perhaps; but there's always a market for that kind of thing. Murder memorabilia, hangman's nooses, pieces of bone; the trappings of notoriety, sold to collectors everywhere.

She had hoped for a better memorial. But this, she thinks, will have to do. For want of proper memories, she will take the clay head cast in bronze, and the letters chiselled into the brass nearly thirty years ago.

First Impressions (the inscription says).
Emily White, aged 3.

Post comment:
blueeyedboy: **Albertine**, *I'm speechless. You have no idea how much this means to me. Will there be more of this? Please?*
Albertine: *Maybe. If you want it so badly . . .*

You are viewing the webjournal of **Albertine** *posting on*:

badguysrock@webjournal.com

Posted at: *22.45 on Thursday, February 7*
Status: *public*
Mood: *determined*

Her mother was an artist. Colours were her whole life. Emily White learnt to crawl on the floor of her mother's workshop; before she could speak she already knew the powdery smell of the watercolours and the chalks, the metallic scent of the acrylics, the smoky reek of the oils. Her mother smelt of turpentine; the child's first word was 'paper'; her first playthings were the rolls of parchment kept under the desk; she remembered their fascinating crinkle, their dusty smell.

As her mother worked Emily learnt to know the sounds of her progress: the fat sloshing of the background brushes; the scratching of nibs; the soft *hishh* of pastels and sponges; the *scree* of scissors; the scrubbing of pencils on art paper.

These were the rhythms of her mother; sometimes accompanied by small sounds of irritation or satisfaction, sometimes by pacing, most often by a running commentary of colour and shade. By the time she was a year old, Emily had still not learnt to walk, but could name all the colours in her mother's box of paints. Their names rang out like chimes in her head: *damson, umber, ochre, gold; madder, violet, crimson, rose.*

Violet was her favourite; the tube had been squeezed almost empty, then curled up like a party favour to eke out the rest. White was full, but only because the tube was new; black was dry and seldom used, pushed to the back of the paintbox among the hairless brushes and cleaning-rags.

'Pat, she's a slow developer. Einstein was the same.' That must be a false memory, she thinks, like so many from those early days: her mother's voice high above her, Daddy's tentative reply.

'But sweetheart, the doctor—'

'Damn the doctor! She can name every colour in the box.'

'She's just repeating what you tell her.'

'She is *not*!'

A familiar high note quivers in her mother's voice, a vinegary note that catches at her sinuses and makes her eyes water. She does not know its name—not yet, though later she will know it as F sharp—but she can pick it out on Daddy's piano. But that's a secret even from her mother; the hours spent together at the old Bechstein, Daddy with his pipe in his mouth, Emily sitting in his lap with her small hands just touching the keyboard as he plays the *Moonlight Sonata* or *Für Elise* and her mother thinks she is in bed.

'Catherine, please—'

'She can see *perfectly*!'

The smell of turpentine intensifies. It is the smell of her mother's distress, and of her terrible disappointment. She scoops the child up in her arms—Emily's face pressed into the front of her overalls—and as she turns, Emily's feet drag across

206

the work-bench, scattering tubes and pots and paintbrushes, *rat-tat-tat* over the parquet floor.

'Catherine, listen—' Her father's voice, as always, is humble, almost apologetic. As always, he smells faintly of Clan tobacco, though officially he never smokes in the house. 'Catherine, please—'

But she is not listening. Instead she holds the child and moans: 'You can see, can't you, Emily, my darling? *Can't* you?'

It *must* be a false memory. Emily was barely a year old; surely she could not have understood or remembered anything so well. And yet she seems to recall it so clearly: her bewildered tears, her mother's cries, and her father's mumbled counterpoint. The smell of the studio and the paint from her mother's overalls sticking her fingertips together, and all the time that high F sharp tremor in her mother's voice, the note of her thwarted expectations, like a persistent harmonic on an over-tightened string.

Daddy knew almost from the first. But he was a meek, reflective little man, a foil to her mother's rages. Even as a small child Emily sensed that she thought him inferior; that he had disappointed her. Perhaps because of his lack of ambition; perhaps because it had taken him ten years to give her the child she longed for. He was a music teacher at St Oswald's; he played several instruments, but the piano was the only one her mother tolerated in the house, and the rest were sold, one by one, to pay for her treatments and therapies.

It was no real sacrifice, Daddy said. After all, he had access to all his department's resources. It was only fair; Emily's mother suffered from headaches, and Emily was a restive infant, apt to wake at the slightest noise. As a result he transferred his records and his music to the school; he could always listen to them at lunchtimes or Break, and besides, school was where he spent most of his time.

You have to understand what it was like for her.

That's Daddy speaking; always making excuses, always ready to stand in her defence, like a tired old knight in the service of a mad queen who has lost her empire. It took Emily a long time to understand the cause of Daddy's subservience. Daddy had been unfaithful once, with a woman who meant nothing to him, but to whom he had given a child. And now he owed Catherine a debt—a debt that could never be repaid—which meant that for the rest of his life he would always accept second place, never complaining, never protesting, never seeming to hope for anything more than to serve her, to give her what she wanted, to redeem the irredeemable.

Babe, you have to understand.

They managed on his salary; she took it as her natural right to pursue her artistic ambitions while Daddy worked to keep them both. From time to time a little gallery sold one of her mother's collages. Little by little her mother's ambition shifted. She was born before her time, she said. Future generations would know her. What might have turned her inwards made her fiercely determined; she threw her heart into having a baby, long after Daddy's small expectations had ceased.

Finally, Emily came. *Oh, the plans we made—* that's Daddy talking, though I doubt whether he was allowed any part in the planning of Emily's young life—*The dreams we had for you, Emily.* For seven and a half months Emily's mother became almost domesticated: knitted bootees in pastel colours; played whale music for a stress-free delivery; wanted a natural birth but took gas at the final moment. So that it was Daddy who counted Emily's fingers and toes, holding his breath at the squalling amazement at his fingertips; the hairless monkey with its eyes squinched shut and its tiny fists clenched.

Darling, she's perfect.

Oh, my God—

But she was nearly two months premature. They gave her too much oxygen; the process detached her retinas. No one noticed straight away; in those days it was enough to know that Emily had all her limbs. When later her blindness became more apparent, Catherine denied it.

Emily was a *special* child, she said. Her gifts would take time to develop. Her mother's friend Feather Dunne—an amateur astrologer—had already predicted a brilliant future: a mystical union between Saturn and the Moon confirmed that she was exceptional. When the doctor became impatient, Emily's mother removed herself to an alternative therapist, who recommended eyebright, massage and colour therapy. For three months she lived in a haze of incense and candles; lost interest in her canvases; never even combed her hair.

Daddy suspected post-natal depression. Catherine denied it, but veered periodically from one extreme to the other: one day protective, refusing to allow him near; the next sitting unresponsive, heedless of the bundle at her side that squalled and squalled.

Sometimes it was worse than that, and Daddy had to turn to the neighbours for help. There had been a mistake, said Catherine; the hospital had mixed up the babies; had somehow given away her perfect baby for this damaged one.

Look at it, Patrick, she would say. *It doesn't even* look *like a baby. It's hideous. Hideous.*

She told Emily that when she was five. There could be no secrets between them, she said; they were part of each other. *Besides, love* is *a kind of madness, isn't it, darling? Love is a kind of possession.*

Yes, that was her voice; that was Catherine White. *She feels things more than the rest of us*, so Emily's father used to say, as if in apology for apparently feeling so much less. And yet it was Daddy who kept things going, during her breakdown and afterwards; Daddy who paid the bills, who cooked and cleaned; who changed and fed; who every day guided Catherine gently into her abandoned studio and showed her the brushes and paints and her baby crawling among the rolls of paper and the crunchy curls of wood.

One day she picked up a paintbrush, inspected it for a moment, then put it down again; but it was the first interest she had shown for months, and Daddy took it as a sign of improvement. It was: by the time Emily was two years old, her mother's creative passion had returned; and although now it was channelled almost exclusively through the child, it was no less ardent than before.

It began with that head in blue clay. But clay, though interesting enough, did not retain her attention for long. Emily wanted new things; she wanted to touch, to smell, to feel. The studio had

210

become too small to contain her; she learnt to follow walls into other rooms; to find the good place under the window where the sun shone; to use the tape-recorder to listen to stories; to open up the piano and to play the notes one-fingered. She loved to play with her mother's tin of loose buttons; to push her hands deep inside; to slither them out on to the floor and arrange them by size, shape and texture.

In every way but one, you see, Emily was an ordinary child. She loved stories, which her father would record for her; she loved to walk in the park; she loved her parents; she loved her dolls. She had a small child's small, infrequent tantrums; she enjoyed her visits to the farm in Pog Hill, and dreamed of getting a puppy.

By the time Emily learnt to walk, her mother had almost accepted her blindness. Specialists were expensive, and their conclusions were inevitably variations on the same theme. Her condition was irreversible; she responded only to the brightest of direct lights, and then only a very, very little. She could not distinguish shapes; could barely recognize movement, and had no awareness of colour.

But Catherine White was not to be defeated. She flung herself into Emily's education with all the energy she had once given to her work. First, clay, to develop spatial awareness and encourage creativity. Next, numbers, on a large wooden abacus with beads that clicked and clacked. Then letters, using a Braille slate and an embossing machine. Then, on Feather's advice, 'colour therapy', designed, so she said, to stimulate the visual parts of the cortex by image association.

211

'If it can work for Gloria's boy, then why can't it work for Emily?'

This was the phrase she used every time Daddy tried to protest. It didn't matter that Gloria's boy was a different case entirely; all that mattered to Catherine White was that Ben—or *Boy X*, as Dr Peacock called him, with typical pretentiousness—had somehow acquired an extra sense; and if the son of a cleaner could do it, then why not little Emily?

Little Emily, of course, had no idea what they were talking about. But she wanted to please; she was eager to learn, and the rest just followed naturally.

The colour therapy worked, to a point. Although the words themselves held no more meaning for Emily than the names of the colours in her paintbox, *green* brings back the memory of summer lawns and cut grass. *Red* is the scent of Bonfire Night; the sound of crackling wood; the heat. *Blue* is water; silent; cool.

'Your name is a colour, too, Emily,' said Feather, who had long, tickly hair that smelt of patchouli and cigarette smoke. 'Emily White. Isn't that lovely?'

White. Snow white. So cold it is almost hot at the fingertips, freezing, burning.

'Emily. Don't you love the pretty snow?'

No, I don't, Emily thinks. Fur is pretty. Silk is pretty. Buttons are pretty in the tin, or rice, or lentils slipping *frrrrrrpp* through the fingers. There's nothing pretty about snow, which hurts your hands and makes the steps slippery. Anyway, white isn't a colour. White is the ugly *brrrrr* you get between radio stations, when the sound breaks up

212

and there's nothing left but noise. White noise. White snow. Snow White, half-dead, half-sleeping under glass.

When she was four, Daddy suggested that Emily might go to school. Maybe in Kirby Edge, he said, where there was a facility. Catherine refused to discuss it, of course. With Feather's help, she said, her teaching had already worked a near-miracle. She had always known Emily was an exceptional child; she was not to waste her gifts in a school for blind children where she would be taught rug-making and self-pity, nor in a mainstream school where she would always be second-rate. No, Emily was to continue to receive tuition from home, so that when she eventually regained her sight—and there was no doubt at all in Catherine's mind that this would happen some day—she would be ready to face whatever the world chanced to offer her.

Daddy protested as strenuously as he could. It was not nearly enough; Feather and Catherine barely heard him. Feather believed in past lives, and thought that if the correct parts of Emily's brain were stimulated, then she would regain her visual memory; and Catherine believed . . .

Well, you know what Catherine believed. She could have lived with an ugly child; even a deformed child. But a blind child? A child with no understanding of colours?

Colours, colours, colours. Green, pink, gold, orange, purple, scarlet, blue. Blue alone has a thousand variations: cerulean, sapphire, cobalt, azure; from sky-blue to deepest midnight, passing through indigo and navy, powder-blue to electric-blue, forget-me-not, turquoise and aqua and Saxe. You see, Emily could understand the *notation* of

213

colours. She knew their terms and their cadences; she learnt to repeat the notes and arpeggios of their seven-tone scale. And yet the *nature* of colours still eluded her. She was like a tone-deaf person who has learnt to play the piano, knowing that what he hears is nothing like music. But she could perform; oh yes; she could.

'See the daffodils, Emily.'

'Pretty daffodils. Sunny yellow-golden daffodils.' As a matter of fact, they felt ugly to the touch; cold and somehow *meaty*, like slices of ham. Emily much preferred the fat silky leaves of the lamb's tongue, or the lavenders with their nubbly flower-heads and sleepy smell.

'Shall we paint the daffodils, sweetheart? Would you like Cathy to help you?'

The easel was set up in the studio. There was a big paintbox on the left, with the colours labelled in Braille. Three pots of water stood to the right, and a selection of brushes. Emily liked the sable brushes best. They were the best quality, and soft as the end of a cat's tail. She liked to run them along the place just underneath her lower lip, a place of such sensitivity that she could feel every hair on a paintbrush, and where the nap of a piece of velvet ribbon was the most exquisitely discerned. The paper—thick, glossy art paper with its new, clean-bedclothes smell—was fastened to the easel with bulldog clips, and was sectioned into squares like a chessboard, by means of wires stretched across the paper. That way, Emily could be sure of not straying outside the picture, or confusing sky with trees.

'Now for the trees, Emily. Good. That's good.'

Trees are tall, Emily thinks. Taller than my

father. Catherine lets her touch them, puts her face to their rough sides, like hugging a beardy man. There's a smell, too, and a hint of movement, far away but still connected, still touching somehow. 'It's windy,' Emily suggests, trying hard. 'The tree's moving in the wind.'

'Good, darling! Very good!'

Splosh, splash. Now the white, no-colour paper is green. She knows this because her mother hugs her. Emily feels her trembling. There is a note in her voice, too—not F sharp this time, but something less shrill and teary—and something in Emily swells with pride and happiness, because she loves her mother; she loves the smell of turpentine because it is the smell of her mother; she loves the painting lessons because they make her mother proud—although later, when it is over and she creeps back to the studio and tries in vain to understand *why* it makes her so happy, Emily can feel only the tiniest roughening and crinkling of the paper, like hands after washing-up. That's all she can feel, even with her lower lip. She tries not to feel too disappointed. There must be something there, she thinks. Her mother says so.

Post comment:
blueeyedboy: *That was beautiful,* **Albertine**.
Albertine: *Glad you liked it,* **blueeyedboy** . . .

You are viewing the webjournal of **blueeyedboy**
posting on:
                        badguysrock@webjournal.com
Posted at: *04.16 on Friday, February 8*
Status: *public*
Mood: *creative*
Listening to: The *Moody Blues*: 'The Story In
Your Eyes'

Poor Emily. Poor Mrs White. So close and yet so
far apart. What had started with Mr White and our
hero's abortive quest for his father had broadened
into a kind of obsession with the whole of the
household: with Mrs White, her husband, and most
of all, with Emily, the little sister he might have
had if things had turned out differently.

And so, all through that summer, the summer of
his eleventh year, *blueeyedboy* followed them in
secret, ritually noting their comings and goings;
their clothes; the things they liked to do; their
haunts, in the cloth-backed Blue Book that served
him as a journal.

He followed them to the sculpture park where
little Emily liked to play; to the open farm with its
piglets and lambs; to the pottery workshop café in
town, where for the price of a cup of tea you could
buy and shape a lump of clay, to be baked in the
oven the same day, then painted and taken home
to take pride of place on some mantelpiece, in

some cabinet.

The Saturday of the blue clay, Emily was four years old. *Blueeyedboy* had spotted her with Mrs White, walking slowly down the hill into Malbry, Emily in a little red coat that made her look like an unseasonal Christmas bauble, her little dark head bobbing up and down, Mrs White in boots and a blue print dress, her long blonde hair trailing down her back. He followed them all the way into town, keeping close to the hedges that lined the road. Mrs White never noticed him, not even when he ventured close, shadowing her blue silhouette with the doggedness of a junior spy.

Blueeyedboy, junior spy. He liked the stealthy sound of the phrase, its pearly string of sibilants, its secret hint of gunsmoke. He followed them into Malbry town centre, and into the pottery workshop, where Feather was waiting at a table for four, a cup of coffee in front of her, a half-smoked cigarette between her elegant fingers.

Blueeyedboy would have liked to have joined them there, but Feather's presence daunted him. Since that first day at the market, he had sensed that she didn't like him somehow, that she thought he wasn't good enough for Mrs White or Emily. So he sat at a table behind them, trying to look casual, as if he had money to spend there and business of his own to conduct.

Feather eyed him suspiciously. She was wearing a brown ethnic-print dress and a lot of tortoiseshell bangles that clattered as she moved the hand holding the half-smoked cigarette.

Blueeyedboy avoided her gaze and pretended to look out of the window. When he dared to look back again, Feather was talking quite loudly to

217

Mrs White, elbows on the table, occasionally tapping a little cone of cigarette ash into her empty teacup.

The pretty waitress came up to him. 'Are you all together?' she said.

Blueeyedboy realized that she had assumed that he had come in with Mrs White, and before he could stop himself, he'd said yes. Against the sound of Feather's voice, his small deception went unnoticed, and in a few moments the waitress had brought him a Pepsi and a lump of clay, with the kindly instruction to call for her if ever he needed anything more.

He was not sure what he'd intended to make. A dog for Ma's collection, perhaps; something to put on the mantelpiece. Something—anything—to draw her away, even for an instant, from the Mansion, Dr Peacock's work, and aspects of synaesthesia.

He watched them over his Pepsi, looking askance at Emily with her starfish hands splayed around her lump of blue clay. Feather was encouraging her, saying: *Make something, darling. Make a shape.* Mrs White was leaning forward, tensed with hope and expectancy, her long hair hanging so close to the clay that it looked as if it might stick there.

'What's it going to be? A face?'

There came a sound from Emily that might have been acquiescence.

'And those are the *eyes*, and there's the *nose*—' said Feather, sounding ecstatic, though *blueeyedboy* couldn't see anything much to provoke such rapt excitement.

Emily's hands moved on the clay, gouging a hole

here and there, exploring with her fingertips, scraping her nails around the back to form the semblance of hair. Now he could see it *was* a head, though primitive and misshapen, with bat's ears and a ludicrous pseudo-scientist's brow that dwarfed the other features. The eyes were shallow thumbprints; barely even visible.

But Feather and Mrs White crowed in delight, and *blueeyedboy* drew closer to them, trying to see what it was in their eyes that made it so remarkable.

Feather gave him a dirty look. He pulled away from the table at once. But Mrs White had noticed him, and instead of pleased recognition, he saw a look of alarm in her eyes, as if she thought he might hurt Emily, as if he could be dangerous—

'What are *you* doing here?' she said.

He gave a shrug. 'N-nothing.'

'Where are your brothers? Your mother?'

He shrugged. Faced with his long-pursued quarry at last, he found that speech had abandoned him, leaving nothing but broken syllables and a stammer that rendered him helpless.

'You're following me,' said Mrs White. 'What do you want?'

Again, he shrugged. He couldn't have explained it to her even if they had been alone, and Feather's presence by her side made it even less possible. He twisted on the seat of his chair, feeling trapped and foolish, with the taste of the vitamin drink in his throat, and his forehead like a squeezed balloon—

Feather narrowed her eyes at him. 'You know this counts as harassment,' she said. 'Catherine could call the police.'

219

'He's only a boy,' said Mrs White.

'Boys grow up,' said Feather darkly.

'What do you want?' said Mrs White again.

'I-I just w-wanted to s-see E-Emily,' said *blueeyedboy*, feeling nauseous. He looked at the lump of untouched clay and the half-drunk Pepsi at his side. He hadn't intended to order them. He had no money to pay for them. And now here was Mrs White's friend talking about calling the police—

He really meant to tell her the truth. But now he hardly knew what that was. He had thought that when he spoke to her he would know what it was that he wanted to say. But now, as the vegetable stink increased and the ache in his head intensified, he knew that what he wanted from her was something far closer to the bone; a word that came clothed in shades of blue . . .

Late that night, alone in his room, he took out the Blue Book from under his bed and, instead of his journal, began to write a story.

Post comment:

ClairDeLune: *Interesting, how this fic explores the evolution of the creative process. If you don't mind, I'd like to circulate this to some of my other students—or maybe we could discuss it here?*

> *You are viewing the webjournal of* **blueeyedboy**.
> **Posted at**: *22.40 on Friday, February 8*
> **Status**: *restricted*
> **Mood**: *ominous*
> **Listening to**: *Jarvis Cocker*: 'I Will Kill Again'

Eleanor Vine called round early tonight while Ma was getting ready to go out, and took the opportunity to take Yours Truly to task again. It seems that my continuing absence from our writing-as-therapy group has been noted and commented upon. She doesn't attend herself, of course—too many people; too much dirt—but I guess Terri must have talked.

People talk to Eleanor. She seems to invite confidences, somehow. And I can see how it's killing her that she has known me all this time and still has no more knowledge of me than when I was four years old—

'You really should go back, you know,' she says. 'You need to get out more. Make new friends. Besides, you owe it to your Ma—'

Owe it to Ma? Don't make me laugh.

I adjusted my iPod earpiece. It's the only way I can deal with her. Through it, in his rasping voice, Jarvis Cocker confided to me what, if given half a chance, he would do to someone like Eleanor—

She gave me a look of fish-eyed reproach. 'I hear there's someone who's missing you.'

'Really?' I feigned innocence.

'Don't be coy. She likes you.' She gave me a nudge. 'You could do worse.'

'Yeah. Thanks, Mrs Vine.'

Interfering old trout. As if that collection of fucktards and losers could ever throw up a live one. I know who she means; I'm not interested. In my earpiece Cocker's voice shifted registers, now soaring plaintively towards the octave:

And don't believe me if I claim to be your friend
'Cos given half the chance I know that I will kill
again . . .

But Eleanor Vine is persistent as glue. 'You could be a nice-looking young man, once those bruises have disappeared. You don't want to be selling yourself short. I've seen you hanging around that girl, and you know as well as I do that if your Ma knew, there'd be hell to pay.'

I flinched at that. 'I don't know what you mean.'

'That girl in the Pink Zebra. The one with all the tattoos,' she said.

'Who, Bethan?' I said. 'She hates me.'

Eleanor raised an eyebrow that was mostly skin and wire. 'On first-name terms, then, are we?' she said.

'I hardly ever speak to her, except to order Earl Grey.'

'That's not what *I've* heard,' said Eleanor.

That'll be Terri, I told myself. She sometimes goes into the Zebra. In fact, I think she follows me. It's getting quite hard to avoid her.

'Bethan's not my type,' I said.

Eleanor seemed to calm down after that, the

roguish expression returning to her sharp and avid features. 'So—you'll think about what I said, then? A girl like our Terri won't wait around for ever. You're going to have to do something soon—'

I gave a sigh. 'All right,' I said.

She gave me an approving look. 'I knew you'd see sense. Now—I have to go. I know your Ma's got her salsa class. But keep me up to date, won't you? And remember what they always say—'

I wondered what cliché she would use this time. *Faint heart never won fair lady*? Or: *Best strike while the iron's hot*?

As it was, she didn't have the chance, because Ma came in just at that moment, all in black, with sequins. Her dancing shoes had six-inch heels. I didn't envy her partner.

'Eleanor! What a surprise!'

'Just having a chat with B.B.,' she said.

'That's nice.' I thought Ma's eyes narrowed a little.

'I'm surprised he doesn't have a girlfriend,' said Eleanor, with a sideways glance. 'If I were twenty years younger,' she said, addressing her words to my mother now, 'I swear I'd marry him myself.'

I considered Mrs Vine in blue. It suited her.

'Really,' said Ma.

I suppose she means well, I told myself, even though she has no idea what she's dealing with. She's only trying to do what's best, as Ma always tries to do what's best for me. But *Our Terri*, as she calls her, is hardly the stuff of fantasy. Besides, I have no time for romance. I have other fish to fry.

Mrs Vine gave me something that I guessed was meant to be a smile. 'Can you drop me off at home? I'd walk, but I know you'll be driving your ma, and—'

'Yes,' I said. 'You have to go.'

You are viewing the webjournal of **blueeyedboy** *posting on*:

badguysrock@webjournal.com

Posted at: *23.49 on Saturday, February 9*
Status: *public*
Mood: *clean*
Listening to: *Genesis*: 'One For The Vine'

He calls her Mrs Chemical Blue. Hygiene and neatness are her concern; something that, in fifteen years, has gone beyond reason—or even a joke. Biscuits eaten over the sink; windows washed daily; dusting ten, twenty times a day; ornaments on the mantelpiece rearranged every quarter of an hour. She was always house-proud—*and what an odd word*, he thinks to himself, recalling what he knows of that house, and the way she used to watch his Ma at work, thin hands clenched in fearful distress, her face rigid with anxiety that a dishtowel might be left disastrously unaligned, or a mat slightly askew to the door, or a speck of dust left on a rug, or even a knick-knack out of place.

Mr Chemical Blue has long gone, taking their teenage son with him. Perhaps she regrets it a little, sometimes; but children are so messy, she thinks, and she never could make him understand how hiring a cleaner only complicated things; caused her, not less, but more work; meant something else to supervise, another person in the house, another set of fingerprints—and although she knew no one was to blame, she found their presence unbearable—yes, even that sweet little boy—until finally they had to go—

Since then, of course, it has worsened. With no one to keep her under control, obsession has taken over her life. No longer content with her spotless house, she has progressed to compulsive hand-washing and near-toxic doses of Listerine. Always slightly neurotic, fifteen years of alcohol and antidepressants have taken their toll on her personality so that now, at fifty-nine years old, she is nothing but twitches and tics, a nervous system out of control, thinly upholstered in wan flesh.

No one would miss her, he tells himself. In fact, it would probably be a relief. An anonymous gift to her family: to her son, who visits twice a year and who can hardly bear to see her like this; to her husband, who has moved on, and whose guilt has grown like a tumour; to her niece, who lives in despair of her perpetual interference and her well-meant but disastrous attempts to fix her up with a nice young man.

Besides, she, too, deserves to die; if only for the waste of time, for sunny days spent indoors, for words unspoken, for smiles unnoticed, for all the things she could have done if only she could have settled for *less*—

Only gossip sustains her now. Gossip, rumour and speculation, disseminated via telephone lines on to the parish grapevine. Behind her lace curtains, she sees all. Nothing goes unnoticed to her; no lingering speck of human dirt. No crime, no secret, no petty aberration goes unreported. Nothing escapes examination. No one evades

226

judgement. Does she sometimes wish that she could put it all aside, throw open the door and breathe the air? Does she sometimes wonder whether her obsessive attention to cleanliness does not hide a different kind of dirt?

She may have done so, long ago. But now all she can do is watch. Like a crab in its shell, like a barnacle, battened tight against the world. What does she do in there all day? No one is allowed to enter the house unless they leave their shoes outside. Teacups are disinfected before and after use. Groceries are delivered to the front porch. Even the postman deposits the mail, not through the door, but into a metal box by the gate, to be retrieved furtively, and at speed, by Mrs Chemical Blue, wearing Marigolds, her pale eyes wide with the daily unease of traversing six feet of unsanitized space . . .

It's a challenge he cannot resist. To erase her like a difficult stain; to oust her like a parasite; to winkle her out of her shell and force her into the open again.

But in the end, it's easy. It requires only subterfuge and some small expense. A hired white minivan, bearing the insignia of an imaginary firm; a baseball cap and a dark-blue jumpsuit with the same firm's logo embroidered on the top pocket; sundry items ordered via the Internet, paid on a borrowed credit card and delivered to a PO box in town; plus a clipboard to give him authority, and a glossy illustrated brochure (wholly produced on his desktop PC) extolling the virtues of an industrial cleaning product of such efficiency that it has only now been granted a licence for (strictly limited) domestic use.

He explains all this through a crack in the door, from which Mrs Chemical Blue's eye watches him with a jellyfish glaze. For a moment, fear outstrips her desire; and then she caves in, as he knows she will, and invites the nice young man inside.

This time, he really wants to watch. So he wears a mask for the crucial part, bought from an Army surplus store. The gas, purchased from a US website claiming to deal with unwanted parasites, remains officially untested on humans, as yet— although a local dog has already contributed to his research, with very promising results. Mrs Chemical Blue should last longer, he thinks; but given her poor immunity and the nervous rise and fall of her chest, he is fairly sure of the outcome.

Still, he expects to feel something more. Guilt, perhaps; even pity. Instead he feels only scientific curiosity mixed with that childlike sense of wonder at the smallness of it all. Death is no big deal, he thinks. The difference between life and its opposite can be as small as a blood clot, as insignificant as a bubble of air. The body is, after all, a machine. He knows a little about machines. The greater the number of moving parts, the greater the chance of things going wrong. And the body has so many moving parts—

Not for long, he tells himself.

The agonal phase (this being the term used by clinicians to describe the visible part of life's attempt to detach itself from protoplasm too compromised to sustain it) lasts for slightly less than two minutes according to his Seiko watch. He tries to observe dispassionately, to avoid the twitching hands and feet of the dying woman on the floor and to try to determine the goings-on behind those peculiar jellyfish eyes, the final, barking gasps for breath—

For a moment the sound makes him queasy, as for a fleeting moment (is there any other kind?) a phantom taste accompanies it—a taste of rotten fruit and dead cabbage—but he forces himself to ignore it by concentrating on Mrs Chemical Blue, whose agonal phase is coming to an end, her floating eyes beginning to glaze, her lips now a shade between cyan and mauve.

In the end, he does not know enough about anatomy to be absolutely certain of the true cause of death. But as Hippocrates used to say: *Man is an obligate aerobe.* Which probably means, he later concludes, that Mrs Chemical Blue died because her aerobically obligated cells failed to receive enough oxygen, thereby resulting in lethal shock.

In other words, therefore, *not my fault.*

His latex gloves have left no prints on the well-polished surfaces. His boots are new, right out of the box, and leave no telltale traces of mud. A window left open will disperse the smell from the offending canister, which he will toss into a skip as he passes the municipal dump before returning the van—minus its logo—to the firm from which he hired it. Her death will look like an accident—a seizure, a stroke, a heart attack—and even if they suspect foul play, there's nothing to make them suspect him.

He burns the jumpsuit and the workman's cap on the bonfire of leaves in his back yard, and the scent of that burning—like Bonfire Night—reminds him of toffee and candyfloss and the turning of fairground wheels in the dark; things that his mother always denied him, though his brothers went to the fair, coming home sticky-fingered and stinking of smoke, and queasy from the carnival rides, while he remained safely indoors, where nothing bad could happen to him.

Today, however, he is free. He rakes the heart of the bonfire and feels its heat against his face; and he feels a surge of sudden release—

And he knows he's going to do it again. He even knows who the next one will be. He breathes in that scent of bonfire smoke, thinks of her face, and smiles to himself—

And all around him, the colours flare like fireworks exploding in the sky.

Post comment:

ClairDeLune: *We need to talk about this, **blueeyedboy**. I think the way in which your fiction is developing sheds interesting insights on your family relationships. Why don't you message me later today? I'd really like to discuss it with you.*

JennyTricks: *(post deleted).*

blueeyedboy: *Hello again. Do I know you?*

JennyTricks: *(post deleted).*

JennyTricks: *(post deleted).*

JennyTricks: *(post deleted).*

blueeyedboy: *Please, Jenny. Do I know you?*

You are viewing the webjournal of **blueeyedboy**.
Posted at: *14.38 on Sunday, February 10*
Status: *restricted*
Mood: *sleepless*
Listening to: *Van Morrison*: 'Wild Night'

Lots of love to my journal today. Mostly in response to my fic, which Clair believes is a breakthrough in style, Toxic assures me *pwns ass*, Cap summarizes as *fuckin' resplendent, man*, and Chryssie, who is still sick, thinks is *awesome (and really hott!)*.

Well, sick she may be, but Chryssie is happy. She has lost six pounds this week—which means, according to her online calorie counter, that, assuming she keeps to her present rate, she will achieve her weight loss goal by this August, rather than July of next year—and she sends love and virtual hugs to her friend *azurechild*, who has always been so supportive.

Clair, however, is upset. She has received an e-mail from Angel Blue. Or rather, from a representative, telling her to cease her correspondence with Angel forthwith, and threatening legal action.

Poor Clair is hurt and indignant. She has never sent any offensive letters or suspicious packages, either to Angel or to his wife. Why would she? She worships Angel. She respects his privacy. She is certain his wife is behind all this. Angel is too nice, she says, to do this to someone who has become, over the months, a friend.

Mrs Angel's jealousy is proof of what she has long since suspected: that Angel's marriage is in crisis; or may even have been a sham from the start. Her online pleas to Angel Blue have begun to attract an audience. Some post to tell her to get a life. Some encourage her to pursue her dream. Some have tales of their own to tell of disappointment, love and revenge. One correspondent, *Hawaiianblue*, urges her to hold fast, to gain her man's attention by force, to show him some token of her love that no one could possibly mistake—

And *Albertine* has been posting fic. I take this as a good sign; now that she has in some way recovered from the shock of my brother's death, she has been online every day.

During their time together, of course, her presence was far less regular. Sometimes several weeks would pass without her even logging on. As webmaster, I can track her movements: how many times she visits the site; what she posts there; what she reads.

I know that she follows everything I write, even the comments. She reads Clair's entries, too, and Chryssie's—I know she is concerned about Chryssie's dieting. She doesn't talk to Cap much— I sense he makes her uncomfortable—but *Toxic69* is a regular correspondent, perhaps because of his handicap. To some, these online friendships can take on a disproportionate significance, especially for those of us for whom the world on screen is more real, more tangible than what lies outside.

Today, she wanted to talk to me. Perhaps it was because of Nigel's funeral, or my last fic. She may have found it disturbing. In fact, I was rather hoping she would. In any case, she came to me, via our private messaging service. Hesitant, shaken, slightly indignant, a child in need of comforting.

Where do you get these stories you write? Why do you have to tell them here?

Ah. The perennial question. Where do stories come from? Are they like dreams, shaped by our subconscious? Do goblins bring them in the night? Or are they all simply forms of the truth, mirror versions of what could have been, twisted and plaited like corn dollies into a plaything for children?

Perhaps I have no choice, I type. It's closer to the truth than she thinks.

A pause. I'm used to her silences. This one goes on a little too long, and I know that she is somehow distressed.

You didn't like my last fic.

It isn't a question. The silence grows. Alone of all my online tribe, *Albertine* has no icon. Where all the others display an image—Clair's picture of Angel Blue, Chryssie's winged child, Cap's cartoon rabbit—she keeps to the default setting: a silhouette in a plain blue square.

The result is oddly disconcerting. Icons and avatars are part of the way we interact. Like the shield designs of mediaeval times, they serve both as a defensive tool and as the image of ourselves we show to the world, cheap escutcheons for those of us with no honour, no king, no country.

So how does *Albertine* see herself?

Time passes, lingering, ticking off the seconds

233

like an impatient schoolmistress. For a while I am sure she has gone.

Then at last she replies. *Your story disturbed me a little*, she says. *The woman reminds me of someone I know. A friend of your mother's, actually.*

Funny, how fact and fic intertwine. I say as much to *Albertine.*

Eleanor Vine's in hospital. She was taken ill late last night. Something to do with her lungs, I heard—

Really? What a coincidence.

If I didn't know any better, she says, *I could almost believe you were somehow involved.*

Could you really? I had to smile.

It sounds just a touch sarcastic to me. But in the absence of facial expressions, there is no way of knowing for sure. If this had been Chryssie or Clair, then she would have followed her comment with a symbol—a smile, a wink, a crying face—to eliminate ambiguity. But *Albertine* does not use emoticons. Their absence makes conversation with her curiously expressionless, and I am never entirely sure if I have understood her fully.

Do you feel guilty, blueeyedboy?

Long pause.

Truth or dare?

Blueeyedboy hesitates, weighing the joy of confiding in her against the danger of saying too much. Fiction is a dangerous friend; a smokescreen that could dissipate and blow away without warning, leaving him naked.

Finally he types: *Yes.*

Maybe that's why you write these things. Maybe you're assuming guilt for something you're not really guilty of.

Hm. What an interesting idea. *You don't think*

I'm guilty of anything?

Everyone's guilty of something, she says. *But sometimes it's easier to confess to something we haven't done than to face up to the truth.*

Now she's trying to profile *me*. I told you she was clever.

So—why do you come here, Albertine? What do you think you're guilty of?

Silence, then, for so long that I'm almost sure she has broken the connection. The cursor blinks, relentlessly. The mailbox *bips*. Once. Twice.

I wonder what I would do now if she simply told the truth. But nothing's ever that easy. Does she even know what she did? Does she *know* that it all started then, at the concert in St Oswald's Chapel, a word that conjures up for me the Christmassy colours of stained glass and the scent of pine and frankincense?

Who are you really, *Albertine*? Plain-vanilla or bad guy at heart? A killer, a coward, a fraudster, a thief? And when I reach the centre of you, will I know if there's anyone home?

And then she replies, and quickly logs off before I can comment or ask for more. In the absence of icons or avatars, I cannot be sure of her motives, but I sense that she is running away, that I have finally touched her somehow—

Truth or dare, Albertine? What have you come here to confess?

Her message to me is just four words long. It simply says:

I told a lie.

You are viewing the webjournal of **blueeyedboy**
posting on:
                              badguysrock@webjournal.com
Posted at: *04.38 on Monday, February 11*
Status: *public*
Mood: *confiding*
Listening to: *Hazel O'Connor*: 'Big Brother'

Everyone does it. Everyone lies. Everyone colours the truth to fit: from the fisherman who exaggerates the length of the carp that got away, to the politician's memoir, transmuting the metal of base experience into the gold of history. Even *blueeyedboy*'s diary (hidden under his mattress at home) was far more wish-fulfilment than fact, detailing with pathetic hopefulness the life of a boy he could never be—a boy with two parents, a boy with friends, a boy who did ordinary things, who went to the seaside on his birthday, a boy who loved his Ma—knowing that the bleaker truth was hiding there under the surface, patiently waiting to be exposed by some casual turn of the tide.

*   *   *

Ben failed the St Oswald's entrance exam. He should have seen it coming, of course, but he'd been told so many times that he would pass that everyone took it for granted, like crossing a friendly border, nothing more than a token gesture to ensure his passage into St Oswald's, and subsequently, his success—

It wasn't that the paper was hard. In fact, he found it quite easy—or would have done, if he'd finished it. But that place, with its smells, unmanned him; and the cavernous room filled with uniforms; and the lists of names tacked to the wall; and the cheesy, hostile faces of the other scholarship boys.

A panic attack, the doctor said. A physical reaction to stress. It began with a nervous headache, which, halfway through the first paper, rapidly grew into something more: a turbulence of colour and scent that drenched him like a tropical storm and bludgeoned him into unconsciousness, there on St Oswald's parquet floor.

They took him to Malbry Infirmary, where he pleaded to be given a bed. He knew his scholarship had sailed, and that Ma was going to be furious, and that the only way to avoid real trouble was by getting the doctors on his side.

But once again, his luck was out. The nurse called Ma straight away, and the teacher who had accompanied him—a Dr Devine, a thin man whose name was a murky dark green—told her what had happened to him.

'You'll let him retake the exam, though?' Ma's first anxious thought was of the longed-for scholarship. To make things worse, by then Ben was feeling fine, with hardly a trace of a headache left. Her berry-black eyes locked briefly on his; long enough, at least, to convey that he was in a world of hurt.

'I'm afraid not,' said Dr Devine. 'That's not St

Oswald's policy. Now, if Benjamin were to sit the common exam—'

'You mean he won't get the scholarship?' Her eyes were narrowed almost to slits.

Dr Devine gave a little shrug. 'I'm afraid the decision isn't mine. Perhaps he could try again next year.'

Ma started forward. 'You don't understand—'

But Dr Devine had had enough. 'I'm sorry, Mrs Winter,' he said, heading for the infirmary door. 'We can't make exceptions for just one boy.'

She kept her calm until they got home. Then she unleashed her rage. First with the piece of electrical cord, then afterwards with her fists and feet, while Nigel and Brendan watched like caged monkeys from the upstairs landing, their faces pressed silently against the bars.

It wasn't the first time she'd beaten him. She'd beaten them all at some time or another—mostly Nigel, but Benjamin too, and even stupid Brendan, who was too scared of everything to ever put a foot wrong—it was her way of keeping them under control.

But this time it was something else. She'd always thought him exceptional. Now, it seemed, he was *just one boy*. The knowledge must have come as a shock, a terrible disappointment to her. Well, that's what *blueeyedboy* thinks now. In fact, he must have known even then that his mother was going insane.

'You lying, malingering little *shit*!'

'No, Ma, please,' whimpered Ben, trying to shield his face with his arms.

'You blew that exam on purpose, Ben! You let me down on purpose!' She grabbed him with one

238

hand by the hair and forced his arm away from his face in readiness for another blow.

He closed his eyes and reached for the words, the magic words to tame the beast. Then came inspiration—

'Please. Ma. It's not my fault. Please, Ma. I love you—'

She stopped. Fist raised like a gauntlet of gems, one eye levelled malignantly.

'What did you say?'

'I love you, Ma—'

Back then, when Ben had gained some ground, he needed to consolidate his position. He was already shaken, already in tears. It didn't take much to summon the rest. And as he clung to her, snivelling, his brothers still watching from the top of the stairs, it struck him that he was good at this, that if he played his cards right, he might just survive. Everyone has an Achilles heel. Ben had just found his mother's.

Then, from behind the bars of the staircase he saw Brendan's eyes go wide. For a moment Brendan held his gaze, and he was suddenly convinced that Bren, who never read anything, had read his mind as easily as he might read a Ladybird book.

His brother looked away at once. But not before Ben had seen that look; that look of understanding. Was it really so obvious? Or had he just been wrong about Bren? For years he had simply dismissed him as a fat and useless waste of space. But how much did Benjamin really know about his backward brother? How much had he taken for granted? He wondered now if he'd made a mistake; if Bren wasn't brighter than he'd thought. Bright enough to have seen through his act. Bright enough to present a threat—

He freed himself from Ma's embrace. Bren was still waiting on the stairs, looking scared and stupid once more. But Benjamin knew he was faking it. Beneath that drab plumage his brother in brown was playing some deeper game of his own. He didn't know what it was—not yet. But from that moment, Benjamin knew that one day he might have to deal with Bren—

Post comment:
Albertine: *Are you sure you know where you're going with this?*
blueeyedboy: *Quite sure. Are you?*
Albertine: *I'm following you. I always have.*
blueeyedboy: *Ah! The snows of yesteryear . . .*

> *You are viewing the webjournal of* **Albertine** *posting on*:
>
> **badguysrock@webjournal.com**
> **Posted at**: *20.14 on Monday, February 11*
> **Status**: *public*
> **Mood**: *mendacious*

Yes, that's where it starts. With a little white lie. White, like the pretty snow. Snow White, like in the story—and who would think snow could be dangerous, that those little wet kisses from the sky could turn into something deadly?

It's all about momentum, you see. Just as that one little, thoughtless lie took on a momentum of its own. A stone can set off an avalanche. A word can sometimes do the same. And a lie can become the avalanche, bringing down everything in its path, bludgeoning, roaring, smothering, reshaping the world in its wake, rewriting the course of our lives.

*   *   *

Emily was five and a half when her father first took her to the school where he taught. Until then it had been a mysterious place (remote and beguiling as all mythical places) which her parents sometimes discussed over the dinner-table. Not often, though: Catherine disliked what she called

'Patrick's shop-talk' and frequently turned the conversation to other matters just as it became most interesting. Emily gathered that 'school' was a place where children came together—to learn, or so her father said, though Catherine seemed to disagree.

'How many children?'

Buttons in a box; beans in a jar. 'Hundreds.'

'Children like me?'

'No, Emily. Not like you. St Oswald's School is just for boys.'

By now she was reading avidly. Braille books for children were hard to find, but her mother had created tactile books from felt and embroidery, and Daddy spent hours every day carefully transcribing stories—all typed in reverse, using the old embossing machine. Emily could already add and subtract as well as divide and multiply. She knew the history of the great artists; she had studied relief maps of the world and of the solar system. She knew the house inside and out. She knew about plants and animals from frequent visits to the children's farm. She could play chess. She could play the piano, too—a pleasure she shared with her father—and her most precious hours were spent with him in his room, learning scales and chords and stretching her small hands in a vain effort to span an octave.

But of other children she knew very little. She heard their voices when she played in the park. She had once petted a baby, which smelt vaguely sour and felt like a sleeping cat. Her next-door neighbour was called Mrs Brannigan, and for some reason she was inferior—perhaps because she was Catholic; or perhaps because she rented her house, whilst theirs was bought and paid for. Mrs Brannigan had a daughter a little older than Emily, with whom she would have liked to play, but who spoke with such a strong accent that the first and only time they had spoken, Emily had not understood a word.

But Emily's father worked in a place where there were hundreds of children, all learning maths and geography and French and Latin and art and history and music and science; as well as fighting in the yard, shouting, talking, making friends, chasing each other, eating dinners in a long room, playing cricket and tennis on the grass.

'I'd like to go to school,' she said.

'You wouldn't.' That was Catherine, with the warning note in her voice. 'Patrick, stop talking shop. You know how it upsets her.'

'It doesn't upset me. I'd like to go.'

'Perhaps I could take her with me one day. Just to see—'

'*Patrick!*'

'Sorry. Just—you know. There's the Christmas concert next month, love. In the school chapel. I'm conducting. She likes—'

'Patrick, I'm not listening!'

'She likes music, Catherine. Let me take her. Just this once.'

And so, just once, Emily went. Perhaps because of Daddy; but mostly because Feather was in favour of the plan. Feather was a staunch believer in the healing powers of music; besides, she had recently read Gide's *La Symphonie Pastorale*, and felt that a concert might boost Emily's flagging colour therapy.

But Catherine didn't like the idea. I think now

that part of it was guilt; the same guilt that had pushed her to remove all traces of Daddy's passion for music from the house. The piano was an exception; even so, it had been relegated to a spare room, where it sat amongst boxes of forgotten papers and old clothes, where Emily was not supposed to venture. But Feather's enthusiasm tipped the balance, and on the evening of the concert they all walked down towards St Oswald's, Catherine smelling of turpentine and rose (*a pink smell*, she tells Emily, *pretty pink roses*), Feather talking high and very fast, and Emily's father guiding her gently by the shoulder, taking care not to let her slip in the wet December snow.

'OK?' he whispered, as they neared the place.

'Mm-mm.'

She had been disappointed to hear that the concert was not to take place in the school itself. She would have liked to visit Daddy's place of work; to have entered the classrooms with their wooden desks, smelt the chalk and the polish; heard the echo of their footsteps against the wooden floors. Later, she was allowed those things. But this event was to take place in the nearby chapel, with the St Oswald's choristers, and her father *conducting*, which she understood to mean guiding, somehow; showing the singers the way.

It was a cold, damp evening that smelt of smoke. From the road came the sounds of cars and bicycle bells and people talking, muffled almost to nothing in the foggy air. In spite of her winter coat she was cold; her thin-soled shoes squelching against the gravel path, and droplets of moisture in her hair. Fog makes the outside feel smaller, somehow; just

244

as the wind expands the world, making the trees rustle and soar. That evening Emily felt very small, squashed down almost to nothing by the dead air. From time to time someone passed her—she felt the swish of a lady's dress, or it might have been a Master's gown—and heard a snatch of conversation before they were once more swept away.

'Won't it be crowded, Patrick? Emily doesn't like crowds.' That was Catherine again, her voice tight as the bodice of Emily's best party dress, which was pretty (and pink) and which had been brought from storage for one last outing before she outgrew it completely.

'It's fine. You've got front-row seats.'

As a matter of fact Emily didn't mind crowds. It was the *noise* she didn't like: those flat and blurry voices that confused everything and turned everything around. She took hold of her father's hand, rather tightly, and squeezed. A single pump meant *I love you*. A double-pump, *I love you, too*. Another of their small secrets, like the fact that she could almost span an octave if she bounced her hand over the keys, and play the lead line of *Für Elise* while her father played the chords.

It was cool inside the chapel. Emily's family didn't attend church—though their neighbour, Mrs Brannigan, did—and she had been inside St Mary's once, just to hear the echo. St Oswald's Chapel sounded like that; their steps *slap-slapped* on the hard, smooth floor, and all the sounds in the place seemed to go *up*, like people climbing an echoey staircase and talking as they went.

Daddy told her later that it was because the ceiling was so high, but at the time she imagined

245

that the choir would be sitting above her, like angels. There was a scent, too; something like Feather's patchouli, but stronger and smokier.

'That's incense,' said her father. 'They burn it in the sanctuary.'

Sanctuary. He'd explained that word. A place to go where you can be safe. Incense and Clan tobacco and angels' voices. Sanctuary.

There was movement all around them now. People were talking, but in lower voices than usual, as if they were afraid of the echoes. As Daddy went to join the choristers and Catherine described the organ and pews and windows for her, Emily heard *wishwishwish* from all around the hall, then a series of settling-down noises, then a hush as the choir began to sing.

It was as if something had broken open inside her. *This*, and not the piece of clay, is Emily's first memory: sitting in St Oswald's Chapel with the tears running down her face and into her smiling mouth, and the music, the lovely music, surging all around her.

Oh, it was not the first time that she had ever heard music; but the homely *rinkety-plink* of their old piano, or the tinny transistors of the kitchen radio, could not convey more than a particle of this. She had no name for what she could hear, no terms with which to describe this new experience. It was, quite simply, an awakening.

Later her mother tried to embellish the tale, as if it needed embellishment. She herself had never really enjoyed religious music—Christmas carols least of all, with their simple tunes and mawkish lyrics. Something by Mozart would have been much more suitable, with its implication of like

246

calling to like, though the legend has a dozen variations—from Mozart to Mahler and even to the inevitable Berlioz—as if the complexity of the music had any bearing on the sounds themselves, or the sensations they evoked.

In fact the piece was nothing more than a four-part a cappella version of an old Christmas carol.

> *In the bleak midwinter,*
> *Frosty wind made moan,*
> *Earth stood hard as iron,*
> *Water like a stone;*

But there is something unique about boys' voices; a tremulous quality, not entirely comfortable, perpetually on the brink of losing pitch. It is a sound that combines an almost inhuman sweetness of tone with a raw edge that is nearly painful.

She listened in silence for the first few bars, unsure of what she was hearing. Then the voices rose again:

> *Snow had fallen, snow on snow,*
> *Snow on snow—*

And on the second *snow* the voices grazed *that* note, the high F sharp that had always been a point of mysterious pressure in her, and Emily began to cry. Not from sorrow or even from emotion; it was simply a reflex, like that cramping of the tastebuds after eating something very sour, or the gasp of fresh chilli against the back of the throat.

Snow on snow, snow on snow they sang, and everything in her responded. She shivered; she smiled; she turned her face to the invisible roof and opened her mouth like a baby bird, half-expecting to *feel* the sounds like snowflakes falling on her tongue. For almost a minute Emily sat trembling on the edge of her seat, and every now and then the boys' voices would rise to that strange F sharp, that magical ice-cream-headache note, and the tears would spill once more from her eyes. Her lower lip tingled; her fingers were numb. She felt as if she were touching God—

'Emily, what is it?'

She could not reply. Only the sounds mattered.

'Emily!'

Every note seemed to cut into her in some delicious way; every chord a miracle of texture and shape. More tears fell.

'Something's wrong.' Catherine's voice came from a great distance. 'Feather, please. I'm taking her home.' Emily felt her starting to move; tugging at her coat, which she had been using as a cushion. 'Get up, sweetheart, we shouldn't have come.'

Was that satisfaction in her voice? Her hand on Emily's forehead was feverish and clammy. 'She's burning up. Feather, give me a hand—'

'No!' whispered Emily.

'Emily, darling, you're upset.'

'Please—' But now her mother was picking her up; Catherine's arms were around her. She caught a fleeting smell of turpentine behind the expensive perfume. Desperately she searched for something, some magic, to make her mother stop: something that would convey the urgency, the imperative to stay, to *listen* . . .

'Please, the music—'

Your mother doesn't care much for music. Daddy's voice; remote but clear.

248

But what *did* Catherine care for? What for her was the language of command?

They were half-out of their seats now. Emily tried to struggle; a seam ripped under the arm of her too-tight dress. Her coat, with its fur collar, smothered her. More of the turpentine smell, the smell of her mother's fever, her madness.

And suddenly Emily understood, with a maturity far beyond her years, that she would never visit her father's school, never go to another concert, just as she would never play with other children in case they hurt or pushed her, never run in the park in case she fell.

If they left now, Emily thought, then her mother would *always* have her way, and the blindness, which had never really troubled her, would finally drag her down like a stone tied to a dog's tail, and she would drown.

There must be words, she told herself; magic words, to make her mother stay. But Emily was five years old; she didn't know any magic words; and now she was moving down the aisle with her mother on one side and Feather on the other, and the lovely voices rolling over them like a river.

In the bleak midwinter,
Lo-ooong ago—

And then it came to her. So simple that she gasped at her own audacity. She *did* know magic words, she realized. Dozens of them; she had learnt them almost from the cradle, but had never really found a use for them until now. She knew their fearsome energy. Emily opened her mouth, stricken with a sudden, demonic inspiration.

249

'The colours,' she whispered.

Catherine White stopped mid-stride. 'What did you say?'

'The colours. Please. I want to stay.' Emily took a deep breath. 'I want to *listen to the colours*.'

Post comment:
blueeyedboy: *How brave of you to post this,* **Albertine**. *You know I'll have to reciprocate . . .*

•

You are viewing the webjournal of **blueeyedboy** *posting on:*

badguysrock@webjournal.com
Posted at: *23.03 on Monday, February 11*
Status: *public*
Mood: *scornful*
Listening to: *Pink Floyd*: 'Any Colour You Like'

Listen to the colours. Oh, please. Don't tell me she was innocent; don't tell me that, even then, she didn't know exactly what she was doing. Mrs White knew all about *Boy X* and his synaesthesia. She knew Dr Peacock would be near by. Easy enough to feed her the line; easier still to believe it when Emily responded by starting to hear the colours.

Ben was in his first year at school. Imagine him then: a chorister, all scrubbed and clean and ready to go in his blue St Oswald's uniform under the frilled white cassock.

I know what you're thinking. He failed the exam. But that was just the scholarship. With money she had set aside, as well as with help from Dr Peacock, Ma had managed to get him into St Oswald's after all, not as a scholar, but as a fee-paying pupil, and here he was in the front row of the school choir, hating every moment of it. And if they didn't already have good enough cause to despise him, he knew that the other boys in his form would never leave him alone after this, not to mention Nigel, who had been dragged along most reluctantly, and who would take it out on him later, he knew, in gibes and kicks and punches.

In the bleak midwinter,
Frosty wind made moan—

He'd prayed in vain for puberty to break his voice and release him. But whilst the other boys in his class were already thickening like palm trees, reeking of teenage civet, Ben remained slim and girlish and pale, with an eerie, off-key treble voice.

Earth stood hard as iron,
Water like a stone—

He could see his mother three rows back, listening for the sound of his voice, and Dr Peacock, behind her; and Nigel, going on seventeen, sprawled and scowling across the bench; and sweaty and malodorous Bren, looking terribly uncomfortable with his lank hair and his pursed-up face, like the world's most enormous baby.

Blueeyedboy tried not to look; to concentrate on the music, but now he caught sight of Mrs White, just a few seats away from him, with Emily by her side—Emily, in her little red coat and her dress of rose-pink, with her hair in bunches and her face illuminated with something half-distress, half-joy—

For a moment he thought her eyes caught his; but the eyes of the blind are like that, aren't they? Emily couldn't see him. Whatever he did, however he tried—Emily never would. And yet, those eyes drew him, skittering from side to side like marbles in a doll's head, like a couple of blue-eye beads,

252

reflecting ill-luck back to the sender.

Blueeyedboy's head was beginning to spin, throbbing in time to the music. A headache was coming; a bad one. He searched for the means to protect himself, imagining a capsule of blue, hard as iron, cold as stone, blue as a block of Arctic ice. But the pain was inescapable. A headache that would escalate until it wrung him like a rag—

It was hot in the choir stalls. Red-faced in their white smocks, the choristers sang like angels. St Oswald's takes its choir seriously: the boys are drilled in obedience. Like soldiers, they are trained to stand and keep their position for hours on end. No one complains. No one dares. *Sing your hearts out, boys, and smile!* bugles the choirmaster during rehearsals. *This is for God and St Oswald's. I don't want to see a single boy letting down the team.*

But now Ben Winter was looking pale. Perhaps the heat; the incense; perhaps the strain of keeping that smile. Remember, he was delicate; Ma always said so. More sensitive than the other two; more prone to illness and accidents—

The angel voices rose again, sweeping towards the crescendo.

Snow had fallen, snow on snow—

And that was when it happened. Almost in slow motion; a thud: a movement in the front row; a pale-faced boy collapsing unseen on to the floor of the chapel; striking his head on the side of a pew, a blow that would require four stitches to mend, a crescent moon on his forehead.

Why did no one notice him? Why was Ben so wholly eclipsed? No one saw him—not even Ma— for just as he fell, a little blind girl in the crowd suffered a kind of panic attack, and all eyes turned

253

to Emily White, Emily in the rose-coloured dress, flailing her arms and shouting out: *Please. I want to stay. I want to—*
  Listen to the colours.

Post comment:
Albertine: *Nice comeback*, **blueeyedboy**.
blueeyedboy: *Glad you liked it,* **Albertine**.
Albertine: *Well*, liked *is maybe not the word—*
blueeyedboy: *Nice comeback*, **Albertine** . . .

You are viewing the webjournal of **Albertine** *posting on:*

                        badguysrock@webjournal.com

Posted at: *23.49 on Monday, February 11*
Status: *public*
Mood: *raw*

Listen to the colours. Maybe you remember the phrase. Glib coming from the mouth of an adult, it must have seemed unbearably poignant from that of a five-year-old blind girl. In any case, it did the trick. *Listen to the colours*. All unknowing, Emily White had opened up a box of magic words, and was drunk with their power and her own, issuing commands like a diminutive general, commands which Catherine and Feather—and later, of course, Dr Peacock—obeyed with unquestioning delight.

'What do you see?'

Diminished chord of F minor. The magic words unfurl like wrapping-paper, every one.

'Pink. Blue. Green. Violet. So pretty.'

Her mother claps her hands in delight. 'More, Emily. Tell me more.'

A chord of F major.

'Red. Orange. Ma-gen-ta. Black.'

It was like an awakening. The infernal power she had discovered in herself had blossomed in an astonishing way, and music was suddenly a part of her curriculum. The piano was brought out of the spare room and re-tuned; her father's secret lessons became official, and Emily was allowed to practise whenever she liked, even when Catherine was working. Then came the local newspapers, and the letters and gifts came pouring in.

The story had plenty of potential. In fact, it had all the ingredients. A Christmas miracle; a photogenic blind girl; music; art; some man-in-the-street science, courtesy of Dr Peacock, and a lot of controversy from the art world that kept the papers wondering on and off for the next three years or so, caught up in speculation. The TV eventually caught on to it; so did the Press. There was even a single—a Top Ten hit—by a rock band whose name I forget. The song was later used in the Hollywood film—an adaptation of the book—starring Robert Redford as Dr Peacock and a young Natalie Portman as the blind girl who sees music.

At first Emily took it for granted. After all, she was very young, and had no basis for comparison. And she was very happy—she listened to music all day long; she studied what she loved most, and everyone was pleased with her.

Over the next twelve months or so Emily attended a number of concerts, as well as performances of *The Magic Flute*, the *Messiah* and *Swan Lake*. She went to her father's school several times, so that she could get to know the instruments by feel.

Flutes, with their slender bodies and intricate keys; pot-bellied cellos and double basses; French horns and tubas like big school canteen-jugs of sound; narrow-waisted violins; icicle bells; fat drums and flat drums; splash cymbals and crash cymbals; triangles and timpani and trumpets and tambourines.

Sometimes her father would play for her. He was different when Catherine was not there: he told jokes; he was exuberant, dancing Emily round and round to the music, making her dizzy with laughter. He would have liked to have been a professional musician: clarinet, and not piano, had been his preferred instrument, but there was little call for a classically trained clarinet player with a lurking passion for Acker Bilk, and his small ambitions had gone unvoiced and unnoticed.

But there was another side to Catherine's conversion. It took Emily months to discover it; longer still to understand. This is where my memories lose all cohesion; reality merges with myth so that I cannot trust myself to be either accurate or truthful. Only the facts speak for themselves; and even they have been so much disputed, queried, misreported, misread that only scraps remain of anything that might show me how it really was.

The facts, then. You must know the tale. In the audience that evening, sitting three rows from the front, at the end, was a man called Graham Peacock. Sixty-seven years old; a well-known local personality; a noted gourmet; a likeable eccentric; a generous patron of the arts. That evening in December, during a recital of Christmas songs in St Oswald's Chapel, Dr Peacock found himself party to an incident that was to change his life.

A small girl—the child of a friend of his—had suffered a kind of panic attack. Her mother began to carry her out, and in the scuffle that ensued—

the child struggling valiantly to stay, the mother trying with equal fortitude to remove her—he heard the child speak a phrase that struck at him like a revelation.

Listen to the colours.

At the time Emily barely understood the significance of what she had said. But Dr Peacock's interest left her mother in a state of near-euphoria; at home, Feather opened a bottle of champagne, and even Daddy seemed pleased, though that might just have been because of the change in Catherine. Nevertheless he did not approve; later, when the thing had begun, his was the only dissenting voice.

Needless to say, no one listened. The very next day little Emily was summoned to the Fireplace House, where every possible test was run to confirm her special talents.

Synaesthesia [writes Dr Peacock in his paper 'Aspects of Modularity'] *is a rare condition where two—or sometimes more—of the five 'normal' senses are apparently fused together. This seems to be related to the concept of modularity. Each of the sensory systems has a corresponding area, or module, of the brain. While there are normal interactions between modules (such as using vision to detect movement), the current understanding of human perception cannot account for the stimulation of one module inducing brain activity in a different module. However, in a synaesthete, this is precisely the case.*

In short, a synaesthete may experience any or all of the following: shape as taste, touch as

258

scent, sound or taste as colour.

All this was new to Emily, if not to Feather and Catherine. But she understood the idea—they all knew about *Boy X*, after all—and from what she'd heard of his special gift, it was not too far removed from the word associations and art lessons and colour therapies she had learnt from her mother. She was five and a half at the time; eager to please; even more so to perform.

The arrangement was simple. In the mornings Emily would go to Dr Peacock's house for her music lesson and her other subjects; and in the afternoons she would play the piano, listen to records, and paint. That was her only duty, and as she was allowed to listen to music as she performed it, it was no great burden. Sometimes Dr Peacock would ask her questions, and record what she said.

Emily, listen. What do you see?

A single note picked out on the clunky old piano in the Fireplace House. G is indigo, almost black. A simple triad takes it further; then a chord— G minor, with a diminished seventh in the bass— resolves in a velvety violet caress.

He marks the result in his notebook.

Very good, Emily. That's my good girl.

Next comes a series of soft chords; C sharp minor; D diminished; E flat minor seventh. Emily points out the colours, marked in Braille on the paintbox.

To Emily it feels almost like playing an instrument, her hands on the little coloured keys; and Dr Peacock notes it down in his scratchy little notepad, and then there is tea by the fireplace,

259

with Dr Peacock's Jack Russell, Patch II, snuffling hopefully after biscuits, tickling Emily's hands, making her laugh. Dr Peacock speaks to his dog as if he, too, is an elderly academic; which makes Emily laugh even more, and which soon becomes part of their lessons together.

'Patch II would like to enquire,' he says in his bassoony voice, 'whether today Miss White feels inclined to peruse my collection of recorded sounds—'

Emily giggles. 'You mean listen to records?'

'My furry colleague would appreciate it.'

On cue, Patch II barks.

Emily laughs. 'OK,' she says.

* * *

Over the thirty months that followed, Dr Peacock became an increasingly large part of all their lives. Catherine was deliriously happy; Emily was an apt pupil, spending three or four hours at the piano every day, and suddenly there was a much-needed focus to all of their lives. I doubt Patrick White could have stopped it, anyway, even if he had wanted to; after all, he too had a stake in the affair. He, too, wanted to believe.

Emily never asked herself why Dr Peacock was so generous. To her he was simply a kind and funny man who spoke in long and ponderous phrases and who never came to see them without bringing some gift of flowers, wine, books. On Emily's sixth birthday he gave her a new piano to replace the old, battered one on which she had learnt; throughout the year there were concert tickets, pastels, paints, easels, canvas, sweets and toys.

And music, of course. Always music. Even now that hurts most of all. To think of a time when Emily could play every day for as long as she liked, when every day was a fanfare, and Mozart, Mahler, Chopin, even Berlioz would line up like suitors for her favour, to be chosen or discarded at whim . . .

'Now, Emily. Listen to the music. Tell me what you hear.'

That was Mendelssohn, *Lieder ohne Worte*, Opus 19, Number 2, in A minor. The left-hand part is difficult to master, with its tight blocks of semi-quavers, but Emily has been practising, and now it's almost perfect. Dr Peacock is pleased. Her mother, too.

'Blue. Quite a dark blue.'

'Show me.'

She has a new paintbox now, sixty-four colours arranged like a chessboard, almost as broad as the desk-top. She cannot see them, but knows them by heart; arranged in order of brightness and tone. F is violet; G is indigo; A is blue; B is green; C is yellow; D is orange; E is red. Sharps are lighter; flats darker. Instruments, too, have their own colours within the orchestral palette: the woodwind section is often green or blue; the strings, brown and orange; the brass, red and yellow.

She picks up her thick brush and daubs it in the paint. She is using watercolours today, and the scent is chalky and grannyish, like Parma violets. Dr Peacock stands to one side, Patch II curled up at his feet. Catherine and Feather stand on the opposite side, ready to pass Emily anything she may need. A sponge; a brush; a smaller brush, a sachet of glitter powder.

The *Andante* is a leisurely abstract, like a day at the seaside. She dabbles her fingers in the paint and strokes them across the smooth untreated paper so that it contracts into ridges, like shallow-water sand, and the paint melts and slides into the gullies her fingers have left. Dr Peacock is pleased; she can hear the smile in his bassoony voice, although much of what he says is incomprehensible to her, swept aside by the lovely music.

Sometimes, other children come by. She remembers a boy, rather older than she is, who is shy, and stammers, and doesn't talk much, but sits on the sofa and reads. In the parlour there are sofas and chairs, a window seat and (her favourite) a swing, suspended from the ceiling on two stout ropes. The room is so large that Emily can swing as high as she likes without hitting anything; besides, everyone knows to keep out of her way, and there are no collisions.

Some days she does not paint at all; instead she sits on her swing in the Fireplace House and listens to sounds. Dr Peacock calls it the Sound Association Game, and if Emily works hard, he says, there will be a present at the end. All she has to do is sit on the swing, listen to the records and tell him the colours she can see. Some are easy—she already has them sorted in her mind like buttons in a box—others not. But she likes Dr Peacock's sound machines, and the records, especially the old ones, with their long-dead voices and wind-up scratchy gramophone strings.

Sometimes there is no music at all, but just a series of sound effects, and these are hardest of all. But Emily still tries her best to satisfy Dr Peacock, who writes down everything she says in a series of cloth-backed notebooks, sometimes with such force that his pencil goes through the paper.

'Listen, Emily. What do you see?'

The sound of a thousand Westerns; a gun fires, a bullet ricochets against a canyon wall; *Gunsmoke*; Bonfire Night and charred potatoes. 'Red.'

'Is that all?'

'Madder red. With a trail of crimson.'

'Good, Emily. Very good.'

It's really very easy; all she has to do is let her mind go. A penny dropped; a man whistling off-key; a single thrush; a door-knocker; the sound of one hand clapping. She goes home with her pockets crammed with sweets. Dr Peacock clack-clacks up his findings every night on a typewriter with a Donald Duck voice. His papers have names like 'Induced Synaesthesia', 'The Colour Complex' and 'Out of Sight, Out of Mind'. His words are like the gas the dentist gives her when he has to drill a tooth; she slides away under its shivery caress, and all the perfumes of the Orient cannot save her.

Post comment:
blueeyedboy: *Oh, yes!*
Albertine: *You mean you want more?*
blueeyedboy: *If you can bear it, then so can I . . .*

You are viewing the webjournal of **Albertine**
posting on:
> **badguysrock@webjournal.com**
Posted at: *01.45 on Tuesday, February 12*
Status: *public*
Mood: *culpable*

Most of this, of course, is speculation. Those
memories are not mine; they belong to Emily
White. As if Emily could be a reliable witness to
anything. And yet her voice—her plaintive treble—
calls to me from over the years. *Help me, please!
I'm still alive! You people buried me alive!*

  'Red. Dark red. Oxblood, with purple streaks.'

  Chopin's Nocturne Number 2 in E flat major.
She has a good ear for music, and at six years old
she can already pick out most of the chords,
although the fretful double-rows of chromatics are
still beyond the skill of her stubby fingers. This
does not trouble Dr Peacock. He is far more
interested in her painting skills than in any musical
talent.

  According to Catherine, he has already framed
and hung half a dozen of Emily's canvases on the
walls of the Fireplace House—including her
Toreador; her *Goldberg Variations*; and (her
mother's favourite) her *Nocturne in Violet Ochre*.

  'There's so much energy in them,' says
Catherine, in a trembling voice. 'So much

experience. It's almost mystic. The way you take the colours from the music and bring them on to the canvas—do you know, Emily? I envy you. I wish I could see what you see now.'

No child could fail to be flattered by such praise. Her paintings make people happy; they earn her rewards from Dr Peacock and the approval of his many friends. She understands that he is planning another book, much of it based on his recent findings.

She knows that she is not the only person he has befriended in his search for synaesthetes. In his book *Beyond Sense*, he explains, he has already written at length about the case of a teenage boy, referred to throughout simply as *Boy X*, who appeared to exhibit signs of olfactory-gustatory acquired synaesthesia.

'What does that mean?' Emily says.

'He experienced things in a special way. Or, at least, he said he could. Now concentrate on the notes, please—'

'What kind of things did he see?' she says.

'I don't think he saw anything.'

Until Emily's appearance on the scene, *Boy X* had been Dr Peacock's pet project. But between a young blind prodigy who can hear colours (and paint them), and a teenage boy with an affinity to smells, there could be no real competition. Besides, the boy was a freeloader, said Catherine; willing to fabricate any number of phoney symptoms to gain attention. The mother was even worse, she said; any fool could see that she'd put her son up to it in the hope of getting her hands on Dr Peacock's money.

'You're too trusting, Gray,' she said. 'Anyone

else would have spotted them a mile off. They saw you coming, dear. They had you fooled.'

'But my tests clearly show that the boy responds—'

'The boy responds to *money*, Gray. And so does his mother. A few quid here, a tenner there. It all builds up, and before you know it—'

'But Cathy—she works on the *market*, for God's sake—she's got three kids, the father's nowhere to be seen. She needs someone—'

'So what? So do half the mothers on the estate. Are you going to pay this boy for the rest of his life?'

Under pressure, Dr Peacock admitted that he had already contributed to the boy's school fees, plus a thousand pounds into a trust fund—*For college, Cathy, the lad's quite bright*—

Catherine White was furious. It wasn't her money, but she resented it as much as if it had been stolen from her own pocket. Besides, it was almost cruel, she said, to have led the boy to expect so much. He'd probably have been happy enough, if no one had tried to give him ideas. But Dr Peacock had encouraged him, had made him into a malcontent.

'That's what you get, Gray,' she said, 'trying to play Pygmalion. Don't expect gratitude from the boy—in fact, you're doing him a disservice, leading him to believe that he can sponge off you instead of getting a proper job. He could even end up being dangerous. Give money to these people, and what do they do? They buy drink and drugs. Things get out of hand. It wouldn't be the first time that some poor benevolent soul has been murdered in his bed by the very people he's trying to help—'

And so on. Finally, following heated discussions between Dr Peacock and Catherine, *Boy X* ceased his visits to the Fireplace House, never to return.

Catherine was magnanimous in victory. *Boy X* had been a mistake, she said. Paid handsomely for his cooperation in Dr Peacock's experiments, it was only natural that a person of his type should try to exploit the situation. But now here was the real thing, that rarest of phenomena: a blind-from-birth true synaesthete, reborn to sight again through music. It was a fabulous story, and deserved to stand alone. There was to be no one to undermine the uniqueness of the Emily White Phenomenon.

Post comment:
blueeyedboy: *Ouch! That was rather below the belt—*
Albertine: *I'll stop whenever you've had enough . . .*
blueeyedboy: *Do you really think you can?*
Albertine: *I don't know,* **blueeyedboy***. The question is: can you?*

You are viewing the webjournal of **blueeyedboy**
posting on:

badguysrock@webjournal.com
Posted at: *01.56 on Tuesday, February 12*
Status: *public*
Mood: *sorry*
Listening to: *Mark Knopfler*: 'The Last Laugh'

That marked the end for Benjamin. He'd sensed it almost immediately, that subtle shift in emphasis, and though it took some time to die, like a flower in a vase, he knew that something had ended for him that night in St Oswald's Chapel. The shadow of little Emily White had eclipsed him almost from the start: from her story, which was sensational, to the undeniable media appeal of the blind girl, whose super-sense was to make her a national superstar.

Now Ben's long days at the Mansion dwindled to an hourly session; time that he shared with Emily, sitting quietly on the couch while Dr Peacock showed her off as if she were some collector's piece—a moth, perhaps, or a figurine—expecting Ben to admire her, to share in his enthusiasm. Worse still, Brendan was there again (to keep an eye on him, Ma said, while she went to work at the market); his gawping, grinning brother in brown with his greasy hair and hangdog look, who rarely spoke, but sat and stared, filling Ben with such hate and shame that sometimes he wanted nothing more than to run away and to leave Bren alone—awkward, boorish, out of place—in that house of delicate things.

Catherine White put a stop to that. It wasn't right for those boys to be there, not without supervision. There were too many valuable things in that house; too many temptations. Benjamin's visits dwindled once again, so that now he dropped by just once a month, and waited with Bren on the front steps until Mrs White was ready to leave, hearing piano music drift out across the lawn, laden with the scent of paint, so that every time *blueeyedboy* hears that sound—be it a Rachmaninoff prelude or the intro to 'Hey Jude'— it brings back the memory of those days and the sorry little lurch of the heart that he felt when he glanced through the parlour window and saw Emily sitting on the swing, pendulum-ing back and forth like a happy little bird—

At first, all he did was watch her. Like everyone else, he was dazzled by her, content to simply admire her ascent, much as Dr Peacock must have watched the Luna moth as she struggled out of the chrysalis, in awe and admiration, coloured, perhaps, with a little regret. She was so pretty, even then. So effortlessly lovable. There was something about the trusting way in which she held her father's hand, face turned up towards him like a flower to the sun; or the monkeyish way in which she would scramble on to the piano stool, one leg tucked in, a sock at half-mast, half-eerie, half-enchanting. She was like a doll that had come to life, all porcelain and ivory, so that Mrs White, who had always liked dolls, could dress her daughter all year round in bright little outfits and matching shoes right out of an old-fashioned storybook.

As for our hero, *blueeyedboy*—

Puberty had hit him hard, with pimples on his back and face, and a half-broken voice that, even now, retains a slightly uneven tone. His childhood stammer had got worse. He lost it later, but that year it got so bad that on some days he could hardly speak. Smells and colours intensified, bringing with them migraines that the doctor promised would fade with time. They never did. He has them still, although his coping strategies have become somewhat more sophisticated.

After the Christmas concert, Emily seemed to spend most of her time at the Mansion. But with so many other people there, *blueeyedboy* rarely spoke to her; besides which, his stammer made him self-conscious, and he preferred to remain in the background, unregarded and unheard. Sometimes he would sit on the porch outside with a comic or a Western, content to be in her orbit, quietly, without fuss. Besides, reading was a pleasure seldom allowed Yours Truly at home, where Ma was always in need of help, and his brothers never left him alone. Reading was for sissies, they said, and whatever he chose—be it *Superman*, *Judge Dredd* or even just the *Beano*—would always incur the ridicule of *blueeyedboy*'s brother in black, who would pester him relentlessly—*Look at the pretty pictures! Aww! So what's your super-power, then?*— until *blueeyedboy* was by turns shamed and coerced into doing something different.

Midweek, between visits to the Mansion, he would sometimes walk past Emily's house in the hope of seeing her playing outside. Occasionally, he saw her in town, but always with her mother: standing to attention like a good little soldier, sometimes flanked by Dr Peacock, who had become her protector, her mentor, her second father. As if she needed *another* one, as if she didn't already have everything.

It probably sounds like he envied her. That isn't altogether true. But somehow he couldn't stop thinking about her, studying her, watching her. His interest gathered momentum. He stole a camera from a second-hand shop, and taught himself to take pictures. He stole a long lens from the same shop, almost getting caught that time, but managing to get away with his trophy before the fat man at the counter—surprisingly speedy for all his bulk—finally gave up the pursuit.

When his mother told him at last that he was no longer welcome at the Mansion, he didn't quite believe her. He'd become so accustomed to his routine—sitting quietly on the couch, reading books, drinking Earl Grey tea, listening to Emily's music—that to be dismissed after all this time felt like an unfair punishment. It wasn't his fault—he'd done nothing wrong. It was surely a misunderstanding. Dr Peacock had always been so kind; why would he turn against him now?

Later, *blueeyedboy* understood. Dr Peacock, for all his kindness, had been just another version of his mother's ladies, who'd been so friendly when he was four, but who had so quickly lost interest. Friendless, starved of affection at home, he'd read too much into those affable ways: the walks around the rose garden; the cups of tea; the sympathy. In short, he'd fallen into the trap of mistaking

271

compassion for caring.

Calling round that evening in the hope of finding out the truth, Yours Truly was met, not by Dr Peacock, but by Mrs White, in a black satin dress with a string of pearls round her long neck, who told him that he shouldn't be there; that he was to leave and never come back, that he was trouble, that she knew his type—

'Is that what Dr Peacock says?'

Well, that was what he *meant* to say. But his stammer was worse than ever that day, closing his mouth with clumsy stitches, and he found he could hardly say a word.

'B-but why?' he asked her.

'Don't try to pretend. Don't think you can get away with it.'

For a moment, shame overwhelmed him. He didn't know what he had done, but Mrs White seemed so sure of his guilt, and his eyes began to sting with tears, and the stink of Ma's vitamin drink in his throat was almost enough to make him gag—

Please don't cry, he told himself. *Not in front of Mrs White.*

She gave him a look of burning contempt. 'Don't think you can get around me like that. You ought to be ashamed of yourself.'

Blueeyedboy was. Ashamed and suddenly angry; and if he could have killed her then, he would have done it without hesitation or remorse. But he was only a schoolboy, and she was from a different sphere, a different class, to be obeyed, no matter what—his mother had trained her sons well—and the sound of her words was like a spike being driven into the side of his head—

'Please,' he said, without stammering.

'Go away,' said Mrs White.

'Please. Mrs White. C-can't we be friends?'

She raised an eyebrow. 'Friends?' she said. 'I don't know what you're talking about. Your mother was my cleaner, that's all. Not even a very good one. And if you think that gives you the right to harass me and my daughter, then think again.'

'I wasn't ha-ha—' he began.

'And what do you call those photographs?' she said, looking him straight in the face.

The shock of it dried his tears at once.

'Ph-photographs?' he said shakily.

Turns out Feather had a friend who worked in the local photo shop. The friend had told Feather, who'd told Mrs White, who'd demanded to see the relevant prints and had taken them straight to the Mansion, where she'd used them to prove her argument that befriending the Winters had been a mistake, one from which Dr Peacock should distance himself without delay—

'Don't think you haven't been seen,' she said. 'Creeping around after Emily. Taking pictures of us both—'

That wasn't true. He never shot *her*. He only ever shot Emily. But he couldn't say that to Mrs White. Nor could he beg her not to tell Ma—

And so he left, dry-eyed with rage, tongue stapled to the roof of his mouth. And as he looked over his shoulder for one last glimpse of the Mansion, he saw a movement in one of the upper windows. He moved away almost at once; but *blueeyedboy* had had time to see Dr Peacock, watching him, warding him off with a sheepish smile—

That was where it really began. That's where *blueeyedboy* was born. Later that night he crept back to the house, armed with a can of peacock-blue paint, and, almost paralysed with fear and guilt, he scrawled his rage on the big front door, the door that had been cruelly shut in his face, and then, alone in his room again, he took out the battered Blue Book to draw up another murder.

Post comment:
Albertine: *Oh please, not another murder. I really thought we were getting somewhere.*
blueeyedboy: *All right, but—you owe me one . . .*

You are viewing the webjournal of **blueeyedboy**
posting on:

badguysrock@webjournal.com

Posted at: *02.05 on Tuesday, February 12*
Status: *public*
Mood: *crushed*
Listening to: *Don Henley*: 'The Boys Of
Summer'

It only started out as that. A journal of his fictional
life. There is a kind of innocence in those early
entries, hidden away between the lines of cramped,
obsessive handwriting. Sometimes he remembers
the truth: the daily disappointments; the rage; the
hurt; the cruelty. The rest of the time he can
almost believe that he was really *blueeyedboy*—that
what was in the Blue Book was real, and Benjamin
Winter and Emily White just figments of some
other person's imagination. The Blue Book helped
him stay sane; in it he wrote his fantasies; his secret
vengeance against all those who hurt and
humiliated him.

As for little Emily—

He watched her more than ever now. In secret,
in envy, in longing, in love. Over the months that
followed his expulsion from the Peacock house, he
followed Emily's career, her life. He took
hundreds of photographs. He collected newspaper
clippings of her. He even befriended the little girl

who lived next door to Mrs White, giving her sweets and calling on her in the hope of a glimpse of Emily.

For some time Dr Peacock had worked to keep Emily's identity secret. In his papers she was simply *Girl Y*—a fitting replacement to *Boy X*—until such time as he and her parents chose to launch her into the world. But *blueeyedboy* knew the truth. *Blueeyedboy* knew what she was. A Luna moth in a glass case, just waiting to fly from the chrysalis straight into the killing jar—

He went on taking photographs, though he learnt to do it with greater stealth. He got two after-school jobs—a newspaper round, a couple of nights washing dishes at a local café—and with his wages he bought himself a second-hand enlarger, a stack of photographic paper and some trays and chemicals. Using books from the library, he learnt to develop the photographs himself, eventually converting the cellar, which his mother never used, into a little darkroom.

He felt like someone who had missed the winning lottery number by a single digit—and it didn't help that Ma never failed to make him feel that somehow it had all been *his* fault, that if he'd been smarter, quicker, better, then it could have been one of her boys scooping up the attention, the praise.

That year, Ma made it clear to her sons that all of them had let her down. Nigel, for failing so miserably to keep the other two in line; Brendan, for his stupidity; but most especially Benjamin, on whom so many hopes had been placed, but who had failed his Ma in every way. At the Mansion; at home; but most of all at St Oswald's. Ben's schooling at that exclusive establishment had proved the greatest setback of all, confounding Ma's expectations that her son was destined for great things. In fact, he'd hated it from the start, and only his relationship with Dr Peacock had prevented him from saying so.

But now everything about it was inimical to him: from the boys, who, just like the ones from the estate, called him *freak* and *loser* and *queer* (albeit in more refined accents), to the pretentious names of the buildings themselves—names like Rotunda and Porte-Cochère—names that tasted of rotten fruit, plummy with self-satisfaction and ripe with the odour of sanctity.

Like the vitamin drink, St Oswald's was meant to be good for his health; to help him achieve his potential. But after three miserable years there, where to some extent he had tried to fit in, he still wanted Dr Peacock's house, with the fireplace and the smell of old books. He missed the Earth globes with their magical names; and most of all he missed the way Dr Peacock used to talk to him, as if he really *cared*—

No one at St Oswald's cared. It was true that no one bullied him—well, not the way his brother did—but all the same he could always feel that undercurrent of contempt. Even the Masters had it, although some were better than others at concealing it.

They called him by his surname, *Winter*, like an Army cadet. They drilled him with tables and irregular verbs. They gave huge, dramatic sighs at his displays of ignorance. They set him to copying lines.

I will keep my schoolbooks in immaculate

condition. (Nigel always found them, however well he hid them away.) *My uniform represents the school. I will wear it always with pride.* (This was when Nigel had scissored his tie, leaving nothing but a stub.) *I will at least pretend to pay attention when a senior Master enters the room.* (This from the ever-sarcastic Dr Devine, who came into his form-room one morning to find him asleep at his desk.)

The worst of it was that he really tried. He tried to excel at his schoolwork. He wanted his teachers to be proud of him. Whereas some boys failed through laziness, he was acutely aware of the hated privilege of attending St Oswald's Grammar School, and he tried very hard to deserve it. But Dr Peacock, with his fine disregard for the curriculum, had coached him in only the subjects he himself valued—art, history, music, English literature—neglecting maths and the sciences, with the result that Ben had lagged behind ever since his first term at school and, in spite of all his efforts, had never recovered the deficit.

When Dr Peacock withdrew from their lives, Benjamin had expected Ma to withdraw him from the grammar school. In fact he prayed for it fervently, but the one time he dared mention the matter to her, she whacked him with the length of electrical cord.

'I've already put too much into you,' she said, as she folded the cord away. 'Far too much, in any case, to let you drop out at this stage.'

After that, he knew better than to complain. He sensed another shift in things as adolescence claimed him. His brothers were growing up fast, and Ma, like an October wasp sensing the coming

278

of winter, had turned vicious overnight, making her sons the target of her frustrations. Suddenly they were all under fire, from the way they spoke to the length of their hair, and *blueeyedboy* realized with growing dismay that Ma's devotion to her sons had been part of a long-term investment plan that now was expected to bear fruit.

Nigel had left school some three months ago, and the urge to make Ben suffer had begun to take second place to finding a flat, a girl, a job, an escape—from Ma, from his brothers, from Malbry.

Now he seemed suddenly older, more distant, more given to dark moods and silences. He'd always been moody and withdrawn. Now he became almost a recluse. He'd bought himself a telescope, and on cloudless nights he took to the moors, coming home in the early hours, which was no bad thing as far as Ben was concerned, but which made Ma anxious and irritable.

If Nigel's escape was in the stars, Brendan had found another route. At sixteen he already outweighed Ben by fifty pounds, and, far from losing his puppy fat, now supplemented his confectionary habit with alarming amounts of junk food. He too had a part-time job, at a fried-chicken place in Malbry town centre, where he could snack all day if he liked, and from which he returned on weekday nights with the Bargain Bucket Meal Deal, which, if he wasn't hungry then, he would have cold for breakfast the following morning, along with a quart of Pepsi, before setting off for Sunnybank Park, where he was in his final year. Ma had hoped that he would at least stay on until his A-levels, but nothing Ma could say or do had any effect on Ben's voracious brother, who seemed to have made it his mission in life to eat his way out of her custody. Ben reckoned it was only a matter of time before Brendan failed his exams and dropped out, then moved away altogether.

Benjamin felt some relief at this. Ever since the St Oswald's entrance exam, he'd had a growing suspicion that Bren was keeping tabs on him. It wasn't anything Ben had said; just the way he looked at him. Sometimes he suspected Bren of following him when he went out; sometimes when he went to his room he was sure his things had been moved about. Books he'd left under his bed would migrate, or vanish for a day or two, then reappear somewhere else. It didn't really make sense, of course. What did Brendan care about books? And yet it made him uneasy to think of someone else going through his things.

But Bren was the least of his worries by then. So much had been invested in him. So much money; so much hope. And now that the returns were about to pay off, there could be no question of retreat. His mother would not submit to the humiliation of hearing the neighbours say that Gloria Winter's boy had dropped out of school—

'You'll do what I tell you and like it,' she said. 'Or I swear I'll make you pay.'

I'll make you pay was Ma's refrain throughout the whole of that year, it seemed. And so, throughout the whole of that year, her sons ran in fear of Gloria.

Blueeyedboy knew he deserved it, at least; *blueeyedboy* knew that he was bad. *How* bad, no one understood. But his mother made it clear to him that there was to be no going back: that to disappoint her at this stage would result in the

280

worst kind of punishment.

'You owe it to me,' Ma said, with a glance at the green ceramic dog. 'What's more, you owe it to *him*. You owe it to your brother.'

Would Malcolm have been a success if he had lived? *Blueeyedboy* often asked himself that. It made him nervous to think of it. As if he were living two lives at once. One for himself, and one for Mal, who would never have the chances he'd had. Fear gnawed at him like a rat in a cage. What if he failed her? What would she do?

His escape from it all was in writing. He kept the Blue Book in the darkroom, where neither Ma nor his brothers would find it, and every night, when things got too bad, he would spin his fear into stories. Always from the point of view of a bad guy, a villain, a murderer—

His victims were many, his methods diverse. No simple shootings for *blueeyedboy*. His style may have been questionable, but his imagination was limitless. His victims died in colourful ways: caught in complex torture machines; buried in wet sand up to their necks; snared in fiendish death traps.

He used the Blue Book as a record of his fictional killings, along with a few actual experiments: Ben had recently moved on from wasps to moths, and later to mice, which were quite easy to obtain, using a simple bottle trap, and whose trapped and fluttering heartbeats— amplified by the resonant glass—echoed the frantic rhythm of his own.

The trap was made from a milk bottle, in which Ben would place a quantity of bait. It was his way of selecting victims; of isolating the guilty from the innocent. The mouse climbs into the bottle, eats

281

the bait, but is unable to climb back up the frictionless wall. It dies quite quickly—of exhaustion and shock—its little pink feet pedalling against the glass as if on an invisible wheel.

The point is, though: they *chose* to die. They chose to enter the baited trap. Their deaths were therefore *not his fault*—

But all that was about to change.

> **Post comment**:
> **JennyTricks**: (*post deleted*).
> **blueeyedboy**: *Jenny? How I've missed you . . .*

You are viewing the webjournal of **Albertine**
posting on:

badguysrock@webjournal.com
Posted at: *03.12 on Tuesday, February 12*
Status: *public*
Mood: *restless*

A lie has a rhythm of its own. Emily's began with a rousing overture; mellowed into a solemn andante; elaborated on several themes and variations; and finally emerged into a triumphant scherzo, to standing ovations and lengthy applause.

It was her grand opening. Her formal presentation to the media. *Girl Y* had served her purpose; now she was ready to take the stage. She was three weeks shy of her eighth birthday; she was clever and articulate; her work was practice-perfect and ready to stand up to scrutiny. As part of the fanfare, the Press had been informed; there was to be an auction of her paintings in a small gallery off Malbry's Kingsgate; Dr Peacock's new book was about to come out, and suddenly, or so it seemed, the whole world was talking about Emily White.

This small figure [said the *Guardian*], *with her bobbed brown hair and wistful face, hardly strikes one as a typical prodigy.* [Why? you wonder. What did they expect?] *In fact at first sight she seems very much like any other eight-year-old, but for the way her eyes skid and skitter, giving this writer the uncomfortable impression that she can see deep into his soul.*

The writer was an ageing journalist called Jeffrey Stuarts, and if he had a soul at all, she never caught a sniff of it. His voice was always a trifle too loud, with a percussive attack like dried peas in a bowl—and his smell was Old Spice aftershave trying too hard to overwhelm an under-scent of sweat and thwarted ambition. That day he was all affability.

It hardly seems conceivable [he goes on to say] *that the canvases that sing and soar from the walls of this tiny gallery off Malbry's Kingsgate can be the unaided work of this shy little girl. And yet there is something eerie about Emily White. The small pale hands flutter restlessly, like moths. The head is cocked just a little to one side, as if she hears something the rest of us do not.*

As a matter of fact she was simply bored.

'Is it true,' he asked, 'that you can actually *see* the music?'

Obediently she nodded; behind him she could hear Dr Peacock's plush laughter above a twittering of white noise. She wondered where her father was; listened for his voice and thought for a second she heard it, all snarled up in the growing cacophony.

'And all these paintings—they actually *represent* what you see?'

Again, she nodded.

284

'So, Emily. How does it feel?'

I may be over-dramatizing, but I feel that there is something of the blank canvas about her; an other-worldly quality that both captivates and repels. Her paintings reflect this; as if the young artist has somehow gained access to another plane of perception.

Oh, my. But the man enjoyed his alliteration. There was much more in the same vein; Rimbaud was mentioned (inevitably); Emily's work was compared to that of Münch and Van Gogh, and it was even suggested that she had experienced what Feather liked to call *channelling*, which meant that she had somehow tuned into some open frequency of talent (possibly linked to artists long-dead) to produce these astonishing paintings.

At first glance [writes Mr Stuarts], *all her canvases seem to be abstracts. Big, bold blocks of colour, some so highly textured as to be almost sculpture. But there are other influences here that surely cannot be coincidental. Emily White's* Eroica *has a look of Picasso's* Guernica; Birthday Bach *is as busy and intricate as a Jackson Pollock, and* Starry Moonlight Sonata *bears more than a passing resemblance to Van Gogh. Could it be, as Graham Peacock suggests, that all art has a common basis in the collective unconscious? Or is this little girl a conduit to something beyond the sensitivity of ordinary mortals?*

There was more—much more—in this vein. A

digested version found its way into the *Daily Mirror* under the headline: BLIND GIRL'S SUPER-SENSE. The *Sun* ran it too, or something very similar, flanked with a photo of Sissy Spacek taken from the film *Carrie*. Shortly afterwards a more extended version was published in a journal called *Aquarius Moon*, alongside an interview with Feather Dunne. The myth was well on its way by then; and although on that particular day there were no signs of the knives that would soon come out in response, I think that even so the attention made her uneasy. Emily hated crowds; hated noise, and all the people who came and went, their voices pecking at her like hungry chickens.

Mr Stuarts was talking to Feather now; Emily could hear her throaty patchouli-dark voice saying something about how *differently able* children were often ideal hosts for benevolent spirits. To her left was her mother, sounding just a little drunk; her laughter too loud in the smoke and the noise.

'I always knew she was an exceptional child,' Emily heard above the noise. 'Who knows? Maybe she's the next step on the evolutionary ladder. One of the Tomorrow Children.'

The Tomorrow Children. God, that phrase. Feather used it in her *Aquarius Moon* interview (for all I know she may have coined it herself), and it alone spawned a dozen theories of which Emily remained mercifully ignorant—at least until the final collapse.

Now it only jarred, and she stood up from her chair and began to move towards the open door, following the smooth line of the wall, feeling soft air on her upturned face. It was warm outside; she could feel the evening sun against her eyelids and smell magnolia from the park across the road.

A white smell, said her mother's voice in her mind. *Magnolia white.* To Emily it sounded soft and chocolatey, like a Chopin nocturne, like *Cinderella,* a scent of magic. The heat from within the gallery was oppressive by comparison; the voices of all those people—guests, academics, journalists, all talking at once and at the tops of their voices—pushing at her like a hot wind. She'd never had an exhibition before. She'd never even had a proper birthday party. She sat down on the gallery step—there was a cast-iron railing, and she pressed her hot cheek against its pockmarked surface and lifted her face towards the white smell.

'Hello, Emily,' someone said.

She turned towards the sound of his voice. He was standing a dozen feet away. A boy—older than she was, she thought; maybe as old as sixteen. His voice sounded oddly flat and tight, like an instrument playing in the wrong register, and Emily could hear caution in it, combined with interest, and something close to hostility.

'What's your name?'

'B.B.,' he said.

'That's not a name,' Emily said.

His shrug was implicit in his tone. 'It's what they call me at home,' he said. There was a rather lengthy pause. Emily could feel him wanting to speak, and sensed he was staring at her. She wished he would either ask his question, or go away and leave her alone. The boy did neither, but just stood there, opening his mouth and then closing it again, like a shop door on a busy day.

'Watch out,' she said. 'You're catching flies.'

She heard his teeth click together. 'I thought

you were supposed to be b-blind.'

'I am, but I can *hear* you all right. You make a noise when you open your mouth. Your breathing changes—' Emily turned away, feeling suddenly impatient. Why did she bother explaining things? He was just another tourist, here to see the freak. In a moment, if he dared, he'd ask her about the colours.

When he did, it took Emily a moment to understand what he was saying. The stammer she'd already noticed in his voice had intensified; not, she realized, through nerves, but from some real conflict that knotted his words into a tangle that for a few seconds even he could not undo.

'You can really *h-* you can *h-h-* you can *hear* c-c—' Emily could hear the frustration in his voice as he struggled with the words. 'You can really hear c-colours?' he said.

She nodded.

'So. What colour am I?'

She shook her head. 'I can't explain. It's like a kind of extra sense.'

The boy laughed. Not a happy sound. 'Malbry smells of shit,' he said in a fast and toneless voice. 'Dr Peacock smells of bubblegum. Mr Pink smells of dentist's gas.' Emily noticed that he hadn't stuttered once throughout this speech, the longest she'd heard him make so far.

'I don't understand,' she said, puzzled.

'You don't know who I am, do you?' he said, with a touch of bitterness. 'All those times I watched you play, or sit in your s-swing in the living-room—'

The penny dropped. 'You're him? *You're Boy X?*'

288

For a long time he said nothing. Perhaps he'd nodded—people forget—and then he just said: 'Yes. That's me.'

'I remember hearing about you,' she said, not wanting him to know that her mother thought he was a fake. 'Where did you go? After Dr Peacock—'

'I didn't go anywhere,' he said. 'We live in White City. The bottom end of the village. Ma works on the m-market. S-selling f-fruit.'

There was a long silence. This time she couldn't hear him struggling to speak, but she could feel his eyes on her. It was uncomfortable; it made her feel indignant and a little guilty at the same time.

'I fucking hate fruit,' he said.

There was another long pause, during which she closed her eyes and wished the boy would go away. Mother was right, she told herself. He wasn't like her. He wasn't even friendly. And yet . . .

'What's it like?' She had to ask.

'What, selling fruit?'

'That—thing you do. The taste-smell-word thing. I don't know the name.'

There was a long silence as, once more, he struggled to explain. 'I don't d-*do* anything,' he said at last. 'It's like—it's just *there*, somehow. Like yours, I guess. I see something, I hear something, and then I get a feeling. Don't ask me why. Weird things. And *it hurts*—'

Another pause. Inside the gallery the sound of voices had dimmed; Emily guessed that someone was getting ready to make a speech.

'You're lucky,' said B.B. 'Yours is a gift. It makes you special. Mine, I'd do without it any day. It hurts, I get these headaches *here*—' He placed a

289

hand on her temple, and another one at the nape of her neck. She felt a tremor go through him then, as if he were actually in pain.

'Plus everyone thinks you're m-mad, or worse, that you're faking it to get attention. I mean, do *you* think I'm faking it?'

For a second she faltered. 'I don't know—'

That laugh again. 'Well, there you go.' Suddenly the pent-up anger Emily had heard in his voice was overlaid with a tremendous weariness. 'At the end, even *I* thought I'd been faking it. And Dr Peacock—don't blame him. I mean, they say it's a gift. But what's it *for*? Yours I can understand. Seeing colours when you're blind. Painting music. It's like a b-bloody miracle. But mine? Imagine what it's like for me, every d-day—' Now he was stuttering again. 'Some d-days it's so bad I can hardly think, and what's it for? What's it even *for*?'

He stopped, and Emily could hear him breathing harshly. 'I used to think there was a cure,' he said finally. 'I used to think that if I did the tests, then Dr Peacock would find a cure. But there isn't a way. It gets everywhere. It gets into everything. TV. Films. You can't get away. From it. From *them*—'

'The smells, you mean?'

He paused. 'Yeah. The smells.'

'What about me?' Emily said. 'Do I have a smell?'

'Sure you do, Emily,' he said, and now she could hear the tiniest hint of a smile in his voice. '*Emily White* smells of roses. That rose that grows by the wall at the edge of the doctor's garden. *Albertine*, that was its name. That's what your name smells like to me.'

Post comment:
JennyTricks: *(post deleted)*.
blueeyedboy: *(post deleted)*.
JennyTricks: *(post deleted)*.
Albertine: *Why, thank you . . .*

15

You are viewing the webjournal of **blueeyedboy**.
Posted at: *04.29 on Tuesday, February 12*
Status: *restricted*
Mood: *good*
Listening to: *Genesis*: 'The Lady Lies'

I knew from that moment she was faking it. Not
quite eight years old, and yet already she was
cleverer than any of those others: the ones in
charge of the media hype; the ones who thought
they'd created her.

What's it like? That—thing you do.

She was so beautiful, even then. Skin like vanilla
ice cream, that smooth dark hair and those sibyl's
eyes. Good breeding makes for good skin. Her
breeding went right down to the bone: forehead,
cheekbones, wrists and neck, collarbones chiselled
and lovely. But—

What's it like? That thing you do?

She would never have asked me otherwise. Not
if she'd been telling the truth. These things we
feel—these things we *sense*—are deeply embedded
inside us, like razor blades in a bar of soap: sharp,
inexplicable edges that cut as keenly as beauty.

That lie of hers confirmed it; but already I knew
she belonged with me. Both of us soulmates in
deceit; both of us bad guys, for ever, at heart.
There was no point in my asking her when—or if—
I could see her again. It would have been difficult

enough with an ordinary child to arrange the kind of clandestine meeting that I had in mind—with this now-famous blind girl, I didn't stand a chance.

That was when the dreams began. No one had really explained to me about hormones, or growing up, or sex. For a woman with three teenage sons, Ma had proved curiously prudish on the subject, and when the relevant time had come, I'd learnt most of the truth from my brothers, a bike-shed education at best, which did not entirely prepare me for the magnitude of the experience.

I'd been a late developer. But that spring I caught up with a vengeance. I grew three inches taller, my skin cleared, and suddenly I was acutely and uncomfortably aware of myself, of the intensity of all my sensations—which seemed, if anything, even stronger than before—to the way I awoke in the mornings with a hard-on that sometimes took hours to subside.

My emotions veered from plummeting misery to absurd elation; all my senses were enhanced; I wanted desperately to be in love, to touch, to kiss, to feel, to *know*—

And through it all were those dreams: vivid, plosive, passionate dreams that I wrote down in my Blue Book, dreams that filled me with shame and despair and a dreadful, lurking sense of joy.

Nigel had told me some months before that it might soon be time for me to do my own laundry. I saw what he meant now, and took his advice, airing my room and washing my bedsheets three times a week in the hope of dispersing the civet smell. Ma never commented; but I felt her disapproval grow, as if it were somehow my fault that I was leaving my boyhood behind.

Ma was looking old, I thought, hard and sour as an under-ripe apple; and there was a sense of desperation in her now, in the way she watched me at the dinner-table, telling me to sit up, to eat properly, to stop *slouching*, for God's sake—

At her insistence I had stayed in school, and had so far managed to conceal the fact that I was lagging far behind. But by Easter the public exams loomed close, and I was failing in most of my subjects. My spelling was awful; maths made my head ache, and the more I tried to concentrate, the more the headaches assaulted me, so that even the sight of my school clothes laid out on the back of a chair was enough to bring it on; torture by association.

There was no one to whom I could go for help. My teachers—even the more well-disposed among them—were inclined to take the view that I just wasn't cut out for academic work. I could hardly explain to them the true reason for my anxiety. I could hardly admit to them that I was afraid of Ma's disappointment.

And so I hid the evidence. I faked my mother's signature on a variety of absence notes. I hid my school reports; I lied; I forged my end-of-term results. But she must have suspected something was wrong, because she began a covert investigation—she must have known that I would lie—first contacting the school by phone to find out what story I'd told, and then making an appointment with my form-teacher and the Head of Year. In which she learnt that since Christmas I had barely attended school at all, due to a prolonged bout of flu which had led to my missing the exams—

I remember the night of that meeting. Ma had cooked my favourite meal—fried chilli chicken and corn on the cob—which I suppose should have alerted me that something serious was afoot. I should have noticed her clothes, too—the dark-blue dress and those high-heeled shoes—but I guess I'd become complacent. I never suspected that I was being lulled into a false sense of security, and I had no inkling of the reprisals that were about to descend on my unsuspecting head.

Maybe I was careless. Maybe I'd underestimated Ma. Or maybe someone saw me in town with my stolen camera—

Anyway, my mother knew. She knew, she watched and she bided her time; then, when she'd spoken to the Head of Year and my teacher, Mrs Platt, she came back home in her interview clothes and cooked me my favourite dinner, and when I'd finished eating it, she left me on the sofa and turned the television on, and then she went into the kitchen (I presumed it was to wash the dishes), and then she came back silently and the first thing I knew was the scent of L'Heure Bleue and her voice in my ear, hissing at me—

'You little *shit*.'

I turned abruptly at the sound, and that was when she hit me. Hit me with the dinner-plate; hit me right in the face with it, and for a second I was torn between the shock of the impact against my eyebrow and cheekbone and simple dismay at the mess of it—at the chicken grease and corn kernels in my face and in my hair, more dismayed at that than the pain, or the blood that was running into my eyes, colouring the world in shades of *escarlata*—

Half-dazed I tried to back away; hit the couch with the small of my back, sending a glassy pain up my spine. She hit me again, in the mouth this time, and then she was on top of me, punching and slapping and screaming at me—

'You lying little shit, you cheating little *bastard*!'

I know you think I could have fought back. With words, if not with my fists and feet. But for me there were no magic words. No specious declaration of love could ward off my mother's fury, and no declaration of innocence could stem the tide of her violent rage.

It was that rage that frightened me—the mad, ballistic anger of her—far, far worse than those punches and slaps, and the sludgy stink of the vitamin drink that was somehow a terrible part of it all, and the way she screamed those things in my ears. Until finally I was crying—*Ma! Please! Ma!*— curled up in a corner beside the couch with my arms wrapped around my head, and blood in my eyes, and blood in my mouth, and that weak and fearful baby-blue word, like the helpless cry of a newborn, punctuating every blow, until the world went by degrees from blood-red to blue-black, and the outburst was finally over.

Afterwards, she made it clear how badly I'd disappointed her. Sitting on the couch with a cloth held up to my cut mouth and another to my eyebrow, I listened to my long list of crimes, and sobbed as I heard the sentence passed.

'I'm going to keep my eye on you, B.B.'

I spy. My mother's eye, like the watchful Eye of God. I felt it like a fresh tattoo, like a graze on my bare skin. Sometimes I see it in my mind: and it's bruise-blue, hospital-blue, faded prison-overall-blue. It marks me, inescapably—the mark of my mother; the mark of Cain, the mark that can never be erased.

Yes, I had disappointed her. First, she told me, with my lies—as if by telling the truth I might have spared myself all this. Then with my many failures: failure to excel at school; failure to be a good son; failure to live up to what she'd always expected of me.

'Please, Ma.' My ribs hurt; later we found out that two of them were broken. My nose, too, was broken—you can see it isn't quite straight—and if you look closely at my lips you can still see the scars, tiny silvery threadneedle scars, like someone's schoolboy stitching.

'You've got no one to blame but yourself,' she said, as if all she'd given me was a maternal slap, something to get my attention. 'And what about that girl, eh?'

The lie was automatic. 'What girl?'

'Don't you look so innocent—' She gave a thin-lipped, vinegary smile, and a finger of ice went down my back. 'I know what you've been up to. Following that blind girl.'

Had Mrs White spoken to her? Had Ma got into my darkroom? Had one of her friends mentioned seeing me with a camera?

But she knew. She always does. The photographs of Emily; the graffiti on Dr Peacock's front door; the weeks of playing truant from school. And the Blue Book, I thought in sudden alarm—could it be that she'd found that, too?

Now my hands began to shake.

'Well, what have you got to say for yourself?'

There was no way I could explain it to her.

297

'Please, M-Ma. I'm s-sorry.'

'What is it with you and that blind girl? What have you two been doing?'

'Nothing. Really. Nothing, Ma. I've never even t-talked to her!'

She gave me one of her freezing smiles. 'So—you've *never* talked to her? Never—not once—in all this time?'

'Just once. Once, in front of the gallery—'

My mother's eyes narrowed abruptly, I saw her hand move upwards, and I knew she was going to slap me again. The thought of those aggressive hands anywhere near my mouth again was suddenly unbearable, and I flinched away defensively and said the first thing that came into my mind:

'Emily's a f-fake,' I said. 'She doesn't hear any colours. She doesn't even know what they are. She's making it up—she told me so—and everybody's c-cashing in—'

Sometimes it takes a new idea to stop a charging juggernaut. She looked at me with those narrowed eyes, as if she were trying to see through the lie. Then, very slowly, she lowered her hand.

'*What* did you say?'

'She makes it up. She tells them what they want to hear. And Mrs White set her up to it—'

The silence simmered around her awhile. I could see the idea taking root in her, supplanting her disappointment, her rage.

'She *told* you that?' she said at last. 'She told you she was making it up?'

I nodded, feeling braver now. My mouth still hurt, and my ribs were sore, but now there was a taste of victory behind that of my suffering. In spite of what my brothers believed, invention at short notice had always been a talent of mine; and now I used it to free myself from my mother's terrible scrutiny.

I told her the lot. I fed her the line. All the things you've ever read about the Emily White affair: every rumour; every gibe; every piece of vitriol. All of that began with *me*—and, like the speck of irritant at the heart of the oyster that hardens to become a pearl, it grew, and bore fruit, and was harvested.

You knew I was a bad guy. What you don't yet know is *how* bad: how there and then I set the course towards this final, fatal act; how little Emily White and I came to be fellow-travellers on this road—

This tortuous road to murder.

You are viewing the webjournal of **Albertine** *posting on:*

badguysrock@webjournal.com
Posted at: *08.37 on Wednesday, February 13*
Status: *public*
Mood: *despondent*

It all began to decline right then, the night of that first exhibition. It took some time for me to realize it, but that was when the Emily White Phenomenon began to take on a disquieting turn. It seemed nothing more than a ripple at first, but especially after the success of Dr Peacock's book, there were more and more people ready to take notice, to believe the worst, to scorn, to envy or to sneer.

In France, a country fond of its child prodigies, *L'Affaire Emily* had attracted more than its share of attention. One of Emily's first patrons—an old Paris friend of Dr Peacock—sold several of her paintings from his gallery on the Left Bank. *Paris-Match* had seized the story, as had *Bild* magazine in Germany, and all of England's tabloid press—not to mention Feather's piece in *Aquarius Moon*.

But then came the scandal. The swift decline. Exposure by the media. Less than six months after that triumphant launch, Emily's career was already foundering.

I never saw it coming, of course. How could I possibly have known? I didn't read papers or magazines. Gossip and rumours passed me by. If there was something in the air, I was too self-absorbed to notice; so deep inside my masquerade that I barely saw what was happening. Daddy knew—he'd known from the start—but he couldn't stop the avalanche. Accusations had been made. Investigations were under way. The papers were filled with conflicting reports, a book was being launched, there was even a film—but one thing was clear to everyone. The bubble had burst. The wonder had gone. The Emily White Phenomenon was well and truly over. And so, with nothing left to lose, like the Snow Child in the fairy tale, we melted away, Daddy and I, leaving no trace of ourselves behind.

At first it seemed like a holiday. *Just until we get back on our feet.* An endless succession of B & Bs. Bacon for breakfast, birdsong at dawn, fresh clean sheets on strange, narrow beds. A holiday from Malbry, he said; and for the first few weeks I believed him, following like a tame sheep until finally we came to rest in a remote little place near the Scottish border, where no one, he said, would recognize us.

I didn't miss my mother at all. I know that must sound terrible. But to have Daddy all to myself like this was such an unusual pleasure that Malbry and my old life seemed to me like something that had happened to someone else, to quite a different girl, long ago. And when finally it became clear to me that something was wrong, that Daddy was slowly losing his mind, that he would never get back on his feet, I covered for him as best I could, until at

301

last they came for us.

He'd always been a quiet man. Now, depression claimed him. At first I'd thought it was loneliness, and I'd tried my best to make it up to him. But as time passed, he grew more remote, more couched in his eccentricities, dependent on his music to such an extent that he forgot to eat, forgot to sleep, telling the same old stories, playing the same old pieces again on the piano in the hall, or on the cracked old stereo, *Für Elise* and *Moonlight Sonata*, and of course the Berlioz, the *Symphonie fantastique* and especially 'The March to the Scaffold'—while I did my best to care for him, and he slipped into silence.

Eighteen months later, he had his first stroke. Lucky I'd been there, they said; lucky I'd found him when I had. It was a mild one, the doctor said; affecting just his speech and his left hand. They didn't seem to understand how important his hands were to Daddy—it was the way he spoke to me when he couldn't express himself with words.

But that was the end of our hideaway. At last, the world had discovered us. They took us to different places—Daddy to a care centre near Malbry, me to another kind of home, where I endured for the next five years without a moment's realization that *someone* had to be paying the bills; that someone was looking out for us, and that Dr Peacock had tracked us down.

Later I learnt of the correspondence between them; of Dr Peacock's repeated attempts to make contact; of Daddy's refusal to answer him. Why did Dr Peacock care? Perhaps it was from a feeling of guilt; or loyalty to an old friend; or pity for the little girl caught up in the tragedy.

In any case, he paid our bills, watched over us from afar, while the house still stood empty, unused and unloved, boxed-up like an unwanted gift, packed to the rafters with memories.

I turned eighteen. I found my own place. There in the centre of Malbry: a tiny cube on a fourth floor, with a living-room-slash-bedroom, a kitchenette and a half-tiled bathroom that smelt of damp. I visited Daddy every week—sometimes he even knew who I was. And though for a while I was sure I'd be recognized, finally I understood. No one cared about Emily White. No one even remembered her.

But nothing ever disappears. Nothing ever really ends. For all the safety and love that Nigel gave me, I realize now—if a little late—that all I had done in following him was to substitute one golden cage for a different set of bars.

But now, at last, I am free of them all. Free of my parents, free of the doctor, free of Nigel. So who am I now? Where do I go? And how many others have to die before I am free of Emily?

Post comment:
blueeyedboy: *Very moving,* **Albertine.** *I sometimes ask myself the same thing—*

PART FOUR

smoke

You are viewing the webjournal of **blueeyedboy**.
Posted at: *15:06 on Wednesday, February 13*
Status: *restricted*
Mood: *mellow*
Listening to: *Voltaire*: 'Blue-eyed Matador'

I slept till long after midday today. Told Ma I'd
taken some time off work. I don't sleep much at
the best of times. But recently I've been averaging
only two or three hours a night, and the latest quid
pro quo with *Albertine* must have taken more out
of me than I'd thought. Still, it was worth it, don't
you think? After twenty silent years, suddenly she
wants to talk.

Can't say I really blame her. Traditionally,
raising the dead has always had serious
consequences. In her case, inevitably, the tabloids
will come out in droves. Money, murder and
madness always make for excellent Press. Can she
survive the exposure? Or will she remain in hiding
here; in tacit, furtive acceptance of a past that
never happened?

When I'd showered and changed my clothes I
went to look for *Albertine*. The Pink Zebra café on
Mill Road; it's where she goes when she feels the
need to be someone else. It was six o'clock. She
was sitting alone at the counter, with a cup of hot
chocolate and a cinnamon bun. Underneath her
red coat, I saw, she was wearing a sky-blue dress.

Albertine *in blue*, I thought. *This may just be my lucky day.*

'May I join you?'

She gave a start at the sound of my voice.

'If you'd rather not socialize, I promise I won't say a word. But that hot chocolate looks wonderful, and—'

'No. Please. I'd like you to stay.'

Grief always gives her face a kind of emotional nakedness. She held out her hand. I took it. A thrill ran through me; a tremor that moved from the soles of my feet right up into the roots of my hair.

I wonder if she felt it too; her fingertips were slightly cold, her small hand not quite steady in mine. There's something almost childlike about her, a kind of passive acceptance that Nigel must have taken for vulnerability. I, of course, know better; but, as she must know, I'm a special case.

'Thank you.' I took a seat next to her. Ordered Earl Grey and whichever pastry was highest in calories. I hadn't eaten for twenty-four hours, and I was suddenly ravenous.

'Lemon meringue pie?' She smiled. 'That seems to be your favourite.'

I ate the pie, and she drank her hot chocolate, leaving the cinnamon bun untouched. The process of eating makes a man look strangely inoffensive, somehow; all weapons laid down in a common purpose.

'How are you coming to terms with it?' I said, when the pie was finished.

'I don't want to talk about that,' she said.

At least she didn't pretend she didn't know what I was talking about. A few days more and she won't have the choice any more. All it will take is a word to the Press, and the story will be out, whether she likes it or not.

'I'm sorry, *Albertine*,' I said.

'It's over, B.B. I've moved on.'

Well, *that* was a lie. No one moves on. The wheel just keeps on turning, that's all, creating the illusion of momentum. Inside it, we are all rats; running in growing desperation towards a painted blue horizon that never gets any closer.

'Lucky you, moving on. At least being dead gives closure.'

'What's that supposed to mean?' she said.

'Well, everyone sides with the victim, of course. Deserving or not, everyone mourns as soon as the mark is safely dead. But what about the rest of us? The ones with problems of our own? Being dead is pretty straightforward. Even my brothers managed that. But living with guilt is something else. It's not easy being the bad guy—'

'Is *that* what you are?' she said mildly.

'I think we've both established that.'

The ghost of a smile crossed her face, like a wisp of cloud on a summer's day. 'What happened between you and Nigel?' she said. 'He never talked about you much.'

Didn't he? Good. 'Does it matter now?'

'I just want to understand. What was it between you two?'

I shrugged. 'We had issues.'

'Don't we all?'

I laughed at that. 'Our issues were different. The whole of our family was different.'

Her eyes skittered for a moment. She has remarkably beautiful eyes; blue as a fairy tale,

309

flecked with gold. Mine are grey in comparison; chilly, they tell me; changeable.

'Nigel didn't tell me much about any of his family,' she said, locating her cup of hot chocolate and bringing it carefully to her lips.

'As I mentioned, we weren't close.'

'It wasn't that. I know families. He couldn't stay away, somehow. As if there were something keeping him here—'

'That would be Ma,' I told her.

'But Nigel *hated* his mother—' She stopped. 'I'm sorry. I know you're devoted to her.'

'Is that what he told you?' My voice was dry.

'I just assumed—well, you live with her.'

'Some people live with cancer,' I said.

Albertine hardly ever smiles. I think she finds it difficult to understand those tiny facial variables, the difference between a smile and a frown, a grimace of pain. Not that her face is expressionless. But social conventions are not for her, and she does not express what she does not feel.

'So why do you stay?' she said at last. 'Why don't you get away, like Nigel?'

'Get away?' I gave a sharp laugh. 'Nigel didn't get away. He ended up half a mile from home. And with the girl next door, no less. You think that counts as getting away? But then, you're hardly an expert. You both ended up in the same gutter, but at least Nigel was looking up at the stars.'

She was silent for such a long time that I wondered if I'd gone too far. But she is tougher than she looks.

'I'm sorry,' I told her. 'Was that too direct?'

'I think I'd like you to go now.' She put down

her cup of chocolate. I could hear the tension in her voice, still under control for the moment, but almost ready to escalate.

I stayed where I was. 'I'm sorry,' I said. 'But Nigel wasn't an innocent. He was playing a game with you. He knew who you were, who you used to be. And he knew that when Dr Peacock died he'd have his ticket out of here.'

'You're lying!'

'No, not this time,' I said.

'Nigel hated liars,' she said. 'That was why he hated you.'

Ouch. That was cruel, Albertine.

'No, he hated me because I was Ma's favourite. He was always jealous of me. Anything I wanted, *he* had to have. Perhaps that's why he wanted you. *And* Dr Peacock's money, of course.' I glanced at the still-untouched cinnamon bun. 'Aren't you going to eat that?'

She ignored me. 'I don't believe you. Nigel would never have lied to me. He was the straightest person I know. That's why I loved him.'

'*Loved* him?' I said. 'You never did. What you loved was being someone else.' I took a bite of the cinnamon bun. 'As for Nigel—who knows? Maybe he wanted to tell you the truth. Maybe he thought you needed time. Or maybe he was enjoying the feeling of power it gave him over you—'

'What?'

'Oh, please. Don't be disingenuous. Some men enjoy being in control. My brother was a control freak—and he had a temper, of course. An uncontrollable temper. I'm sure you must be aware of that.'

'Nigel was a good man,' she said in a low voice.

'There's no such thing,' I told her.

'He was! He was *good*!' Now her voice distressed the air in jagged patterns of green and grey. Soon, I knew, they would bring that scent; but I let the silence roll awhile.

'Sit down. Just for a moment,' I said, and guided her hands towards my face.

For a moment she resisted me. Perhaps it was too much intimacy. But then she must have changed her mind, because at that moment she closed her eyes and put her hands against my face, with cool fingertips that explored me from brow to chin, gently taking in the sutures under my left eye; the still-swollen bruise on my cheekbone; the cut lip, the broken nose—

'Nigel did this?' Her voice was small.

'What do *you* think?'

Now her eyes were open again. God, but they were beautiful. No grief in them now, nor anger, nor love. Just beauty, blank and blameless.

'Nigel was always unstable,' I said. 'I suppose he must have told you that. That he was prone to acts of violence? That he murdered his brother, no less?'

She winced. 'Of course he told me. He said it was an accident.'

'But he told you all about it, right?'

'He got in a fight over twenty years ago. That doesn't make him a murderer.'

'Oh, please,' I interrupted. 'What does it matter how long ago? No one changes. It's a myth. There's no road to Damascus. No path to redemption. Not even the love of a good woman— assuming such a thing exists—can wash the blood from a killer's hands.'

'Stop it!' Her own hands were shaking. 'Can't we just leave this alone?' she said. 'Can't it just stay in the past, for once?'

The *past*? Don't give me that, *Albertine*. You, of all people, should understand that the past is never over. We drag it behind us everywhere, like a can tied to a stray dog's tail. Try to outrun it, it just makes more noise. Until it drives you crazy.

'He never told you, did he?' I said. 'He never said what happened that day?'

'Don't. Please. Leave me alone.'

I could tell from the tone of her voice that she'd given me all she could today. Better than I'd expected, in fact; and besides, the essential part of a game is always knowing when to fold. I paid my bill with a twenty-pound note, leaving it tucked under my plate. She did not respond, or even look up, as I said goodbye to her and left. The last I saw of her as I opened the door and stepped out into the darkness was the fleeting flash of colour as she reached for her red duffel coat hanging behind the counter, and the crescent moon of her profile eclipsed behind the screen of her open hands—

Truth hurts, doesn't it, *Albertine*? Lies are so much safer. But murderers run in our family, and Nigel was no exception. And who would have thought that nice young man could have ever done such a terrible thing? And who would have thought that a little white lie could snowball into murder?

313

> *You are viewing the webjournal of* **blueeyedboy**.
> **Posted at**: *23.25 on Wednesday, February 13*
> **Status**: *restricted*
> **Mood**: *rueful*
> **Listening to**: *Freddie Mercury*: 'The Great
>   Pretender'

It was an accident, they said. A cracked skull, the result of a fall downstairs. Not even the main stairs, as it turned out, but the six stone steps at the front door. Somehow he'd come off the ramp that I'd built, or maybe he had tried to stand, as sometimes he did occasionally; to stand up miraculously and walk across the misty white lawn like Jesus on the water.

That was over three weeks ago. Lots of things have happened since then. My brother's death; the loss of my job; my dialogue with *Albertine*. But don't think I ever forgot. Dr Peacock was always on my mind. Old enough to have been forgotten by almost everyone he'd known; old enough to have outlived his fame, even his notoriety. A pathetic old man, half-blind and confused, who told the same stories again and again and barely recognized my face—

He wrote me into his will, you know. How ironic is that? You'll find me at the end of the list, under *miscellaneous other*. I guess a man who can leave thirty thousand pounds to the animal shelter that supplied his dogs can well afford a couple of grand for the guy who used to clean up for him, and cook his mushy old-man's meals, and wheel him around the garden.

A couple of grand. Less, with tax. Not nearly enough to qualify as a motive. But it's rather nice to be, if not exactly *recognized*, then at least given *some* acknowledgement for all the work I did for him, for my tireless good cheer, for my honesty—

Did he recall my tenth birthday? The candle on the iced bun? I don't suppose so—why should he care? I was nobody; nothing to him. If that day still survived within his damaged memory, it would have been as the day he buried poor old Rover, or Bowser, or Jock, or whatever the hell the dog's name was. To pretend to myself that he might have cared for me, for *blueeyedboy*, is ludicrous. I was simply a project to him, not even the main act of the show. Still, I can't help wondering—

Did he know his murderer? Did he try to call for help? Or was it all just a blur to him, a heap of broken images? Personally, I like to think that, right at the end, he understood. That as he died, his senses returned for just long enough for him to know just *how* he was dying, and *why*. Not everyone gets to know those things. Not everyone gets that privilege. But I like to think that maybe he did, and that the last thing he ever saw, the picture that followed him into eternity, was a familiar face, a more-than-familiar pair of eyes—

The police came round to the house, of course. Eleanor Vine directed them there, though I still have no idea how she found out I was working at the Mansion. For a woman who spent most of her time shut up in her house, cleaning the floors, she seemed to have an uncanny knack for revealing embarrassing secrets. In this case, however, I realized, with some relief, that my cover was only partially blown: she knew I was working for Dr Peacock, but not about my hospital job, though she may have had her suspicions by then, and exposure might have been just a matter of time.

Did she believe I was involved? If so, she was disappointed. There were no handcuffs, there was no interrogation, no trip to the police station. Even the questions they asked me had a tired quality. After all, there was no sign of violence. The victim had merely suffered a fall. The death—the *accidental* death—of one old man (even if he had been famous once) was hardly a matter for much concern.

My mother took it badly, though. It wasn't the thought that I might have killed Dr Peacock, but just the fact that I'd been in the house, had worked in that house for eighteen months without her even suspecting it—and worse, that *Eleanor* had known—

'How could you?' she said, when they had gone. 'How could you set foot in that house again, after everything that's happened?'

There was no point my denying what I'd done. But as any seasoned liar knows, a half-truth can screen a thousand lies. And so I confessed. I'd had no choice. I'd had to take on extra work. It was part of the hospital's outpatient scheme. The fact that I'd got that particular case was nothing but coincidence.

'You could have talked your way out of it. You could talk your way out of a locked *room*—'

'It isn't as easy as that, Ma—'

316

She slapped me then, across the mouth. One of her rings cut my lip. Probably the tourmaline. Its taste was Campari soda with an aluminium chaser of blood.

Tourmaline. Tour. Malign. It sounds like a place of imprisonment, an evil tower from a Perrault fairy tale, and its smell is the same as St Oswald's, a reek of disinfectant and dust and polish and cabbage and chalk and boys.

'Don't you dare patronize me. Don't think I don't know what you're up to.'

My mother has a sixth sense. She always knows when I've done something wrong; when I'm *thinking* of doing something wrong.

'You wanted to see him, didn't you? After everything he's done to us. You wanted his fucking *approval.*' Her camelbacked foot in its slingback heel began to tap a quick, irregular rhythm against the leg of the sofa. The sound of it made my throat go dry, and the vegetable stink of it was enough to make me want to gag.

'Please, Ma.'

'Didn't you?'

'Please, Ma, it's not my fault—'

She is surprisingly quick with her hands. I was expecting the second blow, and still it caught me by surprise, knocking me sideways into the wall. The cabinet with the china dogs shivered once, but nothing fell.

'Then whose fault *is* it, you little shit?'

I put a hand to my cut lip. I knew she hadn't even begun; her face was almost expressionless, but her voice was charged like a battery. I took a step closer to the cabinet. I figured she wouldn't risk anything so close to her china dogs.

317

When she's dead, I thought to myself, *I'm going to take every single one of those fucking dogs out into the back yard and stamp on them with my engineer boots.*

She saw me looking. 'B.B., come *here!*'

Just as I thought, I told myself. She wanted me clear of that cabinet. She'd acquired a new ornament, I saw; an Oriental specimen. I put out my hand and rested it very gently against the pane.

'Don't do that,' my mother snapped. 'You'll leave fingerprints on the glass.'

I could tell she wanted to hit me again. But she didn't—not then—because of those dogs. Still, I couldn't stay there all day. I turned towards the parlour door, hoping to make it upstairs to my room, but Ma grabbed hold of the door-handle and, with one hand in the small of my back, yanked the door open into my face—

After that, it was easy. Once I was down, her feet did the rest, her feet in those fucking sling-backed heels. By the time she was done I was snivelling, and my face was laddered with scratches and cuts.

'*Now* look at you,' Ma said—the violent outburst over now, but still with a trace of impatience, as if this were something I'd brought on myself, some unrelated accident. 'You're a mess. What on earth were you playing at?'

I knew there was no point in trying to explain. Experience has taught me that when Ma gets like this, it's better to stay quiet and hope for the best. Later, she'll fill in the gaps with some kind of plausible story; a fall down the stairs, an accident. Or maybe this time I was mugged, or beaten up on my way from work. I should know. It's happened before. And those sharp little breaks in her memory are getting increasingly frequent, more so since my brother's death.

I tested my ribs. None seemed broken. But my back hurt where she'd kicked me, and there was a deep cut across my eyebrow where the edge of the door had struck. Blood drenched the front of my shirt, and I could already feel one of my headaches coming, arpeggios of coloured light troubling my vision.

'I suppose you'll need stitches now,' said Ma. 'As if I didn't already have enough to do today. Oh, well.' She sighed. 'Boys will be boys. Always up to something. Lucky I was here, eh? I'll come with you to the hospital.'

* * *

OK, so I lied. I'm not proud of the fact. It was Ma, and not Nigel, who messed up my face. Gloria Green; five foot four in her shoes, sixty-nine and built like a bird—

You'll be fine in no time, love, said the pink-haired nurse as she fixed me up. Stupid bitch. As if she cared. I was just a patient to her. *Patient. Penitent.* Words that smell of citrus green and sting like a mouthful of needles. And I have been so patient, Ma, patient for so very long.

I had to quit my job after that. Too many questions; too many lies; too many snares in which to be caught. Having discovered one subterfuge, Ma could so easily have checked me out and exposed the pretence of the past twenty years—

Still, it's a short-term setback. My long-term plan remains unchanged. Enjoy your china dogs,

Ma. Enjoy them while you still can.

I suppose I ought to feel pleased with myself. I'm getting away with murder. A smile, a kiss, and—*Whoops! All gone!*—like a malignant conjuring trick. You don't believe me? Check it out. Search me from all angles. Look for hidden mirrors, for secret compartments, for cards up my sleeve. I promise you I'm totally clean. And yet, it's going to happen, Ma. Just you watch it blow up in your face.

These were my thoughts as I lay there on the hospital trolley, thinking about those china dogs and how I was going to stomp them into powder the minute—the *second*—Ma was dead. And as soon as I let the thought take shape without the comforting blanket of fic, it was almost as if a nuke had gone off inside my skull, tearing into me, wringing me like a wet rag and cramping my jaw in a silent scream—

'I'm sorry, sweetheart. Did that hurt?' The pink-haired nurse, all three of her, swam briefly across my consciousness like a shoal of tropical fish.

'He gets these headaches,' said Ma. 'Don't worry. It's only stress.'

'I can get the doctor to prescribe something—'

'No. Don't bother. It'll pass.'

*   *   *

That was nearly three weeks ago. Forgotten, if not quite forgiven, perhaps, the stitches removed, the bruises now veering from purple and blue to an oil-slick palette of yellows and greens. The headache took three days to subside, during which time Ma fed me home-made soup and watched by my bed

320

as I shivered and moaned. I don't think I said anything aloud. Even in my delirium, I think I was cleverer than that. In any case, by the end of the week, things were back to normal again, and *blueeyedboy* was, if not quite off the hook, then at least back in the net for another spell.

Meanwhile, on the bright side—

Eleanor Vine is most unwell. Taken ill last Saturday, she remains in hospital, on a respirator. Toxic shock, so Terri says, or maybe some kind of allergy. I can't say I'm particularly surprised—with the number of pills Eleanor takes, apparently at random, something like this had to happen some day. Still, it's an odd coincidence that a fic posted in my WeJay should have taken on such a life of its own. It's not the first time this has happened, either; it's almost as if, by some voodoo, I have acquired the ability to delete from the world all those who hurt or threaten me. A stroke of the keys—and *pfft! Delete.*

If only it were as easy as that. If this were simply a matter of wishful thinking, then my troubles would have been over more than twenty years ago. It began with the Blue Book—that catalogue of my hopes and dreams—and followed on into cyberspace, on to my WeJay, and *badguysrock.* But of course it's only fiction. And although it may have been Catherine White in my fic—or Eleanor Vine, or Graham Peacock, or any of those parasites—there was only ever one face in my mind: battered and bleeding, bludgeoned to death, strangled with piano wire; electrocuted in the bath; poisoned; drowned; decapitated, dead in a hundred different ways.

One face. One name.

321

I know. It's unforgivable. To wish for my mother's death in this way—to *long* for it, as one might long for a cool drink on a hot day, to wait with racing heart for the sound of her key in the front door, to hope that today might be the one—

Accidents happen so easily. A hit-and-run; a fall down the stairs; a random act of violence. Then there are the health issues. At sixty-nine, she is already old. Her hands are thick with arthritis; her blood pressure is sky-high. Cancer runs in the family: her own mother died at fifty-five. And the house itself is filled with potential hazards: overloaded electrical sockets; loose carpet runners; plant pots balanced precariously on bedroom window-ledges. Accidents happen all the time; but never, it seems, to Gloria Green. It's enough to drive a boy to despair.

And yet I continue to live in hope. Hope, the most spiteful of all the demons in Pandora's little box of tricks—

You are viewing the webjournal of **blueeyedboy**.
Posted at: *09.55 on Thursday, February 14*
Status: *restricted*
Mood: *romantic*
Listening to: *Boomtown Rats*: 'I Never Loved
                   Eva Braun'

It's February the 14th, Valentine's Day, and love, true love, is in the air. That's why I've left that envelope on the corner of the china cabinet next to the chocolates and flowers. *Not* roses, thank God, nor even orchids, but a nice arrangement nonetheless, lavish enough to be expensive, though not enough to be vulgar.

The card itself is selected with care: no jokey cartoons, no sexual innuendo, no promises of undying affection. Ma knows me better than that. It's the gesture that matters; the triumph that she will feel on her next outing with—for instance— Maureen, Eleanor, or Adèle, whose son lives in London and who rarely even telephones.

We do not fool ourselves, Ma and I. But still the game goes on. We've played the game a long, long time; this game of stealth and strategy. Each of us has had our share of victories and defeats. But now comes the chance to own the field—which is why right now I can't afford to take unnecessary risks. She's suspicious enough of me as it is. Unstable, too, and growing worse. It was bad enough when my brothers were here, but now I am the only one, the last, and she keeps me like one of her china dogs, on display from all angles—

She expresses surprise at the gifts and the card. This, too, is part of the game. If there had been no Valentine, she would have made no comment, but in a few days there would have been consequences. And so it pays to observe the conventions, to play along, to remember the stakes. That's why I've made it this far, of course. By always giving the devil his due.

Online, my friends remember me, too. There are six virtual Valentine's cards, innumerable pictures and banners, including one from Clair, hoping to see me soon, she says, and hoping I find love this year—

Why, how sweet of you, *ClairDeLune*. As it happens I hope so, too. But you have other concerns today—not least, the e-mail you sent from your hotmail account to Angel Blue, bearing a message of undying love, as well as the extra little surprise delivered to his New York address.

I knew that password would come in useful. And, as it happens, I've changed it now, from *clairlovesangel* to *clairhatesangie*, Angie being Mrs Angel Blue. It's cruel, I know. It may cause grief. But as we enter this new phase together, I have become increasingly impatient of time spent away from my main focus. I no longer need my army of mice. Their squeaking has become tiresome. They were a pleasant diversion once. And I needed them to build up this place, to bait my virtual bottle trap, my own private pitcher plant.

But now that *Albertine* and I are entering the final phase of the game, the last thing I want is her

324

wasting her time. Time to concentrate on what really matters; to move in for the tête-à-tête—

And so, of today, all of *badguysrock* has become our private battleground. *Site under construction*, it says, which ought to keep most of our visitors out, while I send out my personal Valentines to deal with the more persistent ones.

Clair's you already know about. Chryssie's takes a different form; that of a dieting challenge—*lose 10lbs in only 3 days!*—a drop in the ocean for Chryssie, of course, but it should keep her out of my hair for a while.

As for Cap, a careless word dropped in his name on a gang message board, followed up by an e-mail inviting him to meet a friend at a certain place, at a certain time, in one of Manhattan's less pleasant districts—

Meanwhile, what of *Albertine*? I hope I haven't upset her. She's very sensitive, of course; recent events must have shaken her. She isn't answering her phone, which implies that she is screening calls. And maybe she lacks the energy, today of all days, when the nation honours a festival, which, though riddled with the pox of merchandising, purports to celebrate true love—

Somehow I don't see Nigel as the type. Then again, I wouldn't. It's hard to visualize one's childhood tormentor as the kind of person who would buy a bunch of red roses, make up a playlist of love songs, or send a Valentine's card to a girl.

Maybe he was, though. Who can say? He may have had hidden depths. He was certainly moody enough as a boy—spending hours alone in his room, looking at his maps of the sky, writing his verses, and listening to rock music that ranted and railed.

Nigel Winter, the poet. Well—you wouldn't have thought it to look at him. But I found some of his poetry, in a book at the bottom of his wardrobe, among the clothes in charcoal and black. A Moleskine notebook—slightly worn—in my brother's colour.

I couldn't help it. I stole the book. Removed myself from the scene of the crime to scrutinize it at leisure. Nigel didn't notice at first; and later, when he discovered the loss, he must have known that there could have been any number of places in which he might have mislaid a small, unobtrusive black notebook. Under his mattress; under the bed; under a fold of carpet. I played the innocent as I watched him search the house in stealth; but I'd hidden the notebook safely away in a box at the back of the garage. Nigel never mentioned to either of us what it was he was looking for, though his face was dark with suspicion as he questioned us—obliquely, and with uncommon restraint.

'Did you go into my stuff?' he said.

'Why? Did you lose something?'

He gave me a look.

'Well?'

He hesitated. 'No.'

I shrugged, but I was grinning inside. Whatever was in that book, I thought, must be something very important. But rather than attract attention to something he clearly wanted to hide, my brother played indifference, hoping perhaps that the notebook would lie for ever undisturbed—

As if. As soon as I could, I retrieved it from its hiding-place. It looked like an astronomy notebook at first; but in between the lists of figures, of

326

sightings of planets and shooting stars and lunar eclipses, I found something else: a journal like mine, but of poetry—

The sweet curve of your back,
Your neck—my fingers walk
A dangerous line.

Poetry? Nigel? Gleefully I read on. Nigel, the poet. What a joke. But my brother was full of contradictions, as well as being almost as cautious as I, and I learnt that behind his sullen façade there lay a few surprises.

The first was that he favoured haikus, those deceptively simple little rhymeless poems of only seventeen syllables. If anything, I would have expected Nigel to have gone for blowsy verses, thumping rhymes, sonnets with rhythms that thundered and rang, bludgeoning blocks of blank verse—

The second surprise was that he was in love— desperately, fiercely in love. It had been going on for months—ever since he'd bought the telescope, in fact, which hobby gave him the perfect excuse to come and go at night as he pleased.

That in itself was amusing enough. I hadn't seen Nigel as the type for romance. But the third surprise was the greatest of all—the thing that killed my amusement cold and made my heart quicken with delayed fear.

I flicked back through the notebook again, my fingers suddenly cold and numb, a cottony, chemical taste in my mouth. Of course, I'd always known that to be caught in possession of Nigel's book might have had serious consequences. But as

327

I read further I understood the terrible risk I'd taken. Because this was something far more incriminating than just a few poems and scribblings. And if Nigel suspected that I was the thief, I'd earn myself more than a beating. If anyone ever found out what I knew—

For that, my brother would kill me.

You are viewing the webjournal of **blueeyedboy**.
Posted at: *21.30 on Thursday, February 14*
Status: *restricted*
Mood: *disappointed*
Listening to: *Blondie*: 'Picture This'

No Valentine yet from *Albertine*. I wonder, *did* he love her? Did they lie side by side in bed, his arm thrown carelessly around her shoulders, her face pressed into the curve of his neck? Did he wake to find her there, and wonder at his good fortune? Did he sometimes forget who he was, imagine that through love of her, some day he could be someone good?

But love is a treacherous animal, a shape-shifter by nature, making the poor man king for a day; transforming the most volatile into paragons of stability; a crutch for the weak, a shield for the craven—at least, until the buzz wears off.

He got it badly. I knew he would. My erstwhile tormentor, who used to force-feed me spiders, had finally, fatally, fallen in love. And with the least likely candidate, in one of those random encounters that even I could not have foreseen.

> *The sweet curve of your back,*
> *Your neck—*

I suppose you could have called her attractive. Not

329

at all my type, of course; but Nigel had always been perverse, and the boy who had spent his childhood trying to escape one older woman had fallen straight into the clutches of another. Her name was Tricia Goldblum; and she was an ex-employer of Ma's. An elegant fifty-something; ice-blonde; and with that air of helplessness that makes them irresistible. Still, there's no accounting for taste, is there? And I suppose she must have felt flattered. Mrs Electric Blue, as was, now divorced from her husband and free to indulge her predilection for nice young men.

Does that sound familiar yet? They always say to write what you know. And fiction is a tower of glass built from a million tiny truths, grains of sand fused together to make a single, gleaming lie—

He'd never really known her from the days when Ma worked as a cleaner. Perhaps he'd encountered her once or twice in one of the cafés or shops in town. But he'd never had reason to speak to her, to understand her, as I had. And as for that day at the market, the day I remembered so vividly—

As far as I was able to tell, Nigel had no memory of it at all. Perhaps that was why he chose her— Malbry's Mrs Robinson, whose furtive collection of young men had coloured her reputation, not blue, but scarlet in the eyes of such folk as Catherine White, Eleanor Vine and, most judgemental of all, Gloria Green.

Not that Nigel cared about *that* at the time. Nigel was besotted. But Mrs Goldblum valued discretion, and their affair was conducted in secret at first, with Mrs Goldblum calling the shots. Still, of course, that journal of his was enough to tell me everything: how cleverly she had reeled him in;

even her penchant for sex toys was there, among the haikus and star charts.

My first impulse, of course, was to tell Ma, who had hated Mrs Goldblum ever since she'd abandoned us, and whose venom was no less lethal for having been stored away. But then I seriously believed that Nigel would have killed me. I knew his temper; and I guessed that Nigel in love, like Nigel at war, was capable of anything.

And so I nursed my discovery until such time as it could be of use. I never told Ma, never mentioned it, not even obliquely, to either of them. I was alone with my secret, a hoard of stolen banknotes that I could never spend without incriminating myself.

But enough of that for the moment. We'll get to that in due course. Suffice it to say that as time passed, the Moleskine diary revealed its use. And now I realized how easily, with the help of a few judicious props, I could set a bottle trap, which hopefully would set me free—

> *You are viewing the webjournal of* **blueeyedboy**.
> **Posted at**: *22.15 on Thursday, February 14*
> **Status**: *restricted*
> **Mood**: *malevolent*
> **Playing**: *Pulp*: 'I Spy'

When Nigel was released from jail, I'd expected him, now he was free, to try again, to rebuild his life, to do all those things he'd always planned, to take the chance he'd been given, and run. But Nigel was never predictable; he was more than usually perverse, seeking out the opposite of whatever he was expected to do. And something in my brother had changed. Not something you could quantify, but something that I recognized. Like a ship in the Sargasso Sea, he had become entangled; enmeshed in himself, swallowed up by the pitcher plant that was Malbry, and our mother.

Oh, yes. Our mother. In spite of it all, he came back home—not to the house, but to Malbry; to Ma. Certainly he had no one else. His friends—such as they were—had moved on. All he had was his family.

My brother was twenty-five by then. He had no money, no prospects, no job. He was taking stabilizing drugs, though he was far from stable. And he blamed me for what had happened to him—blamed me unfairly, but doggedly—although even a headcase like Nigel should have been able to see that it wasn't my fault that he had committed murder—

All that didn't come out at once, of course. But Nigel had never liked me, and now he liked me even less. I suppose he had good reason. To him, I must have seemed a success. By then I was studying—or so he believed—at Malbry Polytechnic, as was, though its status was upgraded a year later to that of a university, much to Ma's satisfaction. I still had money from my part-time job at the electrical shop, though, since I was a student, Ma allowed me to keep all of my salary. The Emily White affair was over, and Ma and I had already moved on.

To look at, Nigel hadn't changed much. His hair was longer than before, and sometimes it was greasy. He had a new tattoo on his arm—a single Chinese character, the symbol for 'courage' in basic black. He was thinner, and somehow smaller, too, as if part of him had been worn away like the end of a pencil eraser. But he still wore black all the time, and he liked the girls as he always had, although, as far as I ever knew, he never kept with the same one for more than a couple of weeks or so, as if trying to keep himself in check; as if he was afraid, somehow, that the rage that had killed a man might some day spring out at someone else.

At first he had no contact with Ma. No surprise, after what he had done. He moved into a flat in town, found himself a job there, and over the next few years lived alone—not happy, perhaps, but free.

And then, somehow, she reeled him back in. That freedom was just an illusion. One day I came home to find him there, sitting with Ma in the parlour, looking like a dead man, and along with that sneaking *Schadenfreude* I felt a sinking sense of doom.

No one escapes the pitcher plant. Not Nigel, not me, not anyone.

It was not a true rapprochement. But over the next eighteen years or so, we saw Nigel three or four times a year. At Christmas; on Ma's birthday; at Easter; on *my* birthday—and every time he came round, he would sit in the same place in the parlour, and stare at the shelf of china dogs—Mal's statuette had been repaired, of course, and had now been joined by a similar one, in the shape of a sleeping puppy.

And every time Nigel visited, he would stare at those fucking china dogs and drink tea from Ma's visitors' cups and listen to her carry on about how much the church had raised this year, and how the hedge needed clipping. And every other Sunday night he would phone at precisely eight thirty (which was when Ma's soaps were over), and stay on until she had finished with him, while the rest of the time he tried to make sense of what was left of his life with therapy and Prozac, working days and spending the nights in his attic flat watching stars that seemed increasingly remote each time, or cruising the streets in his black Toyota and waiting for someone, for *something* . . .

And then, along came *Albertine*. She should never have been there, of course. She didn't belong in that new café, the oddly named Pink Zebra, with its gassy, soporific scent and primary-school colours. And she certainly didn't belong with Nigel, who should have been out of the picture by then, but who had messed up his escape.

334

Maybe I ought to have stopped it then. I knew she was dangerous. But Nigel had already brought her home, like a little stray cat from out of the cold. Nigel was in love, he said. Needless to say, he had to go—

And though it *looked* like an accident, you and I know better, of course. I swallowed him, as I swallowed Mal, as I swallowed all of my brothers. Swallowed them down like the vitamin drink— *One, two, three, gone!*—and the taste may be sour, but the victory is sweeter than a summer rose—

You are viewing the webjournal of **blueeyedboy**
posting on:

badguysrock@webjournal.com

Posted at: *23.25 on Thursday, February 14*
Status: *public*
Mood: *baroque*
Listening to: *The Rolling Stones*: 'Paint It Black'

Let's call him Mr Midnight Blue. A man of moods
and mysteries. A poet and a lover, she thinks; a
gentle man with a head full of stars. The truth is,
she's living in fantasy. A fantasy in which two lost
souls may find each other by happenstance, and be
saved from themselves through true love—

What a joke. Poor girl. In fact her man is a
headcase with blood on his hands; a liar; a coward;
an arrogant thug. What's more, though she thinks
he has chosen her, the truth is *she* was chosen for
him.

You think that isn't possible? People are just
like cards, you know. *Pick a card. Any card.* And
the trick is to make the mark believe that the card
he has picked was his choice, his own particular
Queen of Spades—

He drives a black Toyota. He uses it to cruise
the streets, as he used to do, in the days before.
Still thinks of it as *before* and *after*—as if such a
cataclysmic event could change the predestined
orbit of a man's life, like two planets in collision,

which then go off their separate ways.

Of course, that isn't possible. There is no way to cheat Fate. His crime has become a part of him, like the shape of his face, and the scar on his hand that runs across his heart line, the only physical reminder of that nasty interlude. A shallow cut that healed fast; unlike his victim, poor bastard, who died of a cracked skull a fortnight later.

But of course, Midnight Blue doesn't think of himself as a murderer. It was an accident, he says; an altercation that got out of hand. He never meant to do it, he says—as if that could somehow raise the dead, as if it makes a difference that he acted on impulse, that he was misled, that he was only twenty-one—

His lawyer was inclined to agree. Cited his mental state, which was poor; claimed there were special circumstances, and finally tried for a verdict of misadventure. A piebald word, half-red, half-black, that smells distinctly fishy to me, and sounds almost as if it could be a name: Miss Adventure, like *Boy X*, a comic-book adventuress—

Can any sentence compensate for the loss of a human life? *I'm sorry. I didn't mean it.* All those snivelling, wretched excuses. A five-year stretch—much of it spent in the quilted comfort of a psychiatric ward—discharged Midnight Blue's debt to society—which doesn't mean to say he was cured; or that he didn't deserve to die—

Reader, I killed him. I had no choice. That black Toyota was just too alluring. And I wanted something poetic this time: something to mark the victim's death with a final, triumphant fanfare.

There is a CD deck under the dashboard, on

which he likes to play music as he drives. Midnight Blue favours loud bands, rock music that rants and rails. He likes his music noisy, his vocals raucous, the squeal of guitars; likes to feel the deep punch of the bass in his eardrums and that kick of response in his lower belly, like something there could still be alive.

Some might say that, at his age, he ought to have turned down the volume by now; but Midnight Blue knows that rebellion is something born from experience, a lesson learnt the hard way, wasted on adolescents. Midnight Blue has always been a kind of existentialist; brooding on mortality; taking out on the rest of the world the fact that he is going to die.

A small glass jar under the seat is *blueeyedboy*'s contribution. The rest is all from Midnight Blue: for he is the one who turns up the sound; turns on the heater; drives home in his usual way, by his usual route, at his usual speed. Inside the open jar, a single wasp makes its way sluggishly towards freedom.

A wasp, you say? At this time of year? They are not impossible to find. Under the roof there are often nests, left over from summer, in which the insects lie dormant, waiting for the temperature to rise. Not so hard to climb up there, to ease one out of its padded cell, to transfer it into a glass jar and wait—

The car begins to warm up. Slowly the insect comes to life in an amplified burr of synths and guitars. It crawls towards the source of heat; its stinger begins to pump in time to the rhythm of the bass and drums. Midnight Blue does not hear it. Nor does he see it crawling up the back of the car

338

seat and on to the window, where it slowly unfolds its wings and begins to stutter against the glass—

Two minutes later, the wasp is alert. A combination of music, warmth and light has fully awakened it at last. It takes flight for a moment, hits the glass, rebounds and stubbornly tries again. And then it flies into the windscreen, just at the moment when Midnight Blue approaches the junction, driving with his usual impatience, cursing the other road users, the road, tapping out his frustration on the padded dashboard —

He sees the wasp. It's instinctive. He raises a hand towards his face. The insect, sensing the movement, veers a little closer. Midnight Blue strikes out, keeping one hand on the steering wheel. But the wasp has nowhere to go. It flies back into the windscreen, where it buzzes balefully. Midnight Blue, panicked now, fumbles for the window controls. He misses, and hits the volume instead, bumping up the sound and—

Wham! The volume kicks up from merely loud to an ear-buzzing burst of decibels; a sudden cataclysm of sound that shocks the steering wheel from his hand, sends it jerking spastically, and as Midnight Blue fights for control he slams right across the two lanes, his car tyres squealing soundlessly across the hard shoulder to hell, to the sound of a wailing wall of guitars—

I like to think he thought of me. Right at that moment, when his head smashed through the windscreen, I like to think he saw something more than just a cartoon trail of stars or the shadow of the Reaper. I'd like to think he saw a familiar face, that he knew in that flashgun moment of death *who* had murdered him, and why.

Then again, maybe he didn't. These things are so ephemeral. And Midnight Blue died instantly, or at least within seconds of impact, as the car turned into a fireball, consuming everything inside.

Well—maybe the wasp made it out alive.

It didn't even sting the guy.

Post comment:
Captainbunnykiller: *And he's* back!!!
Toxic69: *You rock!*
chrysalisbaby: *woot woot*
JennyTricks: (*post deleted*).
JennyTricks: (*post deleted*).
JennyTricks: (*post deleted*).
JennyTricks: (*post deleted*).
blueeyedboy: **Albertine?** *Is that you?*
JennyTricks: (*post deleted*).
blueeyedboy: **Albertine?**

You are viewing the webjournal of **Albertine**.
Posted at: *22:46 on Friday, February 15*
Status: *restricted*
Mood: *awake*

It's only fiction, he protests. He never murdered anyone. And yet, there they are—his confessions in fic. Too close to be lies, too vile to be real; Valentines from the other side, picture postcards from the dead.

It *is* only fiction, isn't it? How could it possibly be anything else? This virtual life is so nicely secure, battened against reality. These virtual friends, too, are safely confined behind this screen, this mouse mat. No one expects to encounter the truth in these worlds we build for ourselves. No one expects to feel it this way, through a glass, darkly.

But *blueeyedboy* has a special way of shaping the truth to his purpose. He does the same with people, too: winds them up like clockwork toys and sends them crashing into . . .

Walls? Articulated lorries on a busy main road? *Reader, I killed him.* What dangerous words. What am I meant to do with them? Does he believe what he's telling me, or is he just trying to mess with my mind? Nigel drove a black Toyota. And I know the style in which he drove, and his fear of wasps, and his favourite tracks, and the CD deck under the dashboard. Most of all, I remember how much that letter troubled him, and how he set off to his mother's house to deal with his brother once and for all . . .

Blueeyedboy has been trying to reach me all day. There are five unopened e-mails from him waiting in my inbox. I wonder what he wants from me. Confessions? Lies? Declarations of love?

Well, this time I won't react. I refuse. Because that's what he wants. A dialogue. He's played this game so many times. He admits that he is manipulative. I've watched him do it with Chryssie and Clair. He likes to subject them to mind games, to push them into declaring themselves. Thus, Chryssie is besotted with him; Clair thinks she can heal him; Cap wants to *be* him, and as for myself . . .

What *do* you want of me, *blueeyedboy*? What kind of reaction do you expect? Anger? Scorn? Confusion? Distress? Or could this be something more than that, some declaration of your own? Could it be that, after watching the world through a glass for so long, you finally, desperately want to be *seen*?

*   *   *

At ten o'clock the Zebra shuts. I'm always the last one out of the door. I found him waiting for me outside, under the shelter of the trees.

'Walk you home?' said *blueeyedboy*.

I ignored him. He followed me. I could hear his footsteps behind me, as I've heard them so many times.

'I'm sorry, *Albertine*,' he said. 'Obviously I shouldn't have posted that fic. But you wouldn't

342

answer my e-mails, and—'

'I don't care what you write,' I said.

'That's the spirit, *Albertine*.'

We walked in silence for a while.

'Did I tell you I collect orchids?'

'No.'

'I'd like to show them to you some day. The *Zygopetala* are particularly fragrant. Their scent can fill a whole room. Perhaps I could offer you one as a gift. By way of an apology—'

I shrugged. 'My house plants never survive.'

'Neither do your friends,' he said.

'Nigel's death was an accident.'

'Of course it was. Like Dr Peacock's and Eleanor Vine's—'

I felt my heart give a sick lurch.

'You didn't know?' He sounded surprised. 'She passed away the other night. *Passed away*. What a strange expression. Makes her sound like a parcel. Anyway, she's dead meat. Poor Terri will be inconsolable.'

We walked in silence after that, crossing Mill Road by the traffic lights, listening as the trees came alive over our heads in the rising wind. No snow this year—in fact it is unusually mild, and the air has a milky quality, as if a storm were coming. We passed by the silent nursery school; the shuttered and empty bakery; the Jacadees' house, with its scent of fried garlic and yams and roasting chillies.

At last we paused at the garden gate. By then it felt almost companionable: victim and predator side by side, close enough to touch.

'Can you still do it?' I said at last. 'That—you know—that thing you do.'

He gave a short, percussive laugh. 'It's not a skill you lose,' he said. 'In fact, it gets easier every time.'

'Like murder,' I said.

He laughed again.

I fumbled for the catch on the gate. Around me, the milky, troubled air smelt of fresh earth and rotting leaves. I struggled with myself to keep calm, but I could feel myself slipping away, becoming someone else, as I do every time he looks at me.

'You aren't going to ask me in? Very wise. People might talk.'

'Another time, perhaps,' I said.

'Whenever you want, *Albertine*.'

As I moved towards the house I could feel him watching me, sensed his eyes on the back of my neck as I fumbled for the door key. I can always tell when I am being watched. People give themselves away. He was too silent, too motionless, to be doing anything else but staring.

'I know you're there,' I said, without turning round.

Not a word from *blueeyedboy*.

I was almost tempted to ask him in, then, just to hear his reaction. He thinks I am afraid of him. In fact, the opposite is true. He is like a little boy playing with a wasp in a jar: fascinated, but terribly afraid that at some point the trapped creature will escape its confinement and take revenge. It's hard to believe, isn't it, that something so small could inspire such unease? And yet, Nigel, too, was afraid of wasps. Such a little thing, you'd think, to drive a man into a panic. A blob of fuzz; a drone of wings; armed with nothing more than a sting and a tiny amount of irritant.

You think I don't see how you're playing me. Well, maybe I see more than you think. I see your self-hatred. I see your fear. Most of all, I see what you want, deep down in your secret heart. But what you *want* and what you *need* are not necessarily the same. Desire and compulsion are two different things.

I know you're still out there, watching me. I can almost feel your heart. I can tell how fast it's beating now, like that of an animal caught in a trap. Well, I know how *that* feels. To have to pretend I'm someone else; to live every moment in fear of the past. I've lived this way for over twenty years, hoping to be left alone . . .

But now I'm ready to show myself. At last, from this dried-up chrysalis, something is about to emerge. So—if you're as guilty as you say, you'd better run, while there's still time. Run, like the helpless rat you are. Run as far and as fast as you can—

Run for your life, *blueeyedboy*.

You are viewing the webjournal of **blueeyedboy**.
Posted at: *23.18 on Saturday, February 16*
Status: *restricted*
Mood: *cynical*
Listening to: *Wheatus*: 'Teenage Dirtbag'

I told you before. Nothing ends. Nothing really begins either, except in the kind of story that starts with *Once upon a time, long, long ago*, and in which, in blatant defiance of the human condition, they all live happily ever after. My tastes are rather more humble. I'd settle for outliving Ma. Oh, and the chance to stamp on those dogs. That's all I've ever wanted. The rest of them—my brothers, the Whites, even Dr Peacock—are simply the icing on the cake; a cake long past its sell-by date, and sour under the frosting.

But before I can hope for forgiveness, I have to make the confession. Perhaps that's why I'm here, after all. This screen, like that of the confessional, serves a double purpose. And yes, I'm aware that the fatal flaw in most of our fictional bad guys is that common desire to confess; to strut; to reveal to the hero his master plan, only to be foiled at last—

That's why I'm not going public on this. Not yet, anyway. All of these restricted posts are accessible only by password. But maybe later, when it's done and I'm sitting on a beach somewhere, drinking

Mai Tais and watching the pretty girls go by, I'll mail you the password; I'll give you the truth. Maybe I owe you that, *Albertine*. And maybe one day you'll forgive me for everything I did to you. Most likely you won't. But that's OK. I've been living with guilt for a long time. A little more won't kill me.

Things *really* began to fall apart the summer that followed my brother's death. A long and turbulent summer, all dragonflies and thunderstorms. I was still only seventeen, a month from my eighteenth birthday, and the weight of my mother's attention now sat like a permanent thundercloud over my life. She had always been demanding. Now that my brothers were out of the way, she was viciously critical of every little thing I did, and I dreamed of running away, like Dad—

Ma had been through a difficult patch. The business with Nigel had done something to her. Nothing you would have noticed at first; but living with her as I did, I knew that all was not right with Gloria Green. It had started with lethargy at first; a slow, dull state of recovery. She would sit staring into space for hours; would eat whole packets of biscuits; would talk to people who weren't there; or sleep away whole afternoons before going to bed at eight or nine . . .

Grief sometimes does that to you, Maureen Pike explained to me. Of course, Maureen was in her element then, coming to see us every day, bringing home-made cakes and sound advice. Eleanor, too, offered support, recommending St John's Wort and group therapy. Adèle brought gossip and platitudes. *Time heals all things. Life must go on.*

Tell *that* to the cancer ward.

Then, as the summer waned, Ma had entered another phase. The lethargy had given way to a manic kind of activity. Maureen explained the phenomenon, which she said was called *displacement*; and welcomed it as necessary to the healing process. At that time, Maureen's daughter was doing a degree in psychology, and Maureen had embraced the world of psychoanalysis with the same self-important, lolloping zeal she gave to church fêtes, Junior Fun Days, collections for the elderly, her book group, her work at the coffee shop and ridding Malbry of paedophiles.

In any case, Ma was busy that month: working five days on the market stall, cooking, cleaning, making plans, ticking off time like an impatient schoolmistress—and, of course, keeping an eye on Yours Truly.

I'd had an easy time until then. For nearly a month, enshrouded with grief, she'd barely even noticed me. Now she made up for that in spades: questioning my every move; making the vitamin drink twice a day and worrying about everything. If I coughed, she assumed I was at death's door. If I was late, I'd been murdered or mugged. And when she wasn't fretting over all the things that might happen to me, she was rigid with fear over what I might *do*—that I'd find myself in trouble, somehow, that she'd lose me to drink, or drugs, or a girl—

But there was no escape for *blueeyedboy*. Three months had passed since the incident when Ma had hit me with the plate, and after Nigel failed her, Ma's obsession with success had grown to monstrous proportions. I'd missed my school exams, of course; but an appeal by Ma (on compassionate grounds) had earned me a review of my case. Malbry College was where she believed I should continue my studies. She had it all planned out for me. A year to re-sit those exams; and then I could start afresh, she said. She'd always dreamed of one of her boys entering the medical profession. I was her only hope, she said; and with a ruthless disregard for my wishes—indeed, for my ability—she began to mark out my future career.

I tried to argue with her at first. I had no qualifications. Besides, I wasn't cut out for medicine. Ma was saddened, but took it well—or so I thought in my innocence. I'd expected an outburst at the very least; one of Ma's violent attacks. What I got was a week of redoubled affection and lavishly home-cooked dinners— always my favourites—which she laid on the table with the virtuous air of a long-suffering guardian angel.

Soon after that I fell violently ill, with acute stomach cramps and a fever that brought me to my knees. Even to sit up in bed was to precipitate the most awful spasms of pain and vomiting, and to stand—still less to walk—was wholly out of the question. Ma cared for me with a tenderness that might have made me suspicious if I hadn't been suffering so much. Then, after almost a week, she reverted suddenly to type.

I'd been getting better. I'd lost pounds in weight; I was weak, but at last the pain had gone, and I was able to eat simple food in small quantities. A cup of noodle soup; some bread; a tablespoonful of plain rice; soldiers dipped in egg yolk.

She must have been worried by then, of course.

349

Ma was no doctor; she had no concept of dosage, and the violence of my reaction must have been alarming. Waking up a few nights before from a sleep that was part delirium, I'd heard her talking to herself, arguing fiercely with someone not there:

It serves him right. He needs to learn.

But he's in pain. He's sick—

He'll live. Besides, he should have listened to me—

What had she put in those lavish meals? Ground glass? Rat poison? Whatever it had been, it had worked fast. And the day I was finally able to sit up in bed, even to stand, Ma came in, not with a tray, but with an application form—a form from Malbry College, which she had already filled in for me.

'I hope you've had time to think,' she said in a suspiciously cheery voice. 'Lying in bed doing nothing all day, letting me fetch and carry for you. I hope you've had time to think about everything I've done for you. Everything you owe me—'

'Please. Not now. My stomach hurts—'

'No, it doesn't,' she said. 'In a day or two you'll be good as new, eating me out of house and home, like the ungrateful little bastard you are. Now, have a look at these papers.' Her expression, which had begun to darken, once more took on that look of relentless cheeriness. 'I've been looking at those courses again, and I think you should do the same.'

I looked at her. She was smiling at me, and I felt a pang of guilt in my stomach for letting the thought even cross my mind—

'What was wrong with me?' I said.

I thought her eyes flickered. 'What do you mean?'

'Do you think it was something I ate?' I went on. 'You didn't get sick at all, did you, Ma?'

350

'I can't afford to get sick,' she said. 'I've got you to look after, haven't I?' Then she moved in close to me and fixed me with her espresso eyes. 'I think it's time you got up now,' she said, shoving the papers into my hand. 'You've got a lot of work to do.'

That time I knew better than to protest. I signed up without a word for three subjects I knew nothing about, knowing I could change them later. I was already an accomplished liar; rather than actually take the courses and risk my mother finding out when I failed, I waited until the beginning of term and secretly changed my subject choices to something more suited to my personal talents, then found myself a part-time job in an electrical shop a few miles away, and let her believe I was studying.

After that, it was simply a question of forging my certificates—easy, on a computer—after which I hacked into the Malbry *Examiner*'s computer files and added a single name—my own—to a soon-to-be-published list of results.

*   *   *

I've tried to do my own cooking ever since. But there's always the vitamin drink, of course, which Ma prepares with her own hands, and which keeps me well—or so she says, with a kind of sly innuendo. Every eighteen months or so I come down with a sudden, violent illness characterized by terrible stomach cramps, and my mother cares for me lovingly, and if these bouts of sickness always seem to coincide with moments of tension between Ma and myself, that's just because I am

351

sensitive, and these things have an effect on my health.

I never got away, of course. Some things are inescapable. Even London is too far to go—Hawaii, an impossible dream.

Well, maybe not *quite* impossible. That old blue lamp is still alight. And although it has taken more time than even I imagined it would, I begin to sense that at long last my patience is about to be rewarded.

Patience, too, is a game, of course, a game of skill and endurance. *Solitaire*, the Americans call it, a far less optimistic name, tinged with the grey-green of melancholy. Well, a solitary game it may be; but in my case that's surely a blessing. Besides, in a game that one plays with oneself, can anyone be said to lose?

> *You are viewing the webjournal of* **blueeyedboy**.
> **Posted at**: *23.49 on Saturday, February 16*
> **Status**: *restricted*
> **Mood**: *trapped*
> **Listening to**: *Boomtown Rats*: 'Rat Trap'

'You've got a lot of work to do.'

I'd assumed at first that she meant school. In fact, school was only a part of it. My mother's plans ran deeper than that. It began just after my illness, and hers, in the last days of September, and I remember it all in greys and blues, with a thundery light that hurt my eyes, and a heat that pressed down on to my head, giving me a penitent's slouch, a habit that I never quite lost.

When the police called round for the first time, I assumed it was because of something I'd done. The camera I'd stolen, perhaps; the graffiti on Dr Peacock's door; or maybe finally someone had guessed how I'd disposed of my brother.

But I was not arrested. Instead I sweated it out of doors while Ma entertained in the parlour, bringing out the good biscuits, and the visitors' teacups that usually took pride of place in the cabinet under the china dogs. Then, after what seemed like an interminable wait, the two officers—a man and a woman—came out looking very serious, and the woman said: 'We need to talk.' And I could have passed out with terror and guilt, except that Ma was watching me with that look of expectant pride, and I knew that it wasn't something I'd done, but something she *expected of me*—

Of course, you know what that was. Ma never lets anything go. And what I'd revealed about Emily the day Ma hit me with the plate had festered and borne fruit in her mind, so that now, at last, it was ready for use.

She fixed me with her berry-black eyes. 'I know you don't want to tell them,' she said in a voice like a razor blade hidden inside a toffee apple. 'But I've brought you up to respect the law, and everyone knows it's not your fault—'

For a moment I didn't understand. I must have looked scared, because the policewoman put her arm around me and whispered. 'That's right, son. It's not your fault—' And then I remembered what I'd written that night on Dr Peacock's door, and all the components fell in place like the pieces of a Mouse Trap game, and I understood what my mother had meant—

You've got a lot of work to do.

'Oh, please,' I whispered. 'Please, no.'

'I know you're afraid,' my mother said—in that voice that sounded sweet, but was not. 'But everybody's on your side. No one's going to blame you.' Her eyes, as she spoke, were like steel pins. Her hand on my arm looked gentle, but the next day there would be bruises. 'All we want is the truth, B.B. Just the truth. How hard can that be?'

Well, what could I do? I was alone. Alone with Ma, trapped and afraid. I knew that if I called her bluff, if I disgraced her publicly, she'd find a way to make me pay. So I played the game, telling myself

354

that it was just a white lie; that *their* lies had been much worse than mine; that in any case, I had no choice—

The policewoman's name was Lucy, she said. I guessed her to be very young, maybe just out of training school, still fired with hopeful ideals and convinced that children have no reason to lie. The man was older, more cautious; less likely to show sympathy; but even so, he was gentle enough, allowing her to question me, making notes in his notepad.

'Your mother says you've been ill,' she said.

I nodded, not daring to say it aloud. Beside me, Ma, like a granite cliff face, one arm around my shoulders.

'She says you were delirious. Talking and shouting in your sleep.'

'I guess,' I said. 'It wasn't too bad.'

I felt my mother's bony fingers tighten on my upper arm. 'You say that now you're better,' she said. 'But you don't know the half of it. Until you've got children of your own, you can't imagine how it feels,' she said, without releasing my arm. 'To see my boy in such a bad way, crying like a baby.' She flashed me a brief, unsettling smile. 'You know I lost my other boy,' she said, with a glance at Lucy. 'If anything happened to B.B. now, I think I might go crazy.'

I saw the two officers exchange glances.

'Yes, Mrs Winter. I know. It must have been a terrible time.'

Ma frowned. 'How *could* you know? You're not much older than my son. Do *you* have any children?'

Lucy shook her head.

'Then don't presume to empathize.'

'I'm sorry, Mrs Winter.'

For a moment, Ma was silent, staring vacantly into space. She looked like an unplugged fruit machine; for a second I wondered if she'd had a stroke. Then she went on in a normal voice—at least what passes for normal with her.

'A mother knows these things,' she said. 'A mother senses everything. I knew there was something wrong with him. He started to talk and cry in his sleep. And that's when I began to suspect that something funny was going on.'

Oh, she was clever. She fed them the line. Fed it to them like poisoned bait, watching as I wriggled and squirmed. And the facts were indisputable. Between the ages of seven and thirteen, Ma's youngest son Benjamin had enjoyed a special relationship with Dr Graham Peacock. As payment for helping in his research, the doctor had befriended him, had taken charge of his schooling, had even offered financial aid to Ma, a single parent—

Then suddenly, without warning, Ben had ceased to cooperate. He had become introverted and secretive; had started doing badly at school; had begun to misbehave; above all, he had flatly refused to go back to the Mansion, giving no good reason for his behaviour, so that Dr Peacock had withdrawn his support, leaving Ma to fend alone.

She should have suspected there and then that something had gone seriously wrong, but anger had blinded her to her son's needs, and when, later, graffiti had been scrawled on the door of the Mansion, she had simply seen it as another proof of his growing delinquency. Ben had denied the vandalism. Ma had not believed him. It was only now that she realized what that gesture had really been; a cry for help; a warning—

'What did you write on the door, B.B.?' Her voice was chequered with menace and love.

I looked away. 'Please, M-ma. It was so long ago. I d-don't really think—'

'B.B.' Only I could hear the change in her voice: the vinegary, sour-vegetable tone that brought back the reek of the vitamin drink. Already my head was beginning to throb. I reached for the word that would drive it away. A word that sounds vaguely French, somehow, that makes me think of green summer lawns and the scent of cut grass in the meadows—

'Pervert,' I whispered.

'What?' she said.

I said it again, and she smiled at me.

'And why did you write that, B.B.?' she said.

'Because he is.' I was still feeling trapped, but behind the fear and the guilt of it all there was something almost pleasurable: a sense of perilous ownership.

I thought of Mrs White, and of the way she had looked that day on the steps of the Mansion. I thought of the pity on Mr White's face, that day in St Oswald's schoolyard. I thought of Dr Peacock's face peering through the curtains, and his sheepish smile as I crept away. I thought of the ladies who had spoiled and petted me as a child, only to scorn me when I grew up. I thought of my teachers at school, and my brothers, who'd treated me with such contempt. Then I thought of Emily—

And I saw how easy it would be to take revenge on all those people, to make them pay attention to

357

me, to make them suffer as I had. And for the first time since my earliest childhood, I was conscious of an exhilarating sensation. A feeling of power; an energy rush; a force; a current; a surge; a charge.

Charge. Such an ambivalent word, with its implications of power and blame, attack and detention, payment and cost. And it smells of burnt wiring and solder, and its colour is like a summer's sky, thundery and luminous.

Don't think I'm trying to absolve myself. I told you I was a bad guy. No one forced me to do what I did. I made a conscious decision that day. I could have done the right thing. I could have pulled the plug on it all. Told the truth. Confessed the lie. I had the choice. I could have left home. I could have escaped the pitcher plant.

But Ma was watching, and I knew that I would never do those things. It wasn't that I was afraid of her—although I was, most terribly. It was simply the lure of being in charge—of being the one to whom eyes turned—

I know. Don't think I'm proud of this. It's not exactly my greatest moment. Most crimes are annoyingly petty, and I'm afraid mine was no exception. But I was young, too young in any case to see how cleverly she had handled me, guiding me through a series of hoops to a reward that would ultimately reveal itself to be the worst kind of punishment.

And now she was smiling—a genuine smile, radiating approval. And, at that moment, I wanted it, wanted to hear her say: *well done*, even though I hated her—

'Tell them, B.B.,' she said, pinning me with that brilliant smile. 'Tell them what he did to you.'

358

> *You are viewing the webjournal of* **blueeyedboy**.
> **Posted at**: *03.58 on Sunday, February 17*
> **Status**: *restricted*
> **Mood**: *perverse*
> **Listening to**: *10cc*: 'I'm Not In Love'

The first thing that happened after that was that Emily was taken into protective care. Just as a precaution, they said; just to ensure her safety. Her reluctance to incriminate Dr Peacock was seen as proof of long-term abuse rather than simple innocence, and Catherine's rage and bewilderment when faced with the accusations was seen as further evidence of some kind of collusion. Something had clearly been going on. At best, a cynical fraud. At worst, a large-scale conspiracy.

And now came Yours Truly's testimony. It had started so harmlessly, I said. Dr Peacock had been very kind. Private lessons, cash now and then—that was how he'd reeled us in. And that was how he'd approached Catherine White, a woman with a history of depression, ambitious and easily flattered, so eager to believe that her child was special that she'd managed to blind herself to the truth.

The books in Dr Peacock's library did much to support my claim, of course. Biographies of literature's most notorious synaesthetes. Nabokov; Rimbaud; Baudelaire; De Quincey—self-confessed drug-users, homosexuals, paedophiles. Men whose pursuit of the sublime took precedence to the petty morality of their day. The material seized as evidence was not directly incriminating, but the police are no great connoisseurs of art, and the sheer volume of material in Dr Peacock's collection was enough to convince them that they had the right man. Class photographs of St Oswald's boys taken whilst he was a governor. Volumes of Greek and Roman art; engravings of statues of naked young men. A first edition of Beardsley's *Yellow Book*; a collection of Ovenden prints from *Lolita*; a pencil drawing of a young male nude (attributed to Caravaggio); a lavishly illustrated copy of *The Perfumed Garden*; books of erotic poetry by Verlaine, Swinburne, Rimbaud and the Marquis de Sade—

'You showed this stuff to a seven-year-old?'

Dr Peacock tried to explain. It was part of the boy's education, he said. And Benjamin was interested; he wanted to know what he was—

'And what *was* he, according to you?'

Once more, Dr Peacock struggled to enlighten his audience. But while *Boy X* had been fascinated by case studies of synaesthetes, of music and migraines and orgasms that manifested themselves in trails of colour, the police seemed far more interested in finding out precisely what he and *Boy X* had talked about during all those private lessons. Whether he'd ever been tempted to touch Benjamin; whether he'd ever given him drugs; whether he'd ever spent time alone with him—or his brothers.

And when Dr Peacock finally broke, and vented his rage and frustration, the officers looked at each other and said: 'That's a nasty temper you've got. Did you ever strike the boy? Slap him, correct him in any way?'

Numbly, the doctor shook his head.

'And what about the little girl? It must have been frustrating, having to work with such a young child. Especially when you've been used to teaching boys. Was she ever uncooperative?'

'Never, said Dr Peacock. 'Emily's a sweet little girl.'

'Eager to please?'

He nodded.

'Eager enough to fake a result?'

The doctor denied it vehemently. But the damage was already done. I had painted a more than plausible picture. And if Emily failed to confirm his tale, then that was simply because she was young, confused, and in denial of the way in which she had been used—

They tried to keep it from the Press. Might as well try to stop the tide. The wave of speculation broke just in the wake of the film's release. By the end of that year Emily White was national news; and then, just as suddenly, infamous.

The tabloid headlines came out in force. The *Mail*: *ABUSE CLAIMS IN SUPER-SENSE CASE.* The *Sun*: *SEE EMILY PLAY!* Best of all, from the *Mirror*: *EMILY—WAS SHE A FAKE?*

Jeffrey Stuarts, the journalist who had followed Emily's case throughout, living with the family, attending sessions at the Mansion, answering the sceptics with the keenness of a true fanatic, saw what was coming and quickly changed course, hastily rewriting his book—to be entitled *The Emily Experiment*—to include, not only rumours of

361

sleaze at the Mansion, but strong hints of a darker truth behind the Emily Phenomenon.

The hard, ambitious mother; the weak, ineffectual father; the influential New Age friend; the child-victim, trained to perform; the predatory old man, consumed by his obsessions. And, of course, *Boy X*. Redeemed by what he'd had to endure, he was in it to the hilt. The guileless victim. The innocent. Once again, the blue-eyed boy.

Of course, it never went to court. It never even made it to the magistrate. Whilst still under investigation, Dr Peacock suffered a heart attack that landed him in intensive care. The case was postponed indefinitely.

But just the faintest whiff of smoke was enough to convince the public. Trial by tabloid is swift and sure. Within three months, it was over. *The Emily Experiment* went straight to the top of the best-seller lists. Patrick and Catherine White agreed to a trial separation. Investors withdrew their money; galleries ceased to display Emily's work. Feather moved in with Catherine, while Patrick removed himself to a hostel just outside Malbry.

It wasn't a permanent move, he said. It was simply to give them a little space. A twenty-four-hour police guard was stationed outside the Mansion in the wake of several arson attempts. And the papers were all over Catherine. A row of photographers flanked the house, snapping up anyone who crossed the threshold.

Graffiti appeared on the front door. Hate mail came by the sackful. The *News of the World* ran a picture of Catherine, in tears, with a story (confirmed by Feather, to whom they paid five thousand pounds) that she had suffered a mental breakdown.

Christmas brought little improvement, though Emily was allowed home for the day. Before that the child had remained in the custody of the Social Services, who, failing to detect any signs of abuse, interrogated her kindly but relentlessly until even she began to wonder if she, too, wasn't losing her mind.

Try to remember, Emily.

I know the technique. I know it well. Kindness is a weapon, too, a padded cartoon goofy-stick that batters away at the memory, turning it all into candyfloss.

It's all right. It's not your fault.

Just tell us the truth, Emily.

Imagine what it was like for her. Everything was going wrong. Dr Peacock was under investigation. Her parents were suddenly living apart. People kept asking her questions, and although they kept saying it wasn't her fault, she couldn't help thinking that somehow it was. That somehow, that little snow-white lie had turned into an avalanche—

Listen to the colours.

She wanted to say it was all a mistake, but of course, it was far too late for that. They wanted a demonstration: a once-and-for-all display of her gift, well away from the influence of Dr Peacock or her mother, a performance to confirm or refute for ever the claim that she was a fake, a pawn in their game of deception and greed.

And that was how, in January, on a snowy morning in Manchester, she found herself with her easel and paints, on a sound stage surrounded by

363

cameras, with hot lights battening down on her head and the sound of the *Symphonie fantastique* pouring out of the speakers. And right at that moment the miracle happens and *Emily hears the colours—*

It is by far her most famous work. *Symphonie fantastique in Twenty-four Conflicting Colours* looks something like a Jackson Pollock and something like a Mondrian, with that huge, grey shadow in the far corner reaching into the illuminated canvas like the hand of Death in a field of bright flowers . . .

So says Jeffrey Stuarts, at least, in the follow-up to his best-selling book: *The Emily Enigma*. That, too, raced to the top of the charts, although it was clearly a rehash of the previous one, with an afterword to include the events that followed its publication. After that, of course, the experts pursued the story, with professionals in every associated field from art to child psychology warring with each other to prove their conflicting theories.

Each camp had its adherents, be they cynics or believers. The child psychologists saw Emily's work as a symbolic expression of her fear; the paranormal camp as a harbinger of death; the art experts saw in the change of style a confirmation of what many had already secretly suspected: that Emily's synaesthesia had been a pretence from the start and that Catherine White, and not Emily, had been the creative influence behind such works as *Nocturne in Scarlet Ochre* and *Starry Moonlight Sonata*.

Symphonie fantastique is altogether different. Created in front of an audience on a piece of canvas eight feet square, it almost writhes with energy, so that even a dullard like Jeffrey Stuarts was able to feel its ominous presence. If fear has a colour, then this is it: menacing strings of red, brown and black overlaid with occasional violent patches of light, and that clanging square of blue-grey like the trapdoor to an oubliette—

To me, it smells of Blackpool pier, and my mother, and the vitamin drink. To Emily, it must have been the first step through a looking glass into a world in which nothing was sane, nothing was certain any more.

They tried to hide the truth from her. On compassionate grounds, the experts said. To tell her the truth at such a young age, especially in such circumstances, could prove traumatic in the extreme. But we heard it through the grapevine even before it hit the stands: that Catherine White was in hospital following a failed suicide attempt. And suddenly it seemed that every reporter in the world was heading straight for Malbry, the sleepy little Northern town where everything seemed to be happening, and where the clouds were still gathering for one more cosmic thunderstorm—

> *You are viewing the webjournal of* **blueeyedboy**.
> **Posted at**: *20.55 on Monday, February 18*
> **Status**: *restricted*
> **Mood**: *drained*
> **Listening to**: *Johnny Nash*: 'I Can See Clearly
> Now'

Clair e-mailed me again today. Apparently, she is missing me. And the fic I posted on Valentine's Day has caused more concern than usual. She urges me to return to the fold, to discuss my feelings of alienation and to face up to my responsibilities. The tone of her e-mail is neutral enough; but I sense her disapproval. Maybe she is feeling sensitive; or maybe she feels that my fiction provokes an inappropriate response in subjects such as Toxic and Cap, whose predilection for violence needs no further encouragement.

You need to come back to Group [she says].
Talking online is no substitute. I'd rather see
you face to face. Besides, I'm not sure these
stories of yours are really very helpful. You need
to confront these exhibitionist tendencies of
yours and face up to reality—

Bip! Delete message.
  Now she's gone.
  That's the beauty of e-mail, Clair. That's why I'd

rather meet online than in your little drawing-room with its nice, non-threatening prints on the walls and its scent of cheap pot-pourri. And at the writing group, you're in charge, whereas *badguysrock* belongs to me. Here, I ask the questions; here I am in complete control.

No, I think I'd rather stay and pursue my interests in the comfort and seclusion of my own room. I like myself so much better online. I can express so much more. It was here, and not at that awful school, that I received my classical education. And from here I can crawl into your mind, scent out your little secrets, expose your petty weaknesses, just as you try to find out mine.

Tell me—how *is* Angel Blue these days? I'm sure you must have heard from him. And Chryssie? Still sick? Well, that's too bad. Shouldn't you be talking to *her*, Clair, instead of cross-examining me?

The e-mail *bips*. New message from Clair.

I really think we should talk soon. I know you find our discussions uncomfortable, but I'm getting really worried about you. Please e-mail me back to confirm!

Bip! Delete message.
Whoops, all gone.
If only deleting Clair were as easy.

Still, I have other concerns right now, not least how I stand with *Albertine*. It's not that I hope for forgiveness. Both of us have come too far for that. But her silence is disquieting; and it is all I can do to prevent myself from calling by at her house today. Still, I don't think that would be wise. Too many potential witnesses. Already, I suspect we are being watched. All it would take is a word to Ma, and the house of cards would come tumbling down.

And so half an hour before closing time, I found myself back at the Zebra. My masochistic side so often drives me to that place, that safe little world of which Yours Truly is definitely *not* a part. In passing I noticed, to my annoyance, that Terri was sitting by the door. She looked up hopefully as I came in; I did my best to ignore her. So much for discretion, I thought. Like her aunt, she is an eager observer; a gossip, in spite of her diffidence; the kind of person who stops at the scene of a car crash, not to help, but to participate in the collective misery.

Saxophone Man with the dreadlocks was sitting close by with a pot of coffee at his elbow; he gave me a look designed to convey his contempt for such as I. Maybe Bethan has mentioned me. From time to time she does, you know, in a vain attempt to prove to herself how much she now detests me. *Creepy Dude*, she calls me. I'd hoped for something more imaginative.

I sat down in my usual place; ordered Earl Grey, no lemon, no milk. She brought it on a flowered tray. Lingered just long enough for me to suspect her of having something on her mind, then came to a decision; sat down squarely beside me, looked into my eyes and said:

'What the hell do you *want* from me?'

I poured out the tea. It was fragrant and good. I said: 'I have no idea what you're talking about.'

'Hanging around here all the time. Posting those stories. Raking things up—'

I had to laugh. 'Me? Raking things up? I'm sorry, but when the details of Dr Peacock's will come out, everything you do is going to be news. That isn't my fault, *Albertine*.'

'I wish you wouldn't call me that.'

'You chose it yourself,' I pointed out.

She shrugged. 'You wouldn't understand.'

Well, that's where you're wrong, Albertine. I understand it all too well. The heart's desire to be someone else, to take on a new identity. In a way I've done it myself—

'I don't want his money,' she said. 'I only want to be left alone.'

I grinned. 'Hope *that* works out for you.'

'You talked him into it, didn't you?' Her eyes were dark with anger now. 'Working there, you had the chance. He was old, suggestible. You could have told him anything.'

'Believe me, Bethan, if I had, don't you think I'd have done it for myself?' I let the thought sink in for a while. 'Dear old Dr Peacock. Still trying, after all these years, to make amends. Still half-convinced he could raise the dead. With Patrick gone, there was only you left. Nigel must have been over the moon—'

She looked at me. 'Not *that* again. I tell you, Nigel didn't care about that.'

'Oh, please,' I said. 'Love may be blind, but you'd have to be *really* stupid to think that someone like Nigel wouldn't have cared that his girlfriend was about to inherit a fortune—'

'You told him about Dr Peacock's will?'

'Who knows? I may have let something slip.'

'When?' Her voice was paper-thin.

'Eighteen months ago, maybe more.'

369

Silence. Then: 'You bastard,' she hissed. 'Are you trying to make me believe that this was a set-up from the start?'

'I don't care what you believe,' I said. 'But I'm guessing that he was protective. He didn't like you living alone. He hadn't mentioned marriage yet, but if he had, you would have said yes.' I paused. 'How am I doing so far?'

She fixed me with eyes the colour of murder. 'You know, this is pointless,' she said. 'You're never going to sell me this. Nigel didn't *care* about money.'

'Really? How romantic,' I said. 'Because according to the credit-card statements I came across when I cleared out his flat, when Nigel died he was badly in debt. To the tune of nearly ten thousand pounds—it can't have been easy, making ends meet. Maybe he got impatient. Maybe he got desperate. Dr Peacock was old and sick, but his illness was far from terminal. He could have lived another ten years—'

Now her face was colourless. 'Nigel didn't kill Dr Peacock,' she said, 'any more than you could have done. He wouldn't do a thing like that—' Her voice was wavering. It hurt me to cause her such distress, but she needed to know. To understand.

'Why couldn't he, Bethan? He's done it before.'

She shook her head. 'That was different.'

'Is *that* what he said?'

'Of course it was!'

I grinned.

She stood up abruptly, sending her chair clattering. 'Why on earth does it *matter*?' she cried. 'All that was such a long time ago, so why do you always keep bringing it up? Nigel's *dead*, it's *over*

370

now, so why can't you just leave me alone?'

Her distress was strangely moving, I thought. Her face was bleak and beautiful. The emerald stud in her eyebrow winked at me like an open eye. Suddenly, all I wanted was for her to hold me, to comfort me, to tell me the lies that everyone secretly most wants to hear.

But I had to go on. I owed it to her. 'It's never over, Bethan,' I said. 'There's no going back from murder. Especially when it's a relative—and Benjamin was only sixteen—'

She eyed me with hatred, and now, for the first time, I could almost believe her capable of the act that had already deleted two of Gloria Winter's boys permanently from existence.

'Nigel was right,' she said at last. 'You *are* a twisted bastard.'

'That hurt my feelings, *Albertine*.'

'Don't play the innocent, Brendan.'

I shrugged. 'That's hardly fair,' I said. 'It was *Nigel* who murdered Benjamin. I was lucky I wasn't there. If things had been different, it could have been me.'

PART FIVE

mirrors

> *You are viewing the webjournal of* **blueeyedboy**.
> **Posted at**: *23.40 on Tuesday, February 19*
> **Status**: *restricted*
> **Mood**: *tired*
> **Listening to**: *Cyndi Lauper*: 'True Colours'

All right. You can call me Brendan. Does that make you happy now? *Now* do you think you know me? We choose our names, our identities; just as we choose the lives we lead. I have to believe that, *Albertine*. The alternative—that these things are allocated at birth, or even before, *in utero*—is far too appalling to contemplate.

Someone once told me that seventy per cent of all praise received in the course of an average lifetime is given before the age of five. At five years old, almost anything—eating a mouthful of food; getting dressed; drawing a picture in crayon—can earn the most lavish compliments. Of course, that stops eventually. In my case, when my brother was born—my brother in blue, that is—Benjamin.

Clair, with her love of psychobabble, sometimes speaks of what she calls *the reverse halo* effect; that tendency we all have to assign the colours of villainy on the basis of a single flaw: such as having swallowed a sibling, perhaps, or collected a bucket of sea creatures and left them to die in the scorching sun. When Ben was born, my halo reversed; and henceforth *blueeyedboy* was stripped of all his former privileges.

I saw it coming. At three years old, I already knew that the squalling blue package Ma had brought home would bring me nothing but misery. First came her decision to allocate colours to her three sons. That's where it started, I realize, although she may not have known it then. But that's how I became Brendan Brown—the dull one, neither fish nor fowl—eclipsed on one side by Nigel Black and on the other by Benjamin Blue. No one noticed me any more—unless, of course, I did something wrong, in which case the piece of electrical cord was only too quick to be deployed. No one thought I was special enough to merit any attention.

Still, I've managed to change all that. I've reclaimed my halo—in Ma's eyes, at least. As for you, *Albertine*—or must I call you Bethan now? You always saw more than the others did. You always understood me. You never had the slightest doubt that I, too, was remarkable, that beneath my sensitivity beat the heart of a future murderer. Still—

Everyone knows it wasn't my fault. I never laid a hand on him. In fact, I wasn't even there. I was watching Emily. *All* those times I watched her, followed her to the Mansion and back, felt Dr Peacock's welcoming hug, flew with her on her little swing, felt her mother's hand in mine, heard her say: *Well done, sweetheart*—

My brother never did those things. Perhaps he never needed to. Ben was too busy feeling sorry for himself to take an interest in Emily. *I* was the one who cared for her; took pictures of her from over the hedge; shared the scraps of her strange little

376

life.

Perhaps that was why I loved her then; because she had stolen Benjamin's life just as he had stolen mine. My mother's love; my gift; my chance; all of them passed to Benjamin, as if I'd simply held them in trust until the better man came along.

Ben, the blue-eyed boy. The thief. And what did he do with his big chance? He pissed it away in resentment because somebody else got a bigger break. Everything: his intelligence; his place at St Oswald's; his chance at fame; even his time at the Mansion. All thrown to the winds because Benjamin didn't just want a slice of the cake, he wanted the bloody bakery. Well, that's what it looked like to Brendan Brown, left with only the few crumbs he managed to steal from his brother's plate—

But now, the cake belongs to me. The cake, as well as the bakery. As Cap would say: *Pure pwnage, man*—

I got away with murder.

You are viewing the webjournal of: **blueeyedboy**
posting on:

badguysrock@webjournal.com

Posted at: *23.47 on Tuesday, February 19*
Status: *public*
Mood: *vulnerable*
Listening to: *Johnny Cash*: 'Hurt'

They call him Mr Brendan Brown. Too dull to be gifted; too dull to be seen; too dull even for murder. Shit-brown; donkey-brown; boring, butthead, bastard-brown. All his life he has tried to be blind, an unwilling spectator to everything, watching through interlaced fingers as the action unrolls without him, wincing at the slightest blow, the smallest hint of violence.

Yes, Brendan Brown is sensitive. Action movies frighten him. Wildlife documentaries are out; as are horror movies, video games, cowboy films or combat scenes. He even feels for the bad guy. Sports, too, are a discomfort to him, with their risk of injuries and collisions. Instead he watches cookery shows, or gardening shows, or travelogues, or porn, and dreams of other places; feels printed sunlight on his face—

It's squeamishness, his mother says. *He feels things more than the others do.*

Perhaps he does, thinks Brendan Brown. Perhaps he feels things differently. Because if he watches someone in pain, it makes him so uncomfortable that sometimes he is physically sick, and he cries in frightened confusion at the things the images make him feel—

His brother in blue is aware of this, and makes him watch his experiments with flies and wasps, and then with mice; shows him pictures to make him squirm. Dr Peacock calls it *mirror-touch synaesthesia*, and it presents—in his case, at least— as a kind of pathological sensitivity, in which the optical part of the brain somehow mirrors the physical, so that he can experience what others feel—be it a touch, or a taste, or a blow—as clearly as if it were done to himself.

His brother in black despises him, scorns him for his weakness. Even his mother ignores him now: the middle child, the quiet one, caught between Nigel, the black sheep, and Benjamin, the blue-eyed boy—

Brendan hates his brothers. He hates the way they make him feel. One is angry all the time, the other smug and contemptuous. And Brendan feels for them—too much—whether or not he wants to. They itch; he wants to scratch. They bleed; and Brendan obediently bleeds for them. Truth told, it isn't empathy. It's only a mindless physical response to a series of visual stimuli. He wouldn't care if they both died—as long as they did it far away, where he didn't have to watch it.

Sometimes, when he's alone, he reads. Slowly at first, and in private: books about travel and photography; poems and plays; short stories, novels and dictionaries. The printed word is different from what he sees around him. In his mind, the action unfolds without his body's involvement. He reads in the cellar late at night by the light of the bare bulb; the cellar that, lacking a room of his own, he has secretly converted into a darkroom. Here he reads books that his teachers wouldn't believe he had the wit to understand; books that, if his mates at school were to catch him reading, would make him a target for every joke, for every bully that came along.

But here, in his darkroom, he feels safe; there's no one here to laugh at him when he follows the words with his finger. No one to call him retarded when he reads the words aloud. No, this is Brendan's private place. Here he can do as he pleases. And sometimes, when he's alone, he has dreams. Dreams of dressing in something other than brown, of having people notice him, of showing his true colours.

But that's the problem, isn't it? All his life he has been Brendan Brown; doomed to be dull, to be stupid. In fact, he was never stupid. He simply hid it very well. At school, he did the minimum work, to protect himself from ridicule. At home, he has always pretended to be stolid and unimaginative. He knows that he is safer that way, now that Ben has taken his place, has robbed him of Ma's affection, has swallowed him, as he himself swallowed Mal, in the desperate struggle for dominance—

It isn't fair, thinks Brendan Brown. He, too, has blue eyes. He, too, has special skills. His shyness and his stammer leads them all to assume that he is inarticulate. But words have tremendous power, he knows. He wants to learn how to handle them. And he is good with computers. He knows how to process information. He is fighting his dyslexia with the aid of a special programme. Later, under cover of his part-time job at the fast-food place, he joins a creative-writing class. He isn't very good at first, but he works hard; he wants to learn. Words and their meanings fascinate him. He wants to know more about them. He wants to strip the language down to the very motherboard.

Most importantly, he is discreet. Discreet and very patient. To nail his colours to the mast would be to declare his intentions. Brendan Brown knows better than this. Brendan values camouflage. That is why he has survived this far. By blending into the background; by letting other people shine; by standing on the sidelines to watch while the opposition destroys itself—

Sun Szu says in *The Art Of War: All warfare is based on deception*. Well, if there's anything our boy knows, it's how to deceive and obfuscate.

Hence, when able to attack, we must seem unable; when using our forces, we must seem inactive; when we are near, we must make the enemy believe we are far away; when far away, we must make him believe we are near.

He chooses his moment carefully. He has never been impulsive. Unlike Nigel, who could always be relied upon to act first and think later (if he thought at all), responding to triggers so obvious that even a child could have played him—

If your opponent is of choleric temper, seek to irritate him.

Easily done, where Nigel is concerned. A well-placed word could do it. In this case it leads to violence; to a chain reaction that no one can stop and which ends with the death of his brother in blue and the arrest of his brother in black, and Badass Brendan, free of them both and whiter than the driven snow—

Item One: a black Moleskine notebook.

Item Two: some photographs of his brother in black cavorting with Tricia Goldblum, aka Mrs Electric Blue—some of them nicely intimate, taken with a long lens from the back of the lady's garden and developed in stealth in the darkroom, which no one, not even Ma, knows about—

Put them both together, like nitrogen and glycerine, and—

Wham!

In fact, it was almost too easy. People are so predictable. Nigel was especially, with his moods and his violent temper. Thanks to the reverse-halo effect (Nigel *always* hated Ben), all our hero had to do was to wind him up and put him in place, and the rest was a foregone conclusion. A casual word in Nigel's ear, suggesting that Ben was spying on him; the mention of a secret cache; then planting the evidence for Nigel to find under his brother's mattress, and after that the only thing our boy had to do was to remove himself from the premises while the sordid business of murder unfurled.

Ben denied all knowledge, of course. *That* was the fatal mistake. Brendan knew from experience that the only way to avoid serious hurt is to confess to the crime immediately, even when you're innocent. He'd learnt that lesson early on— thereby earning himself the convenient reputation of being a hopeless liar, whilst taking the blame for a number of things for which he was not responsible. In any case, Ben had no time to explain. Nigel's first blow cracked his skull. After that—well, suffice it to say that Benjamin never stood a chance.

Of course, our hero wasn't there. Like Macavity, the Mystery Cat, he has mastered the difficult technique of eclipsing himself from unpleasantness. It was Brendan's Ma who found her son, who called the police and the ambulance, and then who kept watch at the hospital, and who never cried, not even once, not even when they told her that the damage was irreversible, that Benjamin would never wake up—

Manslaughter, they called it.

Interesting word—*man's laughter*—coloured in shades of lightning-blue and scented with sage and violet. Yes, he sees Ben's colours now. After all, he took his place. It all belongs to Brendan now—his gift; his future; his colours.

It took a little time to adjust. At first our hero was sick for days. His stomach felt like a bottomless pit; his head ached so much that he thought he would die. In one sense, he feels he deserved it. Another part of him grins inside. It's like an evil magic trick. He is innocent of any crime, and yet secretly guilty of murder.

But something is missing nevertheless. Violence is still beyond him. Which is somewhat unfortunate, given the extent of his rage. Without this poison gift, he thinks, anything would be possible. His thoughts are clear and objective. He has no conscience to trouble him. The most terrible things are in his mind, only a blink away from execution. But his body rejects the scenario. Only in fic can he act with impunity. Only then can he be truly free. In life, that surge of victory must always be paid for in the end; paid for in sickness and suffering, just as bad thoughts must be paid for in full—

She still has that piece of electrical cord. Of course, she doesn't use it now. Instead she uses her fists; her feet; she knows that he will never fight back. But he dreams of that piece of electrical cord, and of the china dogs that gape so vapidly from the glass case. The cord would fit snugly around her throat six or seven times at least; after which, the glass case and the china dogs wouldn't stand a fucking chance—

The thought makes him suddenly edgy again. It brings a taste to the back of his throat. It's a taste he ought to know by now: a brackish taste that makes him gag; that makes his mouth go starchy with fear and his heart lurch like a landed fish.

A voice from downstairs. 'Who's there?' she calls.

He gives a sigh. 'It's me, Ma.'

'What are you doing? It's time for your drink.'

He switches off the computer and reaches for his headphones. He likes to listen to music. It gives a different context to things. He wears his iPod all the time, and he has long since mastered the art of *seeming* to listen to what she says, while in his head something else is playing, the secret soundtrack to his life.

He goes downstairs. 'What's that, Ma?'

He watches her mouth moving soundlessly. In his head, the Man in Black sings in a voice so old and broken that he might already be dead. And Brendan feels so empty inside, consumed by such an emptiness, a craving that nothing can satisfy— not food, not love, not murder—like the snake that

384

set out to swallow the world, and ended up by swallowing itself.

And he knows, deep down, that his time has come. Time to take his medicine. Time to do what he has longed to do for the past forty years—practically all of his life. To nail his colours to the mast and to turn and face his enemy. What has he got to lose, after all? His vitamin drink? His empire of dirt?

Post comment:
JennyTricks: (*post deleted*).
Albertine: (*post deleted*).
JennyTricks: (*post deleted*).
blueeyedboy: Albertine?

So that's how a mirror-touch synaesthete got away with murder. A neat trick, you have to admit, which I carried off with my usual flair. Mirrors are very versatile. You can levitate; make things disappear; put swords through the naked lady. Yes, sometimes there are headaches. But *blueeyedboy* has helped me with that. Didn't I say I preferred myself when I was writing as someone else? *Blueeyedboy* has no empathy. He rarely feels for anyone. His cold, dispassionate view of the world is a welcome foil for my tenderness.

Tenderness? I hear you say. Well, yes. I'm *very* sensitive. A mirror-touch synaesthete feels everything he witnesses. As a boy, it took me some time to realize that others did not function this way. Until Dr Peacock arrived on the scene, I'd assumed I was perfectly normal. These things sometimes run in families, I'm told; though even in identical twins the way in which the condition manifests itself is often completely different.

In any case, my brother Ben had no wish to share the limelight. The first time we went to the Mansion, he warned me that if I gave as much as a hint to Dr Peacock that I was not the everyday citizen, the vanilla flavour I seemed to be, then there would be consequences of the most unpleasant kind. At first, I defied the warning. If only because of that sepia print, the picture of Hawaii, and the way Dr Peacock spoke to me, and the thought that I might be remarkable—

I stood my ground for two whole weeks. Nigel was openly scornful—as if Brendan Brown could do anything—and Benjamin watched me resentfully, awaiting his chance to take me down. Even then, he was devious. A casual word or two to Ma; a hint that I was jealous of him; more hints that I was faking my gift and simply copying my brother.

Face it: I never had a chance. I was fat and ungainly; dyslexic; a joke; a stutterer; a disaster at school. Even my eyes were that chilly blue-grey whereas Ben's were a luminous, summery shade that made people want to love him. Of course they believed him. Why wouldn't they?

With the help of the piece of electrical cord, Ma extracted a full confession. In a way I think we were both relieved. I'd known I couldn't compete with Ben. And as for Ma—she'd known from the start; she'd known I couldn't be special. How dare I try to discredit Ben? How dare I tell such lies to her? I snivelled and howled my apologies while my brother watched with a smile on his face, and after that, all it took was the threat of a complaint to Ma to make me his obedient slave.

That was the last time I tried to tell anyone about my gift. Once more, Ben had eclipsed me. I tried to go back to being Brendan Brown, safely less-than-average. But something in Ma had shifted. Perhaps it was the reverse-halo effect. Perhaps the Emily White affair. In any case, from that moment forth, I became the whipping-boy, the butt of her frustration. When Dr Peacock stopped working with Ben, I found that she held me somehow to blame. The year Ben failed at St Oswald's, I was the one who was punished—and yes, I *had* been planning to drop out of school, but both of us knew that if Ben had done well, then no one would have thought twice about me.

Food became my great escape—food, and later, Emily. I ate, not out of hunger or greed, but to cushion myself against a world where everything was dangerous; where every word was a false friend; where even to watch TV was a risk, and every scene a sharp edge just waiting for me to run into it.

Nowadays, I've learnt to cope. Music helps a little; and fic; and now, thanks to the Internet, I have found a means to enjoy my gift. The world online is a medium for every possible kind of porn. And of course, for a mirror-touch synaesthete, that's as good as the real thing. A touch, a kiss, and sometimes I can almost forget that it isn't me on that screen at all, that I am just an observer, a spy, and that the real action is going on somewhere else.

Medium. What an interesting word. It describes at the same time what I *was*—the middle child, the average Joe—and what I am now, a speaker in tongues, a living mouthpiece for the dead.

They say you only have one life. Look online, and you'll see that's not true. Try Googling your name one day, and see how many others share it. All those people who might have been you: the charity case; the sportsman; the almost-famous actor; the one on Death Row; the celebrity chef; the one who shares your birthday—all of them shadows of what might have been if things had been slightly different.

Well, I had the chance to be different. To step out of my own life and into one of my shadows. Wouldn't anyone do the same? Wouldn't *you*, if you had the chance?

You are viewing the webjournal of **blueeyedboy**.
Posted at: *01.04 on Tuesday, February 19*
Status: *restricted*
Mood: *reflective*
Listening to: *Sally Oldfield*: 'Mirrors'

Of course, Ma grieved for Benjamin. In silence, at first—an ominous calm that at first I took for acceptance. Then came the other symptoms; the rage; the forays into insanity. I'd hear her in the middle of the night, dusting the china dogs downstairs or simply walking around the house.

Sometimes she sobbed: *It wasn't your fault.* Sometimes she mistook me for my brother, or ranted at me for my failures. Sometimes she screamed: *It should have been you!* Sometimes she woke me in the night, sobbing—*Oh B.B, I dreamed you'd died*—and it took me some time to understand that we were interchangeable, and that Benjamin Blue and *blueeyedboy* were often, to Ma, one and the same—

Then came the fallout. Inevitably. After the shock came the backlash, and suddenly I was the target once more for all kinds of expectations. With both of my brothers gone from the scene, my role had altered drastically. *I* was now Ma's blue-eyed boy. I was now her only hope. And she felt that I owed it to her to try again, to go back to school; perhaps to study medicine—to do all the things that *he* should have done, and that only I could now achieve.

At first I tried to defend myself. I wasn't cut out for medicine. I'd failed every science subject at Sunnybank Park, and I'd barely scraped through O-level maths. But Ma was having none of it. I had a responsibility. I'd been lazy and slack for far too long; now it was time for me to change . . .

Well, you know what happened then. I fell mysteriously sick. My belly was filled with writhing snakes, pouring their venom into my guts. By the end of it all, I'd lost so much weight that I looked like a clown in my old clothes. I flinched at loud noises, cringed at bright lights. And sometimes I barely remembered the terrible, marvellous thing that I'd done, or where Ben finished and Brendan began—

Well, that's only natural, isn't it? My memories are so nebulous, sneakily substituting second-hand smoke into this game of mirrors. I was feverish; I was in pain; I don't know what I said to her. I don't remember anything—lies, confessions, promises— but when I was fully recovered, and I left my bed for the first time, I knew that something about me had changed. I was no longer Brendan Brown, but something else entirely. And, truth be told, I no longer knew with any kind of certainty whether I had swallowed Ben, or whether he had swallowed *me*—

Of course I don't believe in ghosts. I scarcely believe in the living. And yet, that's just what I became, a shadow of my brother. When the Emily scandal broke, I reinvented his story. I already had his gift, of course, thanks to my own condition. Which made it so much easier to make them believe that I was telling the truth.

I started to wear Ben's colour, his clothes. At first just for practicality's sake, because my own clothes were too big. I didn't wear blue all the time. A sweatshirt here, a T-shirt there. Ma didn't seem to notice. The scandal surrounding Emily White had made me into a hero; people bought me drinks in pubs; girls suddenly found me attractive. I'd started at Malbry College that term. I let Ma believe I was studying medicine. My teenage skin had finally cleared; I'd even lost my stammer. Best of all, I was still losing weight. With my brothers gone, I seemed to have lost that ravenous need to consume, to collect, to swallow everything in sight. What started with Mal had ended with Ben. At last, my craving was satisfied.

You are viewing the webjournal of **blueeyedboy**.
Posted at: *21.56 on Tuesday, February 19*
Status: *restricted*
Mood: *wistful*
Listening to: *Judy Garland*: 'Somewhere Over
                    The Rainbow'

Well, Clair—you got your way. I finally went back
to Group today. With everything going so nicely to
plan, I think I can allow myself a little harmless
distraction. Besides, this may be the last time—

It's a little powder-beige box of a room with a
spider plant on a shelf by the door and a picture of
Angel Blue on the wall. The chairs are orange, and
have been arranged in a circle so that no one feels
inferior. In the middle of the circle is a small table
on which there is a flowered tray with a teapot,
some cups, a plate of biscuits (Bourbon creams—
which I hate, by the way), some lined A4 paper, a
bundle of pens and the obligatory box of tissues.

Well, don't expect any tears from me.
Blueeyedboy never cries.

'Hello! It's so great to see you,' said Clair. (She
always says that to everyone.) 'How are you
feeling?'

'OK, I guess.'

I'm rather less articulate in real life than I am
online. One of the many reasons that I still prefer
to stay at home.

'What happened to your face?' she said. She'd already forgotten my fic, of course—or decided it had to be all in my head.

I shrugged. 'I had an accident.'

She gave me a look of fake sympathy. She looks like her mother, Maureen Pike; especially now that she's reaching that age. Forty-one, forty-two; and suddenly it all moves south, no, not to Hawaii, but to some bleaker territory, a place of dry gulches and fallen rocks and holy rolling wilderness. A far cry, indeed, from *ClairDeLune*, who posts erotic fic on my site and who claims to be only thirty-five. Still, as you must have guessed, who we are on *badguysrock* can differ wildly from our real-life selves. As long as it stays a fantasy, who really cares which role we adopt? Cowboy or Indian, black hat or white, no one makes a judgement.

And yet, these games we like to play are linked to an underlying layer of truth—an untapped stratum of desire. We are what we dream. We know what we want. We know that we are *worth* it—

And if what we want is wickedness? If what we want is iniquity?

Well, maybe we are worth that, too. And the wages of sin is—

'Tea?' Clair indicated the flowered tray.

Tea. The poor man's Prozac. 'No, thanks.'

Terri, who takes her tea black and always ignores the biscuits—but who will eat a whole tub of chocolate-chip ice cream the moment she gets home—patted the chair beside her.

'Hi, Bren,' she simpered.

'Fuck off,' I told her.

I ran my eyes over the rest of the group. Yes,

they were all there. Half a dozen assorted headcases; plus would-be writers; soapbox queens; failed poets (is there any other kind?); all desperate for a chance to be heard. But only one of them matters to me. Bethan, with the Irish eyes, watching me so hungrily—

Today she was wearing a sleeveless grey top that showed the stars tattooed down her arms. *That Irish girl of Nigel's,* Ma calls her, refusing even to mention the name. *The one with all those nasty tattoos.*

Nasty is my mother's word for those things over which she has no control. My photographs. My orchids. My fic. In fact, I rather like Bethan's tattoos, which help to hide the silvery scars that she has had since adolescence, and which criss-cross her arms like spiders' webs. Is *that* what Nigel saw in her? That passion for stars that echoed his own? That furtive, perpetual sense of distress?

In spite of her garish appearance, Bethan hates to be stared at. Perhaps that's why she hides herself beneath so many layers of deception. Tattoos, piercings, identities. As a child, she was docile and shy; mousy; almost invisible. Well, that's Catholicism for you, I suppose. A perpetual war between repression and excess. No wonder Nigel fell for her. She was that rare individual: someone more damaged than he was.

'Stop staring at me, Brendan,' she said.

I wish she wouldn't call me that. *Brendan* has a sour smell, like something damp in the cellar. It makes my mouth go fuzzy-felt dry, and its colour is—well, you know what it is. *Bethan* is no better, with its snuffy scent of church incense. I preferred her as *Albertine*; colourless, immaculate—

395

Clair intervened. 'Now, Bethan, please. You know what we said. I'm sure Bren didn't mean to stare.' She gave me one of her syrupy looks. 'And seeing as you're here, Bren, why don't we start with you today? I hear you've been going out more. That's good.'

I gave a shrug.

'Where have you been going, Bren?'

'Around. You know. Out. Town.'

She gave a wide, approving smile. 'That's really great to hear,' she said. 'And I'm so glad you're writing again. Is there anything you'd like to read for us today?'

I shrugged again.

'Now, don't be shy. You know we're here to help you.' She turned towards the rest of the group. 'Everyone, would you please show Bren how special he is to all of us? How much we want to help him?'

Oh no. Not the fucking group hug. Anything but that. Please.

'I do have a little something—' I said, more to divert their attention than because of any need to confess.

Clair's eyes were fixed upon me now, hungry and expectant. It's the look she gets on her face sometimes when she's telling us about Angel Blue. And I *do* look rather like him, of course—that, at least, was not a lie—which means, thanks to the halo effect, that Clair has a soft spot for me, and a tendency to believe what I say.

'Really? Can we hear it?' she said.

I looked across at Bethan once more. I used to think she hated me, and yet, perhaps she's the only one who really understands what it is to live every moment with the dead, to speak with the dead, to sleep with the dead—

'We'd love to hear it, Bren,' said Clair.

'Are you sure that's what you want?' I said, still directing my gaze towards Bethan. She was watching intently, her blue eyes narrowed like gas flames.

'Of course,' said Clair. 'Don't we, everyone?'

Nods all around the circle. I noticed that Bethan stayed perfectly still.

'It may be a little—edgy,' I said. 'Another murder, I'm afraid.' I smiled at Clair's expression and at the way the others leaned forward, just like pugs at feeding time. 'Sorry about that, guys,' I said. 'You're going to think that's all I do.'

You are viewing the webjournal of **blueeyedboy**, *posting on*:

badguysrock@webjournal.com

Posted at: *22.31 on Tuesday, February 19*
Status: *public*
Mood: *clean*
Listening to: *The Four Seasons*: 'Bye Bye Baby'

He calls her Mrs Baby Blue. She thinks she is an artist. Certainly, she looks like one: her dirt-blonde hair is artistically tousled; she wears paint-spattered jumpsuits and long strings of beads and likes to burn scented candles, which help the creative process, she says (plus they get rid of the smell of paint).

Not that she has accomplished much. No, all her creative passion has gone into raising her daughter. A child is like a work of art, and this one is perfect, she tells herself; perfect and talented and good—

He has been watching her from afar. He thinks how beautiful she is, with her neat little bob and her blanched-almond skin and her little red coat with the pointed hood. She looks nothing like her mother. Everything about her is self-contained. Even her name is beautiful. A name that smells of roses.

Her mother, on the other hand, is everything he most dislikes. Inconstant; pretentious; a parasite, feeding off her daughter, living through her, stealing her life with her expectations—

Blueeyedboy despises her. He thinks of all the harm she has done—to him, to both of them—and he wonders: *Would anyone really care?*

All things considered, he thinks maybe not. The world would be cleaner without her.

Cleaner. What a wonderful word. In blue, it maps out what he does, what he is and what he will achieve, in one. *Cleaner.*

The perfect crime comes in four stages. Stage One is obvious. Stage Two takes time. Stage Three is a little harder, but by now he is getting used to it. Five murders, counting Diesel Blue, and he wonders if he can call himself a serial killer yet, or if he first needs to refine his style.

Style is important to *blueeyedboy*. He wants to feel there's a poetry, a greater purpose in what he does. He would like to do something intricate: a dissection; a beheading; something dramatic, eccentric and strange. Something that will make them shiver; something that will set him apart from the rest. Most importantly, he would like to watch; to see the expression in her eyes; to have her know at last who he is—

He knows from his observation that when she is alone in the house, Mrs Baby Blue likes to take long baths. She stays in the bath for an hour at least, reading magazines—he has seen the telltale watermarks in the bundles of papers she puts out for recycling. He has seen the flicker of candles against the frosted window glass and caught the scent of her bath oil as the water rushes into the drain. Baby Blue bathtime is sacrosanct. She never answers the telephone; never even answers the door. He knows this. He has tried it. She doesn't even lock herself in—

He waits in the garden. He watches the house. Waits for the glow of candles and the sound of water in the pipes. Waits for Mrs Baby Blue; and then, very quietly, lets himself in.

The house has been redecorated. There are new paintings on the walls—abstracts for the most part—a scarlet and brown Axminster carpet in the hall.

Axminster. Ax. Minster. A red word. What does it mean? Axe-murderer. Axe. Minster. Murder in the Cathedral. The thought distracts him for a moment, makes him feel dizzy and remote, brings that taste into his mouth again, that fruity, rotting sweetness that heralds the worst of his headaches. He concentrates on the colour blue; its soothing properties, its calm. Blue is the blanket he reaches for whenever he feels alone or afraid; he closes his eyes, clenches his fists and thinks to himself—

It's not my fault.

When he opens them, the taste and the headache are both gone. He looks around the silent house. The layout is as he remembers it; there's the same lurking scent of turpentine; and those china dollies, *not* thrown away, but under glass in the parlour, all starey-eyed and sinister among their faded ringlets and lace.

The bathroom is tiled in aqua and white. Mrs B is reclining, eyes closed, in the water. Her face is a startling turquoise—some beauty mask, he conjectures. There is a copy of *Vogue* on the floor. Something smells of strawberries. Mrs B favours bath bombs that leave a sparkly residue: a layer of stardust on her skin.

Stellatio: the act of unconsciously transferring bath-bomb glitter on to another person without their knowledge or consent.

Stellata: the tiny fragments of sparkly stuff that find their way into his hair, his skin; three months later, he's still finding those bright flecks around the house, signalling his guilt in Morse code.

He watches her in silence. He could do it now, he tells himself; but sometimes the urge to be seen is too strong; and he wants to see the look in her eyes. He lingers for a moment; and then, some sense alerts her to him. She opens her eyes—for a moment there is no shock at all, just a wide, blank amazement, like that of those dollies in the hall— and then she is sitting up, a surge of water pulling at her, making her heavy, making her slow, and the smell of strawberries is suddenly overwhelming, and the glittery water splashes his face, and he is leaning into the bathtub, and she's punching at him with her helpless fists, and he grabs her by her soapy hair and pushes her under the surface.

It is surprisingly easy. Even so, he dislikes the mess. The woman is covered with glittery stuff that transfers on to his skin. The scent of synthetic strawberry intensifies. She heaves and struggles beneath his weight, but gravity is against her, and the weight of the water holds her down.

He waits for several minutes, thinking of those pink wafers in the tins of Family Circle, and another scent emerges from the lightning chain of words—*Wafer. Communion. Holy Ghost.* He allows himself to relax; gives his breathing time to slow down, then carefully, methodically, he goes about his housework.

No prints will be found at the scene—he is

wearing latex gloves, and has politely removed his shoes in the hall, like a good little boy on a visit. He checks the body. It looks OK. He mops the spilled water from the bathroom floor and leaves the candles burning.

Now he strips off his wet shirt and jeans, balls them up in his gym bag, puts on the clean clothes he has brought. He leaves the house as he found it—takes the wet clothes home with him and puts them in the washing machine.

There, he thinks. *All gone.*

*   *   *

He waits for discovery—no one comes. He has managed it again. But this time, he feels no euphoria. In fact he feels a sense of loss; and that harsh and cuprous dead-vegetable taste, so like that of the vitamin drink, creeps into his throat and fills his mouth, making him gag and grimace.

Why is this one different? he thinks. Why should he feel her absence now, when everything is so close to completion, and why should he feel he has thrown away—to use his Ma's habitual phrase—the baby with the bath water?

Post comment:
ClairDeLune: *Thank you for this,* **blueeyedboy**.
It was wonderful to hear you read this in Group. I hope you won't leave it so long next time!
Remember we're all there for you!
chrysalisbaby: *wish i could have heard U read* ☺

Captainbunnykiller: *Bitchin'—LOL!*
Toxic69: *This is better than sex, man. Still, if you could find your way to writing a bit of both, some day—*

> *You are viewing the webjournal of* **blueeyedboy**.
> **Posted at**: *23.59 on Tuesday, February 19*
> **Status**: *restricted*
> **Mood**: *lonely*
> **Listening to**: *Motorhead*: 'The Ace Of Spades'

Well, of course, one has to allow for poetic licence. But sometimes fiction is better than life. Maybe that's how it *should* have been. Murder is murder—be it by poison, by proxy, by drowning or by the thousand paper-cuts of the Press. Murder is murder, guilt is guilt, and under the fic beats a telltale truth as red and bloody as a heart. Because murder changes everyone—victim, culprit, witness, suspect—in so many unexpected ways. It's a Trojan, which infects the soul, lying dormant for months and years, stealing secrets, severing links, corrupting memories and worse, and finally emerging at last in a system-wide orgy of destruction.

No, I don't feel any remorse. Not for Catherine's death, at least. It was instinct that led me to act as I did; the instinct of a baby bird struggling for survival. Ma's response, too, was instinctive. I was, after all, the only child. I had to succeed, to be the best; discretion was no longer an option. I'd accepted Ben's inheritance. I read his books. I wore his clothes. And when the Peacock scandal broke, I told my brother's story—not as it really happened, of course, but how Ma had imagined it, revealing my brother once and for all as the saint, the victim, the star of the show—

Yes, I do feel sorry for that. Dr Peacock *had* been kind to me. But I had no choice. You know that, right? To refuse would have been unthinkable; I was already caught in the bottle trap, a trap of my own making, and I was fighting for my life by then, the life I'd stolen from Benjamin.

You understand, *Albertine*. You took a life from Emily. Not that I hold it against you. Quite the opposite, in fact. A person who knows how to take a life can always take another. And as I think I said before, what really counts—in murder, as in all affairs of the heart—is not so much knowledge as desire.

Well—may I still call you *Albertine*? *Bethan* never suited you. But the roses that grew up your garden wall—*Albertine*, with their wistful scent—were just the same variety as the ones that grew at the Mansion. I suppose I must have told you that. You always paid attention. Little Bethan Brannigan, with her bobbed brown hair and those slate-blue eyes. You lived next door to Emily, and in a certain kind of light you could almost have been her sister. You might even have been a friend to her, a child of her own age to play with.

But Mrs White was a terrible snob. She despised Mrs Brannigan, with her rented house and her Irish twang and suspiciously absent husband. She worked at the local primary school—in fact, she'd once taught my brother, who dubbed her Mrs Catholic Blue, and poured contempt on her beliefs. And though Patrick White was more tolerant than either Benjamin or Ma, Catherine kept Emily well away from the Irish girl and her family.

But you liked to watch her, didn't you? The little blind girl from over the wall who played the piano so beautifully; who had everything you didn't have, who had tutors and presents and visitors and who never had to go to school? And when I first spoke to you, you were shy; a little suspicious, at least at first, then flattered at the attention. You accepted my gifts first with puzzlement, then finally with gratitude.

Best of all, you never judged me. You never cared that I was fat. You never cared that I stammered, or thought of me as second-rate. You never asked a thing of me, or expected me to be someone else. I was the brother you'd never had. You were the little sister. And it never once occurred to you that you were just an excuse, a stooge; that the main attraction was somewhere else—

Well, now you know how I felt. We don't always get what we want in life. I had Ben, you had Emily; both of us on the sidelines; extras; substitutes for the real thing. Still, I became quite fond of you. Oh, not in the way I loved Emily, the little sister I should have had. But your innocent devotion was something I'd never encountered before. It's true that I was nearly twice your age; but you had a certain quality. You were engaging, obedient. You were unusually bright. And, of course, you desperately longed to be whatever it was that I wanted of you—

Oh, *please*. Don't be disgusting. What kind of a pervert do you take me for? I liked to be with you,

406

that was all, as I liked being close to Emily. Your mother never noticed me, and Mrs White, who knew who I was, never tried to intervene. On weekdays I'd call round after school, before your mother came home from work, and at weekends I'd meet you somewhere, either at the playground on Abbey Road or at the end of your garden, where we were less likely to be seen, and we'd talk about your day and mine; I'd give you sweets and chocolates, and I'd tell you stories about my Ma, my brothers, myself and Emily.

You were an excellent listener. In fact, I sometimes forgot your age and spoke to you as an equal. I told you about my condition—my gift. I showed you my cuts and bruises. I told you about Dr Peacock, and all the tests he'd performed on me before he chose my brother. I showed you some of my photographs, and confessed to you—as I could not to Ma—that all I'd ever wanted in life was to fly as far as Hawaii.

Poor little lonely girl. Who else did you have but me? Who else was there in your life? A working mother, an absent father, no grandparents, no neighbours, no friends. Except for Yours Truly, what did you have? And what wouldn't you have done for me?

Don't ever let them tell you that an eight-year-old child can't feel this way. Those pre-adolescent years are filled with anguish and revolt. Adults try to forget this; to fool themselves into thinking that children feel less strongly than they; that love comes later, with puberty, a kind of compensation for the loss of a state of grace—

Love? Well, yes. There are so many kinds. There's *eros*: simplest and most transient of all.

There's *philia*: friendship; loyalty. There's *storge*: the affection a child gives its parents. There's *thelema*: the desire to perform. Then there's *agape*: platonic love; for a friend; for a world; love for a stranger you've never met; the love of all humanity.

But even the Greeks didn't know everything. Love is like snow: there are so many words, all unique and untranslatable. Is there a word for the love you feel for someone you've hated all your life? Or the love for something that makes you sick? Or that sweet and aching tenderness for the one you're going to kill?

Please believe me, *Albertine*. I'm sorry for all that happened to you. I never wanted you to be hurt. But madness is catching, isn't it? Like love, it believes the impossible. Moves mountains; deals in eternity; sometimes even raises the dead.

You asked me what I wanted of you. Why I couldn't just leave it alone. Well, *Albertine*, here it is. You are going to do for me what I can never do for myself. The single act that can set me free. The act I've been planning for over twenty years. An act I could never carry out, but which *you* could perform so easily—

Pick a card. Any card.

The trick is to make the mark believe that the card he has picked was his own choice, instead of the one that was chosen for him. Any card. *My* card. Which happens to be—

Haven't you guessed?

Then pick a card, *Albertine*.

You are viewing the webjournal of **Albertine**.
Posted at: *23.32 on Tuesday, February 19*
Status: *restricted*
Mood: *tense*

He's playing games with me, of course. That's what *blueeyedboy* does best. We've played so many games, he and I, that the line between truth and fiction has become permanently blurred. I ought to hate him, and yet I know that whatever he *is,* whatever he *does,* I am in part responsible.

Why is he doing this to me? What does he hope to achieve this time? Everyone in this story is dead—Catherine; Daddy; Dr Peacock; Ben; Nigel, and, most importantly, Emily. And yet as he read his story out loud I felt my throat begin to constrict, my nerves to jangle, my head to spin, and soon the chords of the Berlioz would start to tighten in my mind—

'Bethan? Are you all right?' he said. I could hear the little smile in his voice.

'I'm sorry.' I stood up. 'I have to go.'

Clair looked slightly impatient behind her sympathetic façade. I'd interrupted the story, of course, and everyone else was riveted.

'You don't look terribly well,' said Bren. 'I hope it wasn't something I said—'

'Fuck you,' I told him, and made for the door.

He gave me a rueful shrug as I passed. Strange

that, after all he has done, I should feel that sorry little skip of the heart every time he looks at me. He's crazy, and false, and deserves to die, yet there's still something inside me that wants to believe, that still tries to find excuses for him. All that was such a long time ago. We were different people then. And both of us have paid a price, have left a part of ourselves behind, so that neither of us can ever be whole, or escape the ghost of Emily.

For a time, I thought I *had* escaped. Perhaps I might even have managed if he hadn't been there to remind me. Every day in every way, taunting me with his presence until suddenly it all comes out, and the box of delights is broken, and all the demons are free at last, scourging the air with memories.

Funny, where these things can lead us. If Emily had lived, would we have been friends? Would *she* have worn that red coat? Would she have lived in *my* house? Would Nigel have fallen for *her* that night at the Zebra, instead of me? Sometimes I feel I'm in Looking Glass Land, living a life that's not quite mine, a second-hand life that never quite fitted.

Emily's life. Emily's chair. Emily's bed. Emily's house.

But I like it there; it feels right somehow. Not like my old house from so long ago, which is now home to the Jacadees, and which rings with the noise of their cheery lives and the spices of their kitchen. Somehow I couldn't have stayed there. No, Emily's house was the place for me, and I have barely allowed it to change, as if she might come back some day and claim her rightful property.

410

Perhaps that's why Nigel never settled there, preferring to keep to his flat in town. Not that he really remembered her—he missed that business entirely—but I suppose Gloria disapproved, as indeed she disapproved of everything about me. My hair; my accent; my body art; but most of all my proximity to whatever had happened to Emily White, a mystery only half-resolved, in which her son was also enmeshed.

I don't believe in ghosts, of course. *I'm* not the one who's crazy. But all my life I've seen her here: tapping her way round Malbry; walking in the park; by the church; vivid in her bright-red coat. I've seen her; I've *been* her in my mind. How could it have been otherwise? I've been living Emily's life for longer than I have my own. I listen to her music. I grow her favourite flowers. I visited her father every Sunday afternoon, and right until the end he nearly always called me Emily.

Still, the time for nostalgia is long past. My journal now serves a new purpose. Confession is good for the soul, they say, and over time I have acquired the habit of the confessional. It's so much easier this way, of course; there is no priest, no penance. Only the computer screen and the absolution of the *Delete* key. *The moving finger writes, and, having writ*, can be erased at the touch of a hand; unwriting the past, deleting blame, making the sullied spotless again—

Blueeyedboy would understand. *Blueeyedboy*, with his online games. Why does he do it? Because he can. And equally, because he *can't*. And also, of course, because Chryssie believes in happy-ever-after; because Clair buys Bourbon biscuits instead of Family Circle; and because Cap is a fucktard

411

who wouldn't know tough if it jumped up and tore out what's left of his guts—

I know. I'm beginning to sound like him now. I suppose it comes with the territory. And besides, I've always been very good at mimicking other people. It is, you might say, my only skill. My one successful party piece. But this is no time for complacency. This is the time to be most aware. Even at his most vulnerable, *blueeyedboy* is dangerous. He is far from stupid, and he knows how to hit back. Nigel—poor Nigel—is a case in point, deleted just as effectively as if *blueeyedboy* had hit a key.

That's how he does it. That's how he copes. He said as much in his story. That's how a mirror-touch synaesthete orchestrated the death of one brother, by using another as proxy. And that's how he managed to kill Nigel, with the help of an insect in a jar. And if I am to believe him now, that's how he caused those *other* deaths, shielding himself from the consequences by watching it all in reverse, through his fic, like Perseus slaying the Gorgon.

I've thought of going to the police. But it sounds so absurd, doesn't it? I can imagine their faces now; their looks of sympathetic amusement. I could show them his online confessions—if that's what they really are—and I'd be the one to look crazy, lost in a world of fantasy. Like a stage magician as he prepares to saw the lady in half, *blueeyedboy* scrupulously invites us to check that there has been no subterfuge.

Look, no tricks. No hidden trapdoor. There's nothing hidden up his sleeve. His crimes are public, for all to see. To speak up now would simply be to turn the spotlight on myself; to add another scandalous strand to a tale already barbed with lies. I imagine my life with Nigel placed under their scrutiny; I can already see the Press coming like starving rodents out of their holes, swarming over everything, and every little scrap of my life torn up and nibbled at and used to line their filthy nests.

I walked home via the Fireplace House. I knew it so well from his stories. In fact I'd only seen it once, in secret, when I was ten years old. I remembered the garden, all roses, and the bright green lawns, and the big front door, and the fish pond with its fountain. Of course I'd never been inside. But Daddy had told me everything. Over twenty years later, I found my way back with eerie, unsurprising ease. Class had finished at eight o'clock, and a murky dark had fallen, smelling of smoke and sour earth, bracketing the houses and cars in a halo of streetlight-orange.

The house was shut, as I'd thought it would be, but the front gate opened easily and the path had been recently weeded and cleared. Bren's work, I told myself. He has always hated disorder.

Security lights came on as I passed. White spotlights against the green. I could see my giant shadow against the wall of the rose garden, pointing like a finger down the path and across the lawn.

I tried to imagine the house as my own. That gracious house, those gardens. If Emily had lived, I thought, they would have belonged to her now. But Emily had not lived, and the fortune had gone to her family, or at least what was left of it—to her father, Patrick White—and then, at last, from

Daddy to me. I wish I could refuse the gift. But it's too late: wherever I go, Emily White will follow me. Emily White and her circus of horrors: the gloaters, the haters, the stalkers, the Press . . .

The upstairs windows were boarded up. Across the fading front door someone had recently sprayed in blue paint: *ROT IN HELL U PERVERT.*

Nigel? No, surely not. I don't believe Nigel would have harmed the old man, whatever the provocation. And as for Bren's *other* suggestion— that Nigel had never loved me at all, that it had all been because of the money—

No. That's *blueeyedboy* playing games again, trying to poison everything. If Nigel had lied to me, I would have known. And yet I can't help wondering—what was in that letter he got? The letter which sent him off in such a rage? Could Brendan have been blackmailing him? Had he threatened to reveal his plans? Could Nigel really have been involved in something that led to murder?

Click.

A small, but quite familiar sound. For a moment I stood listening, the sound of my blood like surf in my ears, my skin a-prickle with nervous heat. *Could they have found me already?* I thought. Was this the exposure I'd feared?

'Is anyone there?'

No answer. The trees *hisshed* and whispered with the wind.

'Brendan!' I called. 'Bren? Is that you?'

Still nothing moved. There was silence. And yet I could feel him watching me as I've felt him watch me so often before, and the hackles stood up at the back of my neck, and my mouth was suddenly sour and dry.

Then I heard it again. *Click.*

The shutterclick sound of a camera, so dreadfully innocuous, weighted with menace and memories. Then the furtive sound of his retreat, almost inaudible, back through the bushes. He is very quiet, of course. But I can always hear him.

I took a step towards the sound, parted the bushes with my hands.

'Why are you following me?' I said. 'What is it you want, Bren?'

I thought I heard him behind me then, a furtive sound in the undergrowth. I made my voice seductive now, a velvet cat's-paw of a voice, to coax an unsuspecting rat. 'Brendan? Please. We need to talk.'

There was a piece of rock at my feet by the edge of the border. I hefted it. It felt good. I imagined myself bringing it down on his head as he hid there in the bushes.

I stood there, holding the rock in my hand, looking out for a sign of him. 'Brendan? Are you there?' I said. 'Come out. I want to talk to you—'

Once more I heard a rustling, and this time I reacted. I took a step, spun round, and then, as hard as I could, I pitched the rock towards the source of the rustling sound. There came a thud and a muffled cry—and then a terrible silence.

There. You've done it, I told myself.

It didn't feel real; my hands were numb. My ears were filled with white noise. *Was this all I had to do? Is it so easy to kill a man?*

And then it hit me; the horror, the truth. Murder *was* easy, I realized; as easy as throwing a

415

casual punch; as easy as lifting up a stone. I felt empty, amazed at my emptiness. Could this really be all there was?

Then came the opening chords of grief; a swell of love and sickness. I heard a dreadful wounded cry, which for a moment I took to be his voice, but later understood was my own. I took a step towards the place where I'd thrown the rock at Brendan. I called his name. There was no reply. He could be hurt, I told myself. He could be alive, but unconscious. He could be faking it; lying in wait. I didn't care; I had to know. *There*, behind the rose hedge—the briars tore my hands bloody.

And then came a movement behind me. He must have been very silent. He must have crawled on his hands and knees between the herbaceous borders. As I turned I caught a glimpse of his face, his look of pain and disbelief.

'Bren?' I called. 'I didn't mean—'

And then he was running away through the trees, a flash of blue parka against the green. I heard him slip on the dead leaves, sprint across the gravel path, vault over the garden wall and jump down into the alleyway. My heart was pounding furiously. I was shaking with adrenalin. Relief and bitterness warred in me. I hadn't crossed the line, after all. I was not a murderer. Or could it be that the fateful line was not the act, but the *intent*?

Of course, that's academic now. I've shown my hand. The game is on. Like it or not, if he gets the chance, he will try to kill me.

416

You are viewing the webjournal of **blueeyedboy**.
Posted at: *00.07 on Wednesday, February 20*
Status: *restricted*
Mood: *hurt*
Listening to: *Pink Floyd*: 'Run Like Hell'

Bitch. You got me. Right on the wrist—I'm lucky it isn't broken. If you'd hit me in the head—as you undoubtedly meant to—it would have been goodnight, sweet prince, or pick the cliché of your choice.

I have to say I'm a little surprised. I didn't mean any harm, you know. I was only taking photographs. I certainly hadn't expected you to react quite so aggressively. Fortunately I know that garden very well. I know how to move between the beds, and where to watch unnoticed. I knew how to make my escape, too—as I had so many times before—over the wall into the street, with my hurt wrist pressed hard against my stomach and tears of pain half-blinding me, so that everything seemed garlanded with dirty-orange rainbows.

I ran home, trying to tell myself that I *wasn't* running home to Ma, and got back just as she was finishing up in the kitchen.

'How was class?' she called through the door.

'Fine, Ma,' I told her, hoping to get upstairs before she saw me. Mud on my trainers; mud on my jeans; my wrist beginning to swell and throb—

that's why I'm still typing with one hand—and my face a map of where I'd been; of places Ma had warned me against—

'Did you talk to Terri?' she said. 'I'm sure she's upset about Eleanor.'

Surprisingly, Ma has taken it well. Far better than I had expected. Spent most of today looking at hats and choosing hymns for the funeral. Ma enjoys her funerals, of course. She relishes the drama. The trembling hand; the tearful smile; the handkerchief pressed to the lipsticked mouth. Tottering by with Adèle and Maureen, each supporting an elbow:

Gloria's such a survivor.

She stopped me halfway up the stairs. Looking down I could see the top of her head; the parting in her black hair that over time has grown from a narrow path into a four-lane motorway. Ma dyes her hair, of course; it's one of the things I'm not supposed to know about, like the Tena pads in the bathroom, and what happened to my father. But *I'm* not allowed to have secrets from *her*, and she levelled the force of her scrutiny on to my guilty profile as I stood like a deer in the headlights, waiting for the hammer to fall.

But when she spoke, I found that Ma still sounded surprisingly cheery. 'Why don't you have a nice bath?' she said. 'Your dinner's in the oven. There's some of that chilli chicken you like, and some home-made lemon pie.' No mention of the mud on the stairs, or even the fact that I was half an hour late.

Sometimes that's the worst part. I can live with her when she's evil. It's when she's *normal* that it hurts, because that's when the guilt comes creeping

418

back, bringing the headache, the sickness. It's when she's normal that I can feel the bulbs of arthritis in her hands and the way her back aches when she stands up, and that's when I remember what it was like in the old days, before my brother was born, in the days when I was her *blueeyeedboy*—

'I'm not really hungry right now, Ma.'

I expected her to react to that. But this time Ma just smiled and said: 'All right, B.B., you get some rest,' and went back into the kitchen. I was surprised (and oddly disturbed) to be let off the hook so easily; but still, it's good to be back in my room, with a glass of wine and a sandwich, and an ice-pack on my injured hand.

The first thing I did was log on. *Badguysrock* was deserted, although my inbox was filled with messages, mostly from Clair and Chryssie. Nothing from *Albertine*. Oh, well. Perhaps she is feeling shaken. It isn't easy to face the fact that you're capable of murder. But she was always so keen to believe in absolutes. In actual fact the line between good and evil is so blurred as to be almost indistinguishable; and it's only long after you've crossed it that you become aware that it even existed at all.

Albertine, oh *Albertine*. I feel very close to you today. Through the throbbing of my wrist, I can feel the beat of your heart. I wish you all the best, you know. I hope you find what you're looking for. And when it's over, I hope you can find a little place in your heart for me, for *blueeyedboy*, who understands far more than you imagine—

419

Not a word from *blueeyedboy*. Not that I expected one—not so soon, anyway. I'm guessing he'll lie low for a while, like an animal driven to earth. I'm guessing three days before he comes out. The first, to check out the area. The second, to establish a plan of action. The third, to finally make his move. Which is why I made *my* move today—emptying my bank account, setting my things in order, packing away my belongings in preparation for the inevitable.

Don't think this is going to be easy for me. These things are never straightforward. Even less so for him, of course; but his methods are chosen to fool his uniquely cross-wired brain into thinking his actions are not his fault, while the victim walks straight into the trap carefully laid out for them.

What will it be, I wonder? Having now made my intentions so clear, I cannot expect him to make an exception in my case. He'll try to kill me. He has no choice. And his feelings for me—such as they are—are founded on guilt and nostalgia. I've always known what I was to him. A shade; a ghost; a reflection. A substitute for Emily. I knew that, and I didn't care; that was how much he meant to me.

But people are lines of dominoes: one falls, then all the others follow. Emily and Catherine; Daddy, Dr Peacock and me. Nigel and Bren and Benjamin. Where it begins is seldom clear; we own only part of our personal story.

It doesn't seem fair, does it? We all imagine our lives as a story in which we ourselves take centre stage. But what about the extras? What about the substitutes? For every leading role there exist a multitude of expendables, hanging around in the background, never in the spotlight, never speaking a line of dialogue, sometimes not even making the final edit, ending their lives as a single frame on the cutting-room floor. Who cares when an extra bites the dust? Who owns the story of *their* life?

For me it begins at St Oswald's. I can't have been more than seven years old, but I do remember what happened in remarkably vivid detail. Every year my mother and I would go to the Christmas concert in the chapel at St Oswald's at the end of the long winter term. I liked the music, the carols, the hymns, and the organ like a hydra with its shining tongues of brass. She liked the solemnity of the Masters in their black gowns, and the sweetness of the choristers with their angel smocks and candles.

I saw things with such clarity then. The memory loss came afterwards. One moment I was in sunlight; the next in chequered shadows, with only a few flecks of brilliance left to prove that the memories had ever been there. But that day, everything was clear. I remember all of it.

It begins with a little girl crying in the row just in front of me. That was Emily White, of course. Two

421

years younger than I was, and already stealing the limelight. Dr Peacock was there, as well—a large, kind-looking, bearded man with an affable voice like a French horn, whilst elsewhere—another small drama played out, unseen by the major protagonists.

It wasn't much of a drama. Just a blue-eyed boy in the choir pitching forward on to his face. But there was a minor commotion; the music wavered, but did not stop, and a woman—the boy's mother, I assumed—rushed forward into the stalls, her high shoes skidding on the polished floor, her face a lipstick blur of dismay.

My own mother looked disapproving. *She* wouldn't have rushed forward. She would never have made such a fuss—especially not here, in chapel, with everyone so ready to judge and to spread those hateful rumours.

'Gloria Winter. I should have known—'

It was a name I'd heard before. She'd told me the boy had caused trouble at school. In fact, the whole family was bad news: godless, wicked and profane.

Irredeemable, she'd said. It was the word Mother reserved for the worst kind of sinners: rapists, blasphemers, matricides.

Gloria was holding her son. He had cut his head on the side of the pew. Blood—a surprising amount of it—spattered his chorister's surplice. Behind her, two boys, one in black, one in brown, stood by like extras in a game. The black one looked sullen; even bored. The one in brown—a clumsy-looking boy with long, lank hair over his eyes and an oversized sweatshirt that emphasized, rather than hid, his gut—looked distressed, almost dazed.

He put a shaking hand to his head. I wondered if he'd fallen, too.

'What do you think you're playing at? Can't you see I need help?' Gloria Winter's voice was sharp. 'B.B., get a towel, or something. Nigel, call an ambulance.'

Nigel, at sixteen; an innocent. I wish I could say I remembered him. But frankly, I never noticed him; my attention was all on Bren. Perhaps because of the look in his eyes: that trapped and helpless expression. Perhaps because I sensed, even then, a kind of bond between us. First impressions matter so much; they shape us for what comes later.

He raised his hand to his head again. I saw his expression, a rictus of pain as if he'd been hit by something falling from the sky, and then he stumbled against the step and fell to his knees almost at my feet.

My mother had already moved to help, guiding Gloria through the crowd.

I looked down at the boy in brown. 'Are you all right?'

He stared at me in open surprise. To tell the truth, I'd surprised myself. He was so much older than I. I rarely spoke to strangers. But there was something about him that moved me, somehow: an almost childlike quality.

'Are you all right?' I repeated.

He had no time to answer me. Gloria turned impatiently, one arm still supporting Benjamin. It struck me then how tiny she was: wasp-waisted in her pencil skirt, stiletto heels barely grazing the floor. My mother disliked stiletto heels—which she called *slutilloes*—and which, she claimed, were responsible for a variety of conditions ranging from chronic back pain to hammer toes and arthritis. But Gloria moved like a dancer, and her voice was as sharp as those six-inch heels as she snapped at her ungainly son:

'Brendan, get over here right now, or, God help me, I'll wring your fucking *neck*—'

I saw my own mother flinch at that. The F-word was strictly outlawed in our house. And coming from the boy's mother, too—I couldn't help but feel sympathy. He scrambled clumsily to his feet, his face now flushing a dull red. And I could see how troubled he was, how scared and self-conscious and filled with hate.

He wishes she were dead, I thought, with sudden, luminous certainty.

It was a dangerous, powerful thought. It lit up my mind like a beacon. That this boy should wish his mother dead was almost beyond imagining. Surely this was a mortal sin. It meant that he would burn in hell; that he was damned for eternity. And yet, I was drawn to him somehow. He looked so lost and unhappy. Maybe I could save him, I thought. Maybe he was redeemable . . .

You are viewing the webjournal of **Albertine**.
Posted at: *02.04 on Thursday, February 21*
Status: *restricted*
Mood: *anxious*

Let me explain. It's not easy. As a child I was very shy. I was bullied at school. I had no friends. My mother was religious, and her disapproval weighed upon every aspect of my life. She showed me little affection, making it clear to me from the start that only Jesus deserved her love. I was my mother's gift to Him; a soul for His collection, and though I was far from perfect, she said, with His grace and my efforts I might one day be good enough to meet the Saviour's exacting standards.

I don't remember my father at all. Mother never spoke of him, though she wore a wedding ring, and I was left with the vague impression that he had disappointed her, and that she had sent him away, as I too would be sent away if I failed to be good enough.

Well, I tried. I said my prayers. I did my chores. I went to Confession. I never spoke to strangers, or raised my voice, or read comic-books, or took a second slice of cake if Mother invited a friend to tea. But even so, it was never enough. I always fell short of perfection, somehow. There was always a fault in my stubborn clay. Sometimes it was my carelessness; a tear in the hem of my school skirt; a smear of mud on my white socks. Sometimes it was bad thoughts. Sometimes, a song on the radio— Mother detested rock music and called it *Satan's flatulence*—or a passage from a book I'd read. There were so many dangers, Mother said; so many pits on the road to hell. But she tried, in her fashion; she always tried. It wasn't her fault I turned out this way.

There were no toys or dolls in my room, just a blue-eyed Jesus on the cross and a plaster angel (slightly cracked) that was meant to drive away bad thoughts and make me feel safe at night.

In fact, it made me nervous. Its face, neither male nor female, looked like a dead child's. And as for the blue-eyed Jesus, with his head thrown back and his bleeding ribs, he looked neither kind nor compassionate, but angry, tortured and frightening—and why not, I asked myself? If Jesus died to save us all, why wouldn't He be angry? Wouldn't He be furious at what He'd had to endure for our sakes? Wouldn't He want vengeance somehow—for the nails, and the spear, and the crown of thorns?

If I die before I wake, I pray, dear Lord, my soul to take—

And so at night I would lie sleepless for hours, terrified to close my eyes in case the angels took my soul, or, worse still, that Jesus Himself would rise from the dead and come for me, ice-cold and smelling of the grave, and hiss in my ear:

It should have been you.

Bren was dismissive of my fears, and indignant that Mother encouraged them.

'I thought my Ma was bad enough. But yours is a fucking fruitcake.'

426

I sniggered at that. The F-word again. I'd never dared to use it. But Bren was so much older than I; so very much more daring. Those stories he told me about himself—stories of cunning and secret revenge—far from being horrified, I felt a sneaking admiration. My mother believed in humility, Bren in getting even. This was an entirely new concept to me—accustomed as I was to one kind of creed, I was secretly both thrilled and appalled to hear the Gospel of Brendan.

The Gospel of Brendan was simple. Hit back as hard and as low as you can. Forget about turning the other cheek; just get the first punch in and run away. If in doubt, blame someone else. And never confess to *anything*.

Of course I admired him. How could I not? His words made a great deal of sense to me. I was slightly anxious for his soul, but secretly it seemed to me that if Our Saviour had adopted some of Brendan's attitude instead of being *quite* so meek, it might have been better for everyone. Brendan Winter kicked ass. Bren would never let himself be bullied or intimidated. Bren never lay awake in bed, paralysed by fear. Bren hit back at his enemies with the force of angels.

Well, none of that was strictly true. I realized *that* soon enough. Bren told me things as they *ought* to have been, and not precisely as they *were*. Still, I liked him better that way. It made him—if not quite innocent, then at least redeemable. And that's what I wanted—or thought I did. To save him. To fix what was broken inside. To shape him like a piece of clay into the face of innocence.

And I liked to listen. I liked his voice. When he was reading his stories to me, he never used to stutter. Even his tone was different—quiet and cynically humorous, like a woody cor anglais. The violence never troubled me; besides, it was fiction. What harm could it do? The Brothers Grimm had written far worse: babies devoured by ogres, by wolves; mothers deserting their children; sons sent into exile or killed, or cursed by wicked witches.

The moment I first saw him I knew that Bren had a problem with his mother. I'd seen Gloria in the Village, though we didn't have much to do with her. But I knew her through Bren, and hated her—not for my own sake, but for his.

Slowly, I came to know her more: the vitamin drink, and the china dogs, and the piece of electrical cord. Sometimes Bren showed me the marks she had left: the scratches, welts and bruises. He was so much older than I was, and yet on these occasions I felt as if *I* were the grown-up. I comforted him. I listened to him. I gave him unconditional love, sympathy and admiration. And it never once occurred to me that while I thought I was shaping *him*, he was really shaping *me* . . .

You are viewing the webjournal of **Albertine**.
Posted at: *13.57 on Thursday, February 21*
Status: *restricted*
Mood: *melancholy*

Brendan Winter and I became friends five months after the concert. I was going through a difficult time; Mother was always busy at work, and at school I was bullied more than ever. I didn't really understand why. There were other fatherless children in Malbry. Why was I so different? Perhaps it was my fault, I thought, that my Dad had gone away. Perhaps he'd never wanted me in the first place. Maybe neither of my parents had.

That was when Brendan turned up again. I recognized him immediately. Mother was busy, as always. I was alone in the garden. And Emily was in her house, playing the piano—something by Rachmaninov, something sweet and melancholy. I could hear her through the window, which was open, and around which a tangle of roses were in bloom. It looked like a fairy-tale window to me, in which a princess ought to appear: Sleeping Beauty, or Snow White, or maybe the Lady of Shalott.

Brendan was no Lancelot. He was wearing brown cords, and a beige canvas jacket that made him look like a padded envelope. He was carrying a satchel. His hair was longer than before, almost covering his face. He passed by the house, heard the music and stopped, not ten feet away from the garden gate. He hadn't seen me; I was on my swing under the weeping willow tree. But I saw his face as he heard her play, the little smile that touched his mouth. He took out a camera from his satchel, a camera with a long lens; and with a deftness that looked out of place, he clicked off a dozen shots of the house—*clickclickclick*, like dominoes falling—before slipping the camera back into his satchel almost without breaking step.

I left my place on the swing. 'Hey.'

He turned, looking hunted; then seemed to relax when he saw who I was.

'Hey, I'm Bethan,' I said.

'B-Brendan.'

I leaned my elbows on the gate. 'Brendan, why were you taking pictures of the Whites' house?'

He looked alarmed at that. 'Please. If you t-tell anyone, I'll get into trouble. I—just like taking pictures, that's all.'

'Take a picture of me,' I said, showing my teeth like the Cheshire Cat.

Bren looked round, then grinned. 'OK. Just as long as you promise, B-Bethan. Not a word to anyone.'

'Not even Mother?'

'*Especially* not Mother.'

'All right, I promise,' I told him. 'But why do you like taking pictures so much?'

He looked at me and smiled. Behind that graceless curtain of hair his eyes were really quite beautiful, with lashes as long and thick as a girl's. 'This isn't an ordinary camera,' he said, this time, I noticed, without stuttering. 'Through this, I can see right into your heart. I can see what you're

430

hiding from me. I can tell if you're good or bad, if you've said your prayers, if you love your mother—'

My own eyes opened wide at this.

'You can see all that?'

'Of course I can.'

And at that he gave an enormous grin.

And that's how I was collected.

*   *   *

Of course, I didn't see it that way. Not until much later. But that was when I decided that Brendan Winter would be my friend: Bren, whom nobody wanted; Bren, who had asked me to lie for him to keep him out of trouble.

It began like that; with a little white lie. Then, with my curiosity about someone so unlike myself. Then came the wary affection that a child may feel for a dangerous dog. Then, a sense of affinity, in spite of our many differences; and lastly a feeling that blossomed at length into something like infatuation.

I never believed he cared much for me. I knew from the start where his interest lay. But Mrs White was protective. Emily was never alone, never allowed to talk to strangers. A glimpse over the garden wall; a photograph; a vicarious touch was all that Bren could hope for. As far as he was concerned, Emily might as well have been on Mars.

The rest of the time, Brendan was mine; and that was quite enough for me. He didn't even *like* her, I thought. In fact, I believed he hated her. I was naïve. I was very young. And I believed in him—in his *gift*. I'd failed to meet my mother's

431

standards; but maybe, with Bren, I could succeed. I was his guardian angel, he said. Watching him. Protecting him. And so, stepping through the looking glass, I entered the world of *blueeyedboy*, where everything exists in reverse and every sense is twisted and turned, and nothing ever really begins, and nothing ever comes to an end . . .

*   *   *

I was three months shy of twelve years old the summer Brendan's brother died. No one told me what happened, although rumours of varying wildness had been circulating around Malbry for weeks. But the Village has always considered itself above events in White City. Brendan was ill, and at first I assumed that Ben had died of the same sickness. After that, the Emily affair swallowed up most of the details. The scandal, the public breakdown—all of that kept the Press in business for more than long enough to eclipse one dirty little domestic.

Meanwhile, the Fireplace House had become the focus of everything. Emily White's brief moment of fame would have fizzled out long ago, but for the blast of oxygen delivered to it that autumn by Brendan Winter. Those allegations of fraud and abuse did more to raise Emily's profile than Catherine White ever did. Not that Catherine cared by then—her family was breaking apart. She hadn't seen her daughter for weeks, not since the Social Services had decided that the child was at risk. Instead, Emily had been sent to live with Mr White, at a B & B in the Village, with twice-weekly visits from a counsellor, until such time as the business could be properly concluded. Left at home, Catherine was self-medicating with a mixture of alcohol and anti-depressants, which Feather—never a stabilizing influence—supplemented with a variety of herbal remedies, both legal and illegal.

Someone should have noticed the signs. Amazingly, nobody did. And when the thing exploded at last, we were all of us caught by the shrapnel.

Although we were next-door neighbours, I didn't know much about Mr White. I knew he was a quiet man who only played music when Mrs White wasn't around; who sometimes smoked a pipe (again, when his wife wasn't there to nag him); who wore little steel-rimmed glasses and a coat that made him look like a spy. I'd heard him play the organ in church and conduct the choir at St Oswald's. I'd often watched him from over the wall, as he sat in the garden with Emily. She liked him to read aloud to her, and, knowing I liked to listen, Mr White would project his voice so that I could hear the story as well—but for some reason Mrs White disapproved, and always used to call them indoors if ever she noticed me listening, so I never really got the chance to get to know either of them.

After he'd moved, I'd seen him once, in the autumn that followed Benjamin's death. A season, not of mists, but of winds, that stripped the trees of their leaves and made gritty work of the pavements. I was walking home from school through the park that separates Malbry from the Village; the weather was half a degree away from snow, and even in my warmest coat I was already shivering.

I'd heard he'd given up his job to care full-time for Emily. This decision had met with a mixed response: some praised his devotion; others (for instance, Eleanor Vine) felt it wasn't appropriate for a man to be left alone with a girl of Emily's age.

'He'll be having to bathe her, and everything,' she said, with clear disapproval. 'The thought of it! No wonder there's talk.'

Well, if there was, you can bet that Mrs Vine was behind it somehow. Even then, she was poisonous: spreading slime wherever she went. My mother had always blamed her for spreading rumours about my dad; and when once or twice I played truant from school, it was Eleanor Vine who informed the school, rather than telling my mother.

Perhaps that was why I felt a link between myself and Mr White; and when I saw him in the park, Mr White in his Russian-spy coat pushing Emily on the swing, I stopped for a moment to watch them both, thinking how very happy they looked, as if there were no one else in the world.

That's what I remember most. Both of them looking so happy.

I stood on the path for a minute or so. Emily was wearing a red coat, with mittens and a knitted cap. Dead leaves crackled under her feet each time the swing reached its lowest arc. Mr White was laughing, his profile slightly averted so that I had time to look at him; to see him with his defences down.

I'd thought him quite an old man. Older by far than Catherine, with her long, loose hair and girlish ways. Now I saw that I'd been wrong. I'd

434

simply never heard him laugh. It was a young and summery sound, and Emily's voice against it was like a seagull crossing a cloudless sky. I realized that the scandal, far from driving them apart, had strengthened the bond between these two, all alone against the world and glad to be together.

*   *   *

It's snowing outside. Wild, yellow-grey flakes caught in the cone of the corner streetlight. Later, if it settles, then maybe there will be peace over Malbry; all sins past and present reprieved for the day beneath that merciful dusting of white.

It was snowing the night that Emily died. Perhaps if it *hadn't* been snowing then, Emily wouldn't have died at all. Who knows? Nothing ends. Everybody's story starts in the middle of someone else's tale, with messy skeins of narrative just waiting to be unravelled. And whose story is this anyway? Is it mine, or Emily's?

You are viewing the webjournal of **blueeyedboy**.
Posted at: *23.14 on Thursday, February 21*
Status: *restricted*
Mood: *wakeful*
Listening to: *Phil Collins*: 'In The Air Tonight'

They should have seen it coming, of course. Catherine White was unstable. Ready to lash out at the cause of her pain—rather like me, if you think about it. And when Patrick White brought Emily home after her performance—

Well, there was an argument.

I suppose they should have expected it. Tension had been building for months. Emotions ran high in the household. In her husband's absence, Mrs White had been joined by Feather, who, with her alternative therapies, her conspiracy theories, her walk-ins and ghosts and Tomorrow Children, had pushed Catherine White from her volatile state into a full-blown neurosis.

Not that I knew that then, of course. It was late September when Emily left home. Now it was mid-January, with the snowdrops just beginning to push their little green heads through the frozen ground. In all those months of observing the house, I'd barely seen Mrs White. Just once or twice, through the window—a window still hung with Christmas lights, although Twelfth Night was long gone, and the Christmas tree with the tinsel on it was turning brown on the back lawn—I'd seen her standing, looking out, a cigarette trembling at her lips, gazing at nothing but snow and a sky that hissed like white noise.

Feather, on the other hand, was always hanging around the place. I saw her almost every day: fetching the groceries; bringing the mail; dealing with the reporters that still turned up from time to time, hoping for an interview, a word, a picture of Emily—

In actual fact, Emily had barely been seen by anyone. Released by the Social Services when the Peacock case collapsed, she had since moved in with her father, who, every alternate weekend, took her to see her mother in the presence of a social worker, who made careful notes and wrote a report, the gist of which was always that Mrs White was, as yet, unfit to be left alone with Emily.

That night, however, was different. Mr White wasn't thinking clearly. It wasn't the first time that Catherine had threatened to kill herself, but it was her first realistic attempt; averted by Feather's intervention, and by the swift action of the paramedics who had hauled her out of the cooling bath and performed first aid on her slashed wrists.

It could have been worse, the doctor said. It takes a lot of aspirin to actually kill someone outright, and the cuts on her wrists, though fairly deep, had not touched the artery. But it *had* been a serious attempt, grave enough to cause concern— and by the next morning, which happened to be the day of Emily's final performance—the story had reached such giant proportions that it could no longer be contained.

How small are the building-blocks of our fate!

How intricate their workings! Remove just one component, and the whole machine ceases to function. If Catherine had not chosen that particular day to make her suicidal gesture—and who knows what sequence of events led to that final decision—bringing Bodies A, B and C into malign conjunction; if Emily's performance that day had not been quite so compelling; if Patrick White had been stronger, and had not given in to his daughter's pleas; if he hadn't defied the court ruling and taken Emily to see her without a social worker being present; if Mrs White had been in a brighter mood; if Feather had not left them alone; if I had worn a warmer coat; if Bethan had not come outside to look at the newly fallen snow—

If. If. If. A sweetly deceptive word, as light as a snowflake on the tongue. A word that seems too small to contain such a universe of regret. In French, *if* is the yew tree, symbol of mourning and the grave. If a yew tree falls in the woods—

I suppose Mr White meant well. He still loved Catherine, you see. He knew what she meant to Emily. And even though they were living apart, he'd always hoped to move back in, that Feather's influence would fade and that Emily, once the scandal had died, could go back to being a real child instead of a phenomenon.

I'd been watching the house since lunchtime from the coffee shop across the road. I caught it all on camera; the shop had closed at five o'clock, and I was hiding in the garden, where an overgrown clump of leylandii right up by the living-room window offered suitable cover. The trees had a sour and vegetable smell, and where the branches touched my skin they left red marks that itched like nettlerash. But I was nicely shielded from view—on one side by trees—whilst at the window the curtains were drawn, leaving just a tiny gap through which I was able to watch the scene.

That was how it happened. I swear. I never meant to hurt anyone. But standing outside, I heard it all: the recriminations; Mr White's attempt to calm Mrs White down; Feather's interjections; Mrs White's hysterical tears; Emily's hesitant protests. Or maybe I just *thought* I did—in retrospect, Mrs White's voice in my memory now sounds a lot like Ma's voice, and the other voices resonate like something heard from inside a fish tank; creating booming bubbles of sound that burst in nonsense syllables against the whitened glass.

Clickclick. That was the camera. A long lens resting on the sill; the fastest exposure the shot can take. Even so, the pictures, I knew, would be blurry, nebulous, unclear; the colours blooming around the scene like phosphorescence around a shoal of tropical fish.

Clickclick. 'I want her *back*! You can't keep her away—not *now*!'

That was Mrs White, pacing the room, cigarette in one hand, hair like a dirty flag down her back. The bandages on her cut wrists stood out a ghostly, unnatural white.

Clickclick. And the sound tastes like Christmas, with the sappy blue scent of the leylandii, and the numbing cold of the falling snow. *Snow Queen weather*, I thought to myself, and remembered Mrs Electric Blue and the cabbagey reek of the market that day, and the sound her heels had made on the path—*click-click-click*, like my mother's.

'Cathy, please,' said Mr White. 'I had to think of

439

Emily. None of this is good for her. Besides, you needed to rest, and—'

'Don't you fucking *dare* patronize me!' Her voice was rising steadily. 'I know what you're trying to do. You want to get some distance from me. You want to ride the scandal. And when you've pinned the blame on me, then you'll cash in, like all the rest—'

'No one's trying to blame you.' He tried to touch her; she flinched away. Underneath the window, I too flinched; and Emily, her hand at her mouth, stood helplessly to one side, flying her distress like a red flag that only I could see.

Clickclick. I felt the touch on my mouth. I could feel her fingers there. They felt like little butterflies. The intimacy of the gesture made me shiver with tenderness.

Emily. Em-il-y. The scent of roses everywhere. Flecks of light shone through the curtains and scattered the fallen snow with stars.

Em-il-y. *A million lei.*

Clickclick—and now I could almost feel my soul rising out of my body. A million tiny points of light, racing towards oblivion—

And now Feather was joining in, her strident voice drilling through the glass. Somehow, once more, it reminds me of Ma, and the scent that always accompanies her. Cigarette smoke and the lurking scent of L'Heure Bleue and the vitamin drink.

Clickclick, and Feather was in the can.

I imagined her trapped and drowning inside.

'No one asked you to come here,' she said. 'Don't you think you've done enough?'

For a moment I thought she was talking to me.

You little shit, I expected her to say. *Don't you know it's all your fault?* And maybe this time it is, I thought. Maybe this time she knows it, too.

'Don't you think you've humiliated Cathy enough, with your bastard living right next *door*?'

A pause, as cold as snow on snow.

'What?' said Mr White at last.

'That's *right*,' said Feather triumphantly. 'She knows—*we* know—everything. Did you think you could get away with it?'

'I didn't get away with it,' said Mr White to Catherine. 'I told you all about it. I told you straight away, a mistake I've been paying for these past twelve years—'

'You told me it was *over*!' she cried. 'You told me it was a woman at work, a supply teacher who *moved away*—'

For a moment he looked at her, and I was struck by his air of calm. 'Yes, that was a lie,' he said. 'But all the rest of it was true.'

I took a step back. My heart gave a lurch. My breath bloomed huge and monstrous. I knew that I shouldn't be there, that by now Ma would be wondering where I was. But the scene was too much for Yours Truly. *Your bastard.* What a fool I'd been.

'How many *other* people knew?' That was Mrs White again. 'How many people were laughing at me, while that Irish bitch and her fucking *brat*—'

Once more I approached the glass, feeling Emily's hand on my cheek. It was cold, but I could feel her heart beating like a landed fish.

Mum, please. Daddy, please—

No one but I could hear her. No one but I could know how she felt. I stretched out my hand like a starfish, pressing the fingers against the glass.

'Who told you, Cathy?' said Mr White.

Catherine blew smoke into the air. 'You really want to know, Pat?' Her hands were fluttering like birds. 'You want to know who gave you away?'

Behind the window, I shook my head. I already knew who had told her. I knew why I'd seen Mr White giving money to Ma that day; I understood his pity when I'd asked him if he were my father—

'You hypocrite,' she hissed at him. 'Pretending you cared about Emily. You never really wanted her. You never really understood how *special*, how *gifted* Emily was—'

'Oh yes, I did,' said Mr White. His voice was as calm as ever. 'But because of what happened twelve years ago, I've allowed you far too much control. You've made our daughter into a freak. Well, after today's performance, I'm going to stop all that once and for all. No more interviews. No more TV. It's time she had a normal life, and time you learnt to face the facts. She's just a little blind girl who wants to please her mother—'

'She isn't normal,' said Mrs White, her voice beginning to tremble. 'She's *special*! She's *gifted*! I know she is! I'd rather see her dead than be just another handicapped child—'

And at that, the subject under discussion stood up and began to scream: a desperate, penetrating cry that sharpened into a bright point of sound, a laser that sliced through reality with a taste like copper and rotting fruit—

I dropped the camera.

Mиииииии-иииииии-иииииииит!

For a moment, she and I are one. Twins, two hearts that beat as one; a single oscillation. For a

442

moment I know her perfectly; just as Emily knows me. And then, as suddenly, silence. The volume falls. I'm suddenly aware of the vicious cold; I've been standing here for an hour or more. My feet are numb; my hands are sore. Tears are running down my face, but I can barely feel them.

I'm having trouble breathing. I try to move, but it's too late. My body has turned to concrete. The illness I suffered after Ben's death has left me wasted and vulnerable. I have lost too much weight over too short a time; my body's resources are used up.

A wave of terror engulfs me. *I could die here*, I tell myself. *No one knows where I am.* I try to call out, but no sound escapes; my mouth is starchy with fear. I can hardly breathe; my vision is blurred—

Should have listened to Ma, Bren. Ma always knows when you're up to no good. Ma knows you deserve to die—

Please, Ma, I whisper through lips that are papery with cold.

Snow had fallen, snow on snow
Snow on snow—

Silence has enveloped me. Snow deadens everything: sound; light; sensation—

All right, then let me die, I think. *Let me die right here, by her door. At least I'd be free then. Free of her—*

The thought is weirdly exhilarating. To be free of Ma—of everything—seems like the culmination of every desire. Forget Hawaii; all I need is a moment longer in the snow. Just a moment, and

443

then, sleep. Sleep, without hope, without memory—

And then from behind me comes a voice.

'Brendan?'

I open my eyes and turn my head. And it's little Bethan Brannigan, in her red coat and her bobble hat, looking at me from over the wall like something out of a fairy tale. Little Bethan, otherwise known as *Patrick's brat from next door*, and whose parentage—kept secret for years—Ma must have threatened to reveal—

She scrambles over the garden wall. She says: 'Bren, you look *awful.*'

The snow has stolen my voice. Once more I try to move, but my feet are frozen to the ground.

'Wait here. You'll be all right.' Bethan, even at twelve years old, knows how to cope in a crisis. I hear her run to the front door. She rings the bell. Someone comes out. Snow falls from the burdened porch with a dull *ch-thump* on to the step.

Mr White's voice cuts through the night. 'What's happened, Bethan? Is something wrong?'

Bethan's voice: 'It's my friend. He needs help.'

Mrs White, shrill with hysteria: 'Patrick! Don't you *dare* let her in!'

'Cathy. Someone's in trouble—'

'I'm warning you, Patrick!'

'Cathy, please—'

And now, at last, my legs give way. I fall on to my hands and knees. I lift my head and see Emily, at an angle by the door. Syrupy light spills languidly on to the unblemished snow. She is wearing a blue dress, sky-blue, Virgin-blue, and at that moment I love her so much that I would be happy to die in her place—

444

'Emily,' I manage to say.

And then the world shrinks to a speck; the cold rushes in to engulf me, footsteps come running towards me and—

Nothing.

Nothing at all.

14

You are viewing the webjournal of **Albertine**.
Posted at: *00.23 on Friday, February 22*
Status: *restricted*
Mood: *drained*

The Press has a poor vocabulary. It works according to certain rules. A house fire is always described as a *blaze*; a blonde is always *bubbly*. Murders are always *brutal*, as if to distinguish from the more compassionate kind. And the death of a child (better still, a *tot*) is invariably a *tragedy*.

In this case it was almost true: a mother's love tested beyond endurance; friends who failed to notice the signs; a husband too willing to rally round; a freak combination of circumstances.

They blamed the media, of course, as they would for the death of Diana. The ultimate tabloid accolade of being known by one's first name alone is reserved for Jesus, royalty, rock stars, supermodels and little girls who have been kidnapped or killed. Headlines love those dismembered names—those Hayleys and Maddies and Jessicas—implying some kind of shared intimacy, inviting the nation's collective grief. Wreaths and angels and teddy bears; flowers piled knee-high on the street. Emily's legend was reinstated, of course, in the wake of that terrible tragedy.

Tragedy? Well, maybe it was. She had so much
446

to live for. Her talent. Her beauty. Her money. Her fame. So many legends had already grown about her little person. Afterwards, those legends grew into something almost approaching a cult. And the surge of grief that surrounded her death was like a group ululation that mourned and repeated: *Why Emily? Why not some other little girl?*

Well, I, for one, never mourned for her. As *blueeyedboy* might say, shit happens. And she was nothing special, you know; nothing out of the ordinary. He told me himself that she was a fake— a rumour that was buried with her under that white headstone—but death made her untouchable, just one step removed from the holy choir. No one doubts an angel. Emily's status was assured.

Everyone knows the official tale. It needed little embellishment. After her TV performance that night, Emily went home with her father. A quarrel—the cause of which remains unknown— flared up between the estranged couple. Then came one of those incidents that no one could have predicted. A young man—a boy, a neighbour of theirs—collapsed outside the Whites' house. It had been a cold night; snow lay thickly on the ground. The boy—who might have died, they said, if his young friend hadn't asked them for help—was suffering from exposure. Patrick White took both children inside and made them cups of hot tea, and while Feather tried to determine why they'd been there in the garden at all, Catherine White was left alone—for the first time in months—with Emily.

At this point, the time-scale becomes unclear. The sequence of events that night may never be fully understood. Feather Dunne always claimed that she last saw Emily at six o'clock, though

447

forensic evidence suggests that the child was still alive up to an hour later. And Brendan Winter, who saw it all, claims not to remember anything—

In any case, the facts are these. At six or maybe six thirty, while the others were dealing with Brendan, Catherine White ran a bath, in which she drowned nine-year-old Emily before getting in herself and taking a bottle of sleeping pills. And when Patrick went to look for them later, he found them curled up together in the bath, stellated with fragments of glitterbomb—

Oh yes. I was there. I'd refused to leave Brendan alone. And when they discovered Emily, we were peering around the bathroom door; invisible as only children can be in such traumatic circumstances . . .

It took me some time to understand. First, that Emily was dead; next, that her death was no accident. My memory of things exists in a series of images bound together by hindsight; a scent of strawberry bubble bath; glimpses of naked flesh seen through a bathroom mirror; Feather's useless peacock screams and Patrick repeating, *Breathe, baby, breathe!*

And Brendan, watching silently, his eyes reflecting everything . . .

In the bathroom, Patrick White was trying to revive his daughter. *Breathe, dammit, baby, breathe!*—accenting each word with a hard push aimed at the dead girl's heart, as if, by the force of his own desire, he might somehow restart the mechanism. The pushes, increasingly desperate, degenerated into a series of blows as Patrick White lost control and began to flail at the dead girl, thumping her like a pillow.

448

Brendan pressed his hands to his chest.

'Breathe, baby. Breathe!'

Brendan began to gasp for air.

'Patrick!' said Feather. 'Stop it. She's gone.'

'No! I can do it! Emily! *Breathe!*'

Brendan leaned against the door. His face was pale and shiny with sweat; his breathing, rapid and shallow. I knew all about his condition, of course—the mirror-response that made him flinch at the sight of a graze on my knee, and which had caused him such distress the time his brother collapsed in St Oswald's Chapel—but I'd never seen him like this before. It was like a kind of voodoo, I thought; as if, even though she was already dead, Emily was killing him—

Now I knew what I had to do. It was like in the fairy story, I thought, where the boy gets the ice mirror in his eye and can only see everything twisted and warped. *The Snow Queen*, that was the story's name. And the little girl had to save him . . .

I took a step in front of him, blocking his view of Emily. Now it was I who was in his eyes, mirrored there in winter-blue. I could see myself: my little red coat; my bobbed hair, so like Emily's.

'Bren, it wasn't your fault,' I said.

He flung out a hand to ward me off. He looked very near to passing out.

'Brendan, look at me,' I said.

He closed his eyes.

'I said *look* at me!' I grabbed him by the shoulders and held on to him as hard as I could. I could hear him struggling to breathe—

'Please! Just look at me, and *breathe*!'

For a moment I thought I'd lost him. His eyelids fluttered; his legs gave way, and we fell together against the door. And then he opened his eyes again, and Emily was gone from them. Instead there was only my face, reflected in miniature in his eyes. My face, and his eyes. The abyss of his eyes.

I held him at arms' length and *breathed*, just breathed, steadily in and out, and gradually his breathing slowed and shifted gently to match my own, and the colour began to return to his face, and tears spilled from my eyes—and his—and I thought once again of the story where the girl's tears melt the fragment of mirror and free the boy from the Snow Queen's curse—I felt a surge of fierce joy.

I'd saved Brendan. I'd saved his life.

I was there now, in his eyes.

For a moment, I saw myself there, like a mote inside a teardrop. And then he pushed me away and said:

'Emily's dead. It should have been you.'

> *You are viewing the webjournal of* **Albertine**.
> **Posted at**: *00.40 on Friday, February 22*
> **Status**: *restricted*
> **Mood**: *intense*

I really don't remember much about the rest of that evening. I remember running outside in the snow; falling to my knees by the path; seeing the snow angel that Brendan had left by the front door. I ran to my room; lay down on my bed under the blue-eyed Jesus. I don't know how long I stayed there. I was dead; a thing with no voice. My mind kept going back to the fact that Bren had chosen *her*, not *me*; that in spite of everything I'd done, Emily had beaten me.

And then I heard the music . . .

Perhaps that's why I avoid it now. Music brings too many memories. Some mine, some hers, some belonging to both of us. Maybe it was the music that brought me back to life that day. The first movement of the *Symphonie fantastique*, played so loudly from inside the car—a dark-blue four-door Toyota sedan parked in the drive of the White house—that the windows trembled and bulged with the sound, like a heart that was close to breaking.

By then, the ambulance had gone. Feather must have gone with it. Mother was working late that night—something to do with the church, I think.

Bren was nowhere to be seen, and the lights were out in Emily's house. But then came this gust of music, like a black wind set to blow open all the padlocked doors in the world, and I stood up, put on my coat and went outside to the parked car. The engine was running, I noticed, and a rubber pipe fixed on to the exhaust led into the driver's side window, and there was Emily's father, sitting quietly in the driver's seat; not crying, not ranting, just sitting there, listening to music and watching the night.

Through the car window, he looked like a ghost. So did I, against the glass; my pale face reflecting his. All around him, the music swelled. I remember that especially; the Berlioz that haunts me still, and the snow that covered everything.

And I realized that he, too, blamed himself; he thought that if things had been different, then maybe he could have saved Emily. If he hadn't let me in; if he'd left Brendan outside in the snow; if someone else could have taken her place.

Emily's dead. It should have been you.

And now I thought I understood. I saw how I could save us both. Perhaps I could make this *my* story, I thought, instead of it being Emily's. The story of a girl who died, and somehow made it back from the dead. I had no thought of revenge—not then. I didn't want to take her life. All I wanted was to start again, to turn on to a clean page and never think of that girl any more, the girl who had seen and heard too much.

Patrick White was looking at me. He had taken off his glasses, and without them, I thought he looked lost and confused. His eyes without the lenses were a bright—and oddly familiar—blue.

Yesterday he had been someone's daddy— someone who read stories, played games, gave kisses at bedtime, someone who was needed and loved—and who was he now? No one; nothing. A reject, an extra—just like me. Left on the pile while the story goes on somewhere else, without us.

I opened the passenger door on his side. The air was warm inside the car. It smelt of roads and motorways. The hose, attached to the car exhaust, fell out as I released the door.

The music stopped. The engine went off. Patrick was still looking at me. He seemed unable to speak, but his eyes told me all I needed to know.

I closed the door.

I said: 'Daddy, let's go.'

We drove away in silence.

16

No, it wasn't exactly my finest hour. Don't think I'm proud of what I said. But, in my own defence, let me say that I'd suffered a great deal already that day, and that suffering gets passed around in ever-increasing circles, like the ripples from a flung stone as it strikes the water's surface—

It should have been you. Yes, that's what I said. I even meant it at the time. I mean, who would have missed Bethan Brannigan? Who was she in the scheme of things? Emily White was unique; a gift; Bethan was nothing; nobody. Which is why, when Bethan disappeared, she was caught in the headlines, pipped at the *Post*, eclipsed in the mourning for Emily.

Front-page headlines: *EMILY DROWNED! MYSTERY DEATH OF CHILD PRODIGY.*

In the wake of such momentous news, everything else takes second place. *LOCAL GIRL DISAPPEARS* barely makes it to page six. Even Bethan's mother waited until morning before reporting her daughter's absence to the police—

I have very little memory of what happened after that. I made it home; that much I know. Ma noticed I was feverish. She put me to bed, where I was to stay. Headaches, stomach cramps, fever. The police came round eventually, but in the circumstances I was unable to tell them much. As for Mr White, it took them forty-eight hours to realize that he, too, had vanished—

By then, of course, the fugitives were long gone. The trail was cold. And why, they thought, would Patrick White have kidnapped a child he hardly knew? Feather revealed a motive, confirmed by Mrs Brannigan. The news that Bethan was Patrick's child delivered a much-needed blast of oxygen to the story—and once again, the hunt was on for the missing girl and her father.

Patrick's car was found by the road fifty miles north of Hull. Brown hairs taken from the back seat confirmed that Bethan had been in the car, although of course there was no way of knowing how long ago that had been. Meanwhile, bank receipts showed Patrick White emptying his savings account. Then, after three cash withdrawals of ten thousand pounds each, the credit trail stopped abruptly. Patrick was running on cash now. Cash is nicely untraceable. Sightings of a man and a girl were reported to the police from Bath. Two weeks and a city-wide search later, these reports were dismissed as a hoax. More sightings, this time in London, were also judged unreliable. An appeal from Mrs Brannigan met with a similar lack of result.

Nearly three months later, with no solid evidence to the contrary, folk were beginning to wonder whether Patrick, unhinged by the tragedy, hadn't staged a murder-suicide of his own. Ponds were dredged; cliffs investigated. In the Press,

Bethan acquired the first-name status that often precedes a grisly discovery. Candles were lit in Malbry church, *To Angel Beth God Loves You*, et al. Mrs Brannigan led a series of prayer campaigns. Maureen Pike held a jumble sale. Still the Almighty stayed silent. Now they kept the story alive merely on speculation; the life-support of the world's Press, a machine that can be kept running indefinitely (as in the case of Diana—twelve years gone, and still in the headlines) or switched off at the public's whim.

In Bethan's case, the decline was fast. A cut rose swiftly loses its scent. *BETH—STILL MISSING* wasn't a story. Months passed. Then a year. A candlelit vigil in Malbry church marked the anniversary. Mrs Brannigan was diagnosed with Hodgkin's lymphoma, as if her God hadn't tortured her enough. That made the papers for a while—*TRAGIC BETH'S MUM IN CANCER SHOCK*—but everyone knew the story was dead, covered in bedsores and waiting for someone brave enough to turn off the machine at last—

And then they found them. By accident; living in the back of beyond. A man had been rushed to hospital after suffering a sudden stroke. The man had refused to give his name, but the young girl accompanying him had identified him as Patrick White, and herself as his daughter, Emily.

A STROKE OF LUCK! blazoned the Press, never at a loss for a suitable cliché. But the story itself was less easy. Eighteen months had passed since Bethan Brannigan had disappeared. During most of that time she and Patrick had been living in a remote Scottish village, where Patrick had home-schooled the child, and where no one had even suspected that this bookish man and his little girl might be anything other than what they had appeared to be.

And this child—this shy and reticent fourteen-year-old who insisted her name was Emily—was so unlike Bethan Brannigan that even her mother—now bedridden, in the terminal stages of her disease—was hesitant to identify her.

Yes, there were similarities. The colouring was similar. But she played the piano beautifully, although she never had at home; referred to Patrick as *Daddy* and professed to remember nothing at all of the life she had led eighteen months ago—

The papers had a field day. Rumours of sexual abuse were the most common, of course, although there was no reason for any such assumption. Next came the conspiracy theories, digested versions of which were disseminated in all the best journals. After that, the deluge—dumbed-down diagnoses from possession to psychic transference; from schizophrenia to Stockholm syndrome.

Our tabloid culture favours simple solutions. Quick fics. Open-and-shut cases. This case was unsatisfactory; messy and unfathomable. Six weeks into the investigation, Bethan had still not opened up; Patrick White was in hospital, unable—or unwilling—to speak.

Meanwhile Mrs Brannigan—still known to the tabloids as *Bethan's Mum*—had sadly since given up the ghost, giving the papers one more excuse to misappropriate the word *tragedy*, which left poor Bethan alone in the world, except for the man she called *Daddy*—

It must have come as a shock to learn that

Patrick really was her father. Certainly, they mishandled it; and then Dr Peacock compounded the harm, changing his will in her favour, as if that could somehow erase the past and banish the ghost of Emily—

It can't have been easy for her, poor thing. It took years to recover even the semblance of normality. Taken into care at first, then into a foster home, she learnt to fake what she did not feel. Her foster parents, Jeff and Tracey Jones, lived on the White City estate. They'd always wanted a daughter. But Jeff's good humour turned sour when he'd had too many drinks, and Tracey, who'd dreamed of a little girl to dress up in her own image, saw nothing of herself in the silent, sullen teenager. All emotion suppressed and concealed, Bethan found her own ways of coping. You can still see the scars of those early years, their silvery traces down her arms, beneath the ink and filigree.

Talking to her, looking at her, there's always the sense that she's playing a part; that Bethan, just like *Albertine*, is only one of her avatars, a shield thrown up against a world in which nothing is ever certain.

She never told them anything. They assumed she had blocked the memory. I know better, of course; her recent posts confirm it. But her silence ensured Mr White's release; the charges against him were quietly dropped. And although the Malbry gossips never stopped believing the worst, father and daughter were finally left to get on with their lives as best they could.

It was years before I saw her again. By then, like myself, she was someone else. We met almost as strangers; made no reference to the past; talked every week at our creative-writing group; then she wheedled her way into my life until she found the right place to strike—

You thought *she* was in danger from *me*? Quite the opposite, I fear. I told you, I'm incapable of harming as much as a hair on her head. In fiction, I can do as I please; in real life, I'm condemned to grovel before those people I most hate and despise.

Not for very much longer, though. My death list gets shorter day by day. Tricia Goldblum; Eleanor Vine; Graham Peacock; Feather Dunne. Rivals, enemies, parasites—all struck down by the friendly hand of Fate. Well, Fate, or Destiny, or whatever you want to call it. The point is it's never my fault. All I do is write the words.

The moving finger writes, and, having writ—

But that's not strictly true, is it? To wish for the death of an enemy, however well-crafted the fantasy, is not the same as taking a life. Perhaps this is my *real* gift—not the synaesthesia that has caused me so much misery, but this—the power to unleash disaster on those who have offended me—

Have you guessed what I want of you yet, *Albertine*? It really is very simple, you know. As I said, you've done it before. The line between the word and the deed is all about execution.

Execute. Interesting word, with its spiky wintergreen syllables. But the *cute* makes it strangely appealing; sentence to be carried out, not by a man in a black hood, but by an army of puppies . . .

You mean you really haven't guessed what you're going to do for me? Oh, *Albertine*. Shall I tell you? After everything you've done so far, after all we've been through together—*Pick a card, any card*—

You're going to kill my mother.

PART SIX

green

You are viewing the webjournal of **blueeyedboy**
posting on:
badguysrock@webjournal.com
Posted at: *01.39 on Friday, February 22*
Status: *public*
Mood: *nasty*
Listening to: *Gloria Gaynor*: 'I Will Survive'

She has changed her name a number of times, but
folk still call her Gloria Green. Names are like tags
on a suitcase, she thinks, or maps to show people
where you've been, and where you think you're
going. She has never been anywhere. Just round
and round this neighbourhood, like a dog chasing
its tail, running blindly back to herself to start the
whole charade again.

But names are such portentous things. Words
have so much power. The way they roll like sweets
in the mouth; the hidden meanings inside each
one. She has always been good at crosswords, at
acronyms and wordplay. It's a talent she has passed
on to her sons, though only one of them knows it.
And she has an immense respect for books;
although she never reads fiction, preferring to
leave that kind of thing to her middle son, who,
despite his stammer, is brighter than she'll ever
be—too bright, perhaps, for his own good.

His own name, in Anglo-Saxon, means *The*
Flaming One—and though she is terribly proud of

him, she also knows he's dangerous. There's something inside him that doesn't respond; that refuses to see the world as it is. Mrs Brannigan, the schoolteacher at Abbey Road, says he will grow out of it, and tacitly implies that if Gloria attended church on Sundays, then maybe her son would be less troublesome. But as far as *blueeyedboy*'s Ma is concerned, Mrs Brannigan is full of shit. The last thing *blueeyedboy* needs, she thinks, is another helping of fantasy.

She suddenly wonders what things would have been like if Peter Winter hadn't died. Would it have made a difference for *blueeyedboy* and his brothers to have had some fatherly influence in their unruly lives? All those football matches they missed, the games of cricket in the park, the Airfix models, the toy trains, the fry-ups in the mornings?

But there's no use crying over spilt milk. Peter was a parasite, a fat and lazy freeloader good for nothing but spending Gloria's money. The best he could do was die on her, and even then, he'd needed some help. But no one walks out on Gloria Green; and surprisingly, the insurance paid up; and it turned out so easy, after all—just a pinch on a tube between finger and thumb as Peter lay in hospital—

She wonders now if that was a mistake. *Blueeyedboy* needed a father. Someone to sort him out. To teach him a sense of discipline. But Peter couldn't have coped with three boys, let alone such a gifted one. His successor, Mr Blue Eyes, was never even an option. And Patrick White—who, in all ways but one, would have made the perfect father—was, sadly, already spoken for; a gentle, artistic soul whose offence was a lapse of

464

judgement.

Guilt made Patrick vulnerable. Blackmail made him generous. Through a judicious combination of both, he proved a good source of income for years. He found Ma a job; he helped them out; and Gloria never blamed him when, in the end, he let her go. No, she blamed his wife for that, with her candles and her china dolls, and when at last she saw her chance to serve Mrs White a backhanded turn, she told her the secret she'd kept for so long; setting in motion a chain of events that resulted in murder and suicide.

But in spite of his parentage, *blueeyedboy* is different. Perhaps because he feels things more. Perhaps that's why he daydreams so much. God knows, she has tried to protect him. To convince the world he is too dull to hurt. But *blueeyedboy* seeks out suffering like a pig rooting for truffles, and it's all she can do to keep up with him, to correct his mistakes and clean up his mess.

She remembers a day at the seaside once, when all her boys were very young. Nigel is off somewhere on his own. Benjamin is four years old and *blueeyedboy* nearly seven. Both are eating ice cream, and *blueeyedboy* says that his doesn't taste right, as if just watching his brother eat is enough to diminish the flavour.

Blueeyedboy is sensitive. She knows this only too well by now. A slap on another boy's wrist makes him flinch; a crab in a bucket makes him cry. It's like some kind of voodoo; and it brings out at the same time both her cruel and her compassionate side. *How is he going to manage*, she thinks, *if he can't cope with reality?*

You have to remember it's only pretend, she snaps,

more harshly than she means to. He stares at her from round blue eyes as she holds his brother in her arms. At her feet the blue bucket is already beginning to stink.

'Don't play with that. It's nasty,' she says.

But *blueeyedboy* simply looks at her, wiping ice cream from his mouth. He knows dead things are nasty, but he still can't seem to look away. She feels a stab of annoyance. He collected the damn things. What does he want her to do with them now?

'You shouldn't have caught those animals if you didn't want them to die. Now you've upset your brother.'

In fact, little Ben is completely absorbed in finishing his ice cream, which makes her even more annoyed (although she knows it's irrational), because *he* should have been the susceptible one— after all, he is the youngest. *Blueeyedboy* ought to be looking out for *him* instead of making a fuss, she thinks.

But *blueeyedboy* is a special case, pathologically sensitive; and in spite of her efforts to toughen him up, to teach him to look after himself, it never seems to work, somehow, and she always ends up looking after him.

Maureen thinks he is playing games. *Typical middle child*, she says in her supercilious tone. *Jealous, sullen, attention-seeking*. Even Eleanor thinks so; though Catherine White believes there's more to him. Catherine likes to encourage him; which is why Gloria has stopped bringing *blueeyedboy* to work, substituting Benjamin, who plays so nicely with his toys and never seems to get in the way—

'It wasn't my fault,' *blueeyedboy* says. 'I didn't know they were going to die.'

'Everything dies,' Gloria snaps, and now his eyes are swollen with tears and he looks as if he is going to faint.

A part of her wants to comfort him, but knows that this is a dangerous indulgence. To give him attention at this stage is to encourage him in his weakness. Her sons all need to be strong, she thinks. How else will they take care of her?

'Now get rid of that mess,' she tells him, with a nod in the direction of the blue bucket. 'Go put it back in the sea, or something.'

He shakes his head. 'I d-don't want to. It smells.'

'You'd better. Or God help me, you'll pay.'

Blueeyedboy looks at the bucket. Five hours in the sun have brought about a rapid fermentation in the contents. The fishy, salt-water vegetable smell has turned to a suffocating reek. It makes him gag. He begins to whimper helplessly.

'Please, Ma—'

'Don't give me that!'

At last, now, his brother is crying. A high, fretful, icy wail. Gloria turns on her hapless son. '*Now* look what you've done,' she says. 'As if I didn't have enough to deal with already.'

She shoots out a hand to slap his face. She's wearing cork-soled sandals. As she snakes forward to hit him again, she kicks over the blue bucket, spilling the contents over her foot.

To Gloria, this is the final straw. She dumps Benjamin on to the ground and grabs hold of *blueeyedboy* with both hands, the better to take care of business. He tries to escape, but Ma is too strong; Ma is all wire and cables, and she digs her

467

fingers into his hair and forces him down inch by inch, pushing his face into the sand and into that terrible, yeasty mess of dead fish and fake coconut, and there's ice cream melting over his wrist and dripping on to the brown sand, but he dare not let go of his ice cream, because if he does, she'll kill him for sure, just as he killed those things on the beach, the crabs, the shrimp, the snail, and the baby flatfish with its mouth pulled down in a crescent, and he tries very hard not to breathe, but there's sand in his mouth, and sand in his eyes, and he's crying and puking and Ma screams: 'Swallow it, you little shit, just like you swallowed your brother!'

Then, suddenly, it's over. She stops. She wonders what has happened to her. Kids can drive you crazy, she knows, but what on earth was she thinking of?

'Get up,' she says to *blueeyedboy*.

He pushes himself up from the ground, still holding his melted ice-cream cone. His face is smeared with sand and muck. His nose is bleeding a little. He wipes it with his free hand; stares up at Ma with brimming eyes. She says: 'Don't be a baby. No one got killed. Now finish your fucking ice cream.'

Post comment:
Albertine: (*post deleted*).
blueeyedboy: *I know. Most of the time, words fail me, too . . .*

468

2

At last, a version of the truth. Why bother, at this stage in the game? He must know it's too late to go back. Both of us have shown our hand. Is he trying to provoke me again? Or is this a plea for compassion?

For the last two days both of us have stayed indoors, suffering from the same imaginary bout of flu. Clair tells me by e-mail that Brendan hasn't been to work. The Zebra, too, has been closed for two days. I didn't want him coming here. Not before I was ready.

Tonight I came back for the last time. I couldn't sleep in my own bed. My house is too exposed. So easy to start a fire there; to set up a gas leak; an accident. He wouldn't even have to watch. The Zebra is more difficult, built as it is on the main road. Security cameras on the roof. Not that it matters any more. My car is loaded. My things are packed. I could set off immediately.

You thought I'd stay and fight him? I'm afraid I'm not a fighter. I've spent all my life running away, and it's far too late to change that now. But it's strange, to be leaving the Zebra. Strange and sad, after all this time. I'll miss it; more than that,

I'll miss the person I was when I worked there. Even Nigel only half-understood the purpose of that persona; he thought the *real* Bethan was someone else.

The *real* Bethan? Don't make me laugh. Inside the nest of Russian dolls, there's nothing but painted faces. Still, it was a good place. A safe place, while it lasted. I park the car by the side of the church and walk along the deserted street. Most of the houses are dark now, like flowers closing for the night. But the neon sign of the Zebra shines out, spilling its petals of light on the snow; and it feels so good to be coming home, even for a little while—

There was a present waiting for me. An orchid in a pot, with a card that reads: *To Albertine*. He grows them himself; he told me so. Somehow that seems very like him.

I go inside. I log on at once. Sure enough, he's still online.

I hope you like the orchid, he writes.

I wasn't going to answer him. I'd promised myself I wouldn't do that. But what harm could it do now, after all?

It's beautiful, I type. It's true. The flower is green and purple-throated, like a toxic species of bird. And the scent is like that of a hyacinth, but sweeter and more powdery.

Now he knows I'm here, of course. I expect that's why he sent the orchid. But I know he can't leave until his usual time of a quarter to five, not without alerting his Ma. Leave now, and she would ask questions, and *blueeyedboy* would do anything to avoid making Ma suspicious. That keeps me safe till four thirty at least. I can indulge myself awhile.

It's a Zygopetalum *'Brilliant Blue'. One of the fragrant varieties. Try not to kill it, won't you? Oh, and what did you think of my fic, by the way?*

I think you're twisted, I type back.

He answers with an emoticon, a little yellow smiley face.

Why do you tell these stories? I ask.

Because I want you to understand. His voice is very clear in my mind, as clear as if he were in the room. *There's no going back from murder, Beth.*

You should know, I rattle back.

That emoticon again. *I suppose I ought to feel flattered,* he says. *But you know that's only fiction. I could never have done those things, any more than I could have thrown that rock—my wrist still hurts, by the way. I guess I'm lucky it wasn't my head—*

What is he trying to make me believe? That it's all coincidence? Eleanor, Dr Peacock, Nigel—all his enemies wiped from the board by nothing but a lucky chance?

Well, no, not quite, he answers. *Someone was working on my behalf.*

Who?

For a long time he does not reply. There's nothing there but the little blue square of the cursor blinking patiently in the message box. I wonder if his connection has failed. I wonder if I should log on again. Then, just as I am preparing to sign out, a message arrives in my inbox.

You really don't know who I mean?

I have no idea what you're talking about.

Another of those silences. Then comes an automated message from the server—*Someone has posted on badguysrock!*—and a note which simply

471

says:
Read this.

You are viewing the webjournal of **blueeyedboy** *posting on:*

badguysrock@webjournal.com

Posted at: *01.53 on Friday, February 22*
Status: *public*
Mood: *hungry*
Listening to: *The Zombies*: 'She's Not There'

He calls her Miss Chameleon Blue. You can call her *Albertine*. Or Bethan. Or even Emily. Whatever you choose to name her, she has no colour of her own. Like the chameleon, she adapts to suit the situation. And she wants to be all things to all men—saviour, lover, nemesis. She gives them what she thinks they want. She gives them what she thinks they *need*. She likes to cook, and in this way she feeds her need to nurture. She can recognize all of their favourites: knows when to add or hold the cream; senses their cravings almost before they themselves are aware of them.

It is of course for this very reason that *blueeyedboy* avoids her. *Blueeyedboy* used to be fat, and though that was twenty years ago, he knows how easily he could go back to the boy he used to be. Chameleon knows him too well. His fears, his dreams, his appetites. And he knows that certain cravings were never meant to be satisfied. To look at them directly would be to risk the most terrible consequences. So he uses a series of mirrors, like

Perseus with the Gorgon. And, safe behind the darkened glass, he watches, waits, and bides his time.

Some people are born to watch, he knows.

Some people are mirrors, born to reflect.

Some people are weapons, trained to kill.

Does the mirror choose what to reflect? Does the weapon select the victim? Chameleon doesn't know about that. She never had any ideas of her own, not even when she was a child. Let's face it, she barely has memories. She has no idea of who she is, and she changes her role from day to day. But she's trying to make an impression, he knows. She wants to leave her mark on him.

Impress. Impression. Impressionist. What interesting words. To provoke admiration; to make a statement; to leave an indentation. One who pretends to be someone else. One who paints a picture using only little dabs of light. One who creates an illusion—with smoke and mirrors, with portents and dreams.

Yes, dreams. That's where it all begins. In dreams, in fic, in fantasy. And *blueeyedboy*'s business is fantasy; his territory, cyberspace. A place for all seasons, all seasonings; a place for all flavours of desire. Desire creates its own universe; or at least it does here, on *badguysrock*. The name is nicely equivocal—is it an island on to which penitents are cast away, or is it a haven for villains worldwide, in which to indulge our perversions?

Everyone here has something to hide. For one, it is his helplessness, his cowardice, his fear of the world. For another, an upright citizen with a responsible job, a lovely home and a husband as bland as low-fat spread, it's a secret craving for

474

dark meat: for the troubled, the wicked, the dangerous. For a third, who yearns to be thin, it's the fact that her weight is just a kind of excuse; a blubbery blanket against a world she knows will eat her otherwise. For a fourth, it's the girl he killed the day he crashed his motorbike: eight years old, on her way to school, crossing on a blind bend. And along he comes at fifty an hour, still tanked up from last night, and when he skids and hits the wall he thinks: *That's it, game over, dude.* Except that the game keeps on going, and just at the moment he feels his spine give way like a piece of string, he notices a single shoe lying on its side in the road and wonders vaguely who the hell would leave a perfectly good shoe in the gutter like that, and then he sees the rest of her, and twenty years later, that's *all* he can see; and the dreams still come with such clarity, and he hates himself, and he hates the world, but most of all what he really hates is their terrible, fucking sympathy—

And what about *blueeyedboy*? Well, like the rest of the tribe, of course, he's not exactly what he seems. He tells them as much; but the more he does, the more they're prepared to believe the lie.

I never murdered anyone. Of course, he'd never admit the truth. That's why he parades himself online; strutting and strumming his base desires like a peacock's courtship ritual. The others admire his purity. They love him for his candour. *Blueeyedboy* acts out what others barely dare to dream; an avatar, an icon for a lost tribe that even God has turned away—

And what of Chameleon, you ask? She is not one of *blueeyedboy*'s closest friends, but he sees her, if sporadically. They do have a kind of history, but there's nothing much here to move him now; nothing to hold his attention. And yet, as he comes to know her again, he finds her more and more interesting. He used to think she was colourless. In fact, she is merely adaptable. She has been a follower all her life, collecting ideologies; although so far she has never had a single idea of her own. But give her a cause, give her a flag, and she'll give you her devotion.

First she followed Jesus, and prayed to die before she woke. After that, she followed a boy who taught her a different gospel. Then, when she was twelve years old she followed a madman into the snow just for the sake of his blue eyes, and now she follows *blueeyedboy*, like the rest of his little army of mice, and wants nothing more than to dance to his tune all the way to oblivion.

They meet again at her writing class when she is just fifteen years old. Not so much a writing class as a kind of soft-therapy group, which her counsellor recommended to her as a means of better expressing herself. *Blueeyedboy* attends this group primarily to improve his style, of which he has always been ashamed, but also because he has learnt to exploit the appeal of the fictional murder.

There's a woman he knows in the Village. He calls her Mrs Electric Blue. And she's old enough to be his Ma, which makes it quite disgusting. Not that *he* knows what's in her mind. But Mrs Electric is known to have a predilection for nice young men, and *blueeyedboy* is an innocent—at least, he is in matters of love. A nice young man of twenty or so; working in an electrical shop to pay his way through college. Slim in his denim overalls, no pin-up, but still, a far cry from the fat boy he was only a couple of years ago.

Our heroine, in spite of her youth, is far more adept in the ways of the world. After all, she has had to endure a great many things over the years. The death of her mother; her father's stroke; that hellish blaze of publicity. She has been taken into care; she is staying with a family in the White City estate. The man is a plumber; his ugly wife has tried and failed many times to conceive. They are both fervent royalists: the house is filled with images of the Princess of Wales, some of them texturized photographs, others paint-by-numbers kits in acrylic on cheap canvas. Chameleon dislikes them, but says very little, as always. She's found that it pays to keep silent now; to let other people do the talking. This suits the family just fine. Our heroine is a good little girl. Of course, they ought to know by now: it's the good little girls you need to watch.

The man, whom we shall call Diesel Blue and who will die with his wife in a house fire some five or six years later, likes to be seen as a family man; calls Chameleon *Princess* and at weekends takes her to work with him, where she carries his big box of tools and waits while he chats with a series of jaded housewives and their vaguely aggressive husbands, who all think that plumbers are rip-off merchants and that they themselves, if they so desired, could easily fix that gasket, that tap, or put in that new storage heater.

It's only Health and Safety gone mad that does not permit them to do so; and so they are sour and resentful, while the women make tea and bring biscuits and talk to the silent little girl, who rarely answers back, or smiles, but sits with her oversized

477

sweatshirt hiding most of her body, and her little hands poking out of the sleeves like wilted pale-pink rosebuds, and her face as blank as a china doll's under the curtain of dark hair.

It is on one of these visits—to a house in the Village—that our heroine first experiences the furtive joy of homicide. Of course, it wasn't *her* idea; she lifted it from *blueeyedboy* at their creative-writing class. Chameleon has no style of her own. Her claim to creativity is based on imitation. She only attends class because he is there, in the hope that one day he will see her again, that his eyes will meet hers and stay there, transfixed, with no reflection of anyone else to mar his concentration.

He calls her Mrs Electric Blue . . .

Nice move, *blueeyedboy*. All names and identities have been changed in the hope of protecting the innocent. But Chameleon recognizes her; knows the house from her visits. And she knows her reputation, too: her taste for young men; her erstwhile disgusting liaison with our subject's elder brother. She finds her pathetic, pitiable; and when Mrs Electric Blue is found burnt to death in her house a few days later, she cannot find it in herself to grieve, or to even care about it much.

Some people like to play with fire. Other people deserve to die. And how could a tragic accident have anything at all to do with that good little girl who sits so still, and who waits so patiently by the fire while her father fixes the plumbing?

*   *   *

478

At first, even *blueeyedboy* doesn't guess. At first he thinks it's karma. But, with time, as his enemies falter and fall at every stroke of the typewriter key, he begins to see the pattern emerge, clear as the flowered wallpaper in his mother's parlour.

Electric Blue. Diesel Blue. Even poor Mrs Chemical Blue, who set the seal on her own demise by wanting things so nice and clean, beginning with that nice, clean boy in her fat niece's therapy group.

And Dr Peacock, whose only true crime was to find himself in our hero's care; whose mind was half-gone anyway, and whose chair it was so easy to push off the little home-made ramp, so that next morning they found him there, his eyes jacked open, his mouth awry. And if *blueeyedboy* feels anything, it's a dawning sense of hope—

Perhaps it's my guardian angel, he thinks. *Or maybe it's just coincidence.*

Why does she do it, he asks himself? Is it to safeguard his innocence? To take his guilt and make it her own? Or just to attract his attention? Is it because she sees herself as executioner to the world? Is it because of that little girl, whose life she collected so eagerly? Is it because to be someone else is her only means of existing? Or is it because, like *blueeyedboy*, she has no choice but to mirror those around her?

Still, in the end, it's not his fault. He's giving her what she wants, that's all. And if what she wants is guilt, what then? If what she wants is villainy?

Surely, he's not responsible. He never told her what to do. And yet, he feels she wants something more. He senses her impatience. It's always the same: *these women*, he thinks. *These women and*

479

their expectations. He knows that it will end in tears, as it always has before—

But *blueeyedboy* can't blame her now for what she is considering. He was the one who made her, who shaped her from this murderous clay. For years she has been his golem; and now the slave just wants to be free.

How will she do it? he asks himself. Accidents happen so easily. A poison slipped into his drink? A humdrum gas leak? A car crash? A fire? Or will it be something more esoteric: a needle tipped with the venom of a rare South American orchid; a scorpion slipped into a basket of fruit? Whatever it is, *blueeyedboy* expects it to be something special.

And will he see it coming, he thinks? Will he have time to see her eyes? And as she stares into the abyss, what will she see staring back?

Post comment:

JennyTricks: *THINK YOURE SO CLEVER, DONT YOU?*

blueeyedboy: *You didn't like my ficlet? Now why am I not surprised?*

JennyTricks: *BOYS WHO PLAY WITH FIRE GET BURNT.*

blueeyedboy: *Thank you, Jenny. I'll bear it in mind . . .*

You are viewing the webjournal of **Albertine**.
Posted at: *02.37 on Friday, February 22*
Status: *restricted*
Mood: *angry*

He calls me a golem. How hatefully apt. The golem, according to legend, is a creature made from word and clay; a voiceless slave with no purpose but to do its master's bidding. But in one of the stories the slave rebels—did you know that, *blueeyedboy*? It turns against its creator. What then? I don't remember. But I know it ended badly.

Is that what he really thinks of me? He always was conceited. Even when he was a boy, despised by almost everyone, there was always that arrogant side to him; the enduring belief that he was unique, destined some day to be someone. Perhaps his Ma did that to him. Gloria Green and her colours. No, I'm not defending him. But there's something twisted about the idea that boys can be sorted like laundry; that a colour can make you good or bad; that every crime can be washed away and hung out on the line to dry.

It's ironic, isn't it? He hates her, and yet he's incapable of simply walking away. Instead, he has his own means of escape. He's been living inside his head for years. And he has a golem to do his work, moulded to specifications.

He's lying, of course. It's only fic. He's trying to breach my defences. He knows my reluctant memory is like a broken projector, incapable of processing more than a single frame at a time. *Blueeyedboy*'s account of events is always so much better than mine, high-resolution imaging to my grainy black and white. Yes, I was full of confusion and hate. But I was never a murderer.

Of course, he knew that all along. This is his way of taunting me. But he can be very convincing. And he has lied to the police before, incriminating others to hide his guilt. I wonder, will he accuse me now? Has he found anything in Nigel's flat, or at the Fireplace House, that he could present as evidence? Is he trying to play for time by drawing me into a dialogue? Or is he playing the picador, taunting me into making a move?

Boys who play with fire get burnt.

I couldn't have put it better. If this is his plan to disorient me, then he is treading dangerous ground. I know I ought to ignore him now, just get in the car and drive away, but a feeling of outrage consumes me. I have played his mind games for far too long. We all of us have; we indulge him. He can't bear the sight of physical pain, but he thrives on mental suffering. Why do we allow it? I ask. Why has no one rebelled before now?

An e-mail arrived a moment ago. I picked it up on my mobile phone.

Re: Everyday care of orchids.
In my absence, I would be grateful if you might agree to care for my orchid collection. Most orchids do better in a warm, humid environment away from direct sunlight. Water

sparingly. Do not allow the roots to soak.
Thank you. Aloha,
blueeyedboy

I don't know what he means by this. Does he expect me to cut and run? All in all, I don't think so. More likely he is toying with me, trying to put me off my guard. His orchid is on the back seat of my car, anchored between two boxes. Somehow I don't want to leave it behind. It looks so inoffensive, with its clump of little flowers.

And then a thought occurs to me. It comes with the scent of the orchid. And it seems to clear, so beautiful, like a beacon in the smoke.

It has to end somewhere, don't you see? I've followed him down this road too long, like the crippled child after the Pied Piper. He made me like this. I danced to his tune. My skin is a map covered with scars and the marks of what he has done to me. But now I can see him as he is, the boy who cried murder so many times that, finally, someone believed him . . .

*   *   *

I know his routine as well as my own. He'll set off from home at four forty-five, pretending, as always, to go to work. I'm sure that's when he'll make his move. He won't be able to resist the lure of the Pink Zebra, with its warm and welcoming light, and myself, alone and vulnerable, like a moth inside a lantern . . .

He'll be driving his car, a blue Peugeot. He'll drive down Mill Road and park at the corner of All Saints' Church, where the snow has been cleared away. He'll check the street—deserted now—and then he'll walk up to the Zebra, keeping to the shadows around the side of the building. Inside, the radio is playing loudly enough to mask the sound of his entry. *Not* the classical station today, though I have no fear of music. That fear belonged to Emily. Now even the *Symphonie fantastique* has no power over me.

The kitchen door will be on the latch. Easy enough to open it—glancing up at the neon sign as he does—the strobing words; PINK ZEBRA, with their phantom smell of gas.

You see? I know his weaknesses. I'm using his gift against him now, that gift he acquired from his brother, and when the *real* scent assails him, he will simply dismiss the illusion as he has so many times before—at least until he walks inside, and lets the door close after him.

I have made an adjustment to the door. The handle no longer turns from the inside. And the gas will have been on for hours. By five any spark could ignite it: a light switch, a lighter, a mobile phone.

I won't be there to see it, of course. By then I will be long gone. But my mobile can access the Internet, and I have his number. Of course, he has to *choose* to go in. The victim selects his own fate. No one forces him inside; no one else is responsible.

Perhaps, when he's gone, I'll be free again. Free of these desires of his that mirror desires of mine. Where does the reflection go after the mirror is broken? What happens to the lightning after the storm is over? Real life makes so little sense; only fic has meaning. And I have been fictional for so

484

long; a character in one of his stories. I wonder, do fictional characters ever rebel, and turn on their creators?

I only hope it's not over too soon. I hope he has time to understand. Walking blind into the trap, I hope he has a moment or two to cry out, to struggle, to try to escape, to beat his fists against the door, and finally to think of me, the golem who turned on its master . . .

You are viewing the webjournal of **blueeyedboy**.
Posted at: *04.16 on Friday, February 22*
Status: *restricted*
Mood: *optimistic*
Listening to: *Supertramp*: 'Breakfast In
America'

No sleep tonight. Too many dreams. Some people dream in Technicolor. Some only dream in film noir. But I dream in total-immersion: sound, scent, sensation. Some nights I awake half-drowned in sweat; others, I don't sleep at all. Then, too, the Net is my solace; there's always someone awake online. Chat rooms, fan sites, fic sites, porn. But tonight I'm lonesome for my f-list, my little squeaking chorus of mice. Tonight, what I need is to hear someone say: *You're the best, blueeyedboy.*

And so here I am, back on *badguysrock*, watching perfidious *Albertine*. She has come so far—I'm proud of her—and yet she still feels the need to confess, like the good little Catholic girl of old. I've known her password for some time. It's really quite easy to find out, you know. All it takes is a careless gesture: an account left signed in on a desktop while someone pours a cup of tea, and suddenly her private posts are open for that someone to read—

Are you checking your mail, *Albertine*? My inbox is crammed with messages: plaintive whimperings from Cap; tentative noises from Chryssie. From Toxic, some porn, snagged from a site called *Bigjugs.com*. From Clair, one of her *memes*; along with a dull and cretinous post about Angel Blue and his bitchy wife, about my mother's mental health, and about the wonderful progress she thinks I made in my last public confession.

Then, there's the usual junk mail, hate mail, spam: badly spelt letters from Nigeria promising to send me millions of pounds in return for my bank details; offers of Viagra; of sex; of intimate videos of teenage celebs. In short, all the flotsam the Net brings in, and this time I welcome even the spam, because this is my lifeline, this is my world, and to cut me off is to leave me to drown in air like a fish out of water.

At four o'clock, I hear Ma get up. She doesn't sleep well either, these days. Sometimes she sits in the parlour watching satellite TV; sometimes she does housework, or goes for a walk around the block. She likes to be up when I leave for work. She wants to make me breakfast.

I select a clean shirt from my wardrobe—today it's white, with a blue stripe—and dress myself with some care. I take pride in my appearance. It's safer that way, I tell myself; especially when Ma's watching. Of course, I don't *need* to wear a shirt— my uniform at the hospital consists of a grubby navy-blue jumpsuit, engineer boots with steel-capped toes and a pair of heavy-duty gloves—but Ma doesn't need to know that. Ma's so proud of her *blueeyedboy*. And if Ma ever found out the truth—

'B.B.! Is that you?' she calls.

Who else would it be, Ma?

487

'Hurry up! I made breakfast!'

I must be in her good books today. Bacon, eggs, cinnamon toast. I'm not really hungry, but this time I need to humour her. This time tomorrow I'll be having breakfast in America.

She watches me as I fuel up. 'There's my boy. You'll need your strength.'

There's something vaguely disquieting about her mood this morning. To start with, she is fully dressed: discarding her usual dressing gown for a tweed skirt-suit and her crocodile shoes. She's wearing her favourite perfume—L'Heure Bleue, all powdery orange blossom and clove, with that trembling silvery top note that overpowers everything. Most curious of all, she is—what can I say? I can't quite call it *happy*. In Ma's case, you could count those fleeting moments on the fingers of a one-armed man. But there's a cheeriness in her manner today; something I haven't seen since Ben died. Quite ironic, really. Still, it'll soon be over.

'Don't forget your drink,' she says.

This time it's almost a pleasure. The taste is a little better today, perhaps because the fruit is fresh; and there's a different ingredient— blueberries, blackcurrant, perhaps—that gives it a tannic quality.

'I changed the recipe,' she says.

'Mmmm. Nice,' I tell her.

'Feeling better this morning?'

'Fine, Ma.'

Better than fine. I don't even have a headache.

'Good of them to give you time off.'

'Well, Ma, it's a hospital. Can't be bringing germs to work.'

Ma conceded I had a point. For the past few days I've been sick with flu. Well, that's the official story. In fact, I've been otherwise engaged, as I'm sure you can appreciate.

'Sure you're all right? You look a bit pale.'

'Everyone's pale in winter, Ma.'

6

> *You are viewing the webjournal of* **blueeyedboy**.
> **Posted at**: *04.33 on Friday, February 22*
> **Status**: *restricted*
> **Mood**: *excited*
> **Listening to**: *The Beatles*: 'Here Comes The
> Sun'

I bought the tickets on the Net. You get a discount for booking online. You can choose where to sit; order a meal; you can even print out your own boarding card. I chose a seat by the window, where I can watch the ground fall away. I've never been in an aeroplane. I've never even caught a train. The tickets were rather expensive, I thought; but *Albertine*'s credit can stand it. I snagged her details a year ago, when she bought some books from Amazon. Of course, at that time she had fewer funds; but now, with Dr Peacock's legacy, she should be good for a few months, at least. By the time she finds out—if ever she does—I'll be nicely untraceable.

I haven't packed much. Just a satchel with my papers, some cash, my iPod, a change of clothes, a shirt. No, not a blue one this time, Ma. It's orange and pink, with palm trees. Not much in the way of camouflage; but wait till I get there. I'll blend right in.

I log on for the last time, just for luck, before I set off. Simply to read my messages; to see who

490

hasn't slept tonight; to check for any surprises; to find out who loves me and who wants me dead.

No surprises there, then.

'What are you doing up there?' she calls.

'Hang on, Ma. I'll be down in a sec.'

And now there's time for one more mail—to *albertine@yahoo.com*—before I'm ready to go at last; by noon today I'll be on that flight, watching TV and drinking champagne—

Champagne. Sham pain. As if sensation of any kind could ever be anything other than real. My guts are afizz with excitement. It almost hurts for me to breathe. I take a moment to relax and concentrate on the colour blue. Moon-blue, lagoon-blue, ocean, island, Hawaiian blue. Blue, the colour of innocence; blue, the colour of my dreams—

7

You are viewing the webjournal of **blueeyedboy**
posting on:
                    badguysrock@webjournal.com
Posted at: *04.45 on Friday, February 22*
Status: *public*
Mood: *anxious*
Listening to: *Queen*: 'Don't Stop Me Now'

She must have taken off her shoes. He never even heard her. The first he heard was the door as it shut, and the sound of the key as she locked it.

Click.

'Ma?'

No answer. He goes to the door. The keys were in his coat pocket. She must have taken them, thinks *blueeyedboy*, when he went back upstairs. The door is pitch pine; the lock, a Yale. He has always valued his privacy.

'Ma? Please. Talk to me.'

Just that heavy silence, like something buried under snow. Then, the sound of her footsteps receding softly down the carpeted stairs.

Has she guessed? What does she know? A finger of ice slips down his back. A tremor creeps into his voice; the ghost of the stutter he thought was lost.

'Please, Ma!'

In fiction, our hero would break down the door; or failing that, crash through the window to land

492

unharmed on the ground below. In real life, the door is unbreakable—though, sadly, *blueeyedboy* is not, as a leap from the window would surely confirm, sprawling him in agony on to the icy concrete below.

No, he's trapped. He knows that now. Whatever his Ma is planning, he thinks, he's helpless to prevent it. He hears her downstairs; her steps in the hall; her shoes on the polished parquet floor. The rattle of keys. She's going out.

'Ma!' There's a desperate edge to his voice. 'Ma! Don't take the car! *Please!*'

She hardly ever takes the car. Still, today, he knows she will. The café's only a few streets away, down at the corner of Mill Road and All Saints'; but Ma can be so impatient sometimes—and she knows that girl is expecting him, that Irish girl with all the tattoos, the one who has broken her little boy's heart—

How did she know what he was planning? Perhaps it was his mobile phone, left on the hall table. How stupid of him to have left it there so invitingly. So easy to open his inbox; so easy to find the recent dialogue between her son and *Albertine*.

Albertine, she thinks with a sneer. A rose by any other name. And she *knows* that it's that Irish girl, already to blame for the death of one son, now daring to threaten the other. A wasp in a jar may have killed him, but Gloria knows that Nigel's death would never have happened but for *Albertine*. Stupid, jealous Nigel, who first fell for that Irish girl and then, when he found out his brother had been following her, taking photographs, had first threatened, and then used his fists on poor, helpless *blueeyedboy*, so that Ma

493

had had to take action at last, putting Nigel down like a rabid dog lest history repeat itself—

Dear Bethan (if I may),

I suppose you must have heard the news by now. Dr Peacock passed away the other night at the Mansion. Fell out of his wheelchair down the steps, leaving the bulk of his estate—last valued at three million pounds—to you. Congratulations. I suppose the old man felt he owed you something for the Emily White affair.

I have to say I'm surprised, though. Brendan never told me a thing. All that time he was working for Dr Peacock, and never thought to tell me about this. But maybe he mentioned something to you? After all, you're such good friends.

I know our respective families have had our differences over the years. But now that you're seeing both my sons, perhaps we can bury the hatchet. This business comes as a shock to us all. Especially if what I've heard is true; that they're treating the death as suspicious.

Still, I wouldn't lose any sleep over that. These things blow over in time, as you know.
Yours sincerely,
Gloria.

Yes, *Ma* wrote the letter, of course. She has never flinched from her duty. Knowing that Nigel would open it; knowing that he would take the bait. And when Nigel came round that day, demanding to talk to *blueeyedboy*, she was the one who deflected him, who sent him away with a flea in his ear—or at least, with a wasp in a jar—

494

But now her only surviving son owes her a debt that cannot be repaid. He can never leave her now. He can never belong to anyone else. And if he *ever* tries to run—

Post comment:
blueeyedboy: *Comments, anyone? Anyone here?*

You are viewing the webjournal of **blueeyedboy**
posting on:

badguysrock@webjournal.com

Posted at: *04.47 on Friday, February 22*
Status: *public*
Mood: *devious*
Listening to: *My Chemical Romance*: 'Mama'

She ought to have seen it coming, of course. She ought to have known he would end up this way. But Gloria is no expert on child development. To her, *developing* is something he does in his darkroom, alone. She doesn't like to think of it much. It's like the nasty old Blue Book, she thinks, or the games he likes to play online with those invisible friends of his. She has looked into it once or twice, with the same faint dutiful distaste as when she used to wash his sheets, but only for his protection; because other people don't understand that *blueeyedboy* is sensitive; that he is simply incapable of ever standing up for himself—

The thought makes her eyes mist over a little. For all her steely hard-headedness, Gloria can be strangely sentimental at times, and even in her anger, the thought of his helplessness touches her. It's always been at these moments, she thinks, that she loves him best of all: when he's sick, or in tears, or in pain; when everyone else is against him; when there's no one to love him but her; when all the world thinks he's guilty.

Of course, *she* knows he's innocent. Well, of murder, anyway. What *else* he may be guilty of— what crimes of the imagination—is between *blueeyedboy* and his Ma, who has spent her whole life protecting him, even at her own cost. But that's her son all over, she thinks: sitting in the nest she has built, like a fat and flightless cuckoo chick with his beak perpetually open.

No, he wasn't her favourite. But he was always the luckiest of her three unlucky boys: a natural survivor in spite of his gift; a chip, she thinks, off the old block.

And a mother owes it to her son to protect him, no matter what. Sometimes he needs to be punished, she knows; but that's between *blueeyedboy* and his Ma. No stranger raises a hand to him. No one—not his school, not the law—has the right to interfere. Hasn't she always defended him? From bullies and thugs and predators?

Take Tricia Goldblum, the bitch who seduced her elder son—and caused the death of her youngest. It was a pleasure to take care of her. Easy, too: electrical fires are always so reliable.

Then Mrs White's hippie friend, who thought she was better than they were. And Catherine White herself, of course, so easy to destabilize. And Jeff Jones from the estate, the man who fostered that Irish girl, and who some years later, in the pub, dared to raise a hand to her son. Then there was Eleanor Vine, the sneak, spying on Bren at the Mansion, and Graham Peacock, who cheated them, and for whom the boy had *feelings*—

He was the most rewarding of all. Tipped over in his wheelchair and left to die alone on the path,

497

like a tortoise half-out of its shell. Afterwards, she went upstairs and relieved him of his T'ang figurine, the one with which he taunted her all those years ago, and which she carefully placed in her cabinet along with the rest of her china dogs. It isn't stealing, she tells herself. The old man owed her *something*, after all, for all the trouble he has caused her son.

But in spite of everything she has done for him, what gratitude has *blueeyedboy* shown? Instead of supporting his mother, he has dared to transfer his affections to that Irish girl from the village, and worse, has tried to make her believe that *she* could have been his protector—

She'll make him pay for that, she thinks. But first, to take care of business.

Now, from upstairs, she hears his voice, accompanied by a banging and slapping at the bedroom door. 'Ma! Please! Open the *door!*'

'Don't be such a baby,' she says. 'When I get back, *then* we can talk.'

'Ma, *please!*'

'Don't make me come in—'

The sounds from the bedroom cease abruptly.

'That's better,' says Gloria. 'We've got a lot to talk about. Like your job at the hospital. And the way you've been lying to me. And what you've been up to with that girl. That Irish girl with all the tattoos.'

Behind the door, he stiffens. He can feel every hair stiffening. He knows what's in the balance here, and in spite of himself he is afraid. Of course he is. Who wouldn't be? He is caught inside the bottle trap, and the worst of it is, he *needs* to be caught; he needs this feeling of helplessness. But she's there on the other side of the door like a trapdoor spider poised to bite, and if any part of his plan goes wrong, if he has failed to compensate for any one of those minute variables, then—

If. If.

An ominous sound, tinged with the grey-green scent of trees and the dust that accumulates under his bed. It's safe under the bed, he thinks; safe and dark and scentless. He listens as she puts on her boots, fumbles with the front-door key; locks the door behind her. The *crump* of her footsteps in the snow. The sound of the car door opening.

She takes the car, as he knew she would. His begging her not to do so now ensures her cooperation. He closes his eyes. She starts the car. The engine ratchets into life. It would be so ironic, he thinks, if she had an accident. It wouldn't be his fault if she did. And then, at last, he would be *free*—

Post comment:
blueeyedboy: *Still no one here? Right, then. I guess that leaves me all on my own for Stage 4 . . .*

I think you must have guessed by now that this is not an ordinary fic. My other fics are all accounts of things that have already happened—though whether they happened quite as I said is up to you to determine. But this little story is more in the way of being a work-in-progress. An ongoing project, if you like. *A breakthrough in concept*, as Clair might say. And like all conceptual work, it isn't entirely without risk. In fact, I'm more or less convinced that it's all about to end in tears.

Five minutes to drive to the Zebra. Five more to see to business. And after that—*Whoops! All gone!*—here comes the explosive finale.

I hope they'll look after my orchids. They're the only things in this house that I'll miss. The rest can rot, for all I care, except for the china dogs, of course, for which I have special plans of my own.

But first of all, to get out of this room. The door is pinewood, and well-made. In a movie, perhaps, I could break it down. Real life demands a more reasoned approach. A multi-tool with a screwdriver, a file and a short-bladed penknife should help me deal with the hinges, after which I can make my exit unimpeded.

I take a last look at my orchids. I notice that the *Phalaenopsis*—otherwise known as the moth orchid—is in need of re-potting. I know exactly how she feels; I, who have lived for all these years in the same little, airless, toxic space. Time to explore new worlds, I think. Time now to leave the cocoon and to fly . . .

It occurs to me as I work on the door that I ought to be feeling better than this. My stomach is filled with butterflies. I'm even feeling a little sick. My iPod is packed in my travel bag; instead I turn on the radio. From the tinny speakers comes the bubblegum sound of the Rubettes singing 'Sugar Baby Love'.

When I was a little boy, mistaking *baby* for *B.B.*, I always assumed that those songs were for me; that even the folk on the radio *knew* that I was special, somehow. Today the music sounds ominous, a troubling falsetto sweeping across a fat layer of descending chords to a mystic accompaniment of *doop-shoowaddies* and *bop-shoowaddies*; and it tastes sour-sweet like acid drops, the ones that, when you were a child, you poked into the side of your mouth to make your tastebuds shudder and cramp, and if you weren't careful, the tip of your tongue would slide over the boiled-sugar shell and snag on the sharp-edged bubbles there, and your mouth would fill with sweetness and blood, and *that* was the taste of childhood . . .

Nyaaa-haaaa-haaaa-oooooooooooooooh

Today there's something sinister in those

501

soaring, sustained vocals; something that tears at the insides like gravel in a silk purse. The word *sugar* is not sweet: it has a pink and gassy smell, like dentist's anaesthetic, dizzy and intrusive, like something boring its way into my head. And I can almost see her there—right at this moment, *here* and *there*—and the Rubettes are playing at migraine volume in the Zebra's tiny kitchen, and there's a smell, a sickly-sweet, gassy smell that cuts through the scent of fresh coffee, but Ma doesn't really notice that, because fifty years of Marlboros have long since shot her olfactory organs to hell, and only the scent of L'Heure Bleue cuts through, and she opens the door to the kitchen.

Of course I can't *quite* be sure of this. I could be wrong about the radio station. I could be wrong about the time—she might still be in the car park, or by now it might even be over—and yet it feels completely right.

> *Sugar baby love*
> *Sugar baby love*
> *I didn't mean to make you blue—*

Perhaps there was something, after all, in Feather's tales of walk-ins and ghosts and spirits and astral projection; because that's how I feel now, lighter than air, watching the scene from a place somewhere on the ceiling, and the Rubettes are singing—*aaaah-oop shoowaddy-waddy, doop-showaddy-waddy*. And now I can see the top of Ma's head, the parting in her thinning hair; the packet of Marlboros in her hand, the lighter poised above the tip; and I see the superheated air ripple and swell like a balloon inflated beyond its

502

capacity, and she calls out—*Hello? Is anyone there?*—and lights a final cigarette—

*   *   *

She has no time to understand. I never really intended her to. Gloria Green is no wasp in a jar, to be caught and disposed of at leisure. Nor is she a seaside crab, left to die in the simmering sun. Her passing is instantaneous, and the hot draught sweeps her away like a moth—*Pfff!*—into oblivion, so that nothing, not even a finger, remains for *blueeyedboy* to identify, not even a measure of dust large enough to rattle inside a china dog.

From my room I can almost hear the dull *cr-crumpf* of the explosion, and it's like crunching a stick of Blackpool rock, all sharp edges and toothache, and although there's no way I can know for sure, I am suddenly certain, in a surge of wonder and indescribable relief, that I've done it at last. I'm free of her. *I'm finally rid of my mother—*

Don't tell me you're surprised, *Albertine.* Didn't I tell you I knew how to wait? Did you believe, after all this time, that this could have been an *accident*? And did you really believe, Ma, that I didn't know you were watching me, that I hadn't clocked you from the first time you logged on to *badguysrock*?

She appeared on the scene some months ago in response to one of my public posts. Ma isn't what you'd call computer-literate; but she accessed the Net through her mobile phone. After that, it can't have been long before someone, somewhere, steered her towards *badguysrock*. My guess is Maureen, via Clair; or maybe even Eleanor. In any case, I'd expected it; and I'd expected to pay for it, too, though I knew she would never make any direct reference to my online activities. Ma can be strangely prudish at times, and some things are never mentioned. *All your nasty stuff upstairs* is about the closest we ever got to discussing the porn, or the photographs, or the fics that were posted on my site.

I have to admit I enjoyed the game: playing with fire; taking risks; taunting her to reveal herself. Sometimes I went a little too far. Sometimes I got my fingers burnt. But I had to know the boundaries; to see how hard I could push them both; to calculate the precise amount of pressure I could exert over the mechanism before it began to break down. An artist needs to understand the medium in which he works. After that, it was easy.

Don't feel guilty, *Albertine*. You had no way of knowing. Besides, in the end she'd have gone after you, just as she did with those others. Call it self-defence, if you like. Or maybe an act of redemption. Anyway, it's over now. You're free. Goodbye, and thank you. If you're ever in Hawaii, call. And please, look after my orchid.

Post comment:

You are viewing the webjournal of **blueeyedboy**.
Posted at: *05.17 on Friday, February 22*
Status: *restricted*
Mood: *sick*
Listening to: *Voltaire*: 'Snakes'

At last. The door pulls away from the hinge. I'm free to leave. I pick up my bag. But the ache in my guts has worsened; it feels like a piece of bramble scoring my stomach lining. I go to the bathroom; I wash my face; I drink a glass of water.

God, it hurts. What's happening? I'm sweating. I look terrible. In the mirror I look like a corpse: deep shadows around my eyes; mouth bracketed with nausea. What the hell is wrong with me? I felt so good at breakfast.

Breakfast. Ah. I should have known. Too late, I remember the look on her face; that look of almost-happiness. She wanted to make me breakfast today. Cooked me all my favourites. Stood over me while I ate it. The vitamin drink tasted different—and she *said* she'd changed the recipe.

For God's sake, it was obvious. How could I have missed what was happening? Ma up to her old tricks again—how could I have been so *careless*?

And now it feels like shards of glass are grinding away at my insides. I try to stand up, but the pain is too bad; it doubles me up like a penknife. I check the status of my f-list. There has to be someone awake by now. Someone who can help me.

A message through WeJay should bring help. Ma has taken my mobile phone. I type out my SOS and wait. Is there nobody online?

Captainbunnykiller is feeling OK.

Yeah, right. The fucktard. Too scared to leave his house now in case he runs into the boys from the estate. In passing, I notice that *kidcobalt* has been removed from Cap's f-list. Oh, well. Colour me surprised.

ClairDeLune is feeling rejected. Well, yes, probably. Angel has finally had enough, and has written to her personally. His tone, which is cool and professional, leaves Clair with no illusions. Rejection hurts at any age; but to Clair the humiliation is even more of a blow. *sapphiregirl* is gone from her f-list. So, I see, is *blueeyedboy*.

And Chryssie? Once more, she is feeling sick. This time, I almost sympathize. Looking at her f-list this morning, I notice, with diminishing surprise, that *azurechild* has been deleted. I immediately check for *blueeyedboy*. There, too, I am absent.

Three strikes? It's more than coincidence. I scroll quickly through the rest of my f-list, checking accounts and avatars. *BombNumber20. Purepwnage9. Toxic69. All* my friends. As if they had all decided as one to leave me marooned on *badguysrock*—

Of course, there's nothing from *Albertine*. Her Webmail account is marked as *dormant*; her WeJay as *deleted*. I can still look up her old posts— nothing online is ever lost, and every word is

506

hidden away in caches and encrypted files, the ghosts in the machine. But *Albertine* is gone now. For the first time in over twenty years—perhaps for the first time in his *life*—*blueeyedboy* is quite alone.

Alone. A bitter, brown word, like dead leaves caught in a wind trap. It tastes like coffee grounds and dirt, and smells like cigarette ash. Suddenly I feel scared. Not so much of being alone as for the absence of those little voices, the ones that tell me that I'm real, the ones that say they see me—

You understand it was fiction, right? You know I never killed anyone? Yes, some of my fic may have been in bad taste, even a little sick, perhaps, but surely you don't believe I could ever have acted out those things?

Do you, Chryssie?

Do you, Clair?

Seriously. It wasn't real. Artistic licence, anyone? If it sounded genuine, if you were nearly *convinced*, then—surely that's a compliment, proof that *blueeyedboy* kicks ass—

Right, guys? Toxic? Cap?

I try to get down the stairs again. I need to call a taxi. I have to get out. I have to escape. I have to be on that plane at midday. But I feel like I've been cut in half; my legs can barely hold me. I make it to the bathroom again, where I throw up until there's nothing left.

But I know from experience that this doesn't help. Whatever she used is in me now, working its way through my bloodstream, shutting down all systems. Sometimes it lasts for days, sometimes weeks, depending on the dosage. What did she use? I don't know. I have to call that taxi. If I crawl, I can reach the phone. It's in the parlour, with the dogs. But the thought of lying there, helpless, with those china dogs looking down at me, is more than my brutalized nerves can take. The snakes are loose in my belly, and now there is no stopping them—

Damn, I feel sick. I feel dizzy. The room is spinning choppily. Black flowers open behind my eyes. If I just lie here, quietly, then maybe things will be OK. Maybe in time I can regain some strength, enough to get to the airport, at least—

Bip! It's the sound of the mailbox. That bittersweet electronic sound. One of my friends has messaged me. I knew they wouldn't leave me here. I knew they'd come round eventually.

I crawl back to the keyboard. I click on the symbol for *message*.

Someone has commented on your post!

I flick back to my most recent entry. A single line has been added there. No avatar. Just the default pic; a blue silhouette inside a square.

Post comment:
JennyTricks: *NOT BAD AT ALL FOR AN AMATEUR. NOT TOO REALISTIC, THOUGH.*

She ends it with an emoticon: a little winking smiley.

No way. No *way!* A finger of sweat runs down my spine. My stomach's filled with broken glass. It has to be a joke, right? Nothing but a bad joke. Right from the moment she first logged on, thinking she was so clever.

Oh, please. As if I could have missed her, with that ridiculous username—

Jenny Tricks.

Genitrix.

And its colour is sometimes Virgin-blue, and sometimes it's green, like market-stall baize, and it smells of L'Heure Bleue and Marlboros, and cabbage leaves and salt water—

Post comment:
blueeyedboy: *Ma?*

No. No. Of course not. I heard the explosion, for God's sake. Ma isn't coming back, not today, not ever. And even if she had escaped somehow, then why would she choose this medium, instead of simply driving home and dealing with me face to face?

No, someone's trying to mess with my mind. My guess is *Albertine*. Nice try, *Albertine*. But I've been playing these games for much too long to be freaked out by an amateur.

Bip! Someone has commented on your post!

I consider deleting the message unread. But—

Post comment:
JennyTricks: *SO HOW ARE YOU FEELING, blueeyedboy?*
blueeyedboy: *Never felt better, Jenny, thanks.*
JennyTricks: *YOU NEVER COULD LIE TO SAVE YOUR LIFE.*

Well, that's a debatable point, *JennyTricks*. In fact

509

I've survived for as long as I have by doing precisely that. Like the princess Scheherazade, I've consistently lied to save my life for rather more than a thousand and one nights. So, Jenny, whoever you are—

> **Post comment**:
> **blueeyedboy**: *Tell me, do I know you?*
> **JennyTricks**: *NOT AS WELL AS I KNOW YOU.*

Seriously, I doubt that. But now I'm beginning to be intrigued, in spite of the pain that comes and goes like the waves under Blackpool pier. *In pain.* What a phrase. Like a mouse inside a bottle. In any case I'm trapped here, and rather than think about my circumstances—which, let's face it, don't look good—it's easier to stay here, to grab the line that's being offered, to keep up the dialogue, which at least is preferable to silence.

> **Post comment**:
> **blueeyedboy**: *So, you think you know me?*
> **JennyTricks**: *OH YES. I KNOW YOU.*
> **blueeyedboy**: *Is that you,* **Albertine***?*

She responds with another smiley. The pixellated yellow face looks like a grinning goblin. It hurts to type, but the silence is worse.

> **Post comment**:
> **blueeyedboy**: **Albertine***? Is that you?*
> **JennyTricks**: *NO, THAT BITCH IS GONE FOR GOOD.*

Now I'm convinced it's Bethan in there. How did she get Ma's password? Where is she logging on from? It's good she doesn't know I'm sick. She may not even know I'm here. For all she knows I'm at the airport, logging on from the business lounge.

Post comment:
blueeyedboy: *Well, it's been fun, but I have to go.*
JennyTricks: *YOURE NOT GOING ANYWHERE.*
blueeyedboy: *Oh, but I am. I'm flying south.*
JennyTricks: *NOT IN THIS LIFETIME, YOU LITTLE SHIT. WE HAVE THINGS TO TALK ABOUT.*

Bitch, I'm not afraid of you. In fact, I'm feeling better. I'm going to get up in a minute, pick up my bag, call a taxi and then I'll be off to the airport. Who knows, I may even find the time to deal with those dogs before I go. Still, for the moment I think I'll stay here, crunched up like a contortionist, keeping the pain at bay with words as it opens its jaws to swallow me—

Post comment:
JennyTricks: *YOU WAIT HERE. I'M COMING HOME. I'M COMING TO TAKE CARE OF YOU.*

She's bluffing, of course. She has no idea. But if I didn't know better right now, I might even feel a little afraid. She has Ma's voice down so accurately that I can feel my hackles trying to rise, and the back of my shirt is clammy with sweat. But all the same, it's just a bluff, based on what she knows of me. She knows it's a weakness of mine, that's all. She's shooting in the dark. I've won, and there's nothing she can do about it—

Post comment:
JennyTricks: *THINK YOU'RE SO SMART, DON'T YOU? YOU SHOULDN'T HAVE TRIED TO CHEAT ON ME. AND IF I FIND THAT YOU'VE LAID AS MUCH AS A FINGER ON ANY OF MY CERAMICS I'LL BREAK YOUR FUCKING NECK, OK?*

OK, game over, *JennyTricks*. I think I've exhausted my tolerance. Places to go, people to see, crimes to commit, and all that jazz. There are plenty of opportunities for a man of my skills in Hawaii. Plenty of places to explore. Perhaps I'll message you from there. Till then, Jenny, whoever you are—

You are viewing the webjournal of **blueeyedboy**
Posted at: *05.32 on Friday, February 22*
Status: *restricted*
Mood: *scared*
Listening to: *Abba*: 'The Winner Takes It All'

OK. Joke over, thinks *blueeyedboy*. This isn't funny any more. She knows too much about him, of course; it's almost beginning to get to him. He stands up, though it hurts terribly. The room does one of those choppy swoops. He holds on to his desktop to keep from falling over.

Bip! That mailbox sound again. This time he ignores it. He slings his bag across his shoulder, still leaning on to the desk for support.

Bip! Another message. *Someone has posted on badguysrock!*

But he's halfway across the landing now, leaning on the banister. *Badguysrock* is an island from which he is suddenly desperate to escape. Each step he takes is an effort, but he'll walk out if it kills him. No crawling for *blueeyedboy*. He's going to make that fucking plane—

He's concentrating so hard that the sound of the car hardly registers, and when it stops on the driveway it takes him some seconds to react.

Police, here already? thinks *blueeyedboy*.

A car door slams. He hears the crunch of footsteps approaching in the snow. A door key ratchets and turns in the lock. The front door opens quietly. He hears the sound of boots on the mat. A double thud. Then the sound of bare feet across the parquet hall floor.

They found the keys. That's all, he thinks. They let themselves in. Two detectives. He can see them in his mind's eye: a man and a woman (there's always one). He will be plain and businesslike; she will be kinder, more sensitive. But—why did they take their boots off, he thinks? And why on earth didn't they ring the bell?

'Hey!' His voice is rusty. 'Up here!'

No one replies. Instead, a scent of cigarette smoke winds its way up the stairwell. Then comes a small and slithery sound, like a snake—or a long piece of electrical cord sliding across a polished floor.

Panic wrenches at him now. He falls against the banister. He tries to get up, but his legs are on strike. Cursing, he crawls back into his room. Not that *that* will protect him now; the door is off its hinges. But there's always his computer, he thinks; his refuge; his island; his sanctuary.

He logs back on to *badguysrock*. Two messages await him.

He reads them as the room spins dizzily around him. His eyes are streaming; his head sore; his stomach filled with razor blades.

From the stairs, relentlessly, comes the sound of footsteps.

'Who's there?' His voice is raw.

'Ma, please? Is that you?'

No reply but those feet on the stairs, coming up so steadily. With shaking hands, he begins to type. The footsteps reach the landing. A slithery sound on the carpet. *Blueeyedboy* types faster. He cannot, *dare* not, stop typing. Because if he stops, he'll have to turn round, and then he'll have to *look at her*—

But of course, this is only fic. *Blueeyedboy* doesn't believe in ghosts. Even as he types the words he knows that this is *Albertine*. She couldn't leave him after all; she stopped to read her mail, then turned back, knowing that he needed her help. And the phantom reek of Marlboros is only in his mind, he thinks, and the scent of L'Heure Bleue is so powerful that it cannot possibly be real. No, it's only *Albertine*, who has come to save him—

'I knew you wouldn't leave me, Beth.' His voice is weak and grateful.

Albertine makes no reply.

'You gave me a hell of a scare, though. I thought you were my mother.' He tries a laugh, which sounds more like a scream. That slithering sound comes closer.

'I guess that makes us even now. I'll even admit I deserved it.'

Still no reaction from *Albertine*. Behind him the footsteps come to a stop. He can smell her now, a rose in the smoke.

She says: 'I brought your medicine.'

'Ma?' he whispers.

'Ma? *Ma?*'